MOMENT OF DISCOVERY

Petra stood outside Jay Burton's stateroom door for a moment, her hand on the knob. She'd come on impulse—they'd said farewell earlier, and left each other in a storm of passion and frustration. For the first time, a man—her husband-to-be—had seen and touched her naked body. She'd wanted him so, but at the last minute he'd said, "No, Petra my dearest, we must wait ... Suppose I were to die of fever in Panama and leave you bearing our child?"

He'd wanted it to be perfect, this big raw-boned American. But she, with her full, voluptuous body made so perfectly for love had wanted him so desperately. She forced herself back to the present; the decklight glinting on her golden blonde hair, she turned the knob and opened the stateroom door.

Petra could not at first identify the sounds she heard, the soft whispers, the rustlings, and then, as the door opened wider, she stared directly into the eyes of the woman who lay naked in the arms of Jay Burton—her sister Darcie.

Dynasty
of
Desire

Elizabeth Zachary

A DELL/JAMES A. BRYANS BOOK

Published by
Dell Publishing Co., Inc.
1 Dag Hammarskjold Plaza
New York, New York 10017

Dell ® TM 681510, Dell Publishing Co., Inc.

ISBN: 0-440-02024-7

Printed in the United States of America
First printing—November, 1978

Dynasty of Desire

PROLOGUE

"THE GIRL BLAMES herself," Dr. Effram Pettigrew said. "I can find nothing physically wrong with her."

"She refuses to eat," Edward Moncrief said, looking across the dimly lit bedroom to see the closed eyes of his daughter, her normally dark skin showing an ashen pallor. "She spends her time in her room. She has withdrawn, even from Petra."

"I don't want to alarm you unduly," Dr. Pettigrew said, "but it seems that she is literally willing herself to die."

"What can we do?" Edward asked. His voice was low, his eyes showing the effects of his mourning even more vividly than the black armband which he had worn that morning on what he feared was a somewhat selfish trip to his office; in his work he could find a few blessed moments of surcease from his grief.

"In cases of extreme melancholia, it is difficult to determine which actions will help and which will merely make things worse," the doctor mused. "However, in many cases, new surroundings seem to take the patient's mind, as it were, away from his own miseries."

7

"You are suggesting—"

"A trip," Pettigrew said. "The Continent, perhaps. Tire her out physically walking the aisles of museums. Divert her mind from the tragedy."

"I have been invited by Monsieur de Lesseps to attend the grand opening of the Suez Canal," Edward said, feeling a new pang of sadness as he remembered how much Carolle had looked forward to the trip. "We had planned to go as a family."

"If I may give you a further piece of advice," Dr. Pettigrew said, "it would do you good to get away. I don't like the looks of you, sir. I fear you've been trying to lose yourself in your work."

"Guilty, I fear," Edward said.

The two men stood in the doorway, the doctor's back to the bed where Darcie lay, eyes closed, hearing their words but showing no sign of interest.

"Would not the trip to Egypt seem, ah, bittersweet to her?" Edward asked. "After all, her mother was French, and she knows the pride Carolle took in the achievements of her countrymen."

"In this house she is reminded of her mother constantly," Pettigrew said. "A long sea voyage is a standard prescription for many ailments. Moreover, there are excellent doctors in Egypt, should she need professional attention in that country."

"As a matter of fact," Edward said, "my wife's brother is a physician—newly graduated. He is serving—how do you say it—an apprenticeship with Monsieur Roger D'Art, de Lesseps's personal doctor."

"We all know of Dr. D'Art," Pettigrew said. "A man with an excellent reputation—indeed, quite famous. If you could have him look at the girl, the trip would be very much worthwhile, but the main thing is just to get her away. I was in Cairo in '65. Fascinating city. Just the sights and smells are enough to enthrall the girl. A visit to the pyramids. No one can remain steeped in misery when faced with such a sight."

"Perhaps you are right," Edward said. He looked at Darcie and sighed. His dark one, so like her mother with shining black hair, flashing brown eyes, a face which, at fourteen, was already causing interest among the young men. "I will think on it."

Darcie heard it all. But the words were just words. What she had done, what she had seen, those things would not be erased by words or a doctor's prescriptions or a million pyramids. Nothing would ever free her from the reliving of those fatal moments with the thunder rumbling, lightning flashing, the rain beating down, windblown, onto her face. Nothing, not all the perfumes of Arabia, would make her forget the dank, barnyard smell of the deserted sheepcote, the blood, the screams of agony.

Her mother was dead. She, Darcie Eleanora Moncrief, had killed her. She had no reason to live.

BOOK I

1

FROM THE WINDOWS of the spacious Moncrief home, one could look down upon the southern fringe of Kew Gardens, where Carolle Moncrief, six months large with her third child, walked with her two daughters to while away the time before the annual family holiday. It was a difficult time for Edward to be away from his office, but Carolle and the girls did look forward so to their summers in the Norfolk Broads and with Carolle's condition, mid-June was the last possible time for even a short trip. Dr. Pettigrew was not overjoyed at the idea of Carolle's making the journey, but the modern comforts of the good British rail system would smooth the way.

Thus, the doctor gave reluctant consent, and Edward made his arrangements to leave the affairs of Moncrief and Moncrief in the hands of his trusted subordinates.

In June of 1869, the firm was not old, as London firms go, nor was it one of the larger firms in that old section known to the world of finance as The City. However, Edward Moncrief, fifty-two, a vigorous man, large for an Englishman, a true product of the new merchant class which, with the advent of the industrial revolution, had begun to make serious inroads into the power of the old ruling class; had, in the face of disapproval, laughter, and some downright hostility, hitched his wagon to the star of a little Frenchman with a dream. Edward had used his own money to buy Suez stock, had advised all his clients to do the same, and now that the news from Egypt was excellent, the canal to see ship traffic before Christmas, the stock was strong and rising steadily in value. In finance, today's fool is tomorrow's genius—provided that the fool guesses right and a generous God chooses to reward his efforts. Edward Moncrief was being rewarded. His belief in the dream of de Lesseps was making him a wealthy man.

Summer was reluctant in 1869, so that preparations for the holiday were made in weather of dismal variations—one day sunny, the next wet and chill. But not even a new storm from the cold Atlantic could dampen the enthusiasm of Darcie, the oldest Moncrief daughter, who was a great help. She selected clothing to be packed, gave instructions to the members of the staff who would be staying in London to tend the house until the family's return, and did her best to see to it that her mother had little to do. However, Carolle's confinement, during the first six months, had been an easy one; not nearly as difficult as it had been with Petra, the youngest daughter. Petra, Carolle often said, with fond laughter, had been an impatient one with the kick of a French army mule.

This baby she carried, Carolle felt, would be the son her husband desired; he was less active in the womb than either Petra or Darcie. He lay lower. Moreover, she had a boy's name selected. He would be Edward Masters Moncrief III, his name thoroughly English, unlike the names of the two girls who had French names for their French mother.

Darcie's name was apt, for she was truly the little dark one, like her mother. She was small of frame, delicate of figure, had healthy black hair and brown eyes, small and perfect teeth and sensuous lips which belied a forcefulness of character which she displayed, among other ways, in a firm and benevolent dominance of her younger and more temperate sister.

Petra, her name taken from the Greek, the feminine form of Peter, meaning the rock, was her father's daughter with a skin of pure English cream in direct contrast to Darcie's Latin coloration. At twelve, she was as large as her older sister. Early pubescence was adding curves to her body, her hips spreading in a promise of luscious womanhood, her breasts forming into little points the size of lemons. She had her father's golden hair.

Both girls worshiped their father and adored their mother, and in spite of the fact that Darcie was the favorite of both mother and father, Petra loved her sister with an intensity which often approached hero worship. There was no envy in her. When Darcie, the eldest, received the most becoming frocks, Petra lived in reflected glory as Darcie's tiny and perfectly formed body, graceful and feminine, earned compliments. Petra was content to be led, eager to please Darcie. If anyone looked forward more than Darcie to her "season," when she would be introduced to society, it was Petra. She often assured Darcie that she would be the most beautiful girl in all of London.

The future looked bright for the Moncrief family in that spring of 1869, and Edward Moncrief's main worry was whether or not Carolle would birth his son in time for the family to travel together to be with his friend de Lesseps at the most significant event of the century. There were not many in England who had personal invitations from de Lesseps, himself, and Carolle promised not to let having a baby interfere.

Carolle Moncrief had never been able to fit the pattern of the typical English ladies of the age of Victoria. Her lively and impulsive actions often caused

proper English tongues to wag. Firstborn of a prosperous Bordeaux landed gentleman, a sportsman, and
a grower of fine grapes whose wine had been a favorite
at Napoleon's table, she had been, until the birth of
her brother Guy, when she was ten, both daughter
and son to her father. Her mother was of sturdy peasant stock, and she passed along her robust health to
her daughter.

As the wife of an English merchant, Carolle continued to ride, remained active, scorned the popular
feminine pastime of needlework and the gossip of London ladies. She did not feel belittled by getting English
dirt under her fingernails while working in the garden.

It was upon Carolle's insistence that the summer
holiday in Norfolk was not canceled. Even Nanny-
Ruth, the aging nurse-governess, was shocked when
Edward agreed to take a six-months-pregnant woman
on such a journey, but Carolle was firm in stating that
she would not let a large stomach deprive the family
of their yearly treat.

Departure was made in a general air of excitement,
with both Petra and Darcie talking incessantly. The
trip across town to the Liverpool Street Station was
made in the family brougham. While porters loaded
their baggage aboard the train, Darcie and Petra ran
ahead to locate a vacant first-class compartment and
came back to guide Carolle to their selection.

The old Moncrief country home, from which Edward's father had departed to take his place in the
financial life of The City, was on the banks of the
Yare River in a flat and desolate section of Norfolk.
The nearest train stop was the tiny village of Acle,
which was nothing more than a pub, two small shops,
a dozen cottages, and the station set in the flatness of
a peat plain. Family retainers awaited with an open
victoria and a farm cart to carry the not inconsiderable
amount of luggage. The midmorning sky was a mixture
of threat and promise. A bank of dark clouds lined the

western horizon, but after considerable thought and some talk with the local stationmaster about the vagrancies of the weather, it was decided that the drive could be made before the dark clouds moved in from the west.

James, the family footman, neat in his livery, climbed into the driver's seat of the victoria, leaving a younger servant to drive the cart carrying the baggage.

Darcie, like her mother an excellent horsewoman, fancied herself to be an accomplished carriage driver and took every opportunity to have the reins in her hands.

"Please, father," she begged, "let me drive. I know the way. I've been over the road ever so many times."

Edward, in an expansive holiday mood, snug and secure in the bosom of his little family, was in no mood to deny any request from his eldest daughter.

"All right, then, James," he said. "If you'll ride along on the cart."

Petra clambered onto the driver's seat beside Darcie. The team of horses, matched blacks, were lively and well fed. One tossed his head impatiently as Edward assisted Nanny-Ruth and then Carolle into the victoria. Edward loved the old vehicle, admired its fragile but strong lines, liked the comfort of the leather seats. He noted with pleasure that the brass fittings were well polished and made a mental note to praise the old ostler who watched after the country house during the winter, supervised the growing of a bit of corn and a few head of cattle, and generally kept the place going when the family was not in residence.

"Carefully, now," Edward warned, as Darcie clucked the horses into motion and the eager animals started with a jerk.

"The horses seem to be rather spirited," Carolle said.

"Don't worry, *maman,*" Petra said. "Darcie can handle them."

And, indeed, Darcie's firm hand steadied the horses into a distance-eating pace and the carriage wheels rolled smoothly over the well-kept road until, descending the hills, the carriage emerged into the broad, flat pastures. Sheep and cattle grazed peacefully. The harnesses of the spirited blacks jingled merrily, the carriage wheels dug into the soil of the rutted road and the vehicle swayed on its springs, causing Nanny-Ruth to gasp and admonish Darcie to slow down.

Darcie pulled the horses into a walk and allowed her eyes to rove over the lovely countryside.

"I do hope the boat is ready," Petra said, thinking of the slow, calm waters of the Yare and remembering past trips all the way to the large expanse of Breydon Water, near Yarmouth.

"I'm sure it will be," Edward said. "Do you two think you can handle it yourself this year?"

"Darcie can," Petra said.

Carolle laughed. "Is there anything you think your sister cannot do?"

Petra blushed and looked out of the corner of her eye at Darcie, who winked at her.

"If *maman* feels up to it," Edward said, "perhaps we can take the ketch down the Waveney into Oulton Broad this year."

"That would be delightful," Darcie said. "And into Lowestoft, too?"

"Perhaps," Edward said. "We'll have to see how *maman* feels."

"*Maman* feels fine," Carolle said, bracing herself as the carriage wheel slid into a rut and caused her to bounce. "But she would feel even better if the driver of this carriage did not feel compelled to find every rut in the road."

"I'm so sorry, *maman*," Darcie said. "I'll be more careful."

Having passed through the little village of Damgate and arrived in Moulton St. Mary, the family shopped for a meal at a splendid little pub. When they emerged and were seated in the carriage once again, Edward looked toward the west doubtfully. The clouds were higher in the sky. However, there was shelter available at the halfway point, in Freethorpe, so he told Darcie to press onward. The distance went quickly under the feet of the blacks and the spinning wheels of the victoria, the conversation was spirited, the clouds seemed to be no more threatening, so at Freethorpe Edward looked at the sky, laughed, and said, "Onward, brave driver."

Now the countryside flattened into low-lying peat meadows. The last of the country homes had been passed on the outskirts of Freethorpe, and the next shelter was in Reedham Ferry, quite a short distance. The ground leading to the river was sometimes marshy, the land suitable only for the grazing of sheep or cattle, and there were no houses in the flatness of the peat meadows. A brisk wind picked up, and Edward noted with some worry that the clouds to the west now covered half the sky and there was a definite chill in the air.

"Don't concern yourself, *chérie*," Carolle said, noting his bemused attention to the sky. "A drop of rain will not melt me."

Petra cried out in excitement as a flurry of rain was carried on the wind, coming to them with half the sky cloudless and the sun fully visible. To her it was an adventure. Edward wrapped his wife in a carriage blanket. Nanny-Ruth, muttering, hid all but her nose in a coverlet and crouched down, although the flurry of rain was brief.

"It's a race between us and the storm," Darcie cried. She clucked the horses into a trot. The road was rutted, but it was reasonably dry. The carriage swayed only a bit more, and Edward said nothing. He wanted to get his wife in out of the weather before the storm, whose approach now seemed to be quickening, came upon them. There was a nice pub at Reedham where they could be cozy and comfortable until the rain ended, and then it was only a matter of minutes eastward along the river to the house.

Now, with startling swiftness the heavy, black clouds devoured the sky, and the clear areas to the east seemed to coalesce into heavy overcast. The rain came in a solid sheet, and, to the west, there was a clash of air masses, a long, rolling, booming thunder punctuated with flashes of spring lightning. The wind was strong. It blew the rain into horizontal, stinging slashes which caused Petra to cower down and obscured Darcie's vision. The mud of the road, already near saturation, allowed the water to run off quickly, but became quite slick underneath.

On the right there appeared out of the almost solid rain a deserted sheepcote, its thatched roof in disrepair, stone walls sturdy.

"Father," Darcie said, "we can take shelter there."

"No, no," Carolle said, knowing that she was the cause of their concern. "I am already thoroughly wet, and I have no desire to spend hours sitting in a musty shed in the middle of nowhere."

"We're less than a mile from the inn," Edward said. "I suppose we may as well press on."

In her concern for her mother, Darcie decided to quicken the pace. She flicked the whip over the haunches of the blacks, and they leaned into their harness, breaking into a run before Edward could shout a warning. A blaze of lightning crashed immediately overhead, and there was a tremendous clap of thunder. The terrified horses bolted, tossing their heads against Darcie's strong pull on the reins.

"Stop them!" Edward cried, trying to reach over the seat to grab the reins. Nanny-Ruth screamed as she struggled to retain her seat on the bouncing cushions. Carolle, white-faced, clung to the side of the carriage to prevent being thrown out as the wheels careered wildly in and out of the deep ruts and slid on the slick mud.

It happened with a suddenness which gave Darcie no time to be frightened or to scream out. The wheels slid. The carriage fishtailed toward the ditch along the road. The left rear wheel went off the narrow road, sunk to its hub in the mud of the ditch, putting a tremendous drag on the vehicle. The axle snapped at about the same time the trappings parted, freeing the horses and leaving the carriage to tilt wildly and then pitch onto its side.

Petra felt herself flying through the air, and, for a moment, was suspended before she hit the soft ground alongside the road, rolled, and came to her feet crying out in fear. Darcie was pitched forward over the broken tongue. As she flew through the air, she had a clear view, which, although instantaneous, was graven on her memory, of the horses, trailing their harnesses, galloping away down the road. Then she hit the mud of the road on her shoulder and rolled like a tumbler. She, too, was unhurt.

When Edward felt the carriage begin to go, he put his arms around Carolle, as if to protect her, and braced himself with his feet on the forward slope of the carriage. With a shrill cry, Nanny-Ruth was tossed forward, her head striking the front of the carriage with great force. Then Edward was tumbling, holding onto Carolle. He had the presence of mind to twist himself in the air and landed on the ground with a thump that forced all the air from his lungs and left him gasping for long moments before he could get his wind. His first thought was for Carolle, who lay limply atop him, the rain beating down. Now the wind and forceful falling rain were the only sounds until Petra cried out, *"Maman!"*

"My dear, my dear!" Edward gasped. "Are you hurt?"

She was silent. He shook his head to dispel his diz-

ziness and gently pushed her off him, to lie on her back
in the oozing mud, her face pale, her breathing shallow. At least, thank God, she was alive!

Darcie was at his shoulder as he knelt over Carolle.
She was weeping wildly.

"I'm sorry!" she wailed. "Oh, *maman*, I'm so sorry.
Are you all right?"

"She's alive," Edward said. "See to Nanny-Ruth."

Darcie was reluctant to leave the side of her mother,
but she forced herself to move. Nanny-Ruth, her long
skirts askew to show skinny shanks in long stockings,
was trapped under the overturned carriage. There was
a great deal of blood. Her pale old hair was soaked in
the dark, sticky mess, and the falling rain spread it over
the mud of the ditch in shocking profusion. Even as
Darcie leaned down, Nanny-Ruth made a horrible
sound in her throat, jerked convulsively, and died.

Darcie had never seen anyone die. Her one experience with death was attending the funeral of her grandfather, and he had looked almost natural lying in his
casket—not at all horrid and bloody like Nanny-Ruth.

She would never forget the sound, nor the senseless
convulsions which took the old woman's body in those
last seconds.

"Nanny!" she screamed, "Oh, Nanny!"

"Petra," her father was calling. "Petra!"

"Here," Petra cried, from the roadside where she'd
been tossed by the force of the overturning carriage.
"I'm all right."

"She's dead!" Darcie shrieked, and for a moment she
was helpless as hysteria overtook her. It seemed ages,
during which she could only scream senselessly before
her father's voice penetrated the horror.

"Darcie, come here!" he was saying over and over,
forcefully, as thunder rumbled and lightning flashed
and the rain pounded down to spread the ghastly red-
ness from Nanny-Ruth's crushed skull.

She crawled to him, making little mewling sounds in her throat.

"Darcie! Calm yourself!" he ordered. "We must get your mother to shelter."

"Yes, yes," Darcie said, but she was unable to do anything but dig her fingers into the soft, chill mud.

"See to Petra," Edward ordered, standing, picking Carolle up in his arms.

The sheepcote was a few yards back down the road. Although it was in disrepair, it would offer some shelter.

"Get Petra!" Edward yelled at Darcie, still on her hands and knees in the mud. "I'll come back and see to Nanny-Ruth later."

"Darcie, are you all right?" Petra asked, coming up, wading through the now-water-filled ditch to slip and slide up the bank to her sister. "Darcie, please, speak to me."

Darcie wailed. Petra took her arm and lifted her to her feet, seeing her father through the dense rain as he made his way back in the direction of the shed.

Darcie would never remember the walk in the rain down the muddy, rutted road. She allowed Petra to lead her, slipping once to fall heavily in the mud. Then she was inside, out of the rain, and Petra lowered her into a sitting position, her back against a cold stone wall. There was a barnyard smell; old, rotting straw, damp, ancient sheep dung.

Edward placed Carolle down on the cleanest portion of straw. She was still breathing shallowly, her eyes closed. He massaged her hands between his, speaking to her softly, pleadingly.

The shock began to hit Petra. Her limbs seemed to have minds of their own and trembled violently. To halt them, she stood, leaned down over her mother.

"Is she hurt badly?" she asked, the words coming from between teeth which chattered as if with cold.

"Pray God she is not," Edward said. "Petra, we must have help. Do you think you could go—alone—to the inn at Reedham?"

"Yes, father," Petra said, dreading being alone in the storm which still raged, with heavy thunder directly overhead, but knowing the necessity. "I will go."

"Tell them to bring a closed carriage, dry blankets, some brandy," Edward said. He kissed her on the cheek. "That's my brave girl. It's only a short distance."

Petra ran out into the rain, her tremblings lessening in the face of necessity. The road was now covered with water which stood in puddles, deeper in the ruts, and her feet slipped, causing her to fall once or twice; but she ran on, panting, remembering that she had heard Darcie cry out that Nanny-Ruth was dead, and praying for the health of her mother.

In the shed, Carolle opened her eyes, flickeringly, doubtfully.

"Oh, my dear," Edward said.

"Darcie, Petra," Carolle said weakly.

"They're unhurt, thanks be to God."

"And Nanny-Ruth?"

Edward paused for a moment. Carolle was beginning to shiver uncontrollably. He decided that she must not be exposed to the shock of Nanny-Ruth's death.

"Nanny-Ruth and Petra have gone into Reedham for help," he said.

Carolle closed her eyes, shivering. Suddenly a convulsion took her with a force which caused her to cry out. She tried to draw her legs up. Edward clung to her hands, saying, "There, there, my dear."

She collapsed after the convulsion.

"Darcie," Edward said, "go to the carriage and get wraps." Meantime, he removed his light coat and spread it over his wife. "Darcie," he said, louder, turning his head to see Darcie, sitting as if paralyzed, against the stone wall.

"Come on, girl!" he said roughly, as Carolle began to shiver violently again. "Get me the blankets from the carriage."

Darcie nodded, but made no move. Carolle moaned, and her body heaved with another contraction. Edward, helpless, terrified, knowing that the accident had thrown Carolle into premature labor, leaped to slap Darcie sharply on the cheek. Her head jerked. Awareness came into her eyes.

"I need your help, girl. Go to the carriage and get me the blankets."

"They are wet," she said in a dull voice.

"Go! Don't question me!" He jerked her to her feet and thrust her roughly out into the driving rain.

Galvanized into action, Darcie ran to the overturned carriage. She put her hand over her mouth and moaned aloud as she saw Nanny-Ruth, her face now half-covered by a puddle of water made wine-colored by her blood. She tugged on the wet blankets, one of which was caught under the overturned vehicle, and, in desperation, gathered the sodden mass in her arms and ran weeping back to the shed.

Edward spread one of the blankets on the sodden mass of straw and sheep dung, placed Carolle tenderly on it, and covered her with the other wet wrap. She was pale. Pain caused her to bite her lower lip between her even white teeth.

"Our son!" she gasped. "Oh, our son!"

"Calm yourself," Edward said. "Help will be here soon. We'll have dry wraps for you. We'll make you warm, and there will be a covered carriage to take you to the inn."

"Our son," Carolle repeated hopelessly, as a massive pain convulsed her.

"*Maman! Maman!*" Darcie cried, trying to throw herself down to embrace her mother. Edward pushed her aside.

"Darcie," he said, "you must control yourself."

"Oh, God, I've killed her!" Darcie cried.

"Quiet!" Edward said forcefully. "Now listen to me. The baby is coming, and we may have to deliver the child before your sister arrives with help. If that is the case, I want you to do exactly as you're told and to keep quiet. Do you understand?"

"Oh, God!" Darcie sobbed. "Oh, God help us!"

Carolle's body jerked with a new convulsion and there was a soft, plopping sound followed by a gush of water. Carolle screamed. It sent a chill of dread through Edward, for throughout the deliveries of both Darcie and Petra, Carolle had been a tower of strength, grunting with effort, but never screaming out. Edward threw back the wet, sodden blanket which covered her. Her skirts showed a new wetness, and, as he uncovered her, there was blood.

"Darcie," he said, desperation in his voice. "Quickly—remove your petticoat and tear it into strips."

Darcie stood as if stricken.

"Quickly, quickly!" he ordered.

Darcie moved, her limbs shaking, her eyes seeing more blood, her mother's garments now reeking with it. She managed to remove her petticoat, but try as she might, she could not rip the sturdy cloth. Disgustedly, her father jerked it from her hands, having bared Carolle to see a steady ooze of blood. He pressed the white cloth to her, trying to stanch the flow, as she screamed once, twice, as a new convulsion took her and a gush of blood wet the petticoat. In her extreme pain, Carolle flung her hands outward, once of them contacting the rough stone wall, leaving lacerations on her knuckles.

"Hold her hands," Edward ordered. "Hold them tightly!"

Seeing the flow of blood which saturated her petticoat, smelling it, rank and rich over the odors of the sheepcote, Darcie felt blackness closing in.

"Move, Darcie, quickly!" Edward said, as Carolle began to flail her arms in her desperate pain.

The blackness came up slowly, even as Darcie took the first step. Then it was all-encompassing, and she was falling, knowing that she was falling, but unable to stop herself as she pitched, face first, crumpling, into the rank covering of the cote floor.

She awoke to the sound of screaming and tried to crawl away from it. Instead, she had a view of her father's hands. There was something horrid, bloody, shapeless, protruding from her mother's lower body. She retched and lost her stomach.

"Now, again," Edward was saying. "Once more, my darling, and it will be ended."

With a sobbing, shuddering scream, Carolle pushed. Her scream trailed off as Edward's hands worked. The scene was like something out of the most terrible nightmare for Darcie; blood, the screams of dire pain, the odors, the chill, the wetness, the continuing boom of thunder.

Then, in silence, it was over. Darcie crawled to pull herself into a sitting position against the wall, and saw her father looking sadly down at a pathetic mass of bloody flesh in his hands.

"A son," he said. "A son."

The baby had come breech, three months prematurely. He watched it struggle for breath, after he held the tiny thing by its heels and slapped the soft bottom gently. And he watched it die. Then his attentions were for Carolle. The bleeding was severe and he was helpless to do anything but press the sodden petticoat against her.

Petra, arriving, breathless at the inn, was fortunate to find the village midwife, wife of the innkeeper. The capable, buxom woman was gathering her wraps and umbrella before Petra could gasp out her complete story; and the innkeeper was running for the stables to hitch a team of horses to a carriage. The rain was beginning to taper off when they reached the cote, and Petra was first out of the carriage, running into the shed to find her father kneeling over her mother, his hands pressed against the lower part of her body.

Meg Whiting, the midwife, had delivered children in the countryside for thirty years and she'd seen most of the complications which can result from childbirth. She came in, heavy skirts wetted by the rain, her kit in hand, and took in the situation at a glance.

"The baby," Edward said. "Look at the baby."

"Sir," Meg said, "the baby is dead. Now you just move aside and let me see to the poor lady."

Edward, his hands red with blood, stood. He saw Petra. "Oh, Petra," he said.

"And get the children out of here, if you please," Meg ordered, as her husband entered, carrying blankets wrapped in a waterproof.

"I killed her!" Darcie sobbed, as she was lifted to her feet by her father, his hands leaving red marks on her arms. "Oh, God in heaven, I killed her!"

"Come, come," Edward said gently, knowing only a stifling sadness. He stood with them in the rain, light now, with his arm around a shoulder of each. "It was not your fault, but mine," he said. "And your mother is not dead."

"She'll be all right, Darcie," Petra said. "You'll see."

But she was not all right. She lived to make the ride to the village, with Meg Whiting doing her best, using all the skills developed over a quarter of a century of delivering children. She lived to know the comfort of a dry bed, of clean sheets—but the cozy warmth of the room in the inn never penetrated the chill she felt. She died peacefully, falling into a deep sleep from which she did not waken.

"My daughters," Edward said, his head bowed, his face wet with his tears. "God has seen fit to take her from us."

Darcie could not cry. She had wept until her eyes were swollen and red, but now she could not cry. She remembered the frantic moment when she realized that the carriage was going to overturn, and she remembered Nanny-Ruth, skull crushed, blood seeping into the mud and most of all she remembered the smells, the screams, the horrid thing which protruded from her mother's stomach, killing her before her very eyes. And she knew that it was all her fault, that if it had been James or her father at the reins, the horses would not have bolted. She did not want to live, but she could not, although she tried, through a long and sleepless night, die.

The morning brought the perfect June weather to which the whole family only short hours before, had looked forward to, but now all the gay plans were forgotten.

Nanny-Ruth and Carolle Moncrief were buried, side by side, in a small country churchyard. The surviving three members of the Moncrief family left the staff to close the country house. The trip home to London was a sad one. Petra tried to limit her mourning in her concern for Darcie, who, it seemed, threatened to withdraw from the cruel world. Nothing that Petra did was successful in getting more than a monosyllabic answer from Darcie. She curled into a ball of misery in the corner of the compartment, dead eyes watching unseeingly as the once-exciting countryside flashed past the window.

2

IT WAS A troubled Edward Moncrief who joined his younger daughter at table for the evening meal after Dr. Pettigrew's visit. Petra, although red-eyed from weeping, looked well. She wore a rather formal little gown, having dressed for dinner as she would have had her mother been alive to direct her.

"Petra," Edward said, "Dr. Pettigrew thinks it would be wise for us to go ahead with our plans to attend the canal opening."

"I think *maman* would have wanted us to go," Petra said with a maturity which pleased and surprised Edward.

"And Darcie?"

"Poor Darcie," Petra sighed.

"The doctor thinks change would be beneficial to her."

"I don't see how it could harm her," Petra said, "for I fear daily that she will succeed in willing herself to die."

"Yes," Edward said. "There is that. Would you fetch her, please?"

Darcie was in her room, staring blankly at the

closed draperies over her windows. She merely nodded
when Petra said that father wanted to speak with her,
but she followed her younger sister into the parlor.

"Petra and I were thinking of going on with the plan
to go to Egypt," Edward said. "Would you like that?"

"If it pleases you," Darcie said, with total lack of
interest.

"Good, that's settled, then," Edward said, with false
enthusiasm. "Now, there are many things to consider.
First, both of you will need a new wardrobe. I will ask
Adrienne to take you shopping."

"But we must wear mourning," Petra said.

"I have been thinking about that, too," Edward said.
"I, of course, wish to observe the proprieties, but I'm
sure that your mother would not wish you, two handsome young girls, to go off on such an exciting venture
in the weeds of mourning. We shall, then, take a sab-
batical from mourning and, upon our return, resume
it to honor the memory of your mother." He smiled.
"Although black becomes you—both of you—and especially my little dark one with the flashing black eyes."

In the past, such flattery would have roused a blush
and a shy smile in Darcie. As it was, she merely cast
down her eyes and said nothing.

In the following days, Adrienne, once Carolle's personal maid, took the two girls to Harrods, where a
punctilious lady instructed them, sometimes in a severe
voice, on what to wear on a visit to Egypt. She had no
patience with Darcie's phlegmatic acceptance of all her
suggestions. But Petra, excited by the experience of being fitted out for the trip, chattered endlessly about the
various choices. In fact, the lady needled Darcie into
taking some interest, to the point of making some se-
lections herself.

They returned home, after several forays, with
travel frocks and frocks suitable for dining at the captain's table, with ball gowns and light colored, sturdy
skirts for, as the lady at Harrods said, puttering about

in the desert, with lightweight underthings and light wraps for the chill November mornings.

Meanwhile, Edward booked passage on a Cunard liner and set his business affairs in order. There was the matter of engaging a governess; for in the period of mourning he had not found the interest to accomplish the task of replacing Nanny-Ruth. However, after discussing the matter with an interested Petra and a glum Darcie, it was decided to take Adrienne, rather than risk the last-minute gamble of hiring a stranger. The girls knew and liked Adrienne, who had been almost as devastated by her mistress's death as the family.

Adrienne, from a village near the country home of Carolle's father, spoke excellent English. She was short and a trifle stout, being overly fond of sweets. But she had a pleasant disposition, a kind and pretty face and was not too old, at twenty-five, to have forgotten what it was to be a girl the age of Darcie or Petra. When she was informed of the trip, she was ecstatic, and insisted on thanking Monsieur Moncrief in two languages and a bit of a third—the happy tears of a woman.

And so it was decided. Adrienne shared a stateroom with the girls. Edward, having decided to rough it, without benefit of a manservant, had a stateroom of his own, directly next to the one occupied by the women. The trip was timed to put them in Alexandria in early November, with the dedication and formal opening of the canal scheduled for mid-November. There would be time for sightseeing before the trip overland from Cairo to Port Saïd. The voyage was uneventful and rewarding, for slowly, gradually, Darcie began to come out of her retreat and, after an initial bout with *mal de mer,* shared with both Petra and Adrienne, found her appetite. Before the ship docked at Alexandria, Darcie had recovered to the extent of taking delight in the whispered gossip which went around the ship about the tragic young English girl who carried such a heavy load of sorrow.

She did present an appearance worthy of comment, with her dark-circled eyes, her melancholy expression, her somber quietness.

During the last days of the voyage, as the ship sailed into the balmy Mediterranean, Darcie spent much time on deck. Finding her there one day, standing in the bright sun, her face moody, her eyes downcast to watch the swirling water along the side of the ship, Petra stood slightly behind her and considered the situation.

"Ah, la dame aux camélias, n'est-ce pas?" she asked in a soft voice, referring to the tragic heroine of the Dumas *fils* play, which had been read to them by their mother.

Darcie turned, her face forming a frown. Then, seeing the sunny face of her sister, wreathed in smiles, she lightened. The giggle which escaped her, as she imagined herself being the tragic lady, was an outward sign of the beginning of her return to normal. Alexandria did the rest, the very strangeness of the city lifting her out of herself to become, once again, the leader, the instigator, the eternally curious girl who had a thousand and one questions.

3

EDWARD MONCRIEF WAS a methodical man. He had prepared himself for Egypt by reading and studying everything written on the subject onto which he could lay his hands. As the ship approached the low coast, he was able to point out to his daughters the landmarks, the Pharos lighthouse, Pompey's Pillar, Forts Napoleon and Cafferelli.

And then they were in Egypt, amid antiquated windmills, the white palace of Ras-el-Teen, minarets and factory chimneys, clumps of feathery palms and, in the vast harbor, a forest of ships' masts and funnels.

"Napoleon loved this city," Edward told them, as they awaited the time to go ashore. "He said that Alexander the Great rendered himself more illustrious by founding Alexandria, and in proposing to transfer to it the seat of his empire, than by his most brilliant victories. The Little Emperor thought that this city should be the capital of the world, situated between Asia and Africa as it is, within reach of Europe, and, with the canal, now within reach of India. It's the only safe natural harbor in five hundred miles of coastline.

All the navies of the world could find safe harbor
here."

So it was Egypt, if not the Egypt of the pharaohs.
There were older cities in Egypt, but Alexandria was
over a thousand years old before the first brick was
laid in Cairo, and it sported a few ancient ruins worthy
of attention. However, the time spent there was to be
limited. Edward led them on a whirlwind tour, explaining that Pompey's Pillar, a Corinthian column of
red granite rising 99 feet into the air, had nothing to
do with Pompey, but was erected in honor of Diocle-
tian's capture of the city in A.D. 296. Cleopatra's Nee-
dles, which had nothing to do with Cleopatra, had
been looted by Julius Caesar from the ancient city of
Heliopolis, which they would visit, to adorn his own
temple, the Caesarium.

The quick tour began and ended in the same day,
after the family and Adrienne had been whisked away
from the customshouse at breakneck speed in a handsome hackney carriage. Actually, being in Alexandria,
aside from the unseasonable weather, the sapphire sky,
the palm trees along the squares, was much like being
in a French town until, by request from Edward, the
driver took them into the narrow and dirty alleys of
the old native quarter. There they encountered a mot-
ley crowd of turbaned Arabs, jet-black Nubians, and
many races of Europeans in a noisy confusion which
made Petra feel slightly ill at ease and happy to leave
the noise and the throngs for the quiet comfort of a
splendid hotel.

They boarded the morning express to Cairo. The
train picked up speed slowly, passing the village of
Ramleh, rich-looking cultivated land, and then ran past
the eastern shallows of a lake which Edward informed
them was named Mareotis. Water birds rose in dense
white clouds as the train passed marshy areas and
then the track led through a flat expanse of farmlands

dotted by clusters of mud huts and their sheltering clumps of palm trees.

Darcie was intrigued by the little whitewashed cupolas and dumpy minarets, and she was informed, tongue in cheek, that such things were dovecotes, raised to allow the collection of pigeon dung for fertilizer.

"Ugh!" Darcie said, and fell silent for a while—but only for a while. Petra looked at her father and smiled. He winked to show his pleasure at Darcie's new happiness.

The train passed two stations rapidly and then stopped at Damanhour, just thirty-eight miles out of Alexandria. Petra was disappointed by her first view of the famous Nile, until she learned that it was only the Rosetta branch which was crossed to enter the Nile delta. Then, at Benha junction, the train eased over a bridge crossing the Damietta branch and Petra was thoroughly confused, having always thought of the Nile as one huge river.

Before reaching Cairo, there was a view of the eastern desert which stretched away in the direction of the new canal. By far the most exciting view was offered when the giant pyramids came into view, looming against the western horizon, looking disappointingly small until the girls were told that they were a full fifteen or twenty miles away. The pyramids became more solid, more massive, as the train moved on toward them, and then Edward was pointing out the Mokattem hills, on which sat the famous Citadel and the tapering minarets of Mehemet Ali's mosque. A few minutes later the train, slowing, passed one lonely obelisk, which marked the location of ancient Heliopolis, and then continued to slow through a suburban expanse of handsome villas and luxuriant gardens.

Now each hour was filled with wonderful new sights, sounds, smells. It was all so wonderful, so exotic, that both Darcie and Petra were nearly overwhelmed, and would, forever after, carry a collage of impressions; here a file of tall camels laden with merchandise, stalking deliberately, solemnly, step by step through crowded bazaars; a grand native gentleman in all the pride of colorful turban and flowing robes, seated with great dignity on the back of a small donkey; ladies on donkeys, swathed in black garments and white veils. This black *babara* and white veils seemed to be the universal outdoor costume for Egyptian women, and there was visible only two dark eyes, eyes which gleamed out from behind the shroud of the veil. Carriages had the familiarity of home, but they were driven by men in oriental dress and were invariably preceded by a bare-legged Arab who ran ahead shouting to pedestrians to get out of the way. The cries of these *avant-couriers* seemed to fill the streets, ringing forth from every side.

"It would seem," Edward remarked with good humor, "that it would be unhealthy to try to walk the streets, lest one be run over by some cantering donkey or knocked down by a camel."

The railway station was bedlam. There were Greeks, Arabs, soft-featured Syrians. The crowd seemed to ferment before them, men, women, scampering children in a variety of costume and, in the case of some of the children, no costume at all. This last caused both Petra and Darcie to giggle uncontrollably until their father reminded them that they were, after all, proper English young ladies.

Sellers of bread and water and trinkets converged on the party. Ghostly-looking women, determined to be such only by their flashing dark eyes peering out from behind the veils and by their flashing bare feet, flitted in and out of the crowd as if in frantic search. Solemn Turks eyed the two unveiled young girls. Crafty-looking Jews beseeched them to enter tiny shops. A group of recruits for the khedive's army was marched up the platform, Abyssinians, huge, brawny fellows with powerful arms in white tunics, bare black legs, chubby faces and dark, lustrous eyes. A group of Cook's tourists were led away by a guide.

There were kaleidoscopic impressions of olive skin, bronzed skin, black skin. Streets filled with common people, the fellaheen, men short, children thin of limb, bellies distended. The atmosphere was balmy, the sky sapphire, palm trees, dirty alleys, wealth, and utter squalor.

Around the terminal itself a new town was taking shape, with well-laid-out streets and handsome European-type houses and shops. But in the older city, the streets were labyrinthine, dark, dirty, with branching, intricate lanes so narrow that two donkeys could scarcely pass abreast.

They saw it all from the headquarters of Shepheard's Hotel, leaving the hotel after a brief rest to be plunged into the narrow streets with the upper stories of the buildings, seemingly in danger of toppling, closing out all but a narrow slit of cloudless sky.

Among the women, there seemed to be only young and very old. Lower-class women wore blue and carried water jugs on their heads, the long garment revealing the shapely limbs of the young, the deformities of the older women. Black slaves on tall camels wore only white napkins around head and loins. Portly merchants rode donkeys, heads encased in turbans, mouths filled by long pipes. Once a splendid Arab on a shining steed dashed through the crowded streets, not quite at full gallop, scattering pedestrians helter-skelter.

With a guide who spoke English, the Moncriefs spent the first full day exploring the areas nearby the hotel, saw a procession, which the guide explained was a circumcision celebration, moving along, oozing in and out of the crowd to the accompaniment of music which, Edward allowed, would madden a drummer.

Shepheard's Hotel was located on the western side of a park which was a part of an improvement program begun by Mehemet Ali and continued by his

successors. Work was accelerated now, with the canal
completed, and Egypt about to take its place along
modern nations in importance.

Shepheard's Hotel was, of course, filled to overflow-
ing, and it was lucky that de Lesseps himself had made
reservations for the Moncrief party. As it was, once
again Darcie and Petra had to share a small suite of
rooms with Adrienne. The lobby and the dining rooms
were filled with beautiful cosmopolitan people attracted
to the city by the historic event. The excitement of the
canal opening, added to the regular season, which extended from October to April to take advantage of
Cairo's wonderful winter weather, brought people from
all over the world, especially Europe and the United
States. The girls were enthralled by the variety of languages and accents. All over the city there was celebration. Musical cafés offered European bands playing
Strauss and Wagner, native artists performing on weird
and wonderful instruments with even stranger names,
names which made Petra giggle as she tried to pro-
nounce *cka'noon,* or *'oo'd,* or *kemen'geh.*

Shopping was a dizzying pleasure as the merchants of
hundreds of kiosks and booths clamored for their attentions and their money. Petra bought a cunningly carved
ivory box. Darcie purchased a shawl from Persia and
a half dozen ostrich feathers from the Sudan, which she
promptly used to tickle Petra under the chin until Petra
howled with laughter.

Adrienne flirted shamelessly with a handsome French
naval officer, and the new and lively Darcie, having
turned fifteen on October fifth last, dressed in Harrod's
best for young ladies visiting in Egypt, was not unnoticed by young European men who pushed arrogantly
through the crowded streets.

All in all, it was one of the loveliest times in Petra's
life, and she frolicked through the first two full days
in Cairo pausing only now and then to remember that
her mother, bless her memory, would have loved it so.

So, in those cloudless skies, in the balmy temperatures so unlike England in November, there were few moments of sadness. Now and then she'd surprise her father with a faraway look in his eye and once she said, "You were thinking about *maman,* weren't you?"

He smiled a sad little smile. "Lord, how she would have loved it," he said. "And have you noticed, my little Petra, how much your sister resembles her mother?"

Indeed, Petra had, for in the past few months, even the past few weeks, it seemed, Darcie had blossomed. The dark circles had disappeared from under her eyes. There was the usual little smile always ready to beam forth from her full and womanly lips. In her new costumes, her breasts seemed to be emphasized, and her hips spread out from her tiny waist in quite a grown-up manner. She concluded that Petra could never hope to be so feminine, so beautiful. She felt very much the little girl, although her physical size matched Darcie's and she showed signs of growing to be larger and more plush than her tiny sister.

Guy Simel, Carolle's brother, uncle to Darcie and Petra, had sent word from Suez that he would be in Cairo at a given time, and this was an added treat for the girls, for they were very fond of their uncle. When last they saw him, Guy was a fun-loving lad of sixteen, and Darcie was almost six. Petra, who had been only four, remembered Guy as a tall god who invariably caused her to giggle as he hoisted her high into the air.

After a full day of sightseeing, Edward was napping. Darcie and Petra, still too exhilarated to nap, were being prepared for a big evening, during which they would dine in the hotel, go to the opera, and then take a carriage to the house occupied by Monsieur de Lesseps. This prospect excited them more than ever, for it would give Darcie opportunity to wear her first grown-up ball gown and would mark Petra's first appearance at a party which was strictly for adults.

Their room overlooked the street and had a small

balcony from which there was a beautiful view. Throughout the early evening, as Adrienne helped them prepare for the big night, the girls were unable to resist the view of the streets and the park offered by the balcony. Having finished her bath, Petra, in petticoats and wrapper, was leaning on the railing of the balcony when Darcie came up behind her.

"Petra, you must sit down so that Adrienne can finish your hair," Darcie said. "Please do it now." She stepped onto the balcony.

Petra tore herself away and went into the suite. The sun was low, sunken behind the city, and there was a delightful freshness in the evening air. Now and then some exotic smell would flavor the atmosphere, but far from being squeamish, Darcie found herself to be fascinated by the alien aspects of the city. She existed in a state of exhilaration and looked forward to so many things. She felt quite grown up, because she and Petra would accompany their father to the opening night of a new opera house built especially for the inaugural celebrations of the Suez Canal. The famous composer, Verdi, had been commissioned to write an opera for the occasion, but, her father had learned, it was still unfinished, so the first performance was to be *Rigoletto*.

Dinner, then the opera, and then a visit to the villa of her father's friend and business associate, Monsieur de Lesseps himself. It all made her feel so important.

Of late, her father had been treating her with a new respect, almost as if she were fully adult. For example, only that day they had discussed the issue of slavery in Egypt. Darcie expressed shock that it still existed. Her father explained that slavery in Egypt was not the same as that vile institution which had sent African Negroes in the holds of stinking slave ships to the new world to die of fevers in the Caribbean islands and the Americas. According to her father, there were different degrees of slavery in the Arab world, including, he delicately reported, a form of slavery involving European woman. However, almost invariably, a European woman, one of the most valuable of properties, was treated with great consideration and quite often was married to a son of the family which purchased her. True, the black slaves were lowly creatures and suffered the highest death rate in Egypt, but even they were valued properties and treated with consideration and, often, became freedmen.

There was so much to learn, so much food for thought. In a mood of seriousness, Darcie leaned on the rail of the balcony, toes extended over the edge, chin resting on her hands, elbows on the railing. To people who passed on the street below, she gave an appearance of contrast, entrancingly beautiful, still possessed of a childlike innocence, but provocative as she leaned forward to watch the comings and goings at the hotel entrance.

As Darcie watched and Petra called out from inside to demand a running account of what was happening outside, a hackney stopped in front of the steps leading to the terrace. Several European men in distinguished dress descended from the carriage. Two were tall—one an older man with a serious, strong face and straight sandy hair. It was the other tall stranger who caught her eye. He was dressed impeccably in evening clothes and was, by far, the most handsome man she'd ever seen. Darcie turned to call Petra to witness this paragon of manly beauty, but realized that by turning she would have to take her eyes off of the gentleman. She watched, holding her breath, as he led the way, with springing steps, up toward the entrance. A flush lighted her face as, pausing, he turned his face upward and saw her. A pleasant smile greeted her. He doffed his hat to her and she looked into his eyes. He let his eyes linger on her youthful beauty, and she felt her breath leave her as if from a blow to the body. Transfixed, as he seemed to be, they gazed into each other's eyes for

long seconds until, the other tall man having come
abreast, the man reluctantly lowered his eyes and continued toward the entrance.

There was in Darcie a mixture of pleasure and something almost akin to fright as she ducked into the suite.
Petra's hair had been done, and she was twirling gaily
in front of the mirror, making the skirts of her long
gown flare out.

Darcie could not erase the memory of those dark,
flashing eyes, the grace with which the tall, slim, handsome man lifted his hat to her. Musingly, she allowed
Adrienne to arrange her jet-black hair and help her
into her ball gown. In dazzling white, her darkness
was accentuated, and the virginal effect of the gown
was lessened by her mother's ruby brooch, hanging in
red fire just above the point where a quite respectable
decolletage revealed her smooth skin.

Soon there came a knock on the door. Edward, in
evening dress, greeted his daughters with fondness, sincere compliments, and no little surprise in Darcie's
case. Suddenly, she was no longer his little girl but a
dazzling young lady of considerable beauty. For a
moment, his heart ached as he noted her resemblance
to a younger Carolle. Then a glad smile came as he
escorted them, one on each arm, into the dining room,
where, he promised, there would be a surprise.

At the moment of their entry into the dining room,
the band reached the end of a waltz and there was silence, save for the low hum of conversation. Directly
in front of them, a dark-skinned waiter dropped a tray,
causing a loud crash, and all eyes turned, to remain
glued on the trio of handsome Englishman, beautiful
young lady, and pretty child.

"They're all looking at us," Petra whispered.

"I fear," Edward said, casting a sidelong glance at
his Darcie, "that is a condition to which you will have
to become accustomed."

He led the way, following a bowing waiter, toward

a table in a good location. Looking ahead, Darcie felt her pulse begin to pound. There, at a table by himself, was the handsome man of the evening—the one who had tipped his hat to her. She tried to keep her eyes off him, but was not successful, for their path led directly toward his table. And now—oh, God!—he was looking at them, his eyes flicking from Edward's face to Darcie's and back again, a puzzled expression on his face. Then he was leaping to his feet. Edward was beaming and extending his hand.

"This is your surprise," Edward said. "Your Uncle Guy."

"Lord," Guy Simel said, his eyes locked on Darcie, "this can't be little Darcie."

"And Petra," Petra said, dancing about in her excitement.

"Darcie?" Guy asked, smiling, revealing even white teeth in a face of Latin darkness like the faces of his dead sister and his niece Darcie. "Can it be Darcie?"

"And Petra, Uncle Guy," Petra said, thrusting herself between them.

"And Petra," Guy laughed. "My, my, how you've grown. Shall I pick you up and twirl you 'round over my head?"

"You may kiss me on the cheek," Petra said, coquettishly, presenting her face. But, as Guy leaned, she seized him around the neck and hugged him tightly, planting a wet, girlish kiss on his lips.

"That's my little Petra," Guy laughed. Then he was bending over Darcie's hand, all the French gentleman, kissing her hand and smiling up into her eyes. "Never had an uncle two more attractive nieces," he said.

Darcie was flustered. She felt quite guilty for having known such attraction, in a manner quite unfamiliar to her, for her own uncle, and she felt, in a way which she could not explain, as if she had been robbed of something. But then they were seated and talking excitedly, and Guy was telling fantastic stories about being present during the last two years of the canal's construction.

During the meal, the tall, older man who had been with Guy upon his arrival approached the table.

"It is my pleasure," Guy said, standing, "to present to you my mentor and my dear friend, Doctor Roger D'Art."

At thirty-two, Roger D'Art was not really an older man. He only seemed to be to Petra and Darcie, most probably because he assumed a seriousness beyond his years. He bowed politely.

"I have heard so much about you," he said. "About Darcie, who is, indeed, a lovely young lady. About Petra, equally lovely. And you, sir," he said, extending a hand to Edward. "For you, my condolences on your great tragedy, of which Monsieur Simel has told me."

"I thank you, sir," Edward said. "Won't you please join us for dessert and brandy?"

"No, no," D'Art said. "I must be off. I'm sure we'll see each other again. Monsieur de Lesseps speaks highly of you and has reserved a special place for you at the opening ceremonies."

"Doctor D'Art has been kind enough," Guy said, "to offer me a position in his practice when we return to Paris."

"A splendid opportunity, and well deserved," Edward said.

Both Petra and Darcie were allowed one small glass of wine to add to their feeling of being grown up. Then the meal was concluded, and Guy accompanied them to the opera, where they had been assigned a box of only slightly less splendor than the royal boxes and the box of de Lesseps.

Although Darcie knew and loved some of the music from *Rigoletto,* she was impatient. It seemed that the opera would never end. At intermissions, she found Guy close at her side, being solicitous and polite in a way which she had never been treated by a man before.

The villa occupied by Ferdinand de Lesseps had been built to house foreign dignitaries by the khedive and it was among the most splendid in Cairo, with fragrant gardens, spacious rooms, and a ballroom with a marble floor of unparalleled beauty. De Lesseps kissed Edward on both cheeks and greeted him warmly as the family went through the receiving line, and the great engineer had a kiss on the cheek, along with sincere compliments, for both girls.

When they were past, and the men had accepted wine from a magnificently dressed waiter, Edward said, "That is a moment to remember, my daughters. You can tell your grandchildern that you were once received by one of the great men of our time."

Guy laughed. "Oh, he is only human. Do you know that once, as a child, he tried to prove that a falling object accelerates in its fall by leaping from a high window?"

"Oh, no," Darcie said, trying to stop a girlish giggle.

"Broke his arm," Guy said.

"Uncle Guy, you're terrible," Petra said.

"Oh, I don't deny his greatness," Guy said, "but it is also wise to remember, lest he become too godlike for us normal men, that the canal was by no means his idea."

"He pushed the idea through to completion," Edward said.

"Yes, he did that," Guy admitted, "but many men, Napoleon among them, advocated a canal. Monsieur de Lesseps got his inspiration from the writings of Saint-Simon. As I say, I would not wish to detract from his achievement, but consider this: almost three thousand years ago, there was already a canal from the Red Sea to the Mediterranean."

"You must be joking," Darcie said, flushing with her impertinence.

"Not at all," Guy said. "In fact, the canal was in

use, off and on, until it was closed by the second Abbassid caliph to blockade the revolting cities of Mecca and Medina."

"Please tell us about it," Petra said.

"Around two thousand years before Christ," Guy said, "the pharoah Sesostris built a canal which connected the Pelusiac branch of the Nile to the port of Clysma on the Red Sea. Oh, it's quite well documented. Herodotus made the trip, and he wrote that transit from sea to sea took four days, and that the passage could be made by two triremes abreast. So you see, our grand canal is nothing new."

"Still," Edward said, "it is a great achievement."

"Of course. It will change the world," Guy said. "The world will never be the same."

"Would you excuse me for a moment?" Edward said, sighting an old business friend across the ballroom, which was beginning to fill as the band struck up a merry waltz. "Don't feel that you have to play nursemaid, Guy. The girls are quite grown up, and I'll rejoin them shortly, when I've spoken to Gladpay."

"My pleasure," Guy said, smiling at Darcie.

"Uncle Guy, was it very exciting, helping to build the canal?" Petra asked.

"Oh, quite so," Guy said. "And sometimes a deadly bore, having to treat the common laborers. Have you seen much of the city?"

"Not as much as we'd like," Darcie said. "We're going to the pyramids."

"I must warn your father to guard you carefully," Guy said. "Things are much improved, but there are still rogues and scoundrels about." He smiled. "Many a sheik would pay a heavy price in gold for such prizes as you."

"Oh, Uncle Guy!" Petra said. "You're joking."

"Not at all," he said, seriously. "Moreover, robbers teem in the streets. You must always go with a group or with a strong guide. And remember that the common Egyptians—the fellaheen—are nothing more than savages."

"They seem peaceful enough," Darcie said.

"Yes, but they are a strange people," Guy said. "Have you heard the expression 'stick logic'?"

"No," Darcie said.

"It has to do with collecting taxes," Guy said. "You are aware of the great antiquity of the Egyptian civilization?" The girls nodded as one. "Well, perhaps the fellah has more cause to dislike taxes, since he's been paying them, to one tyrant or the other, for thousands of years, but he's quite stubborn. When the tax collector comes around, he hides his money and his goods, and the only way to collect taxes is with a stick. The tax collectors literally beat the poor men, and a fellah is considered to be a great coward—a true poltroon— if he gives in after a mere dozen blows and brings out his hoard, when, by resisting, perhaps, fifty blows, he could have saved the lot."

"How terrible!" Petra said with true compassion.

"But they exist," Guy said, "and they'll continue to exist, just as they have under the pharoahs, the Romans, the Greeks, the Turks, the Arabs, the French. They are a strange people."

"Do tell us more," Darcie said.

"Well, I will shock you," Guy said, with a mischievous grin. "Do you know that the religious sect—the Copts—still practice circumcision?"

"Oh, yes," Petra said, "we saw a circumcision procession."

"Of a boy or a girl?" Guy asked, squinting his eyes with mock evil.

Darcie gasped. Petra said, with a giggle, "Uncle Guy, you are wicked."

"If you were Egyptian, you'd be married by now," Guy said to Petra, "for twelve is the age of marriage."

"I shall move to Egypt," Petra said, feeling very grown up and risqué, to be discussing such forbidden subjects with a man—even if he were her uncle.

"And with good reason," Guy said, "I am referring to the early marriage, for beauty lasts in Egyptian woman only until they reach their eighteenth or nineteenth year. After that, they wither rapidly, and a woman of thirty is a wrinkled and grotesque hag."

"How terrible," Darcie said.

"For this reason, having so few years of beauty," Guy said, looking ever so innocent, "the Egyptian woman is perhaps the most licentious of all females." He looked across the room. "But enough of that. Look yonder."

They followed his indication and saw M. de Lesseps and a stout man in his middle forties, with a strong jaw and clear, expressive eyes.

"That is the khedive," Guy said. "You are in the presence of royalty. Shall I arrange an introduction?"

"Oh, please do," Petra said. "I can hardly wait to tell everyone that I saw the king of Egypt."

It was accomplished, later in the evening, after Guy had danced with both Darcie and Petra. The khedive was a charming man, who complimented both of the young English misses and expressed his gratitude to Edward Moncrief for his help in making the English subscriptions of Suez stock successes.

It was a full evening, which grew late far too quickly. When it ended, Petra and Darcie had been allowed to be up and about longer than ever before, Darcie was feeling a terrible shame at the unwonted feelings engendered in her when she danced with her own uncle, and, although she was half-asleep during the carriage ride back to the hotel, Petra was in a heaven of happy bliss. Not every young English girl had been kissed by a king, and danced with the most handsome man at the ball—Guy, of course—and with the kindly and considerate Roger D'Art, who, although quite serious of mien, was an excellent dancer who treated Petra as if she were the grandest of ladies.

Guy left them in the lobby, telling them that he had to return to Suez in the morning, but that he would reserve them a proper suite for the stay in Suez and would see them when all of the grand company which was gathering in Cairo was transported to the new town for the opening ceremonies.

Then, pulling Edward aside, he said, "My dear brother-in-law, the girls have told me you plan considerable sightseeing. I feel that it is my duty to warn you that although the city gives the impression of being a civilized area, there is still an undercurrent of violence here. Please, as you go about, do not become isolated from others."

"I shall heed your warning with gratitude," Edward said, although he felt that Guy was being overly alarming.

4

In the past, a pilgrimage to the pyramids was a journey of no mean inconvenience. Until very recent times, the trip involved a ferry ride across the Nile and then seven or eight uncomfortable hours aboard pugnacious little donkeys. Now, however, as Egypt opened itself to the world, there was a temporary bridge across the Nile, and, on the other side, there was a comfortable carriage road.

During the first part of the trip, the streets were enlivened by the antics of street performers. The air filled with the calls of merchants from the hundreds of kiosks and booths. The Moncrief family and Adrienne crossed from Kash-en-nil to Ghizeh on the temporary bridge, near which was being constructed a modern iron bridge to make access to the ancient monuments even easier. On the far side of the Nile there was a paved, tree-lined drive leading up from the river through date palms, tamarisks, acacias, sycamores, and figs.

Nearing the pyramids, the huge structures dominating the landscape, they were assailed by dozens of half-naked Arabs, who swarmed around the carriage to offer their services as guides to and up the pyramids. Edward engaged the services of a clean-looking young lad who spoke broken English, but he needed no guide, for he had admired the pyramids from afar for years and was, with his excellent memory, a fount of information. As he stared in awe, he informed his daughters that once the old yellow limestone of the great structures had been covered with a dazzling white facade of pure white stone from the quarries of Tura. What a fantastic sight they must have been.

Their way led first to the largest and most impressive of the pyramids, the tomb of Khufu, or Cheops. There the two girls attempted to scale the huge pile of stone blocks, only to become a bit apprehensive as they climbed.

Most of the day was passed happily. Even from a low point on the pyramids the views were spectacular and utterly alien. From the northern pyramid they could look over the desert toward the distant and strange Blunted Pyramid, lost in a sea of sand and rock, so lonely.

It was possible, Edward found, to become quite melancholy and to remember the words of Shelley, writing of Ozymandias of Egypt:

"My name is Ozymandias, king of kings:
    Look on my works, ye Mighty, and despair!"
Nothing beside remains. Round the decay
Of that colossal wreck, boundless and bare
The lone and level sands stretch far away.

One felt small and insignificant, Edward thought, as he watched his daughters explore, walking through the sands of time which surrounded the monuments to ancient greatness.

Resting, eating the picnic lunch prepared in the hotel kitchen, he talked in a low voice of those who, from the dim beginnings of history, had preceded them in their pilgrimage. Greeks and Romans had come and gone. Millions of people, most of them long dead, had come to wonder, and, in a somewhat pathetic attempt to share the timelessness of the mighty structures, had covered the great pyramids with their carved names and initials. He told an entranced audience of three—Darcie, Petra and Adrienne—how a former circus strongman, Belzoni, had broken into the Second Pyramid in 1818 and not only chisled his name on the entrance, but wrote his name and the date inside the tomb in black paint.

"Caesar and Cleopatra saw them," he told the girls, "as they came up the Nile in the queen's barge. The historian Herodotus was here, as were Plato, Strabo, and Diodorus. And it seems that they all carved their names, although many of the older carvings have since eroded away." He laughed, remembering an amusing story he'd read in his preparation for coming to Egypt. "One of your mother's countrymen, the author François René de Chateaubriand, scorned ordinary tourism, and refused to make what was then a trying trip to the pyramids. Instead, he sent a servant to climb the great pyramid and carve the name Chateaubriand at the top."

A few hundred yards to the southeast of the Great Pyramid, Petra giggled when she faced one of the greater mysteries of Egypt, the enigmatic Sphinx. She listened as her father explained that the monument was in honor of a great pharaoh, Chephren, that the face was Chephren's, the pharaoh portrayed as a great and powerful lion, but she could not get over her amusement at the unworldly thing, half lion, half man.

"You mock the Sphinx?" Edward asked, with a fatherly smile.

"No, it's just that it's so—so—"

"Magnificent," Darcie said.

"Well," Petra agreed. "Yes, it is."

She giggled. "But he's lost his nose," she said.

"Unfortunately," Edward explained, "the entire

monument was carved from soft limestone, and the
elements have not been kind to it. In addition, men
have vandalized it. Some have said that it was Napoleon who knocked off the nose, but it is well recorded that the deed was done in 1496 by a religious
fanatic—a sheik who, in fact, tried to demolish the
Sphinx entirely."

"I'm glad he couldn't do it," Darcie said.

"I still think it's funny-looking," Petra insisted.

"Well, young lady, for you, then"—and he took one
of the books from his pocket—"I cite the historian
Kinglake."

> Upon ancient dynasties of Ethiopian and Egyptian
> kings, upon Greek and Roman, upon Arab and
> Ottoman conquerors, upon Napoleon dreaming of
> an Eastern empire, upon battle and pestilence,
> upon the ceaseless misery of the Egyptian race,
> upon keen-eyed travellers, Herodotus yesterday,
> Warburton today, upon all and more this un-
> worldly Sphinx has watched, and watched like a
> providence, with the same earnest eyes, and the
> same sad, tranquil mien. And we, we shall die,
> and Islam shall wither away; and the Englishman,
> straining far over to hold his loved India, will
> plant a firm foot on the banks of the Nile, and
> sit in the seats of the faithful; and still that shape-
> less rock will lie watching, and watching the
> works of the new, busy race, with those same sad,
> earnest eyes, and the same tranquil mien ever-
> lasting.

He leaned close and whispered, "You dare not mock
the Sphinx."

The long day ended, each of them a bit reddened
by the sun, all tired, all famished and doing great
things to a delicious dinner. Then there was a long and
refreshing night's sleep.

The morning was a ride through fine gardens along the Shoobra Road, with sycamores and acacias lining the way. On this, one of the favorite drives of visiting foreigners, they saw the Shoobra, favorite residence of Mehamet Ali, now owned by the current khedive. The gardens of the Shoobra were among the world's finest.

Now, in their continued quest for antiquity, the way led toward the ancient city of Heliopolis over a fine, newly constructed carriage road. Their regular guide having failed to show up that morning, Edward put his literary knowledge to work, along with a recently drawn map of the city, to act as his own guide. With the perfect weather continuing, they had leased an open victoria.

The eight-mile drive to Heliopolis took them down the Fajala past Abbasieh, the palace of Abbas Pasha, now a barracks and military school, then over a plain on which, Edward informed his audience, Sultan Aliem won all of Egypt in a furious battle in 1517 and where, in 1800, French forces under Kléber beat the Turks to make Cairo, at least temporarily, a French city.

They rested in the jessamine and orange gardens at Mataraeeh. There they paid tribute to the Virgin's Tree, where tradition said that Joseph and Mary sheltered during their flight into Egypt. Less than a mile farther, through a shady acanthus grove, they caught first sight of the lone granite obelisk which was said to be the oldest ancient ruin of the world. There was marked the site of the holy City of the Sun. There, in Heliopolis, Joseph took a wife, Moses studied the wisdom of Egypt, Jeremiah wrote his Lamentations, and Plato formed the doctrine of the immortality of the soul.

Although the pillar was estimated to be over four thousand years old, the hieroglyphics on its surface were sharp, and, had they been able to understand them, readable.

Once again, Edward had his facts ready. The pillar was sixty-two feet high and six feet in diameter at the base. It had been quarried from a single piece of stone over five hundred miles away at Aswan.

Nothing else remained of the ancient city, save the crumbled ruins of walls which served as boundaries for small fields of maize, clover, and cotton.

Not so much impressed by Heliopolis as they had been by the pyramids and the Sphinx, Darcie and Petra, accompanied by Adrienne, reentered the shady and pleasant acanthus grove to rest in the quietness of the fading afternoon while Edward checked his books and tried to make sense of the ruins. Weary, Darcie and Petra sat on the ground with their backs against trees. Adrienne stood, fanning herself with her hand.

Around them there was the total silence of the ages. No other tourists had chosen to visit the site that late in the day; no fellaheen worked in the nearby fields. Edward was walking away from them, some hundred years away, when Petra heard the approach of something through the shady corridors between the trees and, looking up, beheld a sight which both bemused and frightened her.

The sound which first caught Petra's attention was a low babble of voices, speaking the local language. When she first saw the speakers, she went pale, for the leader of a small band which approached them was, she thought for a moment, a child. Upon closer examination, she realized that the turbaned and robed figure was a dwarf with a huge head, short, stubby arms, and short legs which propelled him toward the three girls with stiff, short strides.

The dwarf saw the Englishwoman and halted, turning his almost neckless head to speak in a rough, thick voice, to those who followed him, all five of them of a height, all wearing turbans and the native costume, which reached to the ground.

"Darcie," Petra whispered. Darcie, who had been half-dozing, opened her eyes, and, taking in the bizarre group, stood quickly.

"Where's father?" she asked.

"There," Adrienne said, pointing to Edward, now a hundred yards away, musing over a ruined wall.

Meanwhile, the leader of the group was approaching, his short legs moving him in jerky steps, his large face wreathed in a smile which showed decaying teeth. The girls started to move nervously toward the edge of the grove, but, with a quickness which belied his grotesque, stunted body, the leader blocked their path. Darcie felt Petra's hand in hers and squeezed reassuringly. After all, the sun was bright, the skies cloudless. The day had been a wonderful day, and their father was but a few scant yards away.

"Salaam, English ladies," the dwarf said, his voice harsh and rasping. "Have you alms for the poor and afflicted?"

"I'm sorry," Darcie said, in her most prim and proper voice. "We have no money with us, but perhaps my father can give you a gift." She pointed toward Edward, who was still musing over the ruins near the single granite monument.

"Ah, yessss," the dwarf hissed. "English gentlemen are known for their generosity."

One of the followers leaned close and whispered into the leader's ear. A wide smile, somehow sinister and foreboding, showed the leader's yellowed teeth.

"My poor companions," he said, making a small bow, "suggest that perhaps the generosity of the English ladies might extend so far as to make our poor group very happy with a gift of, perhaps, a small jewel?"

With a gasp, Darcie put her hand up to cover her mother's ruby brooch, which she had chosen to wear to accent her off-white travel costume.

"I'm quite sure that won't do," Adrienne said. "Now, if you'll please stand aside, we must rejoin master Moncrief."

"Ah, English ladies," the dwarf crooned, "we upset you with our shortened limbs, our large heads, our poor, afflicted bodies."

"Not at all," Darcie said. "I think—I think you're quite a nice gentleman, and I'm sure you would not want to upset my father, who is quite an important man, by keeping us from him." She tried to push past, and the dwarf, leaping quickly, laughing, blocked her way again. As she halted, her face pale, the others laughed. One of them spoke in Arabic.

"My poor companions suggest," the dwarf said, "that perhaps you are shy because we have not been properly introduced." He bowed deeply. "I am your humble servant, English ladies, Pasha Olneah Ali." His laugh was rasping, and it drew chuckles from his followers, a grotesque band of midgets and dwarfs ranging in skin tone from honey to jet black.

"It's nice to meet you," Darcie said.

"How is it you speak such excellent English?" Petra asked, becoming emboldened by the fellow's friendly smile.

"Because I am the son of a great king," the dwarf said, then, turning, he translated his remark for the others, who laughed riotously. "Yes, indeed, English ladies, poor Olneah Ali Pasha is the uncrowned prince of all Arabia, neglected, unloved, poor, and for such a prince, I'm sure you would not miss one little trinket." He leaned forward and tried to snatch the brooch from Darcie's breast. She stepped away quickly.

"I suggest," Adienne said, in her charming French accent, "that you gentlemen be gone before we are forced to call the master."

With a snarling smile, Olneah Ali drew a wicked, very sharp scimitar from a sling on his slightly humped back, and, making the blade sing through the air, did a jerky little dance.

"Olneah Ali fears no Englishman!" he shouted.

By this time, Darcie was becoming quite nervous. In French, she spoke quietly to Petra. "Go and fetch father—quickly."

Olneah Ali, sneering, repeated her words, in almost unaccented French. Then; "I suggest, English ladies, that you be generous."

Once again, members of the strange entourage whispered loudly in Arabic. Olneah Ali grinned broadly. "My poor companions suggest that the three English ladies, especially the black-haired one and the fair yellow-haired one, would fetch a great price." He shrugged his deformed little shoulders. "However, it is not the honor of a true pasha—it is not indeed—to sell such gentlewomen into the harem of a sheik. Not when a mere bauble, which means so little to the English ladies and so much to the likes of us, would do as well, and with much less trouble."

"How dare you!" Adrienne gasped. "I command you to leave—this instant."

A black-faced dwarf spoke, laughing loudly.

"Amad suggested that there is fire in the fat one," he said, "and requests my permission to be allowed to sample the fire."

"Oh!" Adrienne gasped.

Darcie noted with relief that her father had apparently completed his musings and was moving with brisk pace toward the grove. She considered crying out, to warn him of possible complications, but the small stature of the little band lulled her into complacency. Her father, big, strong man that he was, could certainly handle a half dozen wizened dwarfs.

But she was not the only one to notice her father's approach. Olneah Ali saw, and he nodded to his followers, who spread themselves to surround the three

now-frightened females. He stationed himself in front
of the girls, his thick shoulders thrown back, the gleaming, evil-looking blade hanging at his side, almost
touching the ground.

"Father," Darcie called, when Edward was a few
paces away, "there are men here."

Edward paused and squinted his eyes to see into
the shadows. The sun was far down the sky, casting
long shades from the grove. Then he came forward.

"English pasha," Olneah Ali said, bowing, "we seek
alms for the poor and afflicted."

"I see," Edward said. "Of course, of course." His
eye took in the situation, but he was not overly concerned. The little fellows looked harmless enough. He
reached into his pocket and brought out a handful of
coins which he extended toward Olneah Ali.

"He tried to take Darcie's brooch," Petra said.

"Is that as far as the English pasha's generosity will
stretch?" Olneah Ali asked, with his sardonic grin.

"Well, perhaps a little more," Edward said, wanting
only to extract his women from the situation and be
on his way back to the point where they'd left the carriage. He fumbled in his other pocket. "I'm afraid this
is all I have," he said, extending coins with both hands.

Unnoticed, the black dwarf had been easing to the
side and was now partially behind Edward, but since
he stood only as high as Edward's knees, he did not
seem to be an overt threat. Olneah Ali took the coins
and looked at them.

"It isn't much," Edward said, "but I don't carry
large amounts of money."

Suddenly the black dwarf moved with surprising
speed.

"Look out, father!" Darcie screamed.

The little man leaped, agile as an acrobat, raising
his weapon, a small and carefully carved club. The club
took Edward on the shoulder and he shouted and
turned to face the attack. Another of the dwarfs leaped,

struck, and the blow made the sound of a melon dropped onto pavement. Edward, senseless before he hit the ground, collapsed weakly.

Adrienne tried to flee, screaming, and was seized, one on each leg, by two of the remaining little men. Others stood menacingly around Petra and Darcie.

"It is said," Olneah Ali said, "that you did not see fit to be generous. Had that been the case, I would have been inclined to be generous in return. Now, I fear, it is too late."

Darcie removed the brooch and, with trembling hands, held it out. "You may have it," she said. "Now may I see to my father, please?"

"Oh, he is alive," Olneah Ali said. "For the moment."

A chill of dread ran up Darcie's spine as the brooch was jerked from her hand. Behind her, Adrienne was screaming. She turned. Adrienne had been brought to the ground by the two dwarfs holding onto her legs and a third dwarf stood over her, laughing, as the two struggled until, with a grunt, the standing dwarf kicked Adrienne in the side and she screamed and ceased her struggles.

The three of them then started tearing at Adrienne's clothing, stripping her rapidly to her petticoats and then, ripping cloth in their eagerness, shreading her undergarments until her ripe, full breasts, her gleaming white stomach, and the shameful dark hair of her mons were exposed. All the while she prayed, sobbing, calling out for help.

Frozen in fear, Darcie watched as Adrienne's nude body was rapidly exposed and then she shrieked in shock as the black dwarf removed his clothing to reveal a misshapen but powerful body accentuated by the vile protrusion of his male organ at full extension, a shocking, huge thing in relation to his body.

"Don't look, Petra!" Darcie cried, but neither of them could take their terrified eyes off the shocking scene as the black dwarf literally dived down into the soft, plush, overly fleshy body of Adrienne, the huge organ finding its sheath as Adrienne shrieked in pain and fear.

"Someone will come to help, Darcie," Petra whispered, her eyes wide, her voice shaking. The terrible scene seemed to be unreal, something out of an unimaginable nightmare. She could not believe that her friend and servant, the gentle Adrienne, was being brutally ravished before her eyes, but then the black dwarf was driving and shuddering and crying out and was being pulled away from Adrienne's cringing body by one of his fellows, already stripped to take his place in the vile abuse of poor Adrienne's body.

"English ladies," Olneah Ali said, with hateful politeness, "perhaps you would like to rest. This will take a while." He chuckled. "You see, we poor devils rarely have such a treat."

"Oh, please," Darcie begged. "Won't you let me tend my father? Won't you please let us alone?"

"Seat yourselves," Olneah Ali ordered. "There." He pointed to a leafy area under a tree. "Perhaps you will learn something by watching closely."

"We will learn only that you are beasts," Petra said bravely. "Have you killed my father?"

"Petra, Petra, we must run," Darcie said. "We must escape."

The leader of the band of ruthless dwarfs was watching a third of his companions ravish Adrienne who, mercifully, had swooned. She awakened, however, as a fourth sturdy, short little man took his place between her outflung legs and entered her roughly with an organ larger than all the rest. She screamed once and then, as the black dwarf slapped her roughly, was quiet.

It was endless. When the five followers had taken their pleasure, one by one, the black dwarf was aroused, once again, and the wanton rape continued until there was a sameness about it, a dull acceptance on the part of the two numbed girls, who sat under the watchful eye of Olneah Ali and could not, no matter how hard they tried, turn their heads and eyes away from the terrible scene.

At last it was over, or so they thought. They had given scant thought to themselves, as they suffered with Adrienne, but now it was over, the lust of the five dwarfs sated. It was growing dark.

"So," Olneah Ali said, "they have plowed the English furrow, planting the good seeds of Egypt in the English belly." Grinning, he moved to stand over the scarcely conscious, dirtied, dampened body of Adrienne. "Now we will harvest the seed," he said, lifting his shining scimitar.

With one powerful slash, he opened Adrienne's belly from navel to mons, vile things springing out to lie exposed in the dusky light as shriek after shriek of terror and unendurable pain escaped Adrienne's lips.

"Mother of God," Darcie moaned, as the blackness came, along with memories of the vile thing which protruded from her mother's lower stomach, killing her, as the swift blade killed Adrienne.

"Help me, oh please, God, help me," Adrienne moaned, reverting to her native language in her extremity. She tried to crawl, the obscene darkness of her intestines dragging on the ground behind her, as the dwarfs laughed and discussed it in their jabber of Arabic.

She died slowly as Petra, shocked into frozen stillness, watched. Her fingers dug into the loose soil, her feet fluttered, and with a final agonized moan she was still.

As darkness fell, the dwarfs set to gathering wood and soon a cheery fire was blazing and they were examining the contents of Edward's pockets. Darcie, reviving, was moaning, leaning against the tree, eyes wide in shock. Edward was beginning to move feebly as he regained consciousness.

Unsatisfied with the contents of Edward's pockets, the dwarfs stripped the rings from Adrienne's dead fingers and quarreled over them. Then two of them, the black one leading, approached the tree where Olneah Ali was guarding Petra and Darcie.

"They want you, dark one," he said to Darcie, after the others spoke. "I have told them you are worth much money, but they do not care for money."

"Oh, no, please," Darcie said. "Please don't."

"You mustn't hurt her," Petra said. "You simply can't."

"Don't worry," Olneah Ali said. "You are too small and too beautiful to kill. We will save you. We will give you much pleasure before we sell you to a brothel."

"Oh, dear God!" Darcie moaned, as the dwarf leered at her.

There was a jabbering from the black dwarf. Olneah Ali moved quickly, the blade slashing, coming within a fraction of an inch of the black's throat. The fellow drew back quickly, the others with him.

"I have told them," Olneah Ali said, with his horrible yellow-toothed leer, "that the pasha himself slices this melon first."

Darcie cringed away as the dwarf's hand reached out, grasped her bodice, and, with a powerful tug, ripped the top of her costume away. Darcie screamed and tried to crawl away, but the dwarf was upon her, riding her on her hands and knees, tugging and ripping at her clothing.

The deed was accomplished within seconds, the cloth rending and tearing, until, with a final flourish of the scimitar, Olneah Ali cut away Darcie's undergarments and looked down upon the delicately colored softness of her breasts, the tiny beauty of waist, the length of shapely leg. He made a strangled sound in his throat and fell upon her.

In a haze of shock and fear, Darcie felt his mouth

at her breasts, sucking, biting painfully, felt his stubby fingers reaching into areas which had known the touch of no man. She screamed out in desperation. With a fierce cry, Petra leaped upon the dwarf's back and dug at him with her fingernails until, amid laughter, she was pulled away from Olneah Ali by the others and roughly subdued.

Darcie fought desperately, her long fingernails slashing down the dwarf's stubbly cheek, leaving red welts, causing the small, thick-bodied man to cry out in anger. She felt a strong blow and was dazed and then she realized that her legs were being parted. Rough hands probed, a cruel finger dug deeply into her softness and she screamed. Looking down the length of her body, she could see her own naked breasts, her indrawn stomach, the light growth of hair on her mons, and near her most intimate parts, the shocking, red, grotesque member of the dwarf, like the others, bigger than one would have believed. Helpless, unable to find strength to fight, half-swooning, she felt the hot thing touch and then push and, with a pain which was like a lance of fire, penetrate, as Olneah Ali grunted with deep satisfaction and began a frantic pounding which numbed Darcie into a state of near-swoon. So powerful was he that in her condition she felt his hot juices jet, pump, spray into her, and she screamed again, defiled, shamed.

Olneah Ali strutted, still mostly naked. He talked to his followers. The black made a move toward Darcie, still lying on the ground, legs spread, dark bush dampened by the dwarf's juices, and, with a curse, Ali struck the black down with a blow of his scimitar which almost severed the fellow's neck. He stood, snarling, ready, daring any of the others to try to avenge the death. They backed away muttering, two of them bowing to the fierce leader.

He turned to Petra, who was leaning over Darcie, sobbing with a broken heart.

"Cleanse her as best you can," he ordered, "for I will use her again."

Petra used a shred of Darcie's petticoat to wipe away the vile-smelling defilement. Then she covered her sister's body with torn clothing and sat there, awaiting her own fate.

The dwarf secured a pipe from his clothing, packed it with a substance and lit it, the smoke smelling strange and unusual. He smiled at Petra and held out the pipe. She shook her head.

"Don't worry, fair one," he said. "This is not for you, this pleasure we have here. For you I have other plans. You will bring many gold pieces at the harem of a sheik. And for that, you must be whole. However, to ease your mind, a whiff of forgetfulness." Once again he extended the pipe. Petra shook her head.

"Take it or I will beat you," he said. "I assure you that I can make it quite painful without leaving marks."

Frightened out of her wits, Petra accepted the pipe. The bite of the smoke caused her to cough. "Breathe deeply, fair one," he said, "and the coming hours will be easy for you."

Not daring to disobey, coughing, feeling a sudden sickness which began to fade as the smoke entered her lungs, she breathed the foul aroma and felt a strange lassitude creep over her.

"What—what is it?" she asked.

"Aboonom," Olneah Ali said, "the father of sleep. You English call it opium."

He forced her to breathe deeply, once more, twice more, and she leaned against the tree, in a strange calm, her senses dulled, eyes seeing color where there was no color, as the dwarf once again used her sister's body with great energy, his short, thick torso heaving, his hairy rump lifting and falling and Darcie's breath being driven from her body with the force of his blows, making a rhythmic sound, a wet, sloppy sound, a plop of flesh against flesh, and Darcie's breaths, harsh, panting.

In the midst of it her father came, rising, swaying, moaning, holding his head and, seeing his daughter being raped, roaring out with anger and desperation.

"Beast!" Edward yelled, throwing himself at the dwarf who was lodged between the outflung legs of his eldest daughter.

Olneah Ali rolled away, seizing the scimitar. On his feet, he dodged a dazed charge and flicked out with the scimitar. A great gash appeared in Edward's trousers. Blood gushed. He fell heavily, still dazed by the cruel blow to his head. But he rose and once again tried to attack the hateful dwarf who had dishonored his daughter and once again he was brought low by the slashing blade.

"You see," Olneah Ali said, bowing to Petra, "he is such a large man that I must cut him down to size."

And so saying, with Edward on his feet again at the cost of a great effort of will and severe pain from an almost-severed leg, Olneah Ali swung the blade with all the power of his muscular arms and Edward toppled to the ground, his left leg severed at the knee.

Through it all Petra was numbly aware, but unable to move, so great was the lassitude which had settled over her, a feeling almost of peace, seeing the blood, but not feeling shock, seeing her father's leg lying on the ground but not realizing the impact of the terror. And still Edward, galvanized by his horror at what had happened to his daughter, came on, crawling toward Olneah Ali to lose his other leg at the knee with a mighty blow of the heavy and deadly sharp blade.

There was much laughter and hooting from the others as Ali leaned, wiped his blade on Edward's shirt, and once again launched himself onto Darcie's body.

Darcie had witnessed the bloody duel and was screaming soundlessly, seeing her father's legs cut off,

seeing the great streams of blood. All her being cried
out to her to run, to escape the horror, but she could
not move.

Then it was too late. The beast was back, his hard
and huge member thrusting once again into the soreness of her, where her own blood marked the loss of
virginity and there was only a numbed acceptance as
she was used, brutally, forcefully, the hardness pounding and penetrating. Then the dwarf used his hands to
push her legs high, rolling her onto her back so that
he could penetrate deeper and as the dwarf's companions began to count the strokes, amid gales of laugh-
ters and hoots of encouragement, she felt a strangeness
in her, something which was not even a part of her,
something hateful and vile and alien, and, as Olneah
Ali punched and forced her legs high and buried his
hardness into her very depths, she exploded in an or-
gasm which was more pain than pleasure and screamed
out, not realizing that deliverance was at hand. A
squad of the khedive's soldiers, sent to look for the
missing English family, from the barracks which they
had passed on the way to Heliopolis, burst into the
grove with shrill cries, slaying the companions of Olneah Ali quickly even as the leader, with that amazing
quickness, left Darcie's body, his member still spurting
his pleasure, and dived naked into the darkness.

In her drugged state, it took Petra a long time to
realize that they were saved. Men were kneeling over
her father, trying to stanch the flow of blood with
tourniquets. Two of the younger soldiers were standing over Darcie, looking with admiration and pity at
Darcie's ravaged but still-beautiful nakedness. Slowly,
willing herself to move, Petra crawled to Darcie and,
with hands which did not seem to want to obey, she
cleaned the smears from Darcie's body and covered it
with her torn clothing.

Somehow Edward Moncrief survived the rough and
rapid ride into the city, where he was hospitalized un-

der the care of Roger D'Art, who was called in by de Lesseps after being notified of the tragedy which had befallen his English friend. D'Art exercised all his skills, fighting a death which was inevitable, for Edward had lost much blood and the shock to his system alone was enough to be fatal.

Edward died just after midnight, but not before he revived long enough to ask about his daughters.

"You may ease your mind, monsieur," D'Art said gently, "for they are both well."

"Darcie," Edward whispered weakly, "he—he—"

"Yes, my dear sir, but she will survive," D'Art said.

"And I?" Edward asked with a clarity of mind which faded gradually.

"There is a chance, monsieur, but only if you have the will to fight," D'Art said.

"My daughters," Edward whispered, growing weaker rapidly, feeling, knowing the approach of death. "Their uncle. Guy Simel. He will care for them."

Once more Edward regained consciousness. He was in great pain. "Doctor," he whispered. "My daughters—"

"Yes, monsieur," D'Art said. "You expressed a wish to leave them in the care of their uncle, Monsieur Simel. Is that still your wish?"

"It is," Edward Moncrief said, in his last moment of rational consciousness. And then, only a moment later, he tried to raise himself, straining with the effort.

"My dear Carolle," he said, his voice soft, weak, loving. "How lovely you look, my dear."

And thus, Roger D'Art, saddened but somehow gratified to be assured, once again, that there was something after death, was left to tell Petra and Darcie of the death of their father.

"They are together now," he told them, Petra seated beside the hospital bed of her sister. "You may be assured of this. For I myself saw the look of happiness on his face as he, once again, looked into her eyes.

You may console yourselves with this pleasant thought, my dear young ladies. They are happily together."

"I would be with them," Darcie said, from the depths of her shame and sorrow.

5

IN THE EARLY morning light, the desert stretched away westward toward the Nile like clouds brought to earth. The rolling dunes were bathed in amethyst light. There was a chill to the November morning. Strange, he thought, as he stepped aside to allow passage to a smiling Nubian on a tall and surly camel, that winter could ever assail this spit of sand and belie the broiling temperatures of August, all the hot, frantic, often tempestuous Augusts of the past ten years.

He walked through the neatly-laid-out streets of a town which might have been in France—a town which he, above all others, had built. When he landed on a narrow strip of sand in April of 1859, there was nothing—only the desert, and, beyond, the shallows of Lake Menzaleh, the first obstacle, the beginning of the unknown which stretched toward the Red Sea, so many miles away.

At that early hour, with the sun a huge red fireball just lifting above the horizon, he had the town to himself—or, at least, he was the only European about among the early rising beggars, black slaves, cheerful labor fellahs, and shrouded women with water jars atop their heads.

He walked toward the site of the ceremonies to come, through neat squares, past the new and luxurious hotels now filled with those who had come to pay tribute to his achievement. Ahead of him the sea, calm, green, that open roadway which led to the ports of Europe, a pathway for the commerce of the world which, now, narrowed into one ultimate exclamation point at the town which he had built.

As he stood overlooking the man-made harbor, he allowed himself a small smile. Now it was done. All the doubts, all the chiding, all the early laughter was wiped away by the accomplishment—the canal. *Le grande Canal Maritime de Suez*—his canal.

Statistics and figures raced through his active brain. The two concrete moles which protected the outer harbor were an engineering achievement to rank with, perhaps, a lesser pyramid; 2,726 yards and 1,962 yards long, built of native materials fabricated on the spot; huge blocks lifted into place to keep out the sea in its angry moods and point the way to the inner harbor and the 300-foot-wide channel capable of taking ships with a draft of 20 feet. And the town itself was built upon land which he himself had created, taking the narrow spit of sand and covering it with tons of dredged argillaceous mud from Lake Menzaleh, using the spoils of deepening the lake to make land for the town named after his dear, departed friend.

Port Said. A lovely sound.

In the harbor and offshore were the ships, two-and three-masters with their tall funnels—one, two, and three to the ship, depending on size—ships which could now cut thousands of miles from the voyage between the busy ports of Europe and the Orient.

Oh, that Mehemet Said had lived to see it.

There was a sadness in it, after all; a bittersweet melancholy which made him, for a moment, lower his head and remember the fat, shy boy whom he had befriended, a boy who had later become viceroy of Egypt, a man who had helped him make possible the greatest engineering feat of modern times.

"Said Pasha," he said aloud, "had you but lived."

Had he lived, the job would have been accomplished perhaps sooner, and at less expense. Had he lived, he could have shared the glory of this day.

Ah, there was so much to remember. The shy, fat boy having difficulty, at first, staying on his horse; but, in his determination, and under the tutelage of the friendly Frenchman, mastering the art to grow not only into an accomplished horseman, but a man among men.

Had he actually been dead six years, his friend Said?

Dear God in Heaven, how the years flew. It seemed only yesterday that he was a child in Egypt, learning wisdom at the knees of his father, a truly wise man who, through the vagaries of a kind fate, was also to be thanked for this day. His father had been instrumental in naming a former Turkish soldier, Mehemet Ali, to be viceroy of Egypt after a small, one-armed Englishman defeated Napoleon's proud fleet and made French withdrawal from Egypt necessary.

It had, after all, been in God's hands from the beginning. He lifted his face to the morning sky, clear, clean, invigorating, and muttered a small prayer of thanks.

So many factors, so much luck, so much divine guidance. Old Claude Henri, Comte de Saint-Simon, and his dream of a world without war and free trade linking the world through two great waterways connecting the Red Sea and the Mediterranean in Egypt and the Pacific and Atlantic in America. His father intervening on behalf of a lowly Turkish soldier, and he himself, befriending a sullen, overweight little prince.

It all ended here, this day. In spite of difficulties, in

spite of the death of Said. In spite of the obstacles
thrown in his path by Ismail Pasha, successor to Said.

He frowned, remembering the difficulties involved
when the new khedive withdrew the agreement to provide 20,000 laborers per month. To a lesser man, that
might have been a deathblow, but to him it was merely
a continuing part of the challenge. Perhaps, he reflected, looking calmly over the harbor and the waiting
ships, which were now beginning to come to life in
preparation for the great day, it was for the best; for
a fellah is a poltroon, at best. Hand labor had been
replaced by the vast machines, the huge dredges, which
had made the job complete.

Yes, it had been for the best, in spite of the difficulties. The second issue of shares, made necessary by
the khedive's treachery, had been a success.

And this brought up other sad memories.

It was not a day for sadness. He made his way back
to the offices of the *Compagnie Universelle du Canal
Maritime de Suez*. His staff was beginning to congre-
gate, in rare mood, looking forward to the festivities.

Young Guy Simel greeted him with a courteous bow.
Then the others gathered around, voicing their congratulations once more, all gay, excited, some a bit
the worse for having celebrated a bit too riotously
during the previous evening.

Roger D'Art, his personal physician, a tall, calm
man with cool gray eyes and straight brown hair, strong
nose, and mature, manly face, examined him.

"You look well, monsieur," D'Art said.

"I feel absolutely marvelous, monsieur," he said.

"Perhaps, with the chill, a light wrap?" D'Art suggested solicitously.

"Roger," he laughed, "I will brook no mothering—
not on this day of all days."

"Well, then," D'Art said, with a smile.

The grand company on hand to pay tribute had
been moved *en masse*, and in the greatest possible

luxury, from Cairo; and all over Egypt there was continuing celebration, grand balls at Port Said, Ismailia, and Suez. Fireworks showered starry fountains of fire into the skies to light the ancient ruins. Monsieur Verdi personally conducted a performance of his not-quite-finished opera, *Aida,* which spoke of the glories of old Egypt. Never had there been such celebration.

At the appointed time, he stood before 6,000 people. He was at home in the illustrious company which included, on the Quai d'Eugénie, the Empress Eugénie herself; Empress Elizabeth of Austria with the Emperor; Prince William of Hesse; the Crown Prince of Prussia; and the Crown Prince of Holland.

A few years in the past, when he was forty years old, his country had discharged him, telling him that his services were no longer needed. But now—now, by his own doing, his country was raised once again into respectability among nations, and he himself stood before the crowned heads of Europe to take their applause.

He was *Le Grand Français,* the greatest engineer of his time. He was Ferdinand de Lesseps, a lowly diplomat whose future had been terminated by his own country. He had, almost single-handedly, restored the lost glory of France. Like France—for he was a true son of France, born during Napoleon's Austrian campaign, son of a man who was Napoleon's personal friend—he had risen above defeat.

The Suez Canal, his personal monument, was now officially opened.

The grand ships sailed up the channel into the lake. They would spend the night at Ismailia, the halfway point, with continued celebration.

As the ships passed, de Lesseps had more time for reflection. Although the years were creeping up on him, he was still young at heart. Money would never again be a problem. The world was his. He would have a young and beautiful wife. He had his strong

son, who would become, more and more, his good
right arm.

With the world at his feet, he had few regrets; but
even in the midst of glory, he could imagine the missing faces. His father would have exulted in the new
glory of both France and Egypt. His friend Said should
have shared the glory. All the missing faces. His wife.
And the latest, his good friend Edward Moncrief, over-
taken by tragedy on the very eve of a triumph in which
he shared.

There were also time for practical thoughts, a glow
of personal satisfaction. Canal company shares were
now worth more than their original value. His own
good fortune would be shared by thousands of people
in Europe and England. The good that he had done
would live in many ways; in the growing volume of
commerce through his canal, and in the increased pros-
perity of those who had believed in him. He was
thankful for many things, and, as he thought once more
of his friend Moncrief, he was doubly thankful that
Moncrief had believed enough to invest heavily in
canal shares. That was small compensation, but the
two parentless girls would, at least, have no financial
worries.

6

IN MANY WAYS, Lyris *Bahala was* a rare woman. In a part of the world where women were considered to be nothing more than property, her very existence at the age of twenty-five was somewhat of a miracle, and the freedom which she had attained was, perhaps, unique in all of the Middle East.

The woman who conceived Lyris, scarcely more than a child at the time, considered her conception a miracle, for, before she had been ushered into the bedchamber of the French pasha, older members of the harem of Hassam Ari Pasha anointed her inner female membranes with the most potent and magical of ancient preventatives, an aromatic mixture of honey and dung from a Nile crocodile. Then, with long and supple fingers, the women of the harem added additional protection by introducing into the young girl's vagina a wad of clean wool impregnated with alum and myrtle oil.

The seed of the French general, Lyris's mother concluded, had a strong will to survive. For, in spite of all the ancient preventions, in spite of the sacred amulet lent to her by the pasha's favorite, the young girl's belly

blossomed at the appointed time; and the use of a slim
ivory wand in the hands of a wise and well-educated
eunuch failed to accomplish the desired abortion.

Thus, a thirteen-year-old honey-skinned, aristocratic
girl whose bloodlines could be traced back to Abbys-
sinian kings labored and delivered a girl, healthy and
vigorous, in spite of the many efforts made to prevent
her birth. Thus, there was to be faced another choice—
that of the oldest of all birth-control methods—in-
fanticide.

The eunuchs who supervised the harem of Hassam
Ari, and who assisted in the delivery, did not bother
the pasha with so trifling a matter, but seized the newly
born child with the intent of mercifully ending the unwanted life by quick immersion in a basin of water.
The wails of the young mother and the intervention of
the other women saved Lyris's life.

In spite of lurid speculation and licentious imaginings, life in a harem was restrictive and unexciting.
Unless a woman adopted the pleasures so well sung
by Sappho, the average member of a harem enjoyed
the attentions of the master less often than the most
moral Victorian lady, and romps with the eunuchs
were less frequent than described by some of the more
sensational writers and were, most often, quite unful-
filling.

The harem of Hassam Ari Pasha was a moral and
orderly establishment. Hassam would not have imagined some of the orgiastic activities conjured up by
sensational writers, for he was a true man of God,
would not think of shaming his wives by licentious behavior, but satisfied his urge for woman and for children by entertaining his wives infrequently and, always,
one at a time. As a matter of fact, Hassam prayed long
and hard before he lowered his moral standards to
pander to the barbaric wishes of his guest, the distinguished French general, but there are times for com-

promise, and Allah will forgive the defilement of one small young girl.

Hassam became aware of the existence of the fruit of the temporary union between the small, shapely girl and the French general when Lyris was six months old and quite spoiled by the attention of the women. Children are rare in a harem; the offspring of the master are removed at an early date. Although she was the seed of a Frenchman, the baby was lively, alert, and endearing. To please the women, Hassam allowed the child to stay. Because of political considerations, he sent the child's mother back, many times, to the bed-chamber of the immoral Frenchman, and it was the child's mother who told the general of the existence of the child. She kept her lips sealed for almost a year, so that when the general first saw his daughter, a pre-cocious child possessed of a bright-eyed and amusing curiosity, he was captivated.

By virtue of birth and by conquest, the general was a wealthy man. Actually, he felt no obligation to the child, but he was, in his own eyes, a man of honor. He broached the subject of the child to his friend, Hassam Ari Pasha, and begged to be allowed to provide the means to rear the child as a European woman —a matter of some difficulty, he was told.

Lyris spent her early years amid scenes which might have been painted by Ingres, who professed, rightly or wrongly, to have been inside a Turkish harem. It was as if she had many mothers, for she was adored by the women and, even at an early age, taught the knowledge which they felt would make her a valued and skillful wife for Hassam Ari Pasha or perhaps one of his sons. That Lyris would have any other fate was beyond the belief of her many "mothers," for, having been born in a harem, they assumed that she would remain there.

However, the general and his money prevailed, and, when she was five, she was tutored by Europeans and

returned to her harem home at the end of the lessons
to regale the women with strange and unbelievable
tales of European customs. By the time she was of
marriagable age, just past twelve, she spoke Arabic,
French, English, a bit of Greek, some Latin, and two
dialects from the African nations to the south of Egypt.
She was also a confirmed sensualist, having fallen early
to the charms of Lesbos under the skillful teachings of
two or three of the younger members of Hassam Ari's
harem. She gave her virginity to a young eunuch slightly older than she, who had been neutered recently
enough for his body to retain the memory and the
ability of manhood, and that encounter opened up a
world of delights.

Lyris's natural wit and her great beauty earned her
a place in Hassam Ari's affections and, before her
father departed Egypt, she also earned a place in his
heart to the point that when he left she was set up well
enough to be that rarity of rarities, an independent
woman in a largely Moslem nation.

Lyris came to consider her first pregnancy a blessing. At thirteen, she seduced a Greek tutor, showed
him a skill which left him gasping, and made lesson
time a time of endless delights—until the tutor left in
the middle of the night, fearful for his life at the hands
of the girl's protector. The attempted and successful
abortion with the long ivory wand set up an infection
which made her desperately ill, but, to her pleasure,
left her barren. Never again would she have to concern
herself with fears of a swollen belly.

As a girl, Lyris possessed a beauty which became
legendary in Cairo and she used that beauty and her
fragile independence to become a part of the gay society of Europeans. She was accepted because of her
apparent wealth, her knowledge of so many things,
and, most of all, for a delicate beauty which, in profile, consisted of the long, slender neck, the proud,
straight nose, the well-formed and sensuous lips, the

beautifully slanted eyes and the strong chin of Akhen-
aten's queen, Nefertiti.

Lyris took the name of her mother, Bahalah. From
her own establishment, she ventured forth like a lovely
bird of prey, seeking pleasure with handsome Frenchmen, Englishmen, and one middle-aged Greek who introduced her, somewhat painfully at first, to a form of
pleasure which she had not known.

Lyris welcomed the return of the French when de
Lesseps landed to begin his canal and attached herself
to them by offering her services as interpreter and, later,
as a valued nurse in the medical services which were
supervised by Roger D'Art. D'Art, a serious man, was
not immune to her ancient and royal beauty, but he
did not allow himself to fall to her charms. It was left
to his young pupil, Guy Simel, to discover that Lyris
was more than just a highly intelligent woman and a
good nurse.

"Ah," Lyris moaned, while they were in the process
of discovering each other, "I was made for you, my
beautiful Frenchman."

For Guy Simel's chief pleasures in life corresponded
with Lyris's own. As a physician, Simel had interested
himself in the little-known pleasure centers of the
human body. In his studies he had devoured all writings on the subject of human sexuality. He knew the
works of the infamous de Sade, and, although he was
neither sadistic nor masochistic, he learned that at
times the application of sharp sensation can accentuate
pleasure. He knew the early writings of Richard von
Krafft-Ebing, had, indeed, corresponded with the gentleman, and he had talked once with a serious young
Englishman named Havelock Ellis about Ellis's plan
to make a scientific study of sexuality. Simel had experimented with great interest, but always with care,
avoiding women of low character who could have
given him the pox. He considered Casanova to be
overrated as a lover, for he felt that any man worthy

of his salt would be aroused when, naked in a bath, an eighteen-year-old girl rubbed him thoroughly all over. He owned a small but growing library on the subject of sensuality and one of the more prized volumes was an early printing of Shaykh Nefzawi's *The Arabian Manual of Love*. He found it to be more entertaining than, for example, the *Kama Sutra,* and when he discovered that Lyris was proficient in the language of the original *Manual,* they spent many hours reading aloud and, when the spirit moved them, which was often, putting the test to the ancient rites.

If Lyris had been made for Guy, as she commented upon first discovering his knowledge of the female anatomy and the secret positioning of certain feminine nerve centers, Guy had most certainly been made for Lyris. For over a year they lived a life of total sensuality as two adepts who experimented and discovered ever-new delights.

Their initial encounter was a delight for Guy. It came about suddenly. He knew Lyris, of course, and respected her ability in aiding in the treatment of workers suffering from fever, dysentery, pox, but he was amazed at the boldness with which she greeted his first tentative suggestions that perhaps they should become better acquainted.

After having arrived in bed with her with a swiftness which made his heart pound, and after having consummated their first hunger, he told her, as she had been told before, that she looked like a queen.

"Nefertiti and I have a common belief," she said, smiling. "Nefertiti worshiped one god." She ducked her head, applying hot and wet lips and tongue to a smooth, round object which was suddenly inbued with new life. "I, too, worship one god," she said, smiling around the object of her worship.

It was Lyris who inspired Guy's early departure from Cairo after his visit with his brother-in-law and his nieces. He was in Port Said, pleased that most of the Europeans were away in Cairo for the festivities, leaving him free to spend much time with Lyris, when word came to him of the disaster which had befallen his kinsman and his oldest niece.

"A most unfortunate thing has occurred," he told Lyris, giving her details. "I must go to Cairo immediately."

"I will go with you," she said.

He frowned doubtfully. In spite of his unending attraction for her, he was a proper Frenchman. Their meetings were always clandestine, more to preserve his own reputation than hers. He knew Roger D'Art as a prudish man who felt that marriage was the only honorable relationship between man and woman, and, since his future was tied to D'Art, he was reluctant to risk D'Art's discovery of his dalliance with the lovely and sensual Lyris.

Guy had, in fact, been undergoing a considerable amount of mental agony, knowing that he would soon be returning to France. He did not know how he could live without Lyris, and he could not imagine any feasible method of having her go with him to France.

"I am a nurse," she said, having suggested that she accompany him to Cairo. "The young girl has been raped. She will need a woman's touch."

"Ah," Guy said, a brilliant plan forming in his mind. "Do you love me, Lyris?"

"For the moment, *mon ami,*" she said, with a frank smile. "For the moment."

"Nor am I ready to give you up," he said. "Now I think I see a way."

"I have seen it before you," she said. "That is why I suggest that I accompany you, as a nurse, to Cairo."

"And then, if I am to be guardian of my two young nieces, to France?" he asked.

"I have not, as yet, seen Paris," she said, with a royal smile.

Dressed as a Western woman, Lyris was a Eurasian

beauty who attracted the eyes of all. D'Art, who was still at the hospital, attending Darcie, who was just beginning to come out of a depression which, at first, had seemed to threaten her sanity, greeted Guy warmly, expressed his sympathy, and then saw Lyris, who had trailed behind upon entering the room.

"And why is Miss Bahalah here?" he asked Guy, his serious face stern.

"I know nothing about the care of young girls," Guy explained with a disarming smile. "I have asked Miss Bahalah to assist me with them—at least until I can return them to France and hire proper attendants."

D'Art was not a man to pay heed to idle gossip, especially when it concerned a colleague. He did not, however, fully approve of Guy's choice of a companion for the two young girls. It was well known that this strange and eerily beautiful woman was independent of mind and action, and there were tales of far more shocking activity. He considered taking Guy aside for a fatherly talk, but, in the end, gave the young man the benefit of the doubt. D'Art was a fair man, and he assumed innocence until guilt was proven.

"I think the first order of business is to get them out of this hospital," D'Art said. "There is nothing physically wrong with Darcie, and Petra was unhurt, although she did, apparently, inhale a dose of opium. I think a total change of climate is in order."

"I do want to attend the opening ceremonies of the canal, if possible," Guy said. "Of course, the welfare of my nieces comes first."

"I don't think that Darcie is quite ready to be out in public," D'Art said.

"Monsieur," Lyris said, "I have the solution. As you may know, I have a house in Cairo. I can take the poor young girls there, and then both of you may attend the ceremonies."

"Kind of you," D'Art said doubtfully.

"Splendid idea," Guy approved. "Just the thing.

Then I shall return after the ceremonies and see to taking them home."

Petra was in Darcie's room, reading aloud to her sister, who had her eyes closed. She looked up when the door opened, saw her uncle, and flew into his arms.

"Oh, Uncle Guy, it was so horrible. They killed father and Adrienne and did horrid things to Darcie."

"I know," Guy said gently. "I know, my darling. They are still searching for the leader of that blood-thirsty band of killers. They will find him and punish him."

"Will that bring them back?" Darcie asked in a low voice.

Guy moved to the side of the bed and took Darcie's hand. "Oh, my poor darling," he said. "Oh, if only I had stayed with you."

Petra had spied Lyris, standing behind Dr. D'Art. Lyris smiled and Petra returned the smile shyly.

"Petra," D'Art said, "this is Miss Bahalah. Your uncle has arranged for her to be with you while he prepares to take you home."

"You are so very beautiful," Petra said, awed by the grace and sophistication of the Eurasian woman.

"And you are quite beautiful, too," Lyris said, moving forward to put her arm around Petra. With mother and father both dead, the show of affection touched Petra, who sniffled and fought back tears.

"But we must get you both out of this dreadful hospital," Lyris said. "I have a wonderful place for you, where we will await your uncle."

"Thank you very much," Petra said. She liked the smell of Lyris—clean, womanly, with a touch of a subtle, unknown essence.

D'Art had Darcie released and rode in the carriage with the group to Lyris's house, in one of the newer sections of the city. It was a pleasant house, a mixture of East and West, and staffed with polite and neat female Egyptian servants. D'Art didn't fully approve of the arrangement, but the place looked spotlessly clean. After all, Lyris Bahalah was an educated and civilized woman. Perhaps it was for the best, he decided.

Dr. D'Art saw to it that Darcie was installed in a bright and sunny room, told her that she was free to move about as she pleased, kissed her on the cheek, and then said his good-byes to Petra. During the period he'd known Petra, and especially in the trying days since the death of her father, he'd come to feel a fatherly affection for the bright-haired girl. He regretted leaving her, but his duty called.

"I will visit you often in France," he promised. "Your uncle and I will be working together. Together we will look after you both and see to it that you have a good life."

With both men off to Port Said for the opening ceremonies, Petra, first, explored the house, with Lyris's permission, found that one of the servants spoke broken French, and then went into the gardens, which were luxurious and well kept. She had dinner, enjoying the strange Arabian dishes. One of them, with chicken and spices, was delicious; the flat, chewy bread which was dipped into the dish was also very good.

Darcie took her dinner in her room.

After dinner, Petra went to the room. "Darcie, are you feeling better?" she asked.

"Should I feel better?" Darcie answered testily.

"Oh, sister," Petra said.

"It's fine for you to feel good," Darcie said. "They didn't rape you."

"Oh, please!" Petra gasped. "Don't say that word!"

"Oh?" Darcie asked archly. "Does it shock you, little sister? It shocked me, too, when he raped me." She put heavy emphasis on the word. "If you'd like to know how it feels, I can probably arrange it," Darcie went on.

"Please, father wouldn't want you to talk like that," Petra said.

"Father's dead."

"Oh, Darcie!" Petra wailed, running to the bed to throw her arms around her sister. "What will we do?"

"I shall have a deformed baby," Darcie said cruelly, for that was deep in her—that fear.

"Oh, God help us!" Petra wailed.

"If you're going to weep, please go away," Darcie said. "I have enough troubles of my own."

Crushed, Petra retreated to her room, there to weep quietly for a while until sleep quieted her.

Darcie was forming mental pictures of a dwarfed baby, twisted and horrible, when the door opened. Lyris, in a long and silken garment, came in, a tray in her hands.

"Do you feel well enough to talk?" Lyris asked. Darcie made a noncommittal movement with her head. "We will talk, then, just two women together."

Lyris sat in the chair beside the bed. There was a strong smell emanating from a container on the tray. "Life is not ended, little one," Lyris said. "I know it must seem so. And it is tragic to have taken from you that which can only be given once, taken by a brute of a man who did not appreciate it."

Darcie turned her head, unwilling to discuss such intimacies.

"Will it embarrass you if I remove your nightdress?" Lyris asked.

"May I ask why you should want to do such a thing?" Darcie asked testily.

"I am a nurse," Lyris said. "Quite a good one, actually. I merely want to treat your bruises. I noticed those places on your arms, and such a brute would not have stopped there."

Darcie was a mass of soreness. The nurses at the hospital had applied salve to some of her bruises, but they were still sore. She sat up, and, holding the sheet in front of her breasts modestly, removed her night-dress.

"There," Lyris said, "that's better." She gently urged Darcie onto her back and, pulling down the sheets, discovered bruises on the elegant little back, and dark fingerprints, livid, in the flesh of Darcie's well-shaped buttock. Deliberately, she dipped her fingers into a fragrant ointment and began there, on the intimate part, on the soft rump flesh. Darcie flinched and tried to pull the sheet up.

"These are the worst," Lyris said. "We will begin with them." She pulled Darcie's arms away and continued her gentle massage, her fingers tender and knowing, working up from the livid marks on the soft rump to the back, the shoulders. Gradually Darcie relaxed.

"He was a beast, and he used you cruelly," Lyris said. "I don't wish to sound callous, but I must tell you, my dear, that it would be unwise to dwell on this unfortunate happening. It could ruin your life."

"I am ruined," Darcie said weakly.

"Not at all," Lyris said. "In fact, there are ways in which you can convince a man, when the time comes, that you are still a virgin."

"I won't concern myself with that," Darcie said forcefully. "I will never allow another man to touch me."

"Ah, such foolish talk," Lyris said, her hands rubbing, rubbing, being gentle, and massaging the bruises on Darcie's back. Then, still talking gently, she turned Darcie over and rubbed the aromatic ointment onto the bruises on Darcie's firm little breasts, her stomach. There were dark and livid bruises on the inside of Darcie's soft thighs, and there Lyris's hands took on an additional gentleness, lingering, caressing, until Darcie dozed languorously.

Before she pulled up the sheet, Lyris stood, her eyes intent on the tiny but perfectly formed body of the young English girl. Then, with a shuddery sigh, she covered Darcie, put out the lamp, and departed.

The application of the fragrant ointment became a twice-daily ritual, Lyris's soft voice soothing as much as her hands soothed as they traversed Darcie's body, the caressing touch lulling Darcie into deep relaxation. Gradually, the bruises began to fade. Gradually, Darcie began to look forward to the treatments. She, like Petra, felt very much alone. She was young, and thus in need of affection. She came to like Lyris very much, but it was three days before she could bring herself to mention her secret fear of being with child by the horrid misshapen dwarf.

"Yes," Lyris said, "there is that possibility, but there are things to be done about it."

She explained. And so, as had Lyris's mother, Darcie was submitted to a series of abortifacients ranging from noxious-smelling applications to vile-tasting liquids.

"Now," Lyris said, "we have only to wait and see." She had administered the last, an oral potion concocted by one of the older servants, a semimagical cure for the disease of pregnancy handed down mouth-to-mouth from the days of the pharaohs. Now she was, once again, massaging the body of her young charge, her hands lingering on buttock and breast without, seemingly, upsetting Darcie.

A true voluptuary, Lyris was, in smoothing her hands over the young and shapely body, reliving certain experiences of her own youth, when she indulged in play with other younger members of Hassam Ari's harem. She noted that when she ran the tips of her fingers lightly over Darcie's stomach, and down into the softness of inner thigh, the girl closed her eyes, breathed deeply, and sighed.

Throughout the three-day period, she'd been talking to Darcie about Darcie's attitude regarding the rape, telling her that it was nothing more than a senseless accident, that Darcie was not to be shamed by it.

And, as she administered the abortifacients, she explained in full how they were supposed to act, telling Darcie things she'd never heard regarding her own body and its mysterious inner works.

Darcie could remember, with a vividness born of nightmare, the dark and horrid blob which had protruded from her mother's lower body as she lay dying, and she could picture herself dying in the same way, being killed by the issue of the terrible dwarf. She found comfort in Lyris's assurances that she would be fine, that the ointments and potions would cause her to abort, and then it would be over and she could resume her life.

"Life is truly wonderful for a woman," Lyris said, her fingers soothing and massaging the fading bruises on Darcie's breast. "You will find a man, love him, and discover that one of life's greatest treasures is man and woman together. You must not let your sad experience spoil that for you."

"Have you been married?" Darcie asked.

"Oh, no," Lyris said.

"Then how do you know?" Darcie flushed and fell silent.

"How do I know about the pleasures of man and woman together?" Lyris laughed. "We come from different cultures, you and I." And then, as she soothed and tickled, she told Darcie of her childhood, of the different values assigned to women by their two societies.

"But isn't it wrong?" Darcie asked. Talking with Lyris took her mind off the horror of her life, her mother's death, her father's murder, the disembowelment of Adrienne, her own brutalization.

"Wrong?" Lyris asked, with a soft laugh. "Who is to say? Would God put into our bodies the desire for pleasure if it were wrong?"

Darcie decided it was too heady a question. She felt

relaxed, languorous, Lyris's gentle hands on her, her body alive to sensation, the soreness gone.

"The youngest girls are taught pleasure in my society," Lyris said. "Are we all wrong?"

"Ummm," Darcie said, as Lyris's soft hands rubbed ointment into the inner thighs. She was unashamed now, accustomed to Lyris, naked, comfortably warm in the balmy evening air.

"The bruises here are much better," Lyris said, touching the region very near Darcie's most intimate parts with her fingertips. Then, with breath held, she bent her lovely graceful neck, her dark hair falling to tickle and caress Darcie's thighs, and kissed the bruises gently with hot, wet lips. Darcie started, then relaxed. She felt warm. She felt an affection for the gentle woman. She said nothing as the lips lingered, caressed, dampened her with warmth on the soft, soft skin.

"Now I want to show you something," Lyris whispered. "Relax and keep an open mind, for it is for your own good. I want you to realize that you have a capacity for pleasure, even after what has happened to you." And, so saying, she placed her flattened hand over Darcie's mons, letting her fingers work gently, gently. "Do you see?"

"Please," Darcie said, a bit frightened by the sudden surge of sensation she felt. "I don't—"

"It is only you and I, little one. It is only Lyris, who shows you, thus, and thus, that you are still a woman, with a woman's capacity."

"But Lyris—"

"Is there harm in a touch between friends?" Lyris asked, letting one finger lower, wet itself, to raise the sweet and oily liquid to a soft-hard spot of bunched nerves.

Darcie's body writhed involuntarily, and she was gasping. And then she felt a new sensation, looked down, opening her eyes, to see the top of Lyris's black-crowned, shapely head, felt a warm and wonderful assault of tongue and lips, and then, with a cry, she abandoned herself to it, her firm young loins heaving up, up, searching, searching and this time, unlike the guilty spasms she'd experienced under the hard and cruel ministrations of the dwarf, the feeling was an upflowing of wonder and a sunrise of bursting gladness. By the time of Guy's return from Port Said, she was reaching out eagerly for the caresses of the sensual Lyris, with no guilt, for Lyris took pains to dispel any hint of guilt, with a joy and an open sensuality which was to remain with her for all the years of her life.

7

THE FIRST SHIP to pay passage through the Suez Canal was British. Although Ferdinand de Lesseps noted the irony, neither he nor anyone connected with the grand venture could know just how prophetic the coincidence was. Nor could de Lesseps imagine that the moment of glory he had given his native country would be short-lived, that soon France was to be plunged to the most shameful depths.

At home, there was a growing feeling of revolution. An epidemic of strikes beset the country. Marxist labor unions preached the doctrine of worker rule. The winds of change were sweeping across all of Europe.

Unwilling to take his three female charges into radical Paris, where political killings were commonplace and huge street demonstrations made the city unsafe for all, Guy Simel landed his little group at Bordeaux shortly after the beginning of the new year of 1870. They traveled by carriage to the family home on the banks of the Garonne River.

Both Petra and Darcie had seen the family home of their mother, but on the occasion of Carolle Moncrief's one trip home Darcie was five and Petra three, so that neither remembered very much about it.

Darcie was in no mood to care. In spite of all of Lyris's efforts, she was definitely with child.

Aside from the unrest in Paris, Darcie's condition was the main factor in Guy's decision to go to the Simel country home instead of to Paris. His decision was eased somewhat by Roger D'Art's decision not to go home directly to Paris, but to remain with de Lesseps as the hero traveled, accepting the plaudits of the world for his triumph at Suez. Thus the joint practice of medicine would be postponed, and there was nothing to lose and much to gain by spending a few months at Chateau du Blanc.

Sometimes wise decisions are formed from materials extraneous from but contemporary with great events. De Lesseps made his decision to travel to England where 40,000 Englishmen jammed the Crystal Palace to applaud him. Roger D'Art, friend and personal physician, decided to accompany de Lesseps. With those reasons added to the condition of his niece Guy Simel decided to take his family and Lyris to the family estate.

When the events which were to sweep away the remnants of the Napoleonic empire began, Simel's group of females was far from the scene of the bloody battles of the War of 1870. When Napoleon III surrendered at Sedan in September, Darcie's ordeal was over. While Moltke besieged Paris, leaving its citizens to eat dogs, cats, and the elephants from the Paris Zoo, Simel and his ladies dined off the fat of the land. The estate was small but prolific, well tended by family retainers.

France's moment of glory had indeed been brief. Now the hated Germans paraded in Paris and forced upon the defeated country an indemnity which, the Germans felt, would keep France subservient for a generation. France was to pay, for the price of having surrendered at Sedan, Metz, and Paris, a sum equal to one billion American dollars. That she paid, and in an incredibly short time. The amount, fully paid by 1873, bespoke of the spirit, the determination, the vitality of the nation so fearfully beset by defeats since the time of Napoleon's triumphs. All those events were to have an effect on the lives of the parentless Moncrief girls, and the civil war which followed the defeats by the Hun legions was to keep them confined at Chateau du Blanc for some time, with varying degrees of personal effect.

At the time of arrival at Chateau du Blanc, Darcie was lost in a conflict of emotional forces. Having been introduced to a life of sensuality by the beautiful Lyris, she abandoned herself to it as an escape from the inescapable fact that life grew in her stomach.

As a physician, Guy had conducted examinations both in Egypt before leaving and aboard ship. When they were snugly and safely tucked into the large white house on the Simel estate on the Garonne, he discussed various possibilities with Lyris, whose ancient methods had failed to abort Darcie. He conducted one final examination.

Medical abortion was not widely practiced. The body of medical knowledge regarding the workings of the female reproductive system was a mixture of science and myth, knowledge and hearsay.

With Darcie in the standard knees-up position, Lyris in attendance, Darcie's upper body sheathed, Guy discovered that, one, Darcie's having become pregnant seemed to be an impossibility; and, two, abortion would not be simple. The problem was in the structure and positioning of Darcie's uterus. It was inverted, the opening which had accepted Olneah Ali's seed seemingly blocked. In order to enter the uterus, it would be necessary, first, to cut or tear it away from the vaginal side walls, position it properly, and then perform the relatively simple task of displacing the embryo which developed within. However, the preliminaries seemed,

to Guy, to be rather severe medical methods, and he
spent long hours with his books, trying to find instances
of similar cases. He was largely on his own.

"The problem, my dear Lyris," he said, "is infection.
Within the heated and fertile confines of the vagina, infection breeds rapidly. So it is that I am hesitant to
perform the necessary operation."

Lyris had a genuine sympathy for Darcie, and she
had developed a sort of love engendered by the heat of
her passions for the smooth, lovely, slim, but perfectly
proportioned body of her young charge. She tried to
explain, amid tender caresses, that bearing the baby
would be only a temporary inconvenience, and must be
endured. The alternative—risking death—was un-
acceptable.

"I would rather die!" Darcie declared.

However, Darcie was helpless. She could not perform the abortion herself, nor could she summon the
necessary courage to wade into the chill Garonne and
end her life.

Meanwhile, Petra was slowly overcoming her grief
at the death of her father and taking great interest in
her new surroundings. She found the vineyards, even
in winter, to be fascinating, asked a million questions
about the winemaking facilities in the sheds, polished
her French by chatting with the servants and the land
workers, and, in general, went her own way, making it
easier for Lyris and Guy to devote most of their time
to Darcie—and, unknown to Petra or Darcie, to their
pursuit of the ultimate sensual experience.

The time spent at Chateau du Blanc was a splendid
time for both Guy and Lyris, their lives one continu-
ous round of sensation, and, for both, there was to be,
soon after arrival, an additional element of pure sensuality and lust.

The idea was put into Lyris's head by Darcie herself.
Although she was three months pregnant, she had not
yet begun to be disfigured by the living embryo in her

womb, her stomach now a pleasant little mound which could have been called, as common men would have said, a pleasure belly—just enough of a rounding to make it noticeable, a smoothness for caressing, a place for hot kisses and tickling fingertips during Darcie and Lyris's frequent bouts of sensualism.

On a day in which Guy was absent, about the fields, followed by a trip into the nearby village, taking Petra with him, Lyris seized the opportunity to spend a languid hour of preparation, a violent moment of completion, and more languid caresses on Darcie's sweet body. Lying side by side, both dusky-skinned, both as beautiful as man could dream, both shamelessly nude in the bedchamber which was heated by a roaring fire in a huge fireplace, Darcie expressed curiosity.

"Is it much different with a man?" she asked, as Lyris's hands continued to keep life in areas which she had thought spent of sensation.

"There is a completion with a man which is not possible in any other way," Lyris said.

"Tell me," Darcie begged, her own hands finding the curves of Lyris's firm, lovely breasts to be quite nice.

Lyris talked in a soft, sultry voice, describing the sensations of love, and Darcie, unwillingly, with repugnance, remembered the wild and unwanted response which her body had made to the thrustings of the dwarf.

"I will never allow a man to touch me," she said, having shuddered away the memory of the painful poundings deep inside her body.

"Ah, my little sweet one," Lyris said. "We cannot allow that."

"But it's so sweet, so gentle with you," Darcie said.

"As it can be with a man who is a gentleman," Lyris said. "Not with an impetuous boy, whose only thought is his own pleasure, who would use you much as the evil one in Egypt used you; but with a man of the world, a man who knows the needs of a woman, you

will find it not at all repulsive, but, rather, a state
much to be desired."

"Perhaps, someday," Darcie said. But then, remembering the hateful life in her womb, she said, "But I
will never risk becoming pregnant again."

While it is true that Lyris's morals were open to
question, certainly unusual for a civilized country in
the nineteenth century, her actions were taken as much
for Darcie's sake as for satisfaction of her own lasciv-
ious desires. She was quite fond of Darcie and had no
desire to see her grow up as a twisted, unhappy, man-
less woman. Now, she concluded, before Darcie's pregnancy developed, while she was immune to the dangers
of fertilization would be the time to demonstrate to
Darcie the wonders of love.

The question was: who was to be the proper instrument of introduction to the joys of lust?

Again, it was Darcie herself who planted the seed.
During one of their endless talks, Darcie confided that
she had felt a thrill on first seeing her Uncle Guy in
Cairo, before she knew that Guy was a kinsman. With
wistful memory, she told how she had felt that Guy
was, by far, the most handsome man she'd ever seen.

Lyris planned carefully. On the evening of her
choice, she laced Darcie's dinner glass of wine with a
strong brandy and refilled the glass twice, telling Darcie that she was pale and needed the strength provided
by a touch of the vine.

Darcie, used only to a single glass of mild wine,
felt her face grow hot and her head dizzy, but thought
only that it was associated with her condition. But
when she rose to leave the table, she was quite tipsy.

"Oh, dear," she said, as she had to hold onto the
side of the table for support.

"I'll help you, dear," Lyris said, going to her side.
She took Darcie to her room, undressed her, and, with
sure knowledge and the aid of the wine and brandy,

quickly brought Darcie to a point of high passion with a skillful use of hands and lips.

"Now I must see to Petra and Guy," Lyris said.

"Oh, no, please, you can't leave now," Darcie begged, clinging to her.

"Think pleasant thoughts, little one," Lyris said, "and I will return to crawl into your bed with you after the others are safely retired."

And so Darcie lay, her body heated, desire a strong force in her, as the house settled down for the night with much creaking and cracking of ancient timbers.

Meanwhile, Lyris quickly saw Petra to her bed, closed the door behind her, and, with a pounding heart and quick little tendrils of anticipation shooting through her lovely body, she joined Guy in his room. There began the usual exploration and stimulation, with Lyris seeming, to Guy, to be more responsive than usual. She seemed, however, to be rushing, and then, with a certain point reached, she withdrew, a strange little smile on her face.

"Tonight," she said, "I have a special treat for you."

"Although it would delight me," he said, caressing her soft thighs with his lips, "I cannot imagine anything untried."

"Will you trust me and do exactly as I say in return for an experience which, I swear to you, will be rewarding and totally new?"

"Of course," he said.

"Then put on only your dressing gown and follow me," she said.

Puzzled but willing, Guy did as he was told. She slipped into a silken robe and led the way down the corridors, past Petra's room, and paused at the entrance to Darcie's chamber.

"Stand here, watch closely, and when I motion to you, come," she said.

"Lyris," he protested, "may I ask—"

"No," she whispered, "trust me. I know what I am doing."

With a mixture of apprehension and lust, he watched as she opened the door. He stood back, in the dark hall, as she entered the room lit by one lamp, making for a pleasant dimness of vision, the glow emphasizing her lustrous flesh as she let the silken gown fall to the floor and approached Darcie's bed to find Darcie awaiting, arms held up to receive her. A bolt of sensual lightning brought every cell in Guy's body to life and froze him there, peering into the room, watching the mingling, the mixture, the folding together of the two bodies, one full and womanly, the other a perfection in miniature.

But she is your niece, he thought, *your dead sister's child.*

The force of his desire was too much for moralizing. On the bed, wanton, loving, Lyris was making love to a girl who ceased to be his niece and became only a lovely young girl who obviously was enjoying Lyris's attentions. Tremors of desire swept through Guy as he watched Lyris doing wonderful things, things which made his blood boil, things which turned Darcie into a wild, heaving mass of passion.

And then, after seeing Lyris apply the favorite method of Lesbos to Darcie's willing body, he heard her speak.

"Now, my little darling," Lyris said. "I have something very, very nice for you."

"Oh, oh," Darcie was moaning, lifting herself as the heated contact was broken. "Don't leave, please, please."

"Close your eyes," Lyris said. "Imagine the nicest things, and they will happen."

"Oh, yes," Darcie breathed, lying on her back, her lovely, shapely legs outflung, her woman's bush dampened by Lyris's kisses, her eyes now closed, her mouth in the form of a kiss, expectant, wildly exciting to Guy, who saw Lyris make a motion with one graceful hand.

He entered the room on silent, bare feet, feeling the sensuous thickness of the carpet, his eyes glued on the trim and beautiful young girl.

"Just keep your eyes closed, darling," Lyris whispered, urging him on with one hand, taking her other hand to open Darcie's outflung legs still wider, Darcie quivering to her touch.

Guy positioned himself. Darcie could feel the movement, thought only in terms of Lyris's sweet weight atop her own body, started to reach up with her arms, but felt Lyris's hands on her wrists, holding her arms down as Lyris's body was poised over her and then lowering, an uncharacteristic panting to her breathing and then she was touched by something firm and hot and she felt herself being opened and, in an instant, it slid into already perfumed and lubricated secret places and, with a thrill of total sensuality, she threw her loins upward and felt her possessed, once again, by man, realizing it with a cry of alarm, opening her mouth to scream and feeling it covered by the hot, soft, wet lips of her female lover and then her eyes looked up past Lyris's black hair into the eyes of Guy.

"Feel," Lyris whispered, her hand going down to smooth, soothe, touch the distended labia pushed out by Guy's hardness. "Experience, little darling, for it is good, it is fitting."

"No, no, please," Darcie moaned, even as her traitorous loins heaved up, with a mind of their own, to feel man squeezed into her depths, to feel the unbelievable thrill of contact and friction. Then she was breathing wildly, her body heaving, unable to get enough, lifting, answering Guy's lunges with upward thrusts, laughing, sobbing with the glory of it as she quickly reached those heights from which she hoped never to fall and it seemed to go on forever. Then, poundingly, it was over, and they were laughing, kissing, fondling, a *ménage à trois* which had been con-

structed so skillfully by Lyris that it seemed natural
to be abed, naked and loving, the three of them spending the sleepless night in endless experimentation. Darcie forgetting, for the moment, her coming trial, knowing only the bliss which came to her when she was
filled by Guy and caressed by the tender Lyris, amazed
to find that Guy and Lyris together, tightly bound,
joined, was a voluptuous sight which heated her own
blood into new and demanding desire.

Now there was a constant undercurrent of lust in
the white house on the Garonne, as winter made a last
assault and there were additional signs of growing life
in Darcie. Now she had something to live for, something which worked a magic and, better than drink or
drugs, took her mind away from the *thing* which grew
in her stomach. The nights were spent in ceaseless
orgy, and she came to resent the daytime presence of
her sister, which prevented her from going to one of
her lovers to express her seemingly boundless lust.

That she felt guilt, at times, added to her resentment
of Petra. Innocent Petra, so blond, so rosy, so childishly naïve, had escaped the horrible scene in the
sheepcote, had not been raped by the maniacal dwarf,
had not been totally and hopelessly debauched by an
Eurasian voluptuary and by her own uncle.

Hateful Petra. Sometimes Darcie wished her dead.
At other times, the child's loving nature overcame
Darcie's resentment and they were almost as close as
once they had been, before the world chose to humili-
ate Darcie and leave her sister untouched.

Summer came, with the war and uncertainty. Darcie
was huge, ungainly. Although she still participated in
the almost nightly bacchanals, she felt ugly and unwanted, although each of her lovers told her she was
still beautiful, and Guy, in particular, explained his
lack of attentions to her by saying that intercourse was
not advisable in her advanced condition. In the end,
she stopped even watching, secluded herself in her

room, and contented herself with imaginings, feeling a new horror at her swollen belly.

August was her time, in the hottest part of the year, sweat and pain and long hours of labor, grunting, ugly, fearful, thinking of seeing that horrible blob coming out of her mother's body, knowing in her heart that she would not survive the ordeal.

Guy himself was concerned, although Darcie's inverted womb had straightened itself during the course of her confinement. She was such a tiny girl. But the genes of Carolle Moncrief were in her daughter. Darcie had Carolle's outflowing hips, a pelvis wide for her size. The birth was uncomplicated and swift, once the initial hours of labor were past. It was over before Darcie could accept the deliverance into sweet, comfortable sleep, her stomach now once more unswollen. She felt free and wonderful, and, upon waking, was not even sure she heard the cry of a child.

It had long since been decided that the child was to be delivered into the keeping of a childless farmer, Francis Freneau, and his wife Marie, whose establishment was but twenty miles away southward along the coast. Only Guy and Lyris knew of the arrangement.

When she awoke, Darcie's first thought was for the new and wonderful flatness of her stomach. She let her hands dwell there, a smile of satisfaction on her face. She saw Lyris's kind and beautiful face bending over her.

"The baby," Darcie asked, "was it, was it—"

"Actually, it was quite a beautiful baby," Lyris said.

"May I see it?" Actually, she didn't want to see it, but there was something, an unexplained urge, which made her curious.

"No, little one, you may not," Lyris said. "She has already been delivered to her new mother."

"She?" Darcie asked. "It was a girl, then?"

"With a headful of dark hair and a pair of lungs which were quite healthy. She screamed quite loudly."

Lyris smiled. "It is for the best, little one. If you never see her, you will not miss her. You are far too young to be burdened with a child. I assure you that she has been delivered into a good home, where she will be loved and cared for tenderly."

"And I'll never know her," Darcie said with a trace of regret.

"No, you will never know her," Lyris said. "And that is as it should be, for someday you will marry and have children with a man of your own choosing."

8

PETRA WAS, ALL agreed, a lovely child, but in the way more and more as Darcie recovered from the birth of her daughter. Paris was still in turmoil, although, from correspondence with D'Art, Guy learned that de Lesseps had returned and taken up residence in an apartment on the Rue Saint Florentin. It was decided to place Petra in a school in Bordeaux, and this was accomplished in time for the fall term.

Life at Chateau du Blanc was now a delight. When, upon examination, which was among the more sensual medical examinations of all time, Guy told Darcie that she never again had to concern herself with fears of pregnancy, she declared a celebration which ended, as all their celebrations ended, in a tangled and very complete *ménage* extending far into the night.

At first, when Roger D'Art wrote and asked permission to call at Chateau du Blanc, Guy considered it an intrusion. However, over a year had been spent in wild and riotous orgy at the country estate, and secretly, Guy was more than ready to return to Paris, if only things would stabilize there.

He met D'Art in Bordeaux, and they talked with great animation on the drive back to the chateau. D'Art was full of news. The Americans had sent a survey party to Darien, in Panama, to examine a possible route for an Atlantic to Pacific canal, and the old war-horse, Ferdinand de Lesseps, had been heard to express great interest.

Neither D'Art nor Simel had had foresight enough to invest in Suez bonds, which, in spite of France's problems, had proven to be a very good investment. In idle speculation, both agreed that should de Lesseps, with his personality of pure magic, engage in a Panama venture, both would invest heavily.

D'Art was urged into spending the Christmas season with them, and, with Petra home for the holidays, the house functioned almost as normally as the average French country home.

In addition to the American expedition to Panama, there had been two French visits in the 1860s, and D'Art was in agreement with de Lesseps that the logical place for a canal was Panama, not Nicaragua, the route most favored by the Americans.

Petra had passsed her fifteenth birthday, and, although she was not as mature in body as Darcie, she was larger; a happy, smiling, blond girl with flowing graceful movements, a honey skin, flashing brown eyes to contrast with her golden hair, full, kissable lips and a laugh which warmed Roger D'Art's heart. Sensing a coldness in the older Moncrief girl, he found himself, during his extended stay, spending more and more time with the laughing Petra. Had he been married, with a daughter of his own, he would have chosen her to be like Petra, and he often told the girl so, to her blushing pleasure.

There was about the house a feeling which did not please D'Art. There was no overt action to enforce his small feeling of doubt, but there was something—an undercurrent of tension—which puzzled him. However, if Petra felt it, she gave no sign of it. She seemed to be a happy, uncomplicated child, eager to resume her schoolwork and even more eagerly looking forward to the time when the family could move to Paris.

When D'Art left after the beginning of the new year, he promised to inform Guy the minute the situation seemed stable enough to set up their joint practice in Paris. Petra went happily back to school. Very unfeminine, said her teachers of her interest in chemistry and the study of medicine. She expressed an interest in becoming a doctor, like her Uncle Guy and her good friend Roger, but she was discouraged. Although Florence Nightingale had established the profession of nursing, first, with her group of women in the Crimea and, secondly, by establishing a highly respectable school of nursing at St. Thomas's Hospital in 1860, the profession was still considered, by many, to be quite unladylike and not at all suited for a girl of good family, such as Petra. Most nursing schools in France were run by the Roman Catholic church, and Petra was not Catholic. Her expressions of interest in becoming a nurse, if not a doctor, earned her pats on the head from Guy and a promise to "talk about it," after they were in Paris, near the larger schools.

Petra had little opportunity to meet boys of her own age during that stay in the provinces; her school was all female, and the only men around the chateau were Guy and the family retainers and workmen. She had little time for thoughts of romance, however, beyond sneaking a quick read of a novel now and then, so engrossed was she in her schoolwork and in the not always simple process of simply growing up.

In March and April of 1871, Paris, long smoldering, erupted into violence. Long the most radical part of France, the city, having survived the four-months-long German siege and the humiliating experience of seeing German troops marching down the boulevards, was taken over by a commune composed of radicals, a

few moderates, and members of the communist First
International. Once again, during Bloody Week, in
May, the city knew the terror of war as the National
Assembly at Versailles sent troops to battle the forces
of the Commune. Victorious, the government forces
visited sanguinary punishment on large numbers of
radicals, deported or exiled others. By summer, Roger
D'Art concluded that it was time for Guy to bring his
small group of attractive females to Paris.

It was a time of excitement. Although he was not a
rich man, Guy had means, derived from Chateau du
Blanc, primarily, and he told his little "family" that
it was important for a physician to put up a good
front. Therefore, he conducted his house-hunting activities in exclusive and expensive areas of the city and
finally purchased an attractive establishment on the
fashionable Avenue Montaigne, quite near the Champs-
Élysées, within easy walking distance of such grand
monuments as the Grand Palais and Petit Palais, Napoleon's Arc de Triomphe, the Place d'Étoile and the
museum established by Napoleon to display his war
booty, the Louvre, on the Quai des Tuileries. One of
the near neighbors was a short, distinguished man with
hair turned almost white, large, black restless eyes, a
tanned and healthy face, an iron-gray moustache—
none other than Ferdinand de Lesseps, the hero of
Suez. The de Lesseps house dwarfed Guy Simel's establishment. All of five stories, in the next few years
it was to become one of the top social gathering places
in all of Paris, with de Lesseps entertaining more and
more as the old warrior's interest in a sea-level canal
at Panama grew with France's return to normal, the
payment of the German war reparations, and the renewed vigor of the economy.

As de Lesseps's personal physician, Roger D'Art
could pick and choose his patients. Quickly after the
establishment of the practice, Dr. Roger D'Art became
the doctor for the wealthy, and his young assistant, the

handsome Guy Simel, was scarcely less in demand—even more so at social occasions. D'Art was somewhat stuffy and altogether too serious by half.

D'Art and Simel were frequent guests at the de Lesseps house and, quite often, it was *en famille,* with de Lesseps's charming and beautiful wife hosting Guy's two pert and pretty nieces. This situation was not to Lyris's liking. For the sake of appearances, her presence in the Simel house was explained by calling her nurse-governess, and servants, even beloved ones, are not invited on social occasions. She contented herself with a life of her own, built around an entirely different circle, peopled, among others, with handsome young army officers who did not ask about the beautiful Eurasian's social standing.

It was Lyris who met and seduced and made talkative a strange and outgoing Hungarian who possessed, perhaps, the largest moustache in all of Paris, and who had ambitions which quickly attracted Lyris's interest. It was not that she was totally tired of Guy, for he still had the capacity to excite her, and to exploit her excitement better than any man she'd ever known. But she was now over twenty-seven years old, and, although she could have returned to Cairo and lived comfortably on her endowment from her French father, she was not content to be a woman in a Moslem country, nor was she content to continue to masquerade as a servant in the household of an up-and-coming young physician.

Like de Lesseps, General Istvan Türr, was a hero of sorts, having acted as second in command to Garibaldi in Sicily and, for a time, representing King Victor Emmanuel II on diplomatic missions. Tall, handsome, always dressed with the utmost elegance, he was a Paris celebrity. When he appeared in public with a beautiful Eurasian on his arm, there was, of course, gossip.

But, Lyris explained to Guy, there was method to her madness. With his powerful connections, General Türr was a man worth knowing—a man who could, if

properly cultivated, lead them into a fortune which
would make all pretense unnecessary forever.

Acting as go-between, Lyris arranged a meeting between Guy and Türr. The Hungarian was often included on the invitation list by de Lesseps, but there
was, at that time, no strong tie between the two men.
It was Guy who was to be instrumental in beginning
the relationship between the socially powerful Hungarian and the even more powerful de Lesseps.

Because of his friendship with de Lesseps, as the
partner of the distinguished old gentleman's best friend,
Roger D'Art, Guy could not openly push toward the
desired end which was to inveigle de Lesseps, hero of
Suez, into heading a consortium aimed at accomplish-
ing the same results in the Panamian isthmus as at
Suez. Nevertheless, with Lyris entertaining Türr, often
between perfumed sheets, and with Guy having de
Lesseps's ear, there came a time for action and the
result was formation of the *Société Civile Internationale
du Canal Interocéanique de Darien*. Powerful men were
members of the company, which was capitalized at
300,000 francs, but neither de Lesseps's nor Simel's
name appeared among the stockholders.

De Lesseps's interest was aroused however, and despite the questions asked by his son Charles, the old
man was almost totally committed to building a second
huge, expensive, and vastly important canal. Guy and
Lyris were sure the stocks would be equally as valuable
as the Suez stocks, which climbed steadily as France
recovered and the English took more interest in Suez,
and which would be their means of becoming so rich
that their lives could be spent in the total pursuit of
pleasure.

9

 "You are far too fat," Darcie scolded Petra.

"I am not fat," Petra said, but she was hurt. More and more of late, her sister seemed to have unkind thinks to say to her. She tried to be patient, not to snap back when Darcie was irritable, but sometimes it was difficult—especially when the attacks seemed to come without cause and, most often, without previous warning.

The occasion was a party for young people to which Petra had been invited. Darcie had not received an invitation, but that seemed natural to Petra, since Darcie had, long since, taken her place in the adult world. She was, after all, eighteen, and quite a grown-up lady, still as slim as she had been at sixteen, and even more beautiful as maturity blessed her with larger breasts, flowing hips, and a rich, smooth skin which was the envy of all other women who saw her.

At sixteen, Petra seemed not half as mature. And yet her body had blossomed, her blond hair was long and luxuriant, her skin equally as smooth, but lighter than Darcie's, a mixture of honey and cream.

Petra was discovering the male sex. To date, her experience, as compared to Darcie's, was nonexistent, Petra having been kissed, twice, by the son of one of M. de Lesseps's friends, who was also an acquaintance of her uncle's.

It seemed to Petra, at times, that she was not really a member of the family, that the others—her uncle, her sister, and Lyris—were always in possession of some secret from which she was excluded. Darcie seemed to be much closer to the adults than she, but there was mixed blessing in that, for their lack of interest in Petra left her free to arrange her own life to please herself. When she started to attend parties, at first she asked permission, and, finding that it was given with a nonchalance bordering on indifference, she took merely to announcing her plans. Had she been inclined to misbehave, she would have been free to do so, but her morals were those of her mother and her father, her companions products of the same stern and Christian upbringing, her follies few, tending toward girlish pranks in school.

But now Petra was in love. She was sure that it was love, that it was eternal, and that there'd never been a woman (giving herself the benefit of the doubt) who had been so much in love.

His name was Charles. He was sixteen, her own age. He lived quite nearby, and it was astounding that she had not met him before. When she first met Charles, she was immediately sorry that she'd kissed the boy in the de Lesseps garden—not once but twice—for her love was so pure, so holy, that she wanted to save all of herself for Charles. It was Charles who was calling for her, in his father's carriage, to take her to the party.

And now, as she was dressed in her newest and nicest frock, her sister was trying to spoil it by saying that she was fat.

She was not fat. She was—one good word for it—plush. Full of feminine delights, with her breasts full, her hips large, her waist small, her limbs full and feminine. True, she was larger than Darcie and did not have Darcie's delicate and fragile beauty, but she was not fat.

She was still pouting when the front doorbell rang and she rushed off to answer it, all asmile as Charles stood, tall and unbelievably handsome, in the doorway. He doffed his hat and bowed, and then, straight again, his eyes met hers for an instant and then shifted suddenly and he was staring, his face going red. Petra turned to see the cause of his discomfort. Darcie was in the entrance hall, a strange little smile on her full lips.

"Will you not introduce me to your friend?" Darcie asked.

"Charles, my sister Darcie," Petra said sullenly, feeling a flash of anger as Charles continued to stare as if mesmerized.

"I am so pleased that my younger sister has such good taste," Darcie said, moving forward, swaying her hips seductively. "Such a handsome young man for such a young girl?"

"Charles, it is time for us to go," Petra said.

"You must come back to visit, Charles," Darcie said.

The party was a total failure. Charles, once so much fun, so attentive, was bemused. Not once but several times, when he should have been dancing with Petra or paying her compliments, he asked questions about her sister.

Petra went home, saddened, angry, but Darcie was sweet and kind and loving, and Petra did not discover for days that Charles had indeed come calling while she was out. She did not have the kind of mind to imagine the astonishment of young Charles when, with a haste which made his head swim, he was hauled off to Darcie's bed, where he was treated to an acrobatic display of sheer womanhood which drove little Petra from his mind forever. Darcie, whose sexual activities

had been limited to experiment with her uncle and
with Lyris, discovered the joy of newness, and only
her quick, flaming nature allowed her to keep pace
with the youthful quickness of Charles.

Unaware of the situation, Petra was in her room
studying when Charles next came calling, but when
she heard the bell, all curious, she went to the top of
the stairs, saw Charles, and started to go down to
greet him. Then, before she could move, she saw Darcie come into the hallway dressed for the street.

Well, Petra told herself, *if he prefers an older woman so be it.* But she was hurt. Her first great love had
lasted for mere days, and then he was stolen by her
sister, who, after using him severely for less than two
weeks, tossed him back, protesting his undying love
for her, to the doubtful joys of youth.

There was a new coldness between the sisters which
went unnoticed by Guy and Lyris, all intent on their
schemes and themselves branching out into new romantic ventures in the city. It was Roger D'Art who
noted, while he was dining alone with the two girls,
that only the necessary conversation passed between
them. At first he said nothing. He was in the habit of
talking with Petra, more so than with Darcie, and quite
often he called for her to take her on excursions into
the city, liking her company, feeling refreshed by her
youthful enthusiasm and not disliking the looks they
received as they walked the boulevards. Serious, yes,
settled, yes, but not so serious or so settled that he did
not enjoy squiring an attractive young lady about the
town.

When Darcie stole away another beau, using the
same tactics which, unknown to Petra, included an
offering of lust which was totally irresistible to the
young man, Petra was angered and engaged in hot
words, threatening, in ladylike language, to "scratch
out some eyes" if it happened again.

More and more it seemed that Darcie said hateful,

taunting things, telling Petra that her large body made her bovine, that blond hair was so cheap, that she had no clothes sense.

"Sister, why do you hate me so?" she asked, after one bitter exchange.

"I don't hate you. Don't give yourself that much importance," Darcie said spitefully. "It's just that your false sweetness makes me sick."

"I am not consciously false," Petra said, "and I do love you, Darcie. Why do you taunt me so?"

"You do make me sick," Darcie said, stalking from the room.

It was as if a wall had been built between them, and Petra had no way of knowing that Darcie, seeing her so young, so innocent, so much enjoying the slow and precious discovery of grown-up pleasures, was envious. She felt as if her own childhood had been stolen from her, first in that dreadful sheepcote in Norfolk, then on the filthy dirt of an Egyptian grove. She knew that she could have any man she wanted, had proven that to herself by so easily luring away Petra's beaux, but she knew, too, that she was using unfair tactics, offering the lads adult pleasure which, surely, they would choose over a sweet little kiss at the door with Petra. Why, she wondered, had it all happened to her? It was easy for her to forget that while her parents were alive she was always given preferential treatment over her sister. It was not easy to forget the horror of her mother's death, Nanny-Ruth lying in the mud with her head cut open, the ooze and blood from Adrienne's opened stomach, the pain and terror of being raped by the horrible dwarf. Why couldn't it have been Petra? Always she had escaped the horrors, smiling and laughing and recovering from her false grief with a quickness which was sickening. Let her one time be forced down into the dirt to have her virginity taken by a beast, and the sweet smiles would fade.

It was a relatively minor incident which alerted

Roger D'Art to the state of affairs between the two sisters. He came calling, unexpectedly, to find them in the hall, heatedly disputing the possession of a new issue of *Le Temps,* which was featuring, in installments, that most popular work by Jules Verne, *Around the World in 80 Days.* Unseen, he stood outside the open door and listened.

At first the argument was mere childishness, he noted with a grim smile, Petra maintaining that she had the paper first, Darcie disputing it. Petra, larger and perhaps stronger, had physical possession of the paper, and Darcie was not going to dispute her physically. Instead, she launched an attack, the ferocity of which startled D'Art.

"I hate you, you little blond bitch," Darcie said with emotion. "You think you have the right to dispute me? You are nothing but a little whore, chasing your pimply-faced boys like a panting bitch. You have no right to live in this house with decent human beings."

"Here, here!" D'Art said, thinking that it was time to intercede.

Darcie looked at him quickly, an expression of pure hate on her face, then fled up the stairs. Petra, near tears, stood, the paper dangling from her limp hand, looking at him without understanding. To try to make her forget the cruel words, he took her to a sidewalk face and ordered chocolate, but it did not cheer her.

"Is she like that often?" he asked, knowing that avoidance of the subject would not help.

"She's never said such horrible things before," Petra said.

"You get along well most of the time?" he asked.

"Well," she said. Then; "We used to."

"And then?"

"And then, oh, I don't know," she said.

"Tell me," he said. "You'll find that I'm a good listener."

"I don't know," she repeated. "It's as if she's come

to hate me, and, oh, Doctor D'Art, I do love her so. Her and Uncle Guy and Lyris, too, and sometimes it's as if they don't even know I'm around. I mean, they laugh and talk, and if I say anything, they all look at me as if I'm intruding."

"Hummm," he said.

"And Darcie has no life of her own, so she steals my beaux, and it's almost as if she does it just to spite me and prove that she can do it."

"Darcie spends a lot of time with your uncle and with Lyris—is that not true?" D'Art asked.

"Yes. I've tried to get her to go to parties with me, but she taunts me about being young and says that she doesn't have time to play with the children."

D'Art didn't know all, but he knew that Darcie was a disturbed young lady. She had good reason to be, true, but it would have been more natural for her to gradually forget the past and to become more gay. She certainly had opportunity, ample invitations, which she most often refused, unless they included Guy, and, of late, Lyris. This puzzled him, the way Lyris, who had been brought to France as a servant, was becoming socially acceptable in more and more places. He had always suspected that the relationship between Guy and the beautiful Eurasian was more than doctor-nurse or master-servant. And yet, they seemed, now, to be going their separate ways, with Lyris seen quite often in the company of rich and powerful men.

Petra was still young and unspoiled, and he determined to do his best to keep her that way, not to allow her to be influenced by Lyris, or touched by Darcie's melancholia. He soon found a way, by arranging for Petra to enter a very good nursing school. When, on a visit to the Simel house, he announced the possibility of Petra's fulfilling one of her ambitions, Petra was overjoyed. The others merely gave curt agreement, as if, D'Art thought, glad to have the bright and happy young girl out of the house.

Now Petra was home only on holidays. D'Art, feeling responsible for her being in the school, visited her, took her on outings, and became, during that period, her most constant companion, outside of her friends in the school.

D'Art had other responsibilities, but he never failed to be available when Petra, perhaps discouraged by the difficult work, needed encouragement or just someone to talk with, and he never failed to remember special days, her vacations, her birthday.

As for Petra, she was engrossed, and wanted, very badly, to continue her work, to become a doctor. She applied herself totally to her schoolwork. It was as if, having had several beaux stolen by Darcie, she did not want to risk further hurt. She saw her "family" seldom, and when she did they were cool and polite. Guy and Lyris were very much involved with the Türr syndicate and when Ferdinand de Lesseps announced to the world that he was vitally interested in building a cross isthmus canal, and cemented his interests by buying the Türr syndicate holdings, the *Société Civile Internationale du Canal Interocéanique de Darien,* whose chief asset was a concession from the Colombian government for such a canal, there was a celebration, the reason for which Petra did not know. The reason was well known to Guy and Lyris. For their services in helping persuade de Lesseps to enter the venture, their reward was measured fivefold.

10

Dressed in morning coat, gray gloves and top hat, Jay Burton lingered behind the American delegation approaching the newly erected headquarters of the French Geographic Society at 184 Boulevard Saint-Germain in the fabled Latin Quarter. Paris, in mid-May 1879, had won his heart. He was not the first, nor would he be the last to fall under the spell of that most seductive of all cities, but, being human, he felt as if he and he alone had made the great discovery. As an engineer, he was impressed by the well-planned city.

At twenty-seven, Burton was one of the younger members of the American delegation, a man of large construction, his body hard, with no surplus fat, but stocky, even for his height of almost six feet. His hair was trim, closely cut, the temples shorn off even with the center of his ears, shorter than was the fashion. He had a strong nose and piercing large gray eyes under expressive brows. The first impression Burton gave was one of masculine strength and confidence. His rudimentary French came from a mouth half-covered by a neatly trimmed moustache a shade darker than his brown hair. He was in Paris as an official representative of the City of San Francisco, which had a vital interest in an Atlantic-Pacific canal.

While others had spent their evenings exploring the gay night life of what was known as the world's most cosmopolitan city, Burton kept to his room studying maps and admiring the work done by Baron Georges Eugène Haussmann, under the administration of Napoleon III, in transforming Paris from a glutted medieval sprawl into the graceful, organized city which allowed a free flow of traffic on wide boulevards. Burton thought it ironic that the creator of modern Paris should bear a Teutonic name, although the good baron was born in Paris. The baron had cut straight avenues through a chaos of meandering streets. The street on which Burton stood, the Boulevard Saint-Germain, was a creation of Haussmann, corresponding to the grand boulevards on the opposite bank of the river.

On the previous evening, Burton had walked along the river to see the magnificent design of Haussmann's bridges, the National, de Solferino, de l'Alma and the Viaduc d'Auteuil. There the engineer of Paris had come into his own, building structures which would carry the unpredictable traffic of the future.

Burton loved his own city, thought it had a splendid future, especially after the opening of a canal in Central America, but its helter-skelter reconstructions after the numerous early fires left much to be desired. He wished fervently, as he studied Haussmann's Paris, for the opportunity of opening up his city as Haussmann had opened Paris. The booming growth of San Francisco occurred so swiftly, however, that planning was difficult, and he did not have the traditions of centuries on which to build.

Burton had come to Paris with an open mind, although he resented, with a thoroughly American pride, the fact that first actions toward building a canal were being taken not by Americans, but by Frenchmen.

However, he realized the value of the hero of Suez, knowing that de Lesseps's great prestige would be invaluable in raising the tremendous sums of money needed for such an undertaking.

Inside the grand hall, a distinguished company was gathering, with delegates from all over Europe, from Guatemala and from Nicaragua, a country which had a great stake in plans for a canal, from Russia and China, and the independent nation of Hawaii. The delegates filled the first few rows, the balance of the lofty hall filled by spectators, including ladies of fashion and members of the press.

Burton had been assigned to the Technical Committee, a large group which, he discovered, was composed of more than 50 percent Frenchmen. Indeed, a solid majority of all delegates were French, and not a quarter of the total number were engineers.

The first session of the grand congress was largely for show, with de Lesseps stating, "The presence of ladies at a scientific gathering is always a good omen."

Among the ladies present was Petra Moncrief, a bosomy beauty with blond curls, dressed in the latest of Paris styles, her full mature beauty making her stand out among the most sophisticated women of the world. Petra was twenty-three in 1879. She had long since finished her training and was working as a nurse in a Paris hospital, finding the work to be both heartbreaking and rewarding. Although she did not lack for male attention, she had not, since her first youthful love for the boy Charles, who had been stolen away so unfairly by her sister, allowed her heart to go out to any male. She was, she knew, well past the usual age for marriage, but she had her work and her friends, chief among them Dr. Roger D'Art, who had become, over the years, very much like the father she did not have.

Petra still lived at home in the Simel house on the Avenue Montaigne, but she was often alone there, with only servants in attendance. Guy, very much involved in the early planning for a canal project, was much away, as was Lyris, who, more and more, was going her own way. Her sister Darcie, like herself, unmarried, came and went with unpredictable impulse, and, to Petra's mixture of shame and pride, had become one of the more famous—or infamous—ladies of Paris. Darcie, slim and utterly lovely, was a fixture at grand social events, often on the arm of her uncle, Guy Simel. Petra was fully aware that there was speculation about the relationship of Darcie and her uncle, but she put it aside as envious gossip.

Over the years of her nurse's training, when she was away in school for long periods, her relationship with Darcie had stabilized into an unsisterlike cool politeness. This was one of Petra's great sadnesses, for she often felt quite alone in the world, having no relatives other than Guy, who seemed to be fond of her but indifferent, and her sister, who, she had to admit, had come to despise her.

Yet there was the work. And there was Roger. When she needed an escort, it was Roger who was always available. When she needed to talk about her work or personal matters, he was always there. As de Lesseps's friend and physician, D'Art was vitally interested in the plans for a Panama canal, and it was his presence among the delegates to the *Congrès Internationale d'Études du Canal Interocéanique* which drew Petra to sit among the spectators during the often boring speeches and discussions.

Although he was a physician and knew little about engineering problems, D'Art had been named by de Lesseps to sit on the Technical Committee, where he soon met and came to like the young American, Jay Burton.

It was at the end of the second session that D'Art met Petra on the stairs, on a pleasant May evening which presented the city in a most favorable light.

Burton, discussing a problem in his accented French, came walking down the stairs with Roger, his hand on the older man's arm, his face bent close as he made a point.

"I quite agree," Roger was saying, as they came abreast of Petra and she, with mild interest, examined the strong, masculine face of the young man she'd noticed among the delegates. "But, my dear Burton," Roger went on, "even you Americans must admit that there is no one in the world with more knowledge, more experience, than Monsieur de Lesseps."

Burton started to speak, and then his eyes fell on Petra, who was moving toward them, her figure displayed to good advantage in a long, pastel gown, her hips accentuated by the protruding bustle, her body showing its shape through a light summer petticoat and the gown. Burton halted, his mouth open, his strong gray eyes locked on Petra's smile.

"Ah, there you are, my dear," Roger said. "May I present, my dear Petra, my friend and colleague, Mr. Jay Burton, from the American city of San Francisco. Mr. Burton, Miss Petra Moncrief."

"*Enchanté*," Petra said. "And how are you finding Paris, Mr. Burton?"

"Lovelier by the minute," Burton said in English, and then his brow furrowed as he tried to find the appropriate words in the unfamiliar language.

"Ah," Petra said, in English. "American men, too, know the art of flattery."

"In fact," D'Art laughed, "Mr. Burton is more a fan of our city than most natives. He is voluble on the subject."

"I can be a bore," Jay said, answering D'Art's laugh, "but I have fallen in love with Paris."

"Many people do," Petra said. "I am still having a love affair with her."

"You are not a native, then?" Jay asked, his eyes locked on hers with a somewhat disturbing intensity.

"Oh, no," she said. "I'm a foreigner, too—a Londoner, as a matter of fact."

"My second favorite city," Jay said.

"I have a splendid idea," D'Art said. "Petra, here, has become an authority on Paris. She spends her time walking the boulevards and visiting historic places. Perhaps she would consent to sharing her knowledge with you."

"Actually," Petra said, preparing to make some excuse.

"Perhaps we presume too much," Jay said with a smile. "I'm sure Miss Moncrief cannot change her plans at such short notice."

Well, she thought, *he seemed civilized, and he was a friend of D'Art.* She had nothing to do. She did not look forward to spending an evening alone in the house.

"Actually," she said, "I'd love it. I'm always pleased to meet a fellow admirer of my city."

"There will be a reception at Monsieur de Lesseps," D'Art said. "Perhaps, after a short tour of the city, you could deliver Miss Moncrief there and I will see her home."

"Yes, of course," Jay said. His smile was broad, his teeth white and strong under his moustache. "And now I place myself in the hands of my lovely guide."

It was a delightful evening, and Petra loved walking. She never tired of it. As she led the way down Saint-Germain and they gained the banks of the river to look across to St.-Louis and Notre Dame, she found that Burton had a solid knowledge of the city from maps and needed only to be oriented. He talked not only of the work done in recent decades to make Paris a modern city, but of his own city, with its hills and the wide bay. Her perfect and clipped English accent contrasted with his broad and slower speech, and she found his voice to have a strange quality. When he spoke, with his natural, sincere enthusiasm, of the structure of the bridge over the Seine, she suddenly found herself, having taken such things for granted, to be vitally interested in bridges. Moreover, his voice seemed to strike a resonance in her, as if some distant drum beat slowly and strongly to cause sensation deep inside her.

Having walked to the island and up it to the impressive facade of Notre Dame, Jay inquired if she were tired, and she said, laughingly, that she was conditioned by long walks alone.

"I can't believe that you would have to walk alone," he said.

Troubled by her response to him, by the feeling she had when he looked at her with those eagle eyes, by the tremors caused inside her by the sound of his voice, she bristled slightly. "It is by choice, monsieur," she said.

"Yes, yes, of course," he said. "Sorry."

Walking was pleasant, but in order to cover more area, she suggested a hackney, and, in an open carriage, they rode in silence, for a while, along the embankment into the huge and impressive Place de la Concorde. Far ahead there appeared Napoleon's monument.

"I do envy you," Jay said, breaking the silence. "Will you stay in Paris? I'm sure I would, if it were possible."

"I am happy here," she said.

Upon her directions, the driver turned left onto the Avenue Montaigne and soon there was, ahead, the activity of comings and goings in front of the impressive de Lesseps house.

"Would I be presuming to ask that you serve as my guide for further exploration, perhaps tomorrow?" Jay asked as the hackney drew up.

Petra was silent for a moment. She had not been affected so by a man since her first childish love, and this one was an American who, within days, would be traveling far away. Discretion dictated that she thank him politely for his interest and get on with her life.

But what was her life? Long hours of work when she actually did not need to work, having enough from her inheritance to allow her to live comfortably? Suddenly, the thought of going back to the hospital, to spend long hours with the sick and the dying, had lost its appeal. She was adult. She could control her emotions. She enjoyed the company of this big, strong American, so why deprive herself of so small a pleasure?

"I would be pleased," she said.

"You will be attending tomorrow's session of the congress?"

"Perhaps I can arrive late," she said. "And if not, Doctor D'Art can supply you with my address."

D'Art delivered her to the house in the early evening, before ten o'clock, and she found herself to be alone. She lingered over her end-of-day toilet, and, once in bed, allowed herself to analyze her feelings about the American.

He was pleasant, handsome, strong, well spoken in his quaint accents, and she would not, very definitely, allow herself to fall in love with him.

Strange, though, the effect his deep, male voice had on her. Thinking of it, she could remember its sound, and could almost feel the response, the little vibrations deep inside her.

She left her work early the next day, and, having stopped off to bathe and dress, arrived just as the day's session was drawing to an end in a discussion of possible routes for the proposed canal. They took a carriage and spent long hours exploring the left bank, ending, once again, on the Champs-Élysées, where they dined and lingered over rich, creamed coffee in a pleasant café.

Jay seemed moody, and when opportunity presented itself, the reason became clear. "Monsieur de Lesseps,

I fear, has made his mind up already," he said. "He seems intent on digging a sea level canal across Panama, and American studies show that this is quite impossible."

"They said Suez was impossible, too," Petra said.

"I don't underestimate the man," Jay said. "But I have read the Wise Report, which is the most complete the French have made, and it does not take into account the geology of Panama. At Suez, the problem was merely moving sand and mud. In Panama, the earth is mostly rock, and conditions are much worse."

"Surely it cannot be so difficult, being such a short distance," Petra said. "Suez was one hundred and five miles. It's only about forty miles across the isthmus."

"Across rivers and mountains," Jay said. "The engineering problems will be a thousand times more difficult than Suez."

"Is this your American pride speaking?" she asked, disarming the barb with a smile. "Are you chagrined because Monsieur de Lesseps won't consider the Nicaraguan route?"

"Perhaps," he said, laughing. "However, on a May night in Paris, with a beautiful lady across the table, I don't care where de Lesseps digs his canal."

As they walked in the cool of the evening, a handsome couple in a city of handsome people, she felt his hand on her arm as they crossed a street, and the touch was a new experience for her—a little jolt of sensation which heightened her awareness of the beauty of the weather, the city, her own sense of well-being.

"You said once that you envied me, living in Paris," she said. "I, on the other hand, envy you, for you will be a part of the great adventure."

"Perhaps," he said. "But if it is totally a French venture—"

"Monsieur de Lesseps considers himself to be a citizen of the world," she said. "Oh, he loves his France, but he would not let your nationality be a factor. He will need good engineers." She smiled up him. "You are a good engineer, are you not?"

Burton grinned, winking at her. "I've got everyone fooled so far."

"And so, you men, you arrogant beasts, will be off for romantic and glamorous places, doing great things, while I remain in Paris and work," she said.

"If I had a choice between Paris and Pamana, there would be no hesitation on my part," he said. "Panama is not exactly romantic and glamorous. In fact, it's somewhat of a hellhole."

"Have you been there, then?"

"Once. I traveled across the isthmus on the Panama Railroad. It is said that there was one dead man for every tie between Colón and Panama City."

"There was also sickness during the construction of Suez."

"Yes, but although Egypt is hot and dry, it is a health resort compared to Panama. If yellow jack doesn't get you, then you're sure to get malaria or dysentery or half a dozen other diseases, including cholera, smallpox and other fevers which don't even have a name."

"Still, I think it would be nice to have a part in something really important," she said.

"You have your work. Doctor D'Art says that you're quite a good nurse, very dedicated."

Petra shrugged. "Sometimes I feel so helpless. We know so little."

"There will be a need for nurses in Panama," he said. And, with his hand on her arm, "I can think of no one I'd rather have at my bedside. It would almost be worth being ill."

"Almost?" she asked, with a laugh.

"If you were by my side, it would unquestionably be worth it," he said, his face turned toward her, as he looked down into her eyes.

A funny little thing happened inside her, almost as if her heart had turned over. She looked away, at a loss for words.

"Petra," he said, "I am undecided as to whether to stay in France when my delegation goes home."

After a pause, she asked, "And what are the elements of your indecision?"

"Mainly you," he said.

"Monsieur," she said, "I fail to see—"

"You could very quickly convince me to stay."

"Well, then, if it is so simple, you will stay."

"Do you want me to?"

"Well, monsieur—"

"My name is Jay," he said.

"Well, Jay, it is not for me to say."

"Do you have other attachments?"

She considered her answer. She was not interested in a brief amour. Nor was she interested in marriage, especially to a foreigner who would be away for long periods of time at his work. And yet she did not want him to go.

"I have no attachments other than my work," she said softly.

"Should I stay, I would not want to spend my time alone in this lovely city."

"Ah, well, a handsome man should never be alone, and I'm sure you would have no difficulty."

"But I don't want to be with just anyone," he said.

They had walked into an area dimly lit by the gas lamps, alongside a grove of huge chestnuts. He, with his hand on her arm, guided her from the sidewalk into the dimness of the grove.

"I want to spend every possible moment with you," he said, pulling her to a halt, facing her in the soft darkness. "If you promise to spend every evening with me, I will stay."

"Well," she said, "perhaps not every evening."

"Most of them?"

"As many as possible," she said, her heart fluttering with his nearness.

"Ah, Petra," he said, drawing her close. At first she made feeble resistance, her hands against his chest. Then, with a real sigh, she allowed herself to be embraced, and, with a weakness coming over her, lifted her face, lips slightly parted, to accept his kiss.

Truly, she had never been kissed before. At least, none of the previous kisses counted, for never had she been immersed so totally in a kiss. It seemed to make her a part of him, a mere extension of his hard, muscular body. It was a roaring, all-consuming thing which closed out the traffic sounds from the boulevard leaving only tiny silver bells ringing in her heart as it went on and on and his strong arms held her close.

At last it was over. Had it continued longer, she was sure she would have swooned. Never had she known such emotion, such yearnings. And, although she would gladly have submitted, he did not kiss her again for days.

The grand congress concluded, with de Lesseps announcing to the world that he was taking command of the enterprise, and that he himself would go to Panama.

Jay Burton, a man in love, allowed his feeling for Petra to influence his thinking. He decided to stay on in Paris and, if possible, become a part of the de Lesseps organization.

Now was the time of triumph for Guy Simel. As a confidant of de Lesseps, he was among some 270 friends of de Lesseps who invested money in a syndicate which provided initial capital. As a founding member, Guy, and, of course, Lyris, who drew on her Egyptian resources to invest in the syndicate, would be sold founders' shares at a bargain price once a Panama company was organized. That this was a triumph was illustrated by Suez shares which had risen from an original price of 500 francs to 2,000 francs. In addition, both Guy and Lyris profited when de Lesseps bought out the Türr syndicate for ten million francs. Having been instrumental in bringing Türr and de Lesseps together, Guy and Lyris were rewarded in two ways: by being made a part of the new enterprise, which, like Suez would bring great profit, and by an unrecorded payment in cash from those who profited greatly by selling the Türr syndicate to the de Lesseps group. Profits on the sale were as high as 3,000 percent.

However, during that summer of Petra and Jay's discovery of each other, things did not always go smoothly. An attempt by de Lesseps to sell shares in a Panama canal company fell far short. Still full of confidence, de Lesseps announced that there would be another issue as soon as the situation was solidified.

De Lesseps was much impressed by the young American engineer who had become a friend of one of his oldest friends, Roger D'Art, and, moreover, it was good politics to have an American on his side, when most other Americans were laughing at his scheme to build a sea-level canal. He invited Jay to his home often, and Jay was invariably accompanied by Petra.

On one quiet evening, when the company present was limited to people quite close to de Lesseps, the old man took Jay and Roger aside where, over brandy, he talked with the usual confidence about the project.

Only D'Art knew that deep inside de Lesseps had doubts. After all, he was not young. He had met one great reverse when his first stock issue was subscribed to a value of only 10 percent. Moreover, D'Art knew that Charles de Lesseps was urging his father to avoid Panama, to let someone else have both the glory and the worry of a new canal project. So, although he was confident to the point of boastfulness on the surface, D'Art knew that de Lesseps had his private doubts, and he realized that, by questioning the young American on the subject, he was seeking confirmation of his own decision to take the Panama route and to aim for a sea-level rather than for a locked canal.

"I understand that you have been to Panama, Monsieur Burton," de Lesseps said. "Were you able to form an opinion during your stay there?"

"I had no opportunity for exhaustive study," Jay said.

"But surely, it is your belief that there is a route— a possible route," D'Art said, wanting to ease the old man's mind, if possible.

"Anything is possible," Jay said, not wanting, at that time, to commit himself. "After all, there is the railroad."

"Ah, yes," de Lesseps said. "And with such men as you, young engineers who do not know the word 'impossible,' and with the miracles of modern technology, we will conquer the isthmus."

"If anyone can do it, sir, it is you," Jay said, sensing that de Lesseps was actually seeking reassurance. "However, I would like to have a more complete survey."

"We shall have it," de Lesseps said. "We shall spare no expense. In fact, Monsieur Burton, I have been seeking an opportunity to ask you if you would care to accompany me and my group when we journey to Panama."

"I would be honored," Jay said.

De Lesseps was summoned by his wife, leaving Jay and Roger seated alone over brandy. "So you will go?" D'Art asked.

"Yes."

"And will you return to France?"

"Of course," Jay said, thinking of Petra.

"It would seem," D'Art said, speaking from his superiority of age, which, although not so vast, was accentuated by D'Art's habitual seriousness of mien, "that you will have some decisions to make."

"Yes," Jay said. "I've been meaning to speak with you, Doctor D'Art. You're quite close to Petra."

"I look upon Petra with the tenderness of a father," D'Art said.

"Yes, sir," Burton said, "and since she has no father, I would like to ask your blessing, sir, on my asking Petra for her hand."

D'Art smiled. "Yes, I suspected it had come to that. Yes, I will give my blessing. Understand, however, that I am not Petra's father. Actually, until she was of age, Doctor Simel was her guardian."

"Then I shall ask his permission, also," Jay said.

"It would be the politic thing to do," D'Art said, "but actually it would be unnecessary. Petra is of age, and she is quite independent. I would think that your main task would be to convince her. Or have you done so already?"

"Perhaps she senses it," Jay said, "but I have not spoken."

"Speak, then," D'Art said, "and I will await her decision with interest. You realize that should you become involved in the canal project, you will be in Panama for many years."

"I've thought of that. In fact, we've discussed it. It seems that she's envious of us men because we will be doing what she calls 'great things.' I see no reason, since she is a capable nurse, that she, too, could not have a part in it."

D'Art frowned. "It's a devilish climate. No place for a woman."

"Won't you be there?" Jay asked.

"I will be with Monsieur de Lesseps."

"Could she have better care than that supplied by yourself?"

"She has told me that you were a flatterer," D'Art said. "Selfishly, I would like to have her with me in Panama. In fact, I would value her as a nurse, as well as for personal reasons."

"Then the decision should be left to her," Jay said.

Jay Burton proposed to Petra as they walked along the embankment on a sweet June night, a lover's moon low in the sky, the air balmy. At first he talked of his plans, how he had been asked to accompany de Lesseps, how de Lesseps had offered him an engineering position in the Panama company to do the work he liked best—field work—actually being on the job to supervise.

"When will you go?" Petra asked, with a little ache in her heart.

"In December," he said.

"We have a little time, then," Petra said.

"Petra, my dear, we have all the time left to us in this world, if you feel the same as I," he said.

"And am I to read your mind?" she asked, with a little smile.

"Read my heart," he said, taking her hand to place it on his chest. "Feel how it beats for you. I want to spend all of my time with you, Petra. I want you, I beg you to be my wife."

"Oh!" she said, for she had, somehow, been expecting it, and she had not been able to make her decision. Now it was there to be made, and she thought of him going away to work on the canal project, perhaps to die from one of the dread diseases which were endemic to Panama.

"Will you say yes?" he asked tenderly, holding both her hands in his.

"You must give me a little time," she said.

"Of course."

"You have not even met my sister, my uncle," she said, talking simply to be able to avoid saying, "Yes, yes, yes," as her heart was saying it.

"I would be honored," he said. "But let me say this, my dear Petra. Perhaps we could make the voyage to Panama our honeymoon trip—the two of us together."

"And then?" she asked.

"You said you would like to be a part of the great adventure. Doctor D'Art has told me that he would value you as a nurse in the hospital which he will set up in Panama."

"Ah, you've spoken with Roger, then?"

"I told him my intentions," Jay said. "He gave me his blessing."

"How nice of him," she said. "But it is my decision."

"Of course."

But the fact that Roger approved of the match could not help but influence her. She respected Roger greatly, and if he thought Jay to be a suitable husband for her, his opinion confirmed her own appraisal of Jay.

But perhaps the most important outside influence which helped her make her decision was Jay's attitude toward her sister. In spite of her maturity, she still remembered how Darcie had stolen away her young beaux with such ease that her pride was forever damaged.

Petra approached the evening when Jay was to meet her family with some agitation. With some difficulty, she had arranged a dinner at which all three of the "family" would be present—a matter of some delicacy, since Lyris was involved with her own social group, Guy was quite busy with his affairs and Darcie had only recently returned from a cruise aboard the yacht of a Prussian nobleman.

Lyris was dressed in black, accented by white trimmings, Darcie in a pastel blue which made her all the more beautiful. Although she was in her best, Petra felt like a barnyard hen among peafowl. However, when Jay entered the parlor, he had eyes only for her. He acknowledged the introductions, shook Guy's hand, kissed the hands of Lyris and Darcie.

With a sinking heart, Petra saw that Jay's strong and handsome appearance appealed to Darcie. She knew her sister's ways, and the immediate change in her showed her interest. She became flirtatious, banter-

ing with Jay, who smiled at Darcie while holding onto
Petra's hand.

Infuriatingly, Darcie changed the seating at table
as planned by Petra. "I'm so interested in your country," she said, so sweetly, taking Jay's arm as dinner
was announced, usurping Petra's place with a superior
glance over her shoulder. "You must sit next to me and
tell me everything."

"Jay's place is set there, beside me," Petra said,
hating herself for it, feeling belittled to have to fight
for her man, once again, not wanting to fight, at the
moment hating both Jay and Darcie.

Jay handled the awkward situation with an insight
which astonished her and pleased her.

"Yes, of course," he said. "My pleasure, for Petra
and I will have the years ahead of us to talk."

"An interesting statement," Guy said as he seated
Lyris at the end of the table.

"With your permission, sir," Jay said, holding Darcie's chair as Petra, smiling, went to the other side of
the table to allow Guy to seat her, "I have more to
say on that subject."

"You are free to speak, sir," Guy said, taking his
chair.

"I have asked your niece to be my wife," Jay said.

"And what did my niece say?" Guy asked, smiling
at Petra.

"She has not spoken as yet," Jay said quickly. "I
think, perhaps, she is waiting for me to observe the
formalities in asking your permission, sir."

"You have it," Guy said curtly.

"So our little Petra is in love," Darcie said, putting
her hand on Jay's arm.

"I pray that she is," Jay said, smiling into Petra's
eyes.

"How romantic," Darcie said.

Jay engaged in a conversation with Guy about his

future plans. Guy very much approved of Jay's interest in the canal.

"I would advise you, sir," he said, "to invest as heavily as possible in the venture, for the shares will rise rapidly."

"Unfortunately," Jay said, "although I earn a respectable salary, I fear that I have little to invest."

"Well, perhaps, should Petra consent to be your wife, you can talk sense to her," Guy said. "I've been telling her to put her holdings into canal stock, and she is somehow reluctant."

"I don't have a head for business," Petra said.

"Then listen to those who do, my dear," Lyris said.

"And when will little Petra make her decision?" Darcie asked, the question aimed at Petra, but spoken directly into Jay's face.

"She has made the decision," Petra said, with sharpness in her voice.

"How unusual," Lyris said with a smile. "A public love scene. May I ask about your decision?"

"Yes," Petra said, as Jay continued to ignore Darcie and look into her eyes. "I will be honored to be your wife, Jay."

Jay smiled. Guy lifted his glass in a toast. Darcie, although she smiled and drank, looked over the top of the glass at Petra, her dark eyes smoldering.

Later Petra walked out with Jay.

"It was a sort of test, wasn't it?" he asked.

"What do you mean?"

"Your sister."

"I'm sorry," she said, "you'll have to make yourself more clear."

"I will, then," he said, pulling her to a halt, holding her in his arms. "Did you believe for one moment that I'd find her more beautiful than you?"

"I don't know what you mean."

"Yes, you do," he said. "You went cold when she

took my arm and asked me to sit beside her. Petra, I don't know what has gone on between you and your sister in the past. I know only that it is you I love. Darcie is quite a beautiful woman, but not so beautiful as you."

Petra felt herself melting. She raised her lips and took his kiss. "Perhaps, without my admitting it, it was a test," she said. "I've never had anyone of my own, Jay. When my parents were alive, Darcie was their favorite. She has always been closer to my uncle than I."

"And I'll bet she used to steal your beaux," Jay said with a laugh.

"As a matter of fact, yes," she said.

"There is one neither she nor anyone can steal," he said, kissing her tenderly.

And as he said it, he meant it, although he had to admit that Lyris and Darcie—especially Darcie—were among the most exciting women he'd ever seen.

That summer was a time of enchantment for Petra. She continued her work at the hospital, for good nurses were scarce and she had her sense of duty. However, she spent every spare hour with Jay and often went in to work feeling almost groggy from lack of sleep after having talked far into the night with Jay. There was so much to learn about each other, two people from two vastly different backgrounds. She listened with doting interest as he talked about his youth in raw California. His father had been a Forty-niner, going west via the grueling overland route through Panama before the building of the Panama Railroad, his mother a Spanish-Irish girl whose Latin ancestors had been among the first settlers of California. He was justly proud of his country and his state, and he believed firmly that future development of the west coast of the United States depended greatly on a Central American canal.

Petra, in her turn, opened her heart to him, telling him all. His strong gray eyes softened when she, in a quiet voice, recounted all of the old bitter memories, the death of her parents and the rape of Darcie. She confided in him her puzzlement at Darcie's apparent hatred for her.

"I think I can understand it," he said. "Her actions, as you have recounted them to me, seem to indicate that she feels that she was ruined forever by the unfortunate incident in Egypt. She has a low opinion of herself, and she uses her beauty to conquer men to prove to herself that she is not—well, a worthless person. Perhaps, together, we might be able to help her."

Jay was so understanding, so gentle. He did not push her to set a date, rather, he let her have all the time she needed to think it over, agreeing with her that she had a duty to the hospital. He said that he would prefer a small and simple wedding, but that was her decision.

'If you want to make a big do of it and have twenty-one-gun salutes, it's all right with me," he said.

Since Guy and Lyris continued to insist that Petra invest her money in the canal company, she asked Jay his opinion. He suggested that they postpone a decision until they knew more about Panama, and that made good sense to her.

After talking with her supervisor at the hospital, she determined that new nurses were to be available near the year's end, and her supervisor requested that she continue to work until that time.

So, although she had no reason to postpone the wedding, Petra told Jay that she would make all preparations and the ceremony would be set for a date soon after his return from the rather quick tour of Panama planned by de Lesseps. Jay agreed reluctantly.

Together, they explored the city, finding quaint little restaurants and hidden byways. Although Jay respected

Petra's desire to observe the proprieties, when he kissed her, her body cried out to his. At such time, in love, in the city of lovers, the waiting seemed senseless.

They spent a few evenings in the company of Guy and Darcie. Darcie continued her flirtatious ways, but Jay was polite and did not respond to Darcie's sometimes provocative actions.

Jay was an accomplished dancer. Petra had not developed her skills at dancing to a great extent, but she found that Jay was so easy to follow that he made her look good—but not as good, she felt, at a ball given in their honor by D'Art, as Darcie looked when she danced with Jay. The small, beautiful girl seemed to become an extension of Jay as they whirled around the floor to a lilting waltz. Petra felt a darkening of her spirits, a sense almost foreboding, but the moment passed and was forgotten.

De Lesseps now had firm plans for a December sailing. As the days passed, Petra began to grow restless, thinking of the long weeks of their coming separation. Her kisses took on a new urgency, as if by clinging to him she could postpone the time of his departure.

Of her family, only Lyris seemed to take an interest in her preparations for the wedding. Without being asked, Lyris helped with preparing the trousseau, and Petra came to know Lyris better during that period than she'd ever known her. Lyris listened with interest and amusement as Petra chattered on about all of her plans and dreams. From that new feeling of closeness, Petra felt free, one day as they worked on the lace for the bridal gown, to ask Lyris why she had never married.

"Because I would not become the property of one man," Lyris said.

"Have you never been in love?" Petra asked.

"Oh, many times," Lyris said with a laugh. "And each time is as exciting as the first."

"You're incorrigible," Petra laughed. "Was there never anyone special?"

"Guy is the most accomplished lover I've ever known," Lyris said matter-of-factly.

Petra blushed. "You and Guy?" she asked.

"Surely you're not pretending that you didn't know?" Lyris asked.

"Why, I never suspected anything like it," Petra said. "You and Guy?"

"Why are you so incredulous? Do you think I am a mere servant?"

"Of course not, Lyris," Petra said. "You've always been like one of the family. But—" She could not find words.

"I have the seed of kings in me," Lyris said. "Guy would have married me. It was I who said no. For some, my dear, one man is not enough."

"Lyris, I've never heard you talk like that!" Petra said.

"Then perhaps it is time we had a talk," Lyris said. "You are happily getting ready to tie yourself to one man for the rest of your life. Are you sure that's what you want?"

"I'm sure."

"The thrill of newness wears off."

"No, it won't. I'll always love him."

Lyris shrugged. "And will he be as true?"

"Yes."

"Ah," Lyris said and would say no more.

Lyris and Guy, Petra was thinking. *All those years, and I didn't suspect.* And then another thought, ugly, shocking, came into her mind. Darcie. They'd always been so close, the three of them, Darcie, Lyris and Guy. Suddenly she could remember many times when, as she came into a room, there would be a sudden silence. Surely not, she told herself. She had no illusions about Darcie. She knew that Darcie had a reputation, that she often went on extended trips with men, but not—surely not—with Guy.

It was disturbing, but if it were true, so many things were answered.

Petra put it out of her mind. Soon she would be married. She would go to Panama with Jay. Then they would be rid of her once and for all. Meantime, she was not going to let anyone or anything infringe on her happiness. Soon she would be Mrs. Jay Burton. Her body quivered at the thought, for she was in love, and she looked forward, with a mixture of pure lust and some apprehension, to being his in both body and spirit.

11

PETRA'S HAPPINESS WAS hateful to Darcie. Once again, the fates were favoring the simpering blond wench. Burton was not all that attractive to Darcie. He was a big, solid slab of a man, so unlike the kind of man she liked, slim, delicate, sophisticated, but the thought of Petra's being happily married, never having to know suffering as she had known it, did not go down easily with her. Throughout the summer, she tried to think of ways to show Petra that life is not so bedamned sweetly romantic. But the big American did not seem to realize that she was alive. Not in all of her experience had she encountered a man who was so immune to her charms. Nothing she did seemed to impress him. This, of course, merely added to her determination to do something about the little blond wench's happiness.

Darcie was bored. There was a sameness to her life. That which once made it all worthwhile, the newness which came when she went into the arms of an attractive man for the first time, was beginning to fade, and if she closed her eyes, one man seemed to be much like the other—perhaps a bit thicker here, a bit thinner there, a bit of difference in voice, smell, in subjects of conversation, but, in the end, all alike, thrusting, driving, selfish, only a few of them, like Guy, interested at all in the woman's need.

Moreover, Darcie was twenty-five. Like Lyris, she had no desire to be married, to be the property of one man; but there were times when champagne seemed to lose its power to bring her forgetfulness, when the thrustings of her current lover seemed to be merely an inconvenience.

She listened to Petra's excited talk about being a part of the great crusade, the building of the Panama canal, with boredom, at first, and then with grudging interest. Perhaps she would travel, see parts of the world. There was America, but from all reports, it was a dull and sluggish country still in the grips of Puritanism. New York might be worthwhile, but with whom?

On one of the rare nights when the three of them were alone, abed after indulging in familiar but still exciting exchanges, enjoying the arcane secrets which only two women and a man know, she suggested that they go together to New York.

"Later, little one," Guy said. "Once the canal is built, we'll be so rich we can go anywhere."

"But that will be so long," Darcie said.

"It is not practical," Guy told her. "We are too involved. We have everything tied up in the canal company, and once the founders' shares are made available, we will be totally dependent on the success of the canal. In view of this, I can't go running off to New York or anywhere else."

"We can use my money," Darcie said.

"My dear, your money is with ours," Lyris said.

"All of it?"

"Most of it," Guy said. "The proceeds of your father's estate, the sale of the English properties—

most of that money is in the syndicate or committed to buy founders' shares."

"Of course," Lyris said, "we won't starve while we await our great riches, but we won't have money to make extended trips, either."

Darcie was not quite sure she liked the idea of having her inheritance tied up, but she had little interest in business. Money was never important with her. She could travel all over Europe and not spend a franc of her own. For Darcie, there was always a gentleman whose pocketbook was open.

So, she thought, *I have a stake in this Panama venture*. But such thoughts did not entertain her for long. As Petra went about picking out feminine petticoats and drawers for her trousseau, so disgustingly happy that it made Darcie sick, she made up her mind that Petra, too, must know the meaning of pain. All her life the little bitch had gotten everything she wanted. The death of their parents had scarcely touched Petra, or so it seemed to Darcie.

Since Darcie knew everyone, it was not difficult to arrange chance meetings with Jay Burton. A few discreet questions established the gentleman's habits. When he visited his favorite little restaurant for lunch, surprise, surprise, there would be Darcie, so unexpectedly, and it would have been rudeness on Jay's part to avoid her, to refuse to join her at her table.

He knew what was happening. He was angered in a way, but he was also flattered. After all, he was a man, and to have a seductive creature like Darcie openly pursuing him did nothing to harm his pride. He was wise enough to conceal the obvious attentions of Darcie from Petra, thinking that it would soon be over, that he would be off on the *Lafayette,* leaving Darcie to play her little games with others.

They were so different, the two sisters. Petra, an armful of girl, delightfully womanly, full-figured, her breasts large and firm, her hips flaring. Darcie, a Venus in miniature, so seductive, a woman who obviously knew how to please a man. Petra's very innocence was endearing, but Darcie's intimations of secret knowledge were exciting. Tempted? Of course he was. He was human, and many men before him had fallen under the spell of a woman who, in earlier times, would have been, perhaps, the greatest courtesan in the world.

It was Darcie herself who brought her pursuit of Jay to Petra's attention.

"Darling," she said, "your Jay is so amusing."

She'd "happened" to bump into Jay that day at a different restaurant, where he had gone hoping to avoid her. It was becoming quite obvious to her that Jay was not telling Petra of their "accidental" encounters, for she knew her sister. Petra would have said something if she knew. This heartened Darcie, for if Jay were being silent, that was a good sign that he was not totally disinterested in what she had to offer.

"Yes, he has a fine sense of humor," Petra said.

"He was telling me today about a man in San Francisco," Darcie said. "The one who rode the mule? Wasn't that funny?"

"Yes," Petra said, but she had not heard about a man in San Francisco riding a mule. "Where did you see Jay today?"

"Why, we had lunch together," Darcie said. She put her hand over her mouth. "Oh, my, he didn't tell you?"

"Yes, of course," Petra said stiffly. "I had forgotten."

Darcie, who had come to Petra's bedchamber after Petra had returned from an evening with Jay, her lips still tingling with his kisses, came close, smiling sweetly.

"He didn't tell you, did he?"

Petra turned away and started to brush her long hair.

"Well, men are naughty that way, aren't they?" Darcie said, turning to leave.

Petra, her face flaming, rose, seized Darcie, and

spun her around. "Darcie," she said, her voice strained, "leave him alone. Will you please leave him alone?"

"Of course," Darcie said. "But will he leave *me* alone?"

"Oh, damn you!" Petra said, whirling away. But, she was telling herself, it had to be Darcie. Jay had talked with her, had sworn to her that he felt no attraction for Darcie. She turned to face her sister. "Darcie, you're up to your old tricks, but it won't do you any good this time. He loves me. He won't fall for your prostitute's tricks."

"You dare call me a whore?" Darcie flared. "Why, you simpering little bitch!"

"Will you please leave my room?"

"Yes, gladly," Darcie said. "But I will show you, damn you. I will show you."

Actually, Petra had no reason to feel that she was less beautiful than Darcie. They were of different types, but they were both beautiful, each in her own way. In fact, Darcie's brittle sophistication, her determination to have her own way in all matters large and small, her reputation as one of the smart set which, even in those conservative times, had the repute of doing many things which were contrary to accepted rules of behavior, all contributed to making Petra seem even more beautiful to those who knew both sisters. Many men had talked about the Moncrief sisters, and seeing them together was, for any man, a pleasant experience, but moral men agreed that of the two, Petra was the choice. Petra, however, was still influenced by having been the awkward, gangling girl when Darcie was already slim and graceful, with having been the second daughter, with having been totally unable to hold onto a beau if Darcie decided that she wanted him.

Now, knowing that Darcie was determined to break up her romance with Jay if at all possible, she considered ways of fighting. She could, of course, talk with Jay, warn him that Darcie was setting out deliberately

to seduce him in order to hurt her. Somehow she could
not bring herself to do that. First, in spite of all, she
felt loyalty to Darcie and could not bring herself to
tell anyone—even the man she intended to marry—
that Darcie was totally amoral. Second, it seemed be-
littling, a blow to her pride, to have to protect the man
she loved from another woman. She did not admit it to
herself, but deep inside she felt that if Jay were so
weak as to fall to Darcie's obvious charms, then his
love for her was not as deep as her love for him.

And so the summer turned into autumn. When Petra
was with Jay, she was happy and confident. It was only
when she was away from him, at her work, or when his
affairs kept him from her that she wondered. She knew
that should Darcie succeed, she would know immediately. Darcie would be only too happy to tell her that
her great love had fallen to her sister, just as all the
young lads had fallen in years past. So, when time
passed and Darcie did not come to crow over her conquest, Petra's confidence grew.

Since Petra was her own woman, with no one to say
no, she spent her time with Jay as she chose, not concerned with appearances, for she knew she was being
honorable. As far as Jay was concerned, he was too
much the gentleman, and he loved her too much, to
make improper advances. It was obvious, for example,
when they spent an evening in the Simel home alone
before a fire which had been kindled to ward off the
November chill, that his blood burned for her as much
as hers for him, for their kisses were heated and his
strong and manly body trembled with his need for her.

The time for his departure came nearer and nearer,
and now all of Petra's wedding plans were complete.
Darcie's threats seemed to have faded. In fact, she was
involved in her own gay social life and seemed, on the
surface, to have forgotten about Jay. But still there was
that fear in Petra when she was alone.

It came to her, on one of those lovely nights alone in

the house, the servants having retired, the three members of her "family" out and unlikely to return until the wee hours of the morning, that she had the same weapon which Darcie was trying to use on Jay.

It was a daring thought, engendered by her love for him, by the way his mere touch caused her to flame with love and desire. Looking back over her life, she was sure now that Darcie had so easily stolen beaux from her by using all of her feminine weapons, by giving the young men and the boys a gift which few young men can refuse: a responsive and eager and lovely female body to use for their own ends.

She could give herself to Jay. By doing so, she would be cementing him to her, and thus nullifying the threat of Darcie forever. She knew how important the pleasures of the flesh were to men. She could give him the ultimate gift, and what would be the harm? They would be married soon, in a matter of mere months.

These thoughts came to her as they sat, he holding her close, on a comfortable chaise in the parlor before the roaring fire. And as they came, her body was alight, for she would not only be pleasing him, she would be answering the wild demands of her own body. The thought of being his, of giving herself gladly, caused her lungs to heave, as if she could not get enough air. She gave him a sweet, hot tongue and tried, as it were, to thrust her entire mouth into his, clinging. pressing her firm breasts against his chest. She was dressed in a neat and simple shirtwaist and skirt, a frilled petticoat and ruffled lawn drawers which came to her knees. She had never bowed to the fashion of wearing heavy corsets, for her figure, although mature and womanly, did not need the cast-iron hardness of a corset to accentuate her waist. Her feet curled under her, leaning against him, her arms as eager and as clinging as his, she abandoned herself to the idea, and he noted the change in her, the sense of urgency in her kiss.

"Soon, my darling, soon," he said, his lips possessing hers, her mouth, her smooth and lovely neck, the hollow of her throat.

"Oh, yes," she whispered, letting her hands know the strength of his shoulders, his back. And she did not break away from the kisses which went on and on until she felt her very blood would boil. She willed him to do something, to touch her, her breasts, her stomach. He, in his dire need, retained his will and allowed himself nothing other than his arms around her and her kisses. Then, with a trembling hand, she unbuttoned her shirtwaist, leaning back, he looking at the swift movements of her fingers as if in a trance. She opened the garment, took his hand in hers and inserted his hand inside her clothing, under the camisole top, and felt his warm hand, for the first time, on her bare breast.

"Oh, God, Petra, how beautiful," Jay breathed, his hand caressing her burning breast, his lips seeking hers.

"I want you, darling," she whispered. "I want you so very much."

"Oh, yes," he said, his mouth going down, hands pushing aside her clothing, his lips burning over her chest, and then, with a gusty sigh, finding the mound of sweetness tipped by engorged erectile tissue. "Oh, yes," he moaned, as he slipped the shirtwaist down off her shoulders, pulled aside the straps of her undergarment—and she was nude from the waist up, her clothing tumbling to bunch at her waist and his lips paying tribute to the two firm, long-nippled mounds as fire and ice competed in her body and she buried her fingers in his hair, pressing his face to her breasts. Never before had any man looked upon those pale mounds, never before had a man's lips touched them, kissed them, caressed them. Never before had she felt so abandoned, so thrillingly womanly. It went on and on, Jay seemingly unable to get enough of her breasts, until, with a shuddering sigh, his lips came back to hers and there was a long, burning kiss.

"This would shock your uncle, should he come home," Jay said, his voice hoarse with passion.

"No one will be home for hours," she whispered, unwilling to allow the passion she felt to die unsatisfied. She was no longer thinking of using her femininity to weld him to her. She thought only of herself, of the thrill of giving herself to him, of the freedom she felt with her breasts bared to him, the surge of desire in her.

"I want you, darling," she whispered, letting her lips touch his ear, his neck. His hands were busy at her breasts.

"Soon," he whispered back. "Soon."

"I am yours," she said. "I'll always be yours. Whatever you desire I cannot refuse."

"Oh, Petra!" he said, his hand going down to fumble with the length of her skirt, to find her legs and the smooth ruffles of her undergarment. Then his hand was under her skirt, separated from her only by the undergarment, and there was a thrill of being possessed in her, as his hand felt her heat through the thin material and she felt her body answering his caress, her loins telling of her desire.

"We must stop this," he said, but he did not remove his hand from within her clothing.

"Not because of me, darling," she said.

"It's not right."

"Whatever you want is right," she whispered. "You will be my husband."

"Are you sure?"

"I'm so very, very sure."

"Not like this, then."

"No."

"Your bed?"

"Come, then," she said, rising, pulling her clothing into some order, and extending her hand to lead him up the stairs into her room. The maid had lit a small lamp, just enough to make the room cozily dim. He undressed her with loving tenderness and many heated kisses and touches. Then she stood before him, proud, womanly, utterly beautiful in her cream-gold skin and her long blond hair now loosened to fall to her shoulders and beyond. He knelt in front of her, his arms around her womanly rump, his face pressed to her stomach. He stayed that way for long moments as she idly let her fingers trail through his hair. And then his lips were teasing her soft womanly bush and she felt thrill after thrill go through her as he gently inserted his hand between her thighs and urged her into a position where she stood with legs apart, her heat and warmth and wetness accessible to his questing tongue.

With urgency now, he lifted her and placed her on her bed, falling down to pay tribute to her most intimate part. A spasm of near-completion caused her to cry out as his mouth closed over her.

Body aflame, she watched as he undressed, her eyes feasting on his masculine chest, the muscles of his arms, and then widening as his passion was revealed. She had never seen such a man nude, much less in a state of arousal and, for a moment, she was frightened. And then he was holding her close and that hard part of his was a hot, protruding pressure on her stomach.

He did not hurry. He was trembling with his need, but he did not hurry, kissing her neck, her breasts and their hard, long nipples, her stomach, and, to her gasp of ecstasy, doing that wonderful thing to her which made her entire body come to life, caused her hips to lift, seeking, seeking, until, with a cry, she felt a sunburst of utter joy in her body and the need came again under his lips, stronger, more urgent.

She felt his hands. She felt his fingers opening her, spreading the flowerlike covering. And then there was a moment of mixed fear and need as he touched her. So big, so demanding.

"Tell me what to do, darling," she whispered, as he hesitated there, just touching her.

"You are perfect," he said.

"I do so want to please you," she said. "And I don't know—"

"Petra?"

"Darling Jay, I know you would never ask, but yes, you are the first. You are the first in everything, darling."

The touch—there in her most secret place—was gone. He put his weight on her and held her close. "Oh, my lovely girl!"

"Did I do something wrong?" she asked, impatient, wanting him in spite of her fear.

"Wrong? It couldn't be more right," he said.

"Why, then?" she asked.

"Oh, Petra. You sweet little dunce."

A moment of irritation. "Do you think you were not the first?"

"Of course not."

"You seemed willing," she said. "And then you stopped."

"It's because I love you so much," he said. "It's because when I marry, it will be forever, and I want it to be perfect."

"Yes, yes."

"And, perhaps, if I took advantage of you now, you would come to regret it. I want nothing to discolor our love."

"I want you so much!"

"I know. I know. And I want you so badly, but there will be time. There will be years when we'll be together."

He removed his body from hers and let his hands wander over her breasts, her stomach, her smooth, strong thighs. "You're so very beautiful, Petra, and I do love you so much, but I will not rush it. I will not satisfy my own passion here, now, and have you feel, in the future, that I dishonored you. Do you understand?"

"I'm trying to," she said, "but it's difficult. A warm and willing woman is offering herself to you, and you're turning her down."

"My dear Lord in Heaven," he said, kissing her again, "you'll never know how difficult it is." But he was covering her naked body with the sheet. "We could," he said, "because it would actually make no difference, would it? What's the difference in my having you now or later, after we're married? Except that we would both know it's wrong, and there would be just a slight tarnish on our love. And, my beautiful girl, what if I should be stricken with fever in Panama? What if our premature union produced a child, and you were left alone?"

"I forbid you to say such things," she said.

"Go with me," he said, as he began to dress. "We'll be married now, and you'll accompany me on the trip."

"Oh, that would be wonderful," she said, "but I've promised the hospital. The plans are all made."

"Yes. Well, then, we will simply have to be strong, won't we?" He raised the sheet, standing beside the bed in only his trousers, and looked down on her perfection. "Just to have the memory of what will be waiting for me when I return," he said.

She reached up and put her arms around his neck, pulling him down on top of her. "I think I shall hate you," she said, but her lips told him differently, and it was with renewed difficulty that he pulled away from her to rush from the house before his will failed, leaving her, heated, naked abed, with the memory of his kisses on her mouth and her body.

She was disappointed, but she was even more pleased. His strength of character, his willpower in resisting his passion for her sake, his love for her made him a man among men. She could do no less than he: control her urges, wait for him. After they were married, she would be to him all that a woman could be.

During the remaining days before his departure, she had a tendency to flush with pleasure when she saw him, for she had the beautiful memories of being naked abed with him. A look from Jay was enough to send her into soaring desire, causing her femininity to flower and express itself in hot, secret liquids which dampened her underthings.

Petra clung to his hand during the train ride to St. Nazaire, where the *Lafayette* awaited. The ship was scheduled to sail in the early evening. The farewell fete was, by necessity, in the grand ballroom of St.-Nazaire's finest hotel. Petra suffered agonies and delights during the entire afternoon, delights at his words, his touch, agonies when Darcie insisted on dancing with Jay and even when he danced with other women, out of politeness.

And then the dreaded time had arrived. They rode together to the ship and she went aboard, with many others, to say her last farewells. One last kiss, as the announcement came for all visitors to go ashore, and she stood on the pier waving to Jay. Sailors moved about, making preparations. She felt a touch on her arm and turned to see Guy.

"So," he said, "your first parting. In spite of what you feel, you'll survive it."

"I'm not at all sure," she said, her smile threatening to contort into tears.

"Come, I'll see you back to the hotel," Guy said.

"Where's Darcie?" Petra asked. The last time she'd seen her sister, she was aboard ship with a handsome man who sported impressive side whiskers.

"She has plans, I believe," Guy said.

Petra waved once more to Jay, who was standing at the rail alongside Roger. Now she would be alone in Paris, both of the men in her life off for distant places.

She was silent during the ride to the hotel. Once there, she accepted Guy's invitation for coffee in the dining room. She knew she would be unable to sleep, so she stayed with Guy as others came to talk and wistfully expressed their desire to be aboard the *Lafayette* for the grand adventure. Shortly before midnight, Lyris appeared, escorted by a distinguished older man who announced that some mechanical problem of a minor nature had delayed the *Lafayette*'s sailing until morning. Petra felt a quick sense of loss. She could have spent hours with Jay. But what was to prevent it, still?

Not wanting to announce her intentions, she said good night to Guy and Lyris and excused herself, making as if to go to her room but, instead, asked the hotel attendant to get a carriage for her. There were still hours of the night left.

Aboard ship, the delay meant little, for most of the company had enjoyed much wine during the bon voyage party, Jay and D'Art, who normally was a very temperate man, among them. At first the announcement said that there would be only an hour or two of delay, so Jay did not consider it worthwhile to think of going to Petra's hotel, or to have her sent for to come to the ship. Then, when it became apparent that sailing would be delayed until the morning, it was late, and he thought that she would already be in bed.

There was a merry group in the ship's lounge, the spirit of celebration continuing to be expressed in the pop of champagne corks and a free and liberal pouring.

Jay had a good head for liquor. In his profession, he encountered some hard-drinking men and often, in the field, relations between supervisor and workers were improved by the boss's bending a bit to have a drink with his men. But the expensive French champagne had, he decided, a hidden kick like a Missouri mule. He confessed as much to D'Art, who admitted that he, too, was feeling the wine.

"I think, sir, that I shall be forced to say good night," Jay said, standing, finding that he had to hold onto the back of a chair to overcome a sudden on-slaught of the drink.

He made his way through the passageways to his cabin, opened the door, surprised to find the light on. He stepped inside, into the sitting room of his small suite, and tosed his hat onto a chair, taking off his coat as he walked, a bit unsteadily, toward the bed-room and bath. His shirt, too, had been taken off when he opened the door to see, languidly posed on his bed, a vision in black silk and lace.

"Hello, Jay," Darcie said, one knee up, the flowing, diaphanous garment molding her perfect body, her taut breasts, and showing a gleaming and enticing length of her leg below.

"Darcie?" Jay said, his head not quite clear.

"I have the suite next to yours," she said. "Isn't that perfect? We can keep each other company during the voyage."

"Darcie, you shouldn't be here, like that," he said, but he was unable to take his eyes off her, as the de-liberately seductive nightgown revealed her lovely form, the upper curve of breast, the shapely legs.

"Don't be so stuffy, Jay," she said. "After all, we'll be members of the same family soon." She rose from the bed, and with flowing motions, smiling at him, she poured champagne from a bottle cooled in a bucket of ice. "Let us drink to your coming marriage," she said.

With some uneasiness, he accepted the glass. She clinked glasses with him, and her eyes measured him speculatively over the rim of the glass.

"And now," he said, "I must insist, for the sake of propriety, that you leave."

"You are most inhospitable," she said, with a fey smile. "And we've had so little opportunity to talk."

She did the talking. He stood, ill at ease, attracted in spite of himself, for she had resumed her position on his bed, leaning on one elbow, toying with her glass and giving him looks that promised him every-thing. To have something to do with his hands, he poured more wine, refilling her glass in the process.

"Sit beside me," she commanded. He sat on the side of the bed. He could smell her perfume, a musky, erotic scent. He could see the rise and fall of her per-fect breasts, and, through the thin material, the outline of the dark circles around her nipples. The nipples themselves were erect, straining against the fabric.

"I'm so happy that you're going on this voyage," she said. "Otherwise I should be lonely and very bored."

"Thank you," he said, "I would like to get to know my future wife's sister."

"I'm quite easy to know," she smiled, "at least for you."

"Darcie—"

"Yes?" She moved her body, pressing her cupped thighs against him. "You're so tense. Here, let me help you to relax."

She put aside her glass and, on her knees, began to use her soft hands to knead the muscles of his neck and shoulders, her hot breasts pressed against his back as she leaned on him, and the smell of her, the feel of her, her obvious willingness, aroused the man in him to the point of aching erectness. When, with a sigh, she fell into his lap and put her arms around him, he was helpless. His own arms went around her, to find her so tiny, so warm, so sweet. And his lips engulfed hers.

Women had never been too important to Jay Bur-ton. He had his goals, and for years he concentrated on them, not dissipating his energies on wenching, as did many young men. Of course, in a raw, frontier town like San Francisco, there were women available, either for money or for their own pleasure, and he was not unfamiliar with the delights of a woman's body. It was just that he had decided early that a man of good character does not patronize prostitutes, except for, perhaps, a few times in the heat of youth, that an hon-

orable man does not risk disgrace or some dire disease
with a free-and-easy woman of the streets. He had always known that he would find the right woman someday, and that he would then, with a woman he loved
as his wife, have ample opportunity to satisfy the
manly needs of his body. He had never known a girl
like Darcie—so beautiful, so clean, so sweet-smelling,
his social equal or better, depending upon one's point
of view. Incensed by the drink, urged on by her seductive willingness, he knew the thrill of her small, taut
body, felt the hot tips of her breasts against his chest,
had her sweet lips and hot, probing tongue to add to
the fire which flowered inside him.

She undressed him eagerly and, nude, he went to
her, removing the delicate garment which covered her
so scantily to see the true beauty of her tiny waist,
long, strong legs, a dense patch of dark hair hiding that
which he would not now be refused.

For one moment, as he went into her, and she, with
a wild cry, threw her shapely legs high to accept him,
he thought of a similar moment, so recently, and there
was a feeling of shame in him—but only for a moment.
And then Petra was not on his mind, only the wild
wanton woman who so eagerly returned his thrusts
with surprisingly strong body movements, clinging
arms, hot breasts against his chest, lips devouring his
as she whispered around their kisses, telling him how
wonderful he was, how huge and hard he was, how she
loved it so.

There was another moment of bittersweet regret
when it ended—ended with a glory which left him
weak and gasping—she bearing his weight uncomplain-
ingly, continued to move her hips as if to milk the last
dram of pleasure from him.

It seemed only a moment later that he was lying on
his back, giving her access to use the same lips which
had kissed him so heatedly to stir new and unexpected
life into him. And then, when he was ready, she

mounted him with a soft laugh of pleasure, using her
hand to guide him into the now deliciously slick and
hot depths and, breasts being fondled by his upreach-
ing hands, used him for her own pleasure, but in doing
so gave him much pleasure in return.

It was in this position that they were seen by Petra,
who had boarded the *Lafayette,* made her way to the
lounge to see but not to be seen by D'Art. Not seeing
Jay in the lounge, she went to his stateroom. At first,
she could not identify the sounds which came from
within, the soft whispers, the low moans. Then, with
a feeling of unreality, she turned the knob, the door
opened a few inches and she looked directly into Darcie's eyes.

Jay was lying on his back with his head toward the
stateroom door, and Darcie was astride him, in the
throes of joy, her tiny, trim body jerking and squirming energetically when she saw the door open and, with
a smile of triumph, saw Petra there. Jay, unaware,
thrust himself up with a moan of bliss.

Numbly Petra watched for long, painful seconds,
seeing the man she loved so obviously enjoying the
exact thing that she had feared—and in that moment
she remembered how she had longed for him, how she
had begged him to take her. He had refused, and now
he was giving to Darcie what he had refused to give
to her. The pain of it was a stab to the heart as she
closed the door quietly and ran, not weeping as yet,
back up the passageway to gain the deck.

Roger D'Art, making his way toward his own cabin,
came out of the lounge to see the familiar figure of
Petra emerge onto the deck.

"Petra," he called. She continued walking swiftly
toward the gangplank. He ran after her, catching her
arm. "Petra, how nice, I didn't know you'd come
back."

"Obviously," she said, "or you would have warned
him."

"I don't understand."

"Oh, Roger, how could you?" she asked, near tears now.

"My dear girl, I have no idea what I've done!"

"Oh, don't lie to me. On top of it all, don't lie! You knew she was aboard. You had to know. You're laughing at me, just like she is. And I hate you. I hate all of you!"

"Petra, Petra," he said, holding onto her arms as she tried to turn away. "I assure you that I have no idea what's wrong. Please tell me."

"It's nothing," she said, turning her head. Tears wet her cheeks.

"No, it is more than nothing," Roger said. "You said I knew she was aboard. Can I guess that you mean Darcie?"

"Please let me go!"

"It is Darcie?"

"Yes, damn you, as if you didn't know. Did you conspire with them to get me out of the way?"

"My dear child," he said. "I will forgive you, for I think I can understand your pain, but how could you think that I would ever do anything to hurt you? If I had known she was here—" He paused. "Is it Jay?"

Petra tried to speak, moving her head back and forth helplessly, fighting the urge to weep, to wail openly.

"My dear, I'm so sorry. I didn't know. If I had, I would have prevented it. I shall have her thrown off the ship."

"Oh, oh, oh," Petra moaned, letting herself fall into his arms, her face against the rough material of his coat.

D'Art, always concerned for propriety, urged Petra down the deck and into his suite. There she continued to cling to him, weeping loudly now.

"She hates me!" she sobbed. "She's always tried to hurt me. And now she's taken the only thing I ever really wanted!"

"There, there," D'Art said, patting her shoulder helplessly.

"I shall tell Monsieur de Lesseps that I cannot accompany him," D'Art said. "I will be with you, my dear."

"No, no," she said, controlling her sobs for a moment. "I can't allow you to do that. The trip means so much to you, and Monsieur de Lesseps would be lost without you."

"But you," he said, "I can't leave you like this."

"I'll be all right," she said, using the large handkerchief he handed her to wipe the tears away. "It hurt for a moment, that's all." And, at the memory, her face contorted.

"Oh, please don't," D'Art said.

"Yes, yes." Petra controlled herself with an effort. "I will work. I will forget. That's all."

"Yes, work. And I'll be back soon, and we'll have gay times. It is not the end of the world, Petra."

"Of course not," she said, but she didn't believe it.

"Is she with him now?" D'Art asked.

"In his stateroom."

"I will inform the captain," he said, his lips tight.

"No, please," she said. "No. Leave them alone. They deserve each other."

"I will be only too happy to have her driven from the ship in disgrace," he said, meaning every word of it, so angered was he to see Petra so hurt.

"No. It's over. And now I must go. I'll look forward to your return, dear Roger. It's wonderful to know that I have one true friend. I want you to know that I feel very warmly toward you."

"And I toward you, my dear," he said. "God, I should stay with you."

"I will not allow it. I'll be fine. I'll have Guy and Lyris. As you say, when you return, we'll have gay times, and I'll have had some time to myself to forget my foolishness."

"I know you're upset," he said, "and perhaps this is not the time to bring up the subject, but I've been meaning to have a talk with you. Now that I'm going away, it seems, suddenly, to be even more important. What I'm trying to say is this; I would like it very much if, while I'm away, you would stay in my apartment."

"But I have my home."

"Your Uncle Guy's home," he said.

She saw the seriousness of his face, his very manner. "Why would you not want me to stay with Guy and Lyris?"

"I am in a difficult position," D'Art said. "Let me say only that—" He paused. "Forgive me."

"I know that Guy and Lyris have lived, at times, as man and wife," she said.

"Ah, there you are," he said.

"I discovered it only recently," she said. "They have always been very discreet."

"You must admit that it isn't the happiest sort of situation for a young lady," he said unhappily. "If you would consent to stay at my apartment—"

"Thank you for your concern, dear Roger, but I'll be fine—really I will. Lyris is a wonderful person, actually."

"Yes, well, then," he said, still uneasy.

"Now, I must go," she said. She tried a smile. "I suppose I still have some girlish tears to shed."

"Oh, dear," he said.

"But I'll spare you," she said, her smile stronger, in spite of her aching inside. She kissed his cheek lightly. "You have a nice trip, and don't concern yourself about me."

She had difficulty, it being so late, in getting a hackney carriage, but, finally, there was one. At home, with only the servants in the house, she fell into her bed and abandoned herself to her pain, for there was no one to hear her sobs.

12

JOHN HUXHAM'S DISEASE struck Paris that December, making the Christmas season a busy one for Petra. As the Italians said, *un influenza di freddo*—the influence of the cold—filled the hospitals with victims suffering from the symptoms which Huxham had noted in 1743 and labeled, after the Italian phrase, influenza. Complications of bronchitis and pneumonia took lives among the elderly and the weak. Since the current medical belief was that the disease was spread by the winds, Parisians kept to their homes as much as possible, doors closed against the noxious cold winds which came with a winter storm bearing heavy snow.

Petra welcomed the hard work, spending long hours at the hospital until, shortly after Christmas, the inevitable caught up with her and she retired to her bed with fever and chills. Since she was young and strong, the influenza merely made her achy and uncomfortable. At first it was impossible to find a position for rest, and then, as the worst of it passed, she slept the days away, being cared for by the staff and by Lyris, who had expressed concern for Petra in her mood of desolation but had made no mention of the fact that she was well aware of the cause.

From the time of the sailing of the *Lafayette,* no one had made mention of Darcie. In her fever and discomfort, Petra could imagine them, Darcie and Jay, on the ship, in the luxury of the suite, endlessly making love. And that did little to lift her spirits.

When she was recovered enough to want to get out of bed, Lyris installed her in front of a roaring fire, with a pretty shawl over her knees, and entertained her with tales of winter society. The first time Petra went downstairs, she stayed only an hour before tiring, and Lyris solicitously helped her back to her bed there to tuck her in with a hot brick at her feet and with tender pats on Petra's shoulders.

Lyris came in shortly after Petra awakened.

"Oh, I ache so!" Petra moaned, trying to find a position of comfort in the bed.

"I can give you a bit of ease," Lyris said, bending down, telling Petra to lie on her stomach. She began to knead Petra's neck, shoulders, and back muscles, her hands firm and comforting through Petra's flannel nightdress. And it was wonderful, her tired and aching muscles feeling the sometimes rather energetic pushing and poundings and squeezings. Petra sighed with relief and made no protest when Lyris removed the coverlet to massage the muscles of her legs.

"That was wonderful," Petra said, when Lyris paused.

The massage had been just that, for Lyris; a massage aimed at easing the aching of Petra's body, but during the course of it, Lyris, always the voluptuary, had been aware of Petra's mature and beautiful figure, the softness of her, the heat of her body through the nightdress.

During the years in which Lyris was a member— often the director—of the *ménage à trois,* she had paid scant attention to Petra. It was only during her participation in the preparations for the wedding, which now would not occur, that she had come to know Petra as a person. She was bemused and somewhat intrigued to think that such a woman could have grown up in the same house with her and a woman like Darcie, for Petra was the soul of convention, with her petty little delusions about morals and the value of one's virginity. Lyris actually felt sorry for Petra when she saw the depth of her sadness. But it was not until she felt the softness and the curves of Petra's body under her hands that she determined, purely for Petra's sake, to teach the girl that society's conventions were formulated by selfish men who felt free to philander but did not want their women to have the same freedom.

As Petra gradually regained her strength, Lyris was very attentive and spent the days entertaining her. Their conversations covered many subjects, but, until Lyris brought it up, Petra carefully avoided mentioning either Jay or Darcie.

Then, during a lull, the fire having built up a huge bed of coals, the heat from it quite comforting against the outside cold and the sound of a cruel wind blowing around the house, Lyris said, "Petra, don't you think it's time you spoke of it?"

"Petra knew immediately what Lyris meant. "You knew, didn't you?" she asked.

"I knew that she was planning to go to Panama on the *Lafayette*," Lyris said.

"You could have told me," Petra said.

"Yes, I could have," Lyris said ruefully, "but I had no idea that she intended to spirit your great lover away from you."

Petra retreated within herself, a bit angered.

"I'm sorry if I've hurt you by speaking lightly of it," Lyris said.

"I understand, I think," Petra said, "for you look upon such things lightly."

"Ah, a barb?"

"A statement of fact. Sometimes, Lyris, I wish I could be like you."

"Well," Lyris said, smiling, thinking that it was going to be easier than she'd expected. "I don't know exactly what happened, but my guess is that you went to the ship and found them together."

"Very much together," Petra said bitterly.

Lyris laughed. "Have you considered, little one, that you could have defused Darcie's weapons by using weapons which you possess in abundance?"

Petra shook her head. "I tried."

"Ah, and he was too honorable. Is that it?"

"So he said. He spoke flowery words about holy matrimony and not soiling our love, but he obviously didn't consider it personally soiling to go to bed with Darcie."

"That's a man for you!" Lyris said. "But perhaps it was not all for the bad. Perhaps you've learned a lesson."

"Oh, I could say that I've learned that men are not to be trusted," Petra said, "but I don't think that's true of all men."

"You are hopeless," Lyris said, shaking her head. "Of course it's true of all men. There isn't a man in the world who could deny the urgings of his loins with the right woman in the proper situation."

"If that's true," Petra said, "then we're very wrong in trying to save ourselves for them."

"Now you are speaking truth. Why should we deny our natural urges simply because men dictate that women must be pure and chaste? It is true that we face some particular difficulties. We must always be on guard against being with child, and, since we are weaker, we must avoid the violent ones. Aside from that, well, consider the fact that the Bible was written by men. It is men who control the various churches of the world. It is men who lay down the rules for us, and we allow them to continue, year after year."

"Yes, it's true," Petra said. "And still—"

"And still you're saturated with romantic drivel," Lyris said. "My dear Petra, when you're well, I'm going to insist that you take a lover."

"Is that Doctor Lyris's advice to cure a broken heart and various other ailments?"

"Absolutely," Lyris said. "In fact, I have someone in mind."

Petra laughed. "Won't I be allowed to make my own choice?"

"*Chérie,* listen to the voice of experience," Lyris laughed.

Since it had been arranged for Petra to be replaced at the hospital, she did not immediately go back to work. She felt she needed some time to herself, and she could always go back when she was ready. Experienced nurses were always in demand. On moderate days, she went out into the city with Lyris, and Lyris, with smirks and smiles, pointed out to her various young men who met Lyris's criteria as potential lovers for Petra. Petra, intrigued but not really interested, played the game, but always found something wrong with Lyris's choices.

At first, Petra was embarrassed by Lyris's frank and open discussion of things sexual. She was astounded by Lyris's knowledge of methods of preventing that most-feared result of illicit sex: pregnancy. When Lyris told her of the ancient Egyptians' use of crocodile dung as a preventative, she laughed outright and made a naughty comment about the smell. Lyris outlined the more successful methods, which included withdrawal by the man, but, laughingly, pointed out that the scoundrels were not to be trusted. All in all, Lyris demonstrated a knowledge which Petra, as a nurse, had never encountered, and, when Lyris explained the way that she could determine her time of fertility by observing her menstrual and ovulation cycles, she was impressed.

As the days went by, Lyris's conversation became

more specific and often, during Lyris's talk about the
joys of love, Petra would remember, with a mixture of
emotions, her need the one time that a man had seen
her naked body: the night when she was in bed with
Jay. However, there was still in her that feeling that
the man-woman relationship was something special,
something sacred, not to be treated lightly, as it was
treated by Lyris and Darcie. She could not bring herself to so much as flirt with any of the handsome men
she knew and met anew as she became a part of Lyris's
social circle. It was reassuring to find that she did not
lack for male attention, and that puzzled her even
more—for men vied for her favors, danced with her,
asked her to dinner, asked permission to call. To the
disgust of Lyris, she declined all invitations.

In the absence of Darcie, her uncle seemed to find
much more time to be with her, and the three of them
often spent quiet evenings at home, with Guy joining
in the bantering conversation which had the intent of
convincing Petra that there was more to life than
mooning over a lost love. Never had Guy been so attentive, and often his compliments, his comments when
she was dressed in something particularly becoming,
seemed almost to be coming from an admirer and not
the man who had been her guardian since she was only
a child.

It was pleasing to find herself truly a part of the family for the first time, and she tried to convince herself
that it was not merely because Darcie was away. She
had to believe that they were fond of her, or else that
left her with no one—only her friend, Roger D'Art,
who was also away. There was in her an insecurity, a
need to be loved, a need which had never been fulfilled. As a child, she had felt that she was second to
Darcie in her parents' affections, and during her years
with Guy and Lyris, there were many times when she
wondered if any of them knew she was alive. Now she
was the center of their attentions.

Lyris's sincere attempts to take Petra's mind off Jay
Burton took them, one day when the wind was less
sharp and a dim winter sun gave the city a hint of its
summertime beauty, to a small shop filled with paintings which, as Petra first viewed them, seemed unfinished and strange. Lyris, however, seemed enthralled,
for she had been in this shop of Julien Tanguy before,
and, in fact, during her solo ventures into the city had
become friendly with several of the artists who defied
convention with their work—some of which could be
seen only in M. Tanguy's establishment.

Tanguy, himself a man with an eye for beauty, soon
came to talk with the two ladies, still bundled in capes
and scarves, and insisted that they make themselves
comfortable by removing their outdoor garments.
Then, over hot cups of aromatic tea, Tanguy, finding
Petra, in particular, unfamiliar with those painters
whom he called Impressionists, began a short course
in modern painting by taking Petra into a back room
where were stored paintings in a wild and colorful style.

Tanguy stated with emotion that the artist Cézanne
would someday be recognized as a master. Petra politely did not express her doubt, but did profess that
she liked better the work of one Pierre Auguste Renoir,
who, she said, seemed to be very fond of women. Indeed some of Renoir's paintings were quite voluptuous;
the compositions composed of nude women in the
classical style, but painted with a wonderfully light and
airy touch which, the more she looked, the more she
liked.

"If you like them so much," Lyris said, "you should
own one."

Although she was by no means poor, Petra had always been conservative with money. Through Guy's
generosity and her saving nature, her inheritance was
untouched. Moreover, she had extra money which she
had saved from her salary. Intrigued by the idea of
buying a painting, she began to look with more in-

terest and was about to decide on a small oil of a lovely young girl shown from the shoulders up when, with a gust of chill air, the door opened and a well-dressed and active-looking man entered with a shout of greeting.

"Ah, Auguste," Tanguy said, "you are just in time. The lovely young lady is about to purchase one of your paintings, and she can't make up her mind."

"My dear," Renoir said, sweeping off his hat and bowing, "you are intelligent as well as beautiful, but if you're thinking of that one, no, by all means, no." Taking Petra's arm with a verve which left Petra laughing, he pulled her along the wall, hung with many paintings, to another study of a young woman, this one more muted, even more airily beautiful. "This one is unquestionably for you."

"It's lovely," Petra said. "Yes, I like it very much."

"For, you see," Renoir said, "she has the same facial structure as you." He traced Petra's cheekbone with his finger. "The same proud, high cheekbones, the same shape of nose. Don't you see?"

Actually, Petra could not, but she nodded and smiled.

Lyris, who had been at the far end of the showroom, came up to them. "Auguste," she said, "how nice. You have won another convert, you see."

"True talent will always out," Renoir said with a bow. "And what a happy chance meeting, my dear Lyris, for I had intended to call on you. There is to be a ball, you see, and Regnault has been asking about you, insisting that you be invited."

"Yes," Tanguy said, "I had forgotten. You were Henri's Salome."

"You never told me you posed for an artist!" Petra said to Lyris.

"My dear," Lyris said, "there are many things I do not tell."

This statement brought a merry laugh from Tanguy and Renoir.

"A lovely painting," Renoir said.

"How exciting," Petra said. "I would so love to see it."

Renoir described the picture to her, Lyris as a gypsy-looking Salome, seated, a yellow blouse hanging on her shoulders, low, to reveal her dusky skin, black hair hanging loosely to her shoulder, a basin containing a sheathed dagger on her knees. As he talked, the artist continued his interested examination of Petra's features and, unable to keep his hands away from the lines of her cheekbones, once again traced them with his gentle fingers, which smelled somewhat of mineral spirits.

"So you think it exciting to be painted?" he asked. "I wanted to paint you, my dear, the moment I saw you."

"Really?" Petra asked, pleased.

"He will first ask you to remove all your clothing," Lyris laughed.

"Ah, well, then," Renoir said. "But it is the face, the face."

"I would be so pleased to be painted, monsieur," Petra said. "The face, the face."

Renoir laughed. "My pleasure," he said, "at your convenience." He gave her the address of his studio in Montmartre and, once again, sincerely expressed his interest in doing her portrait. She promised to call soon.

"And," Renoir said, "you must accompany Lyris to the ball."

"I think I should enjoy that," Petra said.

"What do you think, Julien?" Renoir asked Tanguy, cupping Petra's face in his hands. "Madame Du Barry? Helen of Troy?"

"No," Tanguy said, "I see her beauty as something

more than mere artifice. A modern woman. A lovely
and unspoiled child."

"Yes, yes," Renoir said, and they continued discussing her as if she were not there, somewhat to her embarrassment.

But it was a pleasant experience, and, with her purchase tucked under her arm, she went home with Lyris
to discuss, with some interest, the choice of costume
for the coming ball. With Lyris's help, and remembering
the flattering comments of Julien Tanguy, she fash-
ioned a pastoral costume which might have been worn
by a French peasant girl at a great celebration in the
early eighteenth century: a huge skirt in wine-colored
satin with the lower billows of the skirt decorated in
swirls of silver braid. Over the front of the skirt was
an apron of white silk bordered with ribbon of the
same shade as the skirt. The bodice, which clung tightly
to her torso, was laced, the fichu low to expose a daring décolletage. Her arms were covered by white silk
circled by lace and the costume was topped by a lace
collar tightly around her neck. With her blond hair
piled high in Empire fashion, she made a lovely picture.

The ball was a splendor of costumes. When Lyris
and Petra entered, leaving their wraps in the cloakroom, they were escorted by Guy, dressed as the English King John, in royal red gown and gold cape, a
golden crown on his head.

Lyris was spectacular. She was exposed, in her
scanty costume, to an extent which brought all eyes
toward them. She wore the silken, flowing costume of
a harem dancer, her taut stomach exposed, the billow-
ing pantalets riding very low on her shapely hips, her
breasts covered by a gauze of silk, her dark hair long
and flowing. The contrast—Petra, blond and demure
in her bell-skirted gown. Lyris—as a sensual Eastern
dancer, drew praise as, in the toga of a Roman senator,
Renoir came to them and introduced them to various

people as the dancers whirled on the main floor. The names meant little to Petra at the time, but in years to come she would remember the dark and swarthy face of Edgar Degas, the huge dark beard and large head of Claude Monet, the elegance of Édouard Manet. She was a bit uneasy under the slanted, somewhat satanic eyes of Cézanne. It was the writer Émile Zola who most impressed her that night, however. It was a thrill to dance with one of the best known of all Frenchman, the man who, only the previous year, had shocked the country with his latest sensational novel, *Nana.* Zola was witty and complimentary. Breathlessly, Petra told the famous man that she had read not only *Nana,* but *Une Page d'Amour* as well. Renoir, standing with them, laughed.

"Shame," Renoir said. "You see, Émile, the error of your ways, do you not? Exposing such a charming and innocent young lady to your pornography."

Zola laughed. "Were you corrupted, my dear? If so, I would ask the pleasure of being one of the first to exploit your ruin."

"Not before I capture that look of innocence on canvas, my friend," Renoir said.

Petra danced almost every dance. Names were thrown at her with bewildering swiftness, and, in the end, she ceased trying to remember them. She merely allowed herself to enjoy being sought after by various men, young and middle-aged, laughed with happiness, for the first time since that night on the *Lafayette* able to forget her sadness.

Of course, artists being as they were, there was wine in plenty, quite a potent punch, a selection of delicious food. The evening went on wings, and, heated by the dancing, Petra indulged in champagne.

In the early hours of the morning, with the company gay with the spirit of celebration and no small amount of drink, Lyris was coaxed into taking center stage, the band trying bravely to produce Eastern-sounding music, succeeding, at least, in arriving at the proper rhythm, and Lyris exhibited a suppleness of body which was astounding, with a very sensual Eastern dance which saw her hips gyrate, her stomach muscles do astounding things. Her performance was greeted with cries of "encore" and "bravo" and shrill cries of approval. Then she was swept away by a trio of handsome costumed men, and Petra found herself dancing with Guy.

"She is simply a fantastic woman," Petra said.

"In many ways," Guy agreed, with a smile. "And you, Petra. I've never seen you look more beautiful. With your flushed cheeks, your smile, you look quite kissable."

"Thank you," she said, feeling warm toward him, and very gay. "You may kiss me."

He leaned forward, and, instead of the fatherly peck she expected, received a wet and ardent kiss on the mouth which, for a moment set her aback. She jerked away with a gasp.

"A kiss worth kissing is a kiss worth kissing well," Guy said, laughing as he pulled her close and regained contact with her mouth. However, when he sought entry with his tongue, she pulled away again and put it down to the drink, to the excitement of the night. His arm was close around her and when they touched she could feel the heat of his body.

As the hour grew late, the spirits of the company seemed to lift on the wings of the music and the continued flow of punch and wine. Petra was just a bit dizzied as there swirled around her men and women in oriental costumes, Japanese warriors, Chinese ladies, gentlemen in tights and medieval puffed shoulders, a daring young model in Neoclassic silk which was so thin as to show the curve and dark tips of breast, the dark spot of her pubes. And then, with the sun only an hour below the eastern horizon, they went home, singing and laughing. Petra joined Guy and Lyris in the parlor for a final glass of wine.

There was talk of the ball, and Petra, feeling slightly tipsy and almost happy, was unwilling to call an end to the pleasant night. Guy commented on Lyris's dance, and, with a laugh, Lyris began to do the provocative and sensuous movements, explaining, as she danced without music, the need for perfect muscle control. She could make the muscles of her bared stomach move in waves, and, with a laugh, Guy put his hand on the bare skin to feel the movement.

"Fantastic," he said. "Come here, Petra." He put Petra's hand on Lyris's stomach and she felt the hard muscles writhe like snakes under her palm.

"Can you do it?" Guy asked, putting his hand on Petra's stomach.

"I can't even begin!" she laughed.

"But you kiss well," Guy said, pulling her into his arms and seeking her lips.

"Guy," she wailed, but he was strong and his mouth found hers in a kiss which was anything but the kiss of an uncle.

"She needs only a bit of instruction," Guy said. Lyris, moving sensuously, danced into his arms, and their mouths joined in a long and hungry kiss which made Petra blush.

"You see," Lyris said, "it's easy. Try again."

"No," Petra said, as Guy pulled her into his arms again. "Please, Guy."

"Don't be such a prude," Lyris said, coming to put her hot, bare arm around Petra's shoulders. "It's time you learned the proper technique of kissing."

"I do quite well by myself, thank you," Petra said, then giggled as she realized what she had said.

"That's your problem exactly," Lyris said, "trying to make kissing a one-person thing. It takes two, my darling girl." And so saying, she surprisingly planted her lips on Petra's and, with a gentleness which, for a moment, overcame Petra's shock, moved her lips slowly and exotically. Then Petra jerked her head away, only to be seized, once more, by Guy.

"All right," she said. "I will show you that I know how to kiss, and then I'm going to bed."

"An excellent suggestion," Lyris said.

Petra let her lips part and accepted Guy's kiss, feeling a definite sense of wrongness, but not wanting to be unpleasant—it had been such a wonderful evening. But when the kiss went on and on and became more demanding, she pushed away.

"She doesn't seem to learn," Guy laughed. Lyris came into his arms and molded her body to his. Petra saw Guy's hands go to the bare area of Lyris's back, to the outflow of rump which was visible above the lower part of the costume, and saw Lyris lift herself on her toes in order to press her mons hard against Guy's manhood. Petra wanted to leave the room, but she was feeling a sense of guilty fascination. As she watched, Lyris pulled away and, with graceful movements of her hands, began to loosen her clothing.

"In my country," she said, "the most exotic dances require fewer coverings." She dropped the gauze top, leaving her breasts covered only by a scanty halter-type affair, and, as she began the exotic contortions of the Eastern dance, dropped the pantalets, leaving only a brief and revealing undergarment of silk.

Lyris began to move, slowly, seductively, pouring across the floor, the very picture of feminine grace and seductiveness, and came to stand in front of Petra, her body moving in those well-trained and highly suggestive undulations.

"Petra," she whispered, "it is time. We've talked enough. Now it is time for you to experience life." She moved closer, pressing her body to Petra's, pushing the bell-shaped skirt tightly against Petra's body, her hands moving down Petra's stomach to come suggestively close to her womanhood.

"I've told you that Guy is a wonderful lover," Lyris said. "I can think of no one better qualified to introduce you to the delights of love."

"Lyris!" Petra gasped.

"Watch, Petra, and learn."

Petra could not believe it. She had drunk too much wine. It couldn't be happening—but it was, before her shocked eyes. Lyris, swaying, bumping her hips suggestively, denuded her splendid body and danced toward Guy, who was watching with a pleased smile—stood before him, naked, womanly, her talented body making itself even more voluptuous in the dance. With a gasp, Guy seized her, raining kisses on her mouth, her neck, her bare and swollen breasts, her stomach, which rippled as she continued the motions of the dance.

Then, with a wild cry, Lyris leaped into the air, and came down with her legs spread, arms thrown out, body arched backward. Guy fell to his knees and thrust his head between her legs. Petra gasped in shock. Lyris writhed in pleasure, smiling over her shoulder at Petra.

Her mouth formed words. "It's wonderful, Petra. Come, try it."

With a feeling of fear and revulsion, Petra ran. She stumbled over the long skirt going up the stairs as she heard Lyris calling her name. In her room, she slammed the door and leaned weakly against it. She heard someone coming up the stairs. Then there was a knock on the door.

"Petra," Guy said. "It's all right. Come on back and join us."

Petra was speechless.

"It's time," Lyris said, from outside the door. "It's time, Petra. Join us and we'll make it quite wonderful for you."

"Oh, please!" Petra cried. "Please leave me alone!"

"Yes, all right, then," Guy said. "But think about it, Petra. Think about how wonderful it would be."

"We'll be in my room, Petra," Lyris said. "Think about it and come to us. We'll be gentle. We'll make it so nice for you."

Petra stood, leaning against the door, for long minutes, unable to believe. So it was true. Darcie had been a part of it. Little wonder that she thought nothing of climbing into bed with a man. All these years and she'd been so blind.

Hurriedly, Petra stripped off the costume and left it in a heap on the carpet. She dressed in street clothing, packed a few essentials in a bag, and, after a nervous period of listening at the door, opened it and crept down the hall to hear, as she passed Lyris's room, the soft sounds of uninhibited lovemaking. Then she was down the stairs and outside in the light of dawn, the sun coming up red and weak in the east. She half-ran, half-walked to the only place she had to go: the apartment of Roger D'Art. There she finally aroused the *concierge,* a lady of some years whom she had met on several occasions, and explained that Dr. D'Art had asked her to stay in his apartment while he was away. Although obviously puzzled by Petra's early-morning appearance at her door, the *concierge* admitted her to D'Art's apartment and gave her a spare key for use. The apartment was cold and smelled of disuse. She kindled a fire and, her head aching from too much wine, her good spirits of the night killed by the wanton attempt by her uncle and her friend to seduce her, she fell into D'Art's bed to sleep until late afternoon.

Petra chose her time carefully, a time when both Lyris and Guy were away from the Simel house, and went in with a hired man to get her clothing and her personal things. She was surprised to find that all of her personal possessions could be carried in one load by the man's cart. So little to show for twenty-five years of life! She took the spare bedroom in D'Art's apart-

ment and, aside from her clothing, her presence there
scarcely changed the place. It was time to take stock
of her life. She had lost the man she loved. She had
been alienated from her sister and now from her uncle
and Lyris. She had nothing—nothing but herself and
her skills as a nurse. She went back to the hospital,
where she was welcomed and was going about her life
with a dull acceptance when Roger D'Art returned.

After the ceremonial digging of a shovelful of dirt in
Panama, to indicate the official dedication of the new
canal, de Lesseps had gone to America to try to interest investors there in his plan.

"You should have gone with him," Petra told Roger.

"I could not help thinking of you, my dear girl,"
Roger said. "I was concerned for you, and, apparently,
with good reason."

"No, I'm fine."

"You don't look fine," he said. "There are dark
circles under your eyes. You're thin. And you did not
move into my apartment on a whim."

In the end, Petra had to tell him. Although he had
his suspicions about Guy and Lyris, he was shocked
beyond belief by Petra's recounting of the events following the ball, and by Petra's assumption that Darcie
had been a willing participant in the wild revels in the
Simel house. Roger wanted to set out immediately to
take a horsewhip to Simel. "But it is best," Petra said,
"to leave them to their own ways. I, for my part, do
not care to see them again and they are most certainly
not worth your risking trouble. They did not harm me."

"But they most certainly harmed your sister," he
said. "Do you realize now why she is—well, as she is?"

"Yes, I think so," Petra said, "and I am truly sorry
for her. But it's too late, Roger. It's too late for us to
do anything about it."

"Yes, I must reluctantly admit that you're right," he
said.

D'Art composed a very formal letter in which he informed Guy that it would no longer be possible for them to be associated in the practice of medicine. He gave as his reason his impending departure for Panama, where he would supervise construction of a hospital. However, he was careful, in the days during which he closed his office, to avoid Guy. He did not trust himself to be in Guy's presence. To think that they had tried to debauch his beloved Petra was too much for him to stomach and keep his fists to himself.

But now the honorable and proper D'Art had a problem. In his apartment, in his spare bedroom, was a lady who was no longer a child, but a fully adult woman and, although he felt quite fatherly toward her, she was not his daughter.

"My dear Petra," he said, "it seems that we face a situation. I realize that you yourself, feeling as you do, think nothing wrong with our being alone in an apartment, nor do I care what the world thinks. However, for my own peace of mind, and for the sake of our own honor, we must talk about it."

"I thrust myself upon you," she said. "I'll find an apartment immediately."

"That is not my intention," he said. "Please don't be angry. There is also another problem, which we must face soon. I will be spending quite a number of years in Panama. Do you still profess an interest in being, as you say, a part of the great adventure?"

"I've been thinking about it more and more these days," Petra said. "Yes, I would love to work with you in Panama."

"Well, then, listen, and please don't be shocked and, above all, don't jump to conclusions until you hear me out. You must know, my dear girl, that I look upon you as the daughter I never had. However, you are not my daughter, and that we cannot change. We can change our status in quite an honorable and acceptable, and, I might add, legal way to smooth the way for both of us and to give you a home and a protector." He held up his hands as Petra opened her mouth. "What I am proposing is a *mariage de convenance*." He laughed. "I am too old and set in my ways to propose otherwise, even if our ages were closer—"

"Roger, you're only forty-four," she protested.

"Do not interrupt," he said in a kindly voice. "No, Petra, I offer you only the security of my house and my name."

"It is a very kind offer, Roger," she said.

"Do you accept, then?"

She could see Jay's face before her. For a moment, there was a cold ache in her heart. Then there was the vision of Jay's naked body heaving up to take Darcie in love. No, she would never love again.

"I accept with gratitude, my dear Roger," she said.

"Be assured that I will continue to treat you as my beloved daughter," he said, taking her hand and kissing it. "That does not mean that we cannot have our gay times. We've always had gay times, haven't we?"

"Always," she said. "You have always been my very good and kind friend, Roger."

"And the great adventure together, eh?"

"Yes. I shall enjoy that very much."

"I must warn you, young lady, that I am a stern taskmaster. When we are in hospital, at work, there will be no special status for you, wife or not."

She laughed. "I wouldn't have it any other way."

They were married quietly, with only the required number of legal witnesses. It took a few days to wind up Roger's affairs, to close up the apartment. She discovered that D'Art had not many more items of personal value than she. They could travel light.

Petra said good-bye to her Paris from a train window, and then the great adventure was underway and she was no longer Petra Laurette Moncrief, but Petra Laurette D'Art, Madame Roger D'Art.

The pattern of their marriage had been set during the last days in the apartment: she in her own room, he in his. There were separate staterooms aboard ship, and their time together was spent as it had been in the past, in friendly talk, with a father-daughter closeness. She felt no desire to change it, and apparently neither did he.

BOOK II

1

WHEN ROGER D'ART first saw Panama it was in December, at the height of the dry season when the isthmus puts on its best face with northeast trades blowing freshly, skies clear, the temperatures in the low eighties. Like de Lesseps, he had been warned, especially by those who favored another route for the canal, that Panama was a hellhole. It was natural as they traveled in pleasant temperatures and under azure skies to assume that the situation had been greatly misrepresented.

Perhaps the Spanish, who had been in Panama and other tropical areas of the Americas for centuries, could have warned the optimistic French, but in the 1880s Spain was in the process of being assigned to the backwaters of history and had nothing to do with de Lesseps's grand plan to connect the two great oceans.

The interior of the Panama peninsula was largely unexplored and uncharted, just as it had been when Diego de Nicuesa was sent by King Ferdinand of Spain in 1509 to establish settlements. At that time the area was called Tierra Firme, and the northern coast had

been explored hit-and-miss by Rodrigo de Bastidas in
1501 and by Columbus, on his fourth and last voyage,
in 1502. Had Nicuesa been alive, he could have told
hair-raising tales about the hostility of the natives, the
endless rains, the diseases which made Tierra Firme
untenable for his colonists, but it is doubtful that de
Lesseps would have listened.

The state of European knowledge regarding Panama
was illustrated, perhaps, by the words of the poet, John
Keats:

> —Like stout Cortez when with eagle eyes
> He star'd at the Pacific—and all his men
> Look'd at each other with a wild surmise—
> Silent, upon a peak in Darien.

Keats, by no means an uneducated man, either took
poetic license, since Balboa did not have the proper
meter to fit his verse, or did not know that it was
Vasco Nuñez de Balboa who first saw, not the Pacific,
but the vast mud flats on the Pacific side of the Panama
isthmus.

So little was known about Panama that it came as a
surprise to many that the canal, as proposed by de
Lesseps, would not run directly east-west but, due to
the curvature of the central and narrowest portion of
the isthmus, would be more southerly than westerly in
direction.

De Lesseps made his commitment to build his second great canal without solid knowledge of the year-
round conditions or the height of the interior hills. It
was enough to know that the distance to be covered by
a canal was a mere forty miles—much less than the
"Great Ditch" at Suez.

There were ample warnings in history of the deadli-
ness of the climate there, just nine degrees north of the
equator. The fate of Sir Francis Drake should have
given a medical man like Roger D'Art food for

thought, for it was well recorded that Drake, in his second raid on the Spanish colonies in Panama, failed in an attempt to cross the isthmus for an attack on Old Panama City and died of fever.

So many warnings were ignored. Perhaps the initial coolness of the English to the Panama scheme was the result of a knowledge of history; for William Paterson, founder of the Bank of England, had tried to establish a trading post, only to be defeated by the climate and by rampant disease.

The Americans knew Panama because of the gold rush of 1849, when thousands took the shortcut across Panama to the California gold fields. However, accounts written by gold seekers varied, depending upon the time of year of their crossing, whether it was during the dry or the rainy season. Panama was a Jekyll-Hyde land, presenting different faces in the dry season—mid-December to May, and in the rainy season—May to December.

When Roger D'Art took his wife into Limon Bay, he saw Panama's wet season for the first time. The ship made landfall in a driving rainstorm which swept the decks with the force of a fire hose.

For Petra, product of temperate England and long a resident of France, stepping ashore at Colón was an experience she would never forget. Landing had been made after the rain ceased. The land seemed to steam, heavy vapors rising from the sun-heated rankness, the air still and heavy, no wind, the lungs filling with breath which was much like the product of a vaporizer: hot, steamy. And the town, which from a distance had seemed to be colorful with its white walls and red roofs against the blue of the bay and the green of the foothills, became a horror beyond her experience, worse than the most crowded alleys of Cairo, of which she had memories.

Colón, the eastern terminal of the Panama Railroad, was a new town, built by the men who constructed the railroad. It was low, barely above the moderate tides of the Caribbean, its base a coral flat at the tip of Limon Bay. Streets were dirt and walking them was a hazard, for they served not only as thoroughfares, but as garbage dumps for the populace and were littered with the offal, scraps, dead animals, and useless debris of a society which existed—it could not be said that they lived—in hopeless and grinding poverty.

The smell of the town assaulted Petra's nose, forcing her to cover her nostrils with a handkerchief which was already sodden with perspiration wiped from her face. Huge vultures circled in the muggy sky, perched on the tops of the frame buildings which lined the main street, Front Street, which was bisected by the railroad itself.

The town was the most miserable place Petra had ever seen—a place filled with death and mold, stench and ugliness—and her heart went out to the dazed and helpless look on the faces of blacks, mostly Jamaicans, who had been brought in to build the railroad and remained to exist in terrible squalor.

With some difficulty, Roger arranged for their belongings to be taken to the only acceptable hotel in town, the railroad's Washington House, where a suite of rooms had been reserved for them. In the oppressive heat, Petra had little appetite. Abed, she lay in wakeful thought, sheets soaked with her own sweat. The night brought only a bit of relief from the heat, and the morning was a steam bath until the dark clouds rolled suddenly and thunder crashed with a force which caused Petra to start and cry out in surprise. The sound of the rain itself was a loud rumble on the roof; the town, as seen through her window, disappeared behind a curtain of rain, solid, all-encompassing, so total that for the duration of the shower there existed only the rain, the startlingly vivid lightning, the artillery explosions of the thunder.

Then, as suddenly as it began, it was over, temporarily—but the sky remained filled with clouds which reached to the upper limits of vision, promising the onslaught of another downpour at any time.

It was a relief to be in a carriage; at least the movement of the vehicle gave one an illusion of a breeze. Then, together, they observed the beginnings of the hospital over which D'Art would have jurisdiction. To the credit of de Lesseps and those he chose to run the canal company, construction was well underway not only on the hospital in Colón, but on a larger facility at Panama City, on the Pacific shore.

The visit to the construction site was followed by a visit to the company office, where D'Art was assured that he and his wife would be provided suitable quarters as soon as possible. Already prefabricated houses were being shipped from New Orleans to be erected in a pleasant spot near the water in a new town to be called Christophe-Colombe. Meanwhile they would remain in the Washington House.

Those first weeks were a nightmare for Petra. She seemed to exist in a daze, stunned by the heat, the predictable rains which came every day, her skin ravaged by the bites of insects, and by the heat. She soon discovered that most of her clothing was not suitable for the climate of Panama, and, convention be damned, discarded the heavy underwear, often going about in nothing more than a dress and a thin slip. Even then she was soaked to the skin, either by rain or by her own perspiration before the day was two hours old. Everything seemed to be damp, never drying. A dress taken fresh from the laundry seemed heavy, sodden, and was soon dampened even more as her body fought to cool itself by copious perspiration.

However, Petra gradually began to bear up under the climate. The hospital was now receiving its first patients, and now her days were spent in work, at her husband's side, treating various injuries among the workmen, who had cut a path from Colón to the Pacific.

With the field of tropical medicine in its infancy, they encountered fevers which they could not recognize, snakebite, insect bite, heat prostration. The hours were long, the work often unrewarding because of the high casualty rate among patients. The first malaria cases began to come in immediately.

The name of the disease, malaria, the world's number-one killer, was derived from the Italian *mal'aria,* meaning bad air. The French word for the disease— *paludisme*—means marsh fever. Although, at the time of Petra and Roger's initial encounter with malaria patients in Panama, there were doctors in the world who had solid theories on the nature and cause of the disease, the prevailing opinion was that malaria was caused by the miasma which arose from the swamps and rotting vegetation of tropical areas. With the dreaded yellow fever also thought to be airborne, the cause was attributed to filth such as decaying dead animals or sewage. Thus the only defense against such disease was to be closed up in an airless room, impossible in the tropics—and to be of unreproachable moral fiber. For in the popular belief, those who indulged in excess—of the flesh, of drink or of food—were more likely to be stricken.

There was, however, a defense against malaria which, although not as immediately deadly as yellow fever, had the unfortunate ability to strike a victim more than once. The standard preventive among the people who were beginning to come from all over the world to work on de Lesseps's big ditch was two grains of quinine each morning. Some advocated that the quinine be taken with an ounce of whisky, but Petra did not subscribe to that later view.

At first, the daily doses of quinine tended to make her nauseous, but as the weeks passed, her system became adjusted to it. The only effect was a slight yellowing of her skin which, in the heat of the Panama summer, was blotchy with heat rash and insect bites.

As the hospital at Colón was completed, the beds were almost always filled. Since the fevers were thought to be carried on the wind from the marshes, fever patients were not segregated. Malaria and yellow-fever patients were put into wards with men suffering from broken limbs, and the hospital and the larger facility at Panama soon became known, among the rank-and-file of workers, as deathtraps. If you didn't have fever when you went in, you had it before you came out.

One irritating problem in the hospital was the large and fierce ants which seemed to come from everywhere. To keep them off the patients' beds, the doctors had pans of water put under the legs of the beds. Indeed, on the grounds outside, as the workmen began to beautify them, ringlike containers of water were placed around ornamental plants to prevent their being devoured by the voracious ants.

It was quite perplexing, if one believed in the theory of moral defense against the fever, to see men who were thought to be of the finest moral caliber catch fever and die of it. In that first summer, the diseases did not respect rank or worth, attacking laborers and French engineers alike.

Petra and Roger were now installed in quite a pleasant, if small, cottage. The work on the canal was progressing well, and hundreds of blacks were being imported to do the labor. Meanwhile, opportunists from all over the world were coming into Panama to open gambling houses, saloons, brothels, and to establish what was to become one of the more profitable businesses: coffin making.

Although, as she lived it, that first summer in Panama seemed endless, in retrospect it passed rapidly, with work and heat and death her constant companions. Fighting enemies with which he was unfamiliar,

and against which he had little defense, Roger worked
such long hours that Petra often had to force him to go
to their little cottage for some well-deserved rest. Tired,
beat down by the oppressive heat and humidity, Petra
came out of the cottage one morning in December to
find clear skies, a breathable atmosphere, a strange
lack of the steamy feeling of the summer. Spirits lifted,
she began to feel better as the almost-pleasant dry season established itself, and, indeed, began to take an
interest in her home, hiring a maid to keep it clean,
adding a few civilized touches in the form of curtains
and other decorative items.

The load of fever cases at the hospital began to ease,
and there was time to direct the aides and other help
in a thorough cleaning job, for the summer had left
its mark. The heat and dampness had melted glue in
furniture joints, had grown a layer of mold on almost
everything, seemingly reappearing overnight on items
such as leather. Metal was bright orange with rust. It
was now possible to dry the sheets of the beds, which,
during the summer, seemed always to be damp.

Christmas came and went almost unnoticed. There
was a greater celebration when on a Friday in January,
with a huge blast of explosives, actual digging began
on the canal.

It was shortly after this auspicious beginning that
Roger requested Petra to make the journey to Panama,
on the Pacific shore, to compare notes with the *Filles
de la Charité,* an order of nuns who were handling the
nursing at the large hospital on Ancon Hill overlooking the city and the Bay of Panama. The trip across
the isthmus gave her a better idea of what the men
faced in the jungles of the interior, for the jungle was
like a wall around her as she peered out the window
of the train. She saw the dreaded Chagres River and
the squalid little town of Gatun, overheard two engineers talking about the difficulties faced in the field: the
blue-black mire which could bog down a horse, the

impossibility of ever being dry in the jungle, the incredible amounts of water which had to be controlled in the Chagres before a canal could be possible.

She felt very much alone during the trip, and almost wished herself back in the hospital with Roger. However, the trip did offer a bit of change from the endless day to day grind of the work and the hopelessness as men died. By the time she reached Panama City and was taken to the hospital nestled on the side of a hill, she had a feeling almost of holiday and spent some pleasant hours talking professionally with the nurse-nuns and a few friendly doctors who were interested in Dr. D'Art's conclusions after having practiced medicine in Colón during the rainy season.

It was somewhat depressing to discover that in spite of the splendid facilities of *l'Hôpital Notre Dame du Canal,* the doctors there had no better success in saving the victims of fever than did Roger and Petra, with more limited manpower and facilities. She would have nothing encouraging to report to Roger, and she felt that he had been prepared for exactly that, wanting only to give her a bit of time away from the wards, a small holiday.

She made rounds with Dr. Louis Companyo, who had been in charge of sanitation at Suez, and was further depressed by his contention that nothing could be done to make Panama a fit place for occupation by the Caucasian races.

She was preparing to depart for the trip back to Colón when she saw Jay. She was totally unprepared for her reaction. Dressed in a light-colored shirtwaist dress, her full figure displayed through the dress by the lightness of her underwear, she was walking alone from Dr. Companyo's office down a corridor when she saw the familiar bulk of Burton's large frame coming toward her. She paused in midstep, memories which she had succeeded in hiding coming back in a rush. A flush of anger brightened her cheek, for she had put all of that behind her and he had no right to come back into her life. Seeing him brought back memories of Darcie, who was presumably back in France; of Guy and Lyris, also in France working with de Lesseps to raise the money necessary for building the canal. But most of all, seeing him brought back to her that night aboard the *Lafayette*.

She picked up her step again, head high, her eyes level. Jay was apparently preoccupied, and he was alomst upon her, a bemused look on his face, before he saw her.

He went pale and halted in his tracks. "My God!" he said. "It is. Petra."

"Hello, Jay," she said, not pausing, intending to walk past him.

He caught her arm. "Petra, you look wonderful."

"Thank you. Are you well?"

He shrugged. They stood there awkwardly in the hospital corridor. She made a move to walk on, but he held her, his hand strong on her arm.

"I would like to talk with you," he said.

There was something in his eyes which moved her, a haunted look of sadness. "I must catch the train," she said.

"There's time. Is there a place where we can talk?"

"What is there to say?" she asked.

"Please."

"Yes, well," she said. "I'm sure Dr. Companyo won't mind if we use his office." She led him into the room, sat behind the desk. Jay stood uneasily in front of her.

"Petra, I've heard," he said. "I mean your marriage to D'Art. I want you to know that I'm pleased for both of you. Roger is a fine man."

"Yes."

"So what I have to say comes too late," he said.

"Jay, there's no need to say anything," she said.

"But I must." He spread his hands. "How in hell does a man say that he was seduced?"

"If he is a gentleman," she said coldly, "he does not."

"I was thinking of you, Petra, I—"

"Ha!" she said, with a feeling which surprised her as she remembered how he'd looked.

"I was drinking. We'd been celebrating. She came to my cabin—"

"Jay, it doesn't matter."

"But you must know," he said earnestly. "I had no intention. She came to me and I was—and I know it's no defense—I was drunk. It just happened. I hardly knew what I was doing, and all the time I was, well, all the time, I knew that it was terribly wrong, for I loved you, Petra. I truly loved you."

"Yes, well," she said, trying to hide the flush she felt creeping up her neck, hating herself for feeling, once again, the emotions which she'd thought gone forever. But seeing him, hearing him vow his love, did things to her which she did not choose to accept. Moreover, she'd been exposed to the unashamed sensuality of Guy and Lyris. She knew that they had no morals and, by inference, the same was true of Darcie. It was quite easy to understand how a man could be induced to fall to the charms of a woman as lovely as Darcie, a woman totally amoral, a woman who gave herself for her own pleasure and to hurt her sister.

"And, God help me," Jay said, not looking at her, "I love you still."

"I find this subject too personal and somewhat disgusting," Petra said.

"Yes. I'm very sorry. I wanted you to know. I'll not mention it again, Petra. I wish you all the happiness."

"Thank you. And you? What is your job?"

"I'm in charge of a crew working at the Culebra cut."

"Is it going well?"

"Not well at all," he said. "In fact, it's an impossible task. I'm coming to the belief that it can't be done."

"Oh, it will be done," she said.

"At the cost of how many lives?" he asked. "Do you know that the American press is calling de Lesseps 'The Great Gravedigger'?"

"The Americans are simply jealous that it is not to be a Yankee canal," she said.

"Perhaps," he said, with a smile. "Petra, although it's nice to see you, I'm sorry to see you here. This is no place for a woman. Ever since I heard that you were here, I've been concerned about you. I've questioned Roger's judgment in allowing you to come."

"It isn't your affair, is it?" she asked.

"No, but I'd feel better if you were back in France."

Petra decided that to be rude was not worth it. "Well, I think I'd feel better back in France, without doubt," she said. "Especially when I think that another rainy season is only a few months off. But I have my work. I am making a contribution, however small. That, at least, is something."

"You are not happy?" he asked, and she realized that she'd allowed some of her discouragement to show in her last words.

"Tell me about Culebra," she said.

"Only if you'll have dinner with me."

For a moment she was tempted, but there arose a fear in her, a fear that alone with him she'd be, once again, the helpless little idiot. It was so ironic. She'd been married for almost year, and she was still as she'd been that night when she'd offered herself to this man who stood before her.

"I'm sorry. I must return to Colón. Roger is expecting me."

"Yes," he said. "Well, if you must, you must. I'll give you a lift to the station."

On the way he talked of the work underway at

Culebra, alternating between stubborn insistence that the job could be done and a total despair at its impossibility. At the station, he boarded the train with her and stayed until the hoots of the engine and the jerkings of couplings told him that the train's departure was imminent.

"If I'm in Colón, may I call?"

"I'm sure Roger would be pleased to see you," she said.

Then Petra was alone again. She could not erase the memory of his smile. Once again her body, as if gifted with perfect recall, remembered his touch. Her lips remembered his kisses. He himself had said it. It was too late.

By the time Roger arrived home from the hospital, she had had many hours to think about it. Perhaps it was best that she'd seen Jay. Although she had not allowed herself to think about him, she'd known all along that she'd run into him somewhere if she stayed in Panama. The only surprise was the intensity of her feeling for him. She promised herself she would not go through the rest of her life burning with a love gone sour. Nor, she determined, would she go through the rest of her life like one of the nuns at *l'Hôpital de Notre Dame*. Unlike the nuns, she had a husband.

In the pleasant coolness of the evening, dressed in a light and handsome frock, she greeted Roger with wine and a splendid meal, told him about her visit at the large hospital over the meal, and then, over brandy, sat with him on the veranda to hear the far-off call of nightbirds and the hum of insects. He talked of his work and she listened until, after a few moments of comfortable silence she asked, "Roger, have you ever had the desire to have children?"

He laughed. "I've had scant time to consider it. Why do you ask, my dear?"

"Oh, it's a natural human desire, isn't it?"

"Humm," he said. "Yes, I suppose it is."

"A boy to carry your name? A little girl to pet and spoil?"

"Pleasant thought," he said, "but I'm far too old to think—" He paused. "At any rate, I couldn't ask that of you."

"And if I desire it?"

He cleared his throat uneasily. "Have you thought about it?"

"Quite a lot," she said.

"And your conclusions?"

"I think I would like a girl first," she said. "Then a boy."

"There are many considerations," he said.

"I thought of some of them," she said. "The worst is bringing a child into such a place as this, but then we won't be here forever, will we?"

"If I thought so, I think I should just go to sleep and not wake up," Roger said with a wry laugh.

"I know the feeling," she agreed.

"But most importantly, that was not a part of our agreement."

"I am your wife, Roger. You know I'm very fond of you. And I'm a woman. Do you know that I've never known a man?"

He was silent. They had never discussed what had occurred between her and Jay, nor had he ever questioned her about her life before she met Jay.

"I think I was reminded of this through my contact with the little sisters at *Notre Dame*," she said. "I am a nun out of habit, and that word has a double meaning—out of my own habits and out of the uniform of a nun. I think, my dear Roger, that it is time you put an end to that condition."

"Oh, my dear," he said, at a loss for words. "Can I believe that you mean it?" He rose and took both her hands in his.

"Yes," she said with a smile, "I do mean it. I'm quite sure."

"Do you want some time to think about it?" he asked, his voice showing his nervous state.

"I've had plenty of time." She laughed. "Roger D'Art, what does a woman have to do to get you to seduce her?"

He laughed nervously. "I suppose," he said, "that if my wife—not just a woman, but my wife—came into my bed in, say, ten minutes—?"

Petra discovered that her finest nightdress had been partially devoured by insect, or rot, and she went to him in a plain cambric nightdress which was slightly the worse for wear, but fresh and clean. Her hair, which had been cut to better withstand the heat, was freshly washed, and there was a little tremor of excitement as she saw him, in a robe, standing beside his bed. She kissed him lightly on the lips. Then she climbed into his bed. He put out the light, and she could hear his movements as he discarded the robe.

To her surprise, when he came to her, he was wearing a nightshirt. His hands touched her tentatively, and he leaned over her to kiss her. His kiss was cool, his lips tightly closed. She put her arms around him and pulled him down to her.

"When the time comes, there may be pain."

"I won't mind."

"Should I hurt you, or do anything which displeases you—"

"It's all right," she whispered.

"I confess, my dear Petra, that I am not the most experienced man in the world in these matters," he said.

"Roger, stop talking," she said with a little laugh.

"Oh, my," he said, as his hand closed over her breast, modestly covered by her nightgown. "Oh, my." And now he was breathing with some fervor, his hands moving down to feel the outflow of her hips, to press lightly on her stomach and then under her nightgown onto the heat of her thighs and she, with a sigh, opened

her legs to give him access. There was a small thrill as
his hand touched her heated parts, and his fingers
toyed there. In her mind there leaped pictures: Jay
leaning to kiss her in that spot where Roger's fingers
moved so lightly, the heat of his mouth there, the
overcoming passion she'd felt when Jay mounted her
and she felt his hardness at the very threshold of her
womanhood, and she was willing it to happen again,
with her husband, relaxing her body to give it to him,
wanting to be rid of the encumbering nightclothing
which separated them. She was fond of Roger. He'd
always been so considerate of her. And he was a
doctor. He'd know about a woman's body.

Just beginning to feel the growth of passion, she was
shocked when he lifted her nightgown to her waist, to
leave it there, bunched into an uncomfortable bulge
and, with swift and jerky movements, positioned himself between her outflung legs. *No, no,* she thought,
*it's only beginning. There is all of the lovely prepara-
to be made, all the heated touches, the kisses.* But, instead, he opened her with his fingers and she felt the
heat of him and there was a feeling of being stretched
as he slid into her creamed opening and then a piercing pain which caused her to cry out. He halted immediately, but just as immediately, when she was silent,
shocked by the quickness of his assault, he pushed and
she felt something give, pop, and she was filled with
him and he was moving with a rapidity which forced
the breath from her in panting gasps and then, quickly,
quickly, with short little lunges, he took her and before
she could protest, he was deep, pushing hard, and she
could feel the spasmodic emptyings inside her.

"Oh, Petra, Petra," he moaned, still, his weight on
her. "I never dreamed that it could happen. Oh, how
I've loved you, and how I've wanted you. And to
think you wanted me all the while. You did want me,
didn't you?"

"Yes, my dear," she said, with a sinking heart,

thinking, *Oh, God, is that all there is? Damn, what a farce! All these years they've been telling me how wonderful it was going to be, and now it's done and it's over, and there's only emptiness.*

Now there was a new element in her life. She herself had opened the lid to the Pandora's box of D'Art's emotions, had wrung from him, by giving him her body, the confession that he loved her, not as a father loves a daughter, but as a man loves a woman. And, although he was by no means a demanding man, his passions seeming to run shallow and infrequently, there was, for her, a wifely duty to submit herself, always modestly covered in her nightdress, to him, also and even more modestly covered in his nightshirt, to him and his quick, lunging, gasping releases which, as time went on, became more and more hateful to her. Once having known the wonder of having her emotions heated to a white-hot glow by the skilled lovemaking of Jay, Roger's mechanical and uninspired efforts aroused in her only a sense of disgust, and of utter boredom. As he settled into a predictable routine, requesting her presence in his bed on the first and fifteenth of each month, she came to dread the nights of his passion and left his bed when they were over to wash his sticky juices from her as speedily as possible.

2

THREE OUT OF every five Frenchmen who came to Panama with such high hopes would die. Since many of the Frenchmen brought wives, the death toll included women as well. In the D'Art family, it was to be Petra who first knew the onset of the warning chills which preceded the dreaded forms of fever. They came to her shortly after the onset of her second summer, as she went about her work at the hospital. First, she knew a thirst which was not satisfied, regardless of how much she drank; and then, on a hot and sultry day, her body began to know an arctic cold despite the hothouse atmosphere.

She stood leaning against a wall, her work undone, as the first violent tremblings began and the world seemed to pale around her. The chill passed. She took her temperature and found it to be above normal. Within the next half hour, it rose to a point which made her mind foggy.

Roger was in the operating room. She went to her head nurse, a large, motherly woman who had suffered a bout of malaria herself.

"Anna," Petra said, her voice seeming to come from far away, "I feel quite ill."

Anna halted her ministerings to a fever patient who was dying and turned, concern on her full and pleasant face.

"Ah, no, madame, not you, too," she said, but she was moving, feeling Petra's hot brow and then hustling her away into a private room reserved for high company officials. There she quickly had Petra in bed. Petra was feeling too weak to resist as the chills came again, causing her limbs to jerk and her teeth to chatter as if with cold.

She awoke with Roger bending over her, a look of horror on his face.

"Don't look so sad," she said. "I've never neglected my quinine. It will be a light attack."

"Yes, yes, of course," he said.

When the headache began, the pain was so brutal that she moaned aloud and there were accompanying pains in her back and legs—pains so widespread that her entire body seemed to be a sea of pain and her head so huge, so inflamed with agony that she could not control the moans which came from her lips.

As the fever became more intense, the world seemed to leave her, stranding her in a heated and painful purgatory which was eternal. She was only dimly aware of the comings and goings of Roger and Anna. In lucid moments, a terrible thirst made her agony more unbearable.

Although the choice was a nightmare, Roger hoped that Petra's fever was malaria, for with her heavy doses of quinine she would have a better chance of survival; but, as the long hours went on, it became apparent to his trained eye that she was suffering from the more virulent of the two great fevers.

From the little that was known about yellow fever, Roger knew that the survival rate varied from onset to onset of the disease; at times the mortality rate as low as 15 percent, at times as high as 70. The outbreaks of yellow fever in Panama had been running a mortality rate of approximately 50 percent and a deathly fear almost paralyzed him, caused him to neglect his work, as the swift-acting disease worsened. He spent much of his time in Petra's room, and no little of that time in prayer, for she was in God's hands. The entire medical profession was as ineffectual against yellow fever as a witch doctor waving feathered jujus. He was by her bedside for sleepless hours, bathing her fevered brow with damp cloths, holding her head up so that she could drink.

Thank God, he thought, *that she has not, as yet, been made with child.*

At the height of the fever, Petra alternated between burning and freezing, and when the chills struck, not even the climate, the ever-present heat, the addition of blankets to her coverlets, could help. And then, the chill gone, she would squirm and kick restlessly, seeking escape from the burning fever, weakly tossing aside the coverings.

From grim experience, Roger knew the course of the disease well, and he watched helplessly as it ran its course. Petra grew restless, unable to find ease in the bed, tossing her head, her arms, kicking weakly with her legs. And then came the false recovery, when the fever and chills subsided and, had he not known what could follow, he would have felt vast relief. Petra's face, already slightly yellowed by the constant use of quinine, became more yellow still, and her eyes took on the grim tint of the disease as she entered the last and telling stage.

Drifting in and out of delirium, Petra seemed to relive her life, the memories distorted at times by the fever. Once again she was in the desert watching the dwarf, Hassam Ari, ravish poor Darcie. She saw the slash of Ari's blade as it opened the stomach of the luckless Adrienne, and, in her delirium, could feel the

keen pain in her own body. Once she thought she saw
her mother, pretty, smiling, standing far off, seen
through an obscuring fog, and her mother seemed to
be beckoning to her.

"Come, Petra, come," her mother seemed to be saying.

"No," Petra moaned. "No, *maman,* not yet." And
the feel of coolness on her brow caused her to open
her eyes to see Roger's concerned face. She tried to
smile, and it turned into a grimace as the pain assaulted
her in the head and the fever came and was replaced
by numbing, shaking chill—chill so severe that Roger
feared she would shatter her teeth as they clattered
together.

And in her delirium Guy smiled at her and did
obscene things to her body. And, almost as if she were
real, Darcie was there—a Darcie at the peak of her
mature beauty, tiny, looking delicate and clean even
in the heat.

"Is it very bad, Petra?"

"I hope you'll never know how terrible."

"I forbid you to die."

"You took him from me."

"It doesn't matter anymore, Petra."

"Why should I live?"

"Because I forbid you to die. Do you think you've
known suffering? Ha!"

"Why must I suffer?"

"Why did I have to suffer?"

"You took him. You did it to make me suffer."

"Silly. Mooning over some ox of a man isn't suffering."

"For me it was."

"Well, then. Will you try? I don't want you to die,
Petra."

"I don't want to live."

"You could still have him, you little dunce."

"I'm married."

"So? You can have both of them, if it pleases you."

"Darcie. Darcie."

Darcie.

"I have hope," Roger said. "She has reached the critical point. If, within the next few hours she does not spit up the *vómito negro*—"

"She was always strong," Guy Simel said. "Petra, can you hear me?"

"Yes."

"It's almost over," Guy said. "It's almost over."

Almost over. And the night closing in and a vast and complete lethargy in her, a weakness. She could not lift her head, and the cooling water which gave no relief had to be poured into her mouth where she had difficulty swallowing it and it ran down her face onto the pillow to add to the dampness of her perspiration.

"Come, Petra," her mother said, from far away in the obscuring fog.

You can have both of them, if it pleases you.

"Roger."

"I'm here, my dear."

"I'm so very, very tired."

"Yes. Rest. It's over, my love."

And eons later.

"Roger."

"I'm here."

"I will live."

"Yes, thank God."

The day, hot, heavy. Her sheets dampened and Anna's kind and motherly face. "We'll just change these sheets, madame."

For a few moments a feeling of cleanliness as she was treated to the freshness of the clean linen only to feel it become soggy as she perspired and turned in restlessness.

"Ah," Roger said. "So you're awake."

"Malaria?" she asked, with dread, for having experienced it once, she feared the return of the disease, and malaria can come again and again, even when one is far away from the tropics.

"There is one consolation," he said. "You have survived the worst. You will need have no fear of a repetition of this particular agony."

"Yellow fever?" she asked.

"I fear so."

"Oh, those poor wretches," she said, thinking of the men who had suffered with the disease, many of them not surviving it.

"Rest now. You will have a visitor later in the day."

Jay. It would be Jay. She closed her eyes and let the blessed sleep come.

She surfaced from an exhausted sleep. The heat pressed down upon her. She had kicked off her covers, and the hospital gown was twisted around her uncomfortably. She was so weak that an attempt to straighten the garment left her panting and she gave up, closing her eyes and feeling a depression so intense that tears welled up in her eyes and oozed out her closed lids. She wanted only to go back to sleep, and she did not care if she ever awakened. The thought of getting out of the bed, of going back to her fruitless work, merely saddened her. What was the use? Fifty percent of the men who came into the hospital with fever would die. It was all so futile, the entire attempt. De Lesseps was foolish to think that men could live in such conditions and still function, still do the demanding work. No, all would fail. All would die. And the fever would come to her again—perhaps malaria next time. So heavy was her depression that nothing, no pleasant thought, no effort of will, could lift it. She thought of her life with Roger—a progression of dull and unrewarding days and bouts of his selfish sex—and there was no hope. Jay. Jay would die, along with thousands of others and, in any event, there was no hope there. It was too late, and she had nothing to live for. It would make sense if she died. She willed herself to sleep, to sleep the last and endless sleep, dreamless.

"I forbid you to die," Darcie had said to her in her delirium. So real. And she could, it seemed, still hear Darcie's voice.

"Petra, are you awake?"

"Yes."

"So. You fought it, little sister. You will recover."

She opened her eyes with an effort, and Darcie's face was there, calm, so maturely beautiful. She was dressed in white, a gown suitable for the climate. Her arms were bare. There was a smile on Darcie's face, a cold, speculating smile which made Petra feel uneasy.

"You're not dreaming," Darcie said.

"Go home," Petra said weakly.

"Ah, you don't want me here? Are you not pleased to see your loving sister?"

"Horrible," Petra said. "It's so horrible. Go, please, before you—"

"Why, you're concerned about me," Darcie said.

"No place for civilized people," Petra said.

"How nice of you," Darcie crooned. "To think that you still care for me." There was a taunting, acid tone to her soft voice. "But Guy felt that it was necessary. He's in charge of the Colón office, you know."

"Guy."

"He was here."

"So tired," Petra said.

"Yes, I'll go now. I just wanted you to know that I'm here, little sister. I'm pleased to see that you're well and happy."

"Darcie, why do you hate me so?" But she didn't really care. Nothing mattered.

"Hate you?" She laughed lightly. "Nothing of the sort, little sister. I'm merely here to see that you're taken care of—that's all."

"Go, please. Just go away. I'm so tired."

Endless days. Fits of weeping. Then she was moved

to her cottage. With an effort of will, she could get out of bed and walk about the cottage. And through it all the rains came, heavy, made dramatic by the violent lightning and thunder. Roger was solicitous, talking to her, telling her that her depression was the usual aftermath of the disease, that it would pass.

She feared that it would, that she would live, and she did. Then one day she put on her uniform and went in to work and, thinner, met a smiling Anna, who kissed her cheek and talked about what had happened while she was ill. Nothing. The same. Fever and small-pox and all the ills which beset mankind in that hell-hole of a place.

But there was work, and gradually she regained her strength and her will, and having known the agony of it, was touched even more deeply by those who suffered and died. She was one of the lucky ones. Never again would she have to face yellow fever, for, once people survived the disease, it did not strike them again.

At Roger's insistence, they had dinner at the comfortable home which had been built for the director of the company's Colón operations. Guy was charming and Darcie was the perfect hostess. The visit was necessary, Roger told her, because Guy, in his new position, controlled the funds for the hospital. Roger wanted additional equipment, a building program to add more rooms. He brought up the subject at dinner, and Guy was discouraging.

"Monsieur de Lesseps has made a great mistake," Guy said. "In the beginning, he could have raised an unlimited amount of money through stock issue, for the first issue was oversubscribed. Now, with it becoming evident that all estimates as to cost were much too low, the money is running out. You'll have to get along with what there is for the time being, I'm afraid."

"The old fool will listen to no one," Darcie said.

Petra was shocked to hear The Hero of Suez called an old fool. "Well, the work is going well," she said.

"Estimates of the amount of earth to be moved were so low that it approaches incompetence," Guy said. "At Culebra alone we face almost insurmountable problems. As soon as the diggers remove one lot of earth and stone, the banks slide down, and it's to be dug all over again."

"You seem to know a lot about it," Petra said. "How is it that you've given up medicine and are now so knowledgeable about canal building?" She intended it to be a mild barb, but it did not upset Guy.

"Self-preservation," Guy said, with a shrug of his shoulders. "I believed in the old man." He laughed. "Perhaps you'll turn out to be the smartest of all of us, Petra. At least you didn't invest your money in canal stock."

"Not because I didn't believe," she said.

"With everything we have invested," Guy said, "I felt it necessary to come out and do my part. Monsieur de Lesseps was pleased. I told him I would see to it that no more money is wasted."

"Money spent on health care is hardly wasted," Roger said.

"Of course," Guy said. "We'll not stint you, my dear Roger. But, on the other hand, you'll not find us overgenerous."

"I have neglected to ask about Lyris," Petra said, wanting to change the subject. It made her a little bit angry to see that Roger was now subordinate to Guy. "Is she well?"

"She was the last time I saw her," Darcie said. Then, with a wide smile, she said, "Our Lyris is now in the lobster business."

"Contributing to the morale of our hard-working troops," Guy laughed.

Petra let it pass. She was not exactly sheltered. As a nurse she heard some coarse language, and often, when a worker talked in the delirium of fever, his language was quite earthy. But she had not heard the expression which was common knowledge among the men who worked on the canal. When a new shipment of prostitutes arrived, the word spread quickly all up and down the railroad and to the various worksites on the canal. The phrase "A new shipment of lobsters has arrived" meant, to the men, that there were fresh women coming. Petra took Darcie's statement literally, thinking that Lyris had gone into the food-importing business, specializing in lobsters. She wondered—but only briefly—how Lyris managed to keep the seafood from spoiling rapidly in the terrible climate.

It was obvious to Petra that Darcie and Guy were living as man and wife, although, to others, it seemed that Guy, the uncle and guardian, was providing a home for his unmarried niece. However, it no longer mattered to Petra. She had long since written both of them out of her life, and, in fact, she felt some resentment toward their appearance in the same town where she worked with her husband. She made up her mind to avoid them, but it proved to be unnecessary. The nature of their work left them exhausted at the end of a long day, and neither of them felt like joining in the social life. Neither Guy nor Darcie made an effort to contact them after that dinner.

Since Darcie was beautiful and Guy was the chief executive of the company in Colón, they were much the subject of talk, and from time to time Petra would hear items of gossip. Darcie had gone to Panama City and spent a week there. A gay party had been held at the Simel home. She heard such talk and let it pass in one ear and out the other, for the patient load at the hospital increased in direct ratio to the growing number of men at work on the canal.

Roger gradually became aware of a problem. He did not know, of course, that putting fever patients in the same ward with men who were not feverish was a sure means of spreading both malaria and yellow fever. He did know that the incidence of the disease was in-

creasing and that men who had been in hospital for
other reasons often came down with fever. This fact
was not lost on the workers. It became common knowledge that one sure way to get the fever was to allow a
doctor to send you to a hospital. The wards of the
large hospital on the hill above Panama City were to
become known as The Graveyard because more men
died of fever in that hospital than anywhere else. Con-
sequently, there was a growing revolt among the workers. They resisted being hospitalized, more willing to
chance infection from a minor wound than to go into
the dreaded Graveyards either at Colón or Panama
City.

Although most of the workers were blacks imported
from the Caribbean islands, there was one large con-
tingent of Chinese coolies working with the huge
dredges which were slowly chewing into the soft muck
from the Colón end. There an outbreak of yellow
fever was a severe problem, with a large percentage of
the workers falling to the disease, and all of them re-
fusing to be hospitalized. As the problem grew, Roger
took time from his work to see if he could do anything
about it personally, thinking that a direct appeal to
the Chinese workers might convince them that it was
the best thing to allow themselves to be hospitalized.
He took Petra with him, and it was in the nature of a
holiday as they boarded the train for the short trip to
the small town of Gatun on the Chagres.

If Colón was a hellhole, there was no adequate description for Gatun. It was a small cluster of bedrag-
gled houses on the banks of the river, the jungle behind it, the heat lying over it like an evil miasma. The
Chinese workers were quartered in unbelievable misery,
crowded, with no sanitation. Already their numbers
had been decimated by the fever and other disease,
and, as Roger and Petra arrived, there was underway
one of the more tragic events of all in an area where
death was commonplace. Those who had recovered

from the fever were suffering the usual postfever depression, a feeling Petra knew well. And, the little yellow men, far from home, hopeless, had found a way out of their misery.

It began when a young man sharpened a stake, planted it aslant in the ground, and, with a cry for mercy from his ancestors, ran himself onto the stake, dying slowly and in agony, stuck on the stake like a butterfly on a pin. Others followed, committing suicide in a variety of ways, by drowning in the thick waters of the Chagres, by the knife, slitting wrists and lying peacefully to let life ebb away into a filthy bedmat.

"The Chinese have gone crazy," the work boss informed Roger upon their arrival. "We've got some of them under observation, but every chance they get, they kill themselves."

One middle-aged man had died with his head thrust into a shallow basin of water, breathing in the water in one long gasp and then, with what had to be a great expression of willpower, resisting the temptation, as his lungs spasmed for air, to lift his head and fight for air. In one hovel, six Chinese lay dead, copious amounts of blood having spilled from wrists. One man had slashed his own throat, and the outpouring of blood had splashed against the thatched wall of the hovel.

The ill who were, for the moment, surviving, were forcibly gathered and moved into the hospitals where many died. It was very difficult to communicate with most of them, since they spoke no French and only a bit of pidgin English, but Petra did her best to tell those who survived that the terrible feelings of depression would pass, but her heart went out to them, alone in a strange land, not even able to speak the language.

Behind them, at the place which had become known as Matachín, the nudertakers came en masse to gather the bodies. Guy Simel seemed to take a personal interest in the operation.

In grinding exhaustion, Petra survived the summer. The welcome change in weather came, at last, and life became tolerable. Following her recovery from the fever, the pattern of her married sex life was resumed, and now she prayed that she would not become pregnant. The thought of carrying a child in that terrible climate was too much to bear.

But things eased with the more pleasant weather, and once again there seemed to be reason to live. Once again her thoughts were of Jay, knowing that he was there, only a few miles away, near Panama City. When Roger suggested that she take a holiday and go into the western city for a rest and some shopping, she protested at first, saying that he, too, needed a rest. But he would not hear of it. She said she would not go, thinking that if she did, she would see Jay. In such an event, she did not trust her feelings.

In the end, however, she gave in to her self-indulgent desire just to be away from the cottage and from the hospital. She made her preparations and went to the station to catch the train. A train from the west was being shunted, some cars already being unloaded. Workmen were using a ramp to roll wooden casks from a boxcar. Since she was early, she stood in the shade, a breeze giving an illusion of comfort, watching the men as they proceeded with their strenuous and sweaty work. The casks seemed to be heavy. The men inside the car would position them on the top of the ramp, and others would hold them back as they were allowed to roll, sometimes rather roughly, to the foot of the ramp where they being hoisted into a dray.

She was about to walk on toward the passenger station where the Panama City train awaited when, with a shout of warning, one cask got away from the men at the top of the ramp and rolled off the high side to shatter staves on the dirt. Fortunately, no one was hurt, and she was going to walk on when her eyes fell on the contents of the cask. A small black man lay in a fetal position among the broken staves. Fluid had run out of the broken cask to stain the ground.

Her curiosity aroused, Petra approached the foreman of the crew. "Monsieur," she said, "may I ask why this body was pickled in the cask?"

"May I, madame, ask what concern it is of yours?" the man answered.

"I am Madame D'Art, head nurse at the hospital. My husband is medical director of this area. That is my concern," she said, with acid in her voice.

"Madame," the man said, "you will have to ask that question of the director."

"Monsieur Simel? What has he to do with this?"

"I just do my job, madame," the foreman said. "My job is to load and unload. I don't ask what it is that I am loading and unloading."

"Where, then, is this shipment of casks going?"

"See that ship?" the foreman asked, pointing out into the bay.

Petra counted the casks. There were, on that one boxcar, fifty of them. Fifty bodies pickled in fluid. She was almost ill.

Disposition of bodies had always been a problem. High ground for cemeteries was scarce around Colón. And, with the average worker being nameless, a mere import from some island, with no one to claim the body, burial was often quite casual. In the jungle, it was not unknown for a body to be left to the mercies of the ever-present vultures.

She demanded that she be shown the shipping papers for the casks, and the foreman gave them to her reluctantly. The total shipment consisted of one hundred fifty casks and their destinations were quite interesting; hospitals and schools of medicine in the United States, France, and England. The shipper was listed as M. Guy Simel.

Her train was due to leave in less than fifteen minutes, but Guy Simel's office was quite near. She walked down the muddy street and was admitted to Guy's office immediately.

"Petra, a surprise and a pleasure," Guy said, rising to take her hand.

"I am here on an unpleasant matter," she said. "I come from the railyard, where one of the casks you are shipping to medical schools and hospitals has just been broken, exposing its contents. I assume that the contents of the others are the same."

"Of course," Guy said calmly.

"Guy, those poor men have the right to a decent burial," she said. "I must insist that you stop this macabre dealing in dead bodies."

"My dear Petra," Guy said. "First, it is none of your concern. Second, providing cadavers for research and the training of young doctors is a humanitarian endeavor. Third, it is quite profitable, and I'll thank you to keep your pretty nose out of my business."

"It's loathsome, Guy. When I return from Panama City, I'm going to take it up with Roger."

"I'll remind you that I am the director here," Guy said coldly. "I will not look favorably upon any interference with my activities."

"And if you try to use your authority to make it unpleasant for Roger or me," she said, "I will go directly to Director-General Dingler, and if that fails, to de Lesseps himself."

"Petra, my dear," Guy said more evenly, "you're making such a big thing of this. Those bodies will serve science. I am not the only one who has used the bodies of nameless and homeless workers for such purpose. During the construction of the railroad, one man collected skeletons of each of the racial types working on the project—a museum, as if were, of bones and skulls. It was quite educational, I'm told."

"That does not make it right, Guy," Petra insisted. "And I will discuss it with Roger."

"As you wish," he said, with a shrug. "Now, if you don't mind, I have more important matters."

Petra caught the train just in time, and, the day sullied by the thought of what was in all those casks, which were still being unloaded and transferred to the waiting ship, settled in for the ride across the isthmus.

She spent the evening in her hotel room, content to have someone tend to her needs, ordering her meal to be eaten in privacy. She slept late and then went to Cathedral Plaza to deliver reports and requests from Roger to the headquarters of the canal company. She accomplished the chore, accepting congratulations from the director-general, himself, for a job well done at Colón. Jay was arriving in a carriage as she went out. She did not try to avoid him, but stood, smiling, as he approached. She was sure that she was mature enough to handle any childish fancies she might still retain. She greeted him as one old friend greets another and accepted his invitation to lunch with second thoughts.

Actually, she was glad she'd run into him. She needed to talk with someone. She told him about her discovery of Guy's illicit traffic in bodies.

"I don't quite know what to do about it," she said.

Jay shrugged. "I think that you'd find a sort of blind indifference at the higher levels," he said. "It's a sleazy practice, but Guy is not the first to use it to make money. If that were all your uncle were doing, I think that I could forget it."

"Oh?"

"He also has incoming shipments," Jay said. "Opium for the Orientals, and something for the blacks and Indios, too."

"And what's that?" Petra asked.

"It's an extract from the *coca* bush," Jay said. "It's called cocaine."

"But that's an anesthetic. We just received a paper which detailed the successful use of cocaine as a local anesthetic by Dr. Carl Koller of Vienna. I thought it was a new discovery."

"The Indians of Peru and Bolivia have been chewing the leaves of the *coca* bush for centuries," Jay said. "Perhaps refining cocaine is new—I don't know. I know that your uncle is importing it in hefty quantities, and I know it's becoming a factor. It's highly addictive. One of my foremen had to shoot a man the other day. When they're taking the stuff in regular doses, they become quite fearful, thinking that the whole world is out to get them. They can be quite dangerous. It's spreading rapidly—the use of the drug—especially among the blacks."

"How do you know it's Guy who is bringing it in?"

"It's no secret. He has men out peddling it. It's quite popular because the initial result of sniffing it is a sort of euphoria. It makes a man forget that he may die tomorrow of the fever. It also makes him forget that he's supposed to be working."

"How terrible!" Petra said. "Jay, he must be stopped. I don't understand what's happened to him, but we have to do something—not only about his trade in bodies, but about the drugs."

"I don't know if we can," Jay said. "Your uncle seems to know, as the saying goes, where the bodies are buried."

"I don't understand."

"Well, let me put it this way," Jay said. "It's all falling apart, Petra. The whole grand plan is going to come tumbling down like a house of cards, like the landslides on the Culebra cut. The engineering estimates were so wrong that anyone with good sense knows that it'll take twice the money and twice the time to build the canal—if it can be built at all. We lose men to fever and other diseases faster than we can recruit them. The money is running out. From what I can gather, there have been some pretty un-

believable things going on in France. A lot of the
money from the sale of the stock didn't go into the
canal company at all, but to outsiders. I don't know
the full story, but the word is that there was widespread bribery and political corruption, with everyone
wanting to get a piece of the pie. As a result, millions
were bled off, and it leaves the company short. I don't
know all the details, but I think your uncle does. I
think he was in on some of it because he came up with
large amounts of money—more than he could raise
by mortgaging his holdings in France and by other
means. I know that he was paid off by the people who
formed the first syndicate, the one de Lesseps bought
out. And I suspect that he got his share of the bribes
out of the stock money. I know too—because I've run
into it—that he has quite a bit of influence not only
with Director-General Dingler here, but with the old
boy himself back in France. Guy gets his way, and I
think he does it through blackmail."

"I can't believe it," Petra said.

"He's very scared," Jay said. "He has everything he
owns tied up in the canal. Not only all his holdings,
but all the money from the syndicate and wherever
else he got money. He wants to be director-general,
thinking that he can pull it off, but hell, he's no engineer. Dingler is bad enough, coming over here spending thousands or millions building that monstrosity of
a house of his, but Guy would be impossible. The
whole problem, Petra, is that the project was planned
by non-engineers, and non-engineers have had too
much say in it from the beginning."

"Surely Monsieur de Lesseps would not be involved
in anything dishonorable," Petra said.

"The old man?" Jay shook his head. "No, I suppose
not. But he might look the other way. Or he might be
totally ignorant of any wrongdoing. After all, he's almost eighty. Panama is going to kill him, I'm sure.
There's word in Paris that over three million francs

was paid out in bribes, some of the money going to members of the government. And remember this, Petra; everyone in France who could raise the down payment on a share of stock has money invested in the canal. When the bottom falls out, as it will, there'll be such an uproar that all the dirt will come out. When it does, de Lesseps will bear the brunt of it."

"And men like Guy?"

"They'll probably escape scot-free," Jay said. "Men like Guy operate in secrecy."

"We know he's shipping dead bodies. You know of his drug dealings."

"We could prove the body shipping, perhaps, but that's minor, although repugnant. The drugs? I don't know. Which laws apply—those of Panama or those of France? And, moreover, there's nothing positive to link him with the drug traffic."

Petra was depressed. "Has it all been for nothing?"

"It remains to be seen," Jay said. "Perhaps the old hero will pull another miracle out of his hat. Some of the big machines which are coming in for digging are quite impressive. If we could only solve the fever problem."

"Oh, if we only could," Petra said.

He was silent for a moment. "And Roger?"

"He's well. Very tired. He works far too hard and has had a touch of malaria."

"Haven't we all?" Jay asked.

Her heart leaped. "You?"

"A week in glorious Notre Dame," Jay said with a grin. "A vacation."

"You do take your quinine regularly?" she said, leaning forward.

"Why, Petra, you care," he said. "Yes. My bout was relatively mild. Not nearly so bad as yours."

"How did you know?"

"Oh, it's a small community," he said. "Word travels up and down the railroad."

"You have not yet visited us in Colón," she said.

"One day, one day," he said. "And now, although I regret it, I must be off. Back to Culebra by nightfall."

He kissed her hand and left her. She went back to her hotel, freshened herself, and did some shopping. When she returned to her room once more, Darcie was there, having been admitted by the hotel clerk.

"Hello, Darcie," she said, having recovered from the start she received when she opened the door to see Darcie lying on her bed.

"I thought you'd like some company, little sister," Darcie said.

"How pleasant," Petra said without conviction.

"I have ordered some wine. Will you join me? It should be refreshing after your day of shopping."

"Yes, thank you," Petra said, accepting the glass of wine which had been poured for her. She removed her hat and sat down. "Are you well?" she asked, at a loss for words, wishing only to be alone.

"As well as can be expected in this miserable place," Darcie said.

The wine was refreshing, and Petra drank it down rapidly. She felt a slight dizziness and put it down to the quick consumption of the wine. She went to the washbasin and dampened her wrists, used her fingers to dab water onto her face. She felt quite faint, a roaring noise in her ears.

"I think—I think I shall have to lie down," she said, moving toward the bed to fall onto it weakly. "I feel so very, very—"

After a few moments Darcie lifted Petra's hand and released it. It fell limply to the bed. She rose, arranged her skirts, went out of the room. When she returned, Guy was with her. Between them they half-carried Petra out of the room, down the stairs. The hotel clerk, a fussy little Frenchman, came running over to them.

"Madame D'Art has a touch of fever," Guy said. "We'll just take her to the hospital."

"Oh, yes," the clerk said. "Please." It was bad business to have a fever victim in the hotel, and his only desire was to see her removed. He called a carriage and Petra was lifted limply into it. In the carriage she leaned, only semiconscious, against Darcie.

"Well, little sister," Darcie said. "At last. At last."

3

PETRA AWOKE WITH a terrible taste in her mouth. She licked her dry lips, making a face of distaste, and lifted her head. She was in a small room on a bed which smelled of human sweat and mold. The window was closed and it was quite hot. Her clothing had been removed. She saw her dress thrown carelessly across a chair. She rose, feeling dizzy, and went to a washstand on which stood a pitcher of water. She drank, easing the horrid taste somewhat, and splashed water from the washbasin onto her face. Then she started to dress.

A man's loud and raucous laugh came to her through a thin wall, accompanied by the high-pitched giggle of a woman. Dressed, Petra went to the door. It was locked from the outside. She turned to the window, opened it. She was on the second floor of a wooden house. Below the window was a squalid alley littered with filth and trash. She went back to the door and began to pound on it. She still felt peculiar, but she was not yet frightened. She remembered feeling dizzy in the hotel, but she'd been with Darcie. She assumed that

Darcie had taken her somewhere, perhaps to the home
of a friend.

She heard a bolt being thrown outside the door and
stood back. When the door opened, she looked into
a familiar face.

"Lyris," she said. She started to look past Lyris into
the hallway, but her way was blocked by Lyris, and,
behind her, the form of a large man with a scar on
his face.

"I'm all right now," she said. "I'll just go back to
my hotel."

"Not just yet," Lyris said, pushing her back into the
room, following, closing the door behind her.

"Well, Lyris, you're looking well," Petra said.

"And you," Lyris said with a little smile. "But you're
being unwise, Petra."

"I don't understand."

"Guy thinks you might go to Director-General Dingler with your little suspicions," Lyris said.

"As well I might."

"I think we should talk about it first, don't you?"

"Lyris, are you a part of it?"

"We've always been close, the three of us," Lyris
said. "Petra, as you know, we've invested everything in
the canal company, and it looks bad. You can't blame
us for trying to recover some of our money. After all,
who is hurt? Not the poor wretches who are dead."

"And the poor wretches who take your drugs? Are
they not hurt?"

Lyris frowned. "You are a nosy little wench, aren't
you? What do you know of drugs?"

"Only that Guy is bringing opium and cocaine into
Panama."

"Well, well. And who else knows?"

"I suppose it's general knowledge."

"But no one has yet complained," Lyris said. "At
least not until Little Miss Goodness sticks her nose
into it."

"Lyris, I don't have to stay here and be insulted," Petra said, making a move to pass Lyris and go toward the door.

The violent shove took her by surprise. She stumbled backward and sat down on the soiled bed. "As a matter of fact, you'll stay here until we're damned well ready for you to leave," Lyris said. "Darcie was right. You're not only a prude, you're dangerous."

"Lyris, what's the meaning of this?" Petra demanded.

"The meaning is that you're going to stay here until you get some sense," Lyris said. "Look, *chérie,* I'm not going to let your false morality cost me my last chance to recover some of my losses. Do you know where you are?"

"No," Petra admitted. "But Roger will miss me. When I don't contact him he'll have the police searching for me."

"Let them search," Lyris said. "I pay them enough money so that they'll not search here too closely. In case you don't know it, you're in a bordello. I, Lyris Bahalah, have been reduced to running a whorehouse. After that, do you think I'm going to let you spoil things by running to blab what you think you know to the director-general?"

"All right, Lyris," Petra said. "I can understand your concern. But the canal has not failed. Should it be completed, you'll recover your investment and much more."

"Ha," Lyris said. "Only a fool can believe that it will be completed. No. We're going to bleed every penny we can here, and we're not going to allow you to interfere."

"You can't keep me forever," Petra said defiantly.

"No, that's true. But we can keep you until you die of fever, can't we?"

"Lyris!" Petra gasped. "You wouldn't!"

"Wouldn't I?" Lyris grinned. She had changed since Petra had last seen her. She looked older—her skin, once so lovely and soft, now blotched and rough. There was a look about her eyes which spoke of the effects of malaria. Although still quite a striking woman, she was not beautiful as she once was. "Stay and think about it, Petra. Think very carefully. If, after a few days, you are very, very convincing in your promise that you will tend to your own business, perhaps we will not have to see you dead."

Petra gasped at the threat and drew away, pulling her legs up onto the bed. Then she was alone, not believing that she was being held prisoner by people she had once loved. After long hours, there was a sound at the door. The scar-faced man opened the door and delivered to her a half bottle of red wine and a plate of food. She ate, although she was not hungry, and, after tasting and sniffing it carefully, drank the wine.

This time the drug did not put her all the way out. She was semiconscious, but unable to gather her wits, reluctant to move, having lost all desire to flee, when the door opened again and Lyris entered to sit on the side of the bed.

"Feeling nice?" Lyris asked.

There was a certain dreaminess about it, but Petra could only follow the movement of Lyris's hands as the older woman unbuttoned her dress and pulled it away, then removed her slip, leaving her naked. In a state of dreamy unconcern, Petra felt soft hands on her body, felt her legs being spread so that the soft hands went down to send a warm sensation through the drugged lassitude, causing her to squirm slightly.

"Ah," Lyris said. "So the little prude has, at last, discovered that she is a woman."

It was such a strange feeling. Nothing about it seemed to be real, and yet her body felt the caress and responded to it. There was no thought of rightness or wrongness. It simply was, and there was a sure knowledge in Lyris's hands which roused her inside that shell of indifference and which caused her to gasp in pleasure when Lyris dropped her dark head and began, with warm lips and writhing tongue, to build a desire which, combined with the numbing effect of the drug, reduced Petra to a totally sexual entity which existed only in her feelings.

Nor did it bother her when, with a laugh, Darcie stepped into the room.

"Really, Lyris," Darcie said.

"Laugh if you must," Lyris said.

"And I thought you were beyond such childish pleasures," Darcie said.

"For completion, a man," Lyris said. "For excitement, a beautiful woman. And she is beautiful."

"Yes," Darcie said. And while the talk went on, Lyris continued to do those eerily wonderful things to Petra, and her drugged mind allowed her body to respond, to know the thrill of it, to build in itself the need for totality, a need she had not known since the incomplete experience with Jay, so long ago.

"A bit of sisterly love?" Lyris asked, smiling up at Darcie.

"It would sicken me," Darcie said with disgust.

"Perhaps it would not sicken her," Lyris said with an evil smile.

"Ah," Darcie said. "Perhaps the prude would enjoy."

In that dreamlike state, Petra continued to lift her heated loins to Lyris's wet and wonderful mouth and she could see Darcie's small and perfectly formed body emerging from the clothing. And then Darcie, like her and Lyris, was nude and laughing as she saw Petra's eyes on her.

"So, little sister," Darcie said, "under the proper circumstances you are human."

An element of nightmare entered the dreamy scene as Darcie joined them on the bed and, leaning, thrust one firm breast into Petra's face. Petra tried to turn her head, but it was there, warm, perfumed, insistent.

"Kiss it, little sister," Darcie ordered.

And below, the heat was building as Lyris, doubly excited by seeing Darcie's nude body, darker, slimmer, smaller, alongside the pale, voluptuous softness of Petra. With a gasp, Petra opened her lips and felt the hardness of the long, lovely nipple. Then she was lost in it, kissing, her hands coming up in slow motion, almost uncontrollable, to caress and know the soft-firm mound.

Petra protested once again as Darcie positioned herself over her face, facing Lyris, who was lying on the bed paying heated tribute to femininity. And then Darcie was lowering and there was the close-up view of dark bush and browned labia and she was making a noise, trying to say "No, no," but she was helpless to move and her body was absorbing the thrills of Lyris's expert attentions. Then there was a mellow, buttery feel on her lips and a taste which was new and, in her drug-intoxication, somewhat exciting; and Darcie, laughing, used her mouth, squirming, making it difficult for her to breathe and time stood still with the three of them silent save for the agitated breathing, the rustle of skin on skin, the soft wet sounds. And in Petra's body there was a charge of tension which, when Darcie cried out and moved excitedly on her mouth, sent lightning through her to explode under Lyris's demanding lips and tongue.

Petra could not determine now whether it was real or dream or nightmare, and it didn't matter. Her body screamed out for more, and she was on her hands and knees, willingly doing to Darcie what Lyris was doing to her, moaning now, a totally amoral lust possessing her, her mind still benumbed by the drugs which they had put into her wine. Thrill after thrill ran through her body to detonate inside as Lyris manipulated her soft feminine parts. Then it was over and she lay, half-conscious, until sleep took her. Then there was wakefulness and a memory of what she had done; a taste, a smell on her mouth, which, sobbing, feeling a desperation, she washed and wiped away at the washbasin.

Petra had no idea how long she'd been in the room. She tried once more to open the door, but it was firmly bolted from the other side.

When Darcie came in, Petra was in bed, the sheet up around her neck, suffering agonies of conscience. She knew she'd been drugged, but that was no excuse.

"Well, little sister," Darcie said, "do you know now what you've missed all these years?"

"May God forgive you," Petra said, "for I never shall."

"Merde!" Darcie said.

"If I tell you you've won, will you let me go home?"

"How convincing can you be?" Darcie asked.

"I will speak to no one," Petra said. "I want only to be out of here, to be with normal, decent people. I will wipe all of you from my mind—you and all that you've done."

"You sound convincing."

"I swear to you that I will not speak," Petra said, fighting back her tears.

"Soon, perhaps," Darcie said.

"Oh, please," Petra begged. "Please let me go home."

"But little sister," Darcie said, with a chilling smile, "I don't feel that I've done my best for you. I feel an obligation to make your stay with us more pleasant. Tell me, is the honorable Roger D'Art an adequate lover? Does he lift you into the throes of passion as Lyris did last night?"

"Oh, Darcie, please!"

"Answer me."

"He is—he is. Yes," she said. "He is an adequate lover."

"I think you're lying," Darcie said. "I think, before you go, that you should know a real man."

"Oh, God, Darcie! Please."

"Be patient, little sister. And imagine the perfect man. He will come to you very soon."

Alone in the room Petra ran to the window, looked down. Below the window there was a pile of broken and jagged glass, here wine bottles had been tossed. She considered leaping down—the cuts would be preferable to being held prisoner. But she could not bring herself to do it. She ran to the door and beat on it with her fists until they were bruised and then fell across the bed, weeping. Her clothing had been taken away. When she heard the door opening, she screamed and pulled a sheet over her naked body.

She watched, wide-eyed, as the door opened slowly and then when she saw the creature standing there she screamed again. Her impression was of a huge, bearded head supported by a thick neck and a small, somewhat deformed body, small, thick, powerful-looking. For a moment she was paralyzed with horror, for the dwarf was naked and his penis was hanging, a long, thick lax tube of impressive size.

The dwarf stepped in, looking behind him fearfully. His face was bruised, and there were marks on his arms and legs. When he half-turned, Petra saw cruel whip marks on his naked back and then Darcie was there in the doorway looking over the dwarf's head, laughing merrily as Petra, at last, recognized the creature from the past.

"Little sister, you remember the handsome Hassam Ari Pasha?" Darcie asked. "You met him once in Egypt. I knew him better than you, as you may remember, and I'm sure that you've always felt neglected."

"Darcie, please," Petra moaned.

"The thing is, little sister, that you've never really experienced life, and until you do, your judgment will be distorted. Now, it's cost me considerable money and no little effort to have our mutual friend, the pasha, spirited out of Egypt. I want to make his trip worthwhile. As you can see, he's had some little entertainment already, and he will have more, but now he is to have a small treat. You're Hassam Ari's treat, little sister. Enjoy."

The dwarf looked fearfully up at Darcie. For the first time, Petra noticed that Darcie carried a cruel, many-thonged whip in her hand.

"Hassam Ari," Darcie said, "once, long ago, you had me at your mercy. Did you enjoy it?"

The dwarf fell to his knees. "Mercy, madame, have mercy," he begged.

"Why, of course," Darcie said. "I am giving you, for your own amusement and all for your own, my own sister. What could be more merciful?"

"Don't taunt me, madame, please," Hassam Ari begged. "I was young and fiery then. I knew not what I was doing. Have mercy."

"I will, my good pasha, if you will oblige me. You see, my sister knows little of life, and it is my desire to instruct her, as I was instructed by you when I was a mere girl. Do you think you can bring yourself to enjoy her as you once enjoyed me?"

The dwarf looked fearfully at Darcie, not quite willing to believe. "You taunt me, madame," he said.

"I will observe, to be sure that you leave out nothing," Darcie said. "Now, if you value your hide, sir!"

She laid the lash over Hassam's shoulder, and the dwarf cried out in pain. He moved tentatively toward the bed, looking back at Darcie questioningly.

"Yes, she is yours," Darcie said. "But be fierce, my little lover, as you were fierce with me."

Hassam Ari moved quickly, jerking the sheet from Petra's body. She covered her full breasts with her hands and arms and watched in fear and numbness as Darcie pulled a chair to the wall and sat, a cool smile on her face.

"She is mine?" Hassam Ari asked, looking at Darcie.

"As you wish," Darcie said.

A smile—a grimace—appeared on the dwarf's bruised lips. "Madame, I will do your bidding."

And, incredibly, the thing between his legs began to grow, to straighten, as his eyes, forgetting their former look of pain, took on a gleam of lustful hunger and he moved, squat, powerful, evil, toward the naked Petra, who cowered on the bed.

"Darcie, no," she wailed. "Please tell him to leave me alone!"

"Just this one treat, little sister, and you may go," Darcie said.

In fear and loathing, Petra looked around for a weapon. There was none. However, on a table beside the bed there was an oil lamp, the wick burned low. With a cry of despair, she seized the lamp, and, as the dwarf leaped toward her, she threw it into his face. The fragile globe shattered. The glass base of the lamp, more than half-full of oil, fell to the wooden floor and shattered. The oil splashed up onto the dwarf's naked legs and the low flame of the wick became, with a whoosh of sound and flare of light, a flame which raced across the floor and up the dwarf's legs. He screamed, hoarse, agonized, and tried to beat out the flames which seared him. Fire covered the entire lower half of his body, licking hotly at his genitals.

Darcie yelled a curse and leaped to her feet. The dwarf, maddened by the pain, ran senselessly toward the window, banged into the low sill and, screaming, toppled, falling to the pile of shattered wine bottles in the alley below.

"You crazy bitch." Darcie screamed at Petra.

Petra, galvanized into frenzied motion by the horror of seeing the dwarf burn, by the fear which she had felt, ran at Darcie as Darcie moved toward her threateningly. She hit her sister solidly, and the smaller girl was flung aside to fall into the burning pool of oil, but Petra did not see. She was too intent on escape,

It was only when she opened the door into the hall that she realized she was still naked. She looked around frantically and, as if in answer to her prayers, she saw her clothing hanging on a hook beside the door. She grabbed her dress, and, with trembling hands, threw it over her head. There was no time to concern herself with her underthings. She left them, carrying only her shoes and her handbag, ran down the hall to pause uncertainly. Two women ran into the hall. Behind her she could hear Darcie's screams of pain.

"There's a fire," Petra gasped. "Help Darcie."

The girls ran toward the room and Petra found the stairway leading down, heard sounds of movement, questioning voices, as she gained the entry foyer and fumbled with the front door knob.

She gained the street and looked around. She was in a part of the city she did not know. She paused only long enough to put on her shoes. When she was safely around a corner, she paused to take stock. She looked a mess, she knew. She tried to arrange her hair with her hands. Her hat was missing. She opened her handbag and, miracle of miracles, there was money inside. She walked a block before she could find a carriage and told the driver to take her to her hotel. She cast a fearful look back over her shoulder and saw black smoke rising. There were shouts. People ran toward the fire.

She hoped that Darcie was not burned seriously, and, in fact, she was not quite sure she'd seen her sister fall into the flaming oil. The women who had run into the room would have helped her.

She could not believe that her sister had sunk so low or could hate her so much. Whatever happened, Darcie had brought it on herself. Perhaps the threats against her life had been meant to merely frighten her, but there had been a genuine attempt to shame her, debase her. She had been forced to fight. She would be able to feel sympathy for the dwarf, in spite of the

evil he had done in the past, but she would not feel
sympathy for Darcie or, if the brothel burned, for
Lyris.

Petra felt better when she reached her hotel, dressed
decently, and arranged her hair. She had only one desire, and that was to seek the safety of her home, the
security offered by her husband. She took a carriage
to the station and caught the afternoon train. There
was talk among those at the station about the great
fire which, before it was controlled, burned a large
area of the city.

Her exhaustion allowed her to doze a little on the
ride back to Colón. Once there, she thought about going home, but she needed to see Roger. He would still
be working. She took a carriage to the hospital, paid
the driver, and, safety and security just inside the building, entered it.

Behind her, in Panama City, Petra had left pain and
anger. When Darcie fell into the pool of burning oil,
the oil soaked into her clothing in an area extending
from her armpit to her thigh and immediately began
to blaze. With a scream, she rolled away and began
to beat at the flames with her hands. The fact that she
was wearing a corset saved her from more serious
burns, but the flames reached her in the soft, tender
area under her left arm and on her thigh. She was
screaming in pain when the two women of the house
rushed in, took in the situation at a glance and seized
a blanket from the bed. They smothered the flames
with the blanket and carried her into the hall. Lyris
had appeared and was shouting orders, but the growing crowd of women, some in stages of undress, were
panicked by the smoke which poured from the room
and the sound of the crackling flames from within. Two
patrons of Lyris's establishment, tugging suspenders up
over shirtless shoulders, rushed into the room to find
the flames already too far advanced.

The primitive firefighting equipment available could

not cope with the fire. The upper floor of the brothel was soon a roaring inferno, and there was nothing for the occupants of the house to do but grab what they could and seek the safety of the street. Before the fire consumed the lower floor and spread to adjoining buildings, members of a futile bucket brigade found the dwarf, Hassam Ari, trying to crawl away from the burning building, leaving a trail of blood down the filthy alley.

Darcie was taken immediately to the hospital. In a state of shock, she did not know the pain until she regained consciousness hours later and then, her armpit and thigh aflame, she writhed in agony, cursing her sister.

Lyris stood and watched her establishment burn with a bemused smile on her face. She had not owned the building, merely leasing it. She had lost some furnishings, a few items of clothing, and not much more. There were other buildings, and none of her working girls had been killed in the fire. She gathered them together and lodged them in a cheap hotel and went about the business of finding a new location.

It was not so simple for Darcie. As the days passed and the pain eased, it became evident that her once-perfect body would be marred by a matted, ugly mass of burned flesh under her left arm and on the lower portion of her left thigh. Now she had good reason— evidence which would be with her the rest of her life, something of which she would be reminded every time she removed her clothing—to hate her sister. One day, one day, she would make Petra pay for those terrible scars. One day Petra would know what it meant to know shame and degradation. One day Petra, too, would know pain.

Later, when Darcie was told of Petra's return to the Colón hospital, she laughed. At least Petra had not escaped the incident unscathed.

When Petra entered the hospital she knew that

Roger would be making his rounds. She encountered Anna, the head nurse, and the woman's friendly face went dark at the sight of her. "Oh, Madame D'Art," Anna said. "Oh, my dear lady."

"What's wrong?" Petra asked.

Anna burst into tears. Petra put her hands on her shoulders. "What is it, Anna? Speak to me."

She heard a voice behind her and turned to face Guy. "Please come into the office, Petra," Guy said.

"Where's Roger?" she demanded. "What have you done with him?"

"Come," Guy said, taking her arm. With a sense of foreboding, she allowed herself to be steered into Roger's office.

"My sympathies," Guy said. "It happened suddenly, as it often does. We tried to find you—"

"You lie," she said heatedly. "You knew where I was."

"There is no kind way to say this, Petra," Guy said. He picked up a piece of paper from the desk. She recognized the form immediately and felt faint. Slowly, slowly, she extended her hand and took the hateful paper and looked at it through the beginning of tears.

In capital letters, the form was headed by a number and the ominous words CERTIFICAT DE DÉCÈS, certificate of death. *Nom:* D'Art. *Prénom:* Roger. The cause of death was listed as *fièvre jaune,* yellow fever. The certificate was signed by Dr. Guy Simel.

"I don't believe you," she said. "You're lying. You've taken him away."

"Petra, Petra, we've had our little differences, but do you actually think I would stoop so low? Would you like for me to accompany you to see his grave?"

Petra backed out of the office, her eyes on Guy's face, knowing a real fear, remembering the callousness of both Lyris and Darcie. Now she had no one.

Anna was in the hall.

"When did it happen, Anna?" she asked.

"Only last night, madame," the kindly nurse said. "Oh, madame, we all weep for you. He was a great and gentle man."

So it was true.

Guy took her arm and guided her back into the office. "There will be no more unpleasantness, Petra," he said. "We're all in this together, after all. You're alone now, and I offer the security of family, my dear niece. I am sure you'll want to forget the unpleasantness, won't you, Petra?"

"Yes, yes, of course," she said, feeling helpless. Guy was in a powerful position. There was no one to prevent him having her taken back to that horrible place in Panama City. "May I go home now?"

"Of course, if that is your wish," Guy said. "However, you do not have to be alone. You have your family."

But she had no family. Any blood tie between the brother of her mother and between her and her own sister had been negated in that brothel. "I just need to be by myself," she said, backing away, half-expecting him to stop her.

In the cottage, she locked the doors, and, in spite of the warmth, closed and locked the window. Roger was dead. The effort to build the canal seemed doomed to failure. Her entire world was falling apart along with de Lesseps's grand plan. She had no place to go, no one to turn to for help.

Except Jay. There was Jay, at Culebra or in Panama City. But the last train for the day had left and it was necessary for her to spend the night in the cottage where, in the early hours of the morning, she managed to get a few hours of fitful sleep. In the morning, she was once again at the station and she boarded the train without seeing Guy. At the company office in Panama City, she was given Jay's address. She took a carriage there, was admitted by a middle-aged woman of Spanish blood who, in awkward French, said that she was Jay's housekeeper.

Jay arrived home, just after dark, to be told by an excited housekeeper that a strange lady was asleep in his bed. He tiptoed into the room to see Petra, still dressed, lying across the bed. He woke her gently. At first she did not know where she was. Then, with a cry, she sat up and looked around wildly.

"Petra, it's all right," he said. "It's all right."

She poured her story out to him, and he listened with a growing glower on his face. "No," he said, "I don't think he would have gone so far as to do Roger harm. It had to be the fever."

"But what will I do?" Petra asked. "They've threatened me."

"No harm will come to you—I promise you that," he said darkly. "As to the future, I would guess that we will all be leaving soon."

"But I have no one," she said. "Guy sold the properties in England. I have no family."

"You have me, Petra," Jay said, "if you will have me."

There was a quick leap of joy in her, but it quickly subsided, for—and she'd known it for weeks now—there was another problem. She was now carrying Roger's child.

4

JAY'S COTTAGE HAD only one bedroom. It was one of the prefabricated houses shipped down from New Orleans, and he occupied it by virtue of his rank as a supervising engineer working on the huge cut at Calebra. He moved his things out of the bedroom and slept on a couch in the sitting room.

The housekeeper awakened Petra next morning, and there was the smell of food in the air. She did not think she would be hungry, but, having joined Jay at table, she accepted eggs and salt bacon and found that she was, after all, in need of food. Coffee topped off the breakfast. The housekeeper disappeared into the kitchen.

"I will have to go to work," Jay said.

"Of course. I don't mean to disrupt your life."

"There will be a man outside all day. I've already arranged it. He's an off-duty member of the security force. He'll see to it that no one bothers you."

"That's kind of you, but I don't think they'll harm me now," Petra said. "I shall have to make arrangements."

241

"Please don't make any decisions until I come home," he said. "I want to talk with you."

"At any rate," she said, "my options are limited. I can go back to France and work in Paris. I can stay here. God knows nurses are needed."

"I will not allow you to return to Colón as long as your uncle and your sister are there," he said.

"Allow me?"

"Forgive me." Jay smiled. He had let his moustache grow even bigger and it gave a strength to his masculine face.

"Yes. I'm just upset, that's all."

"With good reason." He sighed. "We've made a proper mess of it, haven't we, Petra?"

She thought of the life which was beginning to form in her. Sitting across the table from him seemed so natural, and she looked at him musingly. If she had it do over again, she decided, she would have ignored the incident on the *Lafayette*. She would have accepted her hurt, ascribing it to the weakness of the male. Then things would have been so different. She tried to imagine life with Jay and felt an immediate onslaught of guilt. Roger was in his grave only a few short days.

She had the day for thinking. For the sake of practicality, she would not wear mourning. It was out of the question to wear heavy black in the climate of Panama. But she did owe something to Roger's memory. In spite of his shortcomings, he had been a good and kind man, always concerned for her. In fact, in retrospect, and in the emotion engendered by his death, in her mind he took on a quality nearing sainthood.

That there was still feeling between her and Jay was obvious. She had only to look into his eyes to see the way he felt about her, and her heart pounded with excitement when he was near. Was she being disloyal to a good husband to dream, to think that, perhaps, in the future, he would speak once again and that she would say yes, yes?

Meantime, she would have to get out of his house. She knew now that her uncle and sister were not to be trusted, but if she avoided them, she should be safe enough. She could return to the hospital, where her services were badly needed. However, the thought of living alone in the cottage she'd shared with Roger was too much to face. It was true that she'd never loved him—not in the way she'd once loved, perhaps still loved, Jay Burton—but he had been dear to her, her best friend, a father. That's how she would remember him, and not as a fumbling, inept lover who invariably left her bored and unsatisfied.

Such thinking made her guilt rise, for that was the thinking of a Lyris, or a Darcie—a woman interested only in her own sexuality.

She would bear Roger's child, and rear the child as a living memorial to him. In the meantime there were things to do. She dressed and journeyed to the large hospital on the hill. There she spoke briefly with the doctor in charge and was told that she would be welcome there. Of the original sisters who had come out to staff the hospital, only a few had survived the fever and there was a shortage of nurses. Moreover, the doctor would send company employees to Colón to move her clothing and her few belongings from the cottage to quarters on the hospital grounds.

Returning to Jay's cottage, she waited until he had returned from his work and announced her decision to work at Notre Dame. He seemed pleased. At least, he thought, she would be near. He, too, knew that it was too soon to speak—her husband had been dead only for days—but he sensed that her grief for Roger was not the terrible pain which a woman in love would have felt.

After a pleasant dinner, he drove her to her quarters at the hospital, kissed her hand, and asked permission to call on her now and then. She agreed.

The pace at the larger hospital was even more hectic than it had been in Colón. Petra threw herself into her work. Days passed rapidly and she saw Jay once, for dinner in the town. She heard, with great relief, that Guy and Darcie had gone back to France. She heard nothing of Lyris, but assumed that she was still operating the brothel. The nurses at the hospital told her about a strange case, an Egyptian dwarf who had been brought in suffering from severe burns and loss of blood, to die of infection. She said a silent prayer for the soul of Hassam Ari Pasha—not without pity—for it had been evident that the little man had been used severely by Darcie. She would always remember the lash marks on his back and would often wonder how her sister could bring herself to torture a man. Surely, she thought, had it been she who was raped in Egypt, she would not have let it embitter her for life. And yet how could she tell? The events in Lyris's brothel seemed to be only a fading nightmare now. She was unchanged. She felt no guilt, for she had been drugged and at their mercy—but what agonies of conscience did Darcie and Lyris suffer?

As the weeks passed, it became customary for her to have dinner once or twice a week with Jay, who was always polite and kind. Petra came to look forward to their evenings together.

Men continued to die, and the mood in the entire canal zone was one of black despair. Entire families were wiped out, one by one, by the fevers. Men who had been off the boat for only days fell ill and died. And the work was not progressing as it should have been.

Nevertheless, Petra came to look forward to the days once more, to the hard and sometimes heartbreaking work, and most of all to the evenings when she and

Jay would visit a restaurant, walk the streets, sit and talk over coffee.

When Jay finally kissed her, Petra was not prepared for the surge of tender emotion which filled her. They had spent the evening in his cottage, talking about the impossibility of his work at the big cut, of the continuing landslides and the continuing deaths and then, having had enough of gloom, they talked of memories, of Paris and the first time they met.

"You were by far the most beautiful girl I'd ever seen," he said. He smiled and took her hand. "And you haven't changed."

"The tropics change everyone," she said.

"You are still the most beautiful girl in the world," he said. He rose and pulled her to her feet, and she did not resist, going into his arms to accept his kiss and not wanting to let him go.

"Petra, Petra," he gasped. "I can wait no longer to speak. I know I should not, out of respect for Roger, but I must. I've never stopped loving you. I love you with all my heart, and I want you. I want you to be my wife."

"It is too soon."

"Yes. It would not be proper. I can bear to wait if only you'll say that you love me, too."

"Yes," Petra whispered. "I love you."

Jay enclosed her in his arms. His kiss was all-devouring, and she let her body mold to him, become a part of him, wished that it would never end. Then, with a sigh, he pushed her away. "I am content," he said. "We will be married after a suitable period."

"Yes," she said, going to him again, demanding his kiss.

"We mustn't," he said, after tasting the inside of her sweet mouth with his tongue.

She would not let him go, holding onto him with her arms and looking up into his serious eyes. "There are two things I must tell you," she said.

"Confessions?" he asked, with a wry grin.

"Yes and no," she said. "First, I carry Roger's child. Three months now."

He touched her cheek. "Of course I wish that it were mine, but it doesn't matter, my darling. Nothing is going to keep us apart now."

"It won't bother you, having to rear another man's child?"

"I shall look upon it as my own," he said. He grinned. "And see to it that he or she has several brothers and sisters."

"Yes," she said. "Two boys, two girls."

"A nice round number," he said.

"Speaking of roundness," she said, "I will be round soon. I'll be heavy and awkward and hot and perspiry, and you won't want to kiss me and I can't stand that, so, sir, I'm going to insist that we store up enough kisses to last me through my confinement."

"With pleasure," he said, suiting action to words.

They sat on the comfortable sofa, and he pulled her across his lap. Her breasts crushed against his chest, and there were long, delicious minutes of kisses.

"You said," he whispered, during a respite, "that you had two things to tell me."

"The second thing is this," she said. "You are all I have in the world now, all I want. Once before I tried to get you to take me, and you refused, out of honor. Tonight I will accept no excuses."

"Ah, Petra," he said, his lips brushing hers as he crushed her to him. "Are you sure?"

"Make love to me, darling. Make love to me as you did on that night so long ago in Paris."

"Yes, yes," he said. He lifted her and carried her tenderly into the bedroom. There, for the second time in her life, she saw a man she loved undress, not bothering to put out the light, and felt his hands on her as he removed her clothing. Then they were together, the soft heat of the night making their skins soft and moist, clinging, a heated tangle of limbs as he embraced her and kissed her breasts, her neck, her stomach and she was caressing him, saying tender things to him, wanting, wanting, wanting. His mouth was delightful, lifting her to the heights from which she reached out, drew him to her, put her hand on his masculinity and guided him into her, feeling the crush of it, the hugeness of her need, clinging to him with her breath fast and short, her heart pounding and her loins reaching up.

"Oh, God, oh, God, at last," she breathed, as she was possessed, as he entered her to the maximum of his ability and clung to her, whispering her name. And then there was an explosion of need in both of them, a tearing, urgent, wild, rough coming together which burst into frenzied reachings and thrustings. With a wild cry, she felt herself melt, ooze around him, take him as her own, the delight of full satisfaction roaring up in waves to build and build until she thought nothing could ever equal it again.

They were together throughout the long night, delighting in the coolness of morning which made their lovemaking even more sensuous, exploring each other's bodies with trembling fingers and avid lips, coming together again and again and then sleeping in each other's arms until the heat of the morning sun came in the window and woke them.

Now Petra lived in a dream world, the days passing in a happy haze, the nights with Jay a sensuous delight. When he announced that he was taking a holiday, going back to his home in San Francisco, that he wanted her to go with him, she accepted eagerly. She was not concerned with propriety. They would be married. Meantime, she didn't care who knew that he was her man and that she loved him. She spent her nights in his cottage and then she boarded a ship with him and discovered that the rocking of a ship at sea is one of nature's finest aphrodisiacs. The tremendous outpouring of sensual love lasted through the voyage and into the pleasant days in the city, where the weather was civilized and there were few insects and the world of the jungle seemed far, far away. Even as her stomach rounded with Roger's child, there was no lessening of their mutual passion; only a new and tender approach to lovemaking by Jay, who enjoyed feeling the baby kick under his hand and, truly, carried on about her as if it were his child.

The lovely, long months passed so swiftly in the healthy atmosphere of San Francisco. Jay's malaria did not bother him. A new feeling of energy and health infused them. They explored the city, walked along the bay, ate seafood and drank wine and loved endlessly until Petra's condition confined her.

She was delivered of a fine and healthy baby girl. Jay wanted to name her Antonia, after his mother, and she agreed. Petra had never been so happy. She loved the small bundle of little girl, took great delight in holding the baby to her breast to see the eagerness of the feeding. Jay found it fascinating, too, and, after some initial male nervousness about handling something so tiny, so helpless, began to play with the baby to the accompaniment of huge chuckles of happiness.

Of course, it had to end. There was the eternal canal. They talked about it, considered not going back, but both somehow felt that they were committed. There was some hesitation about taking Antonia into such a pesthole as Panama, but in the end it had to be done.

Panama struck quickly. Once malaria is in a man's bones, it recurs readily. Jay was stricken with a severe attack within weeks after their return, and Petra used her influence, after the initial onset of the fever had lessened, to have him sent to the convalescent center on the island of Tobago, where sea breezes made the heat bearable. It was a tiring trip, she burdened with a babe in arms and with a sick man, but she bore the burden gladly. With Jay installed in a comfortable room, already feeling better, she went to the head doctor and offered her services. They were accepted gladly. With a Spanish maid caring for Antonia, she began her duties as a nurse and on the first day was making the rounds, acquainting herself with the patients. She followed the doctor into a private room, neat and clean in her uniform, feeling good to be back at work, and halted in mid-stride, her hand flying to her throat. On the bed lay an emaciated man, all skin and bones and burning eyes.

"Roger," she gasped, flying to his side. He turned his head, looking into her face, and then, slowly, turned his face away.

"Do you know him?" the doctor asked.

"Yes. He is Roger D'Art, my husband," she said, a mixture of emotions bringing tears to her eyes.

5

"A VERY STRANGE case," the doctor was saying. "He came to us just as you see him now. The fever seemed to have an unusual effect on him. He doesn't speak. He eats only reluctantly."

Petra, still in shock, was standing beside the bed, holding Roger's hand.

"I was told that he died. I was even shown the death certificate."

"Mix-ups happen," the doctor said. "There are so many of them, poor devils."

"How did he happen to come to you?" Petra asked.

"He was sent to us by Dr. Simel, who was, at the time, director of the Colón office. We were told that the man's identity was not known. He could offer no clue."

Her heart went out to the thin, wasted man on the bed, even as she knew pure hatred for her uncle. To do this to a friend, to exile him from all his friends and loved ones, to draw up a false death certificate. Was it all done to keep her from going to the authori-

ties about Guy's body-smuggling and his drug operations? It made so little sense.

And there were far more important considerations.
For the first time in her life she'd been happy. Within
a short time she would have been married to Jay, which
was all she asked of life. Now it was too late, too late
once again. Roger was alive and he obviously needed
her help.

"Was no effort made to establish his identity?" she
asked.

"Oh, we sent inquiries. But you must know, Madame D'Art, that our workload is not small. We had
scant time to concern ourselves with one poor, ill man,
when there were hundreds in worse condition—if not
mentally, physically."

"I understand. He had no identification on him?"

"Nothing." The doctor looked strange. "Well, there
was something, but I hesitate to mention it to a lady."

"I am his wife," she said. "I demand to know."

"Very well then, if you'll come with me to the office."

She followed. Inside, he took a brown packet from
his locked desk drawer and handed it to her. "I think
you would prefer to be alone," he said, leaving the
office in haste.

Wonderingly, she opened the envelope. Inside were
photographs. The pictures were upside-down, and at
first she had trouble making sense of them. Then she
saw Darcie's familiar face, and with a gasp of shame
and astonishment, she turned the pictures right side up.

They had been taken in Lyris's bordello while she
was under the influence of drugs, and they were quite
vivid and descriptive, showing her, her face contorted
with passion, being loved by Lyris, the back of her
blond head buried into the womanhood of Darcie.
There were six of them, all in various poses, and she
thought, then, that she understood Roger's retreat from
reality.

A thousand thoughts. Had the doctor recognized her? Surely not. The debauched face in the pictures was a parody of passion. Why had Guy given the pictures to Roger? Sheer venom, or some ulterior motive to get him out of the way? Poor, staid, honorable Roger. What a shock it must have been, to see his wife in libertine debauchery with two other women. And underneath it all, *oh, Jay, Jay, what will happen to us now?*

"I will keep these," she told the doctor. He shrugged. She went to Jay's room, found him awake, and broke the news to him. Although he was weak and depressed, he took it well.

"Thank God he's alive," he said.

"Yes." Then she told him of Roger's condition. When he saw the reason for it, he cursed and sat up, in spite of his weakness, and wanted to get dressed immediately, set out for France, there to pummel the treacherous Guy into a pulp.

Calmed, he looked at her. "What about us?" he asked.

"He needs me," she said simply. "I know you'll understand."

"Yes, of course," he said, hitting the bed with his clenched fist. "But it was our turn, Petra. It was our time for happiness."

"I know, my darling, but I couldn't live with myself if I deserted him now."

"And you would not be the woman I love if you did," Jay said grudgingly.

So it was that Jay, recuperated, went back to the isthmus, leaving Petra and Antonia. For months she tried to reach Roger through his glazed indifference. By constant attention, she managed to put some meat on his bones, and he came to be eager to get out of the bed to walk for exercise. But he did it as a zombie, never speaking, never looking directly into her eyes, never acknowledging her. Because of the constant de-

mand for bed space at the convalescent sanitarium,
Petra took her husband to Colón, installed him there
in a cottage like their first home, a Spanish maid to
help her in his care, and to watch him during the day
when Petra was at work in the hospital.

There, to her eternal shame, she made love with
Jay while her husband slept in the next room, knowing
that it was wrong, but tired, discouraged, needing the
reassurance which she gained in his arms. Jay arranged
a transfer to the works nearer to Colón, and her life
was made endurable by his presence. He would come
almost every evening, aid her in bathing Roger. Roger,
with the face of an old, old man, seemed not to recognize either of them.

The first evening she fell to her own desires, making love wildly and noisily in the small living room of
the cottage, she forgot, during the heat of passion, that
her husband, ill as he was, was in the bedroom. When
it was over, she dressed hurriedly and went to him,
but he slept peacefully.

"We must not do this again," she said.

"No," Jay agreed.

But three nights later, with Antonia in bed, with
the maid gone home, Roger sleeping, she went to Jay's
arms and in a frenzy of need stripped his clothing,
urged him, kissed him, fondled his manhood until,
with satisfying lust, he took her, once again, on the
couch.

Their lives were dominated by Roger's illness, by
the continuing problems of the canal, by Petra's work.
She seemed to exist only for her evenings with Jay,
and they were soon to come to an end.

She awoke one night, after Jay had gone to his own
cottage, to hear Roger moving restlessly. And, surprisingly, he was muttering in his sleep. She went to his
bedside. He was saying her name, over and over.
"Petra, Petra, Petra."

She struck a light and sat by his bedside. There was

animation on his face. She put her hand on his shoulder and he awoke with a start. For a moment she thought she saw something in his dead eyes, a glimmer of recognition.

She did not know what had happened to the months. Antonia was two, a happy, healthy little girl who had had a touch of what could have been yellow fever, but a very light case. Two years. Two endless years and more endless, hopeless years stretching ahead of her.

She talked to Roger softly, telling him of the nights in Lyris's bordello, how she'd been drugged, how she'd been forced to do those things against her will. He seemed to listen, but made no response. But one night, desperate, not wanting to spend the rest of her life caring for a mental invalid, knowing gunine concern for Roger, too, she tried a shock treatment. She had kept the pictures, for she wanted to remember the cruelty of her uncle, wanted to feel, at some time in the future when she was in the proper situation, the same hatred and loathing she had felt when she first realized what Guy had done to Roger.

She held the pictures, one by one, in front of Roger's staring eyes. She explained, over and over, that she had been drugged, forced. And there was reaction. His eyes moved; his tongue wet his dry lips. And then, when she came to the picture which showed her face best, he cried out hoarsely and knocked the picture from her hand.

"I was drugged, Roger. Guy did it. He wanted to hurt both of us."

"Told him I was going to go to de Lesseps," Roger croaked, his voice rusty from disuse.

"Roger, Roger, it's Petra. I'm here. Do you hear me?"

"Petra's dead," he said dully.

"They told me *you* were dead," she said. "I'm *alive*, Roger. *You're* alive. You must realize that. You must try, Roger."

"Petra?" There were tears in his eyes. His trembling hand came out to her arm. "Oh, what did they do to you?"

Gradually, reluctantly, he came back from the far place to which he had retreated. He was an old, old man, feeble, frail, wasted, but he came back and then she knew that Roger, too, had accused Guy of illegal traffic in bodies.

Her life entered a new and frustrating phase. No longer was Jay free to visit her nightly. Once, after Roger had regained his mental faculties to a large extent, she went to Jay's cottage, but the guilt was a burden. She kissed him good-bye.

"I'll wait for you," he said.

"You can't wish him dead," she said.

"Heaven forbid. But we're young Petra. There's time."

"Oh, my darling, I hope so," she whispered, and tore herself out of his arms for, perhaps, the last time.

Without Antonia, those would have been wasted years. Her only joy was in watching her daughter develop, in seeing her build a true affection for her father, who doted on her as his mind became more and more sound and he slowly took up his work at the hospital again. Little Antonia, lively, seemingly immune to the various ills which were so prevalent in Panama. A chubby baby who grew into an active and charming child who knew that she was attractive. Spoiled by all— mother, father, the man she called Uncle Jay, by nurses and doctors at the hospital—she was a miniature of Petra, with long blond curls and the honeyed complexion of her English mother.

And so the years passed and people continued to die and the great dream faded until, in February 1889, a liquidator was appointed to bury the *Compagnie Universelle du Canal Interocéanique*. Work came to a virtual standstill, but there were still ill and dying men. Jay Burton was one of a skeleton crew who stayed on to keep the equipment in working order as scandal rocked France and the Americans, once again, began to take an interest in the canal, with moves underway to put Yankee energy and money to work to finish the job which had caused so much misery among the workers in Panama, and so much hardship among the poor stockholders in France who, in many cases, had invested more than a year's income in de Lesseps's canal stock.

6

PETRA WAS LARGELY unaware of the events in France and the United States which would have future bearing on the canal, and upon her life and the life of her daughter. Medical personnel in large numbers had chosen to go back to France along with the disillusioned engineers and administrators, now that the de Lesseps plan was in total collapse. The facility at Colón was operating on less than half staff, and as a result there was little rest, although Petra took every opportunity to insist that Roger, aged beyond his years by his ordeal, have a bit of sleep.

There was a feeling of total futility in Panama. The gangs of black workmen had been returned to their native islands, most generally at the expense of their governments. Equipment was stored all over the canal zone and some huge pieces of expensive machinery had been left in the open, where within weeks the jungle came, sending green tendrils and sucking roots to reclaim that of which it had been robbed, taking the impressive French- and American-built machines with a quiet growth which had the look of inevitability. De Lesseps was no longer the hero. In France, he and those who had worked with him were under attack, for common people had invested millions of francs in the hopes of, as in the case of Suez, making a good profit on their investments.

Now and then, during those unfortunate times, Petra saw Jay. She looked at him always with hungry eyes and with an aching heart, but her duty lay with Roger. It was Jay who kept in contact with events and reported to Petra, who did not really care, and to a bemused Roger that there were moves underway to bring the Americans in, to either finish the canal in Panama or make an entirely new canal across Nicaragua. In fact, Jay told them, there was a political battle going on in Washington and all over the United States regarding the subject of the proper route for a canal. Detractors of Panama laughed at the French, discounting that much had been done during the French years. Although he was an American, Jay had been associated with the French effort and felt somewhat defensive. He always made it a point to show visitors, anyone who would listen, that the French had moved 50,000,000 cubic meters of earth, two-thirds of the total earth moved during the construction of the Suez Canal, that there were ready-made facilities in Panama for a continuation of the work—the hospitals, living quarters, machine shops, millions in equipment.

Meanwhile, progress was being made against the very enemies which were largely responsible for the French failure. As she went about her day to day existence in which there was little joy, save for her bright and charming daughter, Petra filled her hours by reading various medical publications. She began to see a pattern emerging and adopted the views of some medical rebels, who, to date, had been discredited by the establishment, who stated that both yellow fever and malaria were caused by insects, most certainly mosquitoes. She discovered that as early as 1881 an American, Dr. Josiah Clark Nott, had stated that the fevers

were caused by insects. In 1884 Lewis Beauperthuy, in
Venezuela, said with great conviction that the fevers
were injected into a victim by mosquitoes. In Washington, as early as 1882, another American, Dr. Albert
Freeman Africanus King also voiced the mosquito
theory. And Dr. Alphonse Laveran had seen a microbe,
which he believed to be the cause of malaria, under
his microscope in 1880. Incredibly, she was to learn,
as the years went by, that Dr. Carlos Juan Finlay,
working in Havana, had stated and written, in 1881,
that one particular mosquito was the sole carrier of
yellow fever.

She had discussions with Roger and Roger, an old-
school physician, laughed at her newfangled ideas,
said that the mosquito men were a bunch of idealistic
and unscientific dreamers.

Antonia was happy in Panama. She spoke Spanish
as well as French, and her English was tinged with
Americanisms. She continued to flourish, and her developing personality reminded her mother often—sometimes with a tinge of regret and even fear—of Darcie.
Since she was often left in the care of her nurses and
housekeepers, Antonia developed the knack of doing
exactly as she pleased, getting everything she wanted.
Her schooling was a mixture of tutoring and self-edu-
cation under the direction of her parents, with Roger
taking a great interest in her learning. She was a bright
child and advanced for her years. She considered Panama to be her home, and, indeed, Petra had been in
Panama so long that she, too, began to think of herself
as being at home. There was no other place which
qualified. The house in London and the country house
in Norfolk had been sold long ago, her portion of the
revenue deposited in her accounts. Moreover, she had
not seen England since she was thirteen years old. If
anywhere, Paris was home, but there was nothing there
for her—only Guy and Darcie. The two men in her
life chose to stay in Panama and there she stayed and

the years marched on as men in America fought their battles over the proper route for a canal. Meanwhile, less honorable battles were being fought in France, and Petra was to learn of them from a surprising source.

After his partial recovery from the effects of fever and his traumatic shocks, Petra's relationship to her husband was confined to that original regard between them, reverting to a father-daughter relationship, a friendship which was easy and pleasant, a shared joy in watching the growth and development of Antonia. Not once after his recovery did Roger make an attempt to exercise his rights as her husband, which did not displease Petra. They had their work at the hospital, and they often discussed leaving Panama, promising each other that they would, just as soon as the situation allowed. However, the world had abandoned the workers who remained, the few French who conducted the holding operation, hoping against hope that the New Panama Canal Company, which had been formed after the bankruptcy of de Lesseps's company, would find some way to finish the job. Failing that, there was always the chance that the Americans would move in with their unlimited amounts of money and manpower. Petra admitted that she would like to be there, forming a small part of the effort, when the job was finally completed.

A piano, only slightly the worse for the tropical dampness, had been installed in the rather comfortable cottage. Antonia, who seemed to have a natural talent, played it each evening, her skills developing until it was a genuine pleasure for her mother and father to sit quietly, Roger with his eyes closed, very tired, Petra reading, and hear the lovely sounds cascading up from the keyboard. It was on such an evening—another rainy season heavy over the land—that there came a knock on the door.

The larger quarters allowed for a live-in maid, a sturdy half-Indian half-Spanish girl of twenty who had become a favorite of Antonia's and a dependable and stable part of the D'Art establishment. Luisa answered the door and Petra heard a mutter of voices in rapid Spanish. Then Luisa, padding barefoot across the mat carpets, came to whisper quietly. Petra nodded and took the sealed envelope which was handed her.

The writing was feminine and strained, apparently written with a weak hand. Petra had difficulty making out the scrawled words and glanced down to the bottom of the page to see the signature. Once again the past was coming to interfere with her life—the letter was signed by Lyris Bahala.

"My dear Petra," the letter began, "I am ill and fear for my life, but it is not for help that I ask you to come to me, but for other matters of importance. I realize that you have reason to mistrust me, but I beg of you, for the sake of others, to come to me."

"Who brought the message, Luisa?" Petra asked.

Antonia had reached the end of a sprightly Chopin étude and was listening to her mother's halting Spanish.

"A boy of the town," Luisa said. "I did not ask his name."

"And this address?" Petra asked, holding the letter out to Luisa.

"Don't embarrass her, mother," Antonia said. "You know she can't read."

"This address," Petra said, reading the directions included in the letter. "Do you know it?"

"*Si Señora,*" Luisa said. "It is a poor place."

"*Pardon?*" Petra asked, not catching the rapid words.

"A poor place, mother," Antonia said. "Really, I'll be happy to give you Spanish lessons. It would be only fair, since you're always drumming French and English into me."

Petra laughed. "You have a point, dear."

"What is it?" Roger asked, bestirring himself from his doze.

"Lyris Bahalah wants to see me," Petra said. "She's in Colón."

"I forbid it," Roger said.

"She says she is ill, that it is urgent. She intimates that she has important things to tell me."

"I am not interested in anything that woman has to say," Roger said.

"I will go, nevertheless," Petra said.

"I will go with you, then."

"No," she said. *"Su hermano,"* she said to Luisa. Then, with a frown, "Antonia, ask Luisa if she can get her brother to accompany me tomorrow."

Antonia posed the question and Luisa nodded. "Is big and strong," she said in halting English. "No harm come to you."

"Yes," Petra said, "thank you, Luisa."

"I don't like it," Roger said.

"I'll be fine. Luisa's brother is big and strong."

"He can lift a mule on his back," Antonia said. She translated her remark for Luisa, and the dark girl nodded and smiled with pride.

The carriage, with Pedro, Luisa's brother, driving, took her to a section of incredible squalor, decaying shacks perched on pilings in a morass of scum-covered water. "Are you sure this is the place?" Petra asked. Pedro, who spoke a little French, nodded. "Wait for me here," she said, getting out of the carriage to walk carefully along a narrow wooden walkway and climb makeshift steps to the one-room shack. She knocked and there was a faint reply from within. She opened the door—to have her nostrils assaulted by a terrible odor, an odor of rankness and decay. It was dim inside. The room seemed to sag under the oppressive weight of damp and dinginess.

"Lyris?" Petra called, holding up her skirts and stepping into the room.

Lyris was lying on a sodden bed. Her hair was limp. She had changed so since Petra last saw her that she had to look closely to be sure of the woman's identity. She was alone. She lay atop the filthy coverings of the bed, in a dark dress which was darkened, under the arms, by perspiration, the skirts dirty and ragged.

"Petra, thank you for coming," Lyris said, her voice weak. There was an overall air of defeat about her. Age was evident in her wasted face. The sparkling eyes were dulled.

"Do you have the fever?" Petra asked.

"It comes and goes," Lyris said. "I will die soon."

Under the circumstances, seeing the wasted beauty which was still hinted at in the formation of her face, in the still curvaceous, if thin, body, Petra could not halt the surge of sympathy. "No, we'll take you to the hospital."

"It doesn't matter," Lyris said. "I asked you here to talk about Guy." She paused, as if she did not have the energy to go on.

"What about Guy?"

"He must be stopped," Lyris said. "He, and others—" She fell silent again and, clutching her thin body, began to shiver violently. Petra knew that there would be no further talk as long as the attack of fever lasted, and she feared for Lyris's life. She called Pedro, and together they loaded Lyris into the carriage.

In the hospital, Lyris, bathed, dressed in a clean hospital gown, her hair having been washed and arranged, looked somewhat better, but the effects of age and the tropics were to be seen in her wrinkled and wasted face.

"In addition to malaria," Roger told Petra, "she has an advanced case of syphilis. Together, the two have weakened her."

"Will she die?"

"If not now, soon," Roger said.

Only occasionally was Lyris cogent of her surround-

ings. Once, in a moment of clarity, she thanked Petra
for bringing her to the hospital, and, her mind wander-
ing, gave a disjointed account of her recent years.
Her brothel had burned, and with most of the work
force gone, there was no business, no money.

"You wanted to tell me something about Guy?"
Petra said.

"He must be stopped. Stop him. Go to de Lesseps.
Go to the government."

"Yes, yes," Petra said. "But what is he trying to do?"

It took two days, while the fever came and went and
finally subsided, leaving Lyris very, very weak, to get
the story. It came in bits and pieces, poorly organized,
and Petra learned things which once would have
shocked her, but now nothing Darcie, Lyris, and Guy
had done or could do would shock her.

"He used us," Lyris said, "and we cooperated. He
offered our bodies from the beginning, when we were
trying to sell the original syndicate to de Lesseps. If
there was any man who could help Guy achieve his
ends, there was a bribe for him—not only in money,
but in the form of love. Darcie was the more valuable,
bringing several members of the government into the
plan."

"Did de Lesseps know?" Petra asked.

"No, no. But there were others around him who
plotted with Guy. I can give names, dates, places. They
are putting Charles de Lesseps on trial."

"And you want to help him?"

"I don't care about him," Lyris said. "But they—"

"Guy and Darcie?"

"They are once again engaged in manipulations,"
Lyris said. "With Americans."

"What is it?" Petra asked, but Lyris was exhausted
and had fallen into sleep.

Another time. "What are Darcie and Guy plotting
with the Americans?"

"Everyone—all the little people. They're going to be robbed."

"How, Lyris?"

"My money, all in canal common stock," Lyris gasped.

"Yes, I know you put all your money into canal stock," Petra said. "I'm sorry."

"Guy and Darcie have only founders' shares. Must be stopped."

Petra asked Roger to explain the stock situation to her. "When the original company went bankrupt," Roger said, "all those who had bought common stock lost. Shares are worth nothing."

"And the founders' shares?"

"There are efforts underway to try to sell the new company, which has title to the canal concession from the government of Colombia and to the remaining assets, the work already done, the equipment, to the Americans," Roger said.

"And who would get the money?" Petra asked.

"I'm not sure," Roger said, "but I would guess those who hold founders' shares in the old company, for they were the ones who organized the new company."

"Lyris," Petra asked, when next she found Lyris lucid, "are you afraid that Guy and others are going to keep all of the money realized from a sale of the canal holdings and give none of it to the common stockholders?"

"Stop them. I had it written down."

"Where? Where did you write it?"

"All the bribes, all the trickery."

"Where is it, Lyris? Tell me. I'll see that it gets to the proper authorities."

"At the Navaho."

"Your bordello?"

"The Navaho."

But the Navaho had burned, along with a large

section of that part of Panama City. "It's gone, Lyris. Can you tell me some of it? I'll write it down."

"De Lesseps gave Guy money to bribe the press," Lyris said. "Guy kept most of it, put it into shares. Bribes paid to Meyer, Herz, many others.

"Is there proof?"

"Wrote it down as it happened."

But the notes had been destroyed.

"Guy wants to cut the price being asked for the canal," Lyris said. "Only a few would get their money back. Paying bribes to Americans."

"Can you give me names?"

"Deserted me," Lyris said. "Left me to die. Stop them."

Lyris Bahalah's heart, weakened by her diseases, gave out in the late hours of a steamy, insect-ridden night. She was dead when Petra came in to work, and, although Petra was concerned by the things Lyris had said, the information which Lyris had given was so sketchy, so incomplete, that she was helpless.

The nurse who was preparing Lyris for burial stood aside as Petra looked down upon the once-beautiful face, now cold and pale in death.

"I am sorry your friend is dead," the nurse said.

"Thank you," Petra said. Once Lyris had been her friend.

"She said something as she was dying, madame," the nurse said. "I didn't quite understand all of it, but it was something about your mother's brooch. She said, 'Tell Petra.' Her words were disconnected. Something about your mother's brooch, and someone named Freneau. Do you know what she meant?"

"No," Petra said. "Most probably it was merely the ramblings of a dying mind."

Lyris was buried in a driving rain, with only Roger and Petra in attendance. Petra, made melancholy, could not stop the flow of memories: how Lyris had looked when she first became a part of the family, so young, so beautiful and, to a young child, so kind. But then there were all the other memories: Lyris nude, in Guy's house, dancing, trying to coax Petra into being seduced by her own uncle. Lyris in the squalid room of the bordello, arousing feelings in Petra's drugged body which were, although thrilling at the time, against the laws of God and man. Still, Petra felt sad and moody, for it was a terrible waste for so beautiful a woman to die, alone and unloved, in the rains of Panama.

Petra could not forget the urgency which Lyris had seemed to feel about the activities of Guy Simel. She tried to learn as much as she could about the situation in France. The news was, in itself, sad. Charles de Lesseps, the son and good right hand of the old Hero of Suez, was going on trial, as thousands of ordinary citizens who had lost their money in the Panama venture demanded satisfaction. Petra could not grasp the entire situation, for there were conflicting reports of bribery and corruption.

A stream of Americans visited the canal, most of them to scoff at the French efforts and to go home to tout the alternate route through Nicaragua, but powerful forces were at work. A group of American engineers came, and with them were Guy Simel and Darcie. When she heard of the presence of her uncle and her sister, Petra was reminded that she had done nothing, was helpless to do anything, about Lyris's revelations. She did not tell Roger that Guy was back in Panama. It would only upset him. The full story of the false death certificate had never been revealed, but they had been able to determine that Guy had come to the hospital when Roger was very ill with yellow fever and used his authority to take over the case. Roger remembered vaguely that they had argued and that he had threatened to tell the director-general and de Lesseps that Guy was selling bodies pickled in barrels. After that Guy remembered nothing until after Petra found him in the Tobago hospital.

Neither Guy nor Darcie made any attempt to contact Petra, but she received reports of their activities. From what she could gather, Darcie was up to her old tricks, using her sex as a weapon to influence the Americans, who were in Panama to make a study of the work done and the work needed to finish the canal.

One of the visiting Americans had been ill aboard ship. He was an engineer—a middle-aged man with a balding head and a great, graying beard. The heat of the isthmus caused him to feel ill again, and he came to the hospital to see a doctor. Dressed in a gray twill suit with a neat bowtie, the man explained his symptoms to Roger, fearful that he had already contracted one of the dreaded fevers. Roger assured him that it sounded like a matter of indigestion, that he could not have contracted fever so soon, and advised a bland diet and an overnight stay in the hospital. Petra saw to it that he was made comfortable in his bed. He introduced himself as George Appling and asked questions about the country and the work done by the French. Petra answered his questions.

"With such charming nurses," Appling said, "I don't understand why the French failed."

"You are very kind," Petra said. He seemed to be an open man, quite friendly. "Are the Americans coming into Panama, then?" she asked.

"Remains to be seen," Appling said. "This Frenchie, Philippe Bunau-Varilla, he says we'd be getting a bargain if we pay what they're asking. What do you think?"

"I am not an engineer," she said. "But I think it would be almost criminal to waste all the work, all the suffering."

"I hear that fifty percent of the work force died," Appling said.

"Not so terrible as that, but bad enough," Petra said. "If you want to get an educated view of the work done to date, there is a man in Panama City who has been here from the beginning." She gave the American Jay's name and address. "He is an American, like you."

"An American? And you're an English nurse? With help like that, it's a wonder the frogs didn't do the job."

"I'm half-French, monsieur," Petra said, with a little smile.

"Sorry," Appling said, waving his hand. "No offense, just a matter of speaking."

"I've been called worse," she said. "I understand that there is a Frenchman with your party?"

"Yes, a fellow named Simel. With his niece. Quite a beautiful woman."

"I know so little of these affairs," Petra said. "Is it under consideration for the Americans to buy the concession and material and equipment?"

"Well, that's what Simel is pushing for," Appling said. "Ask me, he's looking out for himself. Understand he's got everything he owns tied up in the company, and a sale to the Americans would recover at least some of it."

"And the common stockholders?"

"They gambled and lost," Appling said with a shrug.

"Monsieur de Lesseps?"

"Funny thing there," Appling said. "The old boy didn't have much in it. He'll come out smelling like a rose, as the saying goes, although it will tarnish his image a little. It's his son who is getting the worst end of it. All those frog—'scuse me, those French politicians are looking for a scapegoat, and I think young de Lesseps is it."

"Do you think that Charles de Lesseps was—how shall I say it—mixed up in the crookedness?"

"Not at all. An honorable man, like his father. He just wasn't smart enough. Hell—'scuse me, lady—heck, there was enough money wasted, in bribes and payoffs, to finish the job, if it could be done at all. It's the old story of good men choosing evil men to handle their affairs and then not keeping a close watch on the chicken coop. Now you take this Simel fellow and his so-called niece. It's not only money they're throwing around to try to influence a few men that Panama is the place for a canal."

"I think I understand," Petra said. "And will they succeed?"

"They're trying hard enough. Simel gave the word only a few days ago that the company is willing to settle for a sum which makes the proposition very attractive."

The papers which arrived from France were weeks old, of course, but they, along with the dribble of cabled news from France, told Petra that not only was the reputation of Charles de Lesseps endangered, his freedom was also in doubt. Moreover, books and magazines and newspapers were attacking the old hero himself. It saddened her.

The day after the American rejoined his party, she saw Jay Burton walk into the reception room at the hospital, and, with a pleased smile, for she saw him seldom these days, she went to greet him.

"I had to come over for the day," he said. "I thought perhaps you and Roger could have lunch with me."

Roger was involved, preparing for emergency surgery. He told Jay and Petra to go along and enjoy lunch and invited Jay to spend the night in their cottage.

Petra immediately brought up the subject which was much on her mind, telling Jay of Lyris's half-lucid accusations, of the things the American had said.

"It's true," Jay said. "I think the old boy is going to be touched with the tarbrush of scandal, at the very least, and it's a shame."

"I've been trying to follow the events," Petra said. "I don't quite understand it all, but Lyris gave me some names which have not been mentioned in the press. Do you suppose it would help if I wrote to Monsieur de Lesseps's lawyers, perhaps, and told them what I know?"

"It might help," Jay said.

"I don't knew quite how to put it. Would you help me compose the letter?"

"Sure, I'll be glad to." He looked at his watch and frowned. "I'm supposed to meet the American party at Culebra this afternoon. I wonder if we could get a pen and paper here at the restaurant."

They could not. The waiter was sorry, but no such things were available. "We don't have time to go back to the hospital or to your house," Jay said, "but there's writing material in my hotel room, if you don't think you'll scandalize the town by going into a hotel room with me in broad daylight."

"I think we can let the town follow its own concerns," Petra laughed. "If it is to be done, it should be done quickly."

The room was comfortable; accommodations had improved in the years of their residency in Panama. Alone with Jay Petra felt a feeling of strangeness. It had been a long, long time since she felt the hard strength of his arms. She put such thoughts from her mind and he seated himself at the writing desk. She told him again what she had heard from Lyris, and he organized it, writing in a flowing, strong hand. Finished, he read it back to her and they agreed that it contained all the information she had, which, it seemed, was not much.

Through the letter-writing session, she had been aware of his nearness, and, it was evident, he of hers. Finished, he stood with a sigh. She stood up from where she'd been sitting on the edge of the bed—there was only one chair in the room.

He looked at her, his eyes squinted thoughtfully.

"Oh, God, Petra," he said, with an agony of feeling which stabbed to her heart. And then he was moving toward her and she was helpless to resist as he enfolded her in his arms and found her open and willing mouth.

So long, so long. Her body cried out for him; her

heart yearned for him. Gasping with love and eagerness, he quickly undressed her, and she, pliant, burning, allowed herself to be lowered gently to the bed,
where she awaited him with open arms. It was quick
and almost rough and so very, very wonderful that,
when she cried out her completion, she felt tears of
sadness and joy on her cheeks, for it was so wrong,
and so terribly wonderful.

"God, Petra, I'm sorry. I just—"

"Yes, I know," she said. "It was as much my fault
as yours."

"When I'm near you and can't touch you, I die a
thousand deaths."

"I know," she whispered. "Oh, I know."

"How long?" he asked, his voice hoarse with emotion. "How long?"

"We can't wish him dead." She knew she'd said
those words before, and saying them, she realized with
terrible guilt that a part of her did wish exactly that.

"I know, God help me, I know."

"I must go now," she said, walking unashamed and
nude into the bath to freshen herself. He stood watching as she performed her toilet and there was a smile
on his face as she bent, in that classical feminine pose,
to clean herself.

Then his smile faded. "Petra, does he—do you—"

"We have not lived together as man and wife since
his illness," she said, knowing what he was asking.

"I'm glad, but in a way that makes it even worse.
If you're not man and wife—"

"He needs me in other ways," Petra said. "And there
is Antonia. She loves her father very much."

He seized her. "I'm not going to let you go. To hell
with meeting the Americans. We're going to stay here
for the entire afternoon."

"No, please. I must go."

"I will not let you go," Jay said, lifting her to carry
her to the bed. She struggled, but he was too strong,

his stocky, masculine body too much for her to throw off, and as he made love to her as he so often had, she did not think more of leaving. She was content to let her body enjoy his demanding lust, his passionate kisses and caresses.

It was twilight when she left the hotel, aglow inside, a woman loved, a woman well used and well rewarded. And there was a guilt in her, as she thought of her lovely, fairhaired daughter at home; of Roger, who worked so hard and was so dedicated to his work. She resolved that it would be the last time. She had had enough of guilt. Now she would apply herself to being wife and mother. She was no longer a silly young girl to let her passions rule her.

She was met at the door of her cottage by a distraught Luisa. "Looking everywhere for you, *señora.*"

Hearing the door open, Antonia ran into the room. "Mother, something terrible has happened at the hospital, and Luisa won't let me go. They came for you and they've been looking everywhere for you."

Petra ran to the hospital, her heart pounding. The kind Anna, once her head nurse, had died of malaria, and her place had been taken by another, a woman whom Petra scarcely knew and made no effort to know well. It was too painful to lose friends. Better to keep the working relations on a businesslike basis. Then if someone caught fever and died, there was none of the pain she'd felt when Anna gasped her last and went into everlasting slumber.

"I was told there was something wrong," Petra gasped, winded by her run across the hospital grounds.

"I don't know quite how to say it, madame," the head nurse said.

"As simply as possible," Petra said. "And quickly."

"It was his heart, madame," the nurse said. "We tried to calm him."

"Roger?" She felt a weakness, a terrible feeling that nothing would ever be right again.

"He is dead, some two hours ago."

"Where?"

"Number five."

He was covered, the sheet pulled over his face in finality. Once before she had been told that he was dead. Now there was no doubt, for his body was there, a frail, weak old man, aged beyond his years by the terrible conditions of the isthmus. She pulled back the sheet and there was peace on his face, but there was no peace in her heart. While her husband—her friend —was dying, she'd been rolling in a bed of sin with her lover. God might forgive her, but she would never forgive herself.

A young doctor—one of the few Panamanians who had gone away to get a medical education—came into the room. "How did it happen?" Petra asked.

"A man came, with a handsome woman. They argued. Doctor D'Art seemed to become very excited."

"Was the man's name Simel?"

"I don't know. He was tall. The woman was small and very beautiful, with dark hair and dark eyes."

"Yes," Petra said. "Did you hear what they were saying?"

"No, *señora,*" the doctor said. "We heard only raised voices from the office, and then the man and the woman hurried out, slamming the door behind them. It was then that I went in to find Doctor D'Art in distress. I gave him something to calm him, but he had a massive seizure, and there was nothing we could do. I am sorry."

"Thank you," Petra said. "Thank you for trying."

And now the burden of guilt was unbearable. In sinful lust, she had dallied away the afternoon while Roger, weakened, frail, faced Guy and Darcie. She went into Roger's office and sat at his desk, unable to weep. There was nothing left for her now. She had committed the final folly. Had she been in the hospital, where she belonged, she could have prevented their seeing Roger.

Yes, there was something. There was Antonia. And suddenly, in her daughter, she saw a hope. It was time to leave Panama. Time to give Antonia the life she deserved. Paris, America, England—anywhere but this hellhole whose climate seemed to inflame the passions and lower people, including herself, to the depths of shame. Yes, she would leave.

Oh, Jay!

But he was equally guilty. Together, they had been responsible for Roger's death—if not totally responsible, at least partially responsible, in that their passion had kept Petra from being in a position to prevent the fatal meeting with her uncle and sister.

Still dry-eyed, she began to sort out the things in Roger's desk. The staff had put his personal belongings from his clothing and his pockets into a drawer, his watch—she would save it for Antonia—his cuff links, some little money. His records and notes she would leave for his replacement, if there was to be one. Otherwise there was only a picture of her with Antonia and, in front of the picture, his personal diary. He had hoped someday to write a book about the Panama experiences.

She thumbed through the diary, and phrases etched themselves into her mind. *My beloved Petra. My beloved wife.* And, on the last page, a scrawled line which galvanized her into action, solidified her resolve. He must have written the phrase while suffering the initial pains of his seizure, for the letters were hurried, distorted.

Guy—wanted me to lie about de Lesseps and bribes.

And that was all. But it was enough. Not enough that, after what he'd done to both Petra and Roger, Guy should have the lack of decency to present his face to Roger. No, he had threatened, coaxed, done something, in an effort to further his own ends, and the shock of it had killed Roger. Guy had murdered him as surely as if he'd shot or stabbed him.

They would not get away with it. Now she knew where she would go. Paris. She would seek out Charles de Lesseps and tell him what she knew, to warn him that Simel and others were actively trying to discredit the old man and Charles himself.

Her preparations were brief. After a hurried funeral and a dismal burial, during which Antonia was brave, saving her weeping for the privacy of her bedroom, they packed the few things worth taking back to France, and, luck being with her, boarded the ship which sailed for France that very day.

It was only as the ship cleared harbor and set out into the calm sea that she allowed herself to think of Jay. Looking back, seeing the gay colors which belied the grimness of the town, she wondered where he was.

"Good-bye, my love," she whispered, for she would not allow herself to see him again. It would be wrong —shamefully wrong—to profit with happiness from Roger's death. Never again to feel Jay's lips on hers would be her punishment.

7

BUT PETRA WAS to be rewarded by Roger's death in a way which saddened her. Upon their arrival in Paris with Antonia who, with the resiliency of the young, was only now and then saddened as she remembered her father, she sought out the building in which Roger had maintained his bachelor quarters and found that there was a vacancy. Then it was necessary to buy clothing for herself and for her daughter. Only then did she visit Roger's solicitor, a man who had looked after Roger's affairs in France while he was away. She discovered that Roger was not exceeding wealthy, but that he had several shares of stock in the Suez, worth many thousands of francs, and that he owned not only a business building in the heart of Paris, which returned him sizable rents, but he also owned a sizable farm and a chateau of modest size which had been handed down from his parents. It was, to her, a strange coincidence that the D'Art family farm was on the Garonne, not far from the Chateau du Blanc, the family home of Guy Simel. She knew a moment of regret. She'd never really talked with Roger while he was alive; most of their personal

279

relationship centered around work. There had been so many things she didn't know about him. She knew nothing of his ancestry, and someday Antonia would ask questions.

Petra's own money was safely placed, growing as it earned interest. She had not touched it after leaving Paris for Panama. Money, then, would be no problem. She felt guilty about being Roger's heiress, but, in the end, it would all go to Antonia, and for that she was grateful. She took immediate steps to prepare a will, ensuring that when she died Antonia would get everything.

Personal affairs settled, she and Antonia established in a comfortable apartment, already beginning to forget, in the pleasant French weather, the misery of the tropics, she made an appointment with one of the lawyers working with Charles de Lesseps and told her story. The lawyer was very interested and asked many questions, going over her story time and again.

"I do hope it will help," she said.

"Of course, Madame D'Art, you have given us no proof of anything. However, there are interesting avenues of investigation which are now opened up. I assure you that you have been a help, and I'm sure Monsieur de Lesseps will thank you in person at a latter day, after all this unpleasantness is ended."

The storm raged, and great names were drawn into the debate over blame for the Panama failure. Gustave Eiffel was implicated. The name of the rising politician Georges Clemenceau was mentioned by some as being a part of the conspiracy, for France was convinced that it was a conspiracy to feather the pockets of mystery men like Cornelius Herz and dishonest politicians. Gustave Eiffel was sentenced to prison, as was Charles de Lesseps. Eiffel was freed by the Court of Appeal, and Charles de Lesseps did not serve his full sentence of one year in prison.

Others went to prison, but not one stockholder received a sou for his worthless stock. In the end, Petra saw, it was the common man, who had purchased stock, paying a small down payment and a sum of money every year, who lost. The names of Guy Simel and Darcie were never mentioned, although there were rumors of a beautiful courtesan whose charms had influenced certain central figures in the scandal.

It seemed to Petra that those who profited most and were most guilty escaped. Although the French government fell as a result of the scandal, there was no punishment for Guy Simel, who had been instrumental in coaxing de Lesseps to enter into the venture, who had profited from the sale of the first syndicate, and who would profit again if the Americans bought the assets of the New Canal Company. However, Petra was only a woman alone, and there was no more she could do. Moreover, she had another concern.

At first she thought that her sickness was merely the aftermath of her fever, or from the unhealthy climate of Panama, or from the long voyage home, during which she experienced some seasickness. But it soon became evident that something else had resulted from that last passionate afternoon with Jay. She was with child, and there was no doubt that the child was Jay's.

Petra was not unhappy. To the world, the timing was right for the child to be Roger's. Antonia was bemused when she was told that she would soon have a sister or a brother, and, as the weeks went by and a glorious spring began to leach the fevers and pestilence of the tropics from Petra, Antonia became quite solicitous, making a great show of taking care of her mother. Petra was resigned. Neither happy nor sad, she dressed Antonia in the finest which Paris could offer and entered her into a fine school of music, while continuing her private tutoring.

Petra learned that Guy and Darcie were in America, still trying to convince the Americans to buy the canal holdings. She would be content never to see them again and, in fact, it was when she encountered an engineer she knew from Panama, who told her that her sister and uncle were on the way back to Paris, that she decided to visit Roger's home on the Garonne River. Always ready for novelty and adventure, Antonia was eager to see her father's old home and to enjoy the pleasures of country living during the summer.

The train ride down was pleasant, and they arrived on a glorious day with the sun bright and just warm enough, the breeze pleasant. The D'Art chateau was, like the others in the area, a producer of grapes and a decent wine. The people who had operated the place in Roger's absence, headed by a wizened old man whose name was Louis Desaix, welcomed the two D'Art women with open arms. Louis, insisting on their sampling the product of the chateau after their carriage ride to the house, told them that it was high time a D'Art came to live at the Chateau D'Art.

Antonia, with her bright and charming disposition, had a new bevy of willing slaves and soon went completely native, dressing like the peasant girls who worked in the vineyards, coaxing old Louis into teaching her to ride.

Petra found peace. In the old house, surrounded by furniture, paintings, objects of art which had been accumulated by Roger's family, she at last felt at home. There, she decided, she would spend the rest of her life. There her son—and she was sure, somehow, that it would be a boy—would be born, would grow up to be a gentleman farmer. She felt no guilt, thinking of handing Roger's family home down to a son who was not his, for Roger was the last of the D'Arts, and, somehow, she thought that he would have approved.

One thing bothered her, at first, and that was the nearness of the Chateau du Blanc, Guy's chateau. Then, by casual questioning as neighbors came to call, she learned that Guy had long since sold the chateau. There was no reason for Guy to come back to the Garonne.

Gradually, the yellowish tone which years of taking quinine on a regular basis had engendered in her skin, faded. Petra willed herself to be content, pushing away all thoughts of Jay when they occurred, usually after she had retired for the night. Underweight when she returned from Panama, she filled out as her stomach filled, her full and womanly figure, aside from the distortion in the middle which grew with the weeks, as voluptuous as ever.

The kind sun of France, the generous and cooling breezes, the healthy air, the lack of all the hordes of mosquitoes, ticks, leeches, flies, gnats, spiders, chiggers, and other insects unnamed, all served to restore her health and to cause Antonia to blossom. Fresh vegetables on the table gladdened her, for her appetite was voracious. She had a piano tuner come from the nearest village, and now the house was filled with Antonia's music.

Although she was, in coloration and in her blond hair, much like Petra, Antonia was of a size to the Darcie of her age: tiny, perfectly formed, full of energy and curiosity. Moreover, she was precocious beyond her years and not afraid of anything. She became a splendid horsewoman almost overnight, rode the spirited animals bred on the farm with an abandon which frightened Petra, and was so quick in her studies that she had to spend little time on them during that glorious summer.

Musingly, Petra wondered where the years had gone. It seemed only yesterday that she was not much older than Antonia, setting off, in sadness, from England with her father and sister to begin a life which, at that time, she could not even have imagined. She vowed that life would never be unkind to Antonia. She would devote the rest of her days to that. Soon Antonia would be mature, and she would see to it that a proper match would be made. If Antonia loved, so much the better, for she wished nothing but happiness for her daughter. Sometimes she whiled away the hours dreaming of a Prince Charming for her daughter: a handsome young man of honor and ambition who would give Antonia all the good things of life.

And so Petra was furious when, while walking on a pleasant afternoon, coming from a tour of the vineyards close behind the house, she came near the stables and heard Antonia's voice from within. Antonia was speaking softly, and, although Petra could not catch the words, there was a quality in the tone which aroused her interest. She walked quietly to the door and looked inside. In the dim light she saw only a jumble of riding habit and arms and, as her eyes adjusted to the gloom, saw her daughter, lying on her back on clean straw, kissing the young son of one of the overseers with a passion which shocked her. And, even more shocking, Antonia's legs were spread wide. The lad's hand was buried in her skirts, working with determination as, with each caress, Antonia moaned in pleasure.

Petra did not speak. Near the door hung a riding crop. The son of the overseer, lost in the soft and young lips of Antonia, feeling her young and tender creaminess on his fingers, knew nothing of Petra's presence until, with a strength which made him yell with pain and fear, the riding crop fell over his shoulders.

She beat him out of the stable. Behind her, Antonia was laughing.

Petra turned, fury in her eyes. "You will not laugh in a moment," she cried, raising the crop and bringing it down across Antonia's bare shoulders, for the girl had not yet been able to rearrange her clothing, lowered to expose her pointed, hard young breasts.

Petra saw a bright red welt rise up suddenly and then, with Antonia's laughter changing quickly to tears and cries of pain, she lashed once more, then again and again and then in her mind she saw a picture of Darcie standing over the dwarf beating him with the whip.

Petra sat down weakly and helpless tears shook her body. For a moment, Antonia, smarting, weeping in pain, looked at her in fury. Then her face softened and she knelt beside her mother.

"It was nothing, mother," she said. "Only harmless fun. I would not have—" She paused.

Her words brought on a fresh torrent of sobs. Petra was seeing, in her daughter, the image of Darcie, the small and perfect body, the look of impish mischief, the sensuousness of her lips.

"I didn't mean to upset you, mother, please," Antonia said. "I promise you that I have never done anything more than—well, play, and that I don't intend to. Please?"

Still sobbing, Petra leaned and kissed a welt on Antonia's neck. "Oh, darling," she said. "I'm so sorry I hurt you."

"I guess I was doing wrong," Antonia said. Then, with a wry smile, "I'm sure, from your reaction, that I was doing wrong."

"You mustn't throw yourself away like that," Petra said.

"I won't do it again. I promise."

Later, when Petra was sitting alone in the parlor, remembering and thinking how like Darcie Antonia was, her daughter came in.

"I've been thinking, mother," she said, "and I feel I owe you a complete explanation. You know Louis's granddaughters?"

"Yes."

"They're nice girls."

"They're farm girls, Antonia. You are a lady."

"Well, they're friends. That's all right, isn't it?"

"As long as they keep their station and you yours."

"They do it with boys."

"Do it?"

"You know."

"They told you this?"

"Yes. They laugh about it. They say it's wonderful. They talk about the crop of harvest babies which comes after every harvest festival, and they know ways to keep from getting with child."

"Someday, darling, a man will come along and you'll love him and you'll want to be whole for him," Petra said.

"Oh, I know that," Antonia said impatiently. "I was just curious. I wanted to see how it felt to have a man's hand on my—" She used a common word and Petra gasped.

"It felt good," Antonia said, "but I know what can happen. Now that I know, I'll have something to look forward to, won't I?" There was a twinkle in her eyes.

"You're a devil!" Petra said. "No more experimenting?"

"No more experimenting."

"I want you to become a woman of whom your father would have been proud," Petra said. "You have wealth, my darling. All this will be yours, along with your little brother, when he is born. You'll never want for anything. You have a delightful musical talent and you're quite intelligent. You're going to be a beautiful woman, and you can pick and choose your husband, when the time comes—make a match which will assure that only the best the world has to offer will come to you. At the risk of being pedantic, I will say, once more, that it would be the greatest mistake of your life to throw yourself away on some country swain."

"Were you virgin when you were married, mother?" Antonia asked.

A bit shocked, but hiding it, Petra said, "Yes, of course."

"And is my Aunt Darcie a virgin?" Antonia asked, with a little smile.

"I'm sure that your Aunt Darcie would have to answer that question herself," Petra said, but she wondered about the thinking which led to that question. "Why do you mention Darcie?"

"She's quite beautiful in her pictures," Antonia said. "That's all."

Guided by the direction of the conversation, Petra decided to make one final point. "Your Aunt Darcie was virgin until she was cruelly raped when she was fifteen."

"Tell me about it."

"It's very unpleasant," Petra said, "and no fit subject for your young ears."

Antonia rose, kissing her mother on the cheek. "I'll be good, mother."

"I do hope so."

But at the door, Antonia could not resist. For years she had debated, had questioned the talk she'd heard among the servants in Panama.

"Mother?"

"Yes, darling?"

"When you spent the day with Uncle Jay in the hotel, the day my father died, was that rape or fun?"

Petra gasped, feeling a stab of shock and pain. She put her hand to her breast. How did Antonia know? "Oh, Antonia!" she gasped.

"Please don't faint." Antonia smiled, showing Petra a glimpse of something which frightened her, the young girl so much like Darcie. "I was just asking."

And then she was gone.

Petra did not have the courage to follow her and question her. She was numbed. She had never overcome the heavy burden of guilt she felt at having been with Jay when Roger died. Now it was coming home to her. *Oh, poor Antonia!* she thought. *What she must think.* When she recovered from the shock, she would go to her daughter and make an effort to explain. But somehow she could not bring herself to do it.

Had Petra but known, Antonia was more precocious than her mother could ever imagine. She had no way of knowing that Antonia, with her command of Spanish, had been more friendly with the servants and with children of the servants than Petra realized. Nor could Petra have any way of knowing that the maid, Luisa, a good Catholic, was shocked and revolted during the time when her husband lay ill, an infant daughter slept in the next room, and Jay and Petra made love. To Luisa, to have the man visit in the D'Art home was terrible enough, the poor doctor lying there helpless, but the unmistakable evidence, which Luisa would discover when she did her cleaning the next morning, told her exactly what was happening. And then there were the pictures—hidden securely, Petra thought, but not secure from the curiosity of Luisa.

The young Antonia did not mind Luisa's praying with her and even liked the sound of the words. She joined Luisa in praying for the soul of her mother who, Luisa said, had sinned greatly.

There could have been many explanations for Luisa's telling Antonia of the affair between Jay and Petra. Luisa explained it to herself by thinking that the child had a right to know. That knowing, she would see the shame and horror of it and never, never sin in the same way.

"Pobrecita," Luisa would say as they prayed. "You have so much to overcome. But it is well known that the French are dissolute, and you, with the help of God and good Spanish teachings, can avoid the depravity of the French."

Antonia was too young to know such words as *dissolute* and *depravity,* but she knew, when Luisa, praying God for understanding, showed her the pictures—

which Petra later destroyed—that it was her mother
and her Aunt Darcie doing those strange and, according to Luisa, sinful things. She knew, too, that her
mother and father did not sleep together, doing that
thing which the young children talked of in hushed
voices.

When Luisa blessed the house, trying to drive away
the sin which had accumulated during that time when
Roger lay ill and helpless and the terrible love affair
went on in that very house, Antonia helped.

The greatest sin of all, Luisa said, was that Petra
had spent the afternoon in a hotel room with that man
on the very day the good doctor died.

Antonia did not dwell on it too much. As she grew
older and talked with some of her young friends she
was curious about this sin which seemed to be the
sole property of adults and found that boys were different, having a small appendage which girls did not
have. She played the age-old game of show-and-com-
pare which children the world over begin at an early
age, with no direct results. Most of her friends were
of Luisa's class; children of French workers were rare.
They were an earthy lot, and they whispered of forbidden pleasures. The curious poking of a small male
finger at her femininity left her in puzzlement, and she
often examined herself while in the bath to try to discover the secret. As she grew, she found that a soaped
cloth, rubbed repeatedly and tenderly over certain
areas, produced a pleasurable sensation and the first
time that that sensation grew and became acute she
was frightened, but the memory of it brought a repetition and a discovery of a wondrous capacity.

In France, she was once again thrown into the company of earthy young people of her own age. It was
there that she discovered that a boy's hand can give
the same pleasurable sensation as a soaped cloth or
her own hand—and, in fact, there was an added di-
mension which increased her curiosity.

If it, that forbidden act, was so pleasurable for her mother, so pleasurable that she indulged in it against her marriage vows and on the very day of her father's death, then, Antonia felt, it must be exceedingly powerful. It was, she concluded, merely adult perversity to forbid it to her, simply because she was young.

Antonia had never felt punishment until her mother attacked her with a horsewhip. When she crawled out her bedroom window onto the low roof of the lower story and used a vine-covered drain to reach the ground, she was bent on two things: satisfying her curiosity and punishing her mother for the whip.

Antonia crept through the night to the cottage of the overseer and scratched lightly on Jacques's window until he heard and threw on a few clothes to join her. She led him to the stables.

"Mon Dieu," he said, "I hope your mother is safely in bed. She wields a wicked whip."

"She is asleep," Antonia said. "Did he hurt you badly?"

"Not as badly as she hurt you," he said.

"It is nothing."

Inside the stables, he began kissing her. She kissed back, letting the warm feel of it sweep over her. Whispering, laughing, they climbed into the hayloft. Jacques spread a clean horse blanket, to keep the sharp ends of the hay from sticking into them, and she lay down, allowing him to put his weight on her. His body heat and his kisses soon roused that feeling in her, and she allowed him slowly, a bit at a time, to remove the nightdress in which she had come to him. But when he attempted to mount her quickly, she protested.

"There is no hurry," she said. "I want to experience it all, everything. First, you will kiss my breasts." He did so with gasping pleasure and the feel of his lips, his teeth teasing her erect little nipples, caused her to squirm in need. She cupped her hands around her hard, small breasts and thrust them into his mouth. So this was the forbidden pleasure.

"No, no," she protested, when, once again, he tried to push his body between her soft thighs. "There is more."

"What?" he asked, his breathing harsh.

"My cunt," she whispered, using the vulgar and common term lovingly. "Kiss my cunt. Kiss it well."

With a sigh, Jacques obeyed her. She writhed in pleasure, lifting her slim young loins to his kiss. This was what her mother had done with her Aunt Darcie. Ah, wonderful!

"Oh, come to me," she cried, unable to postpone it.

The horseback riding, the elasticity, the juices engendered by his—for his age—expert ministrations, made the myth of pain laughable, for there was only a feeling of discomfort—and that only for a moment as his juices mingled with hers and made them one, slick, long, sliding deep.

"Remember," she said, as he lunged deep into her. "You must jerk it out quickly before you come."

"Oh, God," Antonia moaned, as she blew sky-high, "Oh, my God—I was made for this!"

8

THE GRAPE FARMER Francis Freneau
had never been a wealthy man. His small holdings,
which produced just enough to assure bread on the
table, clothing on the backs of his wife and his daughter, a few luxuries for his women on birthdays and
Christmas, lay on the banks of the Garonne in fine
grape country. True, he was not rich, but he was rich
in spirit. When Helene came into their lives, which to
that date had been barren of children, Freneau's life
took on a new meaning, and he felt the stirring of
an ambition which he'd never felt.

The small farm, the basic way of life which had
been his and his father's before him, was good enough
for Freneau—in fact, he could ask for nothing better
than to be allowed to rise with the sun, tend his vines
and drink of his own wine over a supper which was
largely produced on his own land. But with a daughter, ah! Such a little jewel she was, and so beloved by
both Freneau and his wife Marie. Their lives were
never the same after Helene came to them, a small,
mewling, kicking, laughing miracle which fulfilled them
and made Freneau think to the future. Had it been a

son, he would have trained the boy in the ways of the farmer and would have been content to leave the small Freneau farm to him, knowing that the boy would have a good life, as he'd had.

But with a girl, ah! Girls were different. From the first, when she was so tiny, holding onto his finger with a strong and pudgy little hand, her undeveloped eyes so small and sweet as they searched for his face, he had wanted more for his daughter.

Ah, his little gypsy. For her, he had ambition. For her, he would make much money. All for her.

The idea came to him when his neighbor, Guy Simel, came to the Garonne to close the sale of the Simel chateau and landholdings. M. Simel had been very kind and very generous with his advice.

"But Monsieur Simel," Freneau had said, "the land has been in your family for generations. How can you part with it?"

"Opportunity, my dear Freneau, opportunity," Simel had said. "For with the money I will invest in Panama Canal stock, and with the profits, I will be able to buy a dozen chateaux, if it pleases me."

"It is so simple, then, this way of making money?" Freneau asked.

"As simple as making a down payment on stock and keeping up the payments," Simel said. "You cannot go wrong, Freneau. Look at the Suez stock. It is worth multiples of its original value. Many who sacrificed to buy Suez stock are now rich."

"And if the Panama stock does not increase in value?"

"Would Monsieur de Lesseps advise everyone to buy Panama stock if it were not a good bargain?" Guy asked.

"Yes, I see," Freneau said. "And I thank you for sharing your wisdom with me."

He did not discuss the matter with Marie. He looked

at his daughter and thought of her future and took his savings into the town, there to join thousands of others in backing de Lesseps's dream. As the splendid news of progress came from Panama, in the form of a small newspaper printed by the company, telling of so many metric tons of earth moved, so much progress, so certain a future, he became even more ambitious. He knew little of money matters, but he discovered that it was quite simple to talk with the friendly and helpful banker and to arrange a certain transaction, which made him the owner of many more shares of canal stock and made the bank the owner of a piece of paper which said that his land and his house would become the bank's property if he should fail to repay the sum borrowed.

Like thousands of others, Francis Freneau could not believe that it could happen. He would not accept the news of the disaster. He could only look at his stock certificates with dulled and wondering eyes, seeing in them all the francs he'd borrowed, all the money he'd saved, and now they were, he was told, nothing more than worthless paper.

He went to the bank and explained. "Here, the stocks are worth so much. I will give you the stocks and you will give me back the piece of paper."

He could not believe that it was not possible. It made sense to him. He had paid good francs for the stocks—why were they now worth nothing? Why would the bank not accept them in place of the money which they represented?

"Monsieur Freneau," the friendly and helpful banker told him, "you have signed a paper. It is backed by all of the laws of the land. It says that you must pay or that you must give us your land."

"How can I give you my land? I live by my land."

"It is a matter of simple business. Life, my friend, is a gamble. It seems that you have lost. But don't fret—many others lost, also. I myself bought canal stock."

"And do you give up your home because you bought stock?"

"No, I did not borrow against my home, Monsieur Freneau. You were the one who borrowed money, with your home as a guarantee that it would be paid. It is a matter of simple business. Unfortunately, I am helpless. We will take your home by such-and-such a date unless you can pay the money."

"My harvest will be in soon," Freneau said. "I will give you all of the money from it."

"And will it pay the amount on the paper?"

"It will pay a small portion of it. I will give you, also, the money from the next harvest and the next until I have paid what it says on the paper."

"I have a responsibility to my bank. If it were left to me, M. Freneau, I would not take your home, but my hands are tied."

"I will shoot to kill any man who tries to put me and my family out of my home," Freneau said calmly, and he was believed by the friendly and helpful banker, for he knew that Freneau still did not understand that his home had gone down the rathole called Panama, and that he was helpless, for the law was on the side of the banker. Oh, well, when the time came, there would be the law, and armed men, if necessary. Then it would be over.

Actually, it never came to that. Francis Freneau died of exhaustion from working to increase his harvest, from worry about losing his home, and from a small virus, which, in that time, was not even known to be the cause of the lung congestion which first made his work a misery, then weakened him to the point where he could not stand, and, in the end, took his life. His wife, suffering from the same congestion of the lungs, and his daughter, a young and gypsy-looking girl, could not know that he was as much a victim of de Lesseps's grand dream as were any of the thousands who had died, far away, in the Panamanian jungles.

9

HELENE FRENEAU WAS a small-boned, delicate girl with a dusky skin and great eyes which contained a host of tiny, sparkling lights to give a vibrancy to her appearance. She had the face and the body to attract attention wherever she went. In the village of Podensac, near her father's farm, there was much talk, as she grew, as to how the plodding Francis and the rather bovine Marie Freneau could produce such a delicate and beautiful creature.

Helene Freneau was the object of serious courtship from her early teens, and she had the pick of the local crop of swains. Yet, despite her popularity with the lads of the area, despite the fact that she was the girl who was always dancing at the harvest festival, while other girls merely looked on, she was also popular with girls of her own age. There seemed to be a sort of magic about her which was large enough, encompassing enough, to allow her to give of herself to all, to be friendly and warm with all of her friends, boys and girls alike.

It was not that she was endearingly and sickeningly sweet. Some had learned—the hard way—that she could have a sharp tongue. Helene offered no offense, but when offended, she was quick to defend herself. This quality won the respect of all her age group and she was also well regarded by the adults of the community.

Her suitors lovingly called her Gypsy, and she did look rather like a gypsy, with her dark, wavy hair, deep brown eyes of exotic shape, tilted and laughing. Her lips, red, full, and kissable, were always curved into an inviting smile, but there were lads with her handprint on their face who knew that it was not a smile of sexual invitation. Her figure was finely formed, a tiny perfection. Her hands were long and graceful, and seemed to be sculpted from smooth marble.

The appearance of her hands belied the fact that she enjoyed being with her father as he worked on the farm, that her delicate appearance did not prevent her from doing her share of the chores: tossing down hay for the cattle, birthing a calf, planting and pruning along with her parents, who had long been browned and wrinkled by their years of exposure to the sun and weather. No matter what Helene did, when freshly washed, her hands were that perfection, that smoothness which would have been the envy of the most pampered woman. Her nails were not always carefully manicured—in fact she was unfamiliar with the term, as were the other women of the area—but they were always clean.

Helene was the joy of her parents' lives. From the first, she was a happy child, so easy to rear. She had taken to farm life as if it were her born station, absorbing everything about working the farm, asking questions even as a child which stumped her father and mother. Nor was her curiosity limited to farm matters.

It became evident early that she had a good mind, and, with her father's ambition for her growing, she was placed in a school. Francis Freneau was not a

wealthy man, but this child, who had come to them
late in life, was a miracle which inspired him. When
she was five, he took her by the hand and walked
into the village to present Helene to the nuns of the
convent. She was to be a day student—walking, in
all weather, to the school, where a new world opened
up to her; a world with all manner of exciting information which she absorbed with an eagerness which
somewhat awed her teachers and gave her parents
much pride.

At first, her mother was against the schooling, telling her husband that he was putting false notions into
the girl's head, for it was not the usual thing for the
daughter of a poor farmer to attend the fine convent
school. Marie told her husband he was trying to give
the girl ideas beyond her station. But even Marie
warmed to the idea as the young girl dived headfirst
into book learning and enlivened the evenings, after
the work was finished, by reading aloud tales of strange
and far places. One of Marie's delights was for Helene
to read to her while she prepared the evening meal.
Helene, accustomed to helping, protested, but soon
accepted the fact that her mother would rather be
hearing about some faraway land or some legendary
monster than to have help in preparing the vegetables
for cooking.

Helene was in no hurry to leave her pleasant life.
She thought that her parents were the world's finest
people and that her mother was, in spite of her age
and her weathering, a truly beautiful woman. She
adored her father. At an age when her friends were all
married—some of them in haste following, perhaps, a
harvest festival—she was content to continue her
schooling, helping the nuns now and then with the
younger students, and to continue her placid life in
her father's house. The subject of Helene's marriage
was a pleasant joke between her and her mother.

"A grown young lady, and still around the house,"

Marie would say. "And I will not live to hold a grand-child in my arms."

"Soon, soon, little mother," Helene would say.

"You're waiting for a prince to come riding through the vines, is that it?"

"Yes. And when he does, I'll make you a dozen grandchildren," Helene would laugh.

"Have you thought about marriage?" her father would ask as she walked with him through the fields.

"Are you tired of me, then?"

"Ah, little gypsy, never," Francis would say, drinking in her young and innocent beauty with grateful eyes.

But all that was before the talk with the friendly and helpful banker, before the rains came when they should not have come and the mildew appeared on the grapes and Francis, in desperation, tried, in driving rain, to clean the grapes by hand, bunch by bunch, patiently moving down the rows in the rain.

Helene knew that something was troubling her father, but he would not have worried her for the world. So it was that she watched, in sadness and puzzlement, as he seemed to shrivel inside his skin, as his hair became more gray. She tried to find ways to force him to smile, and she would be rewarded by a fleeting smile. Then he began to cough and to move very slowly, as if he were in pain. The cough was a small one, at first. Then Helene would see her father put his hand on his chest, struggling for air, as if by pushing on his chest he could force air into his lungs.

On the morning when he was unable to rise from his bed, Helene herself went into the village for the doctor. She found the doctor in a cottage, watching over a woman whose time had come and who was having difficulties. The doctor could not come—perhaps not for a day. She described the symptoms of her father's illness, and the doctor shook his head.

"It is merely a congestion. There is much of it about during this damp and chill weather. Tell him to stay in bed, to keep warm, to rest."

"Will you come as soon as you can?" Helene asked.

"When I can," the doctor said. "There are others."

"We will pay," Helene said.

"With what?" the doctor asked. "A chicken or a goat?" But he lightened the remark with an encouraging smile.

Her father's cough was worse, and he was running a high fever. Moreover, now her mother was coughing and seeming to move with difficulty. Helene put her mother to bed and nursed both of them. The doctor did not come, but he sent word that he would come as soon as possible, and the messenger brought medicine which did not seem to help either of them.

Helene lost count of the hours, knowing only that it was day or it was night. She did not blame the doctor. She knew that he was working day and night, surviving on very little sleep, for the ailment which was afflicting her parents was now quite widespread. Nor did she blame God when, saying that he must see to the harvest, Francis Freneau tried to rise from his bed only to fall back in death.

There was no time for tears. Her mother was worse and her father was dead. In a light rain, Helene walked to the village and left word for the priest, who was off on a similar errand.

With her father's body covered on his bed, she bathed her mother's fevered brow and prayed that at least she might be spared. The tragedy of her father's death had not yet penetrated the exhaustion she felt, the need to stay constantly at her mother's side.

Her mother suffered from the high fever, now and again becoming delirious. She would call out for Francis. In the honesty which had always ruled their family, Helene told her mother that Francis was dead and at times Marie accepted it, but when the fever burned highest, she continued to call out to him, not able to understand why he could not come to her.

Helene, with a peasant sense of acceptance, sat beside her mother's bed mending her father's best clothing for his funeral, listening sadly to the fevered ravings. She did not weep openly, but her face was wet with tears.

Finally the priest came to say the last words over the body of her father and to look with concerned eyes at the failing Marie, who received the last sacrament while Helene let the soft tears roll down her cheeks. Her father's body was removed. Alone with her mother, she gazed out the window at the light rain which was falling, wondering what was happening to her world.

"Helene, Helene," her mother called.

Helene went to the bedside and wiped her mother's brow with a cool cloth.

"I will not live to hold my grandchildren on my knee."

"Yes, yes, you will. I will give you a dozen grandchildren."

Outside, the rain had transformed the usually sunny and green valley into a gray, dripping, dismal scene in which everything drooped, sagged under the weight of the water and the vines were drowned, the crop ruined by the mildew.

A neighbor woman came. She was Jeanine Aumont, a good friend, and she had lost her aged mother to the congestion. She helped Helene give Marie a sponge bath and then had to leave to tend her own family. It was Madame Aumont who sat with Marie while Helene attended to the sad duty of her father's burial. He was put to rest in the little churchyard in the village, where there were already a score of fresh graves.

Helene walked home with a wind blowing in from the distant sea, causing the rain to seek out openings in her clothing and wet her to the skin. She thanked

Madame Aumont and set about making a rich broth for her mother. The wind shrilled around the sturdy house, and, toward morning, as Helene dozed in a chair beside her mother's bed, she was awakened by the crash of a tree limb, torn away by the wind to be dashed against the side of the house. The sound awakened her mother as well, and she looked at Helene with eyes which were, for the moment, bright and aware.

Helene leaped to her feet and felt her mother's brow, praying that the fever had broken. But the fever was still there, very hot. *"Maman,* do you feel better?"

"I dreamed that your father was dead," Marie said in wonder. "It's so foolish. He would not leave me."

Out of kindness, Helene said, "No, he would not leave you."

"He would not leave you alone, my daughter."

"I will have you. I will not be alone."

"No," Marie said, moving her head weakly. "I know he is dead and I know I shall die and I must tell you."

"Tell me what, little mother?"

"Ah, my love, my daughter." The words were faint so that Helene had to lean close. "Francis, my husband, I must tell her."

And then she lapsed into sleep, leaving Helene wondering, only to waken with a start a few minutes later, shivering as if being touched by cold, cold hands. Helene held her hand and whispered to her. One of Marie's weathered hands came up, cupped behind Helene's head, pulled her down. The feel of her mother's lips on her cheek were hot, rough. Marie took a deep, shuddering breath.

"I do not have long, my daughter. And before I join my husband, I ask that you listen." She raised a weak hand. "No, no questions. There is no time. Just listen. Remember that you have been the joy of my life, and the joy of your father as well. You have made our lives so complete, little gypsy, and now you will be alone."

"Ah, no, *maman!*" Helene protested.

"Go," Marie said. "Go to the clothes press. There is a small box at the back of the shelf."

Helene hesitated.

"Go—quickly."

She found the box hidden behind clothes to be mended. She had never seen it before. She carried it carefully and placed it in her mother's hands. She felt a desperate feeling of foreboding. Her lips trembled and questions came to her mind.

"This was to be your wedding present," Marie said. "Ah, that you had married, daughter. Then you would have someone."

"What is it, *maman?*"

"A moment. Before you were born I worked as a cook in the chateau of Monsieur Guy Simel. It was there that I met your father."

For a moment she was lost in her memories, a smile on her lips. "So handsome, Francis Freneau. Ah, you young scamp. Francis, smell the grapes. Ah, Francis, dance with me?" Her voice trailed off.

"*Maman!*" Helene said, squeezing her hand.

It frightened her to see her mother fade off into memory, although it was sweet to think that she was reliving tender moments. She could see them, the young couple, vibrant and full of fire, flushed with wine, dancing, knowing the excitement of the time of the completion of harvest.

"We sat together," Marie said, nodding her head. "And the wind blew a merry tune and everyone was dancing and then he took me quietly off into the shadows—"

"Yes, *maman,* you have told me many times. You thought," and she forced a little laugh, "that he was merely going to try to kiss you, and instead he asked you to marry him."

"Marry," Marie said. "Find a good man, my daughter, and marry."

"Yes, yes," Helene said, holding her mother's hand.

Marie's eyes were open and she was smiling. Helene knew that she was remembering her youth and the touch of her lover's hands and the gaiety of that most exciting time of the year when people from all over the valley got together to celebrate.

"*Maman,* you will have grandchildren," Helene said. "I promise you that you will bounce your grandchildren on your knee and spoil them terribly, just as you spoiled me."

But Marie was lost in her memories, talking in snatches, incoherent, the fever surging up to make her face burn. She heard names—M. Simel—and a name which she thought to be Marcie.

"Chateau du Blanc," Marie said. "Go." And the name Marcie, or something which sounded like it. "The box. The box." Her hands fumbled and she could not open the latch. Helene took the box from her and opened it. The gold brooch inside was so beautiful that she gasped. It was, she realized, quite out of place in the home of a poor farmer. There was a gleaming ruby in the center, and the gold of the brooch and the chain had been polished lovingly over the years.

"What is it, *maman?*"

"Your mother's," Marie said with great difficulty.

"Yes, yours, my mother's."

"No, no, my darling. You must not be alone. Chateau du Blanc. Tell them Marie Freneau—"

Suddenly a look of fear came into Marie's face, and then, with her eyes wide, she began to gasp for breath, the force of her efforts lifting her from the bed. And then she fell back and a deep sigh came from her, continuing on and on as the air was forced from her lungs and the lips, cracked, hot, formed her husband's name and then, like ice freezing quickly on a shallow pond, a glaze covered her eyes and she was still.

Helene sat, dazed, the cooling hand in hers, unable to weep. Lost, alone, the terrible sadness kept her

there for long hours, motionless, quiet tears falling to
wet the front of her dress. Then, as a chill and damp
dawn came in the windows, she rose, tucked the coverlets under her mother's chin, closed the glazed eyes,
and looked around the now very empty room. It had
been her home and she had loved it, but now it seemed
hateful, sad, enclosing. She walked out into the dampness of the morning and watched the sun came up in
a hazy sky. For a long time she did not realize that
she had the golden brooch with its gleaming ruby in
her hand. She looked at it musingly, having difficulty
seeing it through her tears and then she saw that it
opened. She used a short fingernail to open it. Inside
there was a picture of a smiling lady, faded by age,
a lady in the clothing of a generation past but looking, judging from pictures in her books, very English.
And she remembered her mother's words.

"Your mother," Marie had said.

But this woman would have been too old to be
her mother, and it was Marie Freneau who was her
mother and Francis Freneau her father.

Marie had been quite fond of telling her daughter
about her young life and especially about the time she
first met Francis and how he had proposed to her on
festival night. It pleased Helene to remember them
thus—young, full of life and love—and she often
smiled to think that perhaps she was, like many others
in grape country, a harvest baby, for passions bloomed
in the time of celebration, when a year's work was
done. It did not shock her, although she was a God-
fearing girl, to think that she might have been conceived in a glorious moment of young and illicit passion made respectable in haste, with laughter and love.

And now to ponder her mother's words and the
meaning of the locket.

"No," Marie had said. "I am not your mother." Or,
at least, her words had that meaning.

Although it pained Helene to leave her mother's

body alone, she went into the village. The priest came, and once again she stood in the quiet churchyard to hear the hopeful words about a happier life in the hereafter.

With exquisite timing, the friendly and helpful banker had men at the Freneau home when Helene returned from the funeral. She was shocked to learn that her father had borrowed money to buy Panama Canal stock and that now the farm—her home, the only home she'd ever known—was not hers but that it belonged to the bank. However, she was educated and had read. She saw immediately that she was helpless.

"You will give me time to remove my possessions," she said. "It will take some time. I must first find employment and then a place to put the furniture."

"Mademoiselle Freneau," the friendly banker said, "if you will read the contract closely, you will see that it regards not only the house and the land, but the contents of the house as well."

And so it did. So she was not even to have the simple and sturdy furniture with which she had grown up.

"Does it regard my clothing?" she asked coldly.

"The bank would not be so harsh as to take your personal clothing."

"You are most kind," Helene said. "Then you will give me a few hours to pack?"

"One of my men will stay with you."

"Ah," she said bitterly, "to see that I do not steal my own property?"

"Mademoiselle Freneau, it is a matter of business."

Helene packed in haste and with a burning anger, taking her books, her clothing, the few pictures of her mother and father and herself. Daring the watching man to say anything, she also packed the delicate lace tablecloth and napkins made by hand by her mother, and while the man's head was turned, the box containing the brooch. The brooch had taken on a strange

meaning to her. It was mystery, and, in her grief, anything to occupy her mind was welcome.

Then it was done, and all of her life to date was
contained in the old wooden trunk in which Marie
Freneau had brought her trousseau to the farm so
long ago. Helene sat down to look around, for one
last time. The lovely old kitchen with its low beams
and well-worn fixtures, the parlor with chairs gay and
bright in slipcovers made by her mother, the two bed-
rooms, one with the featherbed which had known the
impress of her head from the time when she was a
baby first out of the cradle.

"I am sorry," the man said, "but the hour grows
late."

"I cannot carry the trunk on my back," Helene said.

"If you are ready, I will take the trunk into town
for you."

"You are kind."

He shook his head. "Mademoiselle Freneau, you
know that it is not my doing."

"Yes."

"I am merely a servant of the state, and I have my
orders."

"Yes, I understand. Would you be so kind as to
wait outside? I would like just a moment alone."

"By all means." He closed the door behind him and
she heard, in a few minutes, the jingle of harness as
he brought the surrey in which he had come to the
front door. She quickly opened the trunk, opened the
box, and put the brooch around her neck, letting it
hang inside her dress. She felt more secure, somehow,
having the only thing of value left in her possession
so near to her.

In the village she asked the man to take her to
the convent, where the nuns, having heard of the tragic
deaths of her parents and of the cruel eviction at such
a tragic time, greeted her with kindness, telling her
that she was welcome to stay as long as she wished.

Exhausted from the past few trying days, she slept almost around the clock and then woke to spend long hours in the chapel, praying for the souls of her departed parents.

The weather which, with the unusual rains, had brought hardship to the entire area, now seemed to be trying to make up for its hatefulness by presenting a bright, warm sun to the world. There was a peaceful acceptance in Helene's heart. It was as it was meant to be and, perhaps, God had a purpose in leaving her without a family at so tender an age. It was then up to her to discover his purpose. She considered asking permission to enter the order of nuns, but she knew, even though it was an attractive thought, to find lasting peace and security there with the kind and friendly sisters, that it was not meant to be. She loved the countryside too much, and now she thought longingly of having a place of her own and a man to cook for. First, however, she had a mystery to solve.

In all of her life, she had never traveled more than twenty kilometers from her home. She knew her village and the nearby countryside. To determine her course, she walked through the village, being greeted with sympathy by many who knew her and extending her own condolences to those who had also lost family in the epidemic. At the police station she found the man who had carried her trunk into the village.

"I would like to inquire if you have heard of an establishment called the Chateau du Blanc," she asked.

"Yes. It is not a great distance up the river."

"Could one walk the distance?"

"In half a day, or perhaps a bit more."

"If you would be kind enough to give me directions."

She listened carefully. It sounded simple: merely following the road up the river toward Bordeaux until, before reaching the village of Bègles, a large white house would be seen to the east of the road, near the river. She set out at daybreak, carrying with her a

small lunch packed by the nuns, who were quite concerned with her traveling alone through the countryside, but sympathetic to her stated desire to find employment.

The day was another glorious one, and, as the sun
rose and began to melt away the dew of the night
and birds celebrated the last days of the warm weather
with flittings and glad songs, felt her spirits lifted. She
had not walked more than three kilometers when a
farmer's cart came onto the road behind her and drew
up alongside. The farmer, who reminded her very
much of her father, offered her a ride. He was going
all the way into Bègles and would, he said with self-
conscious politeness, be charmed to have such company. And so Helene found herself riding toward what
would be a new life with coops of chickens on the
cart behind her, the fowl clucking and panting in the
heat of the sun and the old farmer asking her polite
questions and shaking his head in sympathy when she
told him that she had lost both mother and father. He,
too, had been affected by the epidemic: he had lost
his oldest daughter.

She shared her food with the farmer. He knew the
location of the Chateau du Blanc and, before the day
was half gone, pulled the cart to a halt at the entrance
to a side road and pointed down a chestnut-lined avenue to a large white house. He wished her Godspeed
and she thanked him, and, with a feeling of approaching excitement, walked down the rutted road. Workers were in the fields, trying to salvage something from
the ruined harvest. A sturdy woman in heavy clothing, a scarf drawn tightly around her head, was working near the road. She looked up with interest as Helene approached and Helene paused.

The woman was of middle age. They exchanged shy
smiles and Helene spoke first, commenting on the
weather. The woman returned a comment about the
damage done to the grapes.

"I am from the village of Podensac," Helene said. "I am seeking employment."

"These are bad times," the woman said with a shake of her head.

"I understand that the master of the chateau is a Monsieur Simel," Helene said.

"Not for many years," the woman answered. "Monsieur Simel sold the land—oh, let me see—it was the year of the good harvest."

"And is Monsieur Simel still in the area?"

"No, no," the woman said. "I have heard that he went off to help build the canal, the one in Panama. Taking with him his nieces."

"And have you been here for long?" Helene asked.

"I was born nearby," the woman said.

"Then you knew Monsieur Simel."

"Oh, yes. My mother was a member of the household staff."

"I have heard my parents speak of Monsieur Simel," Helene said. "And of someone named Marcie."

"Marcie? Marcie? No there was no one by that name. The niece—the small, dark one—was named Darcie. Perhaps that was the name. In fact," the woman said, looking closely at Helene, "she was much like you—small, dark of skin, very pretty, as you are."

"Thank you."

"Yes, very much like you," the woman said. "And her sister was a beauty, also. But very different, the two. The oldest was small and dark, the youngest a healthy, larger woman with light hair and a happy smile."

"And they are all gone now?"

"Yes, these many years, although I have heard that the younger one—Petra, it was—has returned to France and is living downriver—somewhere near Marmande, I believe."

"You have been very kind, and I thank you,"

Helene said. "There is one more question, if you have the time and the patience."

"I am wasting my time trying to pick these," the woman said, holding a mildewed and runted bunch of grapes disdainfully in her hand.

Helene pulled the brooch out from her clothing and removed it from her neck. Opening it, she extended it toward the woman. "Do you know this lady?"

The woman took the brooch and first turned it, examining the fine workmanship and the gleaming ruby. "It's lovely," she said. Then she looked at the picture. "No, no. But wait. There is a resemblance—something in the face and eyes—to the younger niece, Petra."

"But you think it is not the niece?"

"Oh, no. She would scarcely be this old now. No, the clothing is, I think, quite old."

"Yes. Thank you once again. Could you tell me this Petra's last name?"

"Hummm. It was an English name. Yes, I have it. It was Moncrief."

"English?"

"Of a French mother, sister to Monsieur Simel."

And the picture of the woman in the locket looked quite English. Helene felt a growing excitement. She thanked the woman once again and set out for Podensac, walking the full distance this time and arriving there well after dark, tired and hungry, to be clucked over and fed by the solicitous nuns.

The distance to Marmande was greater than to the Chateau du Blanc, not merely a matter of a day's walk. Helene explained her problem to the nuns and told them that she was seeking a distant relative who might be able to help her find suitable employment. The nuns presented her with a little money and many words of caution. So once again she set out.

The road crossed the river at Langon. She walked to another small village before dark, spent the night in a small hostel, and set out for Marmande the next morning. In Marmande she inquired for the police station, and, having reached it, asked if anyone knew the dwelling of Petra Moncrief. There were negative answers from the man on duty at the station and from two others who came in while Helene was there. In desperation, she said, "The lady is half-English, blond, and, I'm told, quite pretty."

The policeman at the desk fingered his beard. "Yes, there is such a lady. She has only recently returned from abroad to the Chateau D'Art. I know her only as Madame D'Art, but she meets your description."

Chateau D'Art lay but a short distance outside the village, and there was half the afternoon left. Carrying her small bag, Helene set out. Fortunately, the weather was holding, and the walk was pleasant. She found herself, however, slowing her pace as she neared the river—perhaps a bit in dread of what she might discover. But there, ahead, was the chateau. She was walking along a road beside a hedge row, the cloth bag swinging in her hand, her legs making strong strides as she regained her resolution, when she heard the sound of a running horse and quickly looked behind her. There was nothing on the road.

The animal appeared in front of her so suddenly, so unexpectedly, flying over the hedgerow to land not two meters from her. She screamed out and leaped backward. She saw that the rider was a young girl dressed in a handsome riding habit, her blond hair tucked up neatly under the hat. The rider pulled the horse to a halt.

"I'm sorry I frightened you," the rider said, pulling the horse's head up as he pranced excitedly.

"It was a near thing," Helene said. "But it was not your fault. I heard the horse, but could not place the direction from which you were coming. There is no harm done except, perhaps, that I was scared out of my wits for a moment."

"Are you headed for the chateau?"

"I am," Helene said.

"I'm Antonia D'Art," the rider said. "Hop up behind me and I'll give you a ride."

"The horses with which I am familiar pull carts," Helene said with a laugh. "I think I would feel safer walking."

Antonia guided the horse alongside as Helene set out once again.

"Do you know someone here?" Antonia asked.

"No, mademoiselle. I come to seek employment."

"My mother has been talking about taking on a housemaid."

"I am pleased to hear it," Helene said. "Perhaps she will consider me for the position."

"I'll go ahead and tell her you want to see her," Antonia said, kicking the horse into a headlong run, leaving Helene shaking her head in the dust.

It was a lovely place, with neatly kept fields and a pasture in which grazed three horses, a few sheep, and some cows. The barns and outbuildings were pristine in their white paint, and the house, although not so grand as some, had a look of sturdy permanence. Helene approached the front door across a smooth lawn and found the girl, Antonia, there to let her in.

"Mother is on the patio. She will see you."

Helene had never seen such richness as she followed Antonia through the house. The furnishings seemed to be worthy of a palace, the carpeting was rich, with a strange oriental design, the walls hung with drapes and pictures.

Petra was sitting on a lounge in the sun, her bonnet pulled down over her eyes to shade them. She pushed it back when she heard the two girls approaching.

Excitedly, Helene noted that the blond woman, looking so cool, so perfect, so beautiful, resembled the picture in her brooch.

"Madame," Helene said, "thank you for seeing me."

"Antonia says that you seek employment."

"It is true."

"Have you worked elsewhere?" Petra asked, noting the dark prettiness of the girl, the flowing black hair, the dark and slanted eyes, the delicacy of her body even under the concealing peasant dress.

"No, madame, I have not," Helene said. "Except in my own home. However, I am quite good at cleaning and I can cook." She laughed. "I fear that my cooking is limited to very plain dishes. But I am willing, madame, and I would not be afraid to work in the fields, if that should be your wish."

"Tell me about yourself," Petra said, favorably impressed by the girl who did not cower or beg, but simply stated her position in a polite and respectful tone.

"I am from near the village of Podensac. I have only recently lost both father and mother to the epidemic."

"How terrible," Petra said. "You have no home?"

"Unknown to me, my father had borrowed money to buy stock in the Panama Canal. He could not pay the money. They took our home instead."

A flashing thought of Guy and Darcie came into Petra's mind. She felt a flow of sympathy, and, from that moment she was sure that she would take the girl into her household, since she was one of the unfortunates who suffered because of men like Guy.

"As you can see," Petra said, "I am with child. I will need someone to help me with my clothing, my toilet."

"I would gladly do so, madame."

"You would be my personal maid," Petra said. "I will provide you with uniforms."

"That is very kind of you, madame."

"As to salary," and she named a figure which, although small, impressed Helene, who had never had so much money in her life. "When do you wish to begin?"

"At your convenience, madame," Helene said. "I

have only one small problem. My few belongings are with the nuns in Podensac. Perhaps, when I have earned some money, I can send for them."

"We'll take care of that immediately," Petra said. "I will send a man with a cart for your things. In the meantime, Antonia can show you your quarters and you may see if the uniforms there fit. I'd guess they'll be too large, but perhaps we can alter one or two of them until we can have the seamstress make fresh ones for you."

"I am overwhelmed by your kindness," Helene said.

"And I'm sure you're hungry after your walk. Tell the cook to provide you with a snack."

"Yes, madame."

"One more thing," Petra said, with a smile. "It would be helpful to know your name."

"Helene, madame. Helene Freneau."

"Yes, well, thank you, Helene. Be off with you now and get settled in."

She watched the two girls leave, of a size, both small and delicate, one dark, the other blond, and something stirred in her. The beauty of the girl seemed to be unusual for a peasant girl. She was almost gypsy —so dark, the eyes so exotic. And she moved with a grace which reminded Petra of Darcie.

Helene could not give herself any reason why she did not immediately present the brooch and ask Madame D'Art what it meant, if anything. Something told her to bide her time, as she followed the lively Antonia to a pleasant room. As she tried on uniforms, which were too large, Antonia slouched down on the bed, still in her riding habit.

"Helene," Antonia asked, "how did you happen to come to us?"

"I first looked near my home," Helene said. "I was told at the Chateau du Blanc that perhaps help was needed here."

"That was once my great-uncle's chateau," Antonia said.

"Monsieur Simel?"

"Yes, do you know him?"

"Only that he once owned the Chateau du Blanc."

"He's my mother's uncle. He's in America, or somewhere. He was in Panama with my mother and my Aunt Darcie. We haven't seen them in years."

Helene was trying to pin the uniform around her, but it was far too large.

"That's terrible," Antonia said. "Look, I'll tell mother that you'll just have to wear your own clothes until the new uniforms are made."

"Yes, I suppose so."

"In fact," Antonia said. "We look to be about the same size. Since you have so little with you, I'm going to give you a nice dress so that you'll look neat. Not that you don't look fine in your own dress," she added quickly.

"Oh, I couldn't take your clothing," Helene protested.

"Nonsense! I have more than I'll ever wear. Come along." Antonia led the way to her room, where, after diligently searching through her large and varied wardrobe, she placed three simple frocks on the bed. "Try those," she ordered.

"Mademoiselle Antonia, I am very grateful, but may I first retire to my room? I have traveled all day, and I would not want to soil such beautiful dresses with the dust of the road."

"Oh, of course," Antonia said. "Run along, then."

But as Helene started out the door, the dresses folded carefully over her arm, Antonia stopped her. "I'm sure you'll need these," she said, thrusting underthings into Helen's arms. "And some decent shoes. What size?"

Helene told her.

"My size exactly." She rummaged in a wardrobe and came up with two pairs of shoes. "These with the blue and these with the browns," she commanded. Helene nodded.

"You are so kind," Helene said, feeling tears.

"Look, if you're going to get sentimental about a couple of dresses, go to your room to weep," Antonia said, but there was no sting in her words, which were delivered with a glad smile.

In her room, Helene bathed and tried the dresses one by one. She had never had anything so fine, so different from the heavy materials of all of her clothing. They seemed light and airy and so comfortable. In joy, she whirled in front of a mirror. The underthings given to her by Antonia were a perfect fit. She felt naughty, for they were much more brief than the underthings to which she was accustomed.

She chose the blue dress, and, as an afterthought, placed the brooch outside the dress, where it rested between her protruding young breasts. It was difficult to tear herself away from the mirror, because, in the fine dress, she was no longer a peasant gypsy, but a fine lady. It was, she felt, rather amazing.

"I would wager," she thought, "that if a stranger saw Antonia and me together, they would think we were both ladies of quality."

But such thoughts did not make her heady. She knew her station, and, regardless of the outcome, was quite grateful to have a place to stay and a job which would pay her so much money. After one last, fond look at her image in the mirror, she decided that she was rather hungry and went from her quarters across the hall into the kitchen, where a large and motherly woman was elbow-deep in making fresh bread.

"Madame," Helene said, "I was told that I might ask you for a snack."

"And are you the new maid?" the cook asked, unbelieving.

"Yes, madame. I am sorry to bother you. I can come when you are less occupied."

"No bother. If you'll help yourself." She sighed. "What is the world coming to when a housemaid dresses like the mistress?"

Helene laughed. "Mademoiselle Antonia merely gave me a dress to wear until my things arrive."

"I must say it looks well on you," the cook said. "There's a bit of ham in the cupboard, and some sweetbreads. Mind you, don't eat too much, or you'll spoil your dinner. One thing about this place: we eat well."

"Thank you, madame."

"Madame D'Art is called 'madame' here," the cook said. "You may call me Marie."

"That was my mother's name," Helene said.

"Or just 'cook.' I'll answer to either."

"And I would be pleased if you would call me Helene."

"Well, Helene, welcome to Chateau D'Art. It isn't bad. The young girl is a hellion, but pleasant. The mistress is quite considerate. Do your work and mind your manners and you'll find it a pleasant life."

"It's a beautiful place."

"You get used to it. I've been here longer than I like to remember. I was here when the dead master's father was alive, which tells you how old I am."

"You are not over thirty-five," Helene said, placing ham and sweetbreads on a plate.

"Oh, a sweet-talking one," the cook said, with a smile. "Eat your food and be off with you. I have bread to bake."

Now Helene walked tentatively into the parlor through room after room furnished in lovely antique style, the house so rich it took her breath away. Even the walls and ceilings were decorated with lovely gilded intricate swirls. Afraid to touch anything, she walked with her hands behind her back, careful not to let her skirt brush anything, to examine decorative vases of such exquisite design that she wanted to weep for the beauty of them. She did not venture up the stairs. They wound up in a circular shape, the wood of the uprights and rails a deeply polished walnut, the carving lovely. She gasped when she walked into a room which was huge, had a smooth marble floor and wide windows on three sides. It must be a ballroom, although she had never seen one, only pictures.

"Finding your way around?" Antonia asked, having come down the stairs to see Helen in the ballroom. Antonia had changed into a simple dinner dress. Helene thought she was one of the most beautiful girls she'd ever seen.

"I am in total awe," Helene said. "I am quite unaccustomed to such luxury."

"Oh, this is nothing compared to some places," Antonia said offhandedly. "I must say the dress fits you well."

"It's so lovely," Helene said. "I can't thank you enough."

"If I had known it would look so well on you, I might not have given it to you," Antonia said. "I'm supposed to be the young beauty around here."

"You will have no competition from me," Helene said, "for you are quite beautiful."

"Yes, you're going to do," Antonia laughed. "Now, let's go to mother and show her how I've changed the plain brown thrush into a sparkling bluebird."

Petra was still sitting on the sunlit patio, letting her body drink in the lovely day and the cooling of the air as evening approached. She was facing west, and to keep the glare from her eyes, had once again pulled her bonnet down over them. She had her legs stretched out gracefully on the lounge, the shape of the life she carried making a mound of her stomach.

"Mother," Antonia said, as she led Helen across the tiled patio floor, "look what we have here."

Smiling, always pleased to have her daughter come

to her, Petra pushed back her bonnet and turned her head to see.

Helene had pulled her hair up neatly, exposing a slender and splendidly smooth neck. She was smiling—white teeth a contrast to her dusky skin. At first Petra could not believe her eyes. Her heart leaped frighteningly and she sat upright.

"What's wrong?" Antonia asked.

No, it was not Darcie. She could see that now. But why hadn't she seen the resemblance before? But then the girl's hair had been down and she'd been dressed in a colorless, muffling peasant gown.

"See what I've done?" Antonia asked, pushing a shyly smiling Helene forward. Petra stared in amazement.

"Did someone send you here, child?" she asked.

"Madame, I was told you might need help," Helene said, a bit frightened by the look on Petra's face.

"Who are you?"

"Please, madame, I am Helene Freneau, of the village of Podensac."

"Come here," Petra ordered, her voice strained. And when Helene hesitated, looking toward a puzzled Antonia, "Come, I say. Come close." For she had seen something which brought back memories.

"If I have offended you, madame, by wearing your daughter's lovely gown—"

"I said come here," Petra said sternly. She swung her legs to the side of the couch and sat up. As Helene approached uneasily, Petra put out her hand and grasped the brooch. "Where did you get this?" she demanded.

"It is mine, madame," Helene said defiantly, reaching down to dislodge Petra's hand with gentle firmness.

"Yes, of course," Petra said.

Lyris, on her deathbed, had said something about her mother's brooch. At the time, Petra had tried to remember where it had gone, but the last time she

remembered seeing it was in Cairo, on the day of Darcie's rape, when the dwarf, Hassam Ari, had tried to
steal it.

"Of course it's yours. May I see it, please?" she said.

Doubtfully Helene removed it and held it in her
hand. "It is mine, madame. I did not steal it. It came
to me from my dead mother."

A name. Lyris had mentioned a name in association
with her mother's brooch.

"Please," Petra said. "I will return it."

She looked at the locket musingly; then with trembling fingers, she opened it. The smiling face of her
mother caused her to pale. Seeing the girl's agitation,
she closed the brooch and handed it back.

"Now you must tell me, Helene, how you came to
me."

"First, madame, may I ask you a question?"

"You may."

"The brooch seems to mean something to you—am
I right?"

"Perhaps."

"Perhaps you know the woman whose picture is
inside?"

"Perhaps." Petra smiled. "You see, I am reserving
my answers until I hear what caused you to seek me
out."

"As my mother lay dying, she gave me the brooch,"
Helene said. "And she made me promise to go to the
Chateau du Blanc. She mentioned the name of Monsieur Simel and the name of a lady, which I took to
be Marcie."

"Darcie," Petra said. "Your age, Helene?" And
when Helene told her, she counted on her fingers, then
gazed at the setting sun for a moment. "You know
nothing else?"

"Only that I was mystified, madame, and quite concerned, for I loved my mother and my father. I am

here because I was astounded when my dying mother told me that she was not my true mother."

"And the brooch?"

"I had never seen it until the night of my mother's death. Then she gave it to me."

"Your father, Freneau, he was a farmer near the village of Podensac?"

"Yes, madame. He was a good man." She placed the brooch back around her neck. "And now, madame, will you speak?"

"The woman in the picture is my mother," Petra said, "and of course, the mother of my sister Darcie."

Helene felt faint. She backed off a few paces and sat down in a metal chair. "And you, madame," she asked weakly, "are you—" She could not bring herself to say the words.

"No, my dear," Petra said. "Not I. My sister Darcie had a child which was put out to adoption with a farm couple along the Garonne River. I think it is quite likely that you are Darcie's daughter, and my niece."

"That's wonderful," Antonia laughed gaily. "Just like a book. Helene, that would make you my cousin." She turned to her mother. *"Maman,* we can't have family working as a maid."

"Indeed we can't," Petra said. Then, with a great upwelling of sympathy, for Helene's face was twisted with emotion, she rose and pulled the girl to her feet. "There can be no mistake. You are too like her. Oh, my child, you are welcome in our home."

The kindness, the sweet, clean smell of Petra, the soft arms around her loosed the dikes of Helene's emotions and she wept.

"A ready-made older sister," Antonia cried, putting her arms, too, around Helene. "I thought you were too beautiful to be some little peasant girl."

"But that's what I am," Helene sobbed. "That's what I am."

"Well, we'll fix that," Antonia said. "Wait until the boys of the village see us together. *Mon Dieu,* their eyes will pop from their heads!"

It was too much for Helene. Helpless, awed by the sudden revelations, she fainted, and it took both Antonia and Petra to ease her onto the couch. When she had recovered, Petra said, "We have so much to talk about. Do you feel better?"

"Yes, thank you."

"Did you grow up on a farm?" Antonia asked.

"Yes."

"How about beaux?" Antonia asked with a gay laugh.

"Oh, Antonia, be serious," Petra said. "Helene has had a great shock, and, I must admit, so have I."

The cook had appeared in the doorway to announce that the evening meal was ready. With just the two of them on the farm, Petra and Antonia preferred an early dinner, early bedtime, and early rising. Antonia wanted to have as much of the day as possible at her disposal.

Petra wiped away tears with her handkerchief. "Come now," she said, "we will have a peaceful dinner and get to know each other. You must have a thousand questions, my dear."

"How about beaux?" Antonia asked, with an impish grin.

"A few," Helene said, trying to speak without sobbing.

"Antonia, please!" Petra sighed, but she could not help smiling.

10

FOR HELENE, THE NEXT FEW DAYS
were like a dream. She could not believe that, in one
sudden moment of shock, she had ceased to be simple
Helene Freneau and had become, what? She was in
danger of losing her identity, for from the first she saw
that she was not prepared to become—immediately—
the niece of a rich woman—even so kind a rich woman
as Petra. At that first dinner, there were more imple-
ments around her plate than on the entire table in the
home of her youth, and the food was of such bewildering plenty and variety that she did not know what to
eat first. In her excitement, she managed only a few
bites. She had a burning curiosity about her real
mother, but hesitated to ask until Petra brought up
the subject.

"I suppose," Petra said, as the meal was being concluded, "you'd like to know a bit about your mother."

"Yes, please, madame," Helene said.

"First, you must call me Petra, or, if you like, Aunt
Petra. Perhaps the last will be uncomfortable for you,
and it is not necessary."

"Thank you," she swallowed and came out with it. "Aunt Petra."

"Your mother—my sister Darcie—looked much like you, perhaps not quite so dark. But her eyes are much like yours, her lips. She is about your size. She's quite a beautiful woman."

"Where is she now?"

"When last I heard, she was in America. You might as well know early, Helene, that there is bad blood between me and my sister. It has nothing to do with you and will not have any effect on my affection for you."

"I'm sorry," Helene said.

"And so am I," Petra said, "but that's all in the past. I must warn you, also, that there are inevitably some rather unpleasant aspects to your situation, my dear Helene. I hope, when you hear about them, that you will not blame yourself in any way."

In fact, since learning that she was not the daughter of Marie Freneau, Helene had come to think that she was perhaps a harvest baby, born of a moment of passion.

"Your mother was only sixteen when you were born," Petra said. "She was, of course, unmarried. Although it pained her"—a kind little lie would not hurt —"it was decided to adopt you out."

"I'm not sorry," Helene said. "I truly loved my parents."

"I'm happy," Petra said.

"I think I can understand," Helene said. "I won't hate my true mother for it."

"A very good attitude," Petra said.

"I haven't seen Aunt Darcie in years," Antonia said, "but she was very beautiful."

"Who was my father?" Helene asked.

Petra bought some time by drinking wine, looking over the rim of the glass, wondering if it were wise to tell all so quickly. But Helene seemed to be a solid, sensible girl.

"That is one of the unpleasant things," she said. "My sister was the victim of rape."

"How terrible," Helene said. "When she was so young."

"I think it's sort of romantic," Antonia said. "Being raped by an Egyptian sheik."

"You weren't there," Petra said. "It was not romantic. It was brutal." She smiled. "But we can see, now, that even in such things, which seem tragic at the time, there can be good. For if it had not happened, our beautiful Helene would not be here with us."

"How did it happen?" Helene asked.

"My father took us to Egypt for the opening of the Suez Canal," Petra began, and then, as kindly as possible, she told the story.

"A dwarf?" Helene gasped. "Oh, my God." She was thinking of her children—the grandchildren which would come too late for her mother to spoil and pet.

"I know what you're thinking," Petra said, "but you can ease your mind. Such things aren't necessarily hereditary. In most cases, dwarfism is a glandular disorder, and the defect is not passed down to the offspring. As in your case. You're perfectly normal."

"I am small," Helene said.

"As is your mother. And my Antonia."

"Was it so horrible?" Helene asked, trying to envision the scene, so far away, a young girl being ravished in an exotic land.

"It has affected Darcie," Petra said. "She has never been the same since. She has, I'm afraid, not been the perfect lady all of her life, Helene, and as you move about in your new world, you may hear things said about her."

"Poor lady," Helene said.

"Yes, I agree. She has never married. In fact—and this is one of our family skeletons—she has lived with our uncle, Guy Simel, for years."

"Well, they say incest is best," Antonia laughed.

"Really, Antonia!" Petra said harshly.

"Sorry, *maman*. I forget how easily shocked you are," Antonia said, not without venom.

For Petra, the sudden appearance of her long-lost niece was a joy. The girl was so sweet that she rapidly became a valued member of the family. She was always curious and she spent long hours with Petra listening to tales of life in England as a child, the trip to Egypt, the years in Panama.

As for Antonia, she welcomed the presence of a pretty girl who could be her friend, and if she was a bit disappointed to find that Helene was quite a prude, that, too, worked to her advantage. With her mother's attentions so much on Helene, Antonia was free to roam as she pleased. Young Jacques benefited as did three other young men who lived nearby, and Antonia benefited by multiples of four, for she was discovering the true joys of sensuality. Although she did not let it dominate her life, being interested in too many other things, she did raise or remove her pretty skirts quite often and with impunity, since nature did not punish her by giving her a child. In fact, she had come to the conclusion that she was barren, and now did not even insist on the primitive method of birth control in which the boy—or young man—removed himself just before the crucial moment.

Helene, always a quick learner, began to pick up the niceties of gracious living. As the summer ended and Petra began to grow heavy, Helene was her constant companion.

"Helene, you do too much for me," Petra would say. "You are not a servant. Have one of the help do the heavy work, for if you persist, I shall have to hire a personal maid and exile you from my rooms."

"Please," Helene said. "It makes me feel useful, and I enjoy doing for you. It is the only way of showing my gratitude, and I would be bored if I didn't have some work to do."

Nor was Helene jealous of her times and energies when it came to fulfilling a request from Antonia to help in the mending of a favorite riding habit or to prepare Antonia's hair for her Sunday visits to the village.

It pleased Petra that Helene was so conscientious about her churchgoing, although Petra herself had long since ceased regular attendance. It would have pleased her less had she known that Antonia was a faithful churchgoer not out of piety but interest in the tall and handsome son of the town's magistrate. He was a lad of strong physique, clear blue eyes and flaxen hair which might have indicated a contact between some distant female ancestor and a Teutonic invader, and his clear voice was an important part of the small choir which sang at the services. In his clean white smock he was, to Antonia, the ideal of young manhood.

Since she was not yet of an age to be allowed to attend social occasions alone, Antonia's experience had been confined to the rustic lads of the chateau and the surrounding area. Her lusty little heart yearned to discover if more could be offered by an educated, handsome, aristocratic-looking youth with clear blue eyes.

Jean-Charles de Choiseul knew that the pretty young girl from Chateau D'Art had eyes for him. Girls had always been interested in him—he took that to be his right. Descended from a long line of aristocrats, one of his ancestors having been a noteworthy statesman of the eighteenth century, Jean-Charles was destined for the finest of the world's engineering schools, the École Polytechnique. Everyone expected a bright future for him.

To date, Antonia had discovered no reason to speak to the handsome young man. She had to be content with watching his every move as he sang the inspiring old songs, his eyes lifted toward the ornate ceiling of the church. But she determined to remedy the situation. After the services were completed, she dawdled until, having taken off his choir robe, young Jean-Charles came down the center aisle in company with other choir members. Antonia stepped out of her pew directly in front of them, as if she had not seen them, and Jean-Charles, leading the way, had to come to a halt.

"Excuse me," he said, raising a well-shaped eyebrow at one of his companions.

"The fault was mine," Antonia said. "I was lost in thought. But it does give me an opportunity to say how much I enjoyed the choir today. You do sing beautifully." She said it as if it meant the entire choir, but with her eyes on Jean-Charles's face the intent was clear.

"You are most kind, mademoiselle," Jean-Charles said.

"Since my family is new to the area," Antonia said, "I have no one to make introductions for me, so I must introduce myself. I am Antonia D'Art."

Jean-Charles bowed and introduced his companions. "We are pleased to welcome you to Marmande, mademoiselle," he said.

"I was very impressed by the way the bass section handled the chorus on the last hymn," Antonia said. "However, I wonder if it would not be more harmonic if"—and she went on to hum a variation of the bass part, keeping time with her delicate hand.

"We must be off, Jean," one of his companions said. And both expressed the conventional pleasure at having met Antonia, both impressed but knowing, from the way the girl looked at Jean-Charles, that it would do no good to linger.

"Yes," Jean-Charles said, humming along with Antonia. "I shall point it out to our choirmaster. In fact, Mademoiselle D'Art, with your knowledge of music, it would be pleasant if you should join us in the choir."

"Oh, I'm afraid that wouldn't do at all," Antonia laughed. "My voice sounds like a creaking door. I fear that my talent, such as it is, is confined to the piano."

"I should like to hear you play sometime," Jean-Charles said politely. She seemed so young, but there was a certain maturity—and more—in her eyes.

"It would please me greatly if you should call on us," Antonia said. "My mother is eager to meet the worthy people of Marmande, since she plans to make this our permanent home."

"My pleasure," Jean-Charles said, intrigued by the tilt of her saucy young breasts.

"Tea this afternoon?" Antonia asked.

"You observe the English custom?"

"My mother was reared in England," Antonia said. "I fear that we're helpless victims of the tradition."

"I find it," Jean-Charles said, trying out his poor and heavily accented English, "quite—" He had to pause, searching for the word.

"Archaic or charming," Antonia laughed. "Either word will do."

Musingly, Jean-Charles considered. He was not prepared for entanglements, for he had his future ahead of him. However, this pretty, blond, and somewhat forward girl intrigued him.

"I accept with pleasure," he said.

Antonia informed her mother that there would be company for tea. She dressed in a fine pink gown with a neckline as low as her mother allowed. Jean-Charles arrived on a fine Arabian, left the horse with the stableman, and appeared at the door, tall, his hair windblown from his ride. As he brushed it back with one hand, he was, to Antonia, the prettiest man she'd ever seen.

Since the weather had turned, Petra had foregone the pleasant habit of having tea on the patio. It was served in a pleasant room tastefully filled with delicate furniture which made Jean-Charles feel slightly awkward and uncomfortable. He perched on a frail-looking chair as Petra served. He was lifting his small and dainty cup to his lips when Helene entered the room.

"Sorry to be late," she said, then saw that there was a stranger present, and fell silent.

Helene was wearing a white dress with a small, dark shawl thrown over her shoulders against the chill. Her gypsy-black hair was gathered loosely into a mass about her head, exposing her graceful neck and soft throat. Jean-Charles halted the progress of the cup toward his lips, frozen by a vision of loveliness out of his most pleasurable dream.

Unaware of the impact that the first sight of Helene was having on Jean-Charles, Antonia introduced Helene as her cousin. Jean-Charles leaped to his feet, almost spilling his tea. For a moment he was struck dumb, then he regained his tongue and expressed his pleasure.

"Madame D'Art," he said, feeling quite sophisticated, lifted out of himself, somehow, by the presence of the dark and beautiful girl, "I am the most fortunate of men, to be surrounded by three such beautiful ladies."

"How sweet of you," Petra said. "Have you lived in Marmande long?"

"All my life," he said. "But somehow the area has never seemed so attractive to me as it does now."

Antonia smiled, thinking that his flowery talk was aimed at her, but Petra, seeing the direction of his glances, allowed herself a slight frown of misgiving, hidden by the teacup.

"I think we shall like it, too," Antonia said. "It's much more pleasant, climate and everything, than Panama."

"Panama?" Jean-Charles's eyes flashed interest.

"My husband was a physician working in Panama," Petra said. "In fact, Antonia spent all of her early years there."

Antonia's hopes of getting Jean-Charles out of the house for a ride or a walk vanished in his interest in the failed canal project as he asked eager questions and listened politely to Petra's answers. But he could not

keep his eyes off Helene and, after a long discussion
of the reasons for the failure, asked Helene, "And
Mademoiselle Freneau, have you been in Panama?"

"Oh, dear, no," Helene laughed. "My presence here
in my aunt's house represents my greatest journey away
from my native village."

"Jean-Charles," Antonia said, not being able to
stand being closed out of the conversation any longer,
"it's such a lovely day, shall we ride before the coolness of the evening?"

"Perhaps Helene would join us?" Jean-Charles
suggested, looking at Helene with an open smile and
his admiration etched into his blue eyes.

"The horses with which I am familiar pull farm
carts," Helene said.

Antonia made a face. At least the girl could come
up with a new phrase to use when admitting that she
did not ride!

Jean-Charles reluctantly left the parlor and joined
Antonia. They rode side by side, Antonia trying to
make conversation, but it was evident to her that his
thoughts were elsewhere.

"Your cousin," Jean-Charles asked, after it became
evident that he was not interested in small talk, "is she
spoken for?"

Antonia sighed. Strangely, she felt no animosity
toward Helene. She had noticed, during the last part of
the conversations in the parlor, that Jean-Charles's
eyes were always on her cousin. It was not, however,
Helene's fault. *Men!* she thought, as she answered.
"No."

She led the way to a secluded spot by the river and
dismounted. Jean-Charles followed suit and followed
her to stand overlooking the quiet water. There was a
chill in the air which spoke of the coming winter. She
shivered.

"Perhaps we should return to the house," Jean-
Charles said. "You're cold."

"Then warm me," Antonia said, moving to press against him.

Uncomfortably, Jean-Charles looked around. They were hidden from view by the riverside growth and a low rise between them and the chateau.

"With pleasure," he said, putting his arms around her to pull her close. He had to bend to reach her lips. Her kiss was a surprise to him—not the sweet, innocent kiss of a young girl but the deep, wet reachings of a passionate woman. There was a sweet scent coming from her hair, and the feel of her small body against his roused the passions which always sleep lightly in the young. She made no protest as he deepened the kiss and let his hands explore the small of her back and the outflow of her sweet little rump. When, at last, he broke the kiss, with a deep sigh, his masculinity pushing against her, she pressing hard to feel it, she laughed.

"I am not spoken for, either," she said.

For a moment he remembered the dark beauty, the slanted eyes of Helene, but Antonia was in his arms. He lifted her, her toes almost clearing the ground, to press his hardness just under the hard mound of her mons. His need was so great that his arms trembled.

11

THE AMERICAN MILLIONAIRE, An-
drew Carnegie, called the latter half of the nineteenth
century the era of the "philosophy of Grab and Hold."
In the industrialized countries, great fortunes were
being made and the "robber barons" of industry, as
they were to be called by later generations, vied with
each other in an effort to display their riches. In the
United States, the latter part of the century saw the
building of huge pleasure palaces, often in the poorest
of taste, and workers who labored for just enough
money to continue their substandard existence were
treated to newspaper accounts of gala parties at palatial
homes at which the very rich lit their cigars with hun-
dred-dollar bills.

The Panama Scandal in France had its counterparts,
on less spectacular scales, perhaps, in all of the industrial countries.

Since the beginning of oral history, the morality of
power had been in doubt, but the last half of the nineteenth century saw an era in which public morality was
at what some felt to be an all-time low. Materialism
was the motto. Self-service was the aim of all, from

the common man to the most exalted. During the Grant administration, which began when Ferdinand de Lesseps's grand Suez waterway was first being used by the ships of the world, graft was widespread. An entire Congress tried to make a raid on the U.S. Treasury by voting themselves a retroactive pay raise. General Benjamin Butler, a man who had risen to the rank of major general in command of the Union Army—called "Beast" Butler by the South—used his influence as a member of the House of Representatives to pay $100,000 to a cohort. The Whisky Ring successfully bribed treasury officials and defrauded the government of millions. Grant's private secretary was involved in the affair, and his Secretary of War was impeached for accepting bribes from an Indian agent.

It was an age of colorful scoundrels. With information from Grant's brother-in-law, Jay Gould and James Fisk narrowly missed cornering the gold market, bringing on the crash of '69, on Black Friday. Perhaps a diligent historian could find evidence of an honest man in office during those years, but even the honest politician would have been found to hold strange notions of morality. Boss William Tweed and his men, such as "Slippery Dick" Connolly, defrauded the taxpayers of New York of amounts estimated from $45 million to $200 million. Railroad magnates rode roughshod over the rights of the public.

It was the age of the con man, the swindler, the bank robber. The age of *laissez-faire* and let the buyer beware. It was also the age which saw the press come of age as a member of the power structure. The time of the muckraker began shortly after the American Civil War with the cartoons by Thomas Nast attacking Boss Tweed and the Tammany Hall Ring and was definitely established when George Jones, editor of *The New York Times,* turned down a bribe of five million dollars from Tweed and published information which brought Tweed down. Henry Demarest Lloyd

made literary history with the publication of *Wealth
Against Commonwealth,* a carefully documented ex-
posé of the corrupt practices of the Standard Oil Company.

Theodore Roosevelt contemptuously called the muckrakers the creators of "the literature of discontent,"
but did not halt exposés of the insurance industry, high
finance, city vice, filthy and inhumane practices in the
meatpacking industry.

And some of the muckrakers immediately began to
attack the dapper and egocentric Frenchman, Philippe
Bunau-Varilla, when, after the rather strange organization of the *Compagnie Nouvelle*—the new canal
company—Bunau-Varilla, seemingly possessed of unlimited amounts of money, began his effort to sell the
French failure in Panama to the Americans.

However, not even the muckraking American jour-
nalists were ever to guess that the idea of the *Compagnie Nouvelle* came not from Bunea-Varilla or even
from France, but from the plush office of one of the
"Grand Dukes of Fifth Avenue," the *crème de la crème*
of the American Jewish financial elite, in New York
City. Truly, the story would have been sensational; it
involved the head of a large and rich American firm
and a beautiful half-French half-English woman who,
unknown to the son who had inherited the firm, had
known his late father quite well.

Darcie Moncrief saw New York first as a young lady
when she and her uncle, Guy Simel, accompanied de
Lesseps there on his futile and expensive effort to interest American capital in his Panama venture. There
de Lesseps approached Caspar Schumann, head of a
great financial empire. At first, the elder Schumann was
openly contemptuous of de Lesseps's plan for a Panama
route, feeling, like most Americans, that Nicaragua was
the best choice for an interocean canal. De Lesseps
was never to know that application of a warm and soft
poultice to the aging Schumann's body was to have as

much influence on the final decision of Schumann as
the quite substantial amount of money de Lesseps paid
to the Schumann firm. Old Caspar Schumann was a
hard man, but the poultice was soft and in the form
of a young and eager body attached to the most beautiful face he'd ever kissed. After a heated night in his
penthouse with Darcie, Schumann pocketed de Lesseps's money and agreed to use his influence to encourage American investment.

Rarely was so much paid for so little, for practically
no American money was lost in the French failure—
partially because the Schumann firm did nothing to
encourage investment and mostly due to the Americans'
sense of cynicism. The average American saw Panama
from the beginning as a scheme to feather the pockets
of a few, and that cynicism burned even brighter when,
once again, a soft and living poultice was applied to
another Schumann body, money was exchanged, and
the grand new idea was born.

However, quite a few years had passed between
Darcie's seduction of father and son, and the living
poultice, although still in an attractive and mature
package, was no longer quite so lithe and young and
the younger Schumann had to be content with having
a portion of the package hidden from his avid eyes by
a filmy and very sensuous garment which left the stra-
tegic portions of Darcie's body open for admiration
but covered the not-completely-smooth scars under arm
and on thigh.

And, in those intervening years, Darcie's mentor,
her Uncle Guy, had gained valuable experience.

Guy was desperate. Everything he owned was tied
up in founders' shares of the canal company, and, after
the bankruptcy of 1889, they were worthless. History
did not record that it was Guy Simel—and not Philippe
Bunau-Varilla—who first conceived of the plan to interest the Americans in buying the assets of the old
company. To get a foothold, Guy resorted to a varia-

tion of the old badger game. He appeared in Stewart
Schumann's office, Darcie at his side, and introduced
himself as an associate of de Lesseps and an old friend
of Stewart's father, Caspar.

The financier was not in the slightest bit interested
in another ragged Frenchman who had lost shirt and
pants in Panama, but his eye took pleasure in Darcie's
smile. It was not difficult at all for her to arrange for
the American to take her to dinner and even less difficult to lure him into the suite she and Guy had taken
in a fine hotel.

Uncomfortable in a closet, Guy was impatient as
Darcie played coy. "Get on with it," he kept saying as
Darcie teased and ran and urged champagne on Schumann. But Darcie knew what she was doing, for by
the time she had Schumann primed, undressed, panting
for her, he was also past the state of hearing the door
open and the click of Guy's new Premo Sr. Camera
with its fine black leather trim and mahogany frame,
its rack-and-pinion movement for focusing and the
lenses which could gather enough light from the lamps,
which Darcie insisted on having lit, to capture Stewart
Schumann in a variety of compromising poses. Finished, he winked at Darcie over Schumann's heaving
shoulders as the man paid tribute to a lower portion
of Darcie's anatomy with eager tongue. Then he quietly
slipped out the door to have the film processed and
to present it, next day, to an astonished Schumann.

"How much, damn you?" Schumann asked, his bristly moustache quivering.

"Not one penny, sir," Guy said with a disarming
smile.

Darcie had not entered the office with Guy, but she
came in as Schumann looked in puzzlement at the
Frenchman.

"How dare you show your face here?" Schumann
asked Darcie.

"We have business to discuss," Darcie said.

"Ah," Schumann said. "Now we get to it, eh? I warn you in advance. Money I will give you. You leave me no choice, but otherwise—"

"I'm going to say something rather bluntly," Guy said. "Your father cheated us, Mr. Schumann."

"You bounder!" Schumann roared. "You dare attack the memory of my dead father?"

"We paid your father good money to do a job," Guy said. "He didn't do it and he made no effort to do it."

"I don't have to listen—"

"Oh, but you do," Darcie said, waving the photographs.

"I will listen," Schumann said sullenly.

"Your firm was to influence American public opinion," Guy said, "to convince American investors that Panama was a good buy. You did nothing. With a few million in American money, we could have finished the job."

"You're a fool," Schumann said. "De Lesseps was a fool. The job was impossible from the beginning."

"I was there," Guy said. "I say it could be done and can still be done." He sat on the desk and Schumann leaned away from him in disgust. "Now here's what you're going to do. You're going to put every resource this firm has behind an effort to convince the American government that Panama is the proper route for a canald and that it would be a good policy to buy the concession, the equipment, and the work done from the French."

"Impossible," Schumann said. "No American would work there. The fever—"

"I don't care how you do it, I just want you to do it," Guy said. "And I will not accept failure. I will accept no excuse. If you yourself have to start the ball rolling, just take time to estimate how much these pictures are worth to you."

Although he had inherited his position, Schumann was no fool. He could not have survived in the dog-eat-dog world of finance if he had been. "I think I see," he said. "Your main concern is getting your own investments back, is that not correct?"

Guy smiled. "I knew you were an intelligent man, Mr. Schumann."

"Perhaps there is another way," Schumann said. "How much did you sink into the venture?"

"Enough," Guy said. "But you see, Mr. Schumann, I'm greedy. I don't want just what I put into the venture, I want a profit—a large profit—and that requires the canal to be built in Panama."

"The idea of influencing the American government is impossible," Schumann said. "They would never enter into negotiations with men who are being prosecuted by the French government. There will have to be another way."

"You're a man of experience," Darcie said. "Perhaps you can suggest another way."

Schumann tapped a neatly manicured fingernail on a gold tooth. "Do you have access to the liquidator of the company?"

"He is—how shall I say?—on our side."

"Good, good," Schumann said. "It is my understanding that the blame for the failure is still largely unplaced."

"Yes."

"Could, under any conditions, the contractors involved be blamed for any of it?"

"Humm," Guy said. "Perhaps. Most of them failed to live up to their agreements."

"Perhaps, and it's only a wild chance, the American government would consider buying the French holdings from a new company—a company made up of men with clean noses, so to speak."

"Interesting," Guy said.

"Yes, it would be possible," Schumann said, the larceny in his soul excited. "A bit of pressure—"

"Excuse me," Guy said. "I have a poor mind for

finance." He smiled. "On the other hand, Mademoiselle Moncrief is excellent in that field and, ah, in others. Perhaps you would like to discuss your plan with her over dinner and—" He left the sentence unfinished, knowing the value of the carrot-and-stick technique and having successfully applied the stick.

"With or without a camera present?" Schumann asked rather bitterly.

"This time, monsieur, we will check the closets first," Darcie said.

As it turned out, Schumann's impatience had them in the suite before dinner. The most important things concluded to mutual satisfaction, Schumann being a robust and healthy man, they lay side by side and Schumann outlined the plan. Then dinner was served in the suite, there was an encore performance of more important things, and Schumann, preparing for it, tried to remove Darcie's garment.

"Please," he said, "you are so beautiful. I want to see all of you."

"No, leave it alone," she said, clutching the garment, but he had pulled it down enough to see the ridges of keloid tissue which had built up over the scars under her arm.

"Oh, my dear," he said. "You've been burned." He put out his hand to touch the scars and she jerked away. "Please," he said. "I know something of this. I had a son who was badly burned."

"There's nothing to be done," Darcie said.

"But you're wrong. Please let me see. The medical profession have made great strides in correcting the disfigurement caused by burns."

He would not take no for an answer. Darcie submitted and allowed him to remove the garment. The area under her arm, extending downward to the curve of her breast, was a mass of ridged flesh. And on her thigh there was an area of chronic ulceration, caused by an inadequate blood supply to the damaged tissue.

"Do you understand why I didn't want you to see it?" she asked. "It's quite ugly."

"Oh, my poor lady!" he said, touching the scars gently. "How did it happen?"

"An accident," Darcie said, not wanting to discuss it, wanting to hold her hatred of Petra close to her, as if by talking about it the emotion would be diminished.

"A body of such perfection must not be marred," Schumann said. "There is a top man here, in this very city. He did the work on my son. It was marvelous the way he covered the burn scars. I'm sure he can help you."

Darcie refused to allow her hopes to soar. She shrugged.

"Will you see him? I'll call him first thing tomorrow morning."

"There are other considerations," Darcie said. "We must go back to France and—" She paused.

"Is it a matter of money?"

"I, too, invested everything with de Lesseps," Darcie said.

Schumann imagined having this beauty for himself, of keeping her in New York indefinitely while the operations were being performed. "Don't worry about the money."

Tenderly, he applied his lips to the keloid scars under her arm. "Yes, yes," he whispered. "This perfection must not be marred."

Armed with the Schumann plan, Guy went back to France. Darcie stayed, and was moved into a small but plush apartment kept by Schumann for just such purposes.

The doctor who had done plastic surgery on Schumann's son talked to her of the techniques developed by such men as J. Mason Warren of Boston and Jacques Louis Reverdin of France. He expounded on the refinement made by Ollier, Wolfe and Thiersch.

But he was most in praise of Wilhelm Krause, new in the field, and it was the Krause techniques which he put to use in removing areas of soft skin from Darcie's posterior and grafting them onto the cleaned area of her thigh. It was a slow and painful process and the danger of infection made it risky, but, as the weeks passed, she saw the return of smoothness on her thigh. The area under her arm was treated simply by allowing the skin of her inside arm to be flapped down to grow over the burn, from which the keloid scars had been removed. Through it all, Schumann was kind and generous, not demanding her sexual attentions when she was not feeling well. But, between operations, when Darcie was not in pain, she paid him in currency as old as the world and with a skill which made Jules Schumann a willing ally in the effort to sell the *Compagnie Nouvelle,* formed in France following Guy's suggestions, to the American government.

The formation of the *Compagnie Nouvelle* was quite simple, once the basic idea was applied. Gustave Eiffel, for example, was threatened with a breach of contract suit, and he "willingly" invested $2 million in the new company. When approached by the liquidator of the de Lesseps company, other company officials saw the wisdom of financing a new company, including the firm of Bunau-Varilla.

For a while, after Guy returned negatives and prints of the pictures of Darcie and Stewart Schumann, Guy was considered as the front man for the organization. Guy, however, had other plans which would require a certain amount of anonymity. The dedicated Philippe Bunau-Varilla, a man with a view of his own importance to history, solved the problem by appointing himself to be the main influence.

The first offer to the Americans was $109 million. American newspapers greeted the idea with great scorn, and, almost immediately, the offer was lowered to $40 million. The newspaper writers said, with great glee, that the sum represented $20 million for the thieves in Congress who would have to vote a bill and $20 million for the thieves on the other side of the Atlantic who wanted their original investments back.

A commission had been formed to study the various possible canal routes, and it reported in favor of a Nicaraguan canal. The House of Representatives voted 308–2 in favor of Nicaragua. Guy was back in New York, having dinner with Darcie and Schumann, when the news came. It sent him into gloom.

"It's not over yet," Schumann said. "The whole affair will be decided in the Senate. And don't be surprised if there is a change in the Walker Commission's recommendation for a route."

"Do you have reason to think they will change their minds?" Guy asked.

"Hummm," Schumann said, smiling.

Soon his prediction came true. The Walker Commission changed to favor Panama, and Guy's hopes soared. Like Bunau-Varilla, he seemed to be supplied with an endless amount of expense money. And now that the battle in Washington was entering the crucial phase, he wanted to be, with his money, near the area of conflict.

Schumann was unhappy when Guy announced that he and Darcie were going to Washington.

"Don't fret, Stewart," Darcie told him. "I'll be back." For she was grateful. For the first time since the fire in Panama, she did not cringe when she looked at herself in the mirror. Although close examination showed some tiny scars, her voluptuous body was, once again, a thing of beauty.

Resigned, Schumann furnished Guy with a list of senators known to be amenable to a fast dollar. As they left, he smiled sadly. "As for other influences," he said, looking at Darcie, "please be careful, my dear.

To try to influence all members of the Congress would be quite strenuous. There are simply too many of them."

"I shall apply my, ah, influence carefully," Darcie said, smiling back at him.

12

AFTER LONG CONSIDERATION, Petra decided that she was duty-bound to inform her sister that Helene had come to live with them at Chateau D'Art. Through her firm of solicitors in Paris, she obtained the address of the penthouse apartment occupied by Darcie during her long and painful plastic surgery, the solicitors contacting other solicitors involved in the *Compagnie Nouvelle,* with which Guy Simel was known to be associated.

The letter was written after a long talk with Helene. During the last months of Petra's confinement, Helene was at her side constantly, and the girl quite often asked questions about her real mother.

"Perhaps," Petra said, "you would like to correspond with her."

"Would she want to hear from me?" Helene asked doubtfully.

"I'm sure she would," Petra said, although she was not.

And so Petra's letter was written and Helene enclosed a short note expressing an interest in seeing Darcie someday.

Then the time for the birth of Petra's son was upon them. It went well. She named the boy Jason, as near to Jay as she dared. Jason was a healthy, robust baby, always hungry. He was large, showing signs that he would grow up to be a big man, like his father. In the peace of Chateau D'Art, the three of them—Petra, Helene, and Antonia—were relatively content. Petra, still in love with Jay, had long since decided that it was her fate never to have the man she loved. Helene was happy to be with her true family, always busy, always eager to absorb new knowledge. Antonia was content, too—at least for the time being. It had taken her only days to discover that Jean-Charles de Choiseul, handsome as he was, aristocratic as he was, was not as good a lover as the farm boy, Jacques. But now Jean-Charles had gone away to the school in Paris, and Antonia had added to her collection a fine, strong young married man who, by much practice, knew much about how to please a girl.

In the excitement of having a new baby in the house, Petra forgot about the letters to Darcie. Helene did not forget. When the weeks passed without an answer, she assumed that Darcie had no desire to reestablish contact with a baby whom she had given up for adoption.

But the letters had been seen first by Guy, who, seeing their point of origin, opened the envelope. He wanted no complications in his life, in his plans. He had work for Darcie in Washington. He did not want to run the risk of her wanting to go back to France to see her child. There would be time later. Later he would tell her.

As the nineteenth century ended, it was galling to many Europeans to see so much world power being built up in a city which was, by European standards, a new settlement. Of all the major cities of the world, Washington, D.C. was the youngest, and the first city to be created solely as a seat of government. To

Frenchmen, it seemed ironic that the city was the work of one of their own, a French engineer who was a product of the same system which produced the men who strived and failed at Panama. In fact, the city of Pierre Charles L'Enfant, who was commissioned by George Washington to plan and begin construction, reminded Frenchmen of Paris, with the large and open spaces, the wide boulevards, and the sensible street layout.

The thrifty ways of the early Yankees had delayed plans to make Washington a showplace. In the 1840s, the visiting English writer, Charles Dickens, called Washington "The City of Magnificent Intentions," but by the time of Guy and Darcie's visit much had been done. The stately Capitol had been completed during the Civil War, Thomas Crawford's statue of Freedom had been lifted to the top of the dome to the accompaniment of booming cannons. A large building program was conducted during the 1870s. Sculptors worked busily during the last half of the century. Clark Mill's Andrew Jackson on horseback graced Lafayette Square, his statue of George Washington stood in Washington Circle. A host of generals were honored with statues: James McPherson, George Thomas, Winfield Scott, John Logan, Philip Sheridan. David Farragut, the naval hero of Mobile Bay, stood in his place, looking as if he were alive and ready to shout, "Damn the torpedoes." And on the Mall, the stark beauty of the 555-foot tribute to the Father of His Country dominated all.

In the chaos of the Civil War and its aftermath, L'Enfant's plan had been misplaced, however, and the careful observer who was able to tear his eyes away from the beauty of the monuments saw poor shanties and crowded tenements within a stone's throw of the Capitol and the White House. Thousands of blacks and poor whites had crowded into the city after the war to live in a squalor which reminded Darcie of the towns of Panama. The banks of once-beautiful streams became rubbish dumps. Graceful eighteenth century mansions were lost in a sea of helter-skelter urban sprawl, surrounded by ramshackle buildings without sanitary facilities or running water.

There was an undercurrent of vitality, in spite of the scabs of poverty in the heart of the city; Washington was becoming a symbol of power. The world had noted the ease with which the young nation took the measure of poor old Spain, bled through the centuries by her constant wars with England and France. There was a feeling of confidence, of unbounded optimism in Washington. The nation had scarcely flexed its muscles to add to its territory huge pieces of real estate in the Philippines and Cuba. The war had made the United States a world power, and the Caribbean an American lake. The annexation of Hawaii had been hastened by the war. The interest in the navy had been stimulated and the wartime dash of the battleship *Oregon* around the Horn while an entire nation followed its progress breathlessly made the building of an interocean canal a certainty. If the United States were to be a two-ocean power, the canal was a vital necessity, and there was, in its planning, that element which Carnegie called "grab and hold." The tiny voices which questioned the morality of the war with Spain, who questioned the dramatic sinking of the battleship *Maine*, daring even to suggest that the incident was staged to provoke war in order to protect American investments in Cuba, were scarcely heard—and, if heard, decried as traitorous.

The war, of course, had its heroes, as do all wars. Of all of them, Teddy Roosevelt benefited most; and of all the heroes, the human volunteers who, in Cuba, allowed themselves to be chewed upon by a mosquito then called *Stegomyia fasciata*—later to be reclassified as *Aëdes aegypti*—performed the most lasting service to mankind. For while the nation celebrated the defeat of Spain, while Roosevelt made his political plans, while Guy Simel and Darcie Moncrief struggled, in New York and in Washington, to recoup their financial losses, the Yellow Fever Commission, established to find out why the American forces in Cuba lost more men to fever than to the Spanish, finally heeded the words of Carlos Finlay—words spoken unheard in 1881 while French and black workers were dying by the thousands in Panama, and proved beyond doubt that yellow jack was a contagious disease and that it was carried by a mosquito.

And so the stage was set for the final act when Darcie and Guy came to Washington to find the city in the throes of new construction: a new railroad terminal being built, the Mall being opened up by the removal of an old depot and railway tracks. The dome of the Capitol was visible from their hotel window. From names given to them by Stewart Schumann, they gained quick entree into Washington society, where the handsome woman and the graying, aristocratic man, both with interesting tales to tell about Panama, became quick favorites.

In that eternal man-woman relationship which is at the heart of all human activity, nature has made a fortunate provision. Although some mature men yearn for the youthful charms of young women, most are attracted to mature beauty, and of that Darcie Moncrief was possessed in abundance. In spite of the time she had spent in Panama, where the tropic heat ages and weakens, she was still that tiny, perfect Venus, a woman of exquisite figure, the kind of woman for whom the styles of the times were designed. The delicate and ornate silk and velvet waists, designed to emphasize the cinched-in waists, were made for Darcie who needed only a light summer corset underneath. The tight collars served to call attention to her unlined and elegant neck. The capes of winter, with their raised collars, served as a frame for Darcie's face which, with maturity, had a soulful look. Her eyes seemed to express bittersweet experience, leading men to wonder and to go from curiosity to desire.

For dress occasions, Darcie had a selection of the often overstated hats, which tended toward feathers and velvets. In a fine black English felt hat, with a row of fine, twisted jet beads around the crown, she walked the streets in a ladies' suit of wool cheviot serge, and, for less formal outings, was exotic in a simple and unadorned Madrid, a hat patterned after the headgear of a Spanish don. Another of her informal favorites, the Clermont, had a low crown, unadorned, with the brim taking a jaunty tilt upward in the rear. When she could, she wore opera slippers, simple, comfortable, or silk-topped high button shoes when they were called for.

Darcie took care to dress in American style, for a part of the new national pride was a contempt for things foreign. In the eyes of Americans, American things were best, with the possible exception of French champagne. Even her underclothing was not the sometimes daring confections of a Paris designer, but the ruffled and laced creations of Americans.

In her new pose, she neglected to mention her half-French blood. She presented herself as an Englishwoman, making a conscious effort to broaden her accent to make it less grating on the ears of the Washington notables with whom she began to come into contact at various parties, for many of the politicians who would have a vital part in the decision which would affect her financial future were scarcely more than rural bumpkins. True, the caliber of man in office in Washington had improved slightly since the days of U.S. Grant, but there were still a liberal sprinkling of rogues and scoundrels and even more who saw no harm in accepting the hospitality of the rather impressive establishment which Guy set up in a fashionable section of the city. Soon an evening at the

Simel house was a common pastime for dozens of members of the House of Representatives and the Senate. And, while some of them were alienated by the sometimes high-handed ways of Philippe Bunau-Varilla, they found Guy Simel and his charming niece to be "just plain folks." Of course, it became known quite soon that Simel and his niece were lobbying for the Panama route, but then everyone in the city was lobbying for something. It was not dishonorable to try to influence the opinion of a legislator through fine wine and delicious food and charming company.

The guest list at the Simel house was a *Who's Who* in Washington, and it included the crusty old Mark Hanna as well as the chief opponent of the Panama route, the aristocratic Senator John Tyler Morgan. Although both found Darcie to be charming, they were both men of principle, and she realized early on that it would be nothing short of disaster to try to influence either of them with her sexual charms. There were, however, others less principled.

During the period spent in the American capitol, there were times that Darcie thought, with wistfulness, of the peace and quiet of the English countryside, the lovely days of her youth before the tragic death of her mother and the disastrous trip to Egypt. She was often tired. No longer vibrantly young, her energies were stretched to the limit by the round of social activities, by the careful and calculated efforts to influence the coming vote on the canal route. There were times when she wished merely to be allowed to go away, to find a peaceful chateau in the French countryside there to ride, walk the fields, remove her corsets and breathe free. She realized that these ambitions were a sign of her age, and she knew full well that they were unreachable—the money being spent on lavish living would cease if the proponents of the Nicaraguan route won.

Nevertheless, in the quiet moments following a gala

evening during which she had been forced to be charming to a host of people, some with the manners of swineherds, she would review her life, often with bitter regret. More and more, she was becoming the stronger member of the long-lived team of Simel and Moncrief. She knew full well that it was Guy's mis-judgments which had them in their current precarious position, facing the fading years with no means.

Among those who knew of her prime function—that of courtesan—was the lawyer William Nelson Cromwell, an elegant man with silver hair, piercing eyes, modeled nose, and white moustache. Cromwell was a frequent guest, for he, too, had a vital interest in the Panama route. Quick and intelligent, Cromwell also suffered from an overinflated opinion of his own importance, being almost as insufferable in that respect as Philippe Bunau-Varilla, who showed his finesse by going to the home of Senator Morgan and insulting the old man. They were, however, allies, and as such were to be treated with respect.

It was Cromwell who arranged to have members of the most influential committee in the Senate as guests at a gala ball, and it was he who pointed out to Dar-cie a senator who was wavering and, Cromwell thought, could be brought into the fold by the application of, as he put it, "a certain amount of tender care." To his pleased surprise, the good senator found himself to be the target of the full attentions of Darcie, and, to his complete disbelief and joy, heard her agree to a secret rendezvous with him.

That mission accomplished, Darcie turned her at-tentions to others and, at the end of the evening, found herself alone with William Cromwell.

"A job well done, my dear," Cromwell said.

Darcie was tired. She would have to spend an after-noon in the company of a man who chewed tobacco the next day. She wondered if it were worth it. Pre-paring to say good night, her hand was taken by

Cromwell and he beamed a smile at her from behind his silver moustache.

"You are, indeed, lovely," he said. "And I know, my dear, the sacrifices you are making for the cause. I think you deserve a reward. If you are free, I suggest that you and I adjourn to a quiet place for a sip of wine and some relaxing conversation."

"Thank you," Darcie said, "but I'm very tired."

"Oh, the evening is young," Cromwell said. "I promise you that you will find it, ah, interesting."

"Some other time, perhaps," Darcie said.

"My dear," Cromwell said, with a bit of chagrin at being rejected. "You are being paid well to perform your duties."

She turned to face him, her face calm. "It is not for you, sir, to remind me of that, for you and I have much in common. I know what I am, but you, too, are serving the cause for money. It's just that there is no word in the English language for a male whore."

Steaming, mumbling under his breath, Cromwell left. Never again did he make suggestions to Darcie.

In spite of all their efforts, it seemed that the decision was going to go against them. Although Darcie was discouraged, she kept her appointment with the tobacco-chewing southern senator in a sleazy hotel outside the city, exhibited a skill which left the senator gasping with delight and totally sated within the first hour. His male needs satisfied, he offered to get Darcie a carriage back into the city. She was not insulted when he didn't offer to ride with her, for it was the nature of her "work" that it be done in secret.

For the first time, Darcie found her chore to be unpleasant. She couldn't find a particular reason. The man had left his tobacco in his pocket. He was clean. He was undemanding; the event was finished almost before it began, leaving her with nothing more than a feeling of being soiled, which she remedied in the hotel bath. Always, on previous encounters with a man, she had enjoyed her sense of holding power over the man, and nearly always her highly susceptible nature caused her to profit, but not this time. This time there was a dullness in her, and she performed her little contortions automatically. At one point she was reminded of one of Lyris's girls who had worked in the brothel in Panama. Attractive, well-formed, the girl had no interest in her work, living only for her nightly crawling into bed, after business hours, with a thin and surly Spanish girl. While conducting her business, the attractive girl looked at the ceiling, chewed on morsels of food, hummed—in short, did everything she could to separate herself from the rutting creature between her legs. Remembering her as the senator rutted between *her* legs, Darcie could not help but smile. Had it come to that?

It was a glorious spring day. The ride into the city was a pleasant one. She was not ready to go back to the house which Guy had leased, for there would be men there, talking, as ever, making their plans, discussing this senator and that. She was in no mood for it. As the carriage passed through a business area, she tapped on the seat to attract the driver's attention and dismounted, to stroll along the street looking in shop windows. The area was not a rich one, the shops small and poor. One window caught her attention. A curious collection of articles were arrayed therein, among them a selection of metal toys: a nickel-plated model of the *Maine* was a bank for small coins, another bank featured a cannon and a fort, and another had an Indian with bow which shot the coin into the belly of a bear. There were toy steam engines and cast-iron trains and a selection of toys which kept her bemused for long minutes. A mechanical monkey climbed a rope; a chiming toy featured the Rough Riders in colorful uniform.

And, somehow, she was saddened. She realized that she had never bought a toy for a child, had never so much as held an infant in her arms. A feeling of poignant regret rose in her, a strange and eerie feeling which she had never known, and she remembered the hours of pain she'd undergone bearing a child she had never seen.

Bemused, her thoughts going back through the years and across the miles, she at first did not hear when a man of medium height spoke her name.

"Good day, Miss Moncrief," he repeated, bringing her out of her strange reverie.

He was only inches taller than she, dressed in Navy whites, with the insignia of a rear admiral on his shoulders. He looked vaguely familiar. She smiled. When he removed his hat, she saw that his hair was parted down the center, leaving a wide white mark on his skull. His face was clean shaven, his eyes deep-set and strong, their color a deep black.

"Sorry," he said, "you must not remember me. We met at the French embassy."

"Oh, yes," she said. "Of course."

She tried to remember, but that night she'd been paying attention to a ranking member of a House committee.

"David Russell, Ma'am, at your service," he said with a formal bow.

"Of course, Admiral Russell," she said.

"Forgive me for accosting you on the street," he said. She smiled politely. "I was just going in here to buy a birthday gift for my granddaughter."

"Granddaughter?" she asked, with a laugh. "You don't look like a grandfather."

"We Americans believe in getting an early start," Russell said. "Were you going inside?"

"Actually, I was just passing," she said. "Enjoying the excellent weather."

"Ah, yes," he said, his hat still in his hand, a serious expression on his pleasant and somewhat rounded face. "Look, I'm no good at buying gifts for girls. If you have a moment, could I impose on you to offer me some advice?"

"Of course," she said. He opened the door and bowed her into the cluttered little shop. A balding man with a huge beard looked up from a paper, nodded, and said, "Help yourselves, folks. If you need me, holler."

"My wife used to handle such chores," Russell said. "Quite good at it, too."

"I don't know if my advice will be worth much," Darcie said. "I've never been associated with children."

"Too bad," Russell said. "They can be pests at times, but at times they're sheer joy. We had two, my wife and I. A son and a daughter. The girl lives in Georgetown."

"And your son?" Darcie asked idly, as they walked through crowded aisles amid a profusion of toys and hobby items.

"David was killed on San Juan Hill," Russell said, matter-of-factly.

"Oh, I'm so sorry."

"He was a soldier," Russell said, as if that were explanation enough.

Russell picked up a cast-iron fire wagon with a team of horses on wheels. "I don't suppose a little girl would go for something like this."

"Oh, I hardly think so," Darcie said, with a laugh. She pointed to a toy stove complete with pots and kettles. "I should think this would be more like it."

"Excellent," Russell said. He turned toward where the proprietor was still engrossed in his paper. "I think this will do the job, sir."

"You make up your mind quickly," Darcie said.

"Your recommendation is good enough for me," he said. "It hasn't been too long since you were a little girl, yourself."

"Oh, admiral, how wrong you are," Darcie said. "But thank you."

The old man came, put the model stove into a box and rang up the amount on a cash register. Russell was looking at Darcie with a bemused expression. "There's quite a nice little restaurant just down the street," he said. "Could I reward you for your excellent advice with an early dinner?"

"A cup of tea, perhaps," Darcie said, surprising herself. Although he seemed pleasant enough, the admiral was not her type of man. Moreover, in recent years, her association with men had been dictated by practicality, not whim. *But,* she thought, *what would it hurt? A cup of tea with a nice grandfather.*

"Excellent," Russell said. He went to the counter and accepted his package. "By the way, anything new in the way of stamps?"

The bald old man scratched his beard. "Matter of fact, just got in a shipment from the South American missions," he said. "Care to look 'em over?"

"Not today, thank you. But I'll be back."

"Fine, admiral. Nice doing business with you."

"If you want to stay," Darcie said, "I don't mind. I'll take that cup of tea some other time."

"Oh, no," Russell said, taking her arm. "There is no way a batch of used South American stamps can win out over such a beautiful and charming young lady."

"How reassuring," Darcie said. She found herself liking this little man with his ready smile.

"Although," Russell went on, opening the door and seeing her through, "some postage stamps are quite beautiful, also."

"Are you, then, a timbromaniac?" Darcie asked, using the French word.

"We prefer to call ourselves philatelists," Russell said. "Actually, it's much more applicable."

"I'm not familiar with the word."

"Coined by a Frenchman," Russell said. "*Philos,* the Greek for love; *telein,* to tax, since a postage stamp is nothing more than a tax collected in advance. Do you know why stamps were first used?"

"I'm sure I don't," Darcie said.

"For a long time, letters were sent unpaid, so that the receiver had to pay the tax for delivery. Many people, seeing that the letter was from someone they didn't care about, refused to pay, and the postal service was out the cost of delivery. So they printed stamps and required the sender to pay."

"How clever of them."

"Your countrymen," Russell said. "The bloody English."

"Others followed suit quite rapidly," Darcie said.

"Oh, yes. There's no lack of initiative when it comes to new ways to fleece the taxpayer," Russell said.

They walked slowly through the lovely spring late afternoon, the admiral tipping his hat to passing ladies.

"But stamp collecting is a dull subject," Russell said, "except to those who collect them. You, I take it, are not a collector."

"Perhaps I should be, since you find it so interesting."

"A lovely hobby, and quite ladylike." He took her arm to guide her across a street, and they entered a small but well-appointed restaurant.

"Tell me about your grandchildren," Darcie said, when they were seated.

"Oh, don't get a grandfather started on that subject," he said. "I have three, actually; two boys, both hellions, and the little girl."

"And you so young," Darcie said.

"If that's an implied question," he said. "I am forty-nine years old. My oldest grandson is six. My daughter married quite young." He was silent as a waiter served their tea. Then: "You, I believe, have never been married?"

"No," she said simply.

"Would it be presumptuous to ask why?"

She mused.

"It is presumptuous. I'm sorry."

"No," she said, "I was merely thinking about the question."

"And your conclusion?"

"Frankly, I don't know." She looked at him, her teeth nibbling on her lower lip as she thought. "It would be too flip to say that the right man never said the proper words, I suppose."

"Not at all." He sipped his tea. "But there is a sadness in your eyes."

"Oh?"

"A great love gone wrong? A tragic end?"

She laughed. "Nothing so dramatic."

"You can't tell me, Miss Moncrief, that a lady so beautiful has never been in love."

Again she fell into thought. He waited. Had she, she was asking herself, ever been in love? She shook her head in astonishment. Love? She had stolen Jay Burton away from Petra but not for love. She had lived with her uncle, but not for love—for lust, perhaps, but not for love.

"You are a most astonishing lady," Russell said gently.

"You pose questions, admiral, which set me to thinking," she said.

"Well, then, I shall change the subject. I understand that you and your uncle were in Panama during the French years."

"Yes, we were there for a part of the time."

"And you have an interest in seeing that the route for an American canal lies in Panama."

"Yes, that is true."

"Would it impress you at all if I confess that I, too, think Panama to be the best route?"

"It would please me," she said. "Is it true?"

"Absolutely. I told Teddy—" She smiled. "Yes, that's name dropping," he said. "But I told the president just last week it was time to stop lollygagging and get the dirt flying, and in Panama. Actually, if our medical boys can solve the fever problem, we can dig that canal in a few years."

"Are you a friend of the president's?" she asked.

"We don't move in the same social circles," Russell said, "but, yes, I'd say we're friends. Teddy's interested in a strong navy, and so am I."

"And what did the president say?" Darcie asked.

"Nothing. But I think the old boy is leaning toward Panama. If it weren't for the political situation down there, I think he'd have already come out in favor of Panama."

Darcie had finished her tea but, strangely, she was in no hurry. It was pleasant to be talking with David Russell, comfortable, without pressure. She felt that she could be herself and not worry about trying to influence him in any way.

"Miss Moncrief," he said, after a moment's silence. "I must admit that I enjoy your company very much."

"Thank you, sir," Darcie said.

"May I see you to your home?"

"That would be nice of you."

He used bay rum. She could smell it as they sat side by side in a carriage, the clop-clop of the horses' hooves making a nice rhythm, the sunset and the hush of evening coming down over the city. At her door, after talking mainly of the city itself during the drive, he helped her down, bent to kiss her hand, and wished her a pleasant evening. Then he was gone, and for a moment, as she stood on the stoop and watched him climb back into the carriage with the spring of youth, she wanted to call him back. However, it was, she thought, only a momentary whim.

A messenger brought the package shortly after noon the next day. She opened it to find a note, on stationery printed with the admiral's name and address.

Dear Miss Moncrief
*I visited the toy shop this morning to look through
the stamps which were collected from the mail
coming into various South American missions.
Remembering your interest in the subject, I have
taken the liberty of sending you the basic necessities for starting your own stamp collection.*
                                        David Russell

What a pleasant gesture, she thought. *And, most
surprising, he was asking for nothing in return.* That
was quite unlike the men of her experience. There
was an album for mounting the stamps printed by
Justin Lallier in Paris, the English edition; a catalog
printed by Stanley Gibbons in England, gummed
hinges for mounting, and a large envelope of stamps.
Instructions for getting the stamps off paper by soaking
were written on the envelope in Russell's bold hand.
She smiled, pleased with the gift. She spread the
stamps on a table and began to examine them. Some
were American, some English, with a few from the
European countries. Most were from South American
nations. It was quite confusing, for there were so many
of them, and a glance at the Gibbons catalog confused
her even further. She spent a pleasant hour sorting
through the stamps and trying to match them to the
pages in the album.

She was interrupted by the door. There was another
messenger with a huge bouquet of flowers. The note
was from David. It asked simply, "Will you have dinner with me?"

The messenger waited a reply. She wrote quickly.
"David, I'm so sorry. I have previous commitments.
Lunch tomorrow?"

A group of influential men had been invited to the
house. She dressed her part and mingled, but, for some
reason which she could not explain, did not perform

her most valuable duty, although Guy had suggested a suitable target. She awoke earlier than usual, feeling better than usual, feeling, in fact, quite giddy and young. She lingered over her toilet, dressed in a gay and light spring outfit, and found herself flying down the stairs with a haste she had not felt in years when the doorbell announced David's arrival. Although it was some distance away and there were more posh places nearer, he directed the carriage driver to the small restaurant where they had had tea. The food was quite good.

"I have the afternoon ahead of me," he said.

"I have nothing pressing," she said.

"I hoped that would be the case. I have the day planned."

"And I have nothing to say about it?"

"You may protest heartily if you don't approve," he said.

But she approved. They drove into the country and walked a lane which was a glory of green and blooming things, with raucous crows flying overhead, cawing their pleasure in the day, with songbirds competing with each other, with a soft breeze making the day lovely. She asked him about his career in the navy, and, with masculine modesty, he admitted to having been with Dewey at Manila Bay. When she pressed for details, he played down his part in the engagement, although he admitted that his ship was at the heart of the action and had done well.

They rested on a stone wall, David with a fresh blade of grass in his teeth, his deep-set eyes looking out toward the river and the city. There seemed to be no need for talk. She watched him chew happily on his stem of grass and laughed.

"Does it taste good?" she asked.

"Delicious," he grinned. He bent and pulled a stem for her, offering it with a smile. She allowed him to put it into her mouth, and they sat there, grass stems protruding, until she burst out laughing.

"You are an American billygoat," she said, giggling, "and you're teaching me your vile grass-eating habits."

"Good, though," he grinned.

She bit into the grass and it had a fresh and pleasant taste.

"Not on the order with caviar or pâté de foie gras," he said, "but not bad."

"I shall tell the world that American admirals eat grass."

"Oh, don't do that," he said. "That's our secret. Let everyone know about it, and they'll be as good as we are." He stood and began to examine the ground, found what he wanted, plucked it and came back. "But here's our real secret weapon. This is what made us invincible at Manila Bay." He pushed a clover-like plant toward her lips. "Try it."

Laughing, protesting, she allowed him to feed her a bit of the plant, chewed it gingerly with her front teeth, and was rewarded by a surprisingly tart taste which was quite pleasant.

"You are impossible," she said.

"Well, I'm just a country boy," David said. "My old grandmother knew two or three dozen things that grew in the woods and fields that were edible—a green called polk, mushrooms, any number of things."

"We used to dig truffles in France," she said.

"There, you see? Same thing. Truffles or sour grass, all of a kind."

Darcie laughed. "Oh, David. Why do you make me feel so silly?"

"I don't know," he said, coming to sit beside her. "Do I?"

"It's so peaceful here," she said. "And, yes, you do make me feel good. You're a kind and gentle man."

"You tell one of Uncle Sam's fierce warriors that he's kind and gentle," David said, smiting his forehead with his palm. He looked at her. "Coming from you, Miss Moncrief, I like it."

"Shall we walk?" she asked, for he had a look on his face, and she did not want the afternoon to be spoiled, as she felt, somehow, it would be if he kissed her.

"By all means."

He guided her to a wide meadow. A hare ran before them, showing its gay white scut. Meadowlarks, unafraid, sprang into flight at their feet and circled them, coming back to land directly behind them.

When they returned to the carriage, she was pleasantly tired. She was reluctant to see the afternoon end, but it was growing toward evening, and, indeed, as they reached the city, night was falling. In front of her house, she waited for him to pay the hackney and come around to assist her to the sidewalk. As he lifted her, his hands under her arms, she came against his body and felt a jolt of awareness which startled her. She had thought such things to be gone, to be merely a part of her past, her eager youth; yet his touch sent that electricity through her.

"Miss Moncrief," he said, "may I inquire if you are engaged for dinner?"

"Yes, I'm sorry," she said. "My uncle has invited people here. Will you come?"

"I would merely be jealous, seeing you surrounded by others," he said.

"As you please," she said, knowing disappointment. "Oh, I haven't thanked you for your gift. It was lovely, and I do so enjoy looking at the stamps."

"Is that all you've done? *Look* at them?"

"They're devilishly alike," she said. "I can't tell if they're from Argentina or Brazil or whatever."

"Ah, you need the advice of an expert. I offer my services at your convenience." He smiled. "You see, my dear Miss Moncrief, I had motive when I presented you with those stamps."

"Cunning devil," she said.

"Perhaps tomorrow?"

"I should be grateful," she said. "But don't you ever work?"

"I'm taking a short leave," he said.

And then it had to be asked, for he had not mentioned it and her curiosity was merely a facet of this strange relationship, an aspect of her feelings which she could not, as yet, understand. "And your wife?"

"I'm sorry," he said, "I thought you knew. My wife has been dead for two years now."

"Oh, David, I'm sorry," she said.

"What you must have thought of me," he said.

"Oh, no."

"I would not dishonor you by asking for your company if I were a married man," David said, and this, as he left her, concerned her more than anything which had happened.

She was on the stairs when Guy came out of the study. "Ah, there you are," he said. "Where have you been?"

"I've been for a walk in the country to eat sour grass," she said.

"How quaint," Guy said, with some puzzlement. "The admiral again?"

"Yes, as a matter of fact, how did you know?"

"I make it my business to know," Guy said. "And I must say I don't approve, Darcie, when there is so much to do."

"I was not aware that I required your approval," she said.

"Oh, I see." He smiled. "I have been neglecting you, my dear. If you are in need, please come into my room tonight."

"How romantic!"

"My God," Guy said, his face showing amazement. "Don't tell me you're in love, Darcie."

"I don't recall saying anything," Darcie said, but

she paled. Could it be so apparent? Indeed, was that her problem?

"Well, have your little fling, my dear," Guy said. "You will wear the red dress tonight? The senator from New York was quite taken with it, if you remember."

"Yes, all right," she said, starting up the stairs.

"Darcie?"

She paused.

"You won't let your interest in the admiral interfere, will you?"

"I'll do my job."

"We're very close, Darcie. The vote in the Senate is coming soon, and it will be close. If we can, in any fashion, change one vote, such as the senator from New York—"

"I understand."

"I knew you would." He smiled again. "And I'll be in my room when you return, if you need me."

She ran up the stairs. The stamps were still spread on the table. She looked at them, confused by her conflicting emotions. Then, with a shrug, she began to undress. She looked at herself in the mirror and saw a body which was almost flawless, but she was all too familiar with the telltale signs: a sag here, a small indication of a coming wrinkle there.

She thought of David, and a pleasant warmth, not sexual, unlike anything she'd ever known, spread through her. In her bath, she tried to remember all the details of his face: the small mole above his left eye, the way his eyes showed smile and sun lines, the chip on his front tooth. She looked forward to the coming day when he would be there, in her suite, bending his head with that silly part down the middle over the table to look at her stamps.

The gathering that night was typical, except for a growing sense of urgency among those who supported the Panama route. And the senator from New York was not an unattractive man. Darcie forced thoughts

of David from her mind and used her charms to engage
the senator in debate about the various proposed canal
routes, getting in telling points now and then in favor
of Panama. She could tell, for she did not lack experience along those lines, that he was interested in more
than talk about a canal. And, although sexual bribes
were not binding, as were monetary bribes, she knew
their value. She was in the last years of her beauty.
Soon—all too soon—she would begin to age and without money, the process would be a painful one. And
so it was that before midnight, she loosed the hooks
on her light summer corset and performed her duties,
for this bribe which she gave might just turn the vote
of the man who panted and did not rouse her usually
shallow passions. When he bellowed in completion and
used her violently, she saw David's face, and remembered how he'd been concerned to think that she did
not know his wife was dead. What would such an
honorable man think if he could see her now, with the
senator's exhausted body lying limply atop hers, his
head on her shoulder?

She fought back tears and, in anger, told herself,
"Fool, damned fool. Take him to bed, love him, forget
him."

But she knew that she would not ever be able to
forget.

13

"FIRST," DAVID SAID, his head bent over the table showing the silly white mark down the center of his skull, "we will separate them by country." And he proceeded to tell her how to identify the various stamps. "Then we take the country piles and separate them into the various issues."

Darcie was content just to watch him, to see his deft hands handling the tiny pieces of paper, to watch the way his lips moved as he talked.

"Pay attention," he said, with mock severity, and she leaned down, her head close to his.

"You will note," he said, having separated all the stamps to put some of them to soak in water, "that I have brought blotters. They are for drying the stamps." And so saying, he began to pull the wetted stamps from the envelope fragments to which they had been stuck and to place them, face down, on the blotters. "Now, while they dry, perhaps you could supply a thirsty sailor with a drink."

"Thirsty sailor," she smiled, "you've earned it."

"Horrendously difficult labor, stamp sorting," he said.

She gave him whisky and water, a drink favored by Americans, and sat watching him as he leaned back in his chair.

"Take a while to dry, as I said. Care for a walk?"

"If you like," she said. She was dressed in a cream-colored skirt with a brown waist.

"Or, if you don't want to go for a walk, may I suggest that we while away the time by having me kiss you—at least once, perhaps twice."

"I am a believer in the rule of threes," Darcie said.

"So, I shall kiss you three times," he said, his voice low.

"And when, pray tell," she said, with a little smile, "is this great kissing to begin?"

He turned up his glass and finished it. "At this very moment," he said. He rose to stand in front of her chair, neat and small in his white uniform. He took her hands and pulled her to her feet. "I've been dying to kiss you for days."

"I thought sailors were notoriously forward," Darcie said, her voice catching, her heart telling him, *hurry, hurry.*

"I was plain scared," he said.

"Of what?"

"Of your saying no."

"I don't think I could ever say no to you," she said, with an honesty which frightened her. She leaned forward, lifting her face, her eyes closing. She felt his mouth, polite but firm. And then his arms held her, not too tightly, but comfortably. She was at home in his arms. The world lost its importance.

"Oh, Miss Moncrief," he said, breaking the kiss with a sigh.

"Sailors who have kissed me may call me Darcie," she said, speaking lightly to cover the shock she felt at her reaction to his kiss.

"As I count it," he said, "there are two kisses to go."

"Oh, yes!"

And, later, when he tried to pull away: "Who's counting?" she asked.

"I hope," he said, when he did pull away, "that you don't consider me precipitous."

"You are the damnedest man! Can't you tell when a woman wants to be kissed?"

"I haven't had all that much practice," he said with a grin.

She turned away. "Did you have a good marriage?"

"Quite good," he said, "what there was of it. I was away at sea a lot as a young man. I didn't spend as much time with my wife as I would have liked. But now"—he paused—"well, now that she's dead, I'm shore bound."

She had made up her mind. "David," she said, her back to him, looking down at the street from the window. "Before we say anything else, there's something I must tell you."

"All right."

"You said you did not have much practice kissing women."

"Not a lot, no."

"I can't make that statement, David."

"Oh, here now, no confessions. I realize that a woman of your age has, well, has—hell, how can I say it? Been around?"

"I have been around, David."

"You told me you'd never been in love."

"And it was true."

"*Was,* Darcie?"

"I used the past tense."

He moved toward her. She put out her hands and held him from her, her hands on his chest. "I am not finished."

"Yes, yes, you are," he said. "Maybe someday I'll be able to listen and not feel like some bloody-minded idiot, but now I don't want to hear. I don't want to hear about men you've known—or kissed, Darcie."

"David, David," she said, near tears. "That's what I'm trying to tell you. I've done more than kiss."

His face darkened. He shrugged. "Well, so have I." He smiled. "We're not spring chickens, Darcie. But there's still fire in the boiler, right?"

"A lot of fire," she said with a smile.

"So the past is past, and what happens from here on is what counts."

"Can you really mean that?"

"Sure," he said.

"Now I have something else to tell you," she said. He shifted uncomfortably. "I've never—I just realized it in the past few days—I've never been a complete woman, David, because I've never been in love. And now that I am, I'm going to be all the woman you'll ever want. Oh, David, I'm going to love you so much that nothing else will matter. Nothing."

His kiss was long and sweet, his hands staying where a gentleman's hands should stay. "I have a place in Maryland," he said. "Lots of sour grass and mushrooms."

"Oh, yes."

"We'll go there for the honeymoon."

Shocked, she pulled back and looked into his face. "Honeymoon?"

"Of course. That's the thing you have after you're married."

"David, you don't have to—"

He closed her mouth with his hand. "That's the way I want it." He removed his hand and frowned. "You're not saying no."

She laughed. "Say no? God, no, you silly sailor."

"I think a military wedding," he said. "Wanted one when Sally and I got married, but couldn't arrange it. You *will* marry me?"

"Yes," she said, with a happy laugh. "Yes, yes, yes."

"All right," he said. "I'll let you know when. We'll have to arrange the military chapel, and there are men

I'll want to be there." He paused. 'Of course, if you have some preference as to dates?"

"The date doesn't matter, darling."

"Fine. Come along, then—let's see if the stamps are dry."

"Oh, God," she said.

"Look," he said, "if all you're going to want to do is stand around kissing, we'll have a very tiring marriage. Have mercy on an old man."

But he was no more willing to part than she, and when they did, she was limp and he was trembling. His voice was unsteady as he sat at the table and began to look at the stamps.

"Now here's an interesting one," he said. "Nicaragua. We have here the engraved issue of 1900, in denominations of one to fifteen centavos. I think I have the higher denominations in my own collection. Do you see?"

Darcie, her happiness making her misty eyes, took a stamp from David. It was a dark blue, five-centavo value, and it pictured a train on a track extending out into a lake. In the background was a smoking volcano.

"That's Mount Momotombo in the background," David said.

"Are there really active volcanoes in Nicaragua?" Darcie asked, the germ of an idea stirring in her.

"I suppose so," David said. "They seem to be quite proud of the fact, putting one on their stamps."

"And what effect would a volcanic erruption have on an interocean canal through Nicaragua?" Darcie asked.

"Hmmmm," David said. "I see your point. Actually, I don't think there are any volcanoes near the proposed canal route."

"Would the average senator or congressman know that?"

"The average senator or congressman has difficulty knowing his right foot from his left."

Darcie presented the stamp to Guy after David had left. Guy, in turn, went to visit Philippe Bunau-Varilla. Whether or not the picture of an active volcano in Nicaragua influenced votes would become a question for historians, but history recorded that the Senate voted, 42 to 34, to build the American canal in Panama. A swing of five votes would have placed the canal in Nicaragua. Looking back, Darcie could count seven votes which she had, personally and quite intimately, influenced.

14

WHEN IT BECAME apparent, in 1889, that the French effort to build a sea-level canal in Panama was doomed to failure, Jay decided to accept an offer to remain in the country and assist in maintaining equipment pending the formation of a new canal company mainly because Petra was there. A strong man, a big man, Jay was able to fight off the malaria which he had contracted early and which continued to bedevil him from time to time; but in spite of his natural vigor and health, he was reduced in weight, his body solidly muscular and devoid of excess fat.

As a practical-minded engineer he had never subscribed to the belief that de Lesseps was a magician who, with the aid of modern technology, would conquer all. In fact, from the very first time he saw Panama and knew the topography, Jay had begun to state to anyone who would listen that a sea-level canal was impossible, that the only opportunity for victory lay in changing the plan to include locks and a scheme which would harness the Chagres River. As late as 1886, he tried to convince his superiors that it was not too late to alter the plans.

Then, when the French company ran out of money and the bankruptcy scandal began to rock the French nation, Jay stayed, hoping that the Americans would see the value of the work already done and come to the conclusion that it, and some of the machinery left behind, could be utilized in altering the canal into a lock canal and completing the job.

When Petra left, she left without warning, without telling him good-bye. He learned of Roger D'Art's death by way of the greatly diminished grapevine which linked all Europeans in the zone, the news traveling the length of the railway to reach him in Panama City. He rushed to Colón, only to find that Madame D'Art had left for France in great haste. His first impulse was to follow, and then he learned that Roger's death coincided with the passionate afternoon he'd spent with Petra in the hotel room. He knew her and knew that she would have been hard hit by the coincidence. He drafted letter after letter, and, in the end, mailed none of them, partly because he had no way of knowing Petra's whereabouts. She, on the other hand, knew how to contact him. For months he hoped, expected, awaited a communication from her.

Meanwhile, he did his best, as one of the senior men left in the zone, to preserve as much as possible. With the greatly diminished labor force at his disposal, he stored tools, covering them generously with oil as a protection against the insidious dampness, put great locomotives on chocks, the moving parts coated with grease. He could not save everything. Along the route of the canal, huge machines were abandoned, the jungle claiming its own, covering the triumphs of technology with creepers, rusting the metal, freezing moving parts.

Jay was often called upon to escort curious Americans along the canal route, and he never lost the opportunity to point out that the French failure was not indicative of a bad choice in route—only of a bad

choice as to the type of canal to be built. Some news-
papermen were impressed by the work done by the
French, by the care with which equipment was being
preserved. Others called Panama a great ruin, a modern folly.

Jay followed the Panama scandal through cabled
news and weeks-old newspapers and felt strongly that
the wrong men were on trial in France, that the guilty
ones were those who had bled off the cream from the
stock issues in the form of exorbitant interest, bribes
to newspapers for publicity, payments to politicians
and movers and shakers who, more often than not,
merely pocketed the money and did no moving and
shaking in favor of the canal.

Embittered by the failure, he began to transfer some
of his bitterness to Petra, blaming her for leaving without so much as a word, but loving her nevertheless.

His life was tedious. There was no rewarding work
to be done, merely a holding action. The digging which
continued on the Panama City end of the canal was
merely for show and accomplished little, so few were
the machines and the workmen. The jungle and the
hills and the rains and the fever had won. It was over.

Jay wrote letters to the City of San Francisco and
was told that he had a job there anytime he wanted it,
for the city was growing and needed his skills. And yet
something held him.

It was the news of the death of de Lesseps which
finally moved him out of his jungle-induced stupor.
The old man's death seemed to write *finis* to all of it,
for the prevailing opinion was that the United States
would build a canal in Nicaragua. Now there was nothing to keep him in Panama. He packed his few belongings—everyone lived lightly in the tropics—and made
his plans to take ship for San Francisco on the first
available vessel. Instead, he made an instant decision,
took the train to Colón, and boarded ship for France.

Because—and this was not an instant revelation to

382 DYNASTY OF DESIRE

him, but the result of the thinking which occupied his
mind through many a tedious hour and a long, sweaty
evening—he had found the woman he loved.

Jay would have been the first to deny it, but he was
a romantic. A woman, to him, was one of God's greatest miracles. Feminine beauty had always moved him,
from the time he idolized certain actresses as a youth,
loved with a blind passion a young girl when he was
only a boy in school, loved her from afar and never
had the courage to tell her of his devotion. Always,
although he would not have been able to put it into
words, there was in him the determination to marry,
to have children, a home, a woman of his own to love
and protect and to provide for. He was not altogether
chaste, but he was no womanizer. He had known from
the first that Petra was the woman with whom he
wanted to spend his life, and now so much of that life
had been wasted, his chances at happiness ruined by
his moment of drunken abandon aboard the *Lafayette*
with, of all people, the sister of the woman he would
have cut off his right hand for.

The brief period during which they were together
in Panama was the high-water mark of his life, the
happiest period he'd ever known. He remembered it
often, and regretted his sense of honor, which had
caused him to withdraw when Roger was discovered
alive and recovered. And yet, he knew, if he had it to
do again, he would be forced to do the same thing,
for Roger had been his friend.

But now Roger was dead, and regardless of the
wrongs which had been committed—and he did not
forgive himself for leading Petra into adultery on the
day her husband was dying—denying their love did
not make the wrongs right or bring Roger back to life.
Lonely, discouraged, embittered, he saw no virtue in
denying that he loved Petra and she him. He could
almost read her thoughts, although she was thousands
of miles away. He knew that she felt guilt because of

that last day, possibly blaming herself for Roger's death. And, damn it, he would not allow it. The harm was done, and it was past. The years were flying past, too. So, feeling contradictory emotions, anger at Petra for leaving so abruptly without talking with him, a vast yearning to see her face inside him, he took ship and arrived in France in late winter.

Jay started his search in Paris and was finally steered to the firm of solicitors who had handled Roger's estate. He set out for the south, still a bit angry at Petra for depriving them of a happiness which they deserved, and with hidden smiles as he thought of seeing her once again.

At Chateau D'Art, life had settled into a comfortable routine. Upon Helene's insistence, Petra had not hired a woman to help with Jason, for Helene loved the small bundle of boy and took great delight in tending him. Petra, too, found that having a small baby made for a certain feeling of pleasant excitement and so the child had two women to hear his every cry. When Helene placed him on Petra's ample bosom for a feeding, two sets of eyes watched his hungry pawings and smiled at his hunger.

Only Antonia was discontent. Jean-Charles was away in Paris, and she often approached her mother on the subject of sending her away to school in the city. While wanting to please her daughter, Petra was reluctant to send Antonia away to school for both personal and practical reasons. And still she knew that the time was coming when she would have to part with the girl, for Antonia was wise beyond her years and would not suffer much longer being tied to her mother's apron strings.

Jean-Charles found Paris to be much to his liking. A handsome lad with a bit of money in his pocket found any number of interesting things to do, and, although the work at the École Polytechnique was far from easy, he took it in his stride and found plenty of times to sample the pleasures of the city. He discovered that Antonia D'Art was not the only young lady in France who valued the rewards of love, and, indeed, his Paris experiences tended to make him a bit cynical about such women. There was, he discovered, a sameness to them, those who joined him in the pleasures of bed. Not that it wasn't exciting and always new and exceedingly worthwhile, but, he found, if a fellow closed his eyes, it was difficult to remember just which girl writhed and moaned under his heated body.

Although he was not virgin when he first encountered Antonia D'Art, he was relatively inexperienced, and Antonia's eagerness and skill pleased him and made him feel, for a long time, that she was the most beautiful girl in the world and the most passionate, therefore the most desirable. But there were thousands of beautiful girls in Paris, many of them quite willing to dally with a handsome and rich student, including one woman of thirty-five who showed the young Jean-Charles that lovemaking can be an erotic art. Against such experienced competition, the memory of Antonia faded, and, in its place, there came a wistful and romantic memory of Helene. He could remember fully the way he'd felt on first seeing her, before he was diverted by Antonia's quick seduction.

Thus it was, when he journeyed back to Marmande for the Christmas holidays, that he spent a lot of time at Chateau D'Art, and, much to Antonia's chagrin, spent most of it talking with Helene and Petra, his attentions very definitely not on Antonia. Although she had not been bored, finding her young married man to be quite entertaining, Antonia's nose was put out of joint by Jean-Charles's obvious and sometimes unskillful excuses to avoid being alone with her.

"So," she said to him, after he'd made three calls on them without accepting her hints, her invitations to ride, to walk, to be alone, "you're all grown up now that you've been away at school and prefer the company of older women."

At a loss for words, he made some silly excuse about the weather outside and Antonia flounced up to her room, there to lie on her bed, fuming, hearing the merry laughter of the three coming up from the rooms below, wondering if she could, by some ruse, lure her young married lover away from his wife on a fine winter afternoon.

"Darling," Petra told Antonia, "I can't help but notice that there seems to be ill feeling between you and Jean-Charles. Is there anything wrong?" Jean-Charles and Helene were in the drawing room alone.

"Should you leave Helene alone with him?" Antonia asked.

"Shouldn't I?" Petra retorted.

"Mother," Antonia said, "you must remember that Helene has led a rather sheltered life."

"Why, Antonia," Petra said, "are you trying to tell me that Jean-Charles would abuse our hospitality?"

"I think that would depend on how hospitable Helene turned out to be," Antonia said, with an arch smile.

Petra frowned thoughtfully. "Has Jean-Charles given you reason to suspect his motives?"

"Oh, mother, don't be naïve!" Antonia said impatiently. "You, of all people, should know that the motives of all men are suspect."

"On the contrary," Petra said. "I find that most men are honorable. As the old saying goes, it takes two."

"Merde!" Antonia said under her breath. Aloud, she said, "Well, don't say I didn't warn you."

With puzzlement, Petra went back into the room with Helene and Jean-Charles to find them quiet and serious over a game of chess. She smiled. They both looked up and greeted her.

"Don't let me disturb you," she said.

It seemed to Helene that the few months of Jean-Charles's absence had resulted in a filling-out process. No longer did he have the look of an overgrown boy, but, instead, his every characteristic was that of a man. She could see, as she studied his face while he pored over her latest move on the chessboard, the blue tinge of beard under his skin. He had not yet chosen to adorn his face with moustache or beard and his hair was clipped close in the style of the École. In his uniform, he was quite handsome. Her thoughts of him were warm, but she had not, as yet, gone past the pleasure of her new life with the D'Art family in her thinking. She knew only that she looked forward to Jean-Charles's visits and valued his company. His compliments pleased her. She had never considered herself to be more than a peasant girl, and the fact that Petra thought her to be beautiful was sweet knowledge; but to have a handsome and rich young man like Jean-Charles look at her with adoration in his eyes was a heady experience. She wondered, as she watched him, his brow furrowed in thought, his hand making an indecisive movement and then retreating, how it would feel to kiss him.

The thoughts behind Jean-Charles's brow were not, at the moment, wholly confined to chess. He had a problem. His father was giving his annual Christmas ball, and Jean-Charles wanted very desperately to ask Helene. But he was not stupid. He knew that his attentions to Helene were displeasing Antonia, and he shuddered to think of Antonia's reaction if he invited Helene to go with him. He knew from experience that there was more than sexual fire under that pretty exterior. After much thought, he arrived at a compromise. He explained the tradition of the Christmas ball in the Choiseul home and said to Helene, "The affair would not be complete without the presence of both you and your cousin. In fact, I would be honored, as would my entire family, if your aunt would also attend."

At first Petra said no, but seeing that Helene was interested and that Antonia, too, was eager to go, she accepted. It would give her an opportunity to meet some of the ladies of the community, and, in addition, give her a chance to look over the young men of the area, for soon, she knew, Helene would tire of being a companion for her aunt. Moreover, Antonia was soon to be of an age where lads would begin to seriously consider her for matrimony.

Jean-Charles insisted on coming for them, and arrived at his father's home as escort to three lovely women. Petra left word with one of her servants to bring a carriage early so that she could return to Jason, leaving the two girls to be escorted home by Jean-Charles.

It was a pleasant and friendly crowd, and the appearance of the D'Art family caused quite a stir. Not all of the people present had seen all of the females of the Chateau D'Art, but most had heard reports of their beauty. To see them together was an experience. The childlike but blossoming beauty of Antonia, the young sweetness and the gypsy darkness of Helene, complimented and made complete by Petra's blond and mature beauty, made the three of them the center of attention until Petra was swept away by the host to be introduced, Helene was pulled onto the dance floor by Jean-Charles, and Antonia, left alone, began to look around, seeing her young married lover with his doughfaced wife. However, Antonia was not alone long, since women of her type seldom were. There is an air about the promiscuous woman which attracts certain types of men, as if, deep down inside, there is a sixth sense which, with atavistic nostrils, smells the odorless musk radiated by the Antonias of the world.

As she chatted with the host and hostess and others

among their friends, Petra was pleased to note that neither her daughter nor her niece lacked for male attention. That Jean-Charles was constantly at Helene's side did not escape her attention, and she watched closely to see if Antonia seemed to be upset, hiding her frown when Antonia flirted with equal daring with boys of the age of Jean-Charles and older men as well.

Helene, uneasy at first at her first formal ball, soon gained confidence and smiled helplessly when, to Jean-Charles's chagrin, another young man took her away to the dance floor. Understandably, as she experienced her first "belle of the ball" glory, she did not notice either Antonia or her aunt. Thus she did not know what was happening when a woman's voice, shrill and near hysteria, rose above the sound of the music and she noticed a disturbance at the other side of the ballroom.

Hervé Dubois, who had met Antonia first in the bank of which he was chief cashier, had noted the appearance of the D'Art family with great interest, seeing in the childish face of Antonia the familiar face of a lover whose very touch made him forget his humdrum life and the whining voice of his doughfaced wife. Dubois, slickly handsome, with oiled hair and a tightly trimmed moustache, had always fancied himself to be more than a mere cashier and had never forgotten that he married a woman whose beauty was nonexistent simply for his own financial security—her father owned the Bank of Marmande. When he was with Antonia, he fancied himself to be the great lover and adventurer, taking from her not only her eager and youthful sexual charms, but a sense of having traveled with her to such far-off places as exotic Panama.

He had performed his duty dances with his wife and was hoping mightily that someone—anyone—would have the decency to take her off his hands, at least for one dance. He watched, his anger growing, as Antonia danced every number, laughing up into the faces of her partners. And when nature came to his rescue— nature and the punch which was being served in generous quantities—he took advantage of his wife's trip to the bathroom to push between a young and ardent-eyed admirer and Antonia and sweep her onto the floor for a slow and dreamy waltz.

"Aren't you risking rousing her anger?" Antonia asked him. She was fond of teasing him about his wife.

"A mere courtesy dance with a young friend," Hervé said. "I must say you seem to be enjoying yourself."

"Shouldn't I?" she asked, with a little smile.

"I am furiously jealous," he whispered.

"Oh, so am I," she teased. "I cry when I think of you in bed with your wife."

He did not see his wife return, look around for him, and, with tightly set lips, discover him dancing with Antonia. Antonia saw, however.

"You do not have to look as if you're enjoying it so," Hervé told Antonia. "You were dancing so close to that young Gramont that I could scarcely see between you."

Antonia was bored with his jealousy. "It is not for you to say with whom I dance or how closely," she said.

"Oh, please," he begged, "I meant nothing."

"Have care, then, how you speak to me."

"It's just that it pains me to see you in another man's arms," he whispered, "knowing—"

"Knowing?" she asked.

"You know what I mean."

The music ended. Hervé, reluctant to release Antonia, held her arm and guided her toward the punch table. "Go to your wife," Antonia hissed.

"In a moment." He poured her a cup of punch and handed it to her. Then, leaning close, he said, "Can you come tomorrow? I can get away—"

Without noticing it, Hervé had steered Antonia to a

spot quite near Petra, and Petra had begun to move toward them, unseen by either until, just as Hervé was making his proposition—something which definitely was not new with them—Antonia realized that her mother was hearing every whispered word he was saying.

"I can get away at mid-afternoon if you will meet me—"

Thinking quickly, Antonia said, "I find your invitation disgusting and insulting, sir."

There was a stricken look on Dubois's face, and for a moment he did not understand.

"Is there anything wrong, Antonia?" Petra asked, appearing beside them, having heard the words—'I can get away at mid-afternoon if you will meet me.'

"Nothing I can't handle, mother," said Antonia. "I fear, Monsieur Dubois has had too much to drink."

"I—I beg your pardon," Hervé stammered. "I was merely interested, my dear Mademoiselle D'Art, in going over your savings account with you. I had no intention of sounding improper."

"I'm sure you didn't," Petra said coldly, having heard the low and insinuating tone, but not suspecting that her daughter's apparent shock was not genuine.

Instead of fading away, Hervé tried to square things, insisting that he was merely trying to arrange a business conference with the young lady. In the midst of it his wife came, her face dark, lips pinched. She took Hervé's arm, and he, terrified now, could not stop talking.

"I was just telling Madame D'Art, my dear, that her young daughter should have a conference with me at the bank in regard to her savings."

"Why should we have a conference over a mere twenty francs?" Antonia said, beginning to see possibilities in the situation.

"Oh, my dear," Hervé said, "there is no such thing as a mere twenty francs."

"We must go now, Hervé," his wife said.

"A moment, please," Dubois said, desperate, not knowing that prolonging the encounter was a danger to him. "You do understand, Madame D'Art, that my invitation to your daughter was strictly in the line of business."

"Invitation?" Madame Dubois said.

"I merely asked Mademoiselle D'Art to drop by the bank at her convenience," Hervé said, as he saw his wife's eyes narrow. He knew she was insanely jealous.

"Oh, by the *bank*," Madame Dubois said, but her tone made it sound obscene.

Antonia was laughing inside, pleased to see them at each other's throats. Her interest in Hervé was passing, and seeing him as the dominated husband did not endear him to her.

"Business, business," Dubois insisted. "Is the misunderstanding cleared up, then?" he asked, looking at Petra pleadingly.

"There was no misunderstanding on my part, monsieur," Antonia said, stern-faced. "I told you that your invitation was insulting and disgusting, and so it was. Now, if you'll excuse us."

"What did he say?" Madame Dubois demanded.

"For your answer, madame," Antonia said coldly, "look to your husband."

Fury made Madame Dubois's face a reddened mass. "I demand to know—"

"You demand?" Antonia asked, in a voice which Petra recognized as reaching the danger point of anger.

"Come, Antonia," Petra said.

"You dare speak to me in that tone of voice when your disgusting husband has just extended an indecent proposal to me?" Antonia asked, her voice rising.

"Please, please," Hervé Dubois said.

"Shameless hussy!" Madame Dubois said. Petra bristled. But Antonia was too quick. She slapped Madame Dubois full in the face and was preparing to meet the woman's onslaught when Hervé, his face purpled by shame and fear, seized his wife and tried to drag her away.

"I saw you flirting with him, you hussy," Madame Dubois screamed. "I saw you. I've seen you flirting with every man here."

"I think this has gone quite far enough," Petra said. Monsieur de Choiseul, having heard the commotion, was at her side.

"My dear Madame D'Art," Choiseul said, "may I be of assistance?"

"I apologize for the disruption, monsieur," Petra said.

"What is it?" he asked.

"That young slut—" Madame Dubois began, but she was silenced by Hervé's hand over her mouth. She bit his fingers and he yelped, but did not remove his hand as blood ran down onto his wife's lip.

"My wife is upset," Hervé said. "I will see her home."

"Perhaps, Monsieur Dubois," Choiseul said, "that is a good idea."

Petra, pale and upset, watched Dubois struggle to take his wife from the room, and, as they were going into the cloakroom, he freed her mouth.

"Wait until I get you home!" she screamed. And then her voice receded.

"It is nothing," Petra told her host. "Please don't concern yourself. A misunderstanding, that's all."

"Madame Dubois is quite excitable," Choiseul said.

Unable to stand it any longer, Antonia excused herself and those who saw her rush for the powder room thought it was because she, too, was upset. Once inside, however, she held her stomach and let the laughter peel out. She was still laughing when Helene, concerned about her, came into the room.

"Did you see her face?" Antonia gasped. "Oh, did you see her face?"

Helene, who had witnessed the disgraceful exit of the Dubois couple without knowing the entire reason, was astounded by Antonia's reaction. She was going to ask questions when Petra came into the room and suggested, in view of the unpleasant events, that they all go home in the carriage which had arrived for her.

"I will not let a fishwife spoil my evening," Antonia said. "With your permission, Helene and I will stay."

"Will you be all right?" Petra asked nervously, but with the steady and dependable Helene there, she decided that it was all right for the girls to stay, since Antonia wanted to so much. Although she had been impressed by Antonia's maturity in a difficult situation, she questioned the need for violence, and she determined that she would talk with Antonia about the blow which her daughter had delivered.

Petra left and the incident was soon forgotten in the good spirit of the season—forgotten by everyone but Antonia. For her, it was an educational experience. She was already familiar with the power she could wield over men, and now she had discovered that with a straight face and the nerve of—as the saying went—a pirate, she could influence events to her own satisfaction.

Gaily she danced and used her large and lovely eyes to instill wild dreams in the heart of half a dozen young men. It was, for her, a very rewarding evening, and she did not miss the attentions of Jean-Charles. Even at her tender age, she had the happy facility of blaming Jean-Charles for a lack of taste, rather than feeling that Helene had won him away from her. This, too, represented a development in her character which would mark her. For, to use a term only newly defined by a young physician working in Vienna, her ego was such that she would never admit inferiority, in any manner, to another woman.

There was to be one other result of the altercation. Knowing her strength, she would, with confidence and a will which would win out, begin anew her campaign to be sent into Paris to continue her education.

The Christmas ball in the home of Jean-Charles de Choiseul produced other long-lasting emotions. When, at last, Jean-Charles was able to maneuver Helene into an area of privacy, the balcony outside the ballroom, he had to speak quickly, for the night was chill, with a cold wind coming from the river.

"Before we both freeze," he said, laughing, his arm around Helene's shoulders so that he could feel her shiver, "I want to say that you are very beautiful tonight."

"Thank you," Helene said, answering his laugh. "But did you have to bring me to the Arctic to tell me that?"

"No," he said. "I brought you here for this." And so saying, he put his arms around her. Surprised, she tried to turn her lips away, but he put a hand on her cheek and his touch caused her to halt any resistance, let his mouth lower to hers. And then she felt his warmth, and the chill of the night was forgotten.

"Helene," he said. "I must finish my schooling, and so I cannot speak. But I ask a promise of you."

"Yes?" she asked, clinging to him for his warmth and for the pounding of her heart.

"If it is too much to ask, tell me. But will you promise me, my dear Helene, that you will not fall in love while I am away?"

"I think I can safely promise that," she whispered.

"That is all I ask," he said. He kissed her once more, and, his heart singing, took her into the ballroom where she was immediately snatched from his hand by one of his friends. He watched her as she was swirled to the strains of a waltz, thinking that in all his life he had never seen anyone more beautiful.

15

SPRING CAME WITH a giant vial of perfume which she sprinkled liberally over the countryside as flowers celebrated, birds began their annual courtships, and the white, fleecy clouds sailed in azure skies. Petra rediscovered the joys of the country, taking an interest in the running of the farm, with the farm-wise Helene at her side. Now the girl seemed especially dear to her, for Antonia, dressed in a new wardrobe, excited to the point of stumbling over her parting words, had departed for a fine music school in Paris. Little Jason was growing as fast as the fat pigs of the spring litters, as the whole world renewed itself.

With exercise and willpower at the laden table, Petra regained her figure. She was a woman in her full maturity who, with her face as the exception—it was much more beautiful—could have modeled for many of the paintings which were displayed that spring in Paris, or for the full and voluptuous renderings of Liberty which adorned French stamps of that year. A woman at peace with herself at last, she was mother, fond aunt to Helene and she felt like crying with joy when, with a shyness, Helene confessed that Jean-Charles de Choiseul had promised himself to her once he was through with his education. She could have wished no more for the lovely girl and was pleased to think that Helene would escape all of the trials of life, all of the horror which had come to both her mother and to Petra.

"And you," she asked, "do you love him?"

Helene tried to appear to be unflustered, but the nervous movements of her hands belied her calm. "I have asked myself that question. I like being near him. I like the way he looks at me. When he touches me, I feel a slight giddiness."

Petra laughed happily. "A classic description of love," she said. "I fear, my dear niece, that you are lost."

"In Podensac we used to say, 'Don't pick the grapes until they have drunk of the sun,'" Helene said. "He will be away for a long time."

"My wise little oracle," Petra laughed. "But I have a fine feeling about this. I think your Jean-Charles will remember you and come back to you with his ardor undiminished."

"We will see how the grape takes on color," Helene said.

"Oh, Helene, you're impossible!" Petra said, stooping to clutch a handful of field blossoms and toss them into Helene's hair.

"Aha!" Helene laughed, plucking her own flowers.

Petra, seeing her intention, ran. She felt light and young. The spring air was invigorating, and her feet flew over the meadow, with Helene, laughing, close behind, throwing flowers into her hair a few at a time.

To Jay, reining in his horse at the foot of the lane, they looked like Venus and a young nymph, chasing each other across the flower-strewn meadow, skirts flying. His horse, smelling the hay in the stables, neighed and was answered by a pair of horses grazing in the meadow. The two, also feeling the effects of spring, ran, tails high, toward the fence to investigate, passing Petra and Helene, who had stopped, panting, laughing.

"We have company," Helene said, pointing toward the tall, large man on horseback.

Petra looked and her laugh died on her lips, for there was no mistaking the manly bulk, the strong neck, the large head. "Oh, my God!" she said.

"Is something wrong?" Helene asked.

"No, no. It's just an old friend. I haven't seen him in a very long time." And then it was necessary to walk up the slight rise as Jay removed his hat and waited. He was smiling. When they were near, he bowed from the saddle.

"A charming picture," he said.

Petra halted a few feet away. "Hello, Jay."

There were flowering small yellow blossoms caught in her hair. The exercise had flushed her cheeks.

He dismounted. "And is this—" He paused. "No, this is not Antonia."

"My niece," Petra said. "Helene, this is an old friend from Panama, Mr. Jay Burton." Helene made a quick curtsy.

"Charmed," Jay said.

"But where is my sense of hospitality?" Petra asked. "You must be tired. Have you ridden far?"

"Not far," Jay said. They walked up the lane, Jay leading the horse, Petra stealing sidelong glances at him as he told of his trip, of the conditions in Panama.

She ordered food for him and he ate. Helene excused herself, leaving them alone. "God, Petra, you are so beautiful."

"Please!"

"I've come a long way."

"I know," she said. "I know."

"And I've missed you very much."

"Please, Jay. It's too late."

"Yes," he said, "it is much too late—much too late for me to forget you. We've wasted enough time, Petra."

"We will settle it now," she said. "We were wrong, Jay, doing what we did. I have had all the sadness, all the guilt that I can stand in one lifetime. Please feel free to stay until you have rested. Then I must ask you to leave."

"Damn it, Petra," he began.

"No," she said. "Please understand. I am at peace now. I am happy. I have my daughter, Helene—" She started to add, "my son," but she stopped. "Please, Jay, seeing you brings back all the old pain."

He was silent.

"Will you go back to San Francisco?" she asked.

He shrugged. "I have no plans."

There was an uncomfortable silence. Jay toyed with a scrap of food left on his plate. Petra, tension making her hands shake, rose and walked to a window.

"You left without even saying good-bye," he said.

"Do you know how he died?" she asked, not looking at him.

"Only that he died that day," Jay said.

"Guy came to him and tried to get him to do something, I'm not sure what, but he wrote a brief entry in his journal. He said that Guy wanted him to lie about something pertaining to de Lesseps. And, after all that had happened, he hated Guy so much that the excitement—the strain of the argument—caused him to die. Had I been there—"

"You have no way of guessing what might have happened had you been there," Jay said. "It could have been worse. Your presence—seeing you with Guy —might have excited him more."

"No. I would have kept Guy from him."

"Perhaps. But I have to feel that it was God's will, Petra. You know the fever and the aftermath of it weakened Roger terribly. I think his strength merely ran out, that he would have died of something else. Petra, you're being irrational to blame yourself. Roger would not have wanted you to blame yourself."

"Don't try to speak for a dead man," Petra said coldly. She turned to face him. "Listen to me. I'm happy. I'm content. I have the future of two young girls to consider."

Confused thoughts in her. Antonia's frequent cryptic comments attacking her mother's morality. Antonia somehow knew that she had loved Jay, that she had gone to him. And the girl was at a critical stage of her life. She wanted so much for her daughter, and if anything she had done had the influence of bringing to the fore the characteristics of Antonia's personality which were so like Darcie, she would, she felt, simply lie down and die.

"And when they're married and happy and you're alone?" Jay asked. "We're not young anymore, but we have a few good years left, and I want to spend them with you."

For a moment, Petra almost hated him. She remembered the lovely afternoon, the peace, the feeling of exuberance she'd known as she gamboled with Helene in the meadow. Now he was here and his presence brought it all back: all the old hurts and unpleasantness, all the stink and rot of Panama and the feeling of helplessness when Roger was ill, not himself. And then the wrenching pain of his death.

"Petra," he said, rising to come toward her. "I'm sorry. I know that my sudden appearance here must have been a shock to you. I've had a long journey. If you will give me the hospitality of your home, I'll rest, and then, after a good night's sleep, we'll talk. If you still feel the same way tomorrow—"

"Yes, you must be tired," she said.

There was a downstairs room, sometimes used as a servant's quarters. It was small but comfortable. She left Jay there and went to join Helene in the nursery, where she was playing with a happy and cooing Jason. Petra stood in the doorway, watching, seeing in the baby the strong jaw and a hint of the piercing eyes of his father.

He was there, only a short distance away, in the same house. Jay. Oh, God, Jay.

Petra tossed fretfully in her bed, finally sleeping after the entire world had hushed, waking to the sun and the insistence of the roosters from the barnyards. Cook, having a man in the house, served a man-sized breakfast and Jay ate heartily, talking with Helene, answering her curious questions about Panama and the state of things there. Helene was quite impressed by the tall, strong-looking American.

"Oh, I do so wish Jean-Charles were here," she said. "He would enjoy talking with you. He's going to be an engineer, too."

Jay smiled, hearing in her voice a quality which told him much when she spoke of this Jean-Charles. He inquired about Antonia and was told that she was very much involved with her life in Paris, living with several other girls in a sort of foster home presided over by a stern widow who treated the girls as if they were her own; so stern, Petra said, that Antonia was complaining about a lack of freedom.

"But," she said, "I'm sure Antonia has all the freedom I'd like her to have."

"Is she still as full of life as she was?" Jay asked.

"Oh, that girl!" Petra sighed. "You wouldn't even recognize her, Jay. She's grown so. And so full of energy and things to do. Sometimes I feel that she is too precocious, and I worry."

"Antonia has a good head on her shoulders," Helene said. "She may seem to be reckless, at times, but I'm sure that you don't have to worry about her, Aunt Petra."

"I'm sure you're right," Petra said.

They talked of mutual friends and acquaintances

from Panama, and Helene excused herself. There had still been no mention of the baby.

"This is a lovely place," Jay said, when they were alone at the table, with a fresh pot of coffee.

"Roger's family built it and lived in it for generations," Petra said.

"Would you like to show me around the fields?"

"If you like."

"Do you ride?"

"Occasionally."

Petra sent cook to tell the stableman to saddle Jay's horse and her own mare and left him to change into her riding habit. He was in the same clothes he'd worn on arrival when she came downstairs, having carried with him only a small cloth bag of necessities after renting the horse in Marmande. She led the way down to the river and rode along it, and he pulled alongside.

"I can see how you'd be happy here," he said.

"Yes, it's quiet and peaceful."

"And is that what you want?"

"I want no more strife," she said. "Ever."

"Do you hear from Darcie and Guy?"

"No. When Helene came to me and I discovered that she was Darcie's child, we wrote to Darcie, but received no answer."

"I have heard that they are very much involved with Bunau-Varilla in the effort to get the Americans to buy the assets of the canal company."

"I'm not surprised. It sounds like Guy. He sold all his holdings—even his family home—to invest in canal stock. He must be desperate." And for a moment she could feel a bit of sympathy for him, and for Darcie.

The bridle path, worn smooth by Antonia, who loved riding, led to the river's bank in a small glade among chestnuts.

"We'll stop here," Jay said, coming up alongside and catching the bridle of Petra's horse. She did not object. It had to be settled. He had to be convinced that she had no intention of disrupting her life again.

He helped her dismount, his hands under her arms to lift her down and, standing close, facing her, his hands on her shoulders, he looked into her eyes. She turned away.

"Is there someone else?" he asked.

"Oh, no," she said, with involuntary quickness. Then: "There is no one else, nor will there be. Can't you believe that I am content just as I am?"

"No, Petra. I know you. You are a woman who needs love."

"Love, or the wallowing in a man's bed?" she asked bitterly.

"We were going to be married."

"And my husband was alive all the time."

"It is not a sin to love deeply."

"But why is love always associated with lust?"

"Because that is the nature of the world."

"It is not *my* nature," she said heatedly. "Thank God, I've developed past that. I'm not Darcie. I can live and be happy without men."

"If you were like Darcie, I wouldn't be here. You can't push me away again, Petra. I've waited too long. We were meant to be together."

"Will you release me, please?" she asked, trying to move out from under his hands.

"No."

"You are, of course, the stronger."

"Yes, damn it," he said, seizing her roughly and drawing her to him. She made no resistance, but she was limp, unresponding. When he forced her face up, his hand under her chin, she looked at him coldly, and, when his lips came to hers, let her own lips close tightly, accepting his kiss without return.

He released her and walked a few paces away. "I think we'd better go back," she said. "There is Helene.

She is a sweet and loving child. I will do nothing to destroy her faith in me."

"Can you not think of me, of yourself?" he asked in desperation.

"I have. Once there was a chance for us, Jay. It's long past. It's twice past—once because of your actions and once because of mine."

"I will find a place nearby and stay here," he said. "I'll give you some time. I won't take no for an answer until I've had a chance to show my love for you."

"I won't change," she said.

They rode back to the house in silence, approaching it from the rear. The day was sunny and warm, and Helene had taken little Jason to the patio where he wriggled and kicked happily on a quilt placed on the sunny tiles of the floor.

Jay looked at Petra in question. "A sweet and loving child?" he asked.

She flushed, getting his meaning. He had assumed the baby to be Helene's. "He is mine," she said.

"Yours?"

"Yes."

He shook his head. "Oh, my God!" he said. "Petra—"

"And Roger's," she said.

"No. I know that is not true."

"Of course it's true. He was my husband."

Jay moved his horse ahead, tied the reins to a bush behind the patio and walked up to greet the smiling Helene.

"Here's our little darling," Helene said. "Jason D'Art, meet Mr. Jay Burton. He is from America." The baby kicked and cooed. Jay, his face strained, bent and picked Jason up, holding him in his arms in that awkward way men have with babies before they learn by experience that babies don't break easily. Jason made bubbling sounds and reached up a pudgy hand to tug at Jay's moustache. And the picture tore at Petra's heart, seeing them together.

"And how old is he?" Jay asked Helene. She counted on her fingers and gave the figure in months. Jay looked at Petra, his eyes squinted, something like anger in his look. "Jason, is it?" he asked.

"Named for Roger's father," Petra said quickly.

"Oh, I didn't know that, Aunt Petra," Helene said.

"Oh, yes. I suppose I've never mentioned it."

Jason was now trying to pluck Jay's eyes with his uncoordinated little fingers, and there was a smile on the big man's face, a tenderness in his look, which caused Petra to turn away her eyes.

"Mr. Burton was just leaving us," Petra said.

"Not staying for lunch?" Helene said. "Cook will be disappointed. She says that's it nice to cook for a man for a change."

"Well, we wouldn't want to disappoint her, would we?" Jay asked. "I can postpone my departure—at least until after lunch."

After a few minutes, Jay discovered that he could make the baby laugh happily by lifting him into the air and he did so repeatedly, laughing with the boy. And then the inevitable happened. He looked at the growing wet spot on his trousers with a wry laugh. Helene leaped up and took the sodden baby, carrying him inside to make the necessary repairs.

"Petra, Petra," Jay said. "He's a wonderful baby. Why didn't you let me know? God, I would have liked to be here!"

"There was no reason. I've told you—he is Roger's son."

"Lies!" he said harshly. "I can see it in his face. I can see *me* in his face. My God, what do you think I am? Do you think I can walk away from my own son? Now listen to me. Bleed for the past if you must, feel your bedamned guilt if you must, but that is my son. I know it in my very bones. Look me in the eyes and tell me he is not my son."

"It changes nothing."

"It changes everything. Perhaps I might let you deprive us of happiness through guilt and a false sense of atonement for sins which were committed only out of love, but I'm not going to let you deprive me of my son, and my son of his father."

"I must have time to think," Petra said. "Will you please go?"

"Yes," he said. "I'll go. But I'll be back. Tomorrow, and the day after that and the day after that."

He waited until Helene had returned with a dry Jason, bounced the infant on his knee, making silly sounds at him, and then he rode into the village to find a room in a boardinghouse. He spent the next afternoon playing with Jason on the patio and talking with Helene. Petra found something to do in the house. The pattern was established. Each day he would ride out from Marmande. He charmed cook into thinking that he was one of the most witty men in the world, and he ate well as a result, for she loved cooking for a big man with a hearty appetite.

Helene came to like him very much.

"Antonia used to call me Uncle Jay in Panama," he told Helene.

"I've never had a real uncle," she said. "Might I adopt you, too?"

"I'd be honored," he said.

Helene thought it wonderful that the big, strong man loved children so much. He seemed to dote on little Jason and this brought them close, for so did she. As for Petra, she decided on a course of being friendly and informal, as if Jay were merely an old friend. She tried to avoid being alone with him, but it was not always possible. However, he did not try to push her; in fact, he made no mention of their love,

their future, seeming to be content to be a friend of
the family and to have his time with his son.

He was present when the messenger came from the
village with the telegram from Paris. "Daughter ill,"
the telegram said. "Come at once." It was signed by
the widow who ran the home for girls in Paris. In
a panic, Petra found herself relying on Helene to
prepare a bag for her, and on Jay to get her into town
to take a train. She made no objections when Jay said
he was going with her. She sent a telegram telling the
housemother that she was on the way and boarded
the train, Jay at her side, with her fears making her
imagine all sorts of horrors. It seemed ironic that Antonia would survive all the dangers of disease in Panama only to fall ill in Paris. She alternated between
fearing the worst and telling herself that it was merely
influenza, perhaps, that God would not inflict more
sufferings on her. She had been afflicted, she felt, with
more than her share.

16

ANTONIA WAS THE youngest resident of Mme. Tousand's hostel for girls. All of the residents —Antonia soon came to think of herself as an inmate —lived by the rules of the house, and, in Antonia's case, Madame Tousand's already strict rules were augmented by other rules laid down by her mother.

The Tousand establishment had been recommended to Petra by her solicitors. The place had an excellent reputation. It was expensive enough to make a parent feel confident in handing over the care of a daughter to a stranger in a big city.

Mme. Tousand was the widow of an impoverished but highly respectable army officer, and she was of good family. At her receptions, which she gave with clockwork regularity every three months, the young men invited had been screened and would have met the approval—at least on a social level—of all but the most aristocratic parents. Twelve girls lived in the house on the Rue Charlemagne, two to a room. Although the house was old, the rooms were large and airy, with huge windows which allowed plentiful light for the three girls who were studying art.

Antonia's roommate was a bovine and placid girl, daughter of a prosperous wine merchant, who was one of the aspiring artists, so that the room always smelled of mineral spirits and paint, much to Antonia's disgust. Equally disgusting to Antonia was her roommate's name, for never was a girl more mislabeled than fat Babette. However, the girl's easygoing nature allowed her to be easily influenced, and within hours after meeting, the relationship was established, with Antonia being, undoubtedly, the dominating force of the two.

If Mme. Tousand was the warden of what Antonia soon came to think of as a prison, Mlle. Julie was the guard. Mlle. Julie was a cadaverously thin spinster of some sixty years who, Antonia was sure, would faint if a man came within ten feet of her. She took it on herself to keep track of each minute spent by her charges. Indeed, no outing was allowed unless Mlle. Julie was along to prevent the girls from falling into the evil ways of the city, and since she was so old, she complained loudly and piteously if Antonia wanted to walk along the Seine for more than a few minutes at a time.

Early on, Antonia wrote impassioned letters to her mother, telling Petra that she was not a child to be watched each minute, that the lack of freedom was stifling her. However, her pleas for the arrangement of more liberal living arrangements were brushed aside, with Petra's telling her that the young are not always wise enough to know what is best for them.

Antonia's days were exciting. In the very good private music school, she found that she was, if not technically as proficient as some, possessed of a feel for music which impressed her instructors and led to her receiving more than her share of attention.

"Proficiency will come," M. Garlie told her, time and time again. "Technique can be taught. Talent, however, is not teachable, and, my dear girl, you are one of the rare ones."

Antonia did not stint her work. There was quite a good piano in the parlor of the Tousand house and she spent long and rewarding evenings in practice, pleasing Mme. Tousand with her music, often attracting the entire populace of the house to hear her play, and, when she was in the mood, sing some ballad currently popular in a sweet, modulated voice.

There were only two times of the day when Antonia was alone. In the mornings, she walked the short distance to the school, and, after several hours, the schedule varying, she walked home. She was, of course, under strict orders not to tarry along the way and not to deviate from the straight and narrow path between school and her temporary home, but the varying schedule proved to be her salvation. The first time, having left the school a bit earlier than usual, she decided to walk alone along the river and to cross the bridge onto the island, she kept looking over her shoulder as if Mme. Tousand or Mlle. Julie would appear at any instant and reprimand her, but when she spent a lovely hour walking alone and no one seemed to know, it opened up possibilities for her.

Already well founded in the theory of music, she found the classes to be easy. Her compositions received some praise. As she became more established in the regard of her instructors, it was possible for her to leave the school early. It was not M. Garlie's responsibility to see to it that she went directly home. Indeed, once she had left his school, she was, as far as he was concerned, out of sight, out of mind.

Petra was quite generous in giving Antonia spending money, so there was money to take carriages to places not within walking distance. Antonia soon became familiar with the heart of the city, its great monuments, its museums, its parks. The Louvre became one of her favorite places and going there alone, walking if there was time and taking a carriage if not, she felt no guilt. It seemed absolutely silly to her to be

forbidden to take advantage of the cultural and educational opportunities in Paris simply because some
old women thought that she would be sold into white
slavery or something.

It was while examining some of the loot brought
home from Egypt by Napoleon that she met the Baron
Alesia du Cochin. She stood in front of a lovely bust
of an Egyptian woman, wondering at its great age and
exquisite beauty, when a voice behind her interrupted
her musings.

"Life is ever more beautiful than art," the man
said.

She cast a glance and saw a man of, she estimated,
her mother's age. She was wrong, for the baron was
in his early thirties. He carried a handsome cane and
was dressed in a very expensive suit of morning clothes,
a top hat on his well-formed head. In that brief glance,
she saw a clean-shaven face flushed with what she
took to be health. He had a slim, aristocratic nose,
bushy eyebrows, a firm mouth.

"I see her as a queen," he said, when Antonia ignored him.

"Oh, no," she said. "She is merely an attendant to
a queen."

"So young and so knowledgeable?" he asked with
a smile.

"I read it in the guidebook," Antonia said.

"Ah, but I do not have a guidebook," Cochin said.

"They're on sale near the main entrance," Antonia
said.

"Next time, perhaps, I shall buy one. Do you come
here often?"

"Oh, yes. I find it"—she paused—"I find it quite
educational."

"Absolutely. You appear to know much about art."
He laughed. "I, I fear, am quite ignorant in the field."
He gave her a musing look. "In fact, I would be grate-

ful for the company of a beautiful and well-informed guide."

Antonia looked around nervously. This was the very thing which both Mme. Tousand and Mlle. Julie warned against.

"Never, never talk to strange men."

However, people were all around. What could happen in such a public place? She was flattered and she walked around the Egyptian rooms, the baron at her side, explaining the origin of the various displays. In her several trips there, the Egyptians were her favorites, and she had done much reading about them, so that her information was accurate. Cochin was respectful. He asked questions which she was able to answer. She had the feeling of being quite grown-up and wise, pleased to attract the attention of such a distinguished man. She had never known a man with a title.

As they talked, the baron casually threw in personal questions until, by the time they had made the circuit of the Egyptian exhibits, he knew where she was from, where she was staying, her school, her usual hours of finishing at the school. She thought it to be polite curiosity. In return, she gathered some information about the baron. He was, as yet, unmarried, and spent the summer in a house on the Île St.-Louis between the two branches of the Seine, an area which Antonia knew to be quite expensive—very rich, in fact.

The baron was a man of some experience and he was patient. When hunting such young birds of paradise, one had to exercise patience or the bird took flight. He made no move that first day. Instead, on the next day, a sunny and pleasant one, he was standing outside Antonia's school when she came out, a portfolio of music manuscripts under her arm. He tipped his hat and smiled.

"I could say that I just happened to be passing," he said, "but it would be a lie."

"Why, baron," Antonia said, secretly pleased to see him, "what a pleasant surprise."

"Is it the museum today?"

"Actually, I hadn't decided."

"I thought, perhaps, the Greeks today," he said. "And to give us more time, I have my carriage."

Again, he was patient. Although not as familiar with the Greeks as with the Egyptians, Antonia had her guidebook and they pored over it together. After a pleasant hour, she said she had to go.

"I will escort you."

"Thank you," she said. "But you'll have to let me off a block away from the house. My jailors would not approve."

"Then we will make it our secret," the baron said.

It was a lovely secret. It gave her something to look forward to. He did not appear at the school the next day, for he was a patient man and did not want to ruin his chances by haste. But the day after that, his carriage was there and it was the museum again. On subsequent days there were pleasant rides along the wide boulevards, once all the way to the Arc de Triomphe. And, in a pleasant café, she accepted a small glass of sherry.

Two weeks after meeting Cochin, she rode with him along the river. The carriage passed over a bridge onto the island and he ordered the driver to stop in front of an impressive house.

"I thought you might like to see where I live," he said.

"My, it is impressive."

"It is adequate," he said.

She laughed. "Adequate? Many people would consider it to be a palace. Does it have a dungeon?"

"Only a dark and damp basement," he laughed. "But there is said to be a ghost. During the Troubles, it is said that a woman was killed there."

"How terrible. Is it a frightful ghost?"

"A kind one, I think. She does no harm. She mopes about the basement with her head in her hands, or somesuch."

"How exciting," Antonia said, shivering. "Have you seen her?"

"It is said that she makes herself known only to beautiful young women," Cochin said. "Perhaps she would reveal herself to you?"

"Let's try," Antonia said.

"You may take the carriage into the courtyard," he told his driver. "I will call when we are ready."

It was a palace inside, but the baron, seemingly intent on doing only what they had planned to do, escorted her through rich rooms to a stairwell leading down. They had to use candles.

The basement was indeed damp and dark. It was cluttered with the debris of the establishment, some of the discarded or stored pieces looking more valuable, in the flickering light, than anything in Chateau D'Art. Cochin halted in the center of the basement room.

"Now we must blow out the candles."

"Oh," Antonia said, as darkness enfolded them.

"And we must be very quiet."

They stood there for long minutes. She could hear his even breathing. He stood close, but did not touch her. And, after a long time, there was a sound. It could have been a rat, but it was sudden, and, Antonia, startled, let out a cry and reached out her hand for him. He took her hand in his.

"I fear you've frightened her away," he said.

"I think I'm frightened away, too," she laughed.

He lit a candle and led her back up the stairs into a splendid and cozy small room with wide and comfortable sofas. He rang and a maid in uniform came, curtsied at his order to bring tea.

"Perhaps we can try again," he said.

"I've suddenly lost my interest in ghosts." She looked around. "It's all so beautiful."

And so, there was a tour of the house, which was a sort of museum in its own rights, leading Antonia to suspect Cochin's profession to be ignorant of the arts. Then he took her back across the river to let her out a block from her home. He was still patient, but now he moved a bit faster.

The occasion was special. She had agreed to leave school early so that they might have lunch together. It was a splendid meal, served in a small dining room in his house on the island. There was wine. And, afterward, he sat beside her, took her hand and kissed it. There were no words. She saw in his eyes what he intended. In fact, she'd been wondering if he would ever kiss her, and when he did, she answered with wet and seeking lips. The trip to an upstairs bedroom was made swiftly.

He undressed her with loving care, still patient, knowing that the wait would be worthwhile, and by the time he began, ever so slowly, to place kisses on her naked shoulders, she was wet with her passions. However, she was wise beyond her years, and she sensed that a part of her attraction for this elegant and rich older man was her youth and what he must presume to be her innocence.

"I've—I've never done anything like this before," she whispered, allowing her voice to quiver as he began to fondle and kiss her proud young breasts.

"Don't be afraid, little flower," he whispered.

"You won't hurt me?"

"Hurt you? Never, never."

And, later, after she had to fight to prevent her loins from leaping and heaving under his questing tongue. "Is this going to make me with child?"

He laughed lightly. "No, my dear."

"Please don't hurt me," she moaned, as he, at last, with her body crying out in need, came between her soft and firm thighs and began to prepare the way with his fingers.

And he was gentle. And she held her muscles tightly together, moaning as he penetrated, slowly, slowly. Then, with a cry, she heaved and he was thrust in. She screamed.

"It will be but a moment's pain," he whispered, raining kisses on her face.

"Oh, oh, oh!" she moaned, as if in pain, but actually in ecstasy.

She even managed some tears for him, when, in haste and need, he came to a swift completion.

But the afternoon was young, and, in the coming two hours, the Baron Alesia du Cochin displayed a skill and a libido which had Antonia in heaven. With her body tickled and teased with feathers, she writhed and moaned for him, begging him to enter her. Time and again he would lift her to the brink and then ease off—and when, at last, he took her to the end, she sent her voice up, up, in a keening wail of sheer joy and clung to him as heaven came down to earth for what seemed to be an eternity.

"You have given me a great gift," he told her, when they were dressed and it was time to deliver her to the neighborhood of her school. "And so I have a gift for you in return."

The locket was incredibly rich in diamonds. "Oh, I couldn't!" she said.

"Please take it, for it is small payment for your having given me your innocence."

Antonia was laughing inside, and she saw nothing wrong in taking the locket. He could obviously afford it. But she knew that it would be spotted in the hostel, and there would be questions. "It's lovely," she whispered, "but what would I tell my friends? What would Madame Tousand say if she saw it?"

"A good point," he said. "Well, then, leave it with me. It is yours and you shall have it at a later date, when it is safe for you to wear it."

"And I'll come look at it often," she said.

Desire came back to him. "As often as can be arranged, my love."

Other gifts she could take: bottles of exquisite perfume, flowers, a soft leather case in which to carry her music. And the afternoons now had meaning. Two or three times a week, the baron would be waiting for her outside the school. The carriage would take them immediately to the house on the island, and it would be a literal and often laughing race to see who could undress first.

It was Babette's love of perfume which was Antonia's downfall. Not content with a touch, a hint of scent, Babette borrowed from Antonia to splash the heavy scents over her pudgy body, to reek of it.

"Babette, you smell like a perfume shop," Antonia said angrily, when the room was absolutely heavy with it. "If you must steal my perfume, please don't bathe in it."

"I didn't think you'd mind," Babette said. "Did I use too much?"

"You could buy your own perfume," Antonia said angrily. "If you cover your entire fat body with it, it won't last long."

Antonia thought no more about the remark, but without knowing it, she had hit Babette in her most sensitive area. The heavy girl was ashamed of her overweight body. And, underneath her placid exterior, Babette had a streak of spite. She had long suspected that Antonia was not always coming home immediately after school, and she was also aware of the expensive items which had appeared on Antonia's side of the room over the past few weeks.

Babette waited a few days before she hinted to Mlle. Julie that Antonia was acting suspiciously—most probably sneaking off to the shops when she was supposed to be coming directly home. Mlle. Julie paid a call on M. Garlie at Antonia's school and discovered that in recent days Antonia had been unaccounted for

for several hours, having left the school sometimes as much as two hours before she arrived at Mme. Tousand's hostel. Mlle. Julie went pale when, from the cover of lush growth on the school lawn, she waited and saw Antonia enter a carriage with a man much older than herself. She shuffled her cadaverous body home as quickly as possible to report, in great shock and distress, to Mme. Tousand, who made inquiries through a friend who was a member of the Paris police, who followed Antonia and the baron to the baron's house and shook his head, knowing the baron as a notorious preyer on young and defenseless girls.

The end result was an excited conference between Mme. Tousand and Mlle. Julie, in which it was decided that such a girl had no place in a respectable establishment. However, one had to move carefully. Mothers were notorious for believing their precious children in preference to anyone else, and, for all they knew, Madame D'Art was one of those mothers who would never believe that her precious darling would be so brazen as to ride to an older man's house in broad daylight and spent hours inside his house without escort. Nor, they felt, was it wise to put such information into a letter.

"She must see for herself," Mlle. Julie said. "And for that she must come to Paris."

"You are right, my dear," Mme. Tousand said.

"But how will we get her here?"

"We will tell her that her daughter is ill."

"But that's dishonest, madame."

"No, it is true. For the girl is ill. It is the sickness of the fallen woman, the same sickness which is suffered by the *poules* of the street."

The telegram was sent.

Petra arrived, in a state of high agitation, in the early evening. Antonia was in her room, preparing for bed. Petra and Jay were received by Mme. Tousand, who answered Petra's frantic questions with, "It is not

urgent, madame. First, we must have a talk—in my
office, if you please."

"You told me she was ill," Petra said. "Where is
she? I must go to her."

"In a few moments," Mme. Tousand said. "Into my
office, if you please, madame and monsieur."

"Come along," Jay said. "Let's get to the bottom
of this."

And, when the Mme. Tousand told Petra, in a
shocked and disapproving voice, of Antonia's trysts
with an older man of shady reputation, Petra lived up
to her expectation as a mother.

"It can't be true!" Petra gasped. "There must be
some explanation."

"That you must get from your daughter," Mme.
Tousand said. "And the sooner you remove her from
my decent house the better."

"How dare you!" Petra exploded.

"Now let's be calm," Jay said. "I agree that there
must be some explanation."

"I will talk with Antonia," Petra said. "If these people can't fullfil their obligations then she must be removed from"—she spat the words—"this decent
house."

"I do not like being called a liar," Mme. Tousand
said. "I suggest, madame, that you do not talk with
your daughter, that you do as Mademoiselle Julie did
and await outside her school to see for yourself that
your daughter does, indeed, make an illicit rendezvous."

"What? Spy on my own daughter?" Petra asked
with shock.

"Then, unless you want proof for yourself, you will
have to take my word for it," Mme. Tousand snapped.
"At any rate, I have summoned you here to inform
you that your daughter is no longer welcome in my
home."

"Madame," Jay said, "I understand your agitation.

But let me warn you that there is such a thing as slander, and I would advise you to be sure of your facts."

Mme. Tousand sputtered. "Slander? Slander?"

"We must all be calm," Jay said, looking directly at Petra who, a mother animal protecting her young, was near explosion. "I'm sure that if, indeed, young Antonia has erred, her mother will be the first to take steps to correct it. However, for the sake of the child, we must be sure."

"Where is Antonia?" Petra asked. "She will tell us the truth of the matter."

"A member of the police has seen it with his own eyes," Mlle. Julie said.

"Oh, God, the police?" Petra asked.

"In an unofficial capacity," Mme. Tousand said. "We want no scandal, madame."

"It gets more and more insulting," Petra said. "Jay, we will take Antonia out of here."

"And wonder who is wrong?" Jay asked. "Wouldn't it be better to know, now, for her sake as well as your own?"

"Antonia would not lie to me," Petra said.

"Ah, madame," Mlle. Julie said. "I have worked with young girls for forty years. A mother would not be a mother if she did not believe her own child in preference to anyone. Mind you, we do not say that your Antonia has become a fallen woman, but the man she has been seeing has a certain reputation. Our friend with the police says that only his great wealth and his position prevent him from being in serious trouble, because of his preference for very young girls. However, he has, to date, been able to buy himself out of his scrapes."

"He will not buy himself out of this," Petra said.

"He is rich and he has powerful friends," Mme. Tousand said. "It is my belief that your only recourse is to remove your daughter from this situation—if it is not too late already."

"Petra," Jay said. "I'd like to know more about this affair." He looked at Mme. Tousand with a smile. "Madame, would you agree to keeping it quiet for the moment—for a day or two—while I, myself, keep watch and, perhaps, have a private word with this rich and powerful man?"

"But, Jay," Petra said. "We owe it to Antonia—"

"We owe it to Antonia to do what's best for her," Jay said. "And if this pervert, who preys on young girls, has done her any harm—" He left his threat unspoken. "Madame Tousand, I will watch at the school tomorrow and on each subsequent day until the situation is resolved. At that time, we will remove Madame D'Art's daughter from your establishment."

"Very well, monsieur," Mme. Tousand said, thinking that although he spoke accented French, he looked capable enough. She would, she suspected, not want to be in the baron's shoes when this big American caught him with Antonia.

Unsure, but convinced by Jay's confidence and his assumption of control of the situation, Petra allowed herself to be taken to a hotel, where she spent a sleepless night in a room alone. She had breakfast with Jay. Then there was nothing to do but wait. He left her in the hotel, hired a carriage, left it at a distance from the school, and found a concealed spot in a doorway. To avoid missing Antonia, he had arrived early. However, the wait was not unpleasant, for the weather was perfect. He noted with interest when a handsome surrey drew up in front of the school and the driver dismounted to stand respectfully, his hands behind his back, beside the horses. Jay could not see the man inside clearly.

A few minutes later, Antonia came out of the building, so changed that he had to look twice to recognize her. Although youthful, she gave the appearance of a much older woman. Her smile, when she approached the surrey, was a thing of wonder. Quickly, Jay walked back to the carriage which was waiting for him, and, as the surrey moved up the street, ordered the driver to follow at a distance.

The baron's driver took the most direct route to the house on the Île St.-Louis. Jay was fifty yards behind when the baron and Antonia dismounted and ran lightly to the entrance. Telling the driver to wait, Jay walked to the front of the house and took stock. The entrance was solid: huge wooden doors. He knew that they would be locked from the inside. He walked to one side of the house along a high stone fence. At the side, he leaped up, caught the top of the wall, and looked over. He saw a handsome courtyard. The French doors on the side of the house were open. He saw no movement within. He pulled himself to the top of the wall, dropped inside, and then ran quickly across the courtyard to the house. He paused at the windows, looking into what appeared to be a formal parlor. He could hear nothing. He stepped in and crossed the large room, opened a door cautiously, and entered a corridor. Still he could hear nothing. And then, as he moved cautiously along the corridor, he heard the sound of voices and kept going until, outside a closed door, he could clearly hear a man's voice, low, the words not understandable.

Thinking that he'd be in a hell of a pickle if he burst in and found Antonia involved in a simple tea party or something, with several people present, he waited until he heard Antonia's laugh and no other voices. Then, taking a deep breath, he eased the door open.

Antonia lay sprawled on her back on a wide lounge. The baron, on his knees beside the lounge, was enjoying some heated preliminaries before making a quick dash for the upstairs bedchamber, his hands buried in Antonia's clothing, her skirts pulled high.

Jay closed the door behind him. With no attempt
to be quiet, he walked toward them, his blood boil-
ing. His footsteps were quieted by the thick Persian
carpeting, but Antonia, who was facing him, saw him.
Her eyes went wide and she started to scream, but
there was something quite familiar about the man who
had appeared so suddenly. It had been a long time
since she saw him—but, yes, it was. She felt a quick
anger, but it died within a fraction of a second to be
replaced with terror. She was caught!

But Antonia had, in addition to her well-developed
ego, a sharpness of mind and a sense of survival. She
saw the black look on Jay's face. Of course her mother
had sent Jay, although she, at the moment, had no
idea how it had come about. Out of sheer desperation
and no little inspiration, her plan was formed within
the two seconds it took Jay to march from the door
to the center of the room.

"Uncle Jay!" she cried. "Oh, thank God you've
come!"

Cochin leaped to his feet. "What's the meaning of
this?" he demanded, his face white.

"Antonia, make yourself decent," Jay ordered, his
voice shaking with anger.

"Oh, Uncle Jay!" she wailed, pulling down her skirts
and leaping to her feet. "This horrible man was going
to make me—he was going to—oh, oh, oh." And her
fantastic abilities allowed her to cause tears to start
flowing.

"I'm sure this can all be explained," the baron said
smoothly, having regained his composure. He had
heard the words "Uncle Jay," and he knew it could
be a sticky situation, but he'd been in sticky situations before.

"Uncle Jay," Antonia said, through her very real
tears, "he discovered that I was leaving school early
to visit the museum and he said he'd tell Madame

Tousand and get me into trouble unless I came with him and then he—oh, he was making me do horrible things."

"I assure you, monsieur," Cochin said, "no harm has been done to the young lady."

"Is it true?" Jay asked darkly. "Did you blackmail her into coming with you?"

For an instant, the baron considered his reply. "Only because I loved her so much," he said. "I assure you that my intentions are honorable. I had intended to call on her mother at the first opportunity."

"I'll bet you were," Jay said. "This is not the first time."

"He said today was the day, Uncle Jay. Oh, thank God you arrived in time. He was going to make me—make me—do it today, and you've saved me." She ran to him, threw her arms around him.

But Jay had seen her, lying with one leg hanging languidly off the lounge, skirts high, the baron's hand under her drawers. Moreover, he'd seen the look on Antonia's face. Was she so accomplished an actress?

The baron took his hesitation as a good sign.

"I am the Baron Alesia du Cochin," he said. "Any number of men will testify to my character. I realize, my good sir, that the situation looks more evil than it is. A bit of harmless play, that's all. I would not think of sullying this young lady's honor, not when I have every intention—"

"Oh, shut up!" Jay said. "Antonia, has he done anything to you?"

"He touched me," Antonia said, sobbing, with a real hiccup, making it sound ever so convincing. "He touched me all over, and he was going to—"

"There's a carriage out front," Jay said. "Get in it and wait for me."

"What are you going to do?"

"Have a talk with the baron," Jay said.

Antonia ran from the room, but, unknown to Jay, stopped in the hallway and, having left the door open, listened.

"My dear sir," Cochin sighed. "Let's not make this any more unpleasant than it really is."

"A policeman followed you here," Jay said. "I think we shall have a chat with him."

"Will that be necessary?" Cochin asked with an oily smile. "I'm sure that gentlemen of good sense can avoid such obscene public measures. You would not want to expose your niece to the glare of the public eye simply to get revenge for some harmless play."

"If, as you both say, nothing serious has happened, what has my niece to hide?" Jay said. "I think your reputation will help to gain some interested ears with the police."

"My dear sir, let's talk this over. You seem to be a sensible man, and I, sir, am not without means. Perhaps a settlement—not a bribe, mind you, but a settlement between gentlemen? Say fifty thousand francs?"

Jay took one step forward, and, bringing his fist from far behind his shoulder sent the baron reeling to crash against the mantle of the fireplace and slide slowly to the floor. He sat there, his hand to his battered mouth, shaking his head to clear it.

"Hit him again, Uncle Jay!" Antonia said, from the doorway. "Please hit him again!"

"I told you to wait in the carriage," Jay said.

"I had to come back," she said. "I left something. It's mine. It's a locket, and he has it."

"Get it," Jay said to the baron, who rose, shakily. He went to an ornate desk, opened a drawer and took out the locket. With a wry smile, he handed it to Antonia, who took it and cringed, as if in fear of the baron.

"I don't want—ever—to see your face again," Jay told Cochin. "Or to hear your name in connection with my niece."

"I give you my word," Cochin said, with a bow toward them and a smile for Antonia, "for I know when I am hopelessly outclassed by my opponents." The words were meant, of course, for Antonia, and, with Jay glaring at the baron, she smiled back and nodded her head.

She sat contritely in the carriage. "Young lady," Jay said, "I'm not swallowing your story, you know."

"Oh, Uncle Jay, how could you doubt me?"

"Because I saw you there," he said. "But your mother will believe you, and perhaps that's for the best. There's no use in upsetting her further. As it is, you've been tossed out of Madame Tousand's, and I'm sure that your mother is going to insist that you go home."

"Merde!" Antonia said.

"I only hope that this is the end of it," Jay said, "and that no child results from it."

"Oh, Uncle Jay, you shock me!"

"I'm sure I do," he said with a grin of reluctant admiration for her ability to continue to carry it off.

"I was glad to see you, and I'm so glad you're here," she said, for she knew that it was important to her to have him keep his silence. She knew that there is nothing in the world more intolerant than a reformed sinner, and, in addition, her mother's attitude toward loose behavior was also colored by her shame for her sister Darcie.

"You're going to stay, aren't you?" she asked. "Please tell me you'll stay."

"That's up to your mother," he said.

"Don't let her say no. She still loves you, Uncle Jay. I know she does, although she wouldn't admit it."

He was silent. Then: "Are you saying, Antonia, that you would have no objections if I married your mother?"

"Oh, none," she said. And, indeed, it did, at the moment, seem to be an idea which would benefit her.

Perhaps, with a man to tickle her fancy now and then, Petra would remove some of her doting attention from her. She envisioned long years ahead buried at Chateau D'Art, a virtual prisoner, with no one around but lusty farm boys. Cochin had given her a taste for more sophisticated pleasures.

Antonia had managed to work up to quiet tears again by the time Jay led her into the hotel room where Petra paced impatiently, then flew to the door to embrace Antonia. But then she shoved the girl roughly away.

"What's the meaning of this, young lady?" she asked heatedly.

Jay stood to one side, his face impassive, as Antonia gave her performance for Petra, the tears flowing from both, Petra alternating between sympathy and anger, not sure whether to hug Antonia or strike her.

"But nothing happened, mother," Antonia concluded, "because, thank God, Uncle Jay came in time."

"It's true?" Petra asked, looking at Jay. "She was not, ah, harmed?"

"Apparently not," Jay said.

"Oh, Antonia," Petra cried, "how could you? How could you allow yourself to be put into such a terrible situation?"

"I was bad, mother. I wanted to see the museums and the boulevards and I walked by myself and that horrible man was watching me and he knew that I'd be in trouble and oh, I'm so very, very sorry and I'll never disobey again."

"We shall go home," Petra said.

"And Uncle Jay with us?" Antonia asked. "Oh, he was so wonderful, mother. He sent that scoundrel reeling, I tell you, with one mighty blow."

Petra felt her face burn. The question caught her, tugged at her. Jay looked at her and then averted his eyes. The moment seemed to be frozen in time. A storm of emotions flashed through Petra's mind. She could almost feel his arms around her, all the sweet and steamy passion of a tropical night, the strength of his body, his powerful urges which lifted her out of herself and made her forget all. The temptation was to say "yes, yes, of course," but there were other considerations. There had been that terrible moment when she knew that Roger was alive, that she had been deceived by her uncle into thinking that her husband was dead, and thus into adultery even while Roger lay ill and suffering. And there was more—the old, old hurt she'd known, the knife stab of pain when she saw Jay and Darcie together. Life had become for her a clean and simple thing, and her most imperative concern, before having seen Jay again, was in doing her best for Antonia, to assure that her daughter would not make the same mistakes she'd made. Now, with Jay looking at her, waiting for her answer, it was so confused. To what did she owe allegiance? The memory of Roger? Her vow to never, never allow herself to fall prey to her somewhat riotous passions? Or to herself, for even as she hesitated, her body reached out for him. But in the end, in that swift and painful moment of decision, for she knew that she could not resist her natural attraction for Jay if he returned to the chateau with them, the deciding factor was her love for her daughter. She was doing her best, true, but her best, judging from recent events, was lacking. Had it not been for Jay, what terrible fate would have taken Antonia? The girl needed a strong hand, a firm hand.

"That's up to Jay," Petra said.

"Try to keep me away," Jay said.

They were married at the chateau in a lovely but small ceremony, Antonia and Helene members of the wedding, a few selected people from the area as guests. They had been brought together by a scheming young lady for her own purposes, but that did not lessen the happiness of it, when, at long last, there was no reason for them ever again to be apart. Leaving Jason with

Helene and Antonia, they spent a glorious ten days in a small and cozy house on the coast and discovered quickly that age and the years had not dimmed their need for each other.

There were practical considerations to their union. Jay was unemployed. However, since the entire family seemed to love the Chateau D'Art so much, he did not let his pride force him to make a move immediately. There was time now that he was, at last, united with the woman he loved. In that lovely spring and summer, he took an interest in the farm, suggested some improvements, installed windmills to eliminate the need to haul water from the river for the livestock and occasional irrigation, used his massive energies, recovering fully from the drain of the Panama climate and the fever, to make the establishment the neatest and smoothest-functioning farm in the valley.

With no feeling of haste, Jay made some contacts. Good engineers could find work anywhere in the world. There were three or four promising possibilities in France, one project to be undertaken quite nearby: to expand a port on the south coast.

On long and pleasant evenings the family all together listened to a seemingly content Antonia perform. Helene's Jean-Charles visited during a school holiday, and there was an immediate rapport between him and Jay. The men walked together and talked endlessly about problems of engineering. Jean-Charles had his own theories about why the French had failed in Panama, and they coincided with Jay's contention that de Lesseps should have planned a lock canal.

Since Jason was so young, and for considerations of which no one was aware other than Petra and Jay, it was decided that Jay would adopt him, changing his name from D'Art to Burton. Antonia said she preferred, since she was used to it, to keep her own name.

Helene was a delight, and Antonia was, well, Antonia—often fiery. She did not immediately rebel against the restrictions of living back on the farm. Jay watched her closely, and, for a long time, she was well behaved. He had come to a conclusion about her. She was, he decided, a survivor. She would always have her own way in the end. Had he and Petra been married earlier, it might have been different. But now the die was cast. Soon he used his influence with Petra to allow Antonia to enter into the social life of Marmande and, after the summer, she was sent to a convent school, there to finish her formal education.

Time passed, each day golden. For some reason, there were no additions to Petra's family of two children. She did nothing to prevent it, and, God knows, there was plenty of opportunity, but she did not regret not having other children. She was so happy that nothing could dim it. She had made her peace with her memories and the past, and she belonged in Jay's arms. When he worked on the port project for months, she went with him, taking Jason and leaving the girls to manage the chateau. She had everything she wanted. Her life was secure. She and Jay had the same tastes, liked the same pleasures. She read to him in the evenings and worked with him to improve his French. At home, they gardened or walked the fields together. She did not miss having friends, although there were few of them. When they had company in the chateau, she enjoyed it, but was always secretly pleased when they were gone. As long as she was with Jay, her entire life was a source of pleasure. They were seldom apart, so bound up in each other that Petra sometimes wondered if he was too important to her, if he meant more to her than he should. Although she was not deeply religious, she wondered if she were not, after all, living in sin with Jay as her forbidden idol.

For Antonia it worked out well. She was free to attend church and social functions and to visit. She found that there were no Baron Cochins in Marmande and surrounding chateaux, but when one can't have caviar, one does not starve with an abundance of beef on the table.

And so the years passed quietly and happily. Neither Petra nor Jay guessed, during that idyllic interlude, that Panama would come into their lives again.

17

IN WASHINGTON, DARCIE Moncrief was jubilant when the House of Representatives joined the Senate in voting to build an American canal in Panama. Although, in view of her promise to wed Admiral David Russell, it was no longer vital that she regain at least a major portion of her small wealth, which, on Guy's advice, she had invested in French canal shares, she saw no harm in achieving that end, now that victory was so near. Moreover, there was Guy to think about. He had far more invested than she and would be totally ruined if the New Canal Company were not able to sell its Colombia concession to the rich Yankee nation.

Darcie's relationship with Guy had been a close, if rather strange, entanglement. From the time he had taken charge of the two fatherless girls in Egypt, he had been, to Darcie, somewhat of a father figure. That this was later complicated by the sexual relationships which grew among her, Guy, and Lyris, did not diminish her fondness for Guy. And so he had been father, husband, lover to her for so many years that she could not desert him, not even for her own happiness, at such a late hour when only the lack of a United States treaty with Colombia stood in the way of an American canal and the recovery of the major part of their investments.

Preoccupied with her own happiness, spending much time with David, she did not keep abreast of events as well as she had done in the past. When, at last, she deemed it time to tell Guy that she was going to marry David and live with him in the United States, she approached the task with some misgivings.

Guy had aged. His fifty-plus years rode him with a heavy saddle. His slimness had given way to a small pouch, and his sedentary life had softened the once-sinewy strength of him. His sexual appetites had dimmed somewhat, although now and then he would come to her bed and now and again he would conduct an elaborate seduction ritual with a new woman. In the main, however, his energies were devoted to the great cause: publicly called the duty of seeing to it that the French dream was continued and privately admitted to be simply a selfish desire to have his investment back. He had no other hope. He was living on the money supplied by the new company. He would be destitute if he failed.

"Guy," Darcie said, on a rare evening when they were alone, "you've met David Russell, of course."

"Of course," he said without much interest.

"I'm quite fond of him."

"Yes, yes, I can see that."

"Would it upset you terribly if I married him?" She held her breath, waiting for his reaction.

He put down his fork—they were at table—and looked at her. "Are you?"

"Yes."

"Not, I hope, until the job is done."

"But it's done. There will be an American canal."

"There is no treaty," Guy said. "Morgan and his cohorts are waiting in the wings, waiting for a suitable length of time before reviving the Guatemala route again. And there's this bedamned eternal revolution against Colombia. They're saying that the Colombian government doesn't have control of Panama, and therefore a treaty giving the United States rights to build a canal would be meaningless."

"Well," she said, "there's nothing we can do about that, is there?"

He smiled. "On the contrary, the work goes on. We're merely fighting on another front."

"Surely I can be of no help. How can I stop a revolution or influence events in Panama in any way?" she asked.

"You're a powerful weapon, Darcie," he said. "You never know when a woman's smile will turn the tide of a battle."

She was silent for a moment. "Guy, I have promised myself to David. He knows that I have not led the life of a nun, but for my own soul, I will not—ever again—give myself to another man."

He examined her, sucking a tidbit of food from his front teeth. "You really are in love, aren't you?"

"For the first time," she said.

"Promise me only this," he said. "That you will wait only a bit longer, until we see how the tide is running."

"A little longer, then," she said.

David was so kind, so understanding. He did not seem to be upset when she told him that her uncle had requested her to postpone the marriage. Nor did either of them seem to regret the loss of the months, as negotiations seemed to go on endlessly. They had each other, and if their union was not consummated physically, it was completed spiritually, with every minute possible devoted to each other, with lovely picnics in the country and concerts and plays and quiet evenings during which, true to his honor, David allowed himself only kisses which, although it inflamed both of them, seemed only to make the wait even more worthwhile.

In the dead of winter, with Washington cocooned in snow and cold, the United States told Colombia that if the treaty were not signed immediately, the country would begin plans for a Nicaragua canal. Colombia, beset with problems, faced with the loss of great revenue if the canal were not built in Panama, conceded reluctantly to the terms. Congress ratified the treaty by an overwhelming margin in early spring.

Now, truly, it was over. Darcie told Guy that she would marry the admiral in early summer, as soon as he could arrange a short leave, and, although Guy would have preferred her to wait, he said nothing.

Feeling like a young girl, Darcie went about buying a trousseau. Over a weekend, she visited the lovely country home owned by David, and fell in love with it. Full of plans, excited, as David said, she "talked his ears off."

"How can a man ever get in any kissing if you're never quiet?" he asked fondly, closing her mouth with his and leaving her silent for a few moments, her eyes dreamy.

David Russell made the world live for Darcie. For the first time in her memory, she, seeing herself reflected in his eyes, saw herself as something worthwhile, something dear. She did not waste time in wishing that she had met David years before, that he had been the first with her. No, that would be foolish. But she was, at least in spirit, as virginal as the purest young girl, for never before had she kissed a man whom she loved with all her soul. She did not think that she was good enough for David, and she told him so until he hushed her and said, "Don't you dare talk about my girl that way." He loved her. Miracle of miracles, he loved her and she did not think about the past, for he did not.

It was as if she'd been born on a Washington street while looking into the window of a toy store. The Darcie who pined away the hours she had to be away from him was not the Darcie who had been raped on the sands of Egypt and who had accepted countless men into her lovely body in the subsequent years. She was new, whole, pure, for his love made her pure.

She was devastated when David, with a long face, came to tell her that, because of the situation in Panama, he was being put in charge of a ship again, to do duty off the Central American coast until the situation was resolved.

"Oh, David, I've waited so long," she said.

"We can wait a bit longer," he said. "Not that I'm looking forward to it."

"I shall steal a sailor's uniform and stow away aboard your ship," she sighed. "I can't bear the thought of your being so far away."

He laughed. "I could hide you under my bunk."

"Yes, yes," she said. "And then I'll be there every night when you come to bed."

"In order to keep from arousing suspicions, I'd have all my meals in the cabin and share them with you," he said. "But I warn you: I'm a big eater, and you might have nothing but a crust of bread."

"I shall live on your love," she said, then giggled. Was this Darcie Moncrief talking? Oh, God, how she had changed.

"It will be over soon. Then I'll be back and we won't waste a day," he said. "We'll be married the very day I come home."

"Marry me now," she begged.

"It's very tempting," he said.

"Why not? We can be married in secrecy, and, later, have the military wedding you have your heart set on."

"Oh, Darcie."

"Can't we?"

"I'm leaving tonight."

Despondent, alone, she took little interest in events. She knew that Guy and Bunau-Varilla were mixed up in the potential revolution in Panama, but her thoughts

were only for David. She did not know that large sums
of money were changing hands and that Bunau-Varilla
and others—some said extending upward to the presi-
dential level—were encouraging a small group of con-
spirators to wrest the isthmus away from the parent
country, Colombia. It all had nothing to do with her.
She was merely a woman waiting for her man to come
home from the sea.

However, her uncle was to see to it that the revolution was to affect her life. He came to her as she sat
reading the latest batch of letters from David.

"From the admiral?" he asked.

"Ummm, yes," she said, not welcoming the intrusion.

"How much longer is he going to be gone?" Guy
asked.

"He doesn't know."

"Would you like for me to tell you?"

"Oh, how could you?"

"Because I know the date of the revolution."

"Really?"

"It's soon."

"Wonderful."

"You can speed it."

"There's something on your mind, Guy. Out with it."

"The plans are made. We have only one small
problem."

"I will do nothing which would dishonor David,"
she said, anticipating him.

"On the contrary, it would please him. There is a
certain Colombian general, stationed with his troops
in Panama. He is wavering. If we can win him to our
side, the revolution will not only be assured, it will be
bloodless. If he doesn't fight, there will be no fighting."

"Won't Colombia send troops?"

"You know the isthmus, my dear. Any troop movement would have to be by sea. And that's why your

sailor, and others, are off the shores of Panama, to prevent Colombia moving any troops in by ship."

"Are you telling me that the United States is aiding in this revolution?"

"Since the United States holds a concession to build a canal in Panama, it is the responsibility of the United States to preserve order," he said. "To do so, and to prevent bloodshed, the navy will prevent the landing of Colombian troops."

"All right, Guy, why are you telling me all of this?"

"Because we need your help, Darcie. One last job."

"No."

"It's not what you think. The good general will be more easily swayed, I think, with money. In fact, he has named his price, but he wants payment in advance. We'd like you to deliver it to him. In Panama."

"Guy, I can't. I simply can't. I must be here when David returns."

"Unless the money is delivered and the general's loyalty to the new Republic of Panama is assured, there will be no revolution. The situation will remain tense. The picket ships will remain on duty." He spread his hands. "On the other hand, make a simple trip to Panama, see the general, hand him his little packet, and come home to meet your David."

She questioned and protested, but, in the end, she agreed. It was nothing more than a trip, and by some chance, should David have opportunity to come ashore, she might even meet him in Panama.

Although she dreaded going back to that hellhole of the tropics, her stay there would be brief. She would not remain long enough to be exposed to the terrible fevers, the rot and slow death. Unless she could somehow arrange a meeting with David, she would arrive, make her appointment with the general, give him his bribe, and depart.

She wrote to David, but she knew that she would

probably be back in Washington before the mail caught up with him somewhere at sea. The trip was uneventful, the ship comfortable. She stepped ashore at Colón with old and unpleasant memories assailing her. Panama had already claimed one of them, for Lyris, abandoned and forgotten, lay dead there somewhere, perhaps in an unmarked grave. The dwarf, Hassam Ari, was also a victim of Panama, as was Petra's husband Roger.

The town was even more destitute, more rotten than she remembered, and she lost no time in getting a train to Panama City, there checking into the best hotel. Things seemed to be normal. There was none of the excitement she might have expected, knowing that the country was on the verge of revolution.

The small garrison of Colombian troops on the isthmus was stationed at Cuartel de Chiriquí. The barracks were near the seawall. The troops were ill disciplined, some in ill health, and all of them were discontent. Colombian paymasters had not been a model of regularity, and many of the troops had gone for months without spending money in their pockets. Their commander, General Juan Esteban, was in sympathy with the cause of the revolution and made this known to the plotters; but he was also a man who knew that revolutions come and go, while the mighty American dollar is eternal. His price was $50 for each of his men, the equivalent of several months' pay, and a much larger sum for himself; a portion of it in advance, the rest after the revolution was successful.

Darcie did not know how much money she carried in her bag, nor did she want to know. She wanted only to complete the job and take the next ship back to the United States.

Upon arriving in Panama, the first thing she did was to ask the whereabouts of the American ships. She was told that they were offshore, that they rarely sent men to the shore, and that there was no way to contact a particular ship. Her hopes for seeing David thus dashed, she sent a message to General Esteban, requesting that he meet her at the hotel. The reply, several hours later, told her that a meeting at the hotel was impossible. The message named a place—a house near the sea, and a time—early evening.

Darcie was long past the fear of going about alone, so she set out from the hotel in a hired carriage at dusk and gave the driver directions. After a short ride, they arrived at the house, a reminder of the French presence in Panama with a two-story central section flanked by two one-story wings. The tropics had already taken their toll of the structure. Paint flaked off. The garden had not been tended and was being invaded by rank native growth. Mosquitoes buzzed about Darcie's ears as she, having told the carriage to wait for her, walked through the untidy garden. A glow of light came from the main rooms of the central portion of the house. She knocked and was admitted by an officer in uniform and shown into a room which smelled of mildew. Books in the shelves on one wall were covered with mold. The oil lamp gave dim light.

"Buenos noches, señora," the man behind the desk said as he rose.

Darcie was a small woman, but she looked down onto the plumed hat of the little man who bowed to her. In the dim light, he looked like a child playing solider in a comic-opera uniform. Huge epaulets dangled tassels from his shoulders, and his blue jacket was aglow with masses of gold braid down the front, a rope of gold diagonally across his chest, a gold sash from which dangled white gloves at his waist. So long was the jacket that only a few inches of oversized white breeches showed between jacket and huge leather boots of gleaming black which came just below his knees. At his side was a sword which almost dragged the floor.

"You are General Juan Esteban?" she asked.

"I am," the little man said, in a voice which was surprisingly deep. "I think, *señora,* that you have something for me."

She did not correct his mistaken use of the form of address for a married woman. Hearing it she allowed herself to think of David and the fact that soon it would fit.

"I do, general." She put the small cloth bag she carried on the desk. Esteban motioned her toward a chair and opened the bag. She sat on the edge of the chair and watched him count the money. He was not content to find that it was packaged in units of $1,000 each, but took the bands off the packets and counted each bill. All the while, he was silent. When he finished, he looked up, showing his teeth in a grim smile.

"You have done well," he said. "I admire your courage—a mere woman carrying such a large sum of money."

"I am pleased to do my part for a good cause," Darcie said, with a drama she did not feel.

"Yes, now it begins," he said. "Your plans, *señora?*"

"I will return to the United States as soon as possible."

"There will be some little delay, I fear."

"May I ask why?"

He shrugged and things tinkled on his jacket. "It should be obvious. You are the only person alive who knows that I have accepted this money."

"Of course I'm not," she said. "Those who sent me with the money—"

"Know only that you left with it," he said. "Should things go badly in the next few days, I could say, *señora,* that their word was a part of a Yankee plot. But you, you saw me take the money and you watched me count it."

"General Esteban, I thought I was dealing with an honorable man. I demand that I be allowed to go about my business."

"You will come to no harm. The house is quite comfortable. It was built at great expense by a former official of the canal. My men will guard you and there will be servants to attend to your needs. Consider it, my dear *señora,* a vacation at the courtesy of the new Republic of Panama."

"And when will I be allowed to leave?" Darcie asked.

"Only a few days. The great events are quite near." He smiled at her. "I myself will visit you, to see that your hours do not grow lonely."

"That is thoughtful of you," she said, "but not necessary. I'm sure you have important work to do."

"Ah, yes," he said. "Well, as you wish." He stepped to a door and called out. A soldier came. "This man will see you to your room."

She had no choice. She followed. The room was also smelly of mold and disuse, but the bedclothes were fresh. She pushed the latch on the door, placed a chair against it and examined her prison. There were books in a small bookcase, all in French. The lamp was lit. Later, a middle-aged woman who spoke only in monosyllables, and only when spoken to, came with food. She was not hungry. She drank the common red wine, nibbled at the meal, and with resignation prepared herself for bed.

As revolutions go, the Panamanian revolt was almost dull. Thanks to the American ships which prevented landing of any Colombian troops, there were to be no reinforcement for the Colombian forces, weakened to impotency by the defection of General Juan Esteban and the main bulk of the Panama garrison. There was only one moment of tension when Colombians under a young officer named Torres surrounded a stone warehouse in which Americans had taken shelter and were faced by a force of men from the U.S.S *Nashville* who had landed to protect American lives and property. When that tense situation was defused, neither side wishing to fight, there were only minor adjustments to be made and there was a new republic in the isthmus. A sum of American dollars paid to the officer, Torres, had served to be as convincing as a volley from the American guns.

Darcie waited patiently, reasoning that no harm was going to come to her, that she would be released soon. She had been confined to the room for almost a week, but she was not unduly concerned. When she heard sounds of celebration from below and eventually was told that the revolution had been a success, she was pleased. General Juan Esteban himself came to her door late that night and said, *"Señora,* it is over. *Viva La Republica de Panama."*

"Congratulations," Darcie said. "There was no fighting?"

"None," Esteban said. "And now, *señora,* you are free to go."

"Thank you," Darcie said. "I will go first thing in the morning. Is the railroad running?"

"Of course," Esteban said. "All is in order in our new country." He bowed low. "Since you seem to be marooned with us for one more night, *señora,* perhaps you would like to join us in the parlor and drink a toast with us."

She'd been in the room for almost a week, so she welcomed the change. She freshened herself. Her clothing had been washed by the servants and she had facilities for bathing and for her personal toilet, so when she went down the stairs to join a group in the large room, she was at her best. The wives of some of the officers were present, so she was not the only woman there. She accepted a glass of champagne, joined in a series of toasts, flowery and ambitious, promising great things for the new country. She could not help but be affected by the general air of jubilation, and, in fact, began to feel quite gay, for now her future seemed to be assured, the canal to be built, their money recovered through the sale of the French holdings.

More important, she would be on the way home next day and would soon see David. There would be no further impediments to their marriage.

Looking like a proud cock pheasant in his musical-comedy finery, General Esteban bowed low in front of her. A small orchestra was playing. She accepted his invitation to dance, and she was whirled around the floor with some energy, laughing because her future seemed to be bright.

18

THE FINAL CELEBRATION in Washington was still some days away when Guy met Chad Roethke at a party given by Sally Ann Smithers. During Darcie's absence he had turned to Sally Ann, a famous Washington hostess, for company. Sally Ann liked Washington so much that when her congressman husband died, she stayed on and her house continued to be a gathering place for lobbyists, members of the government, and businessmen who found a need to maintain contacts in the city. A portion of the upkeep on Sally Ann's impressive home was paid in under-the-table fees from such businessmen who found it to their advantage to have Sally Ann arrange innocent-looking encounters with certain members of Congress, for example.

A Pennsylvanian, Sally Ann had no desire to leave the gay life of the capitol to return to the small industrial town which had been her home. She fancied herself to be a true sophisticate, and she was greatly impressed by the courtly Frenchman who had known de Lesseps and had been involved in both Suez and the French failure in Panama. She allowed Guy to take her off to bed, but she got no more pleasure out of it than Guy, who, having removed Sally Ann's corsets, found her body to be just a bit too ample for his tastes. Still, he enjoyed her company, and she gave good parties.

Shortly after Darcie had sailed for Panama, Guy was introduced to Chad Roethke. Roethke was a portly man from Sally Ann's home state, and he had made use of her services previously. He was, he liked to say, "in iron." His plant in Pittsburgh fabricated beams and girders, and, due to state-level connections, he sold much of his product to the State of Pennsylvania, sometimes at prices below other bids and more often at prices higher than the lowest bid. He was accustomed to making small and large undercover payments to politicians and was confident that he was ready for bigger things.

Roethke fancied himself to look like the president. He had the same walrus moustache and wore glasses like the president's. But his body was more corpulent, and he lacked the vitality and inner strength of Theodore Roosevelt. However, he made up for that by using the words "capital" and "bully" quite often in his conversation.

"Mr. Simel," Roethke said, after the formalities of introduction and the withdrawal of Sally Ann, "I am told that you had much to do with the victory in Panama."

"It is not yet a victory," Guy said.

"Looks as if it's assured to me," Roethke said. "Of course, I don't have your connections. Is there something I don't know? The revolution is going to go off on schedule, isn't it?"

"I wasn't aware that there was a revolution scheduled," Guy said carefully.

"Capital," Roethke said. "I like a man who knows when to talk and when to be silent. However, Mr. Simel, I know you've done your part. You, sir, are a doer."

"A door?" Guy asked in puzzlement.

"A dooooer," Roethke said. "You make things go. The world needs more of your type of man. I'd like to have a dozen like you in my company."

"Well, thank you," Guy said, looking for a way to escape.

"Now that the canal is assured," Roethke said, "what are your plans?"

"Is it assured?" Guy asked. "If so, then I suppose I will go back to France."

"That would be a great waste of talent," Roethke said. "I have, sir, a small proposition I would like to make you." He smiled. "Unless, of course, you are a man who has no need to think of making a million dollars American."

The phrase penetrated the fuzz in Guy's head. "I don't know of any man who does not have the need to make one million American," he said. "I am at your service."

"Not here," Roethke boomed. "Have had a little too much of the bubbly, old man, to talk business. At your convenience, sir, please call on me at my office. I'm sure that our little chat will interest you."

Guy couldn't remember either the man's name or the address of his Washington office when he awoke the next morning, his stomach sour, his head foul. He forced down coffee, and, remembering only the mention of a million dollars, went to Sally Ann's house to find that good lady also suffering. He joined her over coffee in a formal sitting room.

"I spoke with a gentleman last night," he said. "And I confess that I've forgotten his name."

Sally Ann had to do some thinking, but when Guy described Roethke as looking like Teddy, she knew. The name and address written down, he made his exit, but not before Sally Ann, with a groan, suggested that the only thing which would keep her alive was "the hair of the dog," and he shared a dram of bourbon with

her, felt better, and set out for an office which turned
out to be a cubbyhole in a dingy building in a bad part
of town. Not impressed, he almost turned away, but
since he was there, he went in.

Roethke greeted him with enthusiasm. "Ah, so you
are interested," he said as he greeted Guy.

"I was merely in the neighborhood, and I thought
it polite to listen to what you have in mind."

"Just politeness, huh?" Roethke said. "Well, whatever it is, you're here. As you know, Simel, I'm in
iron."

"I didn't know."

"That's my game," Roethke said, leaning back to
thrust his heavy belly out. "Iron. Structural pieces. Got
a nice little business going, but I'm a man of ambition.
I think there's money to be made once this canal project gets steaming."

"Undoubtedly," Guy said.

"Now my problem," Roethke said, "is that I don't
have the proper contacts. The big boys have all the
ins, and they've got the money to pay off a few politicians. Not that we couldn't come up with a little bit of
grease, you understand—can't do business without it—
but what I need is a man who knows the right people.
You see, I'm getting right to the point. You have been
right in the forefront of this Panama fight, and still
you've kept your skirts clean. Sure, almost everyone
knows you had something to gain, but then who
doesn't? The point is, you're a good man to talk to a
few of the movers and shakers. And if, while talking,
you could interest a few of them in buying a little steel
from the Roethke Company, there'd be a piece of
change in it for you."

"I am not a salesman," Guy said stiffly.

"Now don't go off half-cocked," Roethke said. "You
have any idea how much structural steel is going to
be used in Panama in the next few years?"

"I'm not an engineer," Guy said.

"Tons of it—hundreds of thousands of tons, maybe millions of tons. They'll have to build roads, and that means bridges. There'll be steel in the locks. They'll have to do some renovation of the railroad, tracks, new bridges. The ports. Simel, there are millions to be made."

"I know nothing of steel."

"Hell's fire, man, it's not *what* you know, it's *who* you know."

"I do have some useful contacts," Guy admitted. "But, Mr. Roethke, you spoke of, I believe, one million dollars."

"You bet your boots I did," Roethke said. "Get to the right people, Simel. Get me a contract on the bridge-work alone, and your commissions would be almost that." He leaned forward. "I've developed a process by which I can beat the price of all of them, even the big ones. But merely putting in the lowest bid doesn't guarantee anything. You know that. When you're dealing with politicians, you have to have contacts, influence, grease. You have the contacts. I don't. You can get to the men with influence. I can't. That will be worth a lot of money to me, Mr. Simel. Your position, for the record, would be that of a lobbyist, a paid lobbyist."

"I will say, Mr. Roethke, that you have my attention," Guy said. "But I will have to have more information about your business, and, of course, the entire question is academic at the moment."

"Now we both know the canal is going to be built in Panama," Roethke said. "But as you will, sir. However, while we wait for the revolution and new treaty, there will be ample time for you to acquaint yourself with my operation. I'll pay your expenses. You can visit the plant. I'll give you all the figures. When the time comes, you'll be ready to hit them between the eyes with estimates which will assure us the business. After the corruption in the French deal down there, the whole world will be watching what we do, and you can bet your boots that the low bid will be taken."

"I'm not quite clear why you're so sure that yours will be the low bid," Guy said.

Roethke laughed. "It's my new process, sir. I can make it cheaper and I can sell it cheaper."

"This new process," Guy said. "If it's so good, why don't you have more of a share of the business in the United States?"

"We will talk of that later," Roethke said. "First, sir, you must make up your own mind."

"I will give you my answer within a few days," Guy said.

He talked with some of his American contacts. They knew nothing of a new process wherein steel girders could be made cheaper, but, in an age of technological miracles, they did not doubt it. They told him that if a steel fabricator had such a process, he would become very, very rich.

Since he was privy to inside information, Guy knew, of course, that the final assurances were being laid: that the canal would be in Panama, in a new republic. He was told, too, that preference would be given to American suppliers. Estimates of the amount of steel and iron needed varied, but were uniformly impressive, amounting to millions of dollars. He was very much intrigued. True, he would recover much of his investment, but he had also walked in the corridors of power, near the heart of things, and power is a disease which infects men differently but touches almost all men. The quiet life in France did not appeal to him. How much more exciting to be a part of the new American effort in Panama, for he had been a part of Suez and of the French effort. To see it through appealed to him, and the promise of profit did not make him unhappy. His grand plans for becoming very wealthy had been ruined by de Lesseps, and now there was another chance.

He took a train to Pittsburgh and told Chad Roethke that he was interested. Roethke showed him the company books. There had been a good profit in the last quarter. He was taken on a tour of the plant and shown girders made by the conventional process and by Roethke's "new" process. He couldn't tell the difference, but he was impressed by the difference in price. On single units it was not great, but on the amount of steel needed for a project as great as Panama, the amount would be very impressive.

He sat in Roethke's office and said, "I am with you, sir. I am, I admit, quite impressed."

"Good, good," Roethke said. "Now we go to work." He opened a checkbook, scribbled rapidly. The check was in the amount of $5,000. "This is merely a binder, Mr. Simel. An unwritten contract, so to speak. If you'll just sign this receipt."

"Is that necessary?" Guy asked, suddenly suspicious.

"Ah, yes," Roethke chuckled. "I would have been disappointed in you had you signed without question."

"I think, Mr. Roethke, that there is more to this than I understand."

"You're quite right, sir," Roethke said. "But I assure you that it's all aboveboard and legitimate." He waved his hands. "It's just that some government inspectors are overly zealous."

"I think I understand," Guy said. "This new process—the cheap new process—"

"Because of some rather archaic government regulations, it would not quite meet the standards," Roethke said. He held his finger and thumb just a fraction of an inch apart. "Not that it isn't more than adequate. It is. It's supporting a lot of bridges in Pennsylvania right now."

"Just where is it below standard, Mr. Roethke?" Guy asked.

"Did I say that?" Roethke shoved the receipt toward Guy with his eyebrows raised.

Guy looked at the receipt. Five thousand dollars, and that was just a binder. "Mr. Roethke, I am not against good business—good sharp business—but I have no desire to spend my declining years in a United States federal prison."

"All right," Roethke said. "I am going to show my faith in you, Mr. Simel. Sign the receipt. Then I will give you the full details of the operation, and if you think, then, that you will be compromised by working with me, the five thousand is for services rendered and no hard feelings. The five thousand will also serve, however, as a guarantee that word of my new process does not leak from your lips."

"Fair enough," Guy said, signing and pocketing the check.

"It is in the alloying treatment," Roethke said. "We have found that by using certain alloys, we decrease the strength of the beam only slightly, but the beautiful part of it is the substitution is detectable only by careful laboratory analysis. We have found our product to be quite adequate, and by having tested beams and girders of conventional material, we have avoided any, ah, embarrassment. I assure you that it is merely an overrequirement by governmental agencies which prohibits wide use of our type of steel. I also assure you that our work will stand the test and no one will be hurt. In fact, we will save the taxpayers quite a few dollars, while garnering a handsome profit of our own."

"You sound very convincing," Guy said.

"I knew I could count on you," Roethke said.

"You may, sir," Guy said, rising and extending his hand.

Back in Washington he began, carefully, to ascertain where the power lay, who would have a say in letting contracts when the construction of the canal was begun. And he began to think of Darcie and how useful she would be in this new lobbying effort. *Damn,* he thought, *what a time for her to fall in love.*

Inspiration came to him at one of Sally Ann's parties, a more or less social affair at which he conducted only a bit of business, talking with a minor official from the government who had to do with enforcing standards in manufactured products. The interference of government in private enterprise was on a primitive level, but gradually there was a growing awareness of the need to curb the strength and influence of the large corporations, to protect the consumer against trusts and cabals and sheer dishonesty. He gained little information, but made a lot of assumptions. They could, he thought, get away with it. And if the steel sold by Roethke was as good as Roethke claimed, he had nothing to worry about except getting the contracts. How much of a help Darcie would be! She would have had the information out of the minor official in half the time, with more thrown in simply because a man liked talking with a beautiful woman.

He circulated and was about to make his own way home when he was standing beside the snack table next to a pair of corseted dowagers. He knew neither of them, and they, with a glance at him, continued their conversation in stage whispers which carried better than normal voices would have. To his amusement, Darcie Moncrief was the topic of their talk. It was obvious that they did not know they were being overheard by Darcie's uncle.

"—has the poor man wrapped around her finger."

"And his poor dead wife such a sweet person."

"Well, he's a fool. Everyone in Washington, except him, knows that she's been in more beds than a foot warmer."

"Oh, he knows, all right."

"If he knows, then he's a bigger fool than I thought."

"I told him."

"You? Oh, dear."

"I was poor Ellen's best friend, you know. I told him, 'David Russell, you're making a big fool of yourself running around with that courtesan.'"

"Heavens! What did he say?"

"He told me, not too politely, that if he made a fool of himself, it was his own affair, and he would not listen to slander regarding that woman."

"I know for a fact that she was seen coming out of a senator's house at daybreak."

"Not just one, I'll wager."

But Guy had heard enough. He pulled Sally Ann away from other guests. "That woman," he said, "the big one with the feathers in her hat. What is her name?"

"Navy," Sally Ann said. "Widow of an admiral. Mrs. Agnes McCrom."

19

ALTHOUGH IT WAS good to be back at sea on a good ship and in charge of an important mission, David Russell would have preferred to be in Washington. He missed Darcie. Sometimes he laughed at himself and called himself an old fool on the edge of senility, but he was so much in love that he found himself mooning around like a cadet with his first crush. He wrote to Darcie daily and posted the letters when he had opportunity. Incoming mail was even more irregular and he had received only one batch of letters from Darcie, which he read over and over in the privacy of his quarters.

The command ship stood offshore in the Pacific while the bloodless revolution ran its course and David stayed in close contact with the shore forces who were there simply to protect American lives and property. However, they required contact with command, and therefore small boats came and went quite often. It was one of these messenger boats which brought the cables from Washington among which was one addressed to Admiral David Russell personally. He read the official dispatches first, and then, in privacy, opened the personal cable, thinking, with his heart laughing, that it might be from Darcie.

He skimmed over the address and his eyes froze on the message:

ELLEN'S SAKE. WARNED YOU AGAINST D.M. FIND HER WITH GEN. ESTEBAN PANAMA CITY.

The cable was signed by an old friend of his dead wife's, and the wife of an admiral under whom he had served. He knew her to be a busybody, but this was carrying it too far. He knew that Darcie was not virgin. She had told him so, with great pain, very early in their relationship. He wadded the cable and tossed it into a wastebasket, then pulled it out, looked at it again, and tore it into shreds.

Of course, marrying a woman with a certain reputation would pose problems for him. He had already been warned, obliquely, by a superior in the Navy Department, but he was nearing retirement. He had loved only once in his life—his wife Ellen—and that had not been too successful, for his career kept him at sea for many months out of the year. Ellen had been brave about it at first, and then, in later years, she seemed to lose interest. It had not mattered to her one way or the other whether he was on shore leave or sea duty. In fact, he got the idea at times that when he was at home he was in the way, interfering with the orderly running of the household. It was painful to him to see her growing indifference. He loved her very much and spent long evenings at sea writing to her, thinking of her, dreaming of being alone with her.

In the end, it was only memories of better times which kept them from each other's throats. Indifference on the part of Ellen changed to outright antagonism.

David was a thinking man. He felt that he knew himself as well as any man could know himself, and he knew that the temper which flared under some slight from Ellen was strictly the result of hurt, and it hurt deeply when he realized that Ellen did not love him, and, in fact, had never had the capacity for loving as he understood it. When he committed himself to her, it was once and for all, and from the time that he asked her for her hand and she said yes, he never touched another woman. His entire life was devoted to her. At sea, he hoarded his money, skimping on necessities, rarely indulging in the smallest luxury, for the pay of a junior officer was low enough as it was and he wanted only the best for Ellen and, later, for the two children. He had his career, but that was merely a way of providing a home, good schools, a pony for his daughter on her twelfth birthday. He often wondered if his preoccupation with his family had not slowed his advancement, for others in his class moved up more rapidly, although he was a good and efficient officer. Strangely, however, he had not made admiral until after Ellen's death, after the death of his son at San Juan Hill and after his daughter's marriage, when, Ellen having withdrawn from him, he had nothing left but his work.

David could not bring himself to blame Ellen for their lack of happiness. There had been times when it was very sweet and she seemed to be everything he had ever wanted. At such times there was laughter, and the day-to-day problems seemed to be so minor that, working together, the problems faded. But he was at sea at the time of the birth of his daughter, and it was a hard birth. Ellen never forgave him.

The hours of being without him while he was at sea became an obsession with her, and many times tempers flared as she accused him of not loving her enough to take a job—"My God, Ellen, what job? All I know is the navy,"—where he could be a real husband.

But David thought he was a good husband. He knew that he loved his family and he loved Ellen and would have done anything for her—anything within the realm of practicality. But leaving the navy did not fit into

458   Dynasty of Desire

that category. So it all ended in bitterness, and he felt that he had been wronged. All he had wanted was someone to love him. If she had only understood that he was not staying in the navy simply to spite her, to hurt her! If, just once, she had ever said, "David, you've been a good husband." But no. The later years were attack, attack, attack, and there was no aspect of his character which did not suffer under her sharp tongue. He was helpless to do anything except—and he had to admit that he did it often—lose his temper and attack in turn, knowing all the while that sickness of heart, that regret for something lost.

"Well, Ellen," he told her, when their daughter married and he got a desk job in Washington, "it's just us now. And we'll make the best of the years. There are so many things we can do, just the two of us."

"Maybe you can get around to fixing the screen door," she said, going off into another room to her knitting.

He was, at the time, quite a young man, and with a young man's needs. Ellen was a pretty woman, and during the act of love he felt so close to her, loved her so much, that he could feel his entire body sing out with his love for her. But if he tried to kiss her, she would say, "Oh, David, you're not a boy anymore. Must you always be after me, kissing and handling me?" And if he came to her without the kissing and handling, she would say, "All you care about is my body. You've lost your sense of romance."

But what hurt most of all of the obviousness of her near-hate for him, always criticizing, using some minor incident as an excuse for a screaming, vitriolic tirade, usually about his lack of concern for her.

"You've never loved me! For years you casually went off and left me alone to take care of your children and your house, even when I was ill or tired. You have never even so much as remembered my birthday."

That he may have been in the China Sea at the time

of her birthday didn't matter, nor did her elephantine memory regarding the times he did forget birthdays and anniversaries seem to be capable of remembering the times he did not forget, or the times when, for no reason save for his love for her, he brought gifts on non-birthday-anniversary occasions.

And, in his anger, hurting under her accusations of total worthlessness as a husband, he would say, "Well, since I've never done anything for you, why should I start now?" But he would be the one to try to patch up their frequent quarrels while she seemed to enjoy dragging them on as long as possible, extending a minor spat into days of silence and coldness.

Once, shortly after his daughter was married, he went to the club and got very, very drunk and in his drunkenness told himself maudlinly that he'd somehow missed the finest part of life. It seemed to him that he'd never been appreciated, that all his efforts, all his love, had been tossed down a black hole of self-interest on the part of females. Once his daughter had thought that he was the most wonderful man in the world, but now she was married and another man occupied that position in her heart. There was no one in the world who loved him above all others.

When Ellen died suddenly, he lost everything and was so alone that he became, for a while, a different person. That man went about his work with a ruthless effciency, lost his regard for his fellow men, and his new hardness seemed to impress. At last his long-delayed promotion went through, but there was no one with whom to celebrate. There was no one to say, "David, I'm so proud of you."

Of all the things which attracted him to Darcie Moncrief it was her wide-eyed devotion which impressed him most. She loved him! She thought—and she said so often—that he was the most wonderful man in the world. To Darcie he was a gentleman, a successful man, considerate, handsome, intelligent, a man

among men. To have such a woman, so beautiful, so
wise, so sophisticated, so desirable think that he was
all the things he thought she was was the highest praise
he'd ever enjoyed, and he went about his days smiling
to himself at odd times, not daydreaming, for another
aspect of his love for Darcie was to make him more
ambitious than he'd ever been. He wanted to accomplish impossible things, merely to show her that she
was right in loving him, in thinking that he was quite
a man.

Of course he was troubled by the rumors which he
could not escape. There is a type of person in this
world, he knew, who could not stand seeing others
happy. Ellen's friend Agnes McCrom was one. She
made it a point to try to kill his happiness by telling
him that Darcie was nothing more than a high-class
whore, that he was making a fool of himself.

Even before meeting Darcie in front of the toystore,
he had heard hints regarding her reputation. It was said
that she was not above using the oldest form of bribe
in the world to attain the ends which she and her uncle
desired, and there was even comment on her close relationship with her uncle. That first day when she had
tea with him, he knew that he was attracted to her, but
he had no idea that he would fall in love with her. When
he did, he was a bit frightened. But she was so unlike
any woman he'd ever known. There did not seem to
a selfish bone in her body. Whatever he wanted to do
was not only fine but wonderful with Darcie. Even the
way she looked at him was flattery. All right, so she
was not the model of chastity. The world was changing.
Women were, more and more, taking a place in the
world. She was a woman of the world, and if she had
bedded down with other men, that was long before he
knew her.

When she tried to confess, that day when they'd
been working with the stamps, he felt a moment of
panic. He didn't want to hear. He was afraid of his

own emotions. Just thinking of her in another man's arms was a pain deep in his gut. But she was so sweet about it, so genuinely contrite. And once more she tried to tell him what others had hinted at and what Agnes McCrom had told him openly.

"Oh, David," she whispered, in his arms, his lips close to hers, "I wish to God I'd met you years and years ago. I would so like to be clean and pure, so that I'd be worthy of your love."

"None of that," he said.

"I'm doing you a great harm by marrying you."

"That's crazy."

"No, I'm serious. I feel absolutely suicidal when I think that there are some men who will laugh at you, David. I can't stand that. I can't do that to you. I can't marry you."

"You can't break a promise you've already made," he said. And for a moment he was tempted to say, "What men? Give me their names and I'll go to them. They'll never laugh again." Instead, he soothed her and told her that it didn't matter, because it was so good to be loved so much, so wonderful to know that she loved him enough to want to give up her own happiness for his sake.

"I don't deserve you," she said, tears in her eyes. "But, darling, this I promise you. You are all the world to me. I will never again so much as look at another man."

Find her with Gen. Esteban Panama City.

The words burned holes in his brain. He told himself that it was just another attempt by those who could not abide happiness. But it was so straightforward. It had the unmistakable ring of truth. A navy widow, Agnes McCrom would have access to certain information. The navy would have been keeping a close eye on all those coming and going from Panama during those tense days.

In the end, feeling ashamed, feeling that it was

weakness, he went ashore. A few inquiries pointed
him toward the home of the former French official. He
kept his carriage waiting, walked to the door in his
uniform, to be greeted in a friendly manner by a military guard well into drunkenness, a man who recognized an ally, even a high officer, and threw his arms
around David with flowery Spanish phrases about freedom and friendship. He patted the guard on the back
and went into the house. There was music to guide
him to the ballroom. He stood in the doorway, unnoticed, and let his eyes sweep the room.

She was dancing with Esteban, a little peacock of
a man whose plumed hat came to her head and she
had her head thrown back, exposing the lovely lines
of her throat. And she was laughing merrily, with a
look of abandon on her face—or so it seemed to him
as the scene knifed into his heart.

He was turning to go, his world reeling, when she
saw him and, not believing it, delayed for a moment.
Then he was turning and she saw the dear profile, the
head lowered.

Seeing him set off a sunrise of joy in her. "David,
oh, David!" she cried. "General, excuse me, please."
She left Esteban in the center of the floor and ran
after David, holding up her skirts with one hand. He
was in the entryway, putting his hat on.

"David," she called happily, "oh, darling."

He turned. There was something in his eyes, in the
set of his lips, which brought her to a halt.

"David?"

"I had to see it for myself," he said, his voice cold
and bitter.

"I don't understand," she said, moving toward him
gladly. He put out his hands, and for the first time
touched her breasts, but not in love, in rejection, pushing her away from him.

"What did you have to gain by making me fall in

love with you?" he asked. "How much did they pay you for that?"

"Oh, David!" she cried, trying to hold him, her hands on his arm.

"Go back to your little peacock, whore," David said, pushing her away. She fell against the wall and almost went to the floor, stunned, not believing it.

"David!" she wailed, her voice rising as he hurried off the porch and down the steps. "No, David, no!" and she felt the urge to scream, to beat her head against the wall in protest, for it was so unfair. "It's not what you think, David," she cried, as loudly as she could. "Oh, David, please, please, please!" And the words ran into a wail which became racking sobs.

She felt a hand on her shoulder. "You are ill, *señora?*" Juan Esteban asked drunkenly.

She could not speak. She was sobbing, her entire torso jerking with the force of her grief. Cruel, so cruel, for God to show her happiness and then snatch it away.

"Come, *señora,*" Esteban said, guiding her into a side room to ease her down onto a sofa. "Can you tell me if you're ill?"

She shook her head.

"The American admiral—he did something to you?"

He has only killed me, she thought, but she shook her head. "Please," she sobbed, "may I just be alone?"

"If that is your wish," Esteban said, leaving her, closing the door behind him.

She recovered enough to leave the house and walk the streets of the early-morning town where there were still, now and then, isolated pockets of celebration. She found her way, after long hours, to a hotel and lay there, awake, until morning. On the theory that anything worth while is worth fighting for, she found the headquarters of the naval party which had come ashore and told the officer in charge that she must see

Admiral Russell on a matter of life and death. He was sympathetic, but he told her that the admiral's ship was presently steaming for San Francisco.

There was nothing for her to do. She took passage on the first ship north and rejoined Guy. There she kept to her room, being, Guy thought, quite unlike the Darcie he knew. She was weeping over a bunch of silly used postage stamps. During the following weeks, Guy tried to get her to share his enthusiasm for his new venture, It was looking well. He'd made some good contacts and had used some of Roethke's money to good advantage in the proper places. In advance, he had the estimates—strictly preliminary—of the work to be done and the prices which the government expected to have to pay for various materials. It put him a leg up on everyone, unless, he thought cynically, other steelmakers had done the same thing and bought the same information.

Darcie took no interest. Her only thoughts were for David. She established contact with a clerk at the Navy Department, using her smiles, and, once, a few tears, to get that man to promise her that he would notify her the moment Admiral Russell came back to Washington. However, when word came, it was an additional crushing sadness to her. The clerk sent a message to the effect that Admiral Russell had requested and had been granted a station on the West Coast and that he currently was on a cruise into the Pacific.

As time passed, Darcie began to realize the futility of keeping to her room. Gradually she allowed Guy to involve her in the new business, and, slowly, it began to seem important to her. At least it would give them enough money to do anything they wanted to do with the rest of their lives. Again there were parties at the Simel house, but now the bills were paid by Roethke Steel and Iron.

Thinking that some carnal activity would lighten

Darcie's sadness, Guy made overtures which were firmly refused. And so the months passed. Then, on a night when Darcie had used her charms to squeeze information out of a senior official with inside information about canal plans, on a night when she had drunk much wine, Guy came to her room, a giggling, half-naked young girl of about seventeen on his arm. "We were lonely and decided to join you."

Darcie had undressed and was in her nightgown. She looked at the half-exposed breasts of the young girl, all juice and life. For a moment she resisted the upsurge of lust, but then, with a twist of her head, saying, in effect, "To hell with it," she smiled.

"There is no need for anyone to be lonely," she said, "when there are three of us and I have such a large and comfortable bed."

Once, as she was allowing her basic needs to drive her into position between the young girl's soft and yielding legs, with Guy, made young by drink, driving deeply into her slick cavity from the rear, she thought of Lyris. Was that what she had become? Merely a voluptuary, with no thoughts other than her own carnal pleasure? Ah, Lyris. Dead and rotted in damned Panama, old before her time, deserted by her friends.

Darcie went quite still for a moment and the frantic motion continued around her, the young girl, being treated to the expert ministrations of a woman for the first time, heaving and demanding, Guy driving and gasping. She saw herself as Lyris must have been toward the last; alone, friendless, without money. Well, she determined, it would never happen to her. She did not doubt for a moment that Guy, if occasion demanded, would desert her just as he'd deserted Lyris, but she'd never give him the opportunity. She would be the guiding force and she would make them so rich that, if necessary, she could, in her old age, buy the necessities for happiness: dozens of juicy young girls and passionate young boys. And, with a long sigh, she

arched her back to allow Guy deeper penetration, her
hips, in her hands-and-knees position, flaring out in
a lovely line, and the goodness of it flowed through
her, allowing her to forget, for a time, the face of
that bastard, David Russell.

BOOK III

1

THE HUMAN RACE is advanced not by the efforts of its masses, but on the backs and brains of a few outstanding individuals of the type who, during that long and dreadful dictatorship by the church after the fall of the Roman Empire, were often burned at the stake, boiled in oil, dismembered, stretched on the rack, or drowned. By the time the Englishman, Ronald Ross, won the Nobel Prize for his work in mosquito-carried disease a new idea was no longer punishable by the death penalty or by torture, but for years established scientists called Ross "the outhouse man" because of his study of a particular mosquito which prefers to lay its eggs in filthy water. Even after Ross had proved beyond doubt that his theories were right and that the harmless but pesky little mosquito had done more harm to mankind than all his wars by distributing a host of diseases ranging from the number-one killer, malaria, through elephantiasis, there were those who jokingly held their noses when Ross passed by.

As the twentieth century began, although the cause of yellow fever had been definitely proved by the

Americans in Cuba and Colonel William Gorgas had effectively freed the city of that scourge by killing a type of mosquito which lays eggs only in artificial containers near human habitation, it was still clear to most "thinking" people that such terrors as yellow jack and malaria could not possibly come in so small a package as a single mosquito. Why, one could see the poisons rising from the Chagres River in Panama and could smell them in the reeking jungle.

New ideas are not popular among those who do not create them, and there has always been and always will be a man who will fight to the last to prove that his ways—the traditional ways—are right and that anyone who disputes him is a crackpot. (The fact that the human race has always come up with a large assortment of crackpots does not make the task of the innovator easier.)

In spite of the Cuban experience, where enemy action took only a fraction of the American lives lost to disease, and in spite of Teddy Roosevelt's statement that sanitary and hygienic considerations took first precedent in Panama, there were still lives to be lost because practical-minded men on the commission appointed by Roosevelt to oversee operations in Panama did not see what killing mosquitoes had to do with building a canal.

Gorgas, the man who rid Havana of yellow jack, went to Panama in June 1904, at the height of the rainy season. Having been instructed to make the isthmus safe for Americans, he was given a total force of seven, including one English nurse. Her name was Petra Burton.

During those peaceful and happy years in France on the lands which had belonged to her first husband, Petra seldom thought of Panama. She knew that Jay followed the news from America with much interest, and she was pleased when it was finally decided to finish the French canal instead of starting an entirely new venture in Guatemala. Somehow it seemed fitting. It meant that all those who died had not died in vain, that the grand dream still lived. And, although neither her home country nor France, her adopted country, would have a hand in the glory, the events would, in a way, vindicate de Lesseps, a man for whom she had always had respect.

During those years, Petra had not followed her career of nursing, except in tending the multiple bruises, scrapes, cuts, and bumps which are the inevitable companions of a small and active boy, but she followed the profession in her reading of various medical journals and was aware of the astounding discoveries which had been made by Ross, Walter Reed in Cuba, and others. Now she could see where the French had erred by placing ready-made breeding grounds for the yellow-fever carrier in rings about plants and in pans under the legs of the very bed in which a fever victim lay. Now it made sense as she remembered how men with no signs of fever soon came down with it after having been hospitalized with fever victims. It was tragic that the very institution which had been built to heal—the hospital—had been one of the best spreading agencies of the fevers. Although she could in no way be blamed, she could not help feeling retroactive guilt, having been a part of it.

Thus it was that she was ripe for suggestion when, with a smile on his face, Jay entered her sitting room with the mail and told her he'd been asked to come home to work on the American canal. The letter was from Washington, and the offer was concrete, with salary named, position specified. He would be working against his old enemy, the cut at Culebra, if he accepted the position. First, however, he was requested to come to Washington to give his expert opinions on canal matters.

"Well, the old man has not been forgotten," he grinned.

Petra knew a mixture of emotions. She was pleased for him, but the thought of leaving her home where she had been so happy, the fear of taking her children back into that pesthole, made her doubtful.

"Jay," she said, "don't you feel that we've done our part? Can't we let others do the work now?"

"We could," he said, "but are you sure you want to? You've had a lot of experience with tropical diseases. I wouldn't want you to go back to work full-time, but I'm sure that a person of your experience would be welcome there."

"Now you're trying to flatter me, and I don't want to be flattered. I only want to continue our lives, Jay, to be happy, to make a home for Jason, to see Helene and her Jean-Charles married at last, to see Antonia happy with a good man."

"And rock away the years while you bounce your grandchildren on your knees?" he asked, smiling.

"I'm not young anymore. It's time I was a grandmother."

Jean-Charles had finished his education and was serving his mandatory time in the service of his country. His work kept him mostly on the Mediterranean coast, and his visits were unpredictable. However, it was understood that as soon as possible, he and Helene would be married. Antonia, although she had weathered several tempestuous romances, had shown no indications of wanting to marry.

It was Jean-Charles who turned the tide in favor of Jay, who itched to get back into the action, who yearned for one more chance, with the proper manpower and equipment, to tackle the monster at Culebra. Jean-Charles became wildly excited when he learned that Jay might be going back to Panama, and he immediately set to work to convince his superiors that a Frenchman should be in Panama—if only as an observer. He came for a visit armed with permission to go on detached duty with the Americans, if he himself arranged it.

Then there were two of them, Jay and Jean-Charles. "Madame," Jean-Charles pleaded, "they will need good engineers, and I am a good one, if I can be immodest for a moment, and the pay will be so much more than I earn now. Helene and I could be married."

When the letter came from Colonel William Gorgas, asking Petra if she would care to join the medical mission which would be going to Panama soon, she began to waver.

"It's your work," she said, waving the letter at Jay. "You arranged it."

He grinned. "I may have mentioned in one of my letters that my wife had worked with Doctor Roger D'Art in Colón," he admitted.

Petra did not weep, although she felt like it, when the family, including Jean-Charles, waved good-bye to the servants who were to be left in charge of Chateau D'Art and set out for Washington. She had finally agreed, but on one condition. Until the expectations of Colonel Gorgas were met, and Panama was no longer to be a grave for three out of five white men who went there, she would not allow her family to go. In the meantime, while she went to Panama with Gorgas, the family, Helene and Antonia in charge of Jason, would remain in the United States. Since Jay's work would be keeping him in Washington, he would be with them for a while, until the actual digging began once more.

Petra clung to each day of the sea voyage as if it were to be her last day on earth, filled with misgivings, dreading the time when her family would be separated. Jean-Charles and Helene talked briefly about having the captain of the ship join them in wedlock, but Jean-Charles decided, since he would be going with an advance party of surveyors to Panama, that it would be best to wait until living conditions were right in the new American Canal Zone.

Once they were in the United States, events moved with a rapidity which stunned all of them. One moment they were gaping at the monuments of Washington; the next, settled into a nice house; the next, saying tearful good-byes to Petra.

Petra found Dr. Gorgas to be a charming man, quite considerate, dedicated, and confident that the methods used in Havana would result in a cleanup in Panama, if only he could convince the Canal Commission to give him the proper tools and financing and manpower. She spent nice hours with him discussing his theories and telling him of her experiences with the French.

And then they were in Colón. Almost immediately she was thrust back in time. Conditions were even more miserable than the last time she'd seen the city. And all around there were the swamps and the jungle which now carried a definite threat in their billions of mosquitoes.

Within months, the entire team had been down with malaria, in spite of their daily doses of quinine, and she felt the old, terrible, enervating force of the tropics began to pull on her, to weaken her, to make each day an endless period during which nothing seemed to be accomplished. Jay's arrival gladdened her, of course, and once again they were together, she working in the hospital on the hills overlooking Panama City, he in and out of the town, organizing, placing the workers who began to arrive only to begin to fall to malaria as quickly as the mosquitoes could find them.

Helene, Antonia, and Jason were well placed in Washington, with dependable servants, so there was no worry there. Her concern was the lack of cooperation which Gorgas was getting from his commission and his government.

When Gorgas went back to Washington to plead

for his plan of killing the mosquitoes which carried yellow fever and malaria, at least in the cities and working camps, Petra went with him, spent a lovely holiday with her children. They seemed to be thriving. Antonia was becoming quite the lady about town, quite popular with Washington hostesses, and Helene, sometimes sternly, was keeping an eye on her. Jason was in school and was quickly picking up not only American phrases and expressions, but a definite Southern accent. Petra called him "my little Yankee darling" and almost smothered him with hugs and kisses during the time she was there.

Things did not improve much once they were back in Panama. The Canal Commission wanted to "make the dirt fly," not kill mosquitoes, and the man in charge of the entire operation in Panama agreed with them.

The yellow fever epidemic of 1905 turned the tide. In panic, large numbers of the growing American work force deserted, fleeing Panama on all available transportation. The ineffectual manager was one of those who took ship for the United States. Then, to her great pride, Jay was named to be the engineer in charge. He moved into the offices in Panama City, called in Colonel Gorgas, and told him that whatever he needed, he had only to ask. And, when the commission in Washington questioned his expenditures for mosquito eradication, he told them tersely, "The digging is the easiest part. First we have to make it possible to dig."

Where he had once been limited to dozens, Gorgas now could command hundreds, thousands. Where once he had to justify the purchase of a dozen candles, he now had unlimited funds at his disposal. Fumigation brigades raided dark corners in the towns. Hundreds of workers collected and destroyed possible egg depositories for the carrier of yellow fever. Hundreds of old French wine bottles were collected, drained, broken.

Any container which could collect clean rainwater to attract *Stegomyia fasciata* was destroyed. Jay's work gangs were busy not at digging, but at building suitable quarters, putting screens on the hospital windows, cleaning up the squalid towns.

It took a year and a half, but it was done. There was no way, of course, to kill the billions of insects in the jungles, and there would never be complete assurance that one would not contract a fever, but the towns, the Canal Zone itself, was delivered from the two main scourges: malaria and yellow fever. The pay was good, the dirt was flying, and Uncle Sam's canal was underway. Moreover, Jay was slowly but surely beginning to win an old fight which went back all the way to the first conference in Paris. More and more people were coming to see that a sea-level canal was vastly more complicated and difficult and would be vastly more expensive than a lock canal.

A huge dam would tame the dreaded Chagres, forming a lake to be called Gatun. Because of the lake, the Panama Railroad would have to be relocated, calling for more money and more steel. Locks would be built, more steel, more workers, more material, more money. But now that it was safe to live in Panama, now that there were American goods available in the exchanges, comfortable quarters for executives and workers, health care, lack of fever, payment in gold for Americans, the great rush began. It would not end until the waters of the two great oceans were joined.

Ah, it was an exciting time. The months seemed to race by for Petra, and her work was now rewarding. Medicine was making incredible advances. With no mosquitoes to reinfect her, her malaria was gone, or at least dormant. Cooling fans in the buildings made work bearable, and Jay's progress filled her with pride. There were only a few dark clouds on her horizons. One of them was her uncle, Guy Simel.

"Guess who has the contract to supply steel for the new railroad bridges?" Jay asked her, one night after he'd taken over control.

"I have no idea."

"Your uncle."

"My God!"

"He represents an American company out of Pittsburgh."

"You've seen him, talked with him?"

"He asked about you. He seemed quite changed. He's an old man, Petra, aged beyond his years. He didn't go into detail, but he did say something about being sorry for all the hard feelings of the past. He asked to be allowed to call on you."

"I'm not sure I want to see him." She mused. "Did he mention Darcie?"

"No. It was a brief meeting. There were others there, except for one brief moment."

"I wonder where she is." Petra mused.

"If she's still with Guy, he didn't say. He comes and goes. He's quite an influential man now. The contract for the railroad bridges alone is worth millions, and I understand his company is going to bid on the reinforcements for the locks, if they're ever built. If Darcie is still with him, she has no money problems."

"Well," Petra said, "I suppose, after all these years, I don't begrudge them some success, although I still think it was sinful for the influential people to gain from the sale of the French assets while the little man lost everything."

She thought for a moment. "If he should ask again, tell him I'll see him."

2

ANTONIA D'ART had always known
a certain curiosity about her Aunt Darcie, although it
was quite difficult to get her mother to talk about the
black sheep of the family. Almost immediately, as she
began to get out and around and meet people in Washington, she began to hear of Darcie. She did not reveal
the fact that the lady in question in many gossipy conversations was her aunt; for she was amused to hear
staid little old ladies express shock, all the while with
envy in their voices, as they told of Darcie's influence
in placing the canal in Panama, the wild and wonderful
parties held at the Simel house, the whispers about
Darcie's willingness to jump into the bed of any man
who could help her.

Antonia was no longer an innocent-looking teen-
ager. She was an innocent-looking and very striking
young woman who was old enough be married with
or without the consent of her parents, but not quite
old enough to sign a contract under the law.

The decision to move the family to Washington and
then to Panama had come just in time to prevent her,
she felt, from doing something which might have proven

to be foolish, for she had been on the verge of asserting her age and leaving the dull life of the country. It would have been quite difficult, and it would have precipitated a huge family scene. The difficulty would have been in financing her independence, for her inheritance was not to come to her until her twenty-first birthday, and then it would be in the form of property rather than in money. She loved her family, although she chafed under the restrictions of having to keep up the front of being a virginal young girl.

Judging from what she knew of Darcie, Antonia often felt that she was more like her aunt than her mother. She still harbored some resentment toward her mother —not because she had slept with Jay Burton while her father was still alive, and while he was dying, but because, in her eyes, Petra was so hypocritical about it. Petra's body demanded the same attentions as did, no doubt, Darcie's, and, most certainly, Antonia's—so why deny it?

Some of Antonia's thinking was far ahead of her time. She saw no reason why women should be mere chattels of men. Men had the fredom to go anywhere they pleased, do anything they chose. Oh, society made motions of condemning the out-and-out rake, but in general it winked at the peccadilloes of men while condemning an errant woman to damnation. Had she been a man, she could have long since deserted the day-to-day sameness of country living for Paris or the world, made her own money if necessary, and done exactly as she pleased.

Life in Washington was a constant feast for her. The city was full of life, and there was a growing sense of importance among the citizens of both the city and the country which pleased her. As long as her mother was in the city, she was on good behavior. Aside from having been caught in the act in Paris, she had never given Petra reason to doubt that she was exactly what she appeared to be: a chaste young lady, and, with Jay's tacit help, she had smoothed her way past that one, thank God. For that she owed Jay a debt of gratitude and that aspect of it was another facet in her good behavior. She knew that she had only to step out of line once more, to make her mother unhappy, and Jay would be quite stern with her.

If the extent of Antonia's lust for life had been known to Petra and, indeed, everyone who knew her, they would have been shocked beyond expression. Having discovered early that she was seemingly immune to being implanted with child, she drank life in great gulps, and, although her choice of male companions had been, by necessity, limited, her experiences would have gladdened the hearts of those writers, especially in England, who rebelled against the strict Victorian codes to write some of the most licentious literature the world had ever known. Although Antonia had no opportunity to read all of the secret books which were circulated among the world's sophisticates, she had seen some of them and she agreed with some of the writers that the Good Widow, Victoria herself, having shown that she was a true woman in her love for her dead Albert, was, most certainly, lifting those black skirts of mourning to, first the stout Scot, John Brown, and, later, to the Indian retainer with the impossible name.

Antonia was a natural cynic. She had learned early that the sexual urge is human and that humans succumb to it, as her mother had. Marriage? She had her early affair with the banker to testify to the value of that institution, and, since then, advances from numerous married men did not change her opinion that marriage was merely the male's selfish way of putting a woman in a sort of prison.

But there was nothing truly evil in Antonia's character. She loved her mother enough to go to great lengths to hide her nature from Petra; and if she failed, as she did the night of the ball when she skewered the banker and as she did against the baron, in Paris, when Jay surprised her in a compromising position, she felt no guilt; men brought it on themselves. Had the banker stayed at home with his dough-faced wife, he would have escaped embarrassment. Had the baron been less interested in the seduction of young girls, he would not have been sent reeling by Jay's fist. Antonia had never in her life set out deliberately to hurt anyone. In fact, she was kindhearted to an extreme; considerate, thoughtful of her family in ordinary situations, and she did her share in running the household after Petra went to Panama.

The only thing which set Antonia apart from the average turn-of-the-century girl was her libido. She was definitely not a nymphomanic; for the term, as it was being coined by the followers of Freud, denoted an incapacity to enjoy sex. On the contrary, Antonia was one of those women who, throughout written history, have been gifted with a capacity to take, enjoy, dote on scandalous amounts of lovemaking and enjoy every minute of it. Her entire body was attuned to it, her thoughts never far from it. She was, moreover, eclectic in taste. That most of the men she met at Washington parties were older did not bother her. She asked only that the man be neat, clean, not vulgar—although that was not a dominating requirement, she, like many products of the restrictive age, enjoying a certain amount of vulgarity under certain circumstances—reasonably slim, and, above all, vigorous.

She began branching out as soon as Petra left with the Gorgas party for Panama, was almost immediately a must on many invitation lists. She suspected, from the way Jay looked at her and sometimes made oblique comments, that he was, if not aware, then suspicious of her activities. However, he did not attempt to restrict the freedom she assumed upon the departure of her mother.

She was wise enough to know that total promiscuity would not be acceptable to Washington society, a sophisticated bunch who winked at adultery, but only so long as it was not thrust upon them defiantly. However, by this time she was a mistress of deception and an adept at intrigue. She knew more about how to leave a man's apartment or house without being seen than many women twice her age.

The one complicating factor was Helene. Sometimes the girl's naïveté irked Antonia. There was, in Helene, a country-bred resolution to "keep herself for her husband" and it didn't seem to bother Helene at all that the man she wanted to be her husband did not, in Antonia's opinion, seem too eager to commit matrimony. Helene was, of course, older, but in many ways she was so young.

"Marry him before he goes to Panama," Antonia told Helene. "There's no reason to wait."

"Jean-Charles wants to wait until he can provide a home for us," Helene said.

"You have a home. Married or single, you know you'll always be welcome in our home. In fact, mother would not object to your staying with us always, she loves you so. Marry him. Stay on with us until you can join him in Panama."

"You know men and their silly pride," Helene said. "He would not hear of it. He says he will support his own wife."

"And, meantime, you're growing older," Antonia said. "You're wasting your best years, Helene. You'll be an old maid."

"Oh, Antonia," Helene said, near tears, "I know you're only thinking of me, but please don't say such things."

"I'm sorry, dear Helene." And she truly was, but she was also a bit disgusted with Jean-Charles.

Helene seemed to be content to stay in the com-

fortable house, to tend to Jason, to manage the place
and run the servants and give Antonia advice about
affairs beyond her knowledge.

"Is he of good family?" she would ask, when Antonia had an engagement with a man. "Are his intentions honorable?"

"Americans don't concern themselves about family,"
Antonia said. "Here the measure of a man's worth is
his bank account."

"I do worry about you," Helene would say. "I hear
that some of those parties are quite scandalous."

"Don't worry," Antonia told her. "I can take care
of myself."

From her generous allowance she bought new gowns,
thrilling to the wide selection in the rich and expensive stores which were unlike anything she'd ever seen.
In her enthusiasm, she also bought clothing for Helene,
and saw them only at family dinners. She often urged
Helene to accompany her, especially when she had
nothing definite in the way of an assignation, but
Helene was going to "be true" to Jean-Charles.

As her circle widened, Antonia knew that it was
inevitable for her to meet her aunt, and she was looking forward to the encounter with anticipation. She
didn't know exactly what to expect. She knew that
Darcie had been, according to all reports, a beautiful
girl, but she also did not know exactly how old Darcie
was. Her mother's age she knew, and Darcie was older
by some years, but she did not know how many. She
did not risk having to answer questions by asking about
Darcie, once they were in the city and she knew that
Darcie was, or had been, a rather famous resident.

When it happened, she did not realize, at first, who
Darcie was. Darcie had come out of her grief over the
sad end of her romance with David Russell, and was,
once again, in the thick of a battle, this time to win
contracts for Guy's new partner. The occasion was a
formal ball at the French embassy, Antonia being on

the invitation list because of a brief and pleasant affair
with a senior diplomat whose wife had been in France
for a visit. Surrounded by admirers, the blond girl, in
white, flowing skirts, her hair shortened in the new
fashion, was speaking of her memories of Panama.
Always Panama was a topic of conversation. She had
danced every dance and was sitting one out to catch
her breath. She saw the woman first as a flow of motion, a small, shapely woman in lacy black, her dark
hair highlighted by pearls. She gave her only a passing
glance, admiring her grace and her poise. Then, a bit
later, she was whirled past the woman in black on the
dance floor and saw a face which was mature, but so
beautiful that it made her gasp. And the eyes. The eyes
caught hers for a moment and she smiled spontaneously,
for they were eyes of knowledge and a sadness which
deepened them, made them so striking that they seemed
to burn into one. She was laughing as she danced past,
but her eyes were not, only her lips.

"Who *is* that woman?" Antonia asked her dance
partner.

"Quite a famous Washington beauty," her partner,
a minor government employee, said. "It is said that
she was instrumental in deciding upon a Panama canal
rather than a Guatemala canal."

"Her name?"

"Darcie Moncrief."

The woman in black did not lack for admirers, and
it was some time before Antonia had an opportunity
to speak with her. She was never alone. At worst, it
was Darcie talking seriously to a distinguished-looking
man, her head close to his, her lips smiling, her soulful
eyes stroking him with a skill which, Antonia soon
saw, was beyond her most practiced abilities.

In the end, as the evening latened, Antonia had to
push herself on Darcie; she did not want to have their
meeting come as a result of an introduction. She excused
herself from the gentleman who had just finished a

dance with her, made her way through the crowd to a corner where Darcie was talking with a handsome graying man, and stood close until Darcie looked up questioningly.

"A word with you, *señora*," Antonia said in Spanish.

"Of course," Darcie said, in the same language. "One moment."

Antonia withdrew. Darcie put her hand on the man's shoulder and said something too low for Antonia to hear, then came sweeping toward her, delicate, looking far younger than Petra, although Petra still retained a far from matronly beauty.

"Yes, my dear?" Darcie asked, examining the young girl with obvious approval.

"I just wanted to tell you that you are, by far, the most beautiful woman I've ever seen," Antonia said. She had not planned the remark—it simply came out. "Far more beautiful than I remembered."

"Remembered?" Darcie asked. "Do I know you?"

Antonia smiled. "I've grown a bit since you saw me last, Aunt Darcie."

There was a pretty frown and then a blinding smile. *"Mon Dieu!"* Darcie said. Antonia smiled and nodded "It can't be. Are you—yes, you are. I can see the Moncrief nose. My dear Antonia." And she swept Antonia into her arms, touching her cheek, kissing her lightly. "You've grown a bit?" she laughed. "The understatement of the decade. How beautiful you've become!" She held Antonia at arm's length, looking her up and down. Her eyes held that melancholy sadness, a quality which added to her mystery and endeared her to Antonia on the spot.

"You must tell me everything," Darcie said. "How did you come to be in Washington? Oh, I have a million questions." Her smile faded. She glanced around. "Your mother?"

"She's in Panama," Antonia said.

"Well, not here, not here, my child. I have a splendid idea. If you're as tired of this charade as I, and if you're free to do so, come with me to my home where we can have a long and intimate chat."

"I'd like that," Antonia said.

"You came alone?"

"I was escorted, but no matter. I'll simply tell him I'm going on alone."

Darcie flashed a questioning look and then laughed. "Excellent. You have a certain independence."

"My mother says that in that respect I am like you," Antonia said.

"Well, then, shall we get our wraps?"

Antonia followed Darcie out, impressed by the way Darcie handled herself; the cool assurance of her manner with the servant in the cloakroom, the doorman. A carriage was summoned and they rode through the streets with a light fog making the gaslights cast a roseate glow.

"So Petra is back in Panama," Darcie said, after they were underway.

"With Colonal Gorgas. Together they're going to rid the country of mosquitoes and fever," Antonia said.

"Tell me about her," Darcie said.

Antonia brought her up to date, received a "Well, well," when she told Darcie that Petra was now married to Jay Burton.

"You knew Jay?" Antonia asked.

With a deep and throaty laugh, Darcie said, " I knew him."

"Ah," Antonia said. "Is that the reason for the bad blood between you and mother?"

"Sharp little baggage, aren't you? Hasn't the Snow Maiden told you all about me?"

It was Antonia's turn to laugh. "Only that you're rather terrible, and I have to agree. Did you really seduce poor Jay?"

Taken slightly aback, Darcie tried to examine Antonia's face in the flickering light of a street lamp.

"Poor mother," Antonia went on. "Yes, I can see why you'd call her the Snow Maiden. Pure as the driven snow, that's my mater. Tell me about it."

"*It*, my dear?"

"You and Jay."

"You don't find it shocking?"

"Not at all," Antonia said. "I imagine Jay was quite a stallion when he was younger."

"Humm, trying to shock your aunt?"

"Perhaps," Antonia said in a chilly voice, "I have merely misjudged you, Aunt Darcie." She turned her face away and then, turning, speaking brightly, "Have you knitted anything dear of late, Aunt Darcie?"

Darcie's laugh was so genuine that the driver turned and tried to see what was so amusing. "All right, my dear niece, he was only adequate."

"I'm disappointed," Antonia said.

"You're quite unlike what I would have expected, I must admit," Darcie said. "Are you alone in Washington?"

"No. Jay is here, but he'll be going to Panama. Helene and I will hold down the fort and care for young Jason."

"And who is Helene?"

Under the cover of darkness, Antonia made a face of distaste. More hypocrisy.

"Petra must trust this Helene," Darcie said. "I can't imagine her going off and leaving you if she didn't."

"Oh, yes," Antonia said without enthusiasm.

"She would disapprove of your seeing me, you know."

"She would disapprove of many things."

"I was trying to count on my fingers," Darcie said. "I'm sure you're not of age."

"I'm precocious," Antonia said.

The carriage drew up in front of a handsome house. A servant opened the door, and Darcie led her into a pleasant room. "I'm going to expose one of my secret vices," Darcie said. "I've acquired a taste for American bourbon. Will you join me?"

"A light one," Antonia said, walking around the room, examining furniture and paintings on the wall. "My God, you have a Renoir?" She was captivated by the small portrait. It seemed to glow, to live.

"You're familiar with Renoir?"

"Who isn't?" Antonia asked. "How in the world did you come by it?"

"Actually, I didn't," Darcie said, coming to stand beside her, handing her a glass. "Your mother bought it in Paris many years ago."

"She never mentioned it."

"It's yours rightfully, I suppose," Darcie said. "Would you like to take it with you?"

"I'd love it," Antonia said. "I can't imagine mother buying it."

"She was advised to do so by an old friend."

"Her Uncle Guy?"

"No, a woman named Lyris Bahalah. She's dead now."

Darcie walked away and sat down. "I'll have it sent over if you like."

"It's worth ever so much," Antonia said.

"I know."

"I don't know what mother would say. She's probably forgotten it."

"What will Jay be doing in Panama?" Darcie asked, changing the subject.

"Oh, I don't know. Digging at a place called Culebra, I think."

"Yes. I know the place. Guy is in Panama, too."

"We'll all be going down soon," Antonia said.

"And in the meantime?"

"I think I'd like to get to know you, Aunt Darcie. I'd like to know, for example, why there is that look of melancholy in your eyes."

"I have a feeling you're on your way toward finding out," Darcie said.

"That's quite cryptic. Is that a way of telling me it's none of my business?"

"I find you to be quite refreshing," Darcie said.

"Thank you. May I tell you something?"

"Of course."

"I've been with you for only a brief time, and I feel that you're the first person I've ever known to whom I can talk. Do you find that sentimental or foolish?"

"Not at all. Do you know that you are much like me, at least in looks?"

"So I've been told. The hair is different, but I think your clothing would fit me."

"A bit loose in the bust, perhaps," Darcie said.

"Helene looks very much like you, too," Antonia said, watching for a reaction.

"That's the second time you've mentioned Helene."

With a wry smile, Antonia said archly, "And you have no idea who I'm talking about."

"Frankly, no."

"She was hurt and mother was angry when you didn't answer the letter."

"Darling girl, I am completely mystified."

"I, too, can lie on occasion," Antonia said stiffly.

"Really, I don't know what you're talking about."

"You received no letter?" Antonia asked, having come to that possibility.

"From your mother? I have had no communication with her since Panama."

"I see," Antonia said.

"There is something," Darcie said. "And I think you'd better tell me."

"Did you ever hear the name Freneau? Francis and Marie Freneau?"

Darcie's face went pale and she put a hand quickly to her throat. "Please continue," she said faintly.

"Yes, dear Aunt Darcie, that's who Helene is."

Darcie felt the world spin around her. Quite dizzy, she dropped her drink, heedless as it spilled on her skirts. Both hands gripped the arms of her chair. "Helene is—"

"Are you all right?" Antonia asked, running to use her handkerchief to wipe away the spilled liquid.

"My daughter—she's with you?" Darcie asked, recovering slightly.

"You really didn't know?"

"I swear to you I had no letter. Oh, God, tell me. Is she pretty? Is she happy? How did she come to be with you?"

"Here, I'll mix you another drink, and then I'll tell you all about her." Antonia went to the bar, poured, not quite sure how much of the dark whisky to put in the glass, but she received no complaint. She sat down and told Darcie all about Helene, answering eager questions.

"You can see her if you like," she concluded.

"Oh, yes. No. Oh, God, I don't know. What she must think of me."

"She understands why you had to give her up. She was hurt, as I said, when you didn't answer the letter after she first came to us."

"God forgive me," Darcie said. "I had no letter."

"You do want to see her?"

"Oh, yes, so much. But if she's happy, if she's content, I want to do nothing to harm her. Would it upset her?"

"I'm not sure," Antonia said honestly.

"Perhaps you could arrange for me to see her on the street, a casual meeting so that she won't know who I am. Does she ever ask about me?"

"At first. She was naturally curious. Yes, perhaps that would be best—at least for the moment."

"Would she recognize me?"

"There are some old pictures, but they are dim and faded. I'm not sure. You do have the same nose, the same mouth. She's small, like you, like me. Mother is the only Titian among us. Or the only Renoir."

"Please, Antonia, will you arrange it soon?"

"She likes to walk in the Mall," Antonia said. "If the weather is nice tomorrow, I will see to it that she is there, with me and with Jason. We'll stroll past the Washington Monument as near to three o'clock as I can manage it."

"I will be forever grateful."

"In return, you can teach me that look—the look of the melancholy eyes. It makes men's blood turn to water."

"You are a little beast," Darcie said, laughing. "After seeing you in action at the ball, I'm not sure that I can teach you anything."

"But you'll try," Antonia said.

"With much pleasure."

Helene was only too pleased to take an outing the next day, and the weather cooperated. With Jason covering twice the ground, running what that boundless energy of small boys, they took the sun, strolled, and at three were walking past the tall monolith, Jason craning his head to see the top. Antonia saw Darcie standing near the monument and guided the little group within a few feet of her. Darcie was wearing a veil, looking quite chic, and, somehow, quite lonely. Antonia noted that her head followed their progress, and when they were past, and she looked back, Darcie was still standing there, one hand to her face.

"Helene," Antonia said, "I've met numbers of people who knew your mother."

"Have you?"

"She is quite famous as a great beauty."

"Did they like her?" Helene asked.

"Most of them. The women were jealous, of course."
She called out to Jason to stay near. "Did you think,
before we came to Washington, that someday you
might run into her?"

"I thought about it. Since she does not want to see
me, however, I will make no special effort," Helene
said.

"What if she never got the letter?" Antonia asked.
"Mail does go astray."

"Do you suppose she didn't?" Helene asked with
some interest.

"It's quite possible."

"Oh, I don't know. I would be curious, of course.
I'd like to see her, to talk to her, to see what sort of
person she is. Actually, Antonia, I've thought a lot
about her. It must have been so terrible for her. Do
you suppose she would hate me for reminding her of
all the terrible things?"

"Helene, you're far too nice for anyone to hate. Let's
conjecture. Suppose I should meet Darcie, would you
want me to tell her about you? Would you see her if
she wanted you to see her?"

"Yes, I believe I would like that," Helene said.
"Jason, please don't do that!" she called out, as Jason
ran quite near a family having a picnic on the lawn.

"It wouldn't upset you?"

Helene examined Antonia's face. "You've met her,
haven't you?"

"Would it upset you to see her?"

"No, Antonia. Don't keep it from me. I forbid you
to keep secrets from me."

Antonia mused for a moment. She looked back and
saw the small, forlorn figure, or so it seemed to her,
beside the gleaming white monument. "Come," she said,
taking Helene's arm and turning her around. "Jason,
this way, please."

Darcie saw them turn and started to leave. But then
she thought Antonia was merely being considerate,

parading Helene past her once more. It had been an emotional moment for her. Her eyes misted when she saw the dark-haired, sloe-eyed beauty of her daughter. She could never have imagined anything so delicate, so wonderful having resulted from her forced union with the dwarf. And now they walked back toward her, Helene taking swift, ladylike strides, her long skirts molding gracefully to her legs. Helene seemed to be looking directly at her, and, as they came nearer, there was a look of agitation on the pretty face. Darcie felt her heart leap. And then she felt like running, for she knew that Antonia had told Helene. They were coming directly toward her. Her feet would not move. She had difficulty breathing. And then they were near, so near, and Antonia was smiling, holding Helene's arm. Helene's face was flushed. They came to a halt, so close that she could have reached out and touched Helene.

"Aunt Darcie," Antonia said, her voice choked with emotion.

Darcie's eyes drank in the olive skin, the slanted, huge, lovely eyes, the perfect lips, the slim waist in a light-colored frock.

"Please?" Helene said, gesturing toward Darcie's face.

Slowly Darcie lifted the veil and folded it back over her bonnet. Her eyes were wet.

"Yes," Helene said, "oh, yes, you're just as I always imagined."

"Oh, my God," Darcie said, unable to control the tears.

"Don't cry," Helene said, moving forward. "Please don't cry." And so saying she took Darcie in her arms. A teen-age boy, passing by, snickered. "It wasn't your fault," Helene said.

Darcie swallowed her tears and looked into the young and radiant face. "Forgive me. Please forgive me."

"There is nothing to forgive," Helene said.

"You're so lovely," Darcie said.

"And you. You're beautiful."

"Would you allow me to kiss you?"

"If you like."

Darcie put her hands on either side of Helene's face, looked into her eyes, placed a soft kiss on her cheek.

"You two are going to make me bawl," Antonia said. "Let's go somewhere out of the sun where we can talk."

At Darcie's home, Jason happily went with cook for a piece of cake, and they sat, Darcie unable to see enough of her daughter, to hear enough of the soft voice. Questions, questions, a lifetime to catch up. And then, too soon, it was time to get Jason home for his evening meal. They left, with promises all around to see more of each other.

On the walk home, Antonia said, "I don't think it would be a good idea to tell mother about this by letter."

"I will not deceive her," Helene said. "I love her too much to do that."

"Will you, in the name of love, cause her worry?" Antonia asked. "She has enough worry with her work in Panama."

"Perhaps you're right," Helene said. "Oh, isn't she beautiful?"

"Quite beautiful."

"After seeing her, I just can't believe all the horrible things I've heard about her," Helene said.

"Don't overromanticize her, Helene. She's a woman of the world. She's no saint, she's merely a woman who has seen tragedy, who has been, at times, ill treated by the world."

"Yes, you're right."

"May I speak a bit bluntly?"

"Don't you always, when you're of a mood to?"

"She is not an evil woman," Antonia said. "I think the best word to describe her is 'courtesan.' I'm saying

these things only for your sake, because I don't want
you to be hurt. You know that there is bad feeling between her and my mother. There may be other reasons,
but one of them is that Darcie, at some time, tried to
steal Jay away from my mother."

"Oh, dear, how do you know?"

"She told me," Antonia said. "The thing is, Helene,
you're too sweet, too good, too gentle and pure for
your own good." She laughed. "I've been telling you
for years to let your hair down, but if you don't want
to, that's your choice. You are totally incapable of
understanding a woman like Darcie, like your mother. If
you build her up to be more than she is, you'll be
disappointed. Take her for what she is. She was
genuinely touched by seeing you. Perhaps you can
develop a good relationship with her, a real friendship.
I know that I'm already quite fond of her, but then I
understand her, for we have a lot in common."

"Aunt Petra says that you're a lot like her."

"I think it best that we don't mention this to Jay,
either," Antonia said.

"Oh, Antonia, I'm not sure that would be right."

"Damn, girl, you're no longer a child. You're an
adult woman. You have a right to a bit of privacy."

"Well, I guess you're right," Helene said.

"After Jay goes to Panama, we'll have her to dinner, and then you can get to know her better."

"Yes," Helene said. "I should like that."

3

HELENE HAD DEVELOPED a genuine affection for the big, gentle, but always firm and decisive man who said good-bye to them early one morning, Jason clinging to him, begging to be taken along.

"It won't be long, son," Jay told him. "Soon you'll be getting on a big ship to come and join me and your mother."

"I don't see why I can't go now," Jason said.

"Because we have to wait until your mother has killed all the bad bugs which can make you very ill," Helene said.

"I ain't scared of no bad bugs," Jason said.

"I don't know where he picks up such language," Antonia said. "Don't say 'ain't,' Jason. You should say, 'I'm not afraid of any bad bugs.' "

"I ain't afraid of them neither," Jason said, sniffling.

"We'll spend a part of our time while you're away on grammar lessons," Helene laughed.

"Yes, everyone should speak good English," Antonia said, mimicking Helene's rather charming French accent.

"I like French better anyhow," Jason said.

"All right," Jay said. "You're the man of the house while I'm away, son. Take good care of our ladies."

"Tell them I can stay up until ten o'clock to take care of them," Jason said.

"You will do as Helene says, young man," Jay said. "Or we'll have some serious conversations over a razor strop when you get to Panama."

"Swell," Jason said.

"Don't use that horrid word," Antonia said.

"Enough of this," Jay said. "I have to go."

He embraced each of the girls, kissed them on the cheeks. He held Jason in his arms until the boy started wiggling and then, with a swat to his seat, sent him scurrying.

"As man of the house," Jason said, when his father had gone, "I demand cake twice a day."

"And I demand," Helene said, "that you go to your room and pick up your toys."

"Swell," Jason said, but as Helene looked at him severely, he ran from the room.

Helene laughed. "I think we're going to have our hands full."

"He is a monster," Antonia laughed. She was quite fond of her little brother, although, at times, he could be irksome.

Alone in the house, except for a cook and a man-servant who lived in a small apartment on the grounds, each had her own thoughts. Feeling a heavy responsibility, Helene gave her thoughts to planning how to keep the establishment running properly. Antonia had other plans. Oh, she would do her share, but now, for the first time in her life, she had almost total freedom and she intended to make use of it. Moreover, there was a new and interesting element in her life, and she lost no time in developing the possibilities of getting to know her aunt better. She sent word the day after Jay left that both of them would like Darcie to spend the evening with them.

Helene planned the meal and spent the afternoon working with the cook to be sure everything was just right. She was a bit in awe of Darcie, one of the world's true sophisticates, and she wanted to make a good impression. She dressed in a finely laced gown, had Antonia spent an hour on getting her hair just right, and, nervously, opened the door to let Darcie in.

Darcie was wearing a white duster over her gown, a motoring bonnet on her head. At the curb in front of the house was parked a gleaming Oldsmobile.

"What on earth?" Antonia asked, looking past Helene and Darcie to the automobile.

"My new toy," Darcie said. "It's quite exciting."

"It's yours?" Antonia gasped. "Oh, you must take us to ride in it."

"You are a very daring girl," Darcie laughed. "I'm only learning to drive it, you know."

"Is it difficult?" Helene asked.

"Rather nerve-racking at times, I must admit," Darcie said.

"How fast will it go?" Antonia asked.

"I haven't dared find out."

"Take us for a ride now," Antonia begged.

"Well," Darcie said, uncertainly, looking at Helene.

"There's time before dinner," Helene said. "May Jason go, too? He'd be quite excited."

"Of course," Darcie said.

Excited was not the word for it. Jason had to feel every inch of the motorcar and had to be literally dragged away from the crank, which he insisted he was capable of turning.

"This is the most difficult part," Darcie said, standing in front of the car, blowing on one palm and then seizing the crank firmly. "You must be careful, lest it backfire and break your arm."

"Oh, please be careful!" Helene cried.

The motor started with a swift and energetic crank, and, the car making a frightful noise which caused

Jason to put his hands over his ears and shriek with happiness, Darcie climbed into the driver's seat. With a jerk, she set the vehicle in motion.

"Faster!" Jason cried. "Faster!"

"Young man," Darcie said, "I am working my way into racing by degrees, if you don't mind."

She drove them around several blocks. Traffic was light in the residential neighborhood, but they saw both motorcars and carriages. Jason waved at all passersby and reached over Darcie's shoulder to try to honk the horn. They arrived back at the house in a gay mood, their faces flushed by the wind, and dragged Jason off the motorcar to send him to wash the oil from his hands.

Helene escorted Darcie into a bath so that she could freshen up and stood watching as the small and delicate woman washed her hands, checked her makeup and her hair, and then turned with a smile.

"I did enjoy the ride," Helene said.

"If you like, I'll teach you how to drive it," Darcie said.

"Oh, I'd be terrified."

"It's quite simple, actually."

Antonia poured wine. For a few moments, there was an awkward silence. Antonia broke it by saying, "Helene has worked all afternoon on the meal, Aunt Darcie, so even if you don't like it, you must praise it."

"If Helene did it, I'm sure it will be wonderful," Darcie said. "Do you enjoy cooking, Helene?"

"Oh, yes. When Jean-Charles and I are married I'm going to do all the cooking," Helene said.

"Tell me about your Jean-Charles," Darcie said.

If there was anything Helene enjoyed talking about it was Jean-Charles, so the momentary awkwardness dissolved into a paean dedicated to Jean-Charles, Helene going on until Antonia laughed and said, "I should have warned you. Get her going on that subject and there's no end to it."

"Really, I'm quite interested," Darcie said. "Hush, Antonia."

"Then, since I've heard it all a million times and know that no man could possibly be so wonderful, I shall leave you with it," Antonia said, going into the music room to sit and begin to play.

"—and I have this beautiful wedding gown, which Aunt Petra bought me," Helene was saying. "Would you like to see it? Oh, no, I'm sure you wouldn't."

"I would love to see it," Darcie said, with a fond smile.

And so Darcie Moncrief entered into a period of woman talk and domesticity which would have astounded those, such as Guy, who knew her well. Caught up in Helene's enthusiasm, she oohed and ahed over the lacy and delicate things in Helene's hope chest.

Dinner was lively, with Jason allowed to eat at table with them, entertaining with a tale about his pet frog named Teddy who lived in a rain barrel at the back of the house. Darcie found him to be a charming if lively boy. He had Petra's eyes. She discussed the habits of frogs with a seriousness which convinced Jason to the point of running from the table to bring Teddy, wet and gleaming, cupped in his hands.

"Oh, Jason!" Antonia cried.

But Darcie, with that seriousness which made an instant fan of Jason, took the frog into her hands, examined him with a critical eye, and pronounced him to be the finest frog in the world.

After dinner, Darcie requested that Antonia play for them. Always happy to be seated at the piano, Antonia complied. And the hours passed in woman talk between Helene and Darcie, so that by the time Darcie left there was a bond of understanding between them, and, in Darcie, a love which was an ache of regret.

On the way to her empty house, she tried to speed the feeling away, pushing the Oldsmobile to daring velocity on the wide boulevard, but it was still there as, alone in her bed, she pondered what might have been. To think that she could have been a part of that charming girl's life was pain. She tried to imagine Helene as a toddler, then as child of Jason's age. All that could have been hers. Unable to sleep, she arose, put on a lace wrapper, and went into the study. She poured a small drink and sat at the table, her stamp collection in front of her, idly thumbing through the pages of her album. This, too, reminded her of things she had missed, for she never looked at a stamp without thinking of David. Still, it soothed her. There was, in her collection neatly mounted in the album, an orderliness which was not present in the rest of her life and in times of stress she retreated into the world of stamps with their portraits of the powerful, the kings and queens of the world, their intricate designs, their pictures of far-off and exotic places.

Darcie arrived at the Burton house laden early the next afternoon, having spent the morning shopping. She had gifts for all—Helene, Antonia, Jason—and Jason said it was just like Christmas. Antonia was going to a party that night. Helene asked Darcie if she'd like to spend the evening, and Darcie accepted gladly. She watched, rather helplessly, as Helene saw Jason to bed, checking behind his ears to be sure he'd washed properly. Then they were alone.

"I want to say," Darcie began, "that I am so grateful to you for letting me come into your life."

"And I into yours," Helene said.

"So many things I could say," Darcie mused, "and all of them dreadfully maudlin."

"Feel free to speak," Helene said. "I'm an incurable romantic. In fact, this entire affair is like something out of a fairy tale. First I, a country girl, am taken into a rich and beautiful home by the kindest woman, outside of my mother—" She flushed. "My adopted mother."

"Don't feel embarrassed. She was more your mother than I," Darcie said. "The mere giving of birth does not entitle me to special consideration. I am deeply grateful to your parents, to Monsieur and Madame Freneau, for helping to make you such a delightful person."

"Well," Helene said, "to be taken into a home luxurious beyond my wildest imagination, to be loved, and then to find you and to see that you're so beautiful. I keep going on about that so." She shook her head, flustered.

"It is my understanding that you are postponing your marriage until Jean-Charles can provide a home," Darcie said. "I know that quarters are being built in Panama, but if there is anything I can do—I have some little money. Could I, may I offer—"

"I thank you for the offer," Helene said. "But you know men. Jean-Charles and his fierce pride."

"At least I can see to it that you're the best-dressed bride in Panama," Darcie said. "Having been there, I can be of help in selecting clothing suited to the climate."

"Oh, would you? That would be so nice!"

While Antonia stayed with Jason, Darcie and Helene took the Oldsmobile and went shopping, coming home laden.

Thus the pattern was set. There was only one more awkward snag to get past.

"Helene, I can't help but notice that you do not address me by name," Darcie said, on another evening when Antonia was at a party. "I think it would be embarrassing for both of us to consider a title. Mother? Impossible. Madame? I'm not married. Miss? So, to ease the strain for both of us, will you please just call me Darcie?"

"You're quite perceptive," Helene said. "It has bothered me. Yes, I think Darcie. As between friends."

"My darling girl, if you will be my friend, I will consider it the most wonderful thing which has happened to me in all of my lifetime."

Like Antonia, Helene found Darcie to be easy to

talk to, and, as the days passed, she found herself sharing her most intimate thoughts. There was even a giggly hour during which she asked shy and surprisingly naïve questions about what her life would be as a married woman. Darcie, thinking, with hidden tears, that it was so very, very sweet, talked calmly and sensibly about sex. God knew, she thought wryly, she'd had plenty of education in the field.

Antonia's current escort and bedfellow was a tall and handsome medium-level official from the Department of State. Through him she gained access to the homes of some of the high and mighty and, as always, became a regular on their lists, popular with both men and women, keeping her erotic life carefully hidden.

There were times when she was tempted to risk shocking Helene into instant old age by telling her that she would not be home that night. Now Helene was the only obstacle between her and complete freedom of action. Her diplomat was possessed of a greed and a physical ability to fulfill that greed which often sent her on her way home at an hour which would not upset Helene too much before she was ready to go.

"I'm going to ask your help, Aunt Darcie," she said one afternoon, having dropped by Darcie's house when she knew that Darcie was not with Helene. "Nothing active, just your silence. Tonight I shall tell Helene that I'm going to spend the night with you."

"I see," Darcie said, understanding immediately. "Is that wise?"

"Women are not expected to be wise," Antonia said lightly, "only devious."

"As a matter of fact, Antonia," Darcie said, "I've been looking for an opportunity to have a serious talk with you. Are you aware that you are becoming a topic of gossip in certain quarters?"

"Well, my dear aunt, we can't allow you to be the subject of all conversations, can we?" Antonia asked.

"I'll not humble myself and say you have a right to

say that," Darcie snapped. "Nor have I appointed myself the guardian of your morals. If you have no desire to listen to the voice of experience, then that voice shall be silent."

"That's all I ask," Antonia said and went about her plans.

"Tonight, my great and stalwart stallion," she told Andrew Page, her junior diplomat, when he came for her in his rattling, noisy motorcar, "we shall turn the face of the clock to the wall."

In her eagerness, she rushed him through dinner at a smart restaurant and followed him into his apartment, being careful not to be seen.

Andrew Page was one of Antonia's older men. She found that their lasting abilities were superior to men of or near her own age. Page was a short, sturdy man of some forty years with strong, thick arms, a smiling, rounded face, brown eyes which were clear and lively behind his glasses, a mouth which was either soft or harsh and demanding depending on his immediate emotions and which, when he was not smiling, showed lines descending from the corners. He was a well-educated, cynically humorous man who had once been married and was now widowed. Of all the men Antonia had known, he was by far the most sensual. With libido aroused, Andrew tended to forget his cultured, smooth speech and reverted to the language of the gutter, the harsh four-letter description of anatomical features and actions grating and, somehow, licentiously exciting to Antonia.

"Tell me," she said, having made herself comfortbale in a silken wrapper, her lithe and pinkly healthy skin showing through, her long and lovely nipples engorged by merely being in his presence, so nearly naked, so ready.

And, smilingly, knowing what she wanted, his voice low and suggestive, he used the crude words to tell her what lay in store, describing actions which he had performed with her before, talking, talking, not touching, bringing up the lustful images until she was breathing rapidly and could feel herself loosen, feel the sweet juices begin to flow and her insides seem to melt down, to open her like a flower. She lay on a chaise lounge, a drink in her hand, her head leaning on one hand.

"Oh, God, Andrew," she breathed, "do it. For God's sake do it."

He came to her fully dressed, unbuttoned the silken garment which covered her scantily, rolled her gently to her stomach, and seated on the side of the lounge, began to trail his fingertip up and down her bare back, to the bulge of her buttock, into the smooth crevice there and teasingly, lightly, down to feel her heat, her ready moistness. She accepted his light and tickling caress with eagerness, with liftings and quivers and sighs as his fingertips sought and found areas of extreme sensitivity and the whole of her body seemed to come alive.

And then he was bending over her, his tongue trailing where his fingertips had traveled, her shoulders, her neck, the small of her back and, "ah, ah, ah," into the dry and sensitive cleft between her white buttocks, to fire and flame on the dark and rosy and tightly closed opening, sending the sensation through the meaty membranes separating her two cavities until she was yearning, almost crying out to him. Never before had he prolonged it so, but then never before had they had an entire night ahead of them.

When, at last, he rose and she could hear the rustling of his clothing, hear him moving, she turned her head and watched as he removed his jacket, his shirt, and then his trousers dropping, underthings going with them, to reveal a half-engorged staff which, within seconds, was heatedly pressed to the small of her back as he put his legs on either side of her, riding her, his mouth kissing and soothing her neck and shoulders and then going down, that heated staff moved ahead, seeking the warm indentation and lying there, hard, huge, teasing. He used his hand, sweeping the tip of his hardened flesh down and up, caressing with the meaty glans the tender and silkenly lubricated labia, the brown entrance at the rear until, with a sign of longing, she pushed her hips high, lifting her mons from the couch, sighing, almost sobbing with her need as the stiffness found entrance and slid along the well-prepared channel to drive so deeply into her that the pressure was an exquisite pain. His weight pinned her to the couch, pressing mons and sensitive areas hard into the material and then he was bending to kiss her neck, to turn her face so that a sidelong, sliding kiss wet her lips.

Using the basic four-letter words, he asked her if she liked having him in her and, "Oh, God, yes," she cried, lifting her hips to cup into his loins and drive him ever deeper as he began to move, harder, harder. And she, too, used gutter language, begging for, demanding, pleading for harder and deeper penetration until the pressures, the frictions, the weight of him on her as he rode her, his legs astraddle as he stood on his knees, his hands on her hip bones to lift her rear higher, she felt her first completion and laughed out her pleasure, wiggling, tossing, squirming.

And the glorious thing about it was that there was no hurry, giving him time to pause, mix another drink.

"Three or four ounces of whisky," he told her, "and you'd better be prepared to stay awake all night."

"Promises, promises," she whispered to him, jutting a hard-tipped breast at him as he came to kneel at the foot of the lounge, pull her down, hoist her legs so that her heels were on the edge of the lounge and dive into the heat and sweetness of her with a hunger which soon had her gasping again. Then after long, long minutes during which she hovered on the edge of an abyss of pleasure, the penetrating, the hard, long, magical slide and her legs clamped around his back, soft inner thighs feeling his muscular waist and the long dreamy evening turning into a game during which they decided, somewhat drunkenly after a while, to "initiate" every room in the house, the kitchen work-table cold and hard under her naked back, standing on the veranda, the lights of the city spread below, her hips against the railing and her legs spread wide while he bent his knees and thrust up into her and then at last the bed and positions changing and dear Andrew living up to his promise, going on and on as spasm after spasm of bliss racked her.

She awoke with his entry from the rear into the feel of early morning, not having gotten out of bed when the long and totally erotic session of the evening ended with his completion. She was slick with his residue and he entered. She lay on her side, knees drawn up, his body cupped around her rump, his hard staff thrusting. And then she was rolling, pulling away, only to throw herself onto him, ride the splendid staff, using him for her own enjoyment as she ground and pushed her mons hard against him.

She left just before dawn, each step a delicious little twinge of soreness. And, afterward, she spent at least one night a week with Aunt Darcie, leaving Helene and Jason alone in the house.

The brief and delightful affair with Andrew Page ended when he was posted to the embassy in Rome. At loose ends, Antonia accepted an invitation, swept into the parlor of a lobbyist from New York, to find the party in full swing, the music coming from a piano played by a sad-faced, swarthy man with a cap of tightly curled hair. She recognized the tunes, current-ly popular things, played in a very professional man-ner. After making her pleasantries to the host and hostess and greeting people she knew, she made her way to the piano to lean one elbow on it and watch the talented hands picking out a sprightly melody. The sad-faced man looked up, winked, and examined her. She smiled.

"You're very good," she said.

"Know this one?" he asked, swinging into "Moon-light Bay."

Antonia smiled, stepped away from the piano to do a bit of soft-shoe, then came back to lean.

"We were sailing along, on moonlight bay," she sang, in her clear and melodious voice. And then it was "two live as one, one live as two, under the bamboo tree."

"Let it out," the sad-faced man said. She stood erect and lifted her voice, having fun, liking the glum and glowering man whose fingers could perform such magic on the keyboard. As she sang, people stopped their talking to listen, and, without her noticing it, she became the center of attention. She was feeling it, and when he started "Alexander's Ragtime Band," she marched in place to the intro, and then began to belt out the lyrics with an enthusiasm which brought another wink and a near smile to the man's face. When she finished, there was a round of applause and cries of "Encore, encore."

"Damn," she said. "I didn't know everyone was listening."

"They listen when they have something to listen to," he said. "Name one. We'll give 'em one more."

She named a little French tune and he shrugged. She hummed it for him. He followed, but lost the melody at the bridge. "Take off and I'll fake it," he said.

"It's quite simple," she told him, sliding onto the bench with him. She played the bridge for him as he watched and then, seated beside him, sang the tune, a whimsical and romantic little air, in French. Again the applause.

"Always leave 'em wanting more," the sad-faced man said, rising, giving her his hand. "How come I don't know you? You working Washington?"

"Not exactly," she said with a smile.

"Don't tell me you're not a pro," he said.

"I beg your pardon?"

"You're not in the profession?"

"Hardly," she said, laughing.

"Entertainment," he said, grinning for the first time. "Not the oldest profession."

"Oh. Oh, my, I am flattered. But no, I'm not an entertainer."

He slapped his forehead and groaned. "Jesus, the goddamned amateurs got more talent than the pros around here."

"Is that a compliment, Mr.—Mr.—"

"Young," he said. "Jack Young. You haven't—" He shook his head. "No, you wouldn't have heard of me. I'm working the Capitol."

"The Capitol Theater?"

"Damned well not the Capitol of the United States," he said. "Where can a man get a drink around here?"

"I may not be a professional entertainer," Antonia said, "but I'm the world's best at seeking out the location of the bar." She led him into the large room to one side of the parlor where a liveried servant tended bar. He ordered scotch whiskey, straight, and looked at her. "Mud in your eye," he said.

"Mr. Young—" she began.

"Entertainers are never 'mister,' " he said. "Call me Jack."

"Jack, you play beautifully."

"You didn't do bad yourself."

"It must be exciting, being in the theater."

"It's a pain in the ass."

"Are all entertainers so outspoken?" she asked, with a little laugh.

"It's our way of showing we don't give a damn about what people think," he said. "A form of rebellion. Nice ladies are never seen in our company, so you're compromising your reputation."

"Is that because an actor killed a president?"

"No, it's because actors look at beautiful ladies like you and get the hungries," he said, fixing her with his dark, melancholy eyes.

She laughed. "I like you."

"Mutual," he said. "Well, hell, I'm being paid, so back to the old grindstone. You feel like singing a few more, come on over."

There was something about him which appealed to her. He had a sort of lost-little-boy look. She circulated, danced once or twice as Jack Young played, and then she was back at the piano.

"Are you Jewish?" she asked.

"Nigger," he said.

"You do like to try to shock people," she said.

"Well, my parents were Jewish. Me, I'm nothing."

"I think you're quite something," she said.

"Sing this one," he said, starting a soft and ancient melody. "Sing it soft, just for me." And she put the words, reputedly written by Henry VIII, to the melody of "Greensleeves."

"Jesus God Almighty," he breathed, when she finished and the last lingering note fell away.

"Jews cannot call on our God for help," she said.

"Mimi, that's one advantage of being nothing. You can call on the Great God Buddha if the idea appeals to you. You know I'm in love with you, don't you?"

"You're crazy," she said. "Don't you ever smile?"

"I'm not paid to smile, just play."

"Show me."

He made a grimace, exposing a nice set of teeth.

"You'll have to work on that a little," she said.

"Come over here and do that little French ditty again," he said. She sat down and played it, singing it softly. No one paid any attention. It was almost as if they were alone.

"Pretty," he said. "How long would it take you to teach me them Frenchy words?"

"How long do you have?" she asked, smiling up at him.

"As long as it takes."

She started noodling on the keyboard and her fingers fell into the patterns of one of her own compositions, a sprightly little thing with gaiety and life.

"Not bad," he said. "Where'd you pick that one up?"

"Oh, here and there."

"Never heard it. Not bad." He was a very quick study. He picked it up after one or two tries and added in some raggish styling which enlivened it. "This thing have a name?"

"Not yet," she admitted.

"Now you're not going to tell me you wrote it?" he said incredulously.

"Well, not if you feel so strongly about it."

"Got any more like that?"

"Dozens," she said. "Try this one." She played a sweetly romantic theme, and he was nodding his head in time with the beat.

"Now I *am* in love with you," he said. "Jesus, it just ain't fair. You've got all the looks in the world, sing like a goddamned thrush, and can write music, too. On top of it all, I'll bet you're filthy rich. It's enough to make a man want to shoot himself."

"I'm not rich."

"In that case, let me get those things published for you."

"Really?"

"Mimi, I don't talk just to hear my head rattle."

"But really, are they good enough?"

"I can use that little lively tune. I think we'll call it 'Mimi.' After you."

"My name isn't Mimi."

"It is to me," he said. "You're a Mimi, and if you tell me you're a Sally or a Mary, I won't accept it."

"Mimi Moncrief," she said. "It does have a certain ring."

"You got these things written down?"

"Yes, most of them. They're in France, though."

"Well, no matter. I'm a pretty fast pencil. How's about you and me get together and transcribe a few of them? I'd ask you to my place, but they don't allow women in that fleabag, and there's no piano."

"If you're really serious, you can come to my house."

"No mama and no papa to kick up about an actor in the house?"

"Just my cousin, and she's very understanding."

"Swell," Jack said. "You name it. I got a matinee tomorrow, but any other day except Saturday or Sunday."

"Shall we say Monday, then?"

"Swell. Write down the address, will you, Mimi?"

Helene was quite excited when Antonia told her the story and reminded her of a tune which she hadn't played in a long time. It had the feel of a French cabaret—sprightly, happy, the melody quite tricky. Antonia was playing it on Monday afternoon when the front doorbell rang and Helene escorted Jack Young into the music room.

"Don't stop," he said. "I like it."

She finished and then rose to give him her hand. He had a book of music manuscript paper. He sat beside her, the sheets on the music holder, and began with the little tune she was playing. It took a half hour for him to transcribe it, and he played it back for her to be sure he hadn't missed anything.

Helene brought coffee and lingered, listening as they worked and the hours seemed to fly. He had to rush off to keep from being late for his evening performance, promising to come an hour earlier the next day.

"Mimi," he said, as he came into the music room, "I used your namesake tune in the act last night—"

"Oh, you didn't!" she exclaimed.

"It brought down the house."

"Actually?"

"My, that's thrilling, isn't it?" Helene asked excitedly.

"So I stayed up most of the night putting some words to it. Come over here and see what you think." He seated himself and in a scratchy but somehow entertaining voice he sang a gay little tale about a French girl named Mimi who didn't know how to fall in love. He sang in a comic accent, and the words were so witty that both Antonia and Helene collapsed with laughter.

"You like?" he asked.

"I love it!" Antonia said.

"Mimi," he said, looking at her with a wink, "it's time you and me talked some trash, and I mean serious. You ever hear of an English fellow named George Edwardes?"

"No, I don't think so," Antonia said.

"He was—maybe still is—manager of the Gaiety Theatre in London. He came up with an idea which I think is going to take this country by storm if it's done right. He called it musical comedy. Now what it is is a sort of opera for the common man. Tunes he can whistle. Words he can understand. Like this little Mimi ditty. It has a little bit of the elements of a revue, some burlesque, songs, dances, humor. It has a plot of a sort, but nothing heavy, sort of farce-comedy. But most of all, it has music, songs, lyrics. I've been in this business a long time, and I'm a little tired of this one-night-stand stuff. I've been thinking for a long time in terms of trying this musical-comedy idea and up till now I didn't have the slightest idea where I'd get the original stuff for it. I'm good with words, but I'm not a musical genius. I can't write for split peas when it comes to music. How'd you like to become famous and maybe, if we're lucky, make a dollar or two?"

"I'd love it," Antonia said. "Jack, you're so flattering."

"Straight truth, lady. Just one problem. I don't think the world's ready for a woman composer."

"Humm," Antonia said.

"Hey, hold on. You're thinking that I want to take credit for your music? No, sir. We'll just have to give you a man's name, that's all. It'll all be on the up-and-up. Hell, if you want to, you can call in a battery of law dogs and get it all on paper."

"Well, not this moment," Antonia said.

"While I was laying awake last night, I was thinking," he said. "I came up with sort of a tentative story line. This little French girl, see, she comes to the United States and—"

He went through the story, accenting it with partial renditions of Antonia's songs. "What do you think?" he asked.

"I think it's very nice," Helene said, when Antonia didn't answer immediately.

"I don't know that much about it," Antonia said, still not believing that her compositions were really good.

"Why can't you be nice, like your cousin?" Jack asked.

"She's had longer to practice," Antonia said.

"When Mimi's heart gets broken," Jack said, "we need a love song, a real tearjerker, something romantic young girls can sing and weep over. Know what I mean? Like, 'You never die of a broken heart, but it makes you wish you would.' "

Antonia sat beside him at the piano and began to put chords together, humming. A plaintive little melody formed under her fingers. She sang, "You never die of a broken heart, but sometimes you wish you would."

"Yeah, that's the idea," Jack said. "A love that's lost is sorrow sweet—"

They were still at it when it was time for him to rush to his performance. The love song had become light and farcical, but still had a poignancy.

It was fascinating for Antonia. She spent every afternoon with Jack Young, and not once did she think of him as a man, so engrossed was she in the work. On a

Saturday afternoon, they went to the theater, and Young used two of Antonia's songs in the performance, much to her delight. Hearing her music performed in a professional way before an audience pleased her, and she blushed with pleasure when Helene squeezed her arm and said, "Isn't it thrilling?"

And then Jack Young's engagement was finished.

"Well, Mimi, I'm off to New York. First thing I'm going to do is get your stuff published. We got to have a man's name for you. Any ideas?"

"My father's name? Roger D'Art?"

"No offense, but it doesn't have the right ring. That Moncrief monicker—"

"Mimi Moncrief," she said. "Marcel Moncrief?"

"Fine. Frenchy. The swells in New York go for Frenchies." He bundled the music into a battered portfolio. "You'll be hearing from me, Mimi. Take care of yourself, huh?"

"I will, Jack."

Antonia realized that for a period of thirty days she had not attended a party—had done nothing, in fact, other than work with Jack Young in the afternoons and play the piano and talk with Helene and Jason in the evenings. She was sorry the interlude was over, but it was, and she had doubts that she'd ever hear from Jack Young. Perhaps, she thought, she should have talked with a lawyer before giving him all her music, but it really didn't matter. Gradually she reentered Washington's party whirl and met the nicest man. He was an officer in the Army Corps of Engineers, again an older man with, he confessed, a wife in St. Louis. He was in Washington on temporary duty and would, in all probability, be going to Panama in a few months.

Although Lieutenant-Colonel Arthus Taylor's hair was a gleaming, premature silver, he was far from old. At forty-two, he was a fine specimen of a man, not tall, standing about five-eight, but solidly built and in perfect physical trim. Gentlemanly, courtly, always serious, she encountered him three times before he danced with her and twice more before he asked her to have dinner with him.

For weeks, Antonia found herself checking the post, and when the days continued to go by with no letter from Jack Young, she shrugged mentally and told herself that nothing would come of her work with the entertainer. *Oh, well,* she thought, *best wishes to him. If her songs helped him in his career, no great loss.* Her music was for her own enjoyment and her brief thoughts about a musical career were submerged in her interest in the gentlemanly Colonel Taylor who, after a period of some weeks, finally overcame either his scruples or his shyness and discovered that young Antonia D'Art was quite exciting.

4

IN PANAMA THE dirt was flying. Jay's innovative guidance had made life in the Canal Zone pleasant for the Americans, especially the upper and middle echelons who had private quarters with airy rooms and screens on doors and windows. Now that work was really underway, now that the plans were solidified and the huge dam which would tame the dreaded Chagres was underway, nothing was too good for those who worked on the canal. There were low-priced consumer goods in company stores, clubs, recreation, the best of medical care. Colonel Gorgas's clean-up and mosquito eradication programs had been a great success, and at a family conference attended by Jean-Charles, Petra and Jay decided that it was time to bring the rest of the family to Panama. Quarters would be assigned to Jean-Charles, and he could marry his Helene at long last. The cablegram went out and Petra began to look forward eagerly to having her own with her, made plans to leave her work with Gorgas, and spent her time preparing the house for her girls and her little boy.

When Jay took over as chief engineer, he needed

a good man at Culebra, which was the key to the entire canal. The big cut was the chief problem, for the amount of dirt to be moved was incredible, and the recurrent landslides sometimes made it seem that the cut would never be complete. Although Jean-Charles was young, he had proven to be an excellent man, wise beyond his years, able to give orders with complete confidence to men older than himself. He was put in charge at Culebra and reported directly to Jay.

Jean-Charles loved it. He worked long hours, never asking more of any man than he was willing to give himself, used Jay's system of moving away the soil in railway cars to maximum efficiency and spent his days on the floor of the cut, nothing too minor to merit his personal attention. He selected a house on the hills overlooking Panama City and bought a new suit to be married in. When he slept he always dreamed of Helene.

The relocation of the Panama Railroad was underway, with Guy Simel's firm supplying the steel for bridges, of which there were many. Jay's contacts with Guy were infrequent, and Guy never again mentioned wanting to see Petra. That was somewhat of a relief to her.

Railroad rails were, of course, a big item, for not only were rails required to relocate the railroad but massive amounts of steel were used in building tracks down inside the cut—tracks which were moved by an ingenious rail-moving machine as the need arose. The latest shipment of rails was from Guy's company. Jean-Charles made a special trip into Panama City to report a new problem to Jay.

"We're getting a lot of breakage," he said. "The new rails. When the machine moves them, there's a lot of strain, as you know, and my men have logged a half dozen incidents of rail breakage."

"Maybe they're working too fast," Jay said. "Tell them to be a little more careful." But, at his first opportunity, he visited the big cut and watched the rail-moving crew at work. They had not changed the method of operation, but, as he watched, a rail broke and the breakage cost time and money. He examined the broken rail and it looked normal. But, on the sections of rail which had been installed longer, he noted that the newer rails seemed to collect rust faster than those from an earlier shipment. He made a note to check the specifications and, perhaps, send off to Washington and ask someone to look in on the Roethke Company in Pittsburgh. But, with greater care, the breakage was lessened, and the matter slipped his mind under the pressures of his responsibilities.

The first that Petra knew of a crisis in Washington was a cable from Helene. "SAILING PANAMA MONDAY. ANTONIA STAYS WASHINGTON."

"You can't do this, Antonia," Helene said. "You know how much Aunt Petra has been looking forward to our coming."

"It's only for a little while," Antonia said. "I'll write to her, explaining everything."

"You haven't even explained it to me," Helene said.

"It's quite simple," Antonia said. "I just am not ready to leave Washington."

"Now, Antonia, you know that neither Aunt Petra nor Jay will accept that. You must have a reason."

Antonia turned away and was silent for a long time. "There's someone I don't want to leave," she said softly.

Helene moved swiftly to her side. "Why, you haven't mentioned a word!"

"It's a bit complicated."

"Who is it? Do I know him?"

"No. You don't get out enough to meet anyone."

"Oh, Antonia, can't you tell me?"

"His name is Arthus Taylor. He's in the army, a colonel."

"If you think so much of him, he must be nice."

Antonia turned with a glad smile. "He's unlike any man I've ever met. He's so confident, so sure of himself, so, well I know it sounds silly, but so masterful."

Helene smiled. "Yes, I guess it would take someone like that for you."

"He's trying to get an assignment in Panama. If he does, I shall come down with him."

"Do you have any idea when?"

"No."

"You know that Aunt Petra will be devastated. And we'll all worry about you. I just can't leave you all alone here. Please come with us. Then your Colonel Taylor will have an extra incentive for getting to Panama."

"I'll be all right," Antonia said. "I'll keep the house."

"That will be expensive," Helene said.

"I'll be twenty-one soon," Antonia said. "Then I won't have to depend on mother and Jay for my money."

"Please, please reconsider. How can I ever tell them?"

"You won't have to. I told you I'd write. I'll do it this very evening."

"And what will you tell them?"

"That I am going to stay here so that I can be with Art."

"Has he proposed, then?"

Antonia could not look her in the face. "He's already married, you see."

"Oh, no! Oh, Antonia!"

"He's going to get a divorce. I'm not a home wrecker, if that's what you're thinking. He was determined, when I met him, to end his marriage. Then, when he has the divorce—"

Darcie, too, was upset by Petra's sending for Helene and Jason. She had enjoyed months of sheer happiness, her entire life changed. For the first time in her life, she had someone—her daughter—and to think of having her thousands of miles away was a torment. When she first heard the news, her first thought was that she, too, would go. And then she thought of Petra and what she would think. She reviewed all the old antagonisms. Petra, she felt, had always been the sheltered one, the lucky one, the prude. How could Petra ever understand that she was so fond of Helene that she would never do anything to hurt her?

"Darcie," Helene said, "you must help me talk to Antonia." And she poured out the story. Darcie went to the Burton home and found Antonia preparing for an evening with Art.

"It's none of my business," Darcie began.

"No," Antonia said curtly.

"But I'd think a bit, if I were you. Think of what this is going to do to your mother."

"She's had her life," Antonia said. "She often did things without thinking what it was going to do to others."

"A married man, Antonia? That's a dead-end street, you know."

"He loves me."

"And do you love him?"

"I want him. I want to be with him."

"But you can't say you love him?"

"What difference does it make?"

"Perhaps none, now," Darcie said. "You're being stupid, Antonia."

"Look who's talking," Antonia said. "My God, you find your daughter and all of a sudden you're like my mother. If there's anything I hate it's a damned reformed sinner. Look, you've had yours, my dear Aunt Darcie. Don't try to live my life for me."

"And this romantic older man is going to get a divorce and marry you—is that it?"

"Yes."

"And does he know that you have not been the model of propriety?"

"He knows I wasn't virgin."

"And he doesn't care?"

"No."

"A very wonderful man told me that once," Darcie said. "In the end, however, it ate at him, devoured him. Someday that man will come along for you, Antonia. And when he does, you will be able to say, you'll want to shout it, you'll want to say, 'I love him, I love him.' And it's going to be too late for you, just as it was for me. It's not too late for you, but if you openly consort with a married man—"

"Oh, dear," Antonia said, with false concern, "poor Aunt Darcie, the great courtesan, has her had her little heart broken?"

"Well, I've tried," Darcie said in resignation.

"Yes. If anyone ever asks, I'll tell them you did." She smiled. "Darcie, it's all right. I know what I'm doing. Actually, it's sweet of you to worry about me."

"I see myself in you more and more every day," Darcie said. "It may sound melodramatic, but I wouldn't wish that on anyone. But it's your life, girl. You will do with it as you please, I'm sure."

In Panama City, Petra was raging. "I won't allow her to do this," she said.

"You don't have much choice," Jay said, "unless you go to Washington and drag her down here by her hair."

"We can cut off the money, drop the lease on the house."

"Are you sure you want to do that?" he asked. "You don't even know why she wants to stay in Washington. She may have a good reason."

"It had better be good," Petra said.

But when Antonia's letter arrived, the reason shocked her. Antonia was quite frank. She told her mother that she was in love with a married man, that she was going to stay in Washington until he obtained his divorce. Petra sent a cable.

"COME PANAMA IMMEDIATELY."

Antonia answered, "WILL COME SOON."

Petra, concerned, wanting to do the right thing, worried to distraction, sent: "HOUSE LEASE VOIDED. MONEY STOPPED. COME PANAMA."

And, on the day that Helene and Jason sailed, the cable from Antonia arrived. "HAPPY 21ST TO ME. SEE YOU SOMEDAY."

"Art," Antonia told her colonel, "I am now a homeless waif. My mother is throwing me out of the house as of the last of the month."

Arthus Taylor's handsome face was serious. "You told her about us?"

"Yes."

"Was that wise?"

"She'll have to know sooner or later."

"Yes, I suppose so," he said. "What do you intend doing?"

"I thought you might have a suggestion," she said.

"I'm not a rich man, Antonia. I can't afford to set you up in a place as luxurious as your home."

"You have quarters," she said.

"Impossible."

She bristled. "May I ask why?"

"I have my career to consider."

"And me?"

"You must understand. An army officer is bound by a certain code. If I lived openly with you, I would be in big trouble. My chance of getting the Panama assignment would be nil. I'd never have a chance of promotion. I'd probably be assigned to the most remote post in the command."

"Well, we mustn't jeopardize your precious career," Antonia said, sweeping out of the room to leave him. He appeared at her door the next morning.

"I've been thinking," he said. "I'm sure that I'm going to be given the Panama assignment. Why don't you go on down, join your family? In the meantime, I'll start the divorce proceedings——"

"Start?" she flared. "You told me that you'd already started."

"It's a very serious matter," he said. "Things are changing, and divorce is no longer the scandal it once was, but it's a serious step for a career officer."

Angry, Antonia's first urge was to tell the handsome colonel to go to hell, but, curiously, instead of feeling belittled, her combative instincts were aroused. Since her talk with Darcie, she had done some serious thinking. She had come to the conclusion that she was not completely sure she wanted to spend the rest of her life with Art Taylor, but that her immediate wants were centered on him. She was accustomed to getting what she wanted, and his reluctance to commit himself to her, rather than shaming her, merely made her want him the more. She determened to have him just as long as she wanted him.

"We will go to Panama together," she said. "On the same ship. Oh, don't worry. I'll respect your reputation, damn you."

"And in the meantime?" he asked.

"I won't ask you to support me," she said. "I have my own money."

"You're making me feel like a cad," he said.

"Aren't you?"

He smiled. "In many ways, my love, in many ways."

She would stay in the house until the lease ran out; then she would find other lodging. By that time, perhaps, he would have heard about his Panama assignment. Meanwhile, she said good-bye to Darcie, who, bereft by Helene's leaving, took the next ship for Panama.

"I don't know how it will work out," Darcie said. "I

won't push myself upon your mother and Jay, but I can't bear to think of not seeing Helene for months, years. At least I'll be near her, and perhaps we can arrange something."

5

PETRA SAW THE ship at the entrance to the harbor and she watched it move, with infuriating slowness, toward the docks. She spotted Helene and Jason at the rail while the ship was still moving, and began to wave and call out. Jason saw her and she thought, for one heart-stopping moment, he was going to fall over the rail in his eagerness. And then she was holding him in her arms and weeping happily. She kissed Helene and hugged her, and there were tears of happiness in Helene's eyes, too.

Jason was talking a mile a minute and asking questions as fast as he could form them. Helene had to speak over him. "But where is—where are Jay and Jean-Charles?"

"Oh, I'm sorry. In my excitement I forgot. There's been another slide in the big cut. Several men were buried. They couldn't leave. It happened early this morning. We'll see them before the day is out. In fact, we're to stop at Culebra station—Jean-Charles is as eager to see you as you are to see him."

"Well," Helene said, smiling, "I guess I can survive another few hours."

"I'm sure you can," Petra said.

Jason ran ahead to the carriage. The luggage would be send over to Panama City on the train. Meantime, the afternoon run to Panama City was due to depart, and they had to hurry to catch it.

And, on the train, Petra brought up the painful subject of Antonia, asked questions until she knew as much about the situation as Helene.

"Don't worry about her, Aunt Petra," Helene said. "She's a very mature woman. She'll come out fine. She'll marry her colonel."

"Have you met him?" Petra asked.

"Yes. He's very nice."

"Jay has asked for him," Petra said. "Isn't that a strange coincidence? He's supposed to be quite an expert on hydraulics, and Jay knows little in that field. He's hoping that they can't be married until after Colonel Taylor is down here, or else he might be accused of nepotism."

And then Helene was demanding to know all about Panama, and what each of them had been doing. The ride to Culebra went swiftly.

It was after four o'clock when they arrived. They learned that crews were still working trying to find the bodies of the buried men. Helene was beside herself with eagerness to see her Jean-Charles, so they went out to the cut and walked to the brink, to look far down into the great man-made canyon. A huge steam shovel was buried to its roof. Men worked in the debris of the slide, and Helene's strong young eyes soon spotted Jean-Charles, but he was too far away to hear her call to him. Across the cut, the hill which had been dug away towered over them, its sides stripped bare by the repeated slides.

Jason was prowling around the edge of the cut, but it sloped away gradually at that point, so Petra was not concerned. He was picking up rocks and throwing them down the side to watch them bounce and roll to the depths of the vast excavation. And then he came running, a rock in his hand.

"A fish!" he cried, extending the rock, and they saw the perfect fossil imprint of the skeleton of a fish in the stone.

"Perhaps you can find others," Petra said, and Jason went rushing off.

Below, workers came upon a body and four men carried it out of the jumble of broken timbers, twisted rails, and fallen rocks.

"It's terribly dangerous—the work—isn't it?" Helene asked, watching the dear figure of Jean-Charles, diminished by height and distance, far below her.

"Yes, but he's very careful," Petra said.

"Aunt Petra, if anything happened to him I'd die. I'd just die."

"Nothing is going to happen to him," Petra said, putting her arm around Helene's waist. "He's going to come up out of there soon and meet you, and then you can take a look at the pretty little house which has been assigned to you and spend the evening alone. I've made all the wedding arrangements. I've even got the kitchen equipped with pots and pans and everything you'll need."

"Oh, it sounds so lovely."

"I'm happy for you," Petra said, thinking of Antonia with a twisting feeling in her heart. "Now I think it's time we went back to the station. There's a traveler's rest there where we can wait." She called out to Jason. He came reluctantly, carrying an armful of rocks. He kept looking back at the high side of the cut, where the hill towered over them, and, as they walked through the low ground-cover, he paused.

"Hey, look," he yelled. "The mountain is coming down!"

Startled, Petra turned. The mountain had begun to send a massive slide down the path of the slide of the previous morning. There came to her ears a loud cracking sound, and then the beginnings of a rumble, as a huge section of the hill split away and began to tumble, huge boulders bouncing ahead of the burden of clay and fractured stone which built into a mighty mass as the roar grew and dust rose into the air and, from far below, she could hear men shouting.

She ran to the brink of the cut and watched in helpless terror. Below, men were running, scrambling over the mass of tumbled debris, but behind them, with an ever-growing mass and a roar like low thunder, the side of the cut reached out for them, taking the rearmost as a shrill scream of horror came from Helene.

Helene could see him. He was running, falling over the rocks, scrambling past the almost buried steam shovel with the front edge of the slide closing the distance rapidly. And then he was gone, swallowed up in a vast, heaving sea of clay, dirt, stones as large as a carriage.

"Oh, God, no!" Helene prayed. And, as the dust began to settle in the cut below, she felt the world go out from under her. She did not feel Petra's arms as they clasped her and eased her slowly to the ground.

Men were still running from the slide, although it was now quiet. Only a pall of dust showed where the slide had struck.

"Oh, Jay," Petra was thinking, "Please, God, not Jay, too." And then she felt guilty, praying for her man, when, with her own eyes, she'd seen Jean-Charles swallowed by the advancing avalanche.

"Helene, Helene," she said, patting the girl's cheeks.

"Is she dead?" Jason asked.

"No," Petra said. "Oh, Helene."

Helene opened her eyes and looked around, shaking her head. Then she remembered and leaped to her feet, ran to the brink of the chasm, started to go over the edge onto the sloping side. Petra caught her by the skirts.

"I have to!" Helene wailed. "I have to go to him!"

"No, no," Petra said, pulling her back. "We'll go back to the station. We'll wait there."

"He's dead," Helene said unbelievingly.

"You don't know that."

"I saw it. It covered him," she said, with a rising voice verging on hysteria.

"Perhaps he escaped," Petra said. "We'll go back to the station and await word."

"Oh, God, what am I going to do? What am I going to do without him?"

Helene sat in the waiting room of the traveler's rest, her head in her hands, weeping silently. The news from the cut was grim. Early estimates said that at least a dozen men had been covered by the slide. They were digging now, trying to find survivors, but those who knew had little hope for any of the men caught in the huge slide. A friendly woman came to Petra and aided her in taking Helene to a small room with a bed, where Helene lay, face down, hopeless, sobbing bitterly. She had not spoken since they left the cut.

Not realizing what was happening, Jason was hungry. Petra left Helene and found him some doughnuts. She, herself had coffee. An hour, an eternity. Two injured men were brought up and put aboard a train to be taken to the hospital. Seeing the activity, Petra ran to the station and tried to find someone who knew the situation in the cut.

"Please," she asked a harried man, "my husband was down there. Mr. Burton."

"Hey, you fellows," the harried man called out to the others, "any of you see Mr. Burton after the slide?" They muttered negatives and shook their heads. Petra went back to the traveler's rest and checked on Helene. A merciful nature had brought sleep to her.

Darkness. She sat in dim lamplight, alone in the room. Jason was sleeping on a couch. She put her head back and closed her eyes. She would not let herself think of Jay dead. She prayed for a miracle—for Helene's sake, for both their sakes.

Hearing a commotion outside, she went to the door. Another injured man was being brought up. She ran, skirts flying, to look at his face. A black man.

"Have any of you seen Mr. Burton?"

Negatives.

"Well," a man said, "this is the last of 'em."

"The last of them?" Petra asked. "What do you mean?"

"The last of them that's alive," the man said. "They'll be digging bodies out all night."

Nine o'clock. Ten o'clock. An hour was an eternity. Helene was still sleeping. A doctor had come and given her a sedative. Jason was sleeping soundly now, a blanket covering him. Eyes closed, praying constantly, she heard the door open, looked up. There was the dear, big, bearlike form. His face dusty, the sticky clay of the cut on his clothing.

"Jay—oh, thank God, Jay!" She ran to him, heedless of the dust and clay, clasped him, would not let go.

"I'm all right."

"Oh, God, I didn't know," she sobbed. "I prayed that you were, but then you didn't come and—"

"But I sent word," he said. His face went black. "The bastard didn't find you? Oh, my dear, I'm so sorry. All that needless worry." Then: "Where is Helene?"

"Sleeping. Jean-Charles?"

"I stayed until we found his body," he said grimly.

"Oh, dear Lord. Jay, she saw it. We were on the edge of the cut. She could see Jean-Charles, and she was so happy, and then the slide—"

"Ummm," Jay said, shaking his head. "Poor Helene." He disengaged himself from Petra and went to look down on his sleeping son.

"I think this is the last of it, Petra," he said.

"What do you mean?"

"I brought him here. If it weren't for me, he wouldn't have left France. I've been here long enough. I'm giving it up."

She came to stand beside him, clinging to his arm. "I know it's terrible," she said, "but you mustn't blame yourself. Helene won't blame you. She knows he was doing what he wanted to do, that he was grateful for the opportunity."

"And now he's dead and that poor girl—" He wiped tears from his eyes. "She never even got to know him, Petra. After loving him all this time, waiting, she didn't even get to know the full meaning of love."

Their voices had caused Jason to stir uneasily. Jay put a hand on his shoulder and shook him gently. "Hey, big boy."

Jason came out of sleep slowly, and then, with a final start, he threw his arms around Jay. "Dad, dad."

"My big boy. Lord, it's good to see you."

"Hey, Dad," Jason cried. "We saw it. We saw the mountain come down and smash Jean-Charles like a bug. He's dead, ain't he?"

"Yes, son. He's dead."

"Oh, boy, Helene's going to bawl her eyes out," Jason said, his eyes wide, his face serious. "Can I go out there with you to see those steam shovels?"

"Someday, perhaps," Jay said. "Right now we've got to think of Helene, son. And we have to be careful what we say. No talk about being smashed like a bug. Do you understand?"

"Yeah, I understand," Jason said. "I'll be careful."

"That's my big boy."

The trip into town was accomplished with Helene in a daze, still feeling the effects of the sedative. Then she was put to bed with another pill, and, exhausted, saddened, Jay and Petra caught a few hours sleep.

With Jason and Helene still sleeping, they sat at the table over coffee with the sun coming up. "I meant it last night," he said. "I'm going to ask Washington to replace me."

"Take some time, dear," Petra said. "Be sure."

"I've seen too many men die," he said. "I've done my share. It can be finished by someone else now."

"But you've invested years of your life in it, Jay. Wouldn't you always regret leaving just when victory is within your grasp?"

"I will know what I did," he said. "There are only a few problems to be ironed out. When that's done, we'll leave."

"And where will we go?"

"That will have a lot to do with Helene," Jay said. "Do you think she'll want to go back to France?"

"I don't know," Petra said. She used a rare word of light profanity. "Is it me? Am I the cause? A few months of happiness and contentment and then—"

He smiled wryly. "We can't both go through life feeling guilty," he said.

"Yes, you're right. But sometimes it gets to be just too much. Helene. Poor Jean-Charles. And that hare-brained Antonia."

He laughed. "Of all of them, all of us, I think Antonia is best capable of taking care of herself."

6

THERE WAS NO one to meet Darcie when her ship arrived in Colón. Guy was on a business trip to Pittsburgh and then to Washington. However, the house which the company maintained in Panama City was expecting her, and she would be alone in it with the servants until Guy's return.

The heat and the humid air caused her to breathe deeply, but knowing that she could soon see Helene made it bearable. She had determined that she was not to be deprived of being at Helene's wedding, regardless of what Petra thought. She had missed Helene's childhood partly because she had been so young, so traumatized by the terrible events in Egypt, partly because others made a choice for her. She would not miss this high spot in Helene's life.

From the servants in the house, she learned that the chief engineer lived in a big house on the hill. She sent a messenger with a note addressed to Helene and sat back to await the explosion when Petra learned that she'd not only encountered Helene in Washington, but had come to love the girl. She knew that neither Antonia nor Helene had yet told Petra that Helene even knew her real mother.

She was surprised, and a bit apprehensive, when, two hours later, the servant came to say that a lady wished to see her and immediately recognized Petra's womanly figure outlined against open windows in the parlor. She halted her steps, took a deep breath, and went into the room.

For long moments they stood looking at each other, the two sisters who had last seen each other under strange circumstances in a brothel.

"You haven't changed," Petra said.

"Nor you."

"This has all come as a great shock to me," Petra said, "but perhaps it's for the best. I get the impression that Helene is quite fond of you."

"I love her very deeply," Darcie said simply.

"I wanted to warn you in advance," Petra said. "There's been an accident."

Darcie felt the wind leave her, put her hands to her lips.

"Not Helene," Petra said. "Jean-Charles. He was killed in a landslide in the cut."

"Oh, no," Darcie said, sitting down. "Oh, that poor, poor darling."

"You may go to her if you like."

"Thank you, Petra. Thank you. I—" She paused. There was no way to wipe away the past, no way to erase the memories of Petra naked in the brothel and the dwarf moving toward her.

"But I warn you, Darcie. Helene is as dear to me as my own daughter. I will not see her hurt further."

"You need have no fear of that," Darcie said. "Is she taking it very badly?"

"Quite badly, I'm afraid. She's withdrawn. She speaks only when spoken to. The doctors fear for her sanity. We were standing on the edge of the cut when it happened, and she saw it."

"Oh, my God!"

"Shall we go, then?"

"Oh, yes, yes. Just give me time to find my hat."

They made the trip in silence, each with her own thoughts. The house was silent, as if it were deserted. Petra led the way to an upstairs room, a pleasant and airy room with a veranda, the windows open, screens closing out the ever-present insects. Helene was sitting in a chair, her face blank, her eyes toward the wall. She did not move when they entered. Darcie, her heart aching, knelt beside her.

"My darling," she whispered.

Helene turned her head slowly. "Thank you for coming," she said.

"Oh, Helene, if there were some way for me to take your pain from you, bear it myself—"

"No, no," Helene said, her face twisting, "for it's all I have."

"I won't tell you it will pass," Darcie said. "But it will lessen."

"Yes."

"May I stay with you?" Darcie asked.

"If you like," Helene answered listlessly.

Seeing them together brought mixed emotions to Petra. They were quite alike, both so delicately small, both so dark, both so very pretty. And so unalike in other ways: Darcie the wanton, Helene the innocent. If Petra had her way she would have prevented their meeting, for she knew the dark and corrupt forces which were in her sister, had almost been a victim of them herself. She doubted that Darcie was capable of change, and she would see Darcie dead before she allowed her to influence Helene into her amoral ways.

"Cook has told me that dinner is ready," Petra said.

"I'm not hungry," Helene said.

"Please, you must eat," Petra said.

"For me?" Darcie asked, smiling. "Come down and eat for me?"

Helene rose and followed Petra out of the room. Jay was working late as he did quite often. Jason greeted Darcie eagerly. He liked her. He had told Petra that she was a nice lady who had brought him gifts.

There was little talk between Petra and Darcie, a sort of silent truce between them for the sake of Helene. Jason rambled on and they let him. Now and then one of the women would try to interest Helene in talk, but she would answer as shortly as possible. She toyed with her food and soon begged to be excused. They watched her go up the stairs with equally serious faces. Jason finished and asked to be excused, leaving them alone.

"We're going to be leaving Panama soon," Petra said. "I suspect that Helene will go with us of course. She's become a part of our family."

"You have my thanks for being kind to her," Darcie said.

"She's a woman," Petra said. "And she can choose her own life, her own companions." She paused uncertainly.

"I would not have thrust myself upon you had it not been for her," Darcie said.

"I can't say that you're welcome in my home," Petra said frankly, "but for her sake, please feel free to visit her anytime she wants you." She cleared her throat. "I will warn you, however, that Helene is a decent and innocent girl. Any attempt—"

"I told you that I love her very much," Darcie said.

"As you once loved me?" Petra asked coldly.

Darcie was silent for a moment. "Petra, I've done many things in my life of which I am regretful. At this late date, I won't ask you to forgive me."

"I'm afraid I can't," Petra said.

"I was pleased when I heard that you and Jay were finally married."

"Were you?" Petra asked. Then she sighed. "You're right. It is late. I can't like you, Darcie, and I can't respect you, but I can say, 'Let's let the past lie where it is.' "

"Thank you. There is one thing I must say, however. You have never understood me. You were not there when mother died. You were too young to know the horror—the true horror—of seeing our old nurse dead and of seeing father being mutilated fatally and of being raped by that monster. If you had walked in my shoes—"

"You tried hard enough to put me into them," Petra snapped, her anger growing.

"And I suffered for that, too," Darcie said. "I was terribly burned. I bore the scars for years."

"It was your own doing."

"You know," Darcie said, "you're still insufferable." She rose. "Perhaps it can be arranged for Helene to visit me, rather than have me come here."

"That will be up to Helene," Petra said. "Frankly, I will not encourage it. And now I think you'd better be going."

"Gladly," Darcie said. "I will send for Helene, and if she chooses to come, I don't think it would be wise of you to try to prevent it."

"Darcie, get out," Petra said, seething. "Get out before—"

After a while, Petra went into Helene's room to discover her sitting in the chair, staring at the wall.

"Did Darcie leave?" Helene asked.

"Yes."

"She's coming back, isn't she?"

Petra was caught. She could not bear the thought of hurting Helene by involving her in the old, old disputes between her and Darcie. "She'd like you to visit her when you feel up to it," she said.

"Well—" Helene said, and then fell into silence.

When Jay came home, Helene was still sitting in the chair, and long after the rest of the family was abed, the light was on in her room.

Darcie sent a letter the next morning, saying that circumstances prevented her visiting that day but saying that she would send a carriage for Helene at three in the afternoon, and that if Helene felt like it, she would be ever so happy to see her.

"Aunt Petra," Helene said. "Did you quarrel with her?"

"I fear so," Petra said reluctantly.

"What must I do?"

"My dear Helene, do what your heart tells you to do. The old, old quarrel between me and Darcie has nothing to do with you. If you want to see her, then go."

"You wouldn't mind?"

"No, dear. I wouldn't mind anything which will make you feel a little better."

Guy's house, which was privately owned, was more luxurious than the government quarters of the Burton family, and Helene walked around listlessly, looking at it after arriving, took tea, listened as Darcie, finding it difficult, tried to make conversation. Darcie was relating a minor incident which had happened on her voyage when Helene, obviously not listening, broke in.

"Do you know what I regret most?" she asked.

"What, dear?"

"That he never had a chance to make love to me. He wanted to so badly, and I wanted to. But we were so eternally honorable, both of us. We talked about it, and he would kiss me and tell me how much he wanted me, and I'd tell him, 'Soon, soon,' and then there were times when I felt that waiting was foolish and he'd whisper to me, 'Soon, soon.' And, oh, damn, damn, damn!"

"I know, I know," Darcie said.

"In many ways, I envy you," Helene said. "You wouldn't have waited, and then you would have had that, at least. And maybe even his baby. Oh, God, how I wanted to have his baby."

"Helene, you were right. He was right. He wouldn't have wanted that—you with a baby with no father." She sat beside Helene and took her hand. "It's customary, at times like this, for well-meaning people to say, you're young. You'll love again. To be blunt, that's a lot of nonsense. Love him. Remember him. Memorize every line of his face, every hair on his head, and cling to it and think what a good man he was to love you so much. And then the pain will ease. Then, someday, you can live again." She smiled sadly. "Just don't be like the good Queen Victoria and make mourning a profession for the rest of your life, darling. He wouldn't want that, no more than he would want you to forget him. There's a middle way. Remember him, love him, honor his memory, and do him the service of, someday, finding another man and living your life."

"And I wonder what would have happened if my mother and father had lived, if he hadn't invested all his money in Suez stocks. I'd be in France, living on a nice little farm, with half a dozen children around my skirts." She sobbed. "And I'd never have met him. Oh, God!"

In the early evening, Helene took the carriage back to the Burton house. Now, two or three times a week, she went down the hill to see Darcie, to spend the afternoons talking and, gradually, beginning to pick up her life again, sewing with Darcie, going for a walk, putting on the cumbersome and bulky bathing costume of the times with a white hat, the crown encircled by a black ribbon, the brim wide to keep off the sun, and walking to Toro Point for a dip in the ocean. When, after several months, she agreed to accompany Darcie to one of the Saturday-night dances at the Tivoli Hotel, both Darcie and Petra were pleased. She seemed to be regaining just a bit of her old love for life.

Meanwhile, Jay was having problems. Under a steaming sun, he visited the construction sites along the relocated railway and had concerned engineers point out to him the places where the steel beams and girders seemed to be flaking away. The tropics, he knew, were rough on metals, forming rust overnight. But this was rust on a grand scale, the extreme cases of scaling seemed to be confined to the steel supplied by Roethke Iron and Steel, Guy Simel's company. He made arrangement to have samples sent back to the United States, where the contents of the steel could be checked. Meantime, he was helpless. The contracts for the steel had been let by the Canal Commission, which had the final authority. He wrote letters asking that an investigation be made, but he could not order shipments of Roethke steel stopped—not without higher approval. He made a note to himself to have a chat with Guy when that worthy returned to Panama.

7

CHAD ROETHKE had welcomed Guy to Pittsburgh with a lavish men-only reception at which the entertainment was as risqué as could be provided in the early twentieth century in a somewhat provincial town. Roethke was fully aware that his partner was a *bon vivant* and, even at his age—Guy claimed to be fifty-five, but Darcie or anyone who knew him could put the lie to that by almost a decade—was an admirer of the female form. The strain under which Guy had operated during the long period in which it seemed he would lose everything was definitely past. He had paid out more money in bribes than he had stood to lose in the French failure, and considerably more than that had remained in his various bank accounts. Money, then, would never again be a worry. His natural love of life was revived, the wrinkles of his face were filled in by a healthy increase in weight, making him look like a very vigorous fifty. Money, he would sometimes tell himself, examining his hair—which he tinted—in a mirror, did that for a man.

The next day, both men were suffering the effects of overindulgence and rose late to meet in Roethke's study for a business chat. Roethke had received word that the meddlesome chief engineer in Panama had a shipment of samples of their products on the way to the States for testing.

Guy smiled. "It just so happens that one of my contacts is in charge of the lab which will do the testing. I should not concern myself about it."

"Maybe you'd better drop by and have a talk with him," Roethke said. He reached into a desk drawer and pulled out a banded stack of greenbacks. "This being the subject matter."

"An excellent idea," Guy agreed. "I'll leave for Washington this afternoon."

"I want you to know, my good friend, that you've done an excellent job," Roethke said.

"For which I have been excellently paid, my good friend," Guy said.

"To show my appreciation, here is something for you." Roethke bent and placed a small carrying case on the desk. With a wink, he said, "I advise you to open it in privacy, my friend."

The little case was heavy. Having finished his conference with his partner, Guy took it to his hotel there to open it and discover eleven volumes titled *My Secret Life*. The books were printed in Amsterdam by one Auguste Brancart, and when Guy saw the name he realized the nature of the books, for Brancart was famed as one of the publishers of forbidden books and tabooed literature. He smiled. Roethke had, indeed, presented him with something very special, for he had recently pored over a bibliography by the Englishman Charles Carrington and he specifically remembered the item. The asking price was one hundred pounds sterling, a very respectable sum. Then Guy's eyes narrowed. He might have a look at the books. If Roethke was happy enough with his work to present so expensive a present, he might be making more money for Roethke than he thought.

He kept the first volume out of the bag to read on the way down to Washington the next day and became quite engrossed. In a city he loved, he spent the evening over the books. The anonymous writer of the diaries was a modern Don Juan, a rich Englishman who had spent his life in the pursuit of new and different sexual thrills, and in him, Guy found a kindred spirit.

There were times when he had to chuckle, for the writer suffered remorse and guilt when he departed from so-called accepted standards of behavior—at least in his early years. Guy himself had never felt the least tinge of guilt. He, like the army officer whose case history was cited in Havelock Ellis' *Studies in the Psychology of Sex,* took his pleasures as he found them, with a clear conscience, and would, as the officer said, "as lief couple with my mother" as not.

After a while, the adventures of the Victorian gentleman began to be somewhat repetitious, and Guy found himself skipping. Over a period of the first few days he spent in Washington, he confined himself to his business, spending his evenings chuckling and feeling a bit randy over the eleven volumes in which the anonymous man coupled with some twelve hundred females. Guy learned nothing new until, far into the books, he detected a growing tendency in the writer to praise the virtues of voyeurism coupled with something which made Guy's libido waken and his staff to reach a state of semireadiness. He had not, of course, coupled with twelve hundred women, nor did he have ambitions for sheer numbers, believing in quality rather than quantity. However, the discovery by the writer that there is a certain thrill in going into a previously used woman to feel the slick, hot secretions of her love intrigued him. Guy's threesomes had always been confined to himself and two women, such as Darcie and Lyris back in the good old days.

The idea did not sicken him, as it would many men, for he was the complete voluptuary. Nothing which

gave him pleasure would cause him to regret it the
next morning. It was just that he wasn't quite sure, for
sanitary purposes, that it would be as enjoyable as it
seemed to be to the writer of the diaries.

Business concluded, he was reluctant to return to
Panama. He decided to give himself a holiday. He made
a few inquiries and, on a pleasant late summer evening,
dressed in his best and joined a group of Washington's
elite at one of those parties, one or two of which went
on each evening in the city. He was, of course, interested in feminine companionship, and, with his contacts in the city, knew that the evening would not end
fruitlessly. In fact, he had not been at the party for
more than fifteen minutes when he encountered a
handsome woman in her thirties with whom he had enjoyed the better things of life in the past and quickly
made an assignation. She would, she told him, return
to her home, see to her husband, who was ill, and meet
him.

That important decision made, he circulated and encountered a most charming young girl with saucy blond
curls, bedroom eyes, and a smart line of chatter. He let
his eyes rove up and down her delicate figure. She reminded him very much of a young Darcie, and he
yearned for her. She was with a handsome silver-haired
man dressed in the uniform of the U.S. Army, and he
had to maneuver carefully to have a chance to chat with
her.

Close up, there was something hauntingly familiar
about her, a certain tilt of the eyes and nose, the full
and luscious lips.

"If I had the power of the Creator, I would duplicate
you endlessly," Guy said, having made his way to her
side. "Merely to decorate the world."

"My, my," she smiled, "did you think of that line or
is it from Shakespeare?"

As she looked him full in the face, her eyes teasing,

he racked his brain. She was so familiar. "Do I know you?"

"Oh, I'm disappointed," she laughed. "And you were off to such a nice start."

"No, seriously. Your face is so very familiar."

"I'm afraid I don't know you, sir. But I am Antonia D'Art."

"Well, by God," Guy said. "I can't believe it. Little Antonia?"

"You knew me when I was a child?"

"I'm related to you, my dear girl. In fact, I'm your great-uncle, Guy Simel."

"Well, by God," Antonia said. "No, you're lying. My great-uncle Guy has horns and a scaly tail."

Guy laughed. "Yes, I would imagine some people would describe me so."

"But you seem to be quite harmless," she teased.

"Oh, indeed. My dear Antonia, how lovely you are, and your face is familiar, of course, because it has some of both your mother and your Aunt Darcie in it. Of a size, you're like Darcie."

And, Antonia's colonel having paid his tribute to convention by leaving her, expecting her to come to his quarters later, she spent a pleasant hour with Guy, talking, comparing knowledge of Darcie and the rest of the family. She agreed to have lunch with him the next day.

Antonia was living in quite a nice little apartment in a residential hotel, drawing on her own inheritance now that she had passed her twenty-first birthday. Arthus Taylor had been promoted to full colonel and was, now that Jay Burton was talking about leaving Panama, being considered not for the second-in-command under Jay, but for the big job. In fact, he had told her that very evening that it was almost assured and they would be leaving for Panama shortly.

"And the divorce?" she had asked bluntly.

"Antonia," he said, "these things take time."

"Like the sand in an hourglass," she said, not smiling, "time has a way of running out." So it was a disgruntled Colonel Taylor who went off to his quarters and left the door unlocked so that she might slip in, finding the minutes hanging heavy on his hands as he thought of her slim and lovely body. She was two hours later than she had promised, and he was pacing when he heard her footsteps, heard the door open. The wait, as always, was worthwhile.

Antonia found her great-uncle Guy to be a fascinating man. Still handsome in spite of his gray hair, slim, having the vigor of a much younger man, he was attentive and was always giving her flowery compliments. The lunch was fun, with Guy telling amusing stories of his travels. And that night she did not visit her colonel. She went, instead, with Guy to the performance of a play and laughed at the lines with a youthful exuberance which set Guy's blood stirring. In her apartment, over wine, he asked her how she came to be alone in Washington.

"I was tired of people telling me what to do," Antonia said.

"Yes, it does get to be a bore. That's one thing about your Aunt Darcie. She's always been her own woman."

Antonia laughed archly. "And yours?"

"Why, my dear," he said, with a grin, "you shock me."

But she was, he decided, a cunning little wench, not as innocent as her blond curls and sweet smile might lead one to think. He made some discreet inquiries and found that she was visiting the silver-haired colonel in his quarters regularly. His plan began to form.

How deliciously licentious to think of it. Not Petra, for he had not handled that effort properly so many years ago, but her daughter in his bed. That goal became his obsession. Much later he was to look back and chuckle, to think that he had been so cautious. He began with compliments and attention, and found that she was a fun-loving girl. To help matters, her colonel was often busy, preparing for his great task in Panama, and it was Guy who became her escort. Then there were gifts and flowers and little remarks on the risqúe side which were invariably returned with remarks equally as bold.

In the end it was so easy.

"My dear Antonia," he said, after a night at the theater, a late dinner, and no little wine, "I find myself in a turmoil, feeling very, very guilty."

"That I can't believe," she said.

"Oh, yes. As we sit here, so close together, I find myself having to remind myself that I am your great-uncle and old enough to be your father."

"Grandfather," Antonia said teasingly.

"Ah, how cruel you are," he said. "And so beautiful. God, I would that you were not my great-niece and that I were ten years younger."

"Forty years younger," Antonia said. "But we can fix a part of it." She snapped her fingers. "Presto-changeo, I am no longer Antonia D'Art, I am Mimi, a girl of Paris." She felt a certain sweet wrench. She did not think of Jack Young often.

"Ah, yes," Guy said, his hopes soaring up like fire. "You are a lovely girl, Mimi. Are you a girl of the streets, then?"

"But a very, very expensive one," Antonia said, in French. "Five thousand francs, sir, to kiss my lily-white hand."

"And how much to kiss your red lips?" he asked.

"Hummm," she said. "I'm so new at this business, monsieur, that I have not yet put a price to that." She smiled. "One American penny?"

"I'm not sure I can afford it," Guy said, moving closer to her.

"You seem to be a man of honor, sir. Your credit is good."

550 DYNASTY OF DESIRE

And it was so easy, and so very exciting that, as he tasted her lips and felt her lean into him, her hard little breast pushing against his shoulder, he felt young again, and wished that the night would last forever.

There had been, in Antonia, a growing curiosity. She knew that Darcie and Guy had, for years, lived as man and wife. She had heard the terrible hints from her mother about Guy's total lack of morals. She had heard tales of the beautiful Lyris, now long dead, and how she, too, lived openly with Guy. Moreover, one night during a party, she had conversed with a slightly besotted lady who knew both Darcie and Guy and who, in the strictest confidence, described Guy Simel as, "my dear, the world's most considerate lover."

Besides, Mr. Reluctant, her colonel, needed a lesson. Already she'd stayed away from him for several nights. He would never know she was kissing Guy Simel, but she did, and it served the good colonel right.

And now Guy's kisses rained on her delicate neck and her exposed shoulders and he showed his skill—this brought a secret smile—by the smoothness, the confidence, with which he quickly bared her young and firm breasts with their long, tender nipples already filled with excitement, and smoothly transferred his kisses to them, cupping them in his hands, using his teeth to nibble the sweet protrusions of red at the tips.

"My sweet Mimi," he said, "I would wager that every centimeter of your body is equally as kissable. Shall I see?"

"God, yes," she said, rising to assist him in quickly denuding her eager body to bare it to his lips which, he found, did find every centimeter of her body kissable.

And then she was transported. Literally at first, carried to her bed, then transported into a world which she knew, but which opened up into wider vistas under the ministrations of a true adept, her entire body a flame as his lips, hands, fingers, nose, explored, caressed, brought life into areas which had always been dormant.

When he went into her, she was so ready that her tender young flesh was bathed in her juices and the long delicious slide sent both of them into frantic seekings and plunges which ended quickly, only to begin again with his ability to recover demonstrated to her intense pleasure.

She knew, during that long, lovely evening and into the late hours of the night what both Darcie and Lyris had known: that Guy Simel knew more about a woman and how to arouse her deepest feelings than any man she'd ever had.

"My God," she whispered, when, after thinking that she was totally spent, she was rearoused and it began all over again, "where have you been all of my life?"

"Waiting for this," he whispered, his tongue and lips contacting heated, well used, red-tinged flesh. For she was everything he had hoped: so young, so sweet, so absolutely abandoned. It was Darcie young again, and when he closed his eyes, he could not distinguish the passage of years. But he was once again a young man, going into Darcie's tight and slick orifice with an anticipation and a surplus of energy which sent the firm young body beneath him, over him, atop him, beside him, into responsive movements of equal bliss.

Now Antonia had a double reason for going to Panama. The utter abandonment she enjoyed with Guy and her colonel, who must be taught his lesson. However, the days before the ship sailed, with Colonel Taylor in one stateroom, Guy in another, Antonia next to Guy's in still another, were not wasted. Eager to learn and more than willing to kneel at the feet of a master to watch the soft and strange skin crawl on his scrotum while hands and lips alternated at knowing the wonderful smoothness and the heated wetness of his pleasingly large staff, she became pupil, lover, and sometimes teacher, even to a man who—although he had not coupled with twelve hundred women—had known intimately a number of women in several multiples of Antonia's age. Between bouts of all-out lovemaking, he read aloud to her from an amazing collection of books which were not to be found on the shelves of the public library, and the material he selected was so inflammatory that she could feel her blood rushing through her veins to mass in sensitive areas, to make her swell, pulse, ache for him and in his teasings, preparations, tender kisses, and touches and ticklings she found the utmost in anticipation until, with a cry of delight, she would open to him and take that bigness so deep inside her that she became nothing more than a hollowness for him, surrounding his staff with her entire body and wishing it to be huge, to be so huge that it could take all of her.

With Darcie in Panama, Guy had splendid visions. With that feeling of renewed youth which she gave him, he fantasized the three of them in bed: Darcie, Antonia, himself. He himself had arranged the adjoining staterooms for himself and Antonia. There was an interconnecting door. And down the corridor was her lover, the silver-haired Colonel Taylor.

During the last days in Washington, he knew that Antonia had gone to Taylor, but when she came to him, she was always impeccably fresh. He did not push it. There was time, when they were all aboard ship.

Arthus Tayor was pleased to learn that an uncle of Antonia's would be traveling on the same ship with them. It made the arrangement much more respectable, and he made it a point, once the trip began, to make it clear to Guy that he was welcome at his table in the dining salon. He suspected that Guy knew of his relationship with Antonia and was secretly grateful that Guy was discreet enough not to refer to it. They met, of course, shortly after boarding and had dinner together that first night. There was, for Taylor, only one problem. He did not have a chance to be alone with

Antonia to find out if she would come to his cabin or he to hers. Since her uncle was right next door, he preferred his. His opportunity came toward the end of the evening, while Guy was dancing with a tall and talkative woman who was going to Panama to join her husband, and, perhaps, yearning for a bit of shipboard romance.

"Heard from the lawyers lately?" Antonia asked, when he asked her to come to his cabin.

"Soon," he said. "Soon. I promise. Please?"

"Oh, all right," she said. For he still had to learn his lesson. She had not decided just what she would do, but she would come up with something. Meanwhile, although she would have preferred to stay in her own cabin and open the door into Guy's stateroom, she had to keep him docile.

She pulled Taylor away while Guy was dancing. It had been several days, and he was childishly eager, doing things to please her and being contrite and humble when she was sharp with him. But, although she achieved, it was not in the same class with the thrills she knew when she was with her aging Casanova. He wanted her to stay with him, but, quite frankly, she was bored with him.

"Mustn't shock dear Uncle Guy," she told him.

She rose directly from his bed, using her tight young muscles to keep within her the results of his passion, for there was a sort of sensual satisfaction in knowing that she walked the corridor and nodded at another passenger with the insides of her soft thighs, her bush, her labia still wet with him.

It was not too late. He had been in a hurry. She was not sleepy and looked forward to a nice bath and perhaps some reading. But when she opened the door, Guy was seated in her stateroom, a book on his knee.

"Ah," he said, "have you been for a stroll around the deck?"

"Umm," Antonia said.

He rose and came to her. She gave him her lips, felt his arms around her, and her body responded to him, knowing well the delights which he had given it. And suddenly it was as if she had not already known those rewards of friction and pressure which she'd felt under Art's body, as if she had not known satisfaction in days, weeks, for he had that power—the power to lift her into instant readiness with a few simple caresses, his knowing kiss.

"Umm, you're not sleepy?" she asked him, her eyes feeling heavy, her limbs languorous.

"Far from it," Guy said. "In fact, I've been waiting for you rather impatiently." Indeed, she could feel that his manhood was aroused. He pressed against her tightly, tall enough so that the hard bulge was against her stomach.

"My dear randy Guy," she said. "Leave me for a few minutes and then come back."

"What? Tear myself away from this loveliness?" he asked, his deft hands entering her clothing to find an access to one heated breast. With her desire rising, she allowed him to remove her clothing down to the brief and light lacy drawers.

"No," she whispered, pulling herself away, bowing her back, as he put his hand between her legs. "You must leave me for a few minutes."

Silently he lifted her and placed her on the bed, beginning to pull the undergarment down from her shoulders. "Guy, please," she said. "I must—"

"No, no, it's all right," he said, stripping the garment away from her full but small breasts and falling to cover them, one after the other, with his hungry mouth. And then he was pushing the garment down and away and she held her legs closely together, self-conscious, messy.

"Guy, damn it, I've been trying to tell you," she said, as his hand forced its way between her closely held legs to find the warmth and wetness. "Now let me go wash."

"I *know*," he said. He was, while continuing to caress her soft and silkenly lubricated flesh, unbuttoning his clothing, kicking, wriggling, seemingly in a frenzy to be naked with her. "You've been with the colonel."

"Yes."

He stood and quickly completed the job of denuding himself, his large staff protruding arrogantly, hard and pink-tipped, a drop of moisture telling of his lust. She tried to roll away, but he blocked her. Then his weight was on her and his mouth was on hers, wet, demanding.

Where, only a few minutes before, Arthus Taylor's hard manhood had probed, slid, pushed, Guy's larger and more demanding staff sought, found, made entry on the slickness, the lubricity, and a sense of recklessness swept over Antonia, two men, the juices of two men making her oily and loose. And then she was throwing her small and perfectly formed bottom high to take him, gasping as he entered and possessed her, the depth, the fullness, the thrill of their bodies pounded hard, hard, together and she had never felt him be so excited, his entire body trembling, his efforts hard, fast, selfish, but bringing a response in her which sent her up and over and made her begin to cry out with it as he thrust and strained down that last glorious slope until, together, they plunged over and fell into moaning togetherness.

"You are so terrible," she laughed, when she could breathe again.

But for Guy, it opened new vistas. A new greed was in him; a need to see, to feel, to experience all the aspects of this new and totally abandoned idea. She required little coaxing, having been lifted, by his very lust, to the heights; wanting, as he wanted, to find new and different sensations.

An unwitting tool for two of the world's most abandoned hedonists, Colonel Arthus Taylor allowed himself to be lured into Darcie's stateroom on the very next night, there to find the bliss which kept him attached to this young girl in spite of the dangers to his reputation. In his lust, he had no idea that the interconnecting door was cracked and that a randy and licentious old man was sitting there, his eye glued to the crack to see the mingling of bodies and limbs, to hear the whispers and the wet, slopping sound of it. And, by prearrangement, just as Taylor gasped and emptied his passions into her, Antonia hissed and cautioned him to be quiet.

"My uncle," she said. "I heard him in the next room, and he was supposed to be playing cards until a late hour. You must go quickly. He's very protective toward me."

Taylor leaped to his feet in panic, wanting least of all to be involved in scandal. He dressed in great haste and closed the door into the corridor softly behind him. The door closed only a second before, naked and his staff at the ready, Guy Simel entered the stateroom, a smile of pleasure on his face, to examine at leisure and with panting breaths the soft, wet, used womanhood and then to feel the luxurious slide, the incomparable lubricity of it, for there was, he had discovered, nothing quite like the feel of a tight young woman with the spunk of her lover fresh within her. And to Antonia, the knowledge that she was taking, within a few seconds, perhaps no more than two minutes, one man after the other, the second the most accomplished lover she'd ever known, was a fire which sent her into mindless, lustful, endless spasms.

There was an end to it, of course. It came to an end when the ship pulled up along the docks at Colón and she said good-bye to her colonel. She had had time to make her plans, and she knew now what she would do. It was as if her abandoned behavior with her great-uncle had finally matured her. The fondness which she had felt for Art Taylor was gone, and in its place was a vengeful determination to make him pay for his deceit. She was now sure that he never intended getting a divorce, and, moreover, if he did, he'd be the last person in the world she'd want to marry. She journeyed across the isthmus with Guy to find Darcie and Helene sewing, talking, both very much surprised to see them. There were hugs and kisses around, and then Helene had her questions.

No, she had not notified her mother that she was coming. She would surprise her. No, the colonel had not obtained his divorce and that was over anyhow. She would visit for a while in Panama and then she would go back to Washington. She had no set plans, only knowing that she did not want to spend too much time in the hot and uncomfortable climate of Panama.

Together, she and Helene went to the house on the hill to send Petra into glad cries and happy tears as she embraced her daughter. Then there was an evening of excited talk during which Antonia, to spare her mother's feelings, told her that she had been ill advised, that the matter of the married man was now closed.

Reluctantly, she had told Guy that she would not see him while they were in Panama. "I'm selfish," she told her most wonderful lover, "but mother is such a dear, and you know how she feels about you. As for me, I would couple with you in the middle of the street, but it will not hurt me to be a bit considerate of her, and of Jay. So we'll just have to save it, my dear great-uncle, until we are both back in Washington."

"Since I do business with Jay, perhaps that is the best for both of us," Guy agreed, keeping in mind his fantasy of getting both Antonia and Darcie in a bed.

It was pleasant for Antonia to be with her family again. Jason was so pleased to see her that he would not let go of her hand for the first half hour, and when Jay came home from work, he embraced her quite fondly. The Zone grapevine had been functioning well that day, and he knew that Antonia had arrived in the company of Guy Simel. He had already met and talked with Colonel Arthus Taylor and had arranged a tentative plan wherein Taylor would work with him for a few weeks, or as long as it took before the new man was in a position to take all the vast responsibilities of the overall operation.

It was sort of a sticky situation for Jay, because he knew of Taylor and Antonia's attachment, but he had noted with interest that the colonel had not mentioned his stepdaughter. Still saddened by the death of his young friend Jean-Charles, Jay wanted only to get his family away from Panama, to live a normal life in the pleasant climate of San Francisco. Antonia, he felt, could handle her own affairs; he cared only that she did not hurt Petra with some rash action.

At his first opportunity, he took Antonia to one side. "I met Colonel Taylor today."

"Oh?" she asked.

"He said nothing," Jay said.

"Well, he is not in a position to speak as yet," Antonia said.

"You're of age, Antonia," Jay said, "so I won't presume to give you advice, but I will give you a friendly warning. This entire Canal Zone is like a small village. The entertainment is scarce, so folks amuse themselves by neighbor watching. That's another way of saying that it's damned difficult to hide anything here."

"Thank you. I shall remember that," she said. "However, there is no longer anything to hide."

"Am I to take it that you are no longer interested in the colonel?"

"Exactly."

In spite of his knowledge that Antonia was not as innocent as she seemed, Jay felt a quick and fierce sense of protectiveness. "If he has gone back on his pledge to you—"

"Oh, no," she said, with a little laugh. "It's more the other way around. Jay, I will do nothing to cause you trouble, nor will I hurt mother. Do you believe me?"

"Yes, and I'm grateful for it," he said. "Well, then, what are your plans?"

She shrugged. "No plans past spending some time with the family. Jason has made me promise to take him to the cut and help him look for fossils."

"You know that you're welcome in this house as long as you wish to stay."

"As long as I behave myself?" she asked, smiling archly.

"I didn't say that."

"But you meant it."

"Let's just say that it's nice having the family all together again."

"It is, Jay. It really is."

Jay had to admit to himself that he was proud of them when, Helene going reluctantly, the entire family joined the canal folk in the Saturday-night dance at the Tivoli Hotel. In a group, his three women were spectacular, and when Darcie joined them, brought into the grouping by Helene, the Moncrief women and their daughters made for many whispered comments and for a stream of gallant young men asking for the temporary favors of Helene and Antonia.

Darcie had come with Guy Simel, but Guy did not join the family grouping, nor did anyone ask him to. In the middle of the evening, Jay sought Guy out. After an exchange of rather formal greetings, it was Guy who brought up the subject which was on both their minds.

"I understand that you've had some questions about Roethke steel," Guy said.

"As a matter of fact," Jay said, "I want to have a

talk with you. Can you make yourself available soon?"

"At your service," Guy said. "Would it be possible to see some of this scaling which is concerning you?"

"Come dressed for the bush," Guy said.

"I think you'll find that it's merely the effects of the jungle," Guy said. "All one has to do is visit the site of the French canal and see what the years have done to the abandoned equipment."

"Perhaps," Jay said. "But why aren't the girders bought from other companies showing the same deterioration?"

"In the past few months, I've learned a lot about the product," Guy said. "Let me see the effects before I venture an opinion."

In fact, Guy had already seen some of the scaling in question, having ventured out into the construction sites soon after his arrival to be guided by an engineer who was on his payroll. Huge chips of the seemingly sturdy steel were flaking away. He could see for himself that it was not normal rust, and he had already composed a long letter to Roethke, suggesting that, in the future, the debasing of the alloying process be suspended. The contracts were secure. Profits were already at a point where the company could afford to offer a better product. However, Guy was not overly concerned. He had greased enough palms to feel quite secure. Moreover, he knew that Jay was leaving the canal soon. All he had to do was stall Jay until the army engineer took over, and then he would discover if Colonel Taylor had any ambition about increasing his salary, which, since Taylor was a soldier on detached service, would be about half of Jay's salary as a civilian engineer.

Guy spent a couple of days mending fences in Panama itself, for the new republic was, as yet, poverty stricken, and the men who had formed it, with the aid of United States dollars, still knew the value of the Yankee greenbacks. One of the more cooperative members of the regime was a small peacock of a man, General Juan Esteban. Esteban had built a palatial home in Panama City. In his middle age, he had developed a taste for luxury, and always welcomed a visit from Guy, for Guy always carried a small packet of bills which changed hands discreetly during the evening.

The occasion for his meeting with Esteban was a gala dinner in the house which the Roethke company maintained. Both Americans and Panamanians were invited, with Darcie acting as hostess. Thinking that Antonia and Helene might enjoy meeting some of the high officialdom of the republic, she invited both girls, and Antonia accepted with enthusiasm and coaxed Helene into joining her.

Esteban still remembered his first encounter with the beautiful Darcie, who had aged so well. Having found that money bought more than material luxuries, and having consumed a stream of young and sometimes beautiful girls since his rise to power, he often remembered that lovely woman who had once been in his house. His one regret was that he had not taken advantage of her presence.

In the early evening, Esteban made it a point to seek Darcie out and to make an invitation. There was no missing his meaning, for he had since learned of Darcie's reputation. However, she smiled and said, "Now, general, aren't we both too old for such things?"

This injured Esteban's pride, but the refusal had been delivered with a pleasant smile. With a man of Esteban's ego, her reference to his age was more of a denial than if she had simply said no. And so, in that gala company, he sought for feminine treasures elsewhere. He happened to be near the entrance when Antonia and Helene, somewhat late, came sweeping in to be greeted by Darcie, and his eyes went immediately to the dark, almost Spanish beauty of Helene. When she was introduced by Darcie, not as Darcie's daughter, but as "my dear, dear young friend," he bowed his short body over Helene's hand and made it a point to be by her side often. In fact, he went to Guy and told him that he would consider it a great favor if the seating could be arranged so that he would be next to Helene at table. Guy ordered the servant to make the change in place cards, thus removing Esteban from Guy's right hand and placing him in the center of the long table. Esteban, however, was not concerned with this demotion in protocol—he had eyes only for Helene.

There was more than one reason for having the general at dinner. With his new wealth, Roethke had expanded into shipping, and with a cabal of New York bankers and maritime interests was exploring a new and profitable idea. By registering ships under the flag of the new Republic of Panama, shipowners could escape many of the restrictions and taxes imposed by more industrialized countries, and Guy had been commissioned to explore the idea with the Panamanian officials. As an influential man, General Esteban was Guy's target.

As usual, Esteban took advantage of the free flow of good wine at a Simel party, and by the time Guy was able to get him alone, he was a bit unsteady on his feet, clanking his dangling sword against furniture as he moved about. The man was in no condition to talk business, so Guy merely expressed his wish to have a serious talk at the first opportunity.

"I will talk about anything," Esteban said, "if you will arrange for me to also talk with that lovely creature who is now standing with *Señora* Darcie."

Guy saw that he meant Helene. He, too, had been much impressed by Helene's young, sad-eyed beauty and had entertained thoughts of making her eyes light up through his own actions.

"I fear, general, that you have chosen an unlikely target," he said.

"Still one may hope," Esteban said.

"She is young and innocent," Guy said. "And she had just been exposed to tragedy. No, my good general, I would suggest other interests. For example, that young and beautiful blond girl who is with them."

"Truly a beauty," Esteban said. "But the other, ah," he said, rubbing his genitals suggestively.

Thinking that the general's obsession would fade with the influence of the drink, Guy said, "We will talk about that, too."

All in all, it was a good night for intrigue. As the evening became more gay, with the continued consumption of wine and spirits, Antonia came to Guy.

"Looking at you, my dear great-uncle, my resolution to be a good girl is wavering," she said.

"Where there is a will," he said smiling. "Perhaps you could spend the night. After all, you have your aunt as chaperone."

"No, that wouldn't do," she said. "At least not tonight. Another night, when I've laid the groundwork better." She brushed against him, pushing a taut breast against his arm. "I just wanted you to know that I'm thinking of you."

And he was thinking of her, and of her with Darcie, and of Helene.

"I have a small problem," Antonia said. "And knowing your rather devious mind, perhaps you can help me with it. I had planned to use myself to expose the good colonel, but having seen my mother and Jay I realize that I would be hurting them if I became involved in scandal. I was merely going to go to his quarters and then cry rape."

Guy shook his head. "Remind me—keep reminding me—not to cross you," he said.

"Ah, uncle!"

"The same idea would be workable with another woman," he said.

"But who?"

"Let your old great-uncle think about it. Where there's a will—"

In General Esteban's palatial home the next day,

Guy found that Esteban, rather than forgetting the beauty of Helene, was fairly stewing with it. Guy tried to talk business, and the small man kept coming back to his desire to speak with, to be with, to have the dark, gypsy-looking young lady.

"I've told you it would be impossible," Guy said. "And now, if you please, general, there are important matters to discuss, matters which can mean much profit for both of us and for your country."

"I *have* money," Esteban said.

"All right, general," Guy said with a sigh. "I will speak to Helene. I promise nothing, and I must warn you that she is the ward of a powerful man. Unpleasantness with Jay Burton is something neither of us can afford."

"I ask only that you do your best," Esteban said. "And now a matter of ships, I believe."

At the end of a satisfactory conference, Guy had another thought. "And now, general, I have a small favor to ask of you. I am in need of a pretty young woman with some acting ability to do a chore for me."

"Ah," Esteban said. "I happen to know of several pretty young women. And are not all women natural actresses?"

Without giving names, Guy explained his needs and the general chuckled. "And who, may I ask, is so angry that she seeks such stern revenge?"

"It is better that you don't know," Guy said.

"Yes, perhaps you are right. It will be amusing. I shall await with interest the great scandal. You say the man is quite highly placed?"

"When he is accused of rape, you will know immediately."

The woman Esteban had in mind was, at that time, in his house. She came in, dressed in black lace, with a mantilla over her raven tresses, a shy smile on her young face.

"Quite beautiful," Guy said. "A shame to waste such beauty on an American."

"You will find her to be quite willing to please," Esteban said.

"Your name, child?" Guy asked, in Spanish.

She was Leonela Lopez.

"And your age?" Guy asked.

"Twenty-one," Leonela said. Esteban laughed.

"The truth," Guy said.

"The truth, little one," Esteban said.

"Must I?" she asked.

"For a fact," Esteban said.

"I am almost sixteen," she said. "But I look much older, do I not? And I—"

"Hush," Guy said. "You are exactly the right age, Leonela of the dark hair. Now, can you weep for me?"

Esteban nodded with a smile. The girl took a deep breath and let it out. Then she began to tear at her breast, and the sounds which came from her were the sounds of true anguish. Within seconds, real tears formed in her eyes and began to run down her cheeks.

"Excellent, excellent," Guy said. "My dear child, how would you like to earn for yourself one hundred dollars American?"

"For you, *señor*," she said, wiping away her tears and smiling, "the cost will be much less."

"Ah, yes," Guy said. "Are you brave?"

"When I, ah, discovered her," Esteban said, "she was a motherless waif working the streets of the city."

"But is she well known?"

"Not in your circles," Esteban said. "Fortunately, I saw her before she became too proficient at her trade."

And then Guy explained what was to be done. "Can you do it for me, and for one hundred dollars?" he asked.

"*Señor*," she said with a laugh, "for that much money I will *rape* him."

"I don't think that will be necessary," Guy said.

He took Leonela home with him and sent word to Antonia. She came and he explained the plan. She looked at Leonela with a critical eye and approved. "Yes," she said. "He likes them young. I'm sure it will work. You know what to do, child?"

"I know," Leonela said.

Dressed in the clothes of a low-class Panamanian, Leonela was escorted to Colonel Taylor's quarters that evening.

"I have found a maid for you," Antonia announced.

"Isn't she a bit young?" Taylor wanted to know.

"She is a good worker," Antonia said, "and she needs the position, Art. She's homeless."

"I work hard for you, *señor*," Leonela said seriously.

"Well," Taylor said, "if you think she'll be all right."

Antonia saw that Leonela was settled in the servant's quarters and rejoined Taylor in the sitting room. "Just you behave yourself with that young and pretty girl in the house," she teased.

"Of course," Taylor said stiffly. He was uneasy with her in the house. On the verge of greatness, having been chosen as the man to finish one of the greatest construction projects of all times, he wanted to do nothing to risk failure. He was a good engineer, and he had seen that Burton had solved the unsolvable problems. Now it was simply a matter of following through to the inevitable conclusion. He knew also that the man who finished the canal would be the hero, not those who had laid the groundwork. He could see at least one star on his shoulder, and within a very few short years.

And yet she was so young, so alluring, so awe-inspiring in her appetite for love. In spite of himself, he went to her and put his arms around her, wishing that it were possible for him to get a divorce, but knowing all the while that such a move on his part, at this junc-

ture of his career, would be bad politics. He kissed
her, cursing in his mind the men who forced a double
standard of behavior on the entire officer corps. The
very men who, on holidays, womanized fiercely, talked
about their conquests of some sad little girl of the
streets as if it were the most gallant victory of a
Casanova, were the hypocrites who would frown and
put a mental black mark by his name if he involved
himself in the scandal of divorce.

She allowed his kiss and then pushed him away
with a sweet smile. "Mustn't compromise you, darling,"
she said. And then she was gone.

8

DARCIE COULD NOT pinpoint a moment when she first realized that there was more than friendship between her niece and Guy Simel, but gradually she came to see the looks which passed between them, to feel the heat when they were together and to recognize it. Then she knew that it had been obvious from the first and that she'd been so involved with Helene that she had simply ignored the signs. It was a small sadness for her, but, with Helene beginning to show signs that she was ready to take up living again, she had little time to worry about Antonia. She had long since concluded that Antonia was past saving from the same sort of life which she had led for so long.

Strange, she thought, that for weeks now she had not thought of sex. Had she, all her life, been substituting the pleasures of the flesh for true love? However, there was no time for regrets, either. Nor did she tell herself that it had not been fun. She knew Guy's capabilities full well, from many years of experience, and she knew that young Antonia was being given thrills which few men are capable of giving a woman. She watched for signs of the inevitable coarsening, and saw nothing. On the surface, Antonia was the sweet young lady. That made her one hell of a good actress.

It was inevitable, since she was not welcome in Petra's house, that Helene came into contact with Guy occasionally, but Darcie was very careful not to give Guy an opportunity to be alone with Helene.

As for Guy, his long experience with women warned him, perhaps subconsciously, that there had been a change in Darcie. Once or twice he tried to be affectionate with her, and her reaction was a total lack of interest. He did not push it, although he still, at night, entertained himself, put himself to sleep, with fantasies of having the two of them in his bed: the young and the mature, both receiving his ministrations.

General Esteban was giving Guy problems. Although the general professed to be working hard on the plan to allow ships of other nationalties to register under a quite liberal Panamanian flag, checks with other government officials told Guy that the general was indeed doing nothing. When approached, Esteban said things about one favor calling for another, and, in the end, made it quite clear that the price for his cooperation was Helene.

With great reluctance, Guy began to put his mind to ways of meeting Esteban's price. During his conversations with Helene, always in the presence of others, he had found her to be a charming, shy, modest girl, a girl of, he suspected, militant morality, much as Petra had been at one time in her life. There would be no open way of getting Helene to submit to Esteban's advances. But to a man with a medical education and access, through Esteban, to some rather exotic materials, there was a way. It would be infinitely risky, and he would have to rely on the very morality, the very modesty, which were Helene's strong points. His guess, his hope, was that if Helene were compromised, she would be so shamed that she would not tell even those nearest and dearest to her. He had known girls like that, and had taken advantage of them. Near rape which went unpunished, because the girl would rather keep the shame within her own soul than expose her seducer.

In Paris, Guy had at least one child who was growing up as another man's son: the baby the result of such a near rape accomplished against the girl's will but hidden because she would not bear the shame of having others know of her downfall.

He knew that to accomplish such an outcome, at least two women would have to be taken care of. Darcie, with her fierce love for Helene, would never agree to it, and Petra, he knew, could be expected to become quite violent. Antonia was a question mark. With Darcie and Helene off to one of the government-sponsored shops which sold goods far cheaper than they could be purchased in the United States, Antonia lost her caution and teased him into bed for a quite entertaining hour and after that took advantage of other opportunities. She was dating young men whom she had met through Petra and Jay and their friends and, on the too-infrequent occasions when she could get into bed with Guy, made his blood boil with detailed accounts of her activities with the young men, coming to him once on a happy afternoon, to find Darcie and Helene away, with the fresh lubricity of love in her.

And so the new and exciting perversion which Guy had discovered in a forbidden book by a rich Englishman was, once again, teased, and this brought new thoughts. To have that same pleasure with Helene would be so lovely that it made his heart beat faster just to think of it.

There came a time when Jay Burton was to be put off no longer on the matter of the flaking steel, which, in spite of Jay's continued objections and his frequent protest to Washington, was still arriving in great quan-

tities and being installed in the numerous bridges of
the relocated railroad. Guy, a bit apprehensive, went
to Jay's office early one morning and announced that
he was ready to make his inspection trip. He was dressed
in khaki, wore a sun helmet, and carried an umbrella.
It was the height of the rainy season and he preferred
to stay indoors, with fans to cool him. However, it had
to be done. Although his men in Washington were holding up the reports from the lab, the first of which found
nothing to be wrong with the steel from Roethke's
plant, thanks to his man there, Burton was not to be
put off further.

In cold politeness, they boarded the train in Panama
City and made the crossing, leaving the main track
near the Chagres, which roiled, huge and ugly, glutted
with the torrential rains which fell daily. Workers, often
continuing to labor as the rains came, waved at the
special train which they recognized as the chief engineer's own. The new tracks swung off toward the
north, skirting the low stamps which would be covered by the water of Gatun Lake once the huge
earthen dam was finished, at Gatun. The first of the
bridges was crossed at low speed.

"We've just crossed three bridges built with what
you are calling inferior steel," Guy said. "And safely, I
might add."

"This time," Jay said grimly.

Outside of a small station called Frijoles, the railroad crossed a tributary of the Chagres, a stream swollen and fed by the wet-season downpours falling on the
towering hills to the west of the canal. Having had his
instructions, the engineer stopped the train at the approaches to the bridge and the two men stepped out of
Jay's special car into a dampness which was the result
of a shower having just passed, the thunder and lightning
lingering on the horizon. One of the field engineers
met them, and the three men walked past workers onto
the bridge.

Below them, the stream was the color of the Panama mud. Lowlands all around were flooded, the waters coming in places to the railway embankment. The bridge, one of the longer ones on the relocated route, had been in place for mere months. And yet, when they reached a point above the swollen river and Jay got to his knees and looked down, he could see the girders flaking and peeling.

"For one thing," he said, "it won't hold paint. Paint it today and it rusts away from underneath within weeks."

The engineer, a young man eager to impress the boss, clambered down underneath the track and clung to girders to chip away at a scaly spot with his pocket knife. "I'd estimate that it's lost a good quarter-inch to rust already, Mr. Burton," he called up.

"I don't quite understand," Guy said. "Our own tests showed the steel to be quite resistant to rust."

"Perhaps you weren't testing the same sort of material," Jay said.

"Look here, Burton," Guy said. "You're continually making little hints that something is wrong with our product. And yet your own efforts to hurt us have come to nothing. You've heard the preliminary reports from the lab, I'm sure, for I've had word of them."

"All I know is that this bridge will fall of its own weight in a couple of years," Jay said. "Now you tell me why."

"Would there be a personal motive behind your attacks?" Guy asked, disturbed by the obvious damage already done to Roethke's steel by the elements and the climate of Panama, but operating on the theory that the best defense is a good offense.

"I've struck men for less than that," Jay said angrily. He stood, and the young engineer began to clamber back to the track.

"I just want to tell you, Simel," Jay said, "that I'm going to do everything within my power to have a full investigation of this mess. I don't care how many men you have on your payroll—it'll come out in the end. Any fool fresh out of school can look at this stuff and see it's doctored, and I suspect I know how. I've been doing a little reading on the steelmaking process, and I've come up with some interesting information. I'm sending my ideas along to Washington, and they'll take a look at the source, at the plant itself."

"I can only conclude that you're on some sort of vendetta," Guy blustered. "I can assure you that you won't be allowed to railroad me and my company. I have friends, Burton."

"That's the problem," Jay said. "Friends with their hands out."

"The river's rising pretty good," the young engineer said, coming up to them. "It's been raining up in the hills for about twenty-four hours. Way it looks, she's going to get a pretty good workout."

Jay had seen that the river was rising by the broken tree limbs and other debris which rode the very center of the stream. There was a tremendous difference in water level in the rivers between dry and wet seasons, and if the river were to rise much more, it would be at a level higher than he'd ever seen it. He walked out toward the center of the river. A dead bird floated under the bridge, its bright wings outstretched. The thunder still rumbled from the low mountains. For a moment, in spite of his perpetual tiredness, his being sated with heat and moisture and ever-present insects, he knew that he would miss it, for there was a sort of grandeur about Panama. Never had so large an undertaking been attempted under such intimidating circumstances. To think that men would risk ruining such a grand enterprise for mere greed was beyond his understanding.

Jay was standing alone, looking downstream, when the young engineer came up, put his hand on his arm, and said, "Look, Mr. Burton."

Jay turned. From the upstream side came a mass of tangled trees. They formed a nest of sodden foliage, splintered trunks, protruding limbs which towered over the surface of the water.

"Landslide on some mountain upstream," the young engineer said.

Jay walked farther out to get a better view as the mass of floating trees came slowly closer. At first it appeared that they would pass underneath the bridge between the pilings which held up the trestle. They floated, as the rising water put a bulge in the center of the stream, almost in the exact middle of the river. But as they came slowly downstream, some roiling current, some eddy, began to move the huge mass toward the far bank.

A gang of some fifty Jamaican workmen labored on the bridge past the midpoint. They began to halt their work one by one and look up at the approaching mass. A few began to edge away from what was to be the point of impact.

The floating mass struck with a jar which Jay could feel in his feet. Slowly the tons of fallen trees began to twist, snagged on a group of pilings. The workmen watched nervously. Jay began to run toward the point. When he arrived, the mass of trees seemed to be solidly caught. Other, smaller floating debris began to back up behind the trees.

"Have someone get some lines," Jay ordered the young engineer. He intended to lasso the mass, put men on the end of the lines, and pull it into an opening so that it could drift on beyond the bridge. The young man gave orders.

Guy Simel, who had followed, smiled thinly. "A bridge which can stand up to that isn't built of inferior steel."

Jay was watching upstream. The rains in the hills must have been quite severe, for the bulge in the center of the river was apparent to the naked eye, and more and more floating vegetation was appearing. There was no reason for concern, however. The bridge was built to take much more than a floating mass of trees, even if some of them were three feet thick at the base.

Men came with ropes, and Jay busied himself making nooses to drop down and secure over protruding limbs. He had men on the lines, tugging, when he saw a new logjam of freshly fallen trees bearing down from the upstream side and the same currents or eddy sent the new mass in behind the old. Now there were tons of force being exerted on the one set of pilings.

"Yes, my friend," Guy said. "That is not inferior steel."

"If you're so confident," Jay said, seeing more and more floating limbs, parts of trees, brush coming down the swollen stream, "then you stand right here with me."

"I am confident of my steel," Guy said. "I can't vouch for your design and your engineering."

"If those beams are not porous clean through," Jay said, "so that rust has eaten them away, the bridge will hold. That I guarantee. Can you guarantee the steel?"

"Of course," Guy said.

A new mass lodged behind the huge pile-up with a jolt which sent tremors all the way up to the roadbed on which they stood. New lines were attached, and all available men were pulling, trying to ease the broken and tangled trees away from the pilings. Clouds formed above them, seemingly from relatively clear air, and with a muted roar like a waterfall the rain came down, quickly soaking Jay to the skin. Guy put up his umbrella. And from upstream a huge tree, roots ripped from the ground in a mass, the heavy branches and leaves causing it to float with the root end high, came floating down toward the jam like a battering ram.

"Mr. Burton," the young engineer said, "do you think we'd better get the men off?"

"Let's have one more go at it," Jay said. "All together now, heave."

But the mass was immovable. The huge floating tree came, butt first, ramming into the pile-up with all the force of its tons and momentum. Without warning, steel, weakened at its heart by cheap alloys, bent, then snapped with a sound like the report of a pistol. The track sagged. Three men, off balance as they pulled on the rope, went over the side with a joint shout of alarm, their heads quickly appearing on the other side of the bridge. And the mass was shuddering, moving, grinding.

Guy, white-faced, seeing his ruin in the tilted roadbed, tried to make his way toward the near shore. Jay caught him. "No you don't, mister," he said angrily. "You're staying as long as there's a man on this bridge."

And then: "It's moving, men. One more time—heave."

Another girder snapped with that sharp report, and men dropped their lines, running along the rails toward the shore. Jay grabbed the low rail for balance, seeing the twisted mass of trees directly below him. The mass was moving, moving, and there were grinding and tearing sounds. The three men who had gone into the water were swimming strongly, but being carried downstream.

"All right," Jay said, "let's get the hell out of here."

Guy was already running. Jay followed at a walk and was almost clear of the weakened section when he felt the entire bridge shake. There was a rumbling, and an entire section dropped from under him into the tangled trees, the dark, muddy water. He felt himself falling and reached out, seized something, clung on for dear life as he continued to go down. He was holding a section of rail. It had come loose at a joint, and his hands, made slick by the rain, were slipping as he looked down to see that if he fell, it would be into that mass of broken tree limbs, a deadly mass which was now grinding and moving under the force of the current.

"Simel!" he shouted.

Guy had run ahead and now, in the silence after the crash, he stopped, looked back. Jay Burton was not there. He had to know. He eased back out toward the break, a clean break taking only the center section, and heard Burton's voice shouting for help. He got on his hands and knees and peered over the jumbled and bent edges. Burton was hanging onto one bent rail, the end of it only a foot or so from his hands, which, now and then, slid a bit.

"Simel!" Burton shouted. "Get me a line!"

Below was the floating mass. If Jay fell into that, he would be unable to swim. Guy thought quickly. He had his money. There were many places in a world where a man with money could enjoy it; but if he became involved in criminal proceedings as the result of this bridge collapse, it might drag on for years and might conceivably result in his going to prison.

"A line!" Jay shouted. "Quickly, man!"

Guy pulled back from the edge of the break and looked around. There was a rope within a few feet. He moved toward it slowly. He took his time, coiling the rope in his hand. It was heavy with the water it had absorbed. From the shore, the young engineer and a few of the workmen were starting back toward the break.

He stood over Burton and looked down.

"Throw me the damned line!" Jay yelled, his hands aching, clinging to the very end of the slick rail, the edges of the rail's base cutting into his hands painfully.

Guy looked over his shoulder. The men were within a few yards, running. He dropped the entire coil of rope, holding onto the end of it. The sodden mass hit Jay in the face, and the weight was the last straw.

His hands slipped and he fell, looking down to see the writhing, grinding mass of broken tree limbs, going in feet first.

"It's Burton," Guy said to the young engineer. "I tried to help him. Threw him a line."

Jay had crashed through the tangle of green foliage. There was no sign of him. Then, slowly, the entire mass came free of the pilings and began to drift downstream.

"We've got to do something," Guy said. "He's probably tangled in that mess." And, with cold calculation, he stripped off his light jacket and made as if to dive into the roiling water.

"I can't let you do that, Mr. Simel," the young engineer cried, seizing Guy's arms.

They stood and watched the floating mass of vegetation slide slowly downstream.

"Jesus!" the young engineer said. "I'm going to have to notify the office."

"And his family," Guy said. "Since his wife is my niece, I will take it upon myself to tell her."

"I'd appreciate that, sir."

"I think it's quite clear what happened here," Guy said. "A simple matter of underdesign. The bridge was not constructed to take the possible strains which would be put upon it. Don't you agree?"

"Well," the young engineer said. "I'm not so sure of that." He left Guy and went running back to shore to put out into the river in a rowboat. With two strong workers manning the oars, he caught up with the mass of floating trees, but it was impossible to penetrate it. He saw no signs of Burton and went sadly back to the bridge to board the train for the trip into Panama City to pass the news to the main office that the chief engineer was dead.

9

As Guy rode back into the city, he knew that it was high time to take his gains and get out. Burton's death—and the man was surely dead, drowned in that tangle of brush into which he had fallen—gave him enough time, however, to conclude his current business. If he succeeded in setting up a system for ship registration, with rules liberal enough to please the large shipowners, he would be paid a lump sum in cash. With that and what he had already been paid by Roethke, he could set up an establishment in any country of the world, perhaps with Antonia. That would be a laugh—to steal away Petra's precious daughter. But it would serve Petra right, for if her husband hadn't started trying to make trouble, Guy wouldn't be faced with having to leave a very profitable arrangement. And Jay had brought his own accident on himself. If he'd been in his office, where the chief engineer should be, instead of out in the field looking for trouble, he'd be safe.

Always the opportunist, Guy quickly saw the possibilities engendered by Burton's death. Now he could go through with his plan for Helene, and have only

an irate pair of women—if the girl chose to talk afterward. At least there would be no Jay Burton to worry
about. He would pay General Esteban's price, in the
form of a compliant Helene, as quickly as possible,
for there would surely be an investigation of the bridge
collapse, and he knew that Roethke's steel would not
withstand close examination by experts.

Guy arrived at his home and changed into dry clothing. There was no sign of Darcie. He went to the Burton house to find Petra and Antonia there alone.
Petra greeted him coldly.

"I am here by necessity," Guy said. "And I'm afraid
I have some bad news for you, Petra."

Petra made no reply, but a chill of dread went
through her and she held her breath.

"We pray that he is not dead," Guy said, "but—"

"Is it Jay?" Petra asked.

"I'm sorry," Guy said. Then he told quickly how it
had happened. "There's every chance that he was able
to swim ashore downstream," he said. "In that case,
you know how dense the jungle is, how difficult it
would be for him to walk back. It might be some time
before we know."

"What are you doing, mother?" Antonia asked, as
Petra started to leave the room.

"I'm going out there, of course," she said.

"Is that wise?" Guy asked. "You can do nothing
there, Petra."

"I can be there," Petra said. "I can be there when
he walks out."

"I'll go with you," Antonia said.

"Wait," Guy said. "I think it would be wiser to visit
the office, to check on preparations for a search party.
I'm sure they will send men downstream. In boats,
perhaps along the shore, although it will be rough
going. There were three other men who went into the
water."

"I'll talk with mother," Antonia said. "I think it would be best if you go."

"Yes," Guy said.

"You have my thanks," Antonia said.

"Of course, my dear," he said. "By the way, I'll be leaving Panama. I'd like it very much if you'd go with me."

"We'll talk about that later," Antonia said. "Goodbye."

She went upstairs where Petra was changing into clothing suitable for the jungle. She, too, dressed in sturdy clothing and then convinced Petra that they should go first to the office. There they found that search parties were being organized, but the young engineer who had seen the accident told them reluctantly that there was little hope of Jay's survival.

But Petra would not accept it. She would not allow herself to think of Jay dead. No. He would fight his way out, make his way back to the railroad through the dense jungle and the mucky swamps. Jay was too much man to allow himself to be drowned. She had so much faith that she was very calm. She insisted on being allowed to accompany the search party, but agreed to await in Jay's special car while the party went down-river into the bush. She sent a message to Helene, who was visiting in the home of friends, helping the wife of one of the engineers who had just had twins. Then, with Antonia, she boarded the train.

The messenger reached the home of the proud father of twin girls in the early evening, and Helene, greatly concerned, went to the office, only to find it closed. She knew from the message that Petra and Antonia, were somewhere out on the railroad. Wanting more information, she went to Guy's house to find him there alone. He gave her the story, but did not deny her hope, not wanting her to weep and upset herself, for he saw immediately that this might be his opportunity. He did not know Darcie's whereabouts, but, since it was growing dark, he expected her to be home soon.

"I know you don't want to be alone at a time like this, my dear," he told Helene, "so please stay with me. I'm sure that Darcie will be here shortly, and we can wait word together."

"Yes, I think she was going to do some shopping and then go to the library," Helene said. "Thank you. You're very kind."

"Some wine?" Guy offered.

"Coffee, I think," Helene said.

He took her into his private study, because, he said, it was more cozy. Actually, it was because, through the window, he could watch the street. Within a few minutes, as he chatted comfortingly to Helene, assuring her that Burton had probably made his way to shore and would walk out in time, he saw a carriage. When it stopped in front of the house, he excused himself and went out, closing the door behind him. He met Darcie at the front door.

"Burton's dead," he said brutally. "Petra, Antonia, and Helene have gone to the scene of the accident. I thought you'd want to join them. There'll be another train going out there shortly, with more men for a search party." As he talked, he motioned to the driver of the carriage to wait. Darcie, shocked, allowed herself to be put aboard the carriage, leaving her packages and the books from the library with Guy. When she was gone, Guy secreted the packages and books and went back into the study, hiding a small vial in his jacket pocket. It was a simple matter to offer Helene a second cup of coffee laced with the drug.

When Helen first felt the onset of drowsiness, she attributed it to her nervousness, to the strain of waiting for word which might not come until morning.

"Is there anything wrong?" Guy asked, when she rubbed her eyes and shook her head.

"All of a sudden, I'm very tired," Helene said.

"That's quite a natural reaction. Perhaps you'd like to lie down until Darcie comes?"

"No, no, I'm fine," she said, drinking more of the coffee.

Her eyes were so heavy, so heavy. She leaned her head back and there was such a feeling of comfort in it, just relaxing, closing her eyes. And then she realized that she was going to sleep and tried to lift her head. Her neck seemed to be powerless, her head so heavy. She sighed and gave way to the feeling of overwhelming drowsiness.

With a grim smile, Guy arose, lifted one eyelid. *Yes,* he thought, *just the right amount.* She would sleep for a while and then she would be capable of being awakened to function in a sort of daze—not asleep, but not fully awake, either. He would have preferred her to be fully awake, but that was not practical.

Now, quickly, he called his manservant and instructed him to make all possible haste to General Esteban's house with a note which told the general that what he wanted most of all was awaiting him. If Esteban did not happen to be available, well, it was his loss.

Alone with the sleeping Helene, he allowed himself the luxury of feeling a bulging breast, first through her clothing and then with his hands inside her blouse. And his hand felt, too, the sweet, warm softness of her thighs before he hoisted her into his arms and carried her upstairs to his bed. He stood for a while, panting. Although she was petite, the effort had tired him. He sat in a chair and looked at her, anticipating, tempted to sample the young and helpless body himself but wanting more to experience the thrill of knowing that body as he'd come to like a woman best: freshly used by another man.

He could, and did, remove her clothing. She breathed deeply and evenly, her lovely breasts rising and falling. So soft, so warm under his hands. And the taste of her,

as he allowed himself to know the delicate sweetness of
her, his head thrust between the warm softness of her
thighs. She did not stir as he used her with his eager
mouth, and then he forced himself to stop, for the urge
to mount her was almost irresistible. Better, however,
to wait. Anticipation was becoming with him, more and
more, one of the sweetest parts of the sex act. The
longer the wait, the greater the rewards.

He heard the hooves of a horse at a trot and then he
went downstairs to greet a flushed Esteban. "Is it true?"
Esteban asked.

"Yes. She's upstairs. Come."

She lay with her legs open, as Guy had left her.
Esteban hurried into the room and stopped in mid-
stride, his eyes wide, his heart pounding.

"She's asleep," he said.

"I have administered a drug," Guy said.

"I did not want her this way," Esteban protested.
"Limp, unresponsive. It would seem like making love
to the dead."

"She can be partially awakened," Guy said. "The
drug then will have the effect of merely killing her will.
I assure you that if you are skillful, she will be aroused
and will respond."

"This is true?" Esteban asked, moving to the side of
the bed. He put his hand on one firm breast and
breathed deeply. Then he shook her gently. She stirred
and made a little moaning sound. Guy came to the bedside and put his hand on her shoulder.

"Wake up, Helene," Guy said. "Wake, my dear."

She tried to open her eyes, moving her head. "You
see?" Guy asked. He put his hand between her legs and
used his fingers skillfully.

Helene, only vaguely aware, felt the sensation, much
like the dreams which nature sent to her. With a sigh,
she lifted her loins to press against Guy's hand. "There,"
Guy whispered. "I think you will find it amusing, general. I'll leave you now, but I must tell you that my

niece Darcie will return here in an hour's time, so, although it is regrettable, your time is limited."

"An hour?" Esteban asked, licking his lips as he let his eyes devour the slim and shapely body.

"You must be out of the house and away within something less than an hour," Guy said.

"Well, we must be grateful for what we have," Esteban said.

Guy withdrew. He had made his plans. He left the door slightly ajar, having pulled a chair up close to it. He was in an adjoining bedroom and he watched avidly as Esteban first toyed with Helene, then began eagerly to remove his colorful uniform. Guy hoped that he would hurry, that his greed would cause him to finish quickly. Then Guy would hurry him out of the house and have the rest of the night—or at least several hours —to enjoy his own pleasure with the lovely Helene.

Naked, Esteban looked more like a child, his body small, his already rigid staff the only man-sized thing about him. He fell to his work, kissing Helene's body, chewing lightly on the red, soon-engorged nipples. And his hand worked between her legs until, as if in a dream, she began to make lifting motions. Then it was time. His fingers had churned up sweet moisture in her, wetting the rosy labia, smoothing the point of entry with natural lubrication. He pushed her legs apart, and, on his knees, got between them. He put one hand on his staff to guide it and used the fingers of the other hand to push apart her labia. Then, with a deep breath, with trembling limbs, he pushed toward her.

Darcie had hurried to the railroad station. As Guy had said, men were there organizing a second search party, working rapidly, loading torches and machetes and camping gear. She found a man who looked as if he were in charge.

"Mr. Burton is my brother-in-law," she said. "And I think I should be with my sister and her daughter. May I ride with you?"

"Of course," the man said. In fact, he was the same young man who had been present at the time of the accident. "Yes, I put Mrs. Burton and her daughter on the first train out. She seemed quite calm, as did her daughter. A very brave pair of ladies, I'd say."

"And the other girl? The dark-haired one? Was she all right?" Darcie asked.

"There were only the two," he said. "Mrs. Burton and her daughter Antonia."

"Are you quite sure?" Darcie asked, puzzled. "Perhaps you just did not notice the third girl. Rather small, dark hair?"

"Madame," he said, "I rode to the scene of the accident with Mrs. Burton. I assure you that there were only two of them, as I've said."

Darcie knew then, and a painful spurt of adrenaline went into her stomach. Guy! Guy was using this time of crisis for his own ends, and, knowing Guy quite well, she knew full well what those ends were. She turned and began to run toward the carriage park, where hackneys awaited.

"We'll be leaving quite soon," the young engineer called after her, but she paid no attention.

"Hurry, please!" she told the driver. "Oh, please hurry!"

If it had already happened, she would not be able to forgive herself for being so stupid as to trust Guy, to believe anything he said. She should have checked further instead of allowing him to bundle her into the carriage and get rid of her. Anger burned in her, and she made a resolution. If he had dishonored her daughter, the girl who had saved herself for her Jean-Charles so sweetly only to be deprived of love by his death, if he had, then she would kill him. And she knew how.

She let herself into the house quietly, using her key. The house was very quiet. She tiptoed to the study, where a light burned, and found it empty. Then, with angry resolution, she took Guy's loaded revolver from his desk. Armed, determined to kill Guy if he had raped Helene, she crept up the stairs and stood, for a moment, outside the bedroom door. She heard harsh breathing from within, and her heart sank, for she knew she was too late. She opened the door and cried out as she saw Juan Esteban on his knees between Helene's outflung legs, his huge staff in his hand only inches from Helene.

Esteban, hearing the door open, cursed and turned to see Darcie holding the huge Colt revolver, the muzzle aimed directed at his chest. It all happened quickly. Darcie saw Helene nude, was sure in her heart that it was too late, saw the little man holding his huge staff in his hand, squeezed the trigger just as Esteban, seeing hate in her eyes and the tensing of the finger at the trigger, threw himself toward her—only to meet the bullet. It smashed him, threw him back against the bed, dead before his body slid to the floor.

"Goddamn, Darcie, are you crazy," Guy Simel yelled, throwing open the door. Darcie turned, aiming the pistol at him, her face grim, eyes wet with tears. And Guy looked death in the face as he realized that she was going to shoot him, too, threw himself backward, falling over the chair as the bullet slammed air close by his head, rolled, more frightened than he'd ever been in his life.

Another round smashed the door behind him. But there was hope. In the chest in the bedroom was another gun, a small Belgian automatic. Guy liked guns, owned several of them, carried the little Belgian gun with him when he traveled. He heard Darcie yelling as he scuttled on his hands and knees across the floor, gasping in fright. Then the gun was in his hands and the door was flying open. He saw the muzzle of the Colt, a huge, gaping hole from which would come his death. With a choked cry, he aimed and fired. The bullet took her high, flung her backward, blood beginning to wet her blouse. Guy watched her fall, saw the heavy revolver bounce and skid away, ran to pick it up. A quick glance showed him that the bullet had taken her just above the heart. Esteban was dead. Helene was sitting up, dazed, her mouth open.

"God!" Guy grunted. Esteban, a top figure in the government, dead in his bedroom. Darcie dying. Now, truly, it was over. Now there was nothing to do but flee, and as rapidly as possible. While the drugged girl watched, unable to move, he quickly packed one small bag. His bank accounts were scattered all over the world: in the United States—he might lose that money, but it was a minor part—in France, in Switzerland. He had to get out of the country, out of the Canal Zone. He took a carriage to the docks. He had contacts there. He had money. He had learned long ago never to be without a cash reserve.

He found the man he was looking for, a Panamanian who had once worked with him during the days when, in desperation, he was forced to traffic in drugs. He did not tell the man why he had to get out of Panama, and not aboard a passenger ship, but in a small boat moving along the coast. The man agreed, for a certain sum. And Guy Simel left Panama for the last time aboard a small fishing boat which smelled of the catch, in the company of two men who knew that Señor Simel had much money.

It was a groan from Darcie which finally caused Helene's awareness to break through her stupor. She seemed to move in slow motion. She was naked. She realized that and couldn't understand why. The last thing she remembered was drinking coffee with Guy in the study. She got off the bed, fell forward to her hands and knees, and looked directly into the cold, staring, dead eyes of Juan Esteban. She screamed, and the fright cleared her head further. She heard the groan again and crawled slowly to the door to see Darcie lying on her back, arms and legs akimbo, blood staining her white shirtwaist.

"Darcie!" Helene cried. "Oh, mother, mother!"

10

JAY KEPT HIS feet close together as he fell and brought his arms up to protect his face as he crashed, feet first, into the floating mass of limbs. He heard and felt small limbs breaking, and then he was in the water. Jagged ends scratched at him, and the breath had been knocked out of him. He kept his head and fought his way up, pulling with his hands on the matted limbs, forcing his head up until he found blessed air and held himself there, gasping, making a hoarse croaking sound as his lungs battled to breathe. Above and all around were sodden leaves and small branches.

He knew that if the floating mass shifted, it could pull him under. Slowly he tried to fight his way upward, to be able to see. Two trees shifted and caught his leg painfully between them. It took him long minutes, using all his strength, ducking his head under the water to be able to push with his arms, to free the leg. When at last he was free and able to see, by standing carefully on a partially submerged trunk, he was far downriver from the bridge. Not too far ahead, the tributary joined the Chagres, and the larger river was out of its banks, spreading over miles of marsh and jungle. He'd have to walk out, and if he let himself be carried all the way to the Chagres, it would take days.

Carefully he began to crawl atop the floating mass, sometimes slipping to submerge beneath the tepid, muddy waters until, with a kick, he was free and swimming toward the south bank. The stream was widening and he had not thought to remove his boots. In fact, he needed them, for to be barefoot in the jungle was an impossible thing to contemplate. He was a good swimmer, strong, and he made good progress, although, all the while, he was being swept farther and farther from the bridge and the railroad.

The river had flooded the banks, and he had to push his way through partially submerged brush, watchful for snakes. He crawled up a muddy slope and lay on his stomach, breathing hard. Mosquitoes attacked immediately, giving him no chance to rest. He dug mud with his hands and coated all the exposed areas of his body.

Quite early in the history of Panama, men learned that the jungle can be a formidable foe. The abundant rainfall and year-round growing temperatures encourage an incredible denseness of vegetation in myriad forms, from huge trees through various creepers to thorned things which claw and scratch. Even for an organized party with cutting tools, progress through virgin jungle can be measured in yards for an entire day and a man alone, with only his hands, is at a severe disadvantage.

Jay estimated that he had drifted no more than three miles downstream. At the moment, he had the sun to help establish direction, and even if it had been totally overcast, his knowledge of the terrain would have told him the proper course back to the railroad. If he deviated in an effort to find easier going, he would still hit the railroad simply by traveling northwest.

His progress was made more difficult by the flood-waters which had seeped into the jungle to form stagnant pools. It was necessary to be on guard against snakes, for the jungle was home for several deadly varieties. There were also huge spiders whose bite could be quite serious, if not fatal.

He broke a green branch and stripped the leaves and small twigs from it and used it to beat a way through the most dense portions. As he moved through the brush the vegetation scraped the mud from his exposed body areas and mosquitoes attacked in clouds, so that he expended much energy in brushing and swatting the pesky insects.

He was soon sweating profusely, and that, too, tended to cause his protective coating of mud to slip away so that he was continually replenishing it. He licked and drank relatively fresh rainwater from curled leaves, not daring to drink the plentiful water which was accumulated on the ground.

It seemed, at times, that his movement could be measured in inches, and, when it began to grow dark, he cast around in the immediate area to find a place to spend the night, for it would be foolhardy to try to continue movement after the curtain of darkness made the already dim jungle floor a pitch-black obstacle course. There was no way to clear an area on the ground, so he found a large lignum vitae tree with a huge limb several feet off the ground, coated himself anew with mud, filled his pockets with more mud, and, with some effort, climbed the tree to lie, panting, on the horizontal limb. There he spent a sleepless night, the mud protecting him from the raids of the mosquitoes, except where they found chinks and where they bit through his clothing. Once he dozed and awoke with his mouth open and mosquitoes sucking blood from his exposed lips and tongue. He closed his mouth with a sound of disgust, spat out a buzzing insect, and managed to stay awake as the jungle below came to life with rustlings and the doomed cry of some small animal in the jaws of a predator.

First light found him stiff, cold, red-eyed with fatigue and burning with an anger which boded ill for Guy Simel. Perhaps, he thought, it was mere stupidity which caused the man to throw the full weight of a one-hundred-foot manila rope into his face, but he chose to believe that the act had been deliberate. The thought of putting his fist, quite hard, into Guy's mouth kept him going as he set out once again, fighting his way through tangled growth, sometimes literally crawling atop masses of creepers and low growth.

The night had been a difficult one, too, for Petra. Antonia slept for a while, but Petra managed only to doze, coming out of the light sleep every time she heard men outside the private car only to find, by inquiry, that nothing more encouraging than the return of the three black laborers had been accomplished, and one of the blacks was dying, having been bitten by a deadly snake. It was impossible, of course, for the search parties to stay in the jungle at night. They returned early and spent the night around fires and in the other cars of the train. There was food, but only Antonia ate. Petra contented herself with coffee and, at dawn, was outside, looking down the swollen river, thinking of Jay in that jungle alone at night.

The morning dragged on. Now boats were going up and down the river, searching the banks. Men were cutting their way slowly downstream on land. The heat grew and made the car insufferable, so they sat or stood outside, in the shade made by the train itself. At noon Antonia insisted that Petra eat. She ate sparingly, forcing it down. She overheard men talking. The opinion was that if Burton didn't come out of the jungle soon, he wasn't coming out, and their bet was that he'd never made it out of the river.

By now Petra had heard the entire story. It was Guy's steel, which, the engineers said, was definitely bad, which had been the cause of it all, and now she had real reason to hate her uncle.

In mid-afternoon, men began to straggle out of the jungle, mud-caked, mosquito-bitten, exhausted by the very hard and steamy work. They came a few at a time, vowing never to go back into that hell again—not for anything or for anybody. Work was underway on the bridge, because the canal went on, regardless of who was missing, who was dead. Now Colonel Taylor would be in charge, a bit ahead of schedule. Already men were referring to him as the boss, acknowledging Jay's death.

At four o'clock, the young engineer came to tell Petra that the train was now going to take the search party back to Panama City. "There are a few volunteers still in the bush," he said. "They're going to cut their way down to where the river runs into the Chagres before they give up."

"We'll wait," Petra said.

"Mrs. Burton," the young engineer said. "You're exhausted. You'll make yourself ill. Why don't you go back into the city? If we learn anything, I'll send word to you."

"Yes, thank you," Antonia said. "We'll do that."

She took her mother's arm and led her into the car. Petra went reluctantly. And once the train was in motion she put her head into her hands and let the tears come, for by leaving, she was admitting that Jay was dead.

Antonia, too, had heard the story of the accident from the engineer and was moody. She felt as if it were partly her fault, for she had been an active playmate of the man who had introduced the faulty material onto the job and thus directly contributed to Jay's death. She knew Guy was amoral, but it made her sad and guilty to know that he was also a scoundrel.

But she was not like that, she told herself. She'd never stolen or deliberately tried to hurt anyone.

Except men. Except Arthus Taylor. She knew that the pretty young girl, Leonela, was merely waiting for her opportunity. Wouldn't it be ironic if, on the verge of greatness, her colonel were brought down by a teen-age prostitute?

Ironic? Tragic? Did he actually deserve such a fate?

Well, she would think about it. Meanwhile, she tried to comfort Petra, as the train got underway, telling her without convincing even herself that Jay could still come walking out of the jungle only a bit the worse for wear.

Now the train was gathering speed and Petra was weeping, Antonia holding her close, saying. "Yes, yes, it's all right. It's all right to cry."

There was the sound of the wheels clicking over the rail joints, the chug-chug of the engine as it got up speed, the soft rush of wind past the windows. A hoot of the whistle and then more hoots and a screen of brakes as the train began to stop, the sudden slowing causing them to have to hold on to keep from being pitched forward.

"What is it?" Petra asked.

Sparks flew from locked wheels as the train ground to a halt. There was shouting from the leading end of the train, the back end as it was being pushed backward toward the city, and Petra was first to the door. She saw him, quite near, men jumping down from the cars to assist him up the embankment, his bearlike form unmistakable, although he was sodden, his clothing torn, mud covering him everywhere.

She ran, tripping and almost falling before she gathered up her skirts. Men were shouting and offering him water and he looked up, his eyes red holes in the caked mud of his face. Heedless of the mud and the wetness of his clothing, she ran into his arms and he held her close.

"Oh, Jay," she said, "look what you've done to your clothes!" For there was no way of expressing her feelings to find him alive. There was laughter and back-slapping.

"Thought you were a goner for sure, boss," a man said.

"Take more than a dip in the river and a walk in the jungle to get Old Iron Balls," another man shouted.

Jay grinned, teeth showing whitely through the mud. He knew the men had given him the nickname and he liked it. It showed respect. It showed that he had set out to do a job and that he was getting it done.

He shook off offers of help and walked, his arm around Petra's waist, to the car. Inside, he fell into a seat, not worrying about getting it muddy.

"A drink, a bath and twenty-four hours' sleep," he said. "In that order."

"Quinine," Petra said, holding out a dose to him with a glass of water.

"We were so worried," Antonia said. "And we're so happy you're all right."

"All I need is a blood transfusion," Jay said. "Those little breasts drained quarts of it out of me." And soon he was sleeping, sitting upright in the seat, his head bowed. Petra sat beside him, content to hold his hand.

He awoke before they reached the Panama City station. "Well, it's over," he said, smiling at Petra. "I have only one more chore, and then we're leaving, Petra. San Francisco. Cool mornings. No bugs. There's a hill I know of. We'll build a house there and from the front windows we can look down onto the bay and all the way to the Pacific."

"Yes, I'd like that," she said.

Word traveled ahead of them by the telegraph which kept the office in touch with work crews. They were met at the station by a group of men and women from the office, who cheered as Jay got off the car. He waved and smiled. Then Colonel Arthus Taylor pushed his way to Jay's side.

"I know it's a bad time," Taylor said, "but I've got to have a word with you."

Jay went to one side with him. "We've got a real mess on our hands." Taylor said. And he proceeded to tell Jay about the shootings. A Panamanian general dead in Guy Simel's house. A woman critically wounded. The woman?

"Your wife's sister, Darcie Moncrief," Taylor said. "Now I've given orders to the Canal Zone Police to keep a lid on it, and I'm in touch with the Panamanian government. They agree that it's a good idea to keep it quiet until we find out what happened."

Although exhausted, Jay could not give up, as he would have liked to do. He put Antonia and Petra into a carriage. "Pet," he said, "you know how they say things come in threes?"

"Yes?" she asked, but she thought at first that it was just idle talk. Having him come back, as it were, from the dead, she didn't think anything else could bother her.

"Well, that third one I'm dreading," he said. "Taylor had some bad news."

"What is it?"

"Hang onto yourself," Jay said.

"For heaven's sake," Petra said, beginning to be scared again. Since two of the people she loved were with her, it could only be Jason or Helene.

"It's Helene," Jay said. "She's all right now, but she's in the hospital. There's been some terrible violence."

"Tell me quickly," Petra said.

He told her all he knew. He had given the driver orders to take them to the hospital. Once there, he created quite a stir, for the news of his accident had traveled there, too, and, moreover, the entire staff knew about the beautiful woman who was in critical condition with a gunshot wound in her upper chest.

Since he was still the boss, Jay got immediate attention, first from the surgeon who had treated Darcie's gunshot wound. They were told that it was touch-and-go. Darcie had lost a lot of blood. The wound in itself was not fatal, but she was weakened by loss of blood.

"Her chances?" Petra asked.

"It's hard to say," the surgeon said. "There is an additional complication. She seems quite despondent. During brief periods of consciousness, she kept saying something about being too late. It seems to be that the lady is suffering great feelings of guilt and does not particularly want to live."

From her sketchy information, Petra was puzzled, as were the Canal Zone police. In that hectic time, she seemed to be having information thrown at her from every side. She knew that the Panamanian general, Juan Esteban, had been shot dead and that Darcie was wounded and that Helene was somehow involved and she couldn't get it all together. But one name was conspicuously absent from the reports: Guy Simel.

Darcie had said that she was too late. Did that mean that something had happened to Helene? Torn between the desire to go to Helene and wanting to hear about Darcie, she asked the surgeon about Helene's condition.

"The young lady is going to be all right," he said. "She's under the care of Doctor Foster. She was suffering a bit of shock and hysteria, and I understand, although I have not had time to check, that Doctor Foster is keeping her under sedation for the moment."

Relieved, but still concerned, Petra returned her attention to Dari. "You say she lost much blood. Have you considered a transfusion?"

"We have thought about it," he said, "but it's a very risky procedure. We don't have the facilities nor the time to match blood types. It's quite complicated."

"I know," Petra said. "I'm a nurse. I've followed Dr. Landsteiner's work. Darcie and I are sisters, doctor, and although there's no way, short of testing, to know for sure, it's a good bet that we're of the same blood types."

"Would you be willing, then, to give blood? You know the risks."

"Yes, if it is necessary."

"Let's give it an hour or so, see how she comes along."

"I'll stay here," Petra said. "And now, if you please, I'd like to talk to your Doctor Foster."

Dr. Carl Foster had been in Panama just under a year, having come there directly from his medical training in San Francisco. He was an earnest young man of medium height, unkempt, light-colored hair, a clean shaven face and a pleasing manner.

"I can assure you, Mrs. Burton," he said, when he'd been introduced, "that Miss Freneau is in quite good health. She was semi-hysterical when she was brought to me, and considering the circumstances, I can understand why. It was she who witnessed the shootings and it was she who summoned help for Miss Moncrief." He frowned. "There is one thing I don't understand. She had been administered some sort of drug. Short of exhaustive tests, I can't say what the drug was. Before I could sedate her, I had to be sure that the drug had passed out of her bloodstream, and for a while she was quite agitated. However, she's sleeping now."

"I want to see her as soon as she awakens," Petra said.

"The police want to question her," Foster said. "I've been putting them off. Actually," he said with a shy smile, "I think she could be awakened quite easily now. Having you with her might do her good."

"Yes," Petra said.

They went into Helene's room. The doctor awakened her gently and she came into consciousness slowly, then with a scream and a start. Petra held her in her arms, whispering to her.

"Oh, thank God!" Helene said. "Thank God you're here. He killed her. He killed my mother."

"Hush," Petra hissed, caressing Helene's cheek. "Hush, she's not dead."

"Not dead?" Helene gasped. "She was still and there was blood and he shot her and the man tried to—tried to—"

"Yes, dear," Petra said. "We must know. Can you talk about it now? Did they harm you?"

"I don't know," Helene said, blushing furiously.

"Doctor," Petra asked Foster, "did you conduct a complete examination?"

"I did," Foster said.

"And was there sexual abuse?" Petra asked, holding her breath for the answer.

"There was nothing to indicate it," Foster said quietly. "Since Miss Freneau was nude and in a stage of drugged shock, the question occurred to me. However, the maidenly membrane is intact, and there were no traces of semen in or near the vagina."

Helene had tried to hide her face during this calm discussion. "Did you understand that, dear?" Petra asked. "Nothing happened to you."

"But mother—I mean Darcie—"

"She's hurt very badly," Petra said, "and I must go to her. Do you think you can be a brave girl?"

"Yes, now that you're here."

"All right. But I want to know one thing. Was it Guy?"

"It's all so vague," she said, shaking her head. "It seems like a bad dream. I couldn't move. And then this small and oily man was doing things to me and he was—oh, God, he was going to—when she came in and there was a huge explosion and he fell and I couldn't move and—oh, yes, I remember. Guy shot m-m-Darcie."

"That's enough for now," Petra said. "Don't think about it. The doctor will give you something to let you sleep and we'll be here, all of us, Jay—"

"He's all right?" Helene asked.

"Tired, dirty, but all right. We'll be here with you and we're going to do everything we can to make Darcie well."

"Mrs. Burton," Dr. Foster said. "The police. I can't put them off much longer."

"They can't talk to her if she's asleep," Petra said. "I'll have my husband talk with them."

She went out to Jay. "It was Guy," she said. "Somehow he drugged Helene. Darcie killed Esteban because he was trying to rape Helene, and then Guy shot Darcie."

"That sonofabitch!" Jay growled.

"I'm going to Darcie," Petra said.

"Yes, I suppose you must. But Petra—"

"Yes."

"This transfusion—"

"It's all right. I'm healthy. I suppose I'll be passing along some malaria bugs to her, but she has had malaria, too. It's quite a simple procedure. I'll be weak for a while, but it won't hurt me."

"Take care," he said.

"I have much to live for," Petra said, with a smile. "Keep the police away from Helene for a while. The poor girl has had a terrible experience."

Petra found the surgeon in Darcie's room. Darcie was breathing with difficulty, shallowly, her face ashen. Petra had seen many people near death and she recognized the condition. She bent low over Darcie.

"Darcie," she said. "Darcie, you must listen to me."

There was a flicker of an eyelid. "Do you hear me?"

Darcie moaned softly and tried to move her head.

"Helene is fine. She's safe. You were in time. Do you hear me? You were in time."

There was a flicker as one eyelid raised, a twinge in the lips which could have been an attempt at a smile.

"She loves you, Darcie," Petra said urgently. "She needs you. She wants her mother, Darcie. Her mother."

"Uhhhh," Darcie moaned weakly.

"Doctor, will you please set up for the transfusion?" Petra asked.

Now she lay on a hard bed next to Darcie's, in a hospital gown, the prick of the needle in her arm, the strange and eerie feeling as her life's blood pumped out, traveled the tubing, dripped slowly into Darcie's veins. It took a long time, and she felt the weakness begin, the lightness of head, the urge to sleep.

Much later, she walked unsteadily into Darcie's room. There was a touch of color in the once-ashen cheeks.

"Now we can only wait," the surgeon said.

11

WHILE CANAL ZONE and Panamanian police searched for Guy Simel, a small fishing boat chugged its way down the coast, staying close in. Guy spent a lot of time on deck to escape the stench which permeated the boat, making his plans. He would have his erstwhile confederate in drug traffic put him ashore in the Colombian town of Jurado, for he wanted to be rid of the two men as quickly as possible. They were, he knew, not to be trusted, and he carried a considerable sum of cash. However, he also carried the Belgian automatic, which he displayed with intent, wearing it in his belt.

The area to the west of the canal, mountainous jungle, had resisted penetration by white men for centuries. Small towns and settlements were limited to coastal areas and to navigable streams. Although the distance from the canal to the Colombian border was not great in miles—no more than two hundred—travel by land was impossible. At the time of the revolution, Colombia was helpless because of the difficulty of moving troops through that great and impenetrable wilderness.

Viewing the Pacific coast of the isthmus, Guy shuddered to think of what would have happened to him had he been forced to flee Panama City by land.

Progress was slow. Now and again, the engine of the fishing boat would break down, and the boat would float dead on the water in stifling heat while the two men cursed and slaved in the engine compartment. Gradually, however, distance grew behind the boat, and the coast-hugging voyage brought them to the Golfo de San Miguel, where the boat's owner proposed to put into Patiño for fuel. Guy was watchful, spent the night on the boat alone while his two companions stayed ashore to come back in the early morning hours singing in drunken happiness. The trip continued the next morning, with the Colombian border and Jurado only about sixty miles away.

Perhaps it was tiredness or the nearness of his goal which caused Guy to slacken his vigil. At any rate, he dozed, sitting on the oily deck, and awoke to find the boat's owner looking at him over the sights of his own automatic.

"Give me the gun," Guy said, holding out his hand.

"Perhaps we can make a trade," the swarthy man said. "Your gun for what you carry in your belt."

"Eh, Pedro," Guy said with a smile. "Haven't I paid you well?"

"I think you will pay me better," Pedro said, smiling back at Guy.

"Sure, sure," Guy said. "I'll increase it a bit. Now give me the gun and let's get going. How much further to Jurado?"

"Only a little further, *Señor* Simel," Pedro said. "But the last few miles are the most expensive."

Guy knew that he was in a bad spot. "As an old friend, Pedro, will you leave me enough money to make my way to Cartagena, where I can contact my bankers? You wouldn't want to leave me with nothing down here on the south side of Colombia, where I would be stranded."

"Well, we will see," the man grinned.

"Tell you what. I'll give you half of what I have left. That will leave me just enough to buy horses for the trip to Cartagena. Agreed?"

"Let us count it together, *señor*," Pedro said.

With resignation and some concern, Guy removed his money belt and began to take out the packets of greenbacks. Pedro watched with greedy eyes. "Pedro, I've always dealt squarely with you," Guy said. "Now I'm asking you to be square with me. Look, I'll do better than half. Three-quarters. And I'll send you more when I get back to France. I'll send it to the bank in Panama City in your name, and all you'll have to do is go in and draw it out. It is a deal?"

"Well, you will be far away," Pedro said. "And perhaps your memory will fail you."

"No, no, I promise. Here, take three-quarters. I'll be strapped, but I'll have enough left to get to Cartagena." He pushed the larger pile of bills across the deck toward Pedro's feet.

"I think we take it all," Pedro's companion said.

Pedro nodded. "Yes, I think that would be best."

"Now, look here," Guy said, getting to his feet. Pedro casually slapped him across the face with the pistol, sending him sprawling to the deck. He was not hurt badly, only stunned. But he could do nothing as Pedro and his companion counted the bills and split them fifty-fifty. Then, with Pedro holding the pistol on him, the other man eased the boat in toward the shore where jungle began in mangrove swamps and climbed the hills rising above the shoreline.

"Now you will jump into the water," Pedro said, brandishing the pistol.

"You're killing me, Pedro. A friend. You and I worked together. You always got your share."

"But why was my share always so small and yours
so large?" Pedro asked with a smile which showed his
rotting teeth. *"Adios, Señor* Simel. Perhaps you will not
die. Perhaps you can walk to Jurado, no?"

Well, there was that hope, and if he refused to leave
the boat alive he might leave it dead. Taking a deep
breath he jumped into the water. He was about fifty
yards out from the beginning of the mangroves. He
swam, expecting to feel the smash of a bullet in his
back at any moment. But he gained the shelter of the
trees, crawled, swam, pulled himself shoreward, finally
reached a semblance of high ground, but had to wade
swamps for what seemed to be ages before he was
out of the mangroves and into high jungle which swept
away and up before his eyes, climbing the hills. He
rested. He knew that he had only a slim chance of making his way through that jungle to the nearest settlement which, his memory told him from having studied
maps, was Puerto Piña. He started out resolutely but
was soon near exhaustion from the heat, the sheer
labor of pushing through the dense growth, the attacks
of mosquitoes.

It was growing late in the day when he came across
a trail and, with hope, began to follow it along the
slope of a hill. He knew that some of the Indian tribes
of the unexplored areas of Panama were quite fierce
and always unfriendly, but he knew also that he would
not survive long in the jungle alone. He had his
watch and his ring. Perhaps he could bribe Indians
to take him into civilization with those two items. He
stumbled down the trail, falling now and and then.
And then they appeared around him with a suddenness
which caused him to cry out, little, swarthy men with
oily black hair, wearing nothing more than loincloths,
their skins oiled against the insects.

They were grimly silent, five of them having appeared out of the jungle, two on the trail behind him,

three in front. "Friend," he gasped. "I come as a friend."

One of them, his face expressionless, aimed his bow at Guy and drew it back. The arrow tip, Guy knew, was poisoned. "Friend," he said. "Look, friend." He took out his watch, swung it on its golden chain. "Yours," he said, "if you take me into the nearest town."

One of the Indians came near, took the watch from Guy's hand and stepped back. Guy took off his heavy ring. "Yours, if you take me into the town."

The same Indian, obviously a leader, stepped forward and held out his hand. "Only if you take me into town," Guy said. He saw the kick coming and could not dodge it. It took him in the stomach and he sat down heavily. The Indian held out his hand and Guy gave him the ring. The Indian pointed at Guy's boots. Guy began to take them off. Barefooted, with only his socks, he stood.

"Take friend into town," he said. "Friend give you much money."

The leader silently pointed at Guy's bush jacket. He took it off and handed it over, then followed the same procedure for his shirt and his pants, standing now in his drawers. Then they pushed him and he went with them down the trail to come into a rude village of thatched huts. He was pushed roughly into one of the huts. He sank down onto a molding mass of palm fronds and tried to beat off the mosquitoes which found his exposed skin to be very attractive. He discovered a ragged and filthy blanket and wrapped it around him to keep some of the mosquitoes away.

As darkness fell, the Indians were having some kind of ceremony outside around open fires. A young girl, naked to the waist, came into the hut with a wooden bowl of food. The chunks of meat were tainted. He could not eat.

"I am a friend," he told the girl, who seemed to be

intrigued by his pale white skin. "Take me into the nearest town and I give you much money. You buy nice white man's things."

She giggled. She went away and came back alone. Outside the others were dancing and making sing-song sounds around the fire. The girl carried water and he drank greedily. "You take me town?" he asked.

He had not known, to that time, whether or not any of them spoke Spanish. But when he asked, again, "You take me town?" she shook her head.

"Mañana," she said.

"Ah, tomorrow," he said. "Good, good. I give you much money."

She sat on her heels close to him and put out her hand to feel his white skin, which was, by now, well pocked with insect bites. She giggled. Her hand went down and, through his drawers, seized his penis. She made a two-syllable sound and showed her stained teeth. Good God! Guy thought. *Not now.* He had never expected to see the time when he was not interested, but not now, not with a thousand thorns in his feet from walking without boots, not with his entire body itching with insect bites, his head pounding.

She found the opening in his drawers and pulled out his penis. There was a glow of red light coming from an open fire just outside the hut. She giggled and rolled the limp instrument between her fingers—and the damned thing responded. Amazed, he looked at it and saw it grow as if it had a mind of its own. She slowly skinned back the prepuce and giggled as it grew in her hands until it was a rigid staff. She made that two-syllable sound and lay back on the rotting mass of palm fronds, jerking off her scanty loin covering.

"All right," he said. "If that's what you want. You take me town *mañana?"*

She giggled and reached for his hard staff. He sighed. It might be in the mood, but he wasn't. But it had to be done. He crawled between her sturdy legs. She smelled of rank grease and things unspoken, but she was a woman, if a young one, and she knew what the old tallywhacker was for. She seized it and moved it up and down in her hot and slick slit until it was oiled. And then, making that two-syllable sound, she jerked up to him, driving him into her.

Well, hell, he was thinking, *it's better than being cooked and eaten by the savages.* And he began to match her eagerness, giving her pleasure and, incredibly, beginning to be interested when he heard a guttural, screaming voice behind him and a man was leaping at him to jerk him from between the girl's legs and send a battering blow to his face. He yelped in pain and tried to crawl out the door, but the Indian rode him out, he crawling on his hands and knees. The man was screaming and yelling, and the others came on the run. They were in a frenzy.

The man who had pulled him out of the smelly saddle of the young girl was making an impassioned speech and waving around a mean-looking knife. Guy was sitting on the damp ground, saying, "Friend, friend." The Indian jerked him to his feet. Two fat old women came running, carrying knives and a basin. Guy was thrust to his knees. The women poured scalding water over his head and attacked his hair, cutting, shaving it with the razor-sharp knives until he was bald except for a fringe around the edge. And then there was another steaming basin and he was screaming as the scalding and sticky mass came to sear him, the pain unbearable, the entire top of his denuded head covered with the bubbling, sticky mass and as he screamed and tried to escape the hands of two strong men who held him he saw another woman pour feathers into the tarlike mess atop his head and he was mindless in his pain, the hot, scalding mass running down into his eyes to blind his left eye and burn a scalding streak down his nose and his face and then he was on his feet and a jabbering woman was pulling on his suddenly limp penis and a stab of pain went through him as it was severed at the roots. He screamed, and with a yell of hatred, the woman thrust his severed organ into his open mouth.

Mindless, screaming, but unable to get sound past the disgusting gag which extended far back into his throat, he felt knives being thrust through his shoulders, under the tendons there, and vines were pushed through the holes and he was hoisted on a hastily erected tripod of stripped saplings to hang by his shoulder tendons, his mind now approaching insanity but still conscious as the terrible pains caused him to writhe, thus increasing the pain and then he was drawing up his feet from the ever-increasing agony of the fire which had been built under him.

He lived for most of the night, drifting in and out of coma into incredible pain. And then he died, not even knowing that the cause of his death was his defilement of the village idiot, a girl of moronic mentality who was, because of her affliction, held in awe and reverence, her nubile young body reserved for the elders of the tribe, and then only during sacred ceremonies.

12

AT THE HOSPITAL, Jay was taken in tow by Dr. Foster and a strong-looking nurse. He first soaked away mud and jungle stains in a tub, and then, his clothing having been taken, dressed in a short hospital gown, he was attacked by the grim-faced nurse armed with an antiseptic which burned like fire when she rubbed it into his numerous welts, scratches, and abrasions. He insisted on seeing Petra, who was recovering nicely from having given blood. She told him that Darcie's condition was still critical, but stable. Helene was sleeping, young Dr. Foster looking in on her quite often.

Then Jay allowed himself to sleep and it was sheer heaven—even in a narrow and hard hospital bed. Antonia went home to check on Jason and found him to be quite happy, for he'd been told that his father was all right and would be home shortly. The day was spent. Antonia had things to do, but they would have to wait for the morning. Exhausted, she went to bed early.

Colonel Arthus Taylor had also had quite a day. In the absence of Burton, he'd been called when Canal

Zone police discovered the potentially internationally scandalous situation in Guy Simel's house and he'd spent most of the day doing his best to hush it up. The last thing he needed, when he was on the verge of taking charge of the canal, was a tense relationship with the new Panama Republic. He pointed out to members of the government that the general had been killed with his pants down—in the process, apparently, of debauching a young girl who had been drugged, so that there was no problem with the Panamanians, who were just as eager to avoid a scandal which would rock their young regime.

There was those in the Zone, however, God-fearing, Bible reading men, who questioned the involvement of the chief engineer's young ward and his wife's sister. Their fine religious reasoning was that since two women who were connected with Burton were involved, Burton could not be totally innocent. It was the old, old doctrine of guilt by association.

Taylor threatened to bring reprisals in the form of the most unfavorable assignments. "The shitty end of the stick will be in your hand during the rest of your stay in Panama," he told one army officer on detached duty with the engineering section, "if you breathe so much as one word of this to the press." With others he used logic. "The canal is the thing and it's too important, too big, to allow the ideal to be besmirched with petty scandal."

He ordered an all-out effort to apprehend Guy Simel, when the police finally were able to question Helene and got the whole story. And then, tired, looking forward to being the most powerful man in the Zone, he went to his home.

But there, too, he had a situation. The young girl whom Antonia had forced upon him had been nothing but trouble. Not that she didn't do her work. No. She was a good worker, kept the house spotless and was

always clean and neat herself. No, it was something
else.

Taylor had three servants: a cook, a man who slept
in a small room over the stables, and Leonela Lopez,
the housekeeper and maid. The cook was an older
woman who, when it became dark, took to her room
off the kitchen and could not be awakened by anything short of an act of Congress. Leonela, however,
seemed never to sleep. No matter what time he came
home, she was waiting for him. And it became quite
obvious, from almost the very first, that she wanted
something more than an employer-servant relationship.
She quite obviously and openly flirted, made it understandable that she was willing to serve her master in
ways not covered by the employment agreement, and
although Taylor could not fail to note the very feminine
form under her clothing, he was not the type of man
to take advantage of a young servant girl.

Leonela was growing desperate. Never before had
she failed to interest a man when she had the opportunity and the desire to interest him. However, she'd done
everything but crawl naked into this white man's bed.
She'd used her most seductive voice, her most studied
poses, her most flirtatious glances, her dark eyes telling
the tale of passion through her long lashes, and this
white-haired colonel merely nodded and said, "Thank
you, Leonela, that will be all."

She had gone to him one night in a very brief
nightgown as he sat reading in his study. "Colonel,
sir," she'd said, "I fix you coffee before I go to bed?"

"No, thank you," he said.

"Tea, maybe. A drink of whisky?"

"No, nothing," he said.

"Maybe you just lonely and like Leonela to keep you
company for a while?" she asked, moving so that she
stood in front of him, for he had not bothered to look
up. But now he looked up and saw that her white,

fragile sleeping costume was very revealing of the young and taut breasts and that through the thinness he could see the dark vee of her mound of Venus.

"Thank you, Leonela," he said, "but I have work to do. Now you run along to bed."

Damn, she thought. *What am I going to have to do?* And on the night after so much had happened she, unaware of the events, of the fact that her protector was dead and the man who had promised to pay her $100 was no longer in the city, decided that the most drastic measures were called for. She undressed and crawled into Taylor's bed and waited there, sneaking just a little drink or two of his whisky to keep herself awake. It was late when he came home, and he did not come directly to bed. For the longest time she heard him moving around in the house and then, at last, the door to the bedroom opened. He came in, head down, and did not see her at first. Then he saw her and froze.

"What on God's earth!" he asked.

"Colonel, sir," she whispered, looking at him through those long lashes.

"Get out of my bed this instant!" he ordered. "And I must ask you, Leonela, to find other employment."

"But colonel, sir," she said, becoming slightly worried, "it is only because I love you so much. I want to do nice things for you, sir." Slowly she let the sheet fall away to expose her jutting breasts, small, excitingly dark, tipped by dark red moons centered with jutting, long nipples.

"Get your clothes on, damn you!" Taylor yelled. He left the room. "When I come back, in three minutes, you're to be dressed and ready to leave my house."

She could not understand it. She got out of the bed, wondering how she'd failed. She dressed quickly and went to find him in his study. "Colonel, I am sorry," she said, still unwilling to give up. "You must forgive a foolish young girl who has fallen in love with you." And her ability to cry at will was put to use.

"All right," he said. "I guess you understand now. I tell you what, Leonela, if you think you can behave yourself, you may keep your position. But the next time you make one of these childish attempts to seduce me, that's it—do you understand? Hell's bells, girl, you're only a child. You could get me into all kinds of trouble."

"I would never get you in trouble, sir," she sobbed. If he felt kindly enough toward her to talk with her, let her stay, perhaps he was weakening and she could still get her hundred dollars. "If you want to kiss me, to make love to me, no one would ever know, for I would not hurt the man I love."

"All right, that's it," Taylor said. "Go pack your clothing. I'll put you up in a hotel for the night."

"You can't mean it, sir," she wailed, her tears becoming genuine.

"I *do* mean it. Now go get packed. I'll give you just fifteen minutes and if you're not ready I'll call a policeman to help you."

Well, she knew it was over. She had failed, and she was not used to failure. Her lovely little body had never before failed to interest a man who had seen it. Quick Latin anger changed her. "Lover of little boys!" she spat at him in Spanish. "We should have known you would not be interested in a real woman." The "we" slipped out. She knew it was a mistake when he looked at her, eyes narrowing.

"We?" he asked. He rose and came toward her.

"All right," she said. "I will pack and I will go."

"Hold it," he said. "Who put you up to this?"

"I am leaving."

He seized her arm. "Not before you tell me what you meant," he said, his voice harsh.

"You let me go," she said. "I have powerful friends."

"And these powerful friends sent you to me?" he asked. "Did Antonia have anything to do with this?

Were you supposed to seduce me and then run out yelling rape?"

She was shocked by his accurate guess. She went silent. "You will tell me," he said. "Or I will send for the police and they will put you in jail." She was, after all, only a child and, he suspected, could be frightened. "I will tell them that you plotted against me, and they'll put you in a cell all alone and keep you there until you tell who put you up to this."

"Please, Colonel," she begged. "I meant no harm. Just let me go. I will bother you no more."

"I will let you go when you tell me who sent you to me," he said. And when she did not speak, he started pulling her toward the front door. "So, we go to the police station."

"No, no," she cried. "I will tell you. *Señor* Simel, he promised to give me one hundred dollars."

"Simel? Why?"

"The Yankee lady, *Senorita* Antonia, she wanted it," Leonela said. "Now may I go?"

"Antonia wanted what?" he demanded.

"I was to tell the police that you raped me," she said sullenly.

"Ah, and it was Antonia's idea?"

"Yes. *Señor* Simel was to pay me. He promised me. And the general would have seen to it that he did."

"Which general is that?" Taylor asked.

"General Juan Esteban."

"You poor little wench," Taylor said. "You've done it all for nothing. General Esteban is dead and Guy Simel is a fugitive from the law." And Antonia? He had no idea that she was so vengeful. True, he'd lied to her, but that didn't give her the right to try to ruin him. Hell, he'd taken nothing from her that she hadn't given quite willingly to God only knew how many other men. Well, he'd see to her. She was not going to get away with it, by God—not when he was on the

verge of one of the greatest achievements any army engineer had ever accomplished.

He watched as Leonela packed her few belongings.
Then he took her to a hotel and left her with instructions to stay there until he told her it was all right to
leave. And then, knowing that Burton and his wife
were at the hospital, he went to the Burton house
and banged on the door until a servant came, frightened and sleepy, to let him in. He gave the woman orders to wake Miss Antonia and waited, pacing angrily.

She came in with her hair up, wrapped in a dressing gown. "I hope there's good reason for this, Art,"
she said icily. Their relationship had disintegrated into
a coldness. She had not been to him in weeks.

"Damned good reason," he said. "I'm onto your little
game. The little Panamanian bitch confessed, Antonia.
And she's willing to tell her story to the police and in
court."

Antonia laughed. "Well, well, you're smarter than I
thought, but still pretty stupid. So you're going to go
into court?"

"I don't want trouble with Burton," he said. "Here's
what you're going to do—"

"Now just a minute," Antonia said sharply. "Don't
think for one minute, you strutting ass, that you can
tell me what to do."

"You will leave Panama on the first ship," Taylor
said. "And you will not come back as long as I am
here."

He looked so funny, Antonia thought. *What had she
ever seen in him? And this foolish little man thought
that he was in control.* "My, my," she said. "Our little
boy is angry." She whirled and sat down, exposing a
length of lovely leg. "While I tremble in fear, tell me
how you're going to force me to do this."

"If you don't, I'll have the girl tell the whole story,"
he said. "How you plotted with Simel and Esteban to

frame me. It will rub off onto your entire family. I'm sure you don't want that."

"No, I will not allow that," she said. "In fact, my dear colonel, had not our little girl of the streets moved tonight, as she apparently did, I was going to withdraw her tomorrow."

"Well, I choose not to believe that, and you're too late. The harm's done," he said. "Now do you leave Panama or do I bring out the whole sordid story?"

Before she answered, she reached for a decanter and poured a glass of brandy, offering one to him. He shook his head angrily and she sipped. "I will leave Panama, little man, when I am good and goddamned ready, and not before."

"You leave me no choice," he said, white-faced, becoming a bit unsure of himself in view of her calmness.

"Actually," Antonia said, "I'm ashamed of myself. I lowered myself to your level, Art. You were amusing and fairly competent in bed, and I should have just let it go at that instead of taking it on myself to teach you that lying to a woman is not advisable. Now here's what you're going to do. You're going to haul your great, boring ass out of this house, send that poor girl back to wherever it is she wants to go, and forget the whole incident."

"Never," he said. "You attacked my honor."

"Honor?" she laughed. "Oh, well. You want to make it public, then?"

"I've given you your choices. Leave and don't come back, or I will let it be known how the stepdaughter of the chief engineer conspired against an officer and a representative of the United States government."

"Well," Antonia said. She finished the bit of brandy and stood up. "If we're to have a public scandal, let's make it an interesting one." Quickly she threw off her dressing gown and seized her nightdress, ripping it to expose one of her breasts. Then she threw back her head and screamed. "Help, oh, help! Oh, help, he's killing me!"

She smiled. "There's young Jason and two servants in the house. They'll be here within seconds." And then, while he was frozen, she threw herself on him and began to struggle so that to someone running into the room, it would appear that she was trying to escape his grasp when, in fact, it was she who was clinging and he who was trying to push her away.

He thought quickly, panic rising. "Please," he said, "all right, you win. I'll go."

"And forget the whole thing?"

"Yes, yes, damn you."

There was a patter of footsteps in the hall. Antonia quickly picked up her wrapper and put it on. "Remember, dear colonel, that I can cause you more trouble than you could ever imagine."

"Señorita," the maid cried, running into the room. "I heard screaming."

"Oh?" Antonia asked. "Oh, I'm sure what you heard was me laughing. Colonel Taylor just told me something quite funny."

"You are all right?" the woman asked, looking from one to the other.

"Don't I look all right?" Antonia asked. "Go on back to bed. I'm sorry I awakened you."

"Yes, yes," the woman said doubtfully, backing away.

"And now, Colonel Taylor, you were about to say good night," Antonia said.

"Yes."

"I would advise you," she said, as he walked stiff-backed toward the door, "to reconcile yourself with your wife. You're a bit naïve for modern women."

But she was not proud of herself. She poured another glass of brandy—a full one this time—and sat there in the parlor, huddled into a chair, her feet under her. Not proud at all. She had joined them—the schemers, the people who preyed on others. She felt dirtied. And, as she sat and drank without feeling the effects, she thought about her life. She had used various excuses to do as she pleased, to give her highly excitable nature a vent, and that vent invariably took the form of sexual activity. Of that she was not ashamed, only of some of the things which had resulted from it: the continual deceiving of her mother who was, after all, only human loving her Jay, being separated from him by circumstances and then breaking the rules a bit by loving him while she was married to Roger D'Art.

Of all of them, Helene was, perhaps, the most worthwhile, with her decent peasant background, her genuine sweetness, her great love for the entire family. And look what had almost happened to Helene!

What would she do? She didn't know. Stay with them, help if she could. At least until Darcie recovered and her mother and Jay left the hot and humid place which seemed to bring out the worst in everyone. And then? Well, there was a wide world out there, and she had some money. Her music. Suddenly she had the urge to play, and she went to the piano and began softly, then was seized by it, taken by the music, sending it thundering out in a flood of sadness and emotion until her fingers found a new and powerful theme which seemed to grow magically and developed as she repeated it again and again, tears coursing silently down her cheeks.

She did not know that Jason had come into the room until, spent, she let her arms fall to her sides and sat there, head hanging, hair falling.

"Boy!" Jason said. "You sure play loud!"

"Oh, Jason," she said. "I'm so sorry I awakened you."

"I don't mind," he said. "Hey, that was great. It was real sad."

"Yes," she said, "but that's all over now. There's none of us ever going to have reason to be sad again."

She went to him and hugged him. "And now, young man, back to bed."

"My dad's all right?"

"He's fine. He'll be home to see you in the morning."

13

TEDDY ROOSEVELT WAS furious. He had spent a long weekend with his closest advisers and friends at Sagamore Hill going over the situation in Panama. Now he was back in Washington.

"This whole situation came about because we tried to run the job with a committee," he told the men whom he had gathered in the White House. He paced in front of the windows, a big, active man who seemed to radiate energy. "We find a man who can make the dirt fly, and we don't give him enough authority. I have on my desk a half-dozen communications from Burton complaining about the quality of steel from a primary supplier. And was anything done about it?"

John Hay, a sharp-eyed little man with a massive and bristly beard, cleared this throat. "The attorney general is presently drawing up charges against the Roethke company and its officials."

"Bully," Teddy said, with some sarcasm. "We lock the barn door now, eh? And we lose a good man. Yes, Burton is definitely quitting. I don't like it. The man is a leader, but he has chosen to desert his troops just when the battle is at a height. Well, so be it. But

no more committees. I've called you all here for one
reason. You and you and you I have appointed to the
Canal Commission, but don't let it go to your heads.
You're there for one reason: because Congress says
the job has to be done by a committee. But understand
this. You will agree with the man whom I put in
charge, without question, without reservation. You will
agree or you will be immediately replaced. Hell, you
can't fight a war with a committee. One man. One man
gives the orders. And that man is going to make the
dirt fly, believe me."

All eyes turned toward a serene and dignified man
with white hair who sat, dressed in a white suit, with
one leg crossed casually, his back straight, his lips
unsmiling.

"Yes, gentlemen, that's the man," Roosevelt said.
"The czar of Panama. His word is law. When he says
'frog,' everyone jumps. And we'll get the job done."

"Hear, hear," John Hay said. The others nodded
and joined in the "hear, hears." Teddy Roosevelt
angry was an awesome sight. There was not a man
present who would have questioned his decision. Seeing him aroused, they were sure that all those who had
conspired to defraud the government would be punished.
They were sure, to a man, that not even that august
body, the Congress of the United States, would dare
stand in Teddy's way.

Perhaps a few of them were in doubt about the ability of the man whom Teddy had chosen to be the ab-
solute dictator within the Canal Zone, although he had
a fine record in the Corps of Engineers. Perhaps some
felt sympathy for Colonel Arthus Taylor, who would
be notified shortly that his verbal appointment to be
chief engineer in Panama had been rescinded and that
the man who would reap the harvest of glory was another army career man, Colonel George Washington
Goethals, who sat with his legs crossed and watched
with hidden amusement as Teddy laid down the law.

14

For over seventy-two hours Darcie Moncrief hovered between life and death. Once more Petra lay beside her, a complicated grouping of tubes connecting her veins with Darcie's, and felt that slowly growing weakness which is the result of giving blood. Helene was fully recovered, her full attention now being given to Darcie. She insisted on alternating sitting with Darcie and it was her presence which finally burned through into Darcie's pain-hazed mind to give her the will to fight. In fact, it was one word which made Darcie weep—and not with pain.

The word was "mother," spoken softly into Darcie's ear. And repeated until Darcie heard and smiled and felt the pressure of Helene's hand in hers.

After spending one night in the hospital and praying fervently that his stay in the mosquito-ridden jungle would not bring on another attack of malaria, Jay went back to his work, directing that the bridges built with Roethke steel be dismantled. His resignation had been accepted with a cool letter from Teddy Roosevelt, but he no longer cared. He knew his contribution. That was enough. Now all he wanted was to live in peace and comfort with his son and his wife.

He greeted the advance party of Goethal's new command with politeness and did everything he could to make the changeover orderly. Two of the men impressed him very much: Lieutenant-Colonel David D. Gaillard, who would, under Goethals, be in charge of Culebra; and a navy man who would be a sort of chief of staff under Goethals. It quickly was brought out that the navy man knew of him, and when he asked a shyly worded question about his sister-in-law, Jay told him that Darcie had been wounded badly while saving his young ward from a savage attack. The man seemed to be quite preoccupied for a while after that and soon asked to be excused.

Thus it was that Darcie awoke, very weak, to see the face of David Russell looking down on her. She saw his slightly sunken eyes looking at her and that silly, dear part down the center of his head. He was holding a hat in his hand.

She closed her eyes. "So," she muttered weakly, "I am dead and dreaming."

"She's still very ill," Petra told David. "I'm not sure she recognized you."

"Are you dead, too, Petra?" Darcie asked.

"No, dear. We're not dead. We're all very much alive, and Admiral Russell is here to see you."

"David?" she asked, opening her eyes.

"I hope you don't mind," David said uncertainly. "I—I wanted to see you, to tell you to get well."

"Kind," Darcie said, closing her eyes.

"May I come again?" David asked Petra. Petra put her finger to her lips and led him out of the room.

"I'd like to see her again," David said. "If it won't upset her."

Petra, sensing something, asked, "Should it upset her, admiral?"

He tried to form words, turning his hat in his hands. "It might. You see——"

Petra smiled. "Admiral, I will leave it to you. I'm sure you'll do the right thing."

"Yes, thank you," he said.

He had come for curiosity, no more. He had been impelled to come, for Burton had told him that it was still a question whether Darcie would live. He told himself that he wanted to see her one more time, to convince himself that he'd been right in breaking off with her, for on long and lonely nights he could not forget her, and it was often difficult to convince himself that he'd been right.

And it was a mistake, seeing her. He knew that as he went out of the hospital, for he could never forget her.

Never had a patient so devoted a staff of nurses. The overworked nursing staff of the hospital gladly took the family's offer to have Petra, Antonia, and Helene alternate sitting with Darcie, and she never opened her eyes without seeing one of their faces.

When next David Russell came, Darcie was able to stay awake for hours at a time and was eating well. The terrible wound had been repaired during two operations, the last of which required still another blood transfusion from Petra. But her recovery from the second operation was much more swift, and now it was apparent that if infection didn't set in, she would live. She now had heard the full story and she knew that another chapter in her life had ended. Guy Simel was gone and would never dare show his face in Panama or the United States again. And Helene called her, quite naturally now, "mother." It was mother this and mother that, the girl seemingly taking every opportunity to use the word. And she also had the care of two of the finest doctors: the surgeon who had repaired her wound and the bright and handsome young Dr. Carl Foster.

Darcie was not too ill to notice, however, that Dr. Foster's visits with her always coincided with Helene's presence, and, as the days went on, she smiled as she saw the way the young man looked at Helene. She was pleased to see Helene blush prettily when Foster paid her a compliment and did not mind at all that the doctor's attention was more on her daughter than on the patient.

And then David was back. Helene had fixed her hair and she looked quite pretty, even with her sunken eyes and dark circles and wan complexion. He brought flowers. She introduced him to Helene and surprised Helene by telling the admiral, "This is my dear and sweet daughter."

There had been much discussion among Helene, Petra, and Antonia about the mysterious admiral. Antonia had heard a bit in Washington about a romance involving the Moncrief woman, as Darcie was called in some circles, and they speculated endlessly about what had happened. So, although Helene was naturally curious, she left the room to leave them alone.

"It's so nice of you to visit me, David," Darcie said.

"It seems foolish to say it, in view of what you're suffering," he said, with a wry smile, "but I've been going through hell these last few days, Darcie."

"I'm sorry."

"Are you feeling well enough to listen to some foolish talk from a stupid old man?"

"You're neither stupid nor old."

"Stupid to let you get away from me. I should have stopped you from coming to Panama."

"David, David," she said. "I can't blame you. I know what you thought. I've always wished for a chance to talk with you, to explain."

"There is no need for explanation, other than from me," he said. "I let a false masculine pride influence me, Darcie."

"I will tell you. From the time you asked me to marry you, no man touched me. And most certainly not General Esteban. You saw me dancing and—"

"I saw you dancing and celebrating the new republic," he said, "and I jumped to conclusions. I was afraid, Darcie, afraid of what my fellow officers would say. I don't give a damn about them anymore. Darcie, can you ever forgive me, give me another chance?"

"With all my heart," Darcie said.

And now that she had double reason to live, she astounded everyone by getting up and walking weakly, leaning on Helene's shoulder.

When Darcie was well enough, she was moved to the Burton house to a bright and airy room. By then Goethals was in Panama and Jay was going through his last few days as a canal employee. David Russell was a constant visitor. And Dr. Carl Foster, on the excuse of checking on Darcie, was there at least once a day. When at last he kissed Helene, she had one fleeting thought of Jean-Charles, and then it seemed that his memory smiled at her. When Carl Foster asked for her hand, she said, "Oh, yes."

Petra cried at the wedding, but they were tears of happiness for Helene as well as tears of regret. She would be leaving, would not be there to see Helene as a young married woman. But Darcie would be there. For there had been an earlier and less public wedding in which Darcie Moncrief, leaning on a cane and being supported by her distinguished admiral, became Mrs. David Russell.

And before Petra, Jason, and Jay stood on the rail of a ship and looked down on a huge crowd gathered on the pier at Cristobal, another event occurred which saddened Petra.

The cablegram came to the office and was lost for a while among the stream of communications coming into the office of the new director. Finally, however, it was noticed, opened, and discovered to be of a personal nature. In due time, it was, delivered to Burton's house.

It read: IF WHEREABOUTS ANTONIA D'ART KNOWN, INFORM "MIMI" REHEARSALS START MID-APRIL. HER PRESENCE REQUIRED.

Signed Jack Young, the message galvanized Antonia into frenzied action and excitement. She made tearful good-byes and, it seemed to Petra, sailed out of her life. Her work in the theater would be done in New York, with the rest of the family far away across the country in San Francisco. Petra's world was falling apart, but she had her son, a stout and lively boy who was growing like a weed, and she had her husband. Panama would still have a hold on her, for Helene was there, with her doctor. And Darcie was there, a changed woman who had come to Petra and talked softly about all the sad times, both of them agreeing that the past was past.

So it was with a mixture of joy and sadness that Petra waved to the crowd who had gathered into one of the Zone's greatest send-offs, a crowd who knew Jay Burton's contribution to the great endeavor. They were singing "Auld Lang Syne" when the ship was pulled away from the pier by its tugs.

15

IN THE SPRING of 1914 a big bear of a gray-haired man made the trip across the United States in the company of a handsome silver-haired lady and a young man of twenty-one years who was as tall as he, but not as bulky. In New York, they checked into the finest of hotels and, using tickets which had been mailed to them in advance, attended the evening performance of a new musical.

Jason Burton was one of those young men whom Mark Twain spoke about. Jason was astounded to realize how much his father had learned in the past five years, or so he laughingly said in different words.

"Dad, when I was sixteen, I knew that you were hopelessly old-fashioned and ignorant. You've sure learned a lot in five years."

But Jason had always thought his mother to be among the beauties of the world, and he was sure that she was the most handsome matron in the theater.

"Silly, you're not supposed to cry," he whispered to Petra, when she first saw Mimi Moncrief—or Antonia —come onto the stage in costume, her lovely voice raised in a happy little song.

The show was a hit to rival another opening of the season, Jerome Kern's *The Girl from Utah*. Music by Moncrief and lyrics by Young were sung, whistled, and hummed all over the country, and, Petra thought, Antonia had to be the most beautiful of all. She was, in fact, majestic, with her hair piled high, in daring costumes which set off her perfect figure. And she was good. Petra had a scrapbook at home filled with pictures and newspaper stories about Mimi Moncrief. She wasn't sure what to believe: the news stories which painted Antonia as one of the world's great actress-courtesans, or Antonia, who said, "Oh, mother, it's only publicity. You know, I don't care what they say, just so they're talking about me."

Ah, the years since leaving Panama had been good. And it was good to see Antonia again, although she made regular trips to California, once in a road show of *Mimi* and once to act in an Adolph Zukor film, the new craze of motion pictures becoming more and more a force in show business.

Afterward, Jack Young embraced Petra and said, "I have a role for you in my next show, young lady."

"As someone's grandmother?" Petra laughed.

"A mature queen," Jack said.

And Antonia's hug, she smelling of makeup. Jason telling her that she had been smashing.

"Oh, I'll bet you're making some little feminine hearts quiver," Antonia laughed, kissing Jason's cheek.

Lovely days, exciting nights, as Jack and Antonia "painted the town red" for them, causing Petra to plea for one good night's rest. But it was over too soon. Amid threatening rumbles from Europe, they sailed south and found a changed Canal Zone, modern, clean, and the huge impressive locks now finished. Many men remembered Jay Burton. They spoke with Philippe Bunau-Varilla, who stood at the rail of the *Cristobal,* a lowly cement carrier, the ship which made the first ocean-to-ocean transit of the canal on the same day,

August 3, that the Great War began in Europe, pushing the official opening of the canal, on August 15, to back pages of newspapers the world over.

It was the *Ancon* which officially opened the canal, and on her were Jay and Petra and others, including Helene Foster and three stair-step boys named, in order of height, Jay Carl, Paige, and Cordell.

It all seemed anticlimactic. In the home of Dr. and Mrs. Carl Foster they gathered, Darcie and her admiral among them, the three boys squirming in their company clothes.

At dinner, Carl Foster offered a toast. "To the man who got it started and made it possible," he said. "To Jay Burton."

"Hear, hear," they all said.

"To all those who had a part in it," Jay responded, standing, his glass high. "To all who died. And to the old man who dreamed it, to Ferdinand de Lesseps."

"Hear, hear," they said.

To Petra's vast delight, Helene and Carl announced that they were leaving the canal and would set up a practice in California. "You're my family," Helene said. "We do so want to be near you."

Darcie and David were going to New York, first, and then travel across country. During his time of service in California, David had come to like it, and, Darcie said, she would not allow him to keep her away from her grandchildren too long.

Without consciously seeking it, Darcie and Petra found themselves alone on the screened veranda. The men were outside in the yard, examining the results of Carl Foster's hobby, growing exotic plants.

"Look at him," Darcie said, nodding toward Jason. "I can't believe it. A man. As tall as his father. Where have the years gone?"

"Into two great ditches," Petra said.

"Yes. God, so long ago. Do you know I can still close my eyes and see father's face? In fact, your

Jason has some of him, in the way he holds his mouth and chin."

"Yes," Petra said.

"And we're just two old ladies looking forward to watching our grandchildren grow," Darcie said.

"Speak for yourself," Petra laughed. "Although the coals may not be arranged as neatly as they once were, there's still fire in this old furnace."

Darcie chuckled and fell into silence. And from below the male voices came.

"We'll be in it within a year."

"Damned Huns!"

And Jason's voice, strong, youthful, clear. "I've been meaning to tell you, Dad. I've contacted the Canadian War Office. They're forming a squadron of Americans and Canadians to fight in France."

Petra's face went white.

"Don't rush it, son," Jay said. "You'll have your chance, under American commanders."

"But those are my mother's countries fighting," Jason said. "And our politicians are falling all over themselves promising to keep us out of it."

"Oh, God!" Petra said.

"You're of age," Jay said. "There's no way I can stop you. But think of what this will do to your mother."

"Mother's tough," Jason said with a laugh. "She'll understand."

"My dear God!" Petra said.

IF YOU ENJOYED THIS NOVEL HERE'S ANOTHER BIG ROMANTIC "READ" FROM DELL

Passion's Pawn

Annabella

"A sensuous yet spunky heroine . . . exciting, elegant, exotic . . . Move over, Rosemary Rogers," says George McNeill, author of THE PLANTATION and RAFAELLA.

This is the story of Elizabeth Stewart, an orphan schoolgirl of mysterious parentage, who lost her heart to the Lord of Polreath Manor the first time she saw him.

Bizarre twists and turns of destiny flung them together, then tore them apart—first at the Manor where beautiful Elizabeth is cruelly tortured and forced to flee for her life, then in London where she becomes the toast of high society and is courted by a Prince of Hanover, finally as a princeling's love slave in the Taj Mahal.

Unable to resist the one man she could never have, was Elizabeth fated forever to be passion's pawn?

A DELL BOOK on sale now